Praise for the Novels of S. M. Stirling

The Tears of the Sun

"The emerging kingdom of Montival is a damn cool place to hang out. In this postapocalyptic North America, Stirling has cherry-picked everything a fan might wish for in a high fantasy/apocalypse/alternate history mashup. You've got heroes, horses, swordplay, kings, siege engines, and mystics. And all with (somewhat) less patriarchy, because the postmodern world that spawned Montival—our world—has left a big stamp of twentieth-century social progress on the society rising from its ashes."

—Tor.com

The High King of Montival

"Filled with plenty of action, intrigue, and a touch of romance. . . . S. M. Stirling provides another fabulous postapocalyptic thriller to his Change saga."

—Alternative Worlds

"Stirling's series combines the best of fantasy and post-apocalyptic genres but rises above them both with his long vision and skill in creating compelling characters, no matter how large or small their role."   —Fresh Fiction

The Sword of the Lady

"This new novel of the Change is quite probably the finest by an author who has been growing in skill and imagination for more than twenty-five years."

—*Booklist* (starred review)

"Well written. Stirling has the ability to make the commonplace exciting and to dribble out the information needed to complete the tapestry of understanding . . . a good tale."   —SFRevu

continued . . .

"Absolutely stunning work [that] proves again why people say that Stirling is the best postapocalyptic writer today. There are enough twists and turns to keep fans of the series happy." —Bitten by Books

"A thrilling, action-packed, and suspenseful quest narrative that takes place in a vividly described postapocalyptic world." —*Romantic Times*

The Scourge of God

"Vivid. . . . Stirling eloquently describes a devastated, mystical world that will appeal to fans of traditional fantasy as well as postapocalyptic SF." —*Publishers Weekly* (starred review)

"Stirling is a perfect master of keep-them-up-all-night pacing, possibly the best in American SF, quite capable of sweeping readers all the way to the end." —*Booklist* (starred review)

"I liked this book. . . . Stirling is a master of world building. This series has gone a long way from its point of departure, but still keeps a horde of fans wanting more." —SFRevu

"Stirling has crafted a complex follow-up to *The Sunrise Lands* that vividly describes the political landscape." —Monsters and Critics

The Sunrise Lands

"Combines vigorous military adventure with cleverly packaged political idealism. . . . Stirling's narrative deftly balances sharply contrasting ideologies. . . . The thought-provoking and engaging storytelling should please Stirling's many fans." —*Publishers Weekly*

"Brilliant action." —*Booklist*

"Fast-paced." —*Futures Mystery Anthology Magazine*

"A master of speculative fiction and alternate history, Stirling delivers another chapter in an epic of survival and rebirth." —*Library Journal*

A Meeting at Corvallis

"[A] richly realized story of swordplay and intrigue."
—*Entertainment Weekly*

"Stirling concludes his alternative history trilogy in high style. . . . [The story] resembles one of the cavalry charges the novel describes—gorgeous, stirring, and gathering such earth-pounding momentum that it's difficult to resist."
—*Publishers Weekly*

"A fascinating glimpse into a future transformed by the lack of easy solutions to both human and technological dilemmas."
—*Library Journal*

The Protector's War

"Absorbing."
—*The San Diego Union-Tribune*

"[A] vivid portrait of a world gone insane . . . it also has human warmth and courage. . . . It is full of bloody action, exposition that expands character, and telling detail that makes it all seem very real.
—*Statesman Journal* (Salem, OR)

"Reminds me of Poul Anderson at his best."
—David Drake, author of *What Distant Deeps*

"Rousing. . . . Without a doubt [*The Protector's War*] will raise the bar for alternate universe fiction."
—John Ringo, *New York Times* bestselling
author of *Citadel*

Dies the Fire

"*Dies the Fire* kept me reading till five in the morning so I could finish at one great gulp. . . . Don't miss it."
—Harry Turtledove

"Gritty, realistic, apocalyptic, yet a grim hopefulness pervades it like a fog of light. The characters are multidimensional, unusual, and so very human. Buy *Dies the Fire*. Sell your house; sell your soul; get the book. You won't be sorry."
—John Ringo

"A stunning speculative vision of a near-future bereft of modern conveniences but filled with human hope and determination. Highly recommended."
—*Library Journal*

ALSO BY S. M. STIRLING

The
Tears of the Sun

A NOVEL OF THE CHANGE

S. M. STIRLING

A ROC BOOK

ROC
Published by New American Library, a division of
Penguin Group (USA) Inc., 375 Hudson Street,
New York, New York 10014, USA
Penguin Group (Canada), 90 Eglinton Avenue East, Suite 700, Toronto,
Ontario M4P 2Y3, Canada (a division of Pearson Penguin Canada Inc.)
Penguin Books Ltd., 80 Strand, London WC2R 0RL, England
Penguin Ireland, 25 St. Stephen's Green, Dublin 2,
Ireland (a division of Penguin Books Ltd.)
Penguin Group (Australia), 250 Camberwell Road, Camberwell, Victoria 3124,
Australia (a division of Pearson Australia Group Pty. Ltd.)
Penguin Books India Pvt. Ltd., 11 Community Centre, Panchsheel Park,
New Delhi - 110 017, India
Penguin Group (NZ), 67 Apollo Drive, Rosedale, Auckland 0632,
New Zealand (a division of Pearson New Zealand Ltd.)
Penguin Books (South Africa) (Pty.) Ltd., 24 Sturdee Avenue,
Rosebank, Johannesburg 2196, South Africa

Penguin Books Ltd., Registered Offices:
80 Strand, London WC2R 0RL, England

Published by Roc, an imprint of New American Library, a division of Penguin
Group (USA) Inc. Previously published in a Roc hardcover edition.

First Roc Mass Market Printing, September 2012
10 9 8 7 6 5 4 3

Copyright © S. M. Stirling, 2011
Map by Courtney Skinner

 REGISTERED TRADEMARK—MARCA REGISTRADA

Printed in the United States of America

PUBLISHER'S NOTE
This is a work of fiction. Names, characters, places, and incidents either are the
product of the author's imagination or are used fictitiously, and any resemblance
to actual persons, living or dead, business establishments, events, or locales is
entirely coincidental.
    The publisher does not have any control over and does not assume any re-
sponsibility for author or third-party Web sites or their content.

ALWAYS LEARNING   PEARSON

This one's for Kier

Acknowledgments

Yet more!

Thanks to my friends who are also first readers:

To Steve Brady, for assistance with dialects and British background, and also natural history of all sorts.

Thanks also to Kier Salmon, insufficiently credited collaborator, for once again helping with the beautiful complexities of the Old Religion, and with . . . well, all sorts of stuff! Sometimes I feel guilty about not paying her.

To Diana L. Paxson, for help and advice, and for writing the beautiful Westria books, among many others. If you liked the Change novels, you'll probably enjoy the hell out of the Westria books—I certainly did, and they were one of the inspirations for this series; and her *Essential Asatru* and recommendation of *Our Troth* were extremely helpful . . . and fascinating reading.

To Dale Price, help with Catholic organization, theology and praxis; and for his entertaining blog, Dyspeptic Mutterings, which can be read at http://dprice.blogspot.com/.

To Brenda Sutton, for multitudinous advice.

To Melinda Snodgrass, Emily Mah, Terry England, George R. R. Martin, Walter Jon Williams, Vic Milan, Jan Stirling and Ian Tregellis of Critical Mass, for constant help and advice as the book was under construction.

Thanks to John Miller, good friend, writer and scholar, for many useful discussions, for lending me some great books, and for some really, really cool old movies.

Special thanks to Heather Alexander, bard and balladeer, for permission to use the lyrics from her beautiful songs, which can be—and should be!—ordered at www.heath erlands.com. Run, do not walk, to do so.

Thanks again to William Pint and Felicia Dale, for permission to use their music, which can be found at www .pintndale.com and should be, for anyone with an ear and salt water in their veins.

And to Three Weird Sisters—Gwen Knighton, Mary Crowell, Brenda Sutton and Teresa Powell—whose alternately funny and beautiful music can be found at http:// www.threeweirdsisters.com/.

And to Heather Dale for permission to quote the lyrics of her songs, whose beautiful (and strangely appropriate!) music can be found at www.HeatherDale.com, and is highly recommended. The lyrics are wonderful and the tunes make it even better.

To S. J. Tucker for permission to use the lyrics of her beautiful songs, which can be found at www.skinnywhite chick.com, and should be.

Thanks again to Russell Galen, my agent, who has been an invaluable help and friend for a decade now, and never more than in these difficult times.

All mistakes, infelicities and errors are of course my own.

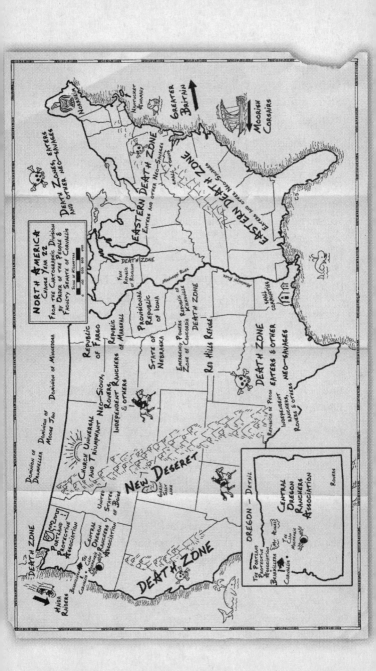

CHAPTER ONE

DUN JUNIPER
DÙTHCHAS OF THE CLAN MACKENZIE
(FORMERLY THE EAST-CENTRAL WILLAMETTE VALLEY,
OREGON)
HIGH KINGDOM OF MONTIVAL
(FORMERLY WESTERN NORTH AMERICA)
JULY 31, CHANGE YEAR 25/2023 AD

Rudi Mackenzie—Artos the First, High King of Montival though yet to be formally crowned—finished the last crusty bite of the ham sandwich, savoring the smoky taste of the cured meat and sharp cheese, and washed it down with the last swallow in the clay crock of beer. Then he leaned back against the smooth-worn roots of the gnarled wild apple tree and sighed, listening to the soft sough of wind in branches, the hum of bees. A sharp *tup-tup* came from a flock of little yellow-faced warblers diving through a cloud of mayflies, and then a buzzing *zee-zee-zee-bzz-zee* as they swarmed off like swooping dots of sunlight into the Douglas firs above.

"Now this," he said, "is something on the order of a homecoming, so it is. Or close enough for government work, until the war is over. Which is appropriate, since now we *are* the government."

His newly handfasted bride Mathilda Arminger snuggled into the curve of his shoulder, a pleasant solid burden, her brown hair smelling of summer like the sun-warmed grass in which they rested, and her strong not-quite-pretty features relaxed as she turned her face towards the sun. The weight didn't bother him, though Mathilda was a rangy five-nine and had the leanly solid build of someone who'd trained to fight in armor most of her life. He was a tall man, born late in the first year of the Change—which made him a few months older than his bride—long-limbed, broad in the shoulders and narrow in the waist, with a regular high-cheeked face just on the edge of beauty, a shoulder-length mane of hair a color just halfway between gold and molten copper, and light eyes of a changeable blue-green-gray.

"It's fair beyond bearing, this is. We've seen everything from the Sunset Ocean to the lands of Sunrise and nothing can quite compare," he said softly.

He pulled a strand of long grass free and chewed meditatively on the stem as they looked down through the screen of firs to the open benchland below that made an irregular oval of grassland running east-west along the side of the hill, about a mile long and half a mile wide at its broadest. Most of it was rolling meadowland where horses and red-coated cattle grazed thick green grass starred with pink lupine and white daisies, separated by hawthorn hedge and white board fence into paddocks studded with great garry oaks or the tall black walnuts his mother's great-uncle had planted long before the Change. Beyond that the forested ground fell away steeply and blocked sight of the little valley of Artemis Creek flowing westward into the great green-gold quilt of the Willamette lowlands. Those faded in turn to the blue line of the Coast Range on the very edge of sight, even to keen young eyes on a day cloudless from horizon to horizon.

Mathilda crossed herself and touched her crucifix to her lips for an instant.

"God made all lands beautiful in their own way," she said. "But this is *our* way, or part of it. For Rudi and Mathilda, not just the King and Queen."

"It's a good thing to have your heartstrings rooted in one place, small and very dear," he agreed. "You build from there, but it's the foundation, as the love of your kin is the starting place for a regard for folk in general."

When he'd left this place two years ago to journey to the Sunrise lands and return, there had still been a good deal of boy in his face. Though he'd already been a warrior of note and chosen tanist of the Clan, successor to his mother as Chief. There was little of that lad left, though the man the boy had become was contentedly relaxed for the moment. Living out a prophecy every day was much more wearing, he found, than simply living with one looming in his future had been, and he needed to take the moments of peace when he could.

"I like the beard," Mathilda said, tickling his jaw; he arched his neck and purred like a cat. "Very distinguished looking. This time. Not mangy, like the previous attempts."

"Like a wheat field struck by rust and weevils and blight that was, the black sorrow and shame of it, but the third's the charm."

"I remember when you were sixteen and tried for a mustache. Your mother said: *And aren't you getting old enough to shave that peach fuzz on your lip now, boyo?* You blushed crimson."

The short-cropped growth was a slightly darker shade than his head hair, and had come in dense and even this time.

It adds a few years to my looks, Rudi thought. *Which*

4 S. M. STIRLING

*cannot hurt when I'm dealing with so many touchy men
and women of power. Human beings are like that; buried
memories of our childhoods, perhaps, when age is authority.*

She sighed. "Remember how we used to come up here
as kids and lie finding shapes in the clouds?"

"It drove your attendants mad. Not that some of them
ever liked your spending part of the year here."

"Those ones didn't last. Anyway, it was in the treaty."

Off to the left was the little waterfall, falling like a
strand of silver lace over a lip of rock and into its pool,
and below it the dam and querning gristmill, busy with
grain from the just-completed harvest. Beyond that the
distant snow peaks of the High Cascades glittered like
islands of white against blue heaven in the east; the enemy held the Bend country overmountain, up to the forts
in the passes. To his right he could just see the white
stucco on the walls of Dun Juniper, and over it a blink of
paint and gilding from the Chief's Hall. The wind down
from the crags carried a hint of the glaciers, and the
strong wild scent of the great fir-forests that rolled mile
after mile along the west-facing scarps.

"We're still driving them all crazy," Mathilda said.
"Just in different ways."

The oval of pastureland and garden on the knee of the
hill below was a little crowded, with tents in many of the
paddocks and far more horses than usual, including those
of Dun Juniper's share of the eastern refugees quartered
in every Mackenzie settlement.

"I wish we'd been able to do more than a flying visit
in Portland and Castle Todenangst, though," she added.
"They're home too."

She was in a kilt and plaid herself, not for the first time.
She'd spent half of every year here since they were both

ten, back at the end of the War of the Eye, and had often gone in Mackenzie dress for convenience's sake. Now it was also a statement that the High Queen belonged to all her peoples, not just her native Portland Protective Association, the same reason she'd taken to wearing jeans and turtleneck when they were in Corvallis.

Which was wise, given the long and well-merited grudges many bore from her ghastly *bachlach* of a father's reign and the wars against the Association; there were still people to whom the sight of a cote-hardie or hose and houppelande were like a red rag to a bull. Some simply feared the Colossus of the North because it had more territory and as many people as all the rest put together. The War of the Eye had trimmed it back, but it had recovered quickly and had been growing steadily stronger in numbers and wealth and power all three under Sandra Arminger's farsighted rule. That had made everyone nervous until the rise of the Prophet and the Church Universal and Triumphant had buried old feuds in a common fear.

"Or the PPA outweighed all the other powers before we proclaimed Montival," Mathilda murmured. "If you look at it in terms of everything from the Pacific to the Sioux country and not just as far as the Rockies, then the Association is cut down to size . . . and people may learn to relax about it a little."

Rudi chuckled. Their minds did tend to run alike. He'd heard that long-married couples were often so. They'd been wed about one turning of the Moon, but he supposed being friends from childhood as well as lovers now hastened the process. Plus both being the children of rulers, and extremely shrewd ones.

"But we have to win the war to make that more than a claim," he said, and kissed her. The touch was soft and sweet, and he murmured: "In the meantime, your wearing a kilt *does* have its merits . . ."

"Eeek! *Rudi!*"

He stopped, a little unwillingly even though he'd been playing.

"But we have permission from the Gods themselves now," he said, teasing. "Yours in particular, since we were married in a Catholic church."

"Not in the open air. Someone might come by! I *am* Catholic, remember, not a witch-girl."

"Nobody's coming by, not with Edain and a score of the High King's Archers on guard."

"And *they're* too close!"

He sighed dramatically. "Alas, it's right you are; their silent presence just out of sight would make for a little constraint?"

"*Just* a little!"

They rose, brushing bits of grass and the odd leaf off each other; Rudi put on his flat Scots bonnet with the spray of raven feathers in its clasp. There was a clump of meadowsweet growing half a pace away; he made a sign of apology and murmured: "Let us share your beauty for a while, little sisters," as he bent and plucked them and wove a garland. "My thanks to you and Her."

"There," he said, setting the lacy cream-white flowers on her head, binding the long seal-brown hair that fell past her shoulders. "Queen of the Meadow to crown my Queen."

She kissed him again, and the sweet almond smell of the flowers encompassed them both.

"Duty calls," she said a moment later.

"In a shrill unpleasant voice," he agreed mournfully.

Reflex as deep as instinct made them reach for their sheathed swords where they leaned against the tree with the belts wound around the tooled black leather of the scabbards; you didn't go a step without steel in reach. Rudi felt a slight sudden cold *shock* as he touched his and swung the belt around his waist, doubling it and tucking the tongue under and settling the weight on his right hip with a twitch.

He'd borne the Sword of the Lady for more than a year now, since that memorable day on Nantucket, and it still made the little hairs prickle along his spine every time he put his flesh to it anew. It was quiet today, or as much as the Sword ever was. There were times a casual eye might have mistaken it for an ordinary weapon of extraordinary quality. The form was that of a knight's weapon, a yard of straight two-edged tapering blade with a slightly crescent-shaped guard and a double-lobed hilt of black staghorn. He gripped it and drew it slightly, enough for a handspan to gleam above the silver of the chape. Steel, at first glance. Then you could see the rippling, curling marks on it weren't damascene work. They drew the eye inward, every pattern repeating, down and down and down, as if it were a window *through* the world.

And the pommel, a sphere of crystalline moon-opal gripped in antlers. Light swirled in it—

"Rudi!"

Mathilda's voice was sharp as she called him back to the world of common day. He snapped the weapon home with a *click* of guard against chape.

"It's so *creepy* when you . . . go away like that."

He looked up at her and smiled. "Don't say it's always bad, acushla," he said. "Here, put your hand on mine, and we'll see together what I glimpsed."

She did, where his left—his sword-hand, since the wound that nearly killed him leached a hair-fine edge of the strength and speed from his right—rested on the hilt. Then she gasped.

Rudi went on one knee in this very spot, sinewy wedge-shaped torso brown and bare above his kilt. But older, a little, with scars she didn't recognize, and his hair longer and worn Mackenzie-style, tied back with a spare bowstring into a queue. He smiled as he extended his arms, and a two-year-old toddled towards him, a girl in a yellow shift, chubby feet bare, white-silk hair falling around her shoulders, huge turquoise eyes sparkling above a gap-toothed elfin grin. Rudi seized her beneath the arms and tossed her high, catching her and tossing her again.

Mathilda watched, laughing, an infant in her arms . . .

They took their hands from the Sword and looked at each other, wondering.

"Is . . . that what will be?" she asked.

"No. It's what *might very well be*, though, which is close enough for government work, which is appropriate, eh? Making it so is up to us."

"Two children," she said wonderingly; he could hear happiness bubbling up beneath it. "In a few years from now, at least, and maybe more later. Oh, thank you, Holy Mary, mother of God. *My* children! *Our* children!"

"A daughter and a son," Rudi added, nodding; then his mouth quirked. "Crown Princess Órlaith, and little Prince John."

Mathilda looked at him sharply; the order of succession hadn't been settled yet, whether it should be the eldest or the eldest *son*. The conservative nobility of the Association mostly wanted the latter, of course; and he knew she was ambivalent herself. Then her eyes went wider.

"You know their *names*. The *Sword* knows their names?"

"Well, we *could* choose others now, just to spite it, so.

But they have a nice ring to them, don't they? So we might as well . . . though it's most surely a matter of the snake biting its own tail . . ."

"Órlaith," Mathilda said. "That means . . . *Golden Princess*, doesn't it?"

"So it does, in the ancient tongue. Her hair will be like white gold as a child, and palest yellow when she's grown, with eyes like the sunlit sea; she'll be tall and graceful as a willow-wand, stronger than sword steel."

He frowned seriously. "And she'll be mad for strawberries and cream in season, and love cats, and play the mandolin—"

Mathilda mock-punched him in the chest. "Now you're making it up!"

"That I am. It's true about the hair and all that, though."

She paused for a moment. "And John . . . that was Dad's middle name."

"And so it was," Rudi said mildly, meeting her eyes.

"I wouldn't have dared suggest naming him *Norman*. I know that's impossible. The politics."

"Your father did great things, my heart, for good and ill. Let that part of him which did well and saved lives and built for the ages be remembered with the name, and the part of him that loved your mother and you. Let all else . . . be forgotten."

Mathilda looked away for a moment. "Thank you," she whispered.

Her father Norman John Arminger, the first Lord Protector and founder of the PPA, had been a very able man. A warrior to be feared with his own hands, and himself fearless as a lion, and still more to be respected as a battle-leader. Intelligent and quick-witted enough to see immediately what the Change that stopped the machines meant, while others dithered and denied and died. And with power of will enough to inspire and bully others into following him. Without him most of what became the PPA would have been ruins and charred bones split for marrow and wilderness long since. He'd truly loved Mathilda also, and in his odd way her mother Sandra.

A strong man, Rudi thought. *Even a great one, but bad at the heart; though no man is all one thing.*

As a ruler he'd also been a brutal terrorist and outright tyrant both from policy and by natural inclination, and from a half-mad determination to bring his obsessions to life and impose them as far as his sword's writ reached. One who killed with a relish and delight that would probably have appalled even his idols and models, William the Bastard and Strongbow and Bohemond and Godfrey de Bouillon. Opportunities for that had been many in those early years of chaos and despair, when the most of human kind perished in a welter of famine and plague and desperate violence.

And ten years after the Change he'd have killed me, *if Matti's mother hadn't hustled us out of his way after Tiphaine d'Ath rescued Matti from us Mackenzies, and captured me in turn. Killed me with embellishments, just to give Mother anguish, I think. His mind worked that way, the creature. But Sandra saw she might have use for me, even then.*

Lady Regent Sandra Arminger was just as ruthless as her spouse had been. She was also even more intelligent, vastly more patient, and not hag-ridden by his inner demons. Since Norman's death at the end of the War of the Eye she'd even been a good overlord to the Association from pure rational calculation; a hard ruler, very hard indeed, but not vicious. She had men killed without passion when she thought it necessary, like a croft-wife picking a chicken for the pot, and with as little regret; in just the same spirit as she calculated taxes or which bridges needed repair or how to balance factions in the dance of intrigue. She was even popular with the commons in the PPA territories, because the Counts and barons feared and obeyed her and she kept them in check and enforced the law on high and low alike.

Out of . . . craftsmanship, I think. It's with good reason they call her the Spider of the Silver Tower. Yet she wept tears of joy when she saw Mathilda again; and she raised Mathilda . . . me too, when I was spending those months there every year after the war . . . as well as could be asked. Certainly we both learned much of kingcraft from her. We can never know the whole inwardness of another, nor all the paths their souls take from the Eastern to the Western gate. Not even our own, until the Dread Lord comes for us, and we stand before the Guardians in the place where Truth is seen whole.

"Our children," Mathilda said again, leaning against him.

"When we've made a world safe for them," he said. "So, let's be about it, eh? We've troops to muster. Nearly as important, we need to get a better handle on what's been going on here while we were away questing for the Sword."

Mathilda nodded vigorously, her eyes going narrow with calculation. When she did that, she could look disquietingly like her mother. Rudi knew he was quick-witted; he suspected that in her way his handfasted wife was more intelligent still. More subtle, certainly, and perhaps a little more systematic.

"And not just the big things, battles won or lost, castles defended or not," she said. "All the details. It's going to be crucial to manage the politics properly from the start and we can't assume things stood still while we were gone."

"That's my girl!" he laughed. "Though Chancellor Ignatius will have to take most of the burden perforce . . . and I'll need him in the field eventually."

"He's a very able man. And *not* from the Protectorate."

"Sure, and that's one reason I appointed him. That and being absolutely sure of him."

She frowned, still lost in thought. "And that's why I'm glad we sent your Aunt Astrid off on Operation Lúthien."

"I took your advice on that, acushla, though it's a thin chance, but what's the relation?"

"Mom always said you have to remember that individual people exist in themselves, but things like nations and clans and armies and classes and religions only exist because people *think* they exist. They're not rocks, they're a swarm of people all flocking in the same direction. I mean, think of Montival—it didn't exist two years ago, and now it does, and that's because we pretty much *talked* people into thinking it did. By letter, at that."

"A point, though we were pushing on an open door. The folk *wanted* to believe in a . . . dream of greatness. When people by the scores of thousands are convinced something is true, that truth can hit you very much *like* a rock. Hence our problems with the Church Universal and Triumphant and its Prophet Sethaz, the creature."

She nodded. "That's so. But Mom also always said that when bunches of people are fighting against each other, whether it's with arms or words, you have to remember that they're not rocks colliding. They're *people* colliding. Every helmet has a head under it, and the head can think. The whole point of politics is to get people to do what you think they should. Bashing them is just one way of doing that. That's why Operation Lúthien is so important. I think it might help us . . . talk some people out of thinking that a certain set of rocks exist. And make them believe in *our* rocks."

"With the Sword in my left hand, and you at my right, I'm going to be invincible," Rudi grinned. Then more soberly: "Though we'd best remember this is far bigger than either of us the now, the story of many and not ours alone. We may be at the center, but it's the wheel that matters, not just the hub."

One arm went around her shoulders. He put the other hand's thumb and forefinger to his lips and whistled sharply. There was a moment's silence, and then figures with long yew bows in their hands came trotting down out of the trees, hard to see at first in their green-covered brigandines and Mackenzie-tartan kilts and plaids. As they formed up around the High King and Queen for the walk back to Dun Juniper one began to sing, and they all took it up. When he recognized the tune so did Rudi, despite Mathilda's laughing gesture of protest:

> *"Near Sutterdown, in the country round*
> *One morning last Beltaine*
> *Down a boreen green came a sweet colleen*
> *And she was whistlin' Rudi's Tain.*
> *She looked so sweet from her sandaled feet*
> *To the sheen of her nut-brown hair*
> *Such a coaxing elf, sure I shook myself*
> *To see if I was really there!"*

"That song's a mutilation!" Mathilda said. "I've heard the original."

"I call it an improvement," Rudi said. "This isn't Erin, after all!"

And he continued in a strong tenor:

> *"From Ashland's plays up to Portland's quays*
> *From Bend down to Coos Bay town*
> *No maid I've seen like the fair colleen*
> *That I met near Sutterdown!*
> *As she onward sped I shook my head*
> *And I gazed with a feeling rare*
> *And I said, says I, to a passerby*
> *'Who's the maid with the nut-brown hair?'*
> *He smiled at me, and with pride says he,*
> *'That's the gem of our own Clan's crown . . .'"*

CHAPTER TWO

SHATTUCK HALL, TEMPORARY CHANCELLERY
CROWN CITY OF PORTLAND
(FORMERLY PORTLAND, OREGON)
PORTLAND PROTECTIVE ASSOCIATION
HIGH KINGDOM OF MONTIVAL
(FORMERLY WESTERN NORTH AMERICA)
JULY 31, CHANGE YEAR 25/2023 AD

"**M**y Lord Chancellor," his executive assistant said. "Abbot-Bishop Dmwoski to see you."

"Thank you, Ms. Wong," Ignatius said, with a polite nod.

Many hats to keep straight, he thought; the title still felt a little unnatural.

Though at present, with the hood of his scapular thrown back, there was nothing between his tonsured head with its rim of raven hair and the ceiling. He was a slim broad-shouldered man of medium height, with a pale weathered regular face and slightly tilted black eyes, the legacy of a Vietnamese grandmother brought back here after some half-forgotten war of the ancient world.

Knight-brother of the Order of the Shield of St. Benedict, priest, Lord Chancellor of Montival. Remember that names do not make the man. You are a human soul like uncounted millions more, the smallholder's boy baptized Karl Berg-fried; as precious to God as they, and no more so.

"Please send him through immediately," he went on. "Then the mustering reports from the Ashland . . . no, it's the Liu matter, isn't it?"

He concealed a rush of embarrassment at her raised eyebrow. Adjunct Professor Felicia Wong was from Corvallis, part of the University Faculty of Administration there—which meant that she was a junior-to-middling-level bureaucrat on secondment from the city-state's government, and hoping to get in on the ground floor of the new High Kingdom's administration. *Faculties* were the term Corvallans used for what most people called *guilds*; a little confusingly they were also part of the University's teaching structure. Like their terminology, they also insisted on dressing in what Ignatius considered an absurdly archaic manner; in her case, a button-down dress shirt, a tweed jacket with leather patches on the elbows, blue denim trousers and a painstaking modern re-creation of an old-world type of shoe known, for no discernible reason, as a *sneaker*.

She was also hard-working and efficient, and everyone was entitled to their foibles. Even if she was in her early thirties, scarcely older than he. Effectively they were as much Changelings as those born after that day in 1998.

"Yes, my lord Chancellor. The Liu children are expected momentarily."

"Notify me when they arrive."

I have been lurching from emergency to emergency all month. This lack of system wastes time, but there is no time to introduce a system! I must delegate more! But there is no time to test and come to know my subordinates. I must know more, *I have been absent for two years, but there is scarcely a moment to spare to read, think or question people.*

She left and held the door for the next entrant; a clicking noise of counting-boards and scritch of pens came through from the open-plan spaces beyond, and the clatter and ring of typewriters and adding machines. Ignatius rose from behind his desk and advanced with a smile of relief. The man was in his sixties, twice Ignatius' age, balding and white-haired with penetrating blue eyes under tufted brows, but likewise in the simple black Benedictine habit. Around his waist was a broad leather belt with a plain cross-hilted long sword, a dagger, a rosary and crucifix; the buckle bore a shield-and-raven badge that was the emblem of the Order of the Shield of St. Benedict that he had founded.

Don't be excessive, Ignatius, he told himself. *Yes, he is a very intelligent and holy man. But you are not the hero-worshipping novice Karl Bergfried anymore. You have your own tasks to do and cannot always run to the Reverend Father for reassurance.*

Dmwoski had been thicker-set than the younger man but was growing gaunt, and stooped a very little now. Ignatius bowed and kissed his bishop's ring.

"Are you well, Most Reverend Father in God?"

Dmwoski shrugged. "At my age and in this world of ours, a man is either well, or dead, my son," he said. "At present I am consumed with curiosity at this task you have for me. Curiosity and eagerness."

Ignatius indicated a chair and poured cool water before he resumed his seat behind the desk; the day was hot for Portland, probably over eighty. Dmwoski removed his sword belt and racked it beside Ignatius' on the stand to the left of the door before he sat.

"I ask you only because, Reverend Father, you are one of the few able men I know who is *not* impossibly busy. Merely *very* busy."

Dmwoski nodded. "The forces of the Order and of the lay militia of the Queen of Angels Commonwealth march even as we speak; the Abbey and its daughter-houses and the civil administration are functioning well."

"I expected nothing else," Ignatius said. "It's not the first time we've marched north towards Portland."

They both appreciated the irony of that; the last time it had been to fight the Association, at the Field of the Cloth of Gold, at the end of the War of the Eye.

"And now . . ."

He indicated his desk as he sat behind it. It wasn't precisely cluttered; he was a man of painstaking neatness, the habits of a monk and a soldier and an engineer combined. But it was certainly *crowded*, and it also held a tray with the remains of a working lunch of bread, butter, cheese, sausage and a vegetable salad. The room was brightly lit by an overhead skylight, but the shabbiness of long disuse lingered in corners that had evaded a whirlwind of hasty patching and renovation.

"I am in the midst of trying to erect the skeleton of an administrative structure to coordinate our efforts while His Majesty fights a major war. All in the course of a month and without a legal or constitutional framework as yet. Not to mention no source of funds once what we brought from Iowa runs out."

"I *hope* that is not self-pity I hear in your tone, my son. The reward for work well done . . ."

"Is more work, yes."

"It seems the Association is providing generous assistance," Dmwoski said, a slight dryness in his tone.

"As you see, rather too much so; that is why I picked this building, unused since the Change and obviously temporary. It would have been easier just to use the Lady Regent's administrative apparatus . . ."

". . . which would have meant a most unfortunate precedent, and all the other states would be justly terrified that the new kingdom is the Association in disguise, yes," Dmwoski said.

"Your lecture to the novices on that curious old concept of *initial path dependency* suddenly seems much more relevant," Ignatius said.

They shared a brief chuckle. The Order was a militant offshoot of the original Benedictine house at Mt. Angel; that mutation had been a necessity of survival in the terrible years, approved by the Church a decade later when contact had been restored with the new Pope and Curia in Badia. It had organized an enclave of survival, and it had played a significant role in the wars against the Association and Norman Arminger's schismatic antipope Leo. In the years since the Order had helped bring civilization back to remote areas, spreading skills, teaching and guarding. That necessarily meant a fairly close acquaintance with politics, if only to protect their bailiwick around Mt. Angel and the daughter-houses.

In all that time since the War of the Eye, Sandra Arminger had played the part of a loyal daughter of the Faith with smooth skill and used the Church in the PPA lands as an instrument of her rule whenever she could. The arrangement wasn't completely one-sided; it had kept up and consolidated in less violent form the momentum of conversion that had started with Norman Arminger's motto of *kiss the cross or kiss the sword*. The dangers were still all too apparent.

They were both morally certain that she had had Leo assassinated, as well, during her housecleaning after Norman Arminger's death. The timing of his mysterious collapse had simply been too convenient. That knowledge went silently between them in a glance, and Ignatius murmured: "When a man causes you a problem—"

"—remember, no man, no problem," Dmwoski finished for him.

"Fortunately, our new High Queen will be quite a different type of ruler. And she is now very close indeed to her delayed majority. Early next year, in fact. That will make her Lady Protector of the Association as well as High Queen of Montival."

"Yes," Dmwoski said. "And she really *is* a loyal daughter of Holy Mother Church."

"Which does not mean she will necessarily defer to a cleric's political opinions, of course," Ignatius said. "I know her, and believe me, that *is* the case."

"Nor should she. However, she will not necessarily defer to her *mother's* opinions, either, close as they are. Yet the Association's apparatus is one designed by and loyal to her mother; even when Norman Arminger was Lord Protector she managed the detail work. It is a tool shaped and fitted to her hand. You do quite right to build anew, my son, even in these desperate circumstances. Institutional inertia is a very powerful force—which, as Catholic clerics and heirs to two thousand years of it, is something we should know down in our bones."

Ignatius nodded. "I am improvising, and pulling in whatever personnel I can from wherever I can get them, but there is method in my madness. It keeps things fluid. And every power in our new Montival is of course fully occupied with mobilization for the campaign to come, down to the littlest autonomous village. If it were not for the fact that all the other powers were jealous of the Association—"

"And each other," Dmwoski added.

"—and each other, and hence anxious to have their

people involved, I could never have pried loose a single clerk."

"And I am *whatever you can get* as well, my son?"

Ignatius flushed slightly, despite the detached amusement in the Abbot-Bishop's voice.

"I am attending to political tasks His Majesty understandably cannot do in his own person yet recognizes are utterly essential. He must have the support of the realm, and what is that if not a political matter? And for that, I need your help."

Dmwoski nodded slowly. "Which speaks well of him," the older cleric said. "I knew he was a very able field commander, but a King requires far more than that. More than a charismatic presence, as well. He must be able to *govern*, or he is a disaster in the making. Especially in a new kingdom without a cushion of institutions and traditions."

Ignatius spread his hands. "Even before the Sword, his grasp of detail was phenomenal. Since then . . . miraculous. And I mean that in a fairly literal manner, Reverend Father. Yet he can still only be in one place at a time."

"I presume from the files you sent me that your request has something to do with the problem of the false Church Universal and Triumphant's infiltrations here."

Ignatius nodded. "Precisely. Most particularly, the matter of House Liu. This is not simply a political matter, either. Their mother's machinations may have begun that way, as a plan to make their brother Odard Lord Protector, but her contacts with the Church Universal and Triumphant quickly became more than that . . . spiritual elements seem to have been involved."

"Infernal elements, and there is no spoon long enough to sup safely in that company. She went from ally to unwitting tool to *possessed* rather quickly," Dmwoski said grimly. "I understand that you had direct experience with agents of the CUT."

Ignatius crossed himself and shivered slightly. "And only by the very great mercy of God and the Virgin was I able to cope with them."

"You are fortunate, my son. The Queen of Angels has taken a very personal interest in you, and you are hence protected against this . . . filth. For those less armored in Faith it is a contagious foul leprosy of the soul."

Ignatius blinked at the choice of words. Dmwoski was usually a very temperate man. Then he recalled looking into eyes that were windows into nothing, whose very existence was a wound in the fabric of the world and an invitation to the mortal sin of despair . . .

He shook his head, refusing to be daunted. "The matter of the Liu family is very delicate. Baron Gervais, Odard Liu, was one of our companions on the Quest. By the end of it, at least, he was a *true* comrade; and he saved us all several times."

"This bureaucratic morass must seem infuriating beyond bearing by contrast!" Dmwoski said.

"Am I so obvious?" Ignatius said. "It is valuable work. And the Quest was . . . often a nightmare. Hunger, thirst, heat, cold, battle and perils, constant fear for my companions, constant worry for those back here at home facing the enemy."

"A single, comprehensible aim to which you could devote heart and soul; the company of honorable friends who became as dear to you as brothers and sisters; each day a new vista and a new challenge; the inexpressible glory of a direct vision of the Virgin calling you to be *her* chosen knight . . ."

Ignatius laughed. "I *am* so obvious, then! Yes, this is almost squalid by contrast. Absolutely essential, though.

And I must *not* let my life be one long declension from a moment of glory. I must make that a beginning and this work also an offering to Him, the Cross I am called to carry up to Heaven's gate."

Dmwoski nodded. "I do not blame you in the least if you find that difficult. Let difficulty be a spur to effort. And even in your very bare-bones reports, my son, it is obvious that everyone on that quest—with the exception of Baron Odard's traitorous servant Alex—saved each other many times. I was a soldier before I became a monk or a priest; and then after the Change, soldier and monk and priest as well, as you are now. I know the strength of those bonds. The exhilaration of shared danger is not necessarily sinful, so long as it does not become an addiction."

"Even Alex Vinton saved the Princess . . . the High Queen . . . at least once, though without intending anything but treachery."

"So does God turn even evil to the service of good," Dmwoski agreed.

"And I am doing essential work here. Yet it will be a relief beyond expressing if you can lift some of that burden from me. And frankly, the tale of the Quest to Nantucket and the Sword of the Lady is also an important element in rallying support to the new kingdom."

"What *is* a kingdom, if not a tale that many agree is true? Or a nation, if not a collection of shared stories? To lead is to tell stories through action. To embody them and give them substance. We shape them; and then they shape us."

Ignatius nodded. "So if we emphasize the, ummm, cleanness and loyalty of the younger generation of House Liu, it will be useful politically. It will also show that the High King is not biased *against* the Association's nobility either. They are half at least of Montival's military power and must be, ummmm, kept sweet."

"I should be glad to help, my son."

Ignatius sighed slightly. *I expected that, but it is so good to hear it! And the Abbot has always had a gift for dealing with the young.*

"I knew a little of these matters as they occurred," Dmwoski said. "And I have studied the papers you forwarded. The Lady Regent Sandra was always a little obsessive about complete files on every conceivable matter!"

"For which, thank God," Ignatius said sincerely, and crossed himself again. "This matter is personally important to the High King and Her Majesty as well—they have sworn to protect Baron Odard's younger brother and sister. Her Majesty promised it to him as he lay dying. But it is also important that they gain an overview of how it relates to the larger problem. We *must* defeat the CUT in battle, but in the longer run its remnants will be a severe problem, perhaps even a mortal threat . . . ah, the children have arrived."

Though they were not really children anymore. Yseult was a striking yellow-haired maiden of seventeen with delicate umber-tinted features very slightly marred by four small deep pinhead-sized scars on the left side of her face, one at the corner of her eye. She wore a plain gray robe and white wimple, the habit of a lay oblate of the Sisters of Compassion. Her long, slanted blue eyes were slightly haunted, and she was limping a little from an injury about which the records told a remarkable story. Huon was younger and darker, fifteen and obviously shooting up, in a page's outfit with the arms of the Barons of Mollala on its chest, the Lion-and-Assegai quartered with the *mon* symbol of House Liu. Both of them looked more than a little apprehensive as they made their curtsy and leg-forward bow respectively, and then turned to kiss the bishop's ring. Their past year had been traumatic, to say the least.

"You are not in trouble, my children," Ignatius said warmly. "Quite the contrary. I was with your brother Odard for over a year, all the way from Odell to the Sunrise Ocean. The second Baron of Gervais was a very brave man, a loyal comrade and a true knight whose name will live forever when honor's praise is sung, one whom the High King has several times said to me he sorely misses at his right hand. I heard his last confession and administered the Sacraments to him. He died in great hope, and I think that hope was justified. His last request to the Princess . . . High Queen . . . was that she take you under her protection, and that she swore to do."

The youngsters relaxed a little, though both were still a little wary under impeccable manners.

Their lives have been much disrupted, Ignatius thought. *Their brother gone, their mother a traitor . . . to God as well as the Realm . . . and unpleasantly dead, themselves under virtual house arrest, and then the direct attack of the CUT's powers. Also the result of their mother's folly, ably abetted by her brother.*

"Young lord Huon, I am directed by Their Majesties to assure you that you are confirmed as heir to the Barony and lands of Gervais upon reaching your majority, and that there is no question of attainture for the actions of your mother and uncle. You will understand that the Lady Regent felt this matter had to be reserved for Their Majesties' final judgment."

"Yes, my lord Chancellor."

"Furthermore, your education has been severely disrupted by . . . the unfortunate events. Her Majesty is now forming her own household—a riding household, primarily, a fighting *menie*, for the duration of the war. You have completed your time as a page and Lord Chaka gives you excellent recommendations. It would therefore please Her Majesty to take your oath as squire."

Ignatius folded his hands on the desk and went on gravely: "I can testify from personal experience that Her Majesty is a knight of no mean skill with her own hands, and she will often be in the forefront at the High King's side, or on independent commands of her own. As her squire you would share her perils and her achievements. This is a post of both honor and danger, in which you will be given the opportunity to show what is in you. Do you accept?"

Huon flushed crimson, stammered, nodded wordlessly and then nodded quickly again. It was also a public affirmation of his family's loyalty and a promise of great preferment, if he showed well; a plum position at which any young nobleman would jump.

After a moment he spoke: "Yes, my lord Chancellor, that is, if Lord Chaka agrees. Lord Chaka has been very kind to me when it was, ummm, politically and physically dangerous to be anywhere near me, and I would not desert him."

"He has given his consent, and"—Ignatius looked down at a letter—"says you show promise and that he wishes he could have been a better master for you as a page, for your brother's sake and your own. Do sit, young man."

Huon sat, nearly collapsing into the chair and looking rather stunned. Ignatius turned his attention to the boy's sister, standing with her hands modestly clasped before her and obviously happy for Huon.

"My child, I understand that you have a special devotion for St. Bernadette of Lourdes. I take it you do not feel a vocation for the life of a religious, though?"

"No, Father . . . my lord Chancellor. That is, I've wondered, and prayed, but . . . I want to be married and have children and a home of my own someday. Though I've been glad to be useful with the Sisters."

"It is good that you know your mind and heart," Ignatius said robustly. "We are not all called to make the same sacrifices and a vocation must be firm and unambiguous; if there is doubt, the answer is *no*. According to your superiors you have worked well and uncomplainingly with the wounded. Her Majesty instructs me to tell you that when matters are more settled—"

When we know we're going to survive the next year as something besides guerillas in the hills, went unspoken among them.

"—she will take you into her own household as lady-in-waiting. Furthermore, she will settle lands on you from the Crown demesne, several manors, to be held by you in your own right for life as a tenant-in-chief of the Crown, and to descend to the heirs of your body. As to the matter of your marriage, that will be taken under consideration in due course in consultation with you and your brother. There's no hurry; Her Majesty does not approve of early marriages. And in memory of your elder brother, Their Majesties will stand godparents to your children and your brother's, when they come, which God grant."

It was Yseult's turn to flush and look dazed; she'd been turned from a dubious prospect to a prize catch in one stroke, and given a promise she could take her pick of the suitors she'd eventually have rather than be played as a card in the game of politics. In fact, with manors of her own she could take a landless man if she preferred him. Godparenthood was also something their generation took very seriously indeed; it was called *compadrazgo* in the Association territories, and established lifelong bonds almost as strong as kinship by blood. To have the right to call the High Queen *comadre* was a *cadeau* of incredible value.

Ignatius chuckled slightly. "Don't look quite so stunned, my children. I didn't speak lightly when I said how highly Their Majesties held your brother in their esteem. He is sorely missed in this time of war and trial. He would have been trusted with the most vital missions and highest offices if he had lived."

Then gravely: "Take him as your example in loyalty and service, and you will find the High King and Queen very faithful friends and good lords, and House Liu will rest secure in their favor."

"I . . . we will, my lord Chancellor," Huon said fervently.

"And your service can begin now. Abbot-Bishop Dmwoski has kindly agreed to take charge of preparing a full report on the attacks by the CUT on your family. On the Quest we suffered from the attentions of the diabolists, but you fought the same fight here."

Which is a tactful way to put it. But for the best. We need to draw a line beneath the machinations of their mother and uncles.

"Lord Huon, you'll need a few days to outfit yourself before you join Her Majesty, probably in Goldendale. Here is a letter of credit for arms, horses and field gear, and a note giving you precedence. I would appreciate it if you and your sister would cooperate with the good Abbot while you're preparing."

"We will stop at the inn where I am staying, for a little while," Dmwoski said, as they made their way out onto

Park and turned onto the thronged sidewalks of Broadway.

Shattuck Hall was near the southern part of modern Portland, where the city wall curved in towards the Willamette along the eastern edge of the old Interstate 405. The shadow of the great works of the Barbur Gate reached almost as far as the street where they stood, and you could see the towers of the outworks on the other side of the highway, tall on the hills that guarded the approaches. Edged metal blinked there as sentries paced the ramparts, and a blimp-shaped observation balloon floated in the sky above at the end of the long graceful curve of its tethering cable.

"I will return you to good Sister Cecilia at the War Ministry, and she can escort you back to Bethany Refuge when we are done for today, Lady Yseult. Or your brother could escort you, if you feel the need for some private conversation."

Huon Liu nodded. *He seems OK,* he thought.

The Order of the Shield of St. Benedict had a reputation for severity in the Association territories, but its founder scarcely seemed the ogre that legend made him. If you subtracted the black robe and the sword belt, he seemed like everyone's favorite uncle, in fact, or a good-natured but shrewd teacher. Huon exchanged a quick glance with his sister, and they shared a wary nod.

We've always been close, Huon thought. *After the last couple of years, we're each about all the other has left, though.*

"I am not simply going to ask you questions, my children. I am going to tell you things as well. Nothing will be withheld. You have a right to know the whole story of what has happened to your family, and how it bears on the kingdom and yourselves. I have the time for this, you understand, while Friar Ignatius . . ."

They both nodded; the Lord Chancellor had been opening a new file even as they left, gnawing absently on a heel of bread as he did.

The office building that he'd picked was a little out of the way and had been vacant since the Change, a low nondescript brick structure convenient because of its location, its position on the preventative maintenance list, and the fact that the pipes could be turned back on for city water. Huon was glad to be out of the slightly musty scent of a building unoccupied for twenty-five years. Most of the time his generation was thoroughly indifferent to the world before the Change, but settings like that could give you a slight subliminal knowledge that the present was built on the bones of six billion dead.

And . . .

Told everything! That's a change from being treated like a mushroom, he thought, with a sudden eagerness. *It's going to be fun being the High Queen's squire, but I'm still sort of burning a bit over the way we were kept in the dark about things. I suppose it was necessary, but that doesn't mean I have to* like *it. The Spider . . . the Lady Regent . . . is tighter with information than she is with money, and that's saying something.*

He felt a slight guilty spurt of pleasure when he thought of the letter of credit in his belt-pouch, after years on a close allowance while Barony Gervais was under Crown wardship. He could run amok through the quality armorers that catered to the nobility, even with the war. No need to accept good-enough Armory standard gear. It was even *justified*, since he was going to be a *royal* squire. He had to show well to do his patron credit!

And horses, he thought. *A pair of rouncies and a good courser . . . maybe even a destrier—*

Destriers were the ultimate luxury; they cost many times what a suit of plate armor did, and wore out much faster.

If I bought a young one, just out of a training farm, he would still be in his prime when I'm old enough to fight as a man-at-arms; that's only three years or so from now . . . and he'd be really well-used to me by then.

Yseult gave him a sharp elbow in the ribs and he glared back; they knew each other too well to hide much, even of their thoughts. Then he smoothed his expression. He had a feeling that the elderly cleric didn't miss much either.

Most of the gathering troops were passing directly east, or were being held in tented camps outside the city walls, but there were armed men in plenty—noblemen and officers clutching papers as often as swords, afoot or on horseback or in pedicabs, with sergeants on bicycles or trotting doggedly with a rasp of hobnails on asphalt and cement. Most of the traffic was freight, though; endless wagons of grain, barreled hardtack, racked armor, crossbows, and the salvage metal and timber and leather that the city's craft guilds and factories would transform into the sinews of war.

The noise was a continuous grumbling roar, voices and steel-shod hooves clattering hollowly on pavement, and steel wheels grinding on the steel rails of the city's horsecar network. The inn was not far away and had been a hotel before the Change, called the Benson after some lord of old. It occupied most of a block, three stories of pale terra-cotta and many more of brick above, graded by ease of access. The reception rooms and dining chambers and kitchens were on the first two, the guests of rank on the next pair, those of more humble background on the three above that, and the rest fading up through servants and attendants to the hotel staff themselves.

Right now more than a dozen miniature heraldic shields were hung beside the main doors, showing that guests of armigerous family were staying—knights and lesser nobles who had no town houses of their own and rented suites here instead for themselves and their families and retinues when duty or pleasure called them in from their estates. Huon read them as casually and automatically as he would have so many printed signs. They flanked a larger fixed shield bearing a Madonna and Child; the Virgin was Portland's patron.

The staff were dashing around looked harried themselves, but one man with a towel over his shoulder showed the bishop and his party to a corner booth of the big common room with its cut-glass wall at one end. The good odors of cooking overrode the city-smells of smoke and horses and sweat and wool; they were not far from the riverside docks where barges and the craft that plied the Columbia above its joining with the Willamette unloaded. Even oceangoing ships came upstream from Astoria sometimes, and they added their tang of bulk produce and salt fish and exotics like sugar and coffee and indigo and tea to the symphony of scents.

It was all exciting, and would be even in peacetime compared to the quiet routine of a castle or manor, though he didn't think he'd like it for more than a visit. The great walls and towers that surrounded Portland made it immensely strong, but they also gave an uncomfortable sense of confinement. You could get out of a castle quickly, at least, and most of them had green fields right up to the moat.

A swift look at the menu chalked on a blackboard

made him dither a bit, but Yseult had been teasing him about always getting the same thing; he forewent the double-bacon cheeseburger and had the souvlaki and pita with fries and a Portland Crown Ale. Yseult chose the batter-fried sturgeon with a salad and a glass of white wine, and Dmwoski settled for bread and a piece of grilled fish.

"It's not a fast-day, is it, Most Reverend Father?" Huon asked, with a prickle of stricken embarrassment.

He wasn't as devout as his sister, but he tried to do the right thing. Yseult shook her head doubtfully, then pulled out a little bound Book of Hours and checked the reference table at the back as the platters arrived to be sure. Dmwoski chuckled.

"Just *Father* will do, my children. No, it's simply that at my age the fire needs less fuel. Fat monks are figures of fun for good reason."

He pronounced a short brisk grace and they fell to; Huon was feeling hungrier than usual, since he'd been too nervous to do breakfast any justice. Dmwoski nodded at his appetite.

"You, on the other hand, are building bone and muscle yet, my son. Give me your hand for a moment."

He did, and they squeezed. The soldier-monk's grip was astonishingly strong for a man his age, and felt as if it had been carved from an ancient dry-cured ham.

"Good," the cleric said. "Lord Chaka's report did say that you were shaping well. What is the first thing you wish to know?"

Huon opened his mouth, closed it again, and thought. He was warmed and irritated both when Yseult gave him an approving look, and though Dmwoski's face was calm he thought there was something similar in the monk's blue eyes.

"I'd like to know what really happened with our—
with Barony Gervais—contingent at the Battle of Pendleton. With my uncle."

"Sir Guelf Mortimer, your mother's brother."

"Yes. I know *something* went badly wrong, Father, at
the battle or just after, and there are all sorts of rumors.
But our men are *not* cowards!"

"No, they are not," Dmwoski said. He frowned, tapping his fingers together. "In fact, they did rather well."

When he went on his tone was dry, the voice he would
have used to speak to an adult: "What happened was this:
the allied powers of the Corvallis Meeting—we were not
yet Montival then, Rudi Mackenzie and the Princess and
the other questers were still struggling through eastern
Idaho—tried to steal a march on the CUT and Boise and
seize Pendleton. That was just a little under two years ago
now. We meant to strike before its Bossman could make
a pact with them and they could send troops to secure the
city and its territories. Unfortunately, it turned out that
they had stolen a march on *us*. As nearly as we can tell,
from reports and interrogations later, what happened
is . . ."

Huon leaned forward as the old soldier-monk spoke.
The room around them faded away; he could smell the
oiled metal of armor, feel the fierce interior sun—

PENDLETON ROUND-UP TERRITORY
CITY OF PENDLETON
(FORMERLY NORTHEASTERN OREGON)
SEPTEMBER 15, CHANGE YEAR 23/2021 AD

This is not going to be a good day.
Sir Guelf Mortimer of Loiston Manor frowned down
at the map spread over the gritty soil and weighed down

at the corners with chunks of volcanic rock. It showed the city of Pendleton, capital of the Round-Up territory, or the Associated Communities of the Pendleton Emergency Area if you wanted to be technical, which he didn't. He could look up and south across the river and see the low rough-built walls with bits of rusty iron showing where the reinforcement cropped out through the concrete and rubble and odd angles where buildings had been incorporated into the defenses. Modern Pendleton was a rectangle, roughly, on the south bank of the Umatilla River; that acted as a natural moat on three sides.

Sir Ruffin Velin was delivering the bad news. He was the Grand Constable's second-in-command right now, a hard-looking man in his thirties with thinning brown hair, and one of her vassals and hatchet men. You had to be careful around them. They'd been the Lady Regent's kill-squad before Baroness d'Ath went into the mainline military. He wasn't going to take Ruffin on lightly. Tiphaine d'Ath . . . made his skin crawl. He wasn't the only one. Nor was the Regent called *the Spider* without good reason.

In fact, it's going to be a very bad day, Guelf thought.

He was head of the Barony Gervais contingent here today, as senior fighting vassal in the absence of his nephew Baron Odard . . . who was off somewhere to the east on a quest like something out of one of the Dúnedain storybooks, hopefully making the runaway Princess Mathilda helpless with admiration of his heroism as they tailed along behind the Mackenzie brat.

And what I'm doing today won't be in front of a beautiful . . . well, passably good-looking . . . Princess who's heir to immense wealth and power. Hell, let Odard get her flat and I'll be content to be his uncle and shake the patronage tree in his shade.

They'd been up before the dawn, working like mules to set up the siege machinery along the bank of the Umatilla. He was sweating like a pig inside his suit of plate and wishing he'd switched to an old-fashioned mail hauberk; the interior was still beastly hot this time of year, and they were a long way from the Pacific's cool breezes. Plate might as well be waxed canvas as far as keeping the air out was concerned. All he was getting was the occasional tantalizing draught through the joints when he moved. Little metallic clanks sounded as men jostled around the map and their harness rattled, or the leather straps and padding beneath creaked.

The stated objective—*Right up till now,* thought Guelf, casting an irritated eye at the quarter high sun—had been to install the machines to sweep the bridges across the river, then advance to take out the city wall of Pendleton by the Emigrant Gate when the beaten forces of the Round-Up tried to hold the city. Meanwhile the rumor was that the Dúnedain were to do something unspecified but wonderful, if it worked.

"The whole operation got blown," Ruffin said bluntly. "They pushed in more forces at precisely the wrong time for us. We don't have very much information yet, mostly from enemy deserters, but the Grand Constable . . ."

Sir Ruffin was looking at Sir Érard Renfrew, who was also Viscount Chenoweth, heir to the Count of Odell, and his younger brother, Sir Thierry Renfrew, who was something of an artillery specialist.

Sir Guelf allowed himself the luxury of a grimace of distaste and a quick turn of his head and spit. With enough dust to make your teeth gritty every time you swallowed no one could prove it was a statement of opinion. Of the Grand Constable, and of House Odell, d'Ath had been Conrad Renfrew's protégé as well as the Lady

Regent's; the families were tight, part of the glacis around the Lady Regent's position.

". . . says we also have intelligence that we are facing almost twice the numbers we expected, say two or three thousand men each from Boise and the Church Universal and Triumphant as well as the Pendleton troops we knew about."

That brought grunts. Everyone here could add.

"They suckered us and got their forces in here first. We can't fight this one and win with what we've got here and there's no way to get meaningful reinforcements in time to do any good. We need to break contact and re- treat as far as Castle Hermiston, on the old border. The fortifications there will give us an edge and we can put in enough additional forces to make them think three times about trying to invest the castle."

Guelf growled at the thought of giving ground. He knelt next to Thierry and traced the bridges over the Umatilla north of the walled city of Pendleton.

"They can cross these and flank us. We control the 18th Street bridge and the footbridge next to it. But 10th, 8th and Main are weak points. If we can cut those off, they'll have to go all the way up to Fulton"—his gloved finger traced north, over the river and then back down—"and sneak back down Highway 37 to get near us. Which will give us the time we need."

Sir Ruffin nodded. "So, here's what we'll do—Sir Guelf, you'll take your men and neutralize those bridges. Caltrops, barbed wire, oil slicks, burn them, saw them, fucking *piss* on them, whatever it takes. Just make them impassable for long enough if you can't destroy them."

He turned to the scions of House Renfrew. "Sir Thi- erry, we're abandoning the siege engines, so you can start the teams and limbers out now, at least we can save the horses. You'll hold this headland until the evacuation is complete. Breaking contact is going to be a bitch."

Thierry thought for a moment, then grinned like a coyote scenting a housecat.

"I think we can get some use out of the engines first, Sir Ruffin. There's only a couple of ways they can get at us here; if a place is hard to get into it's usually hard to get out of as well. And if we channel them a bit that narrows it even more. Done right we can turn it into a real killing ground and they'll lose all interest in chasing us for a while."

Sir Ruffin nodded. "Good, use your discretion. I need you and you, my lord Viscount, to hold here and get as much matériel out as possible as well as the troops. We've got the pedal cars all set up; they'll go to Hermiston and return for a second trip if possible, and anyone marching in that direction can hop on when they reach them. When you leave, take out these three bridges over the Umatilla . . ."

Sir Ruffin marked a cross on the bridges at Highway 84, the Westgate Bridge and the rail bridge.

"They have to be impassable for at least twelve hours, more if possible. That'll bottleneck the enemy long enough, hopefully."

The elder Renfrew brother looked east. "We don't have enough men for that, Sir Ruffin. If there's a sortie in any strength from the city to capture the engines, we'll be up Shit Creek, not the Umatilla River!"

The Grand Constable's right-hand man nodded. "I'll send a couple of *conroi* of men-at-arms and infantry to help you hold. Most of the fighting is down around the John Day Highway and south of the old Highway 84 and 30, that's where it looks like the battle line is shaping up. The enemy is anchoring their right on the city and trying to swing up north. We'll have to rock them back on their heels there, that's where we've got most of our lancers and the Mackenzie longbowmen, but this position has to be secured or they can use their reserves to flank us out too soon. As soon as I can spring the men I'll send them to you."

"What forces specifically, Sir Ruffin?" the Viscount asked a little more formally.

Ruffin chewed his lip and shook his head. "How good are you at kicking butt? The only one I think we can detach is going to be from House Stavarov's contingent from County Chehalis; Sir Constantine and his *menie*, you know."

"Piotr's brat? He'd better not mess with me. But he won't."

"His reputation isn't long on discipline."

The heir to Odell snorted. "To hell with discipline, Sir Ruffin. He likes to *fight*. He's a complete loss at knightly courtesy and social graces, in fact his vocabulary is limited to variations on *drink* and *fuck* and *kill*, but give him a chance to charge screaming at the head of his men-at-arms and he's happy as a drunken pig in a grape-vat. That maneuver is the limit of his military knowledge but he does it well. *And* he'll take my orders."

Guelf glanced curiously over at the iron expression on Viscount Chenoweth's face, but decided not to ask. Sir Ruffin nodded and picked up the yard square map. Guelf hurried to help him shake it gently and roll it up. Map paper was horribly difficult to press evenly and cost the earth. Only the Albany presses of Corvallis made this grade of paper. He tapped it very carefully and slid it into the carry tube for Ruffin.

The Viscount took off his helmet with a single pungent word as Ruffin mounted and left in a spurt of pebbles and dust, the pennants of his escort flapping as the lance heads glittered in the sunlight. He scrubbed his short, light-brown hair and growled.

"Thank you so very much for this gift of a helmet full of horse turds, Sir Ruffin! Guelf, get your men; take out those bridges. I don't need to teach you how to suck eggs. What the *hell* happened to the Dúnedain? That op was tricky, but they've pulled off harder. Beelzebub's arse with piles the size of plums, I wish I knew the details!"

Guelf didn't answer, limiting himself to a duck of the head and thump of fist on breastplate in salute. He took off looking for Sir Harold Czarnecki, the other Gervais knight here, and waved their squires forward. But he bared his teeth in a sudden angry grin.

The Dúnedain, huh? Hope that bitch and her sidekicks all bought it. That would be a nice little dividend on Gervais' arrears of revenge for my brother Jason's death back in the Protector's War! Baroness Mary will be pleased. And they *promised me,* uncle to the King, *they did indeed promise me that. Which doesn't mean throwing this fight. Uncle to the King of As Much As Possible, that's the thing.*

"Chezzy! Get the *menie* together; we're on dirty tricks! Grab some mantlets, one of Thierry's engineering wagons and let's go burn and destroy!"

His men-at-arms and footmen . . .

Odard's men! he thought. *But I'm here and my nephew isn't.*

. . . roared with pleasure.

"Valentine! Valentine! St. Valentine for Gervais! Let the arrows fly! Valentine will suck them up! *Face Gervais, face Death!*"

The battle banner of the barony waved in the hot sun with its black-and-red image of St. Valentine, transfixed with arrows, on a yellow background.

Looks painful, he thought, not for the first time.

The crossbowmen slung their weapons and put their shoulders to the heavy wheeled shields, heaving them up on their props like wheelbarrows.

"Six men pulling, six pushing on each!" Guelf snapped. "Get to it!"

The spearmen moved their shields to their right shoulders and fanned out in a protective screen between the mantlets and the city walls.

"Dismount the lancers," he decided. "We won't have time to get the mounts out and warhorses can't be wasted."

There was grumbling at that, but Association knights trained to fight on foot when they had to, and being armored cap-a-pie the men-at-arms would stiffen the footmen nicely. The mantlets trundled along, bouncing on their spoked steel wheels over the irregular ground.

"Idle bastards," Guelf said, looking around at the ruins of what had been Pendleton's northern half.

Nobody had to ask whom he meant. The wreckage of the suburbs here had mostly been left to decay naturally, with only occasional efforts to clear a field of fire on the north bank of the river—or perhaps that was simply people salvaging building material. Concrete floor-pads and basements and the ruins of burnt-out houses were still thick, and others had been converted into workshops or storage or piles of rubble had been shoved aside for truck gardens and turnout pasture. There were even occasional rusted automobile hulks littering the dirt-drifted, sagebrush-grown roadways, though they'd been stripped of useful items like springs and glass windows. Anywhere in the Association territories—or at least anywhere with an inhabited countryside and a city in the middle of it—would have been a lot neater.

The wagon with the engineering supplies followed behind, lurching and jerking as the heavy horses dragged it up the footpath east along the bank opposite Pendleton's walls.

"Keep going!" Guelf called. "Eighth Street first, then work your way back!"

They broke out into open country as they traveled, east of the ruined suburb. There was the Eighth Street bridge, the last one actually fronted by the wall of the smaller modern city on the south bank. A couple of sentries pelted back across it, their yells thin with distance; a sally port beside the main gate opened for a second to their frantic pounding, and then slammed with a hollow boom as they dashed through. That looked as if everyone in the city was firmly focused on the battle shaping up to the southwest.

Good.

"My lord, where should I put this stuff?" a sergeant asked, gingerly holding a cloth tube of the mixture of powdered aluminum and iron oxide.

"The thermite? See there, where the crossbeams are riveted to the main support pillars? Pack it in there. Crossbowmen here, ready to give covering fire!"

The mantlets swiveled to face the city walls, trundled forward and dropped on their support props with a *thunk*. The crossbowmen took position behind them, thumbing bolts into the grooves of their weapons and leveling them through the firing slits. Working parties scrambled down the steep slope to the foundations of the bridge, men standing on each other's shoulders to reach the vulnerable part he'd pointed out.

Guelf sweated more than running around in a sixty-pound suit of plate and carrying a fifteen-pound shield in ninety-degree heat demanded. Pendleton was notoriously sloppy, but Boise was equally notorious for paying tight-arsed attention to detail. And the CUT . . .

His mind seemed to skip a beat. He blinked in confusion. *What was I about to think? What—*

"Done!" the sergeant called.

"Light the fuse. Back west, next bridge!"

The river turned a little south of west; the Main Street bridge was absurdly wide in the fashion of pre-Change construction, and the banks of the Umatilla were forested here.

"Sentries!" yelled Sir Harold, pointing.

Guelf looked up. Several men were standing on the wall, visible between the crenellations as light flashed off field glasses. One had a transverse crest of scarlet-dyed horsehair on his helmet.

Boise centurion, that one, he thought. *The rest are Registered Refugee Regiment, no mistaking the red pants. The Pendleton Bossman, Carl Peters, must have ordered some of his household troops to stay back and protect his precious hide.*

"Get going! They're not going to stay asleep forever!"

Damn! he thought. *It made sense to rush to the end of the job and work my way back, I thought; we have to take these down so they use the ones we want when they sally. At five hundred feet from the wall to us this one isn't safe, that's a long crossbow shot. Much less the next one, it's barely half that. Should have taken the nearer ones out first before they got men here to harass the working parties. Crap! No help for it, got to get it done. They'll be waiting for us at 10th; might even defend it.*

"Chezzy! Grab thirty men and the wagon and go start on 10th Street! Be careful; be smart, but get it down. Take two of the mantlets!"

He turned back to the Main Street bridge, wishing he

had Thierry's training as a field engineer. Crossbows began to twang and thump from the wall; most of the bolts fell short, but he ordered spearmen forward to hold their shields up to protect the working parties. Just as they finished the work and were forming up, a scorpion was wrestled up onto the wall. Men looked up and yelled in alarm; they were well within range of the four-foot bolts and you couldn't count on a siege mantlet stopping them.

Guelf laughed; it was even mostly genuine.

"They haven't fastened that thing down, men!"

Recoil would buck it right off the wall if they tried to fire it without a solid anchor. Pendleton was short of artillery; the Boise army had probably brought in a lot, but there wouldn't be pre-fitted bolts ready to secure them on the walls. There were men working around it, probably trying to improvise braces.

"Give them a salute, boys!"

He turned his back on the wall, pulled the knot on his trews' waistband and mooned the useless scorpion; a knight's plate armor left the seat bare to grip the saddle.

Dangerous, he thought. *But it puts fresh heart in the men.*

The Gervais contingent roared and laughed and followed suit, waggling and slapping their buttocks at the wall and shouting remarks that started with *shoot this, you sheep-fuckers* and went downhill from there. The thermite charges lit with a hissing dragon's roar, and off-white smoke poured heavenward. Metal bubbled and ran, and concrete broke with a snapping crackle. Guelf yanked his trews up, pulled a new slip knot and pointed his sword west . . .

"Back! Let's help Chezzy stick it to them again!"

He led the way down the old footpath, mantlets clanking and rattling beside them. Over the rattling sound of his men double-timing in pounding unison and the banging of the mantlet's steel wheels came a sudden *wheep*, like an arrow hugely magnified.

"Hurry!" he roared.

The muffled impact came with a scream, high and pain-laden. Guelf pounded up onto 10th Street, into chaos. The men he'd sent were milling about, on the ground . . . he clenched his jaw against the welling of despair—Chezzy and Chezzy's squire, Terry Reddings, a huge bolt transfixing his body. Terry was his wife's younger brother and as like to Layella as a twin.

God! Thank you! He's facedown. I couldn't bear to see his dead face . . . her face—dead . . . She's not dead, she's not!

He laid about with the flat of his sword, banging on mail and shocking men back into sense.

"Get that mantlet set up, get us some cover!"

He turned to see Father Stanyon working on Chezzy.

"He's alive? What's happened to him?"

"Crossbow bolt in the scapular." The doctor-priest jerked a thumb to the right. "They got a man over the wall and he sneaked up close enough to take a shot. Young Reddings is dead, and Sir Czarnecki isn't. But the bolt hit a vein; luckily not an artery. I can't budge it and we need it out to cauterize it. I have to get him back to the cars. Probably need to get him to Hermiston before we can do anything."

Guelf nodded. "Brandon! Take three men for stretcher duty. Take Chezzy and . . . and . . . Terry, Terry's *body*, back to the rail head. Evacuate all nonessential personnel, *now*. Charlmain! Get those drums unloaded all over the bridge, spill the oil, now!"

The flat *tung* of the scorpion twanged again and every-

body threw themselves flat. This one *was* properly anchored, which meant they could reload it quickly. The
bolt went overhead with a tooth-grating *wheep* and then
a *whunk* of impact as it buried half its length in the soil.
They worked, using the mantlets as best they could to
shield themselves. Another bolt hit one, and half the shaft
stood through it; a man stumbled back swearing as the
sharp three-sided head stopped a handsbreadth from his
face, then dropped flat with a yell as crossbowmen vol-
leyed at his suddenly exposed form.

Beyond the walls a slowly growing brabble sounded;
pounding feet, equipment clanging and thumping against
other men or walls and stairs, shouts loud enough to be
almost comprehensible. That meant hundreds of men at
least, massing in the open space just inside the walls.
When there were enough of them the gates would spring
open.

"They're getting ready to sortie," he muttered to himself.

*And there's nothing much we can do but wait for it, and
hope those Stavarov men get here the way Ruffin promised.*

He looked up and was shocked to see the morning was
gone and the sun was in the west. A squire handed him a
couple of hardtack biscuits and a lump of rock-hard
cheese strong enough to make you feel that it was biting
you, and the sight brought on a sudden raw hunger that
had nothing to do with taste and everything with fuel.
He worried at both, and drank from a canteen of Umatilla water cut one-to-five with bad brandy to kill the
bugs.

Then the banners of House Stavarov, a glitter of lance-
points and footmen trotting behind; just far enough away
to see clearly, as they reined in beside the flag of House
Odell. He breathed out in relief—they might not be

enough, but he *certainly* didn't have enough without them.

"Pile it all up!" he shouted. "The tents, the food, tear down those corrugated-iron sheds. There, there, there! We'll stop them in these ruined streets just north of here!"

The stink of blood, sweat, spoiling food, dust, oils and distillates was compounded by the filth three hundred men could void in a single day of hard and ceaseless work.

Go ahead and shit, pee, spit and foul the nest. We'll either lie in our filth with the coming of dark, or leave them lying in it.

The last pedal cars were already pulling up on the rail line to the west, ready to take them out. Viscount Chenoweth, Thierry and Guelf met at the railhead; it was close to sundown.

"Are we 'bout ready?" Chenoweth asked.

"Yes," Guelf answered shortly. Then, seeing anger begin to darken the other's eyes, he apologized. "Too long a day and too much sun, my lord. What's the plan, now?"

To his relief, Chenoweth nodded an acceptance for the implied apology.

"They're going to launch an attack soon; it must have taken this long to get enough troops up from the main battle south of town. Thierry's specialists will fire the Highway 84 bridge the moment they do, then double-time over to the Westgate Bridge and fire it with incendiary bolts from the prearranged positions. It's thick with the HD40 now. We'll all converge on the railcars."

Constantine Stavarov's face fell. "Well, fuck your mother, don't I get to *fight*?"

"Yes, you do, Sir Constantine," the Viscount said patiently. "You have to hit the head of their column when they come out of the city and across the bridge. Hold them. Then I hit them. Then Sir Guelf hits them in the flank. Then you withdraw, we withdraw, and we spring our little surprise on them when they're nicely stalled just where we want them. Understand, my lord?"

"Da, da. They come out and I charge them down this street here."

The heir to Odell sighed. "Exactly. My lords, Sir Constantine and his people will hold until we get there and then take the first pedal cars off. Most of Thierry's specialists will follow in the next two cars. They won't need their reloading crews and the machines will be laid in advance."

Guelf nodded, frowning as he looked for his squires. Brandon and Charlmain were . . . *back by the rails, arguing*? He strode back, a blistering rebuke behind his teeth. They were confronting a child of eleven. Odo Reddings, his wife's youngest brother and his youngest page.

"God's *teeth*, Odo! I sent you back to Hermiston with orders to accompany the wounded into Portland, *hours* ago! *This* is no place for a page!"

Odo looked up at his lord, his defiant, angry attitude towards the squires crumbling. "I missed the train, sir. Do I take the one with the Chehalis *menie*?"

God, of course not! One of Constantine's knights, I know his reputation. I can't tell them Odo hid from his brother's dead body, but I'm sure that was it! Damn! I didn't think of that!

"Brandon, detail someone to get this brat on the train with you—"

"And what is going on here?"

At the angry voice, Guelf turned, baring his teeth at Thierry. "A little bit of a snaggle. My page is still here!"

"Get your men into position, Mortimer. I'm going up."

Guelf nodded, his cheeks burning with embarrassment. *And Odo's butt is going to burn!*

"Brandon, Charlmain; back to your position. Sir Thierry, the padre will be at your orders. I'll see you at the rendezvous."

Guelf and his squires double-timed it to the formation point in the tangle of dead streets. As Guelf strode up the line, checking his men's readiness, he saw many reach for their scapular or the saint's medal they wore around their necks, murmur a brief prayer and tuck it back.

With a sour smile, he did the same. The plain gold disk dangling on a fine gold chain around his neck was set with a small piece of jasper. Unless somebody took it in hand and looked at it, they wouldn't realize his old St. Valentine medal was gone, nor what the new one signified.

The Ascended masters are real. *So is their power.*

Then a shout of: "Here they come!"

He skipped backward a few steps to get a line of sight. The city gates were open, and at least two hundred men were quickstepping out with more behind; the assault party was Pendleton city militia from the looks, wildly mismatched armor but long pikes, coming straight down the road to the bridge and heading equally straight for Constantine's banner. His position would be invisible to them . . . hopefully until too late.

"Face forward, all of you. When the signal comes we're going to run down this street, turn right—that's *right*, everyone—into the cross street and hit, in a wedge, splitting the join between the Chehalis men and the enemy. I want you all to think that you're wild Celts! Like the McClintock woodsrunners from the far south, fangs out and hair on fire. We have to hit them like a sledgehammer; it's our asses if we don't. Charlmain, you're there! Brandon, there!"

He took his place at the head of the lines, spearmen

and men-at-arms with their shields forward, the lighter-armed crossbowmen on the flanks.

"Nobody look back! Everybody, eyes front! You'll follow me!"

He turned his head over his right shoulder, waiting for the flash of red, stamping his feet rhythmically and hearing the whole *menie* take it up as they jogged in place. Just a few feet forward was the entrance to the north-south alley they had numbered *two*. He could hear the fight struggling back and forth, like the sound of sea surf in storm as a bristle of long Pendleton pikes slammed up against the County Chehalis men-at-arms and spearmen. Chenoweth was at the other end, though he couldn't see him. Thierry's flag signal would synchronize the attack.

Thierry's squire swung the red flag from his position on top of the post and Guelf lifted his sword and knocked down his visor. The world shrank to a bright slit, and he put his left fist four inches below his chin. The shield covered him from face to knee, and he tucked his shoulder into it, making his armored body into a battering ram. Then he filled his lungs and screamed the order:

"With me, *forward*."

Everyone stepped off together, synchronized by their stamping unison. He moved at a trot, building momentum and speed as his *menie* came behind him in a thick wedge of muscle and bone and steel and wood and leather, a harsh stink of sweat and oiled metal like a wave moving with them, a crashing rhythm of hobnailed boots and clattering steel. Voices echoed, muffled by the visors and booming from the curved inner surfaces of the big kite-shaped shields:

"Forward for Portland! Haro! *Face Gervais, face Death!* St. Valentine protect us! *Haro!*"

Ahead the clatter and thump of close-quarter combat,

the unmusical crash of steel on steel, like scrap falling on a stone floor. The grunting and panting of the heaving shoving match, shield against point or shield, men crushed forward by the weight at their backs and forced into the enemy ahead. Shocked screams of pain as steel bit home, shrieks of animal rage and fear, the patterned bellow of war shouts from the men of County Odell:

"Dismas, Dismas, Saint Dismas protect! Odell, Odell, *Odell!* Haro! Haro!"

They hit the enemy force locked with the Odell and Chehalis men, and the sound turned shrill as they realized they were being flanked and the crossbow volleys struck home. He rammed his shield into a pikeman's unguarded right side with an impact that knocked into all his joints and the small of his back, smashed him off his feet and into the press of stamping boots below and thrust over and down into a man's neck above the breastplate. The points of spears and gisarmes slammed past him from behind, thudding home in faces and guts or screeching off armor with tooth-grating tortured squeals.

Odell's oliphants were sounding *retreat*. Guelf kept his head moving as he fought; you had no peripheral vision with a visor down, but he could feel the Pendleton men crumbling. He could also see Constantine Stavarov, shieldless, his visor knocked away, with blood spattered across his flushed high-cheeked, snub-nosed face and the white showing all around his eyes as he swung a two-handed war hammer with a thick spike on the other side in a blur of smashing, stabbing motion.

He was either laughing or just giving a bestial roar of joy, mouth like a red-and-white cavern. It was impossible to hear him in the tumult, but it was utterly obvious he wasn't going to obey any trumpet-call to retreat and probably hadn't even heard it. Two of his squires grabbed him neatly in what was obviously a rehearsed maneuver, each throwing an arm about him to pin his arms to his sides, pushing their shields forward to guard all three as they backed up with their lord's feet almost off the ground as he screamed and struggled wildly.

Stavarov's *menie* turned and ran west, to the waiting railcars and retreat. Viscount Chenoweth's men and Guelf's plugged the hole at the intersection, holding the enemy at bay while Thierry's siege engineers and artillerists worked behind them in a ratcheting clack and clatter of machinery.

Smoke billowed upward as the bridge was fired, black and oily and rank with a scent of burning petroleum seldom smelled these days. The Pendleton men crumbled away, but behind them were ranks of oval hemispherical shields like sections of tower wall, each marked alike with an eagle and thunderbolts. The grim faces behind the low domed helmets and face-guards looked completely unfazed by being cut off from reinforcements by the fire. They moved in unison like the bristle of a porcupine's quills around an eagle standard, and the points of long javelins cocked backward with a ripple on brawny thick-muscled arms.

"Ware spears! Up shields!" Guelf shouted, and he wasn't the only one.

The kite shields came up and the crossbowmen ducked and grabbed for their small steel bucklers. From the other side, a steady unhurried bellow of:

"Pila . . . ready . . . front   rank . . . *throw*.   Second rank . . . *throw*. Third rank . . . *throw*."

A whistle of six-foot throwing spears at fewer than ten yards distance. Guelf grunted and took a step back as two hammered into his shield, then cursed and threw it aside as the long soft-iron shanks bent, making the defense useless. He tossed his long sword up, settling it in the two-handed grip and working his fingers in the armored gauntlets. The setting sun cast long shadows, and the rusty patchwork of the sheet metal building beside him reflected the red rays. Guelf felt squeezed like grapes in a press as the close quarters caused the sound to echo and re-echo up and down the hot, airless, man-made canyons.

"Charge!" the enemy commander shouted, and the blatting tubae echoed it.

The eagle standard moved forward, carried by a man with a lion's-skin headdress over his helmet.

"Hooh-RAH! Hooh-rah!" chanted the Boise infantry, pushing forward, their short swords flickering out from the wall of shields. "USA! USA!"

"CUT! CUT! CUT!" came the eerie scream of the Church Universal and Triumphant's men, somewhere not far distant.

Guelf wondered if any red-robed Seekers were with them, but he was too busy flexing with his line. Swaying aside from the glaive that poked over his shoulder at the shield in front of him, the hook catching it and pulling it down. Delivering a sweeping overarm cut onto a low-crowned helmet with all his strength, and feeling something snap. The man in hoop armor fell, and the one behind him stepped forward into his position with stolid speed. No time to really think through the implications.

Like two turtles, he thought as the lines drew apart for a few seconds, breathing hard.

The dust, the smell of blood, voided bowels and urine rasped at his throat, and the burning oil made him cough. He panted, mouth hanging open, ignoring the taste on his tongue. In front of him he could see a Boise sergeant rallying his men for the next push, more confident as the PPA ranks moved back. They flexed, swords poked out, pole arms reached over the shields; individuals pushed harder, probed for openings. Guelf grinned savagely as he lifted his sword overhand. The late sun was in the enemy's eyes and he stabbed at a face. Chenoweth was by his side as they worked in tandem to hold the plug until Thierry's men had done their work. He watched for the swath of whitewash on a wall by the side of the road that marked the prearranged spot. The Boise men paused to regroup, wounded dragged back and fresh men stepping forward, new pila handed forward too.

Five, four, three . . . wait for it, two, one . . .

The oliphants screamed. "Back!" he shouted.

The Gervais men skipped backward, shields up but moving fast; then in one fluid motion the PPA men threw themselves down; the front rank holding up their shields as they went to one knee.

The Boise men drew back, paused, and in the instant, were lost. All the siege machinery that would be abandoned had been pre-sighted on this spot; behind each crouched a gunner with a lanyard in his hand. They jerked the cords in unison, and the murder-machines flung their loads in a chorus like the harps of tone-deaf demons. Cast-iron round shot, darts, incendiaries lashed down on the small crowd of warriors. Men screamed as napalm ran down their shields and under their armor in splashes of clinging fire. Shields cracked under the round shot and legs snapped like twigs as the twelve-pound balls bounced and spun. At this range four-foot darts nailed men together through armor and shields both.

Guelf stood, his balls crawling up inside as he saw what remained of the enemy rank; smoke and flame billowed up behind them. Even if the asphalt of the surface didn't catch, it would be a while before anyone could cross that bridge.

It only takes one dart thrower . . . he thought.

"Back, retreat!" he shouted, and the oliphants echoed it. He stooped and snatched up an intact shield someone had dropped. "Back! This place is rigged to burn. Fast, fast!"

The men turned and trotted away; some of them had the arms of wounded comrades over their shoulders, and others were making rough carrying seats from two pairs of crossed hands. One giant even had an armored form slung across his back. The knights and squires were last, backing in a controlled rush and trusting to their fuller armor to shield their subordinates.

Chenoweth's eyes flicked back and forth over the broken bodies they left behind. Guelf was doing the same. Stopping to pick up the dead was out of the question; even the wounded weren't always possible. If they could recognize the fallen, it made it easier later to compile the lists of the dead.

Then they were out, running, running for their lives to the rail bridge, 84 to the left and Westbridge dead ahead, engulfed in flames. The warehouses behind them burst open like an overripe watermelon dropped off a castle's battlements, the stacked incendiaries collapsing as the thermite charges ruptured their glass walls. A *wave* of liquid fire poured out of the ruined buildings, running knee-high like surf on a beach.

The screams of the enemy rose to a peak and then died as the fire ripped the air out of the narrow alley. Men fled burning; even Boise's discipline couldn't take this.

Guelf leapt aboard the first of his contingent's pedal cars, ignoring the Odell brothers doing likewise ahead of him.

"Push, damn you!" Guelf screamed. "Half push, half pedal!"

His men threw their weapons and shields on the cars; some clambered aboard and threw themselves into the recliner seats, booted feet searching for the pedals. The rest rammed their shoulders into the sides, so enthusiastically that Guelf had to grab for a support as his car almost came off the tracks. It began to rock forward with the rough, irregular neglected bed giving it a sickening side-to-side motion as it gathered speed. He and a few others went around the edge, bending and straining to get the now-trotting groundlings up and onto the surface.

"Pull your arms and legs in, don't get in the way of the men pedaling!"

"Too close!"

More stacks of incendiary shot and barrels of the noxious stuff were going up in the warehouses to either side. The wave of heat washed over them. Men covered their faces and held their breaths and pedaled even while they coughed and retched. The heat seared the membranes of their noses and throats, and hoarse screams sounded. Fortunately the only way to panic was to pedal harder.

Guelf felt dizziness edging his vision with gray, sparks and black spots dancing before his eyes. He drew a cautious breath in and then another. Hot, but not hot enough to burn his lungs. Around him men were fainting or breathing cautiously through wet cloths that lay over the train.

He could hear the rough jeers and laughter from the ones who'd stayed conscious. *They'll rib their mates for days,* he thought. *It will keep them all alert.*

Someone shoved a canteen of improved river water into his hand; he drank, coughed liquid out through his nose, spat and drank again despite the savage pain as the diluted alcohol struck the damaged membranes, and passed it along. They pedaled onward into the setting sun, bloodred sunset to the fore; bloodred fire to the rear.

Huon Liu frowned. "So . . . so he didn't really do anything bad there?"

"Not there," Dmwoski said grimly. "Your uncle was no coward and not a bad soldier. It was his bad judgment that gave the enemy their opening; his refusal to let go of hatred and the desire for revenge. We learned the details of that later; from his deeds, and his words."

CHAPTER THREE

DUN JUNIPER TO DUN FAIRFAX
DÙTHCHAS OF THE CLAN MACKENZIE
(FORMERLY THE EAST-CENTRAL WILLAMETTE VALLEY,
OREGON)
HIGH KINGDOM OF MONTIVAL
(FORMERLY WESTERN NORTH AMERICA)
JULY 31, CHANGE YEAR 25/2023 AD

"It's by you my place is, Chief," Edain Aylward Mackenzie said.

Rudi Mackenzie cocked an eyebrow. The commander of his guard regiment continued stolidly, his feet planted apart and hands on his sword belt, his gray eyes steady in his square young face: "I'm Bow-Captain of the High King's Archers. You can dismiss me if you've a mind to; but until you do, I'll do my job whether you find it suits your whim or not. Your Majesty."

"You never call me that save when you're going to defy me," Rudi laughed.

"With all due respect—"

"And you never say *that* unless you're going to be disrespectful, either. I've a sufficiency of armed men to guard me here in Dun Juniper, don't you think? *And* this."

He slapped a hand to the Sword of the Lady, and went on: "And I'll have you remember I put your face in the midden more than once when we were boys together. I can do it again if I must."

Despite himself, Edain laughed. At the High King's inquiring glance he admitted: "That is most exactly what I said to me little brother Dickie when we got home, word for word, midden and all. And him grown so tall and roynish while we were gone."

"Then be off. We'll have our fill of risk this year, and you can throw yourself between it and me. This day I'm going to spend with my mother and stepfather and my sisters in the place I was born. You and your bride the sword-maiden go down to Dun Fairfax and do likewise!"

Edain chuckled as he set foot on the steep path that led down from the plateau of Dun Juniper to Dun Fairfax, where it was tucked away in the valley of Artemis Creek. The quiet of the hillside forest swallowed it, green-umber distances between the tall candle-straight trunks of the Douglas fir and Ponderosa pine, red cedar and hemlock, with the odd big-leaf maple or garry oak, and black walnut thickly planted long ago for variety. A jay went *sheunk-sheunk-sheunk*, squirrels ran chattering like gray streaks, and a hedgehog scuttled off into the underbrush.

Asgerd Karlsdottir looked at him and raised one yellow brow. She was only a finger shorter than his five-nine, but with a slender strength in contrast to his broad-shouldered, thick-armed, barrel-chested build; she wore breeks and tunic rather than the kilt, a seax-knife and Norrheimer broadsword at her belt but a Mackenzie-style quiver on her back. They both took the steep way effortlessly, ducking and twisting now and then when tree branches or undergrowth nearly caught at the arrows in their quivers, their feet making little sound despite the boots they wore. Now and then one would bend a fern gently aside with the tip of the long-bows they both carried in their left hands, leaving no trace of their passing.

Neither was conscious of taking care not to make noise or leave trail. It was a manner you learned when you hunted for food's sake, not to mention scouting and tracking and skirmishing across a continent with life and death for the table stakes.

"What's the jest?" she asked.

"No jest; just thinking that I'm a lucky man."

"Lucky in your lord, or your wife?"

He grinned at her; freed from the helmet his oak-colored curls tossed around his tanned face, and she re-strained an impulse to smooth them back.

"The both, which is as much luck as a man can decently ask of the Powers, eh?"

They both made protective signs, though different ones; he the Invoking Pentagram, she Thor's Hammer.

"And I was happy that the Sword gave Rudi a happy vision for once, those children he told us of. It'll be a fine rare thing to have a little princess and prince about."

Asgerd sighed. "I wish *we* had such a foretelling," she said.

"Well, as a general rule folk don't need a vision from a magic sword to produce children, you see. The usual way suffices," he said solemnly.

A glint came into Edain's gray eyes as he deliberately looked her up and down. "We'll just have to keep practic-ing over and over until we get it right, so to say . . ."

He dodged as she pretended to clout him along the head with her bow, then said more seriously: "Though we've plenty of time; we're both of us younger than Rudi and his lady. Why, look at me ma and da; I come back after only two years away, and I've a new brother and sister tumbling about the place like puppies. Twins, I admit, and born no more than nine months after I left almost to a day, but it's scarce daycent, at their ages. Da'll be seventy, come Samhain and a bit!"

Asgerd snorted. "Your mother is younger, and that's what counts."

"Aye, eighteen year younger, near nineteen; she lost her first man in the Change, my half sister Tamar's father, he was some place far away. And Tamar was nobbut a wee one then. Not that I'm not glad to have little Nigel and Nola, of course. The more Aylwards the better for the Clan and the world—"

"They do set an example of modesty," Asgerd said in a pawky tone.

"Modesty is a vice I leave to Christians, as the Chief likes to say. But it's odd to think they're younger than Tamar's children, my nieces and nephews. It's taken a good deal out of Ma, too. Fifty is old to be brought to bed of a hard labor, and they say it was painful hard. Thank Brigid we have fine midwives and healers."

Asgerd shivered a little inwardly; her people did too, but you went to the mouth of Hela's realm to bring forth life, nonetheless. Then her mouth quirked. "And she's not all that happy you've brought a foreign wife home, and one who follows other Gods than hers."

Edain shrugged. "Could be worse, darlin'; you're not of the Old Religion, but you're not quite a cowan either. Now if you'd been a Christian, one of the ones who *scorns* all other Gods and won't so much as set aside a bowl of milk for the house-hob . . . *that* would have put the manure-fork in the soup kettle, right and proper it would."

Asgerd wore the triple interlinked triangles of Odin on a thong around her neck, the Valknut; she was Asatru, like most of the folk in her distant homeland of Nor-rheim, what had once been northernmost Maine.

Her man went on: "*And* she's not overhappy her grown children are near all off to the war—Tamar's man Eochu, and me, and Dickie, and even young Fand as an *eòghann*. Tamar would be too, except that she has a babe at the breast. We'd best remember that there's been war here, with battles and all, while we made our way to Nantucket and back, tricking and twisting and fighting. Not to mention runnin' like buggery when we could, though the bards will leave that out, I'm thinking."

"Only from Norrheim to Nantucket and all the way back here, for me, but that was long enough! Three thousand miles, is it?"

A chill ran down her back as she remembered what had happened on Nantucket. The details were hazy, as if in a fever-dream that slipped away when you woke; but she knew she had stepped out of the light of Midgard's common day there. And the Sword . . . she could hear the seeress' voice, deepened and roughened as the All-Father took hold of her on the high seat of *seidh* in the hall at Eriksgarth: *More potent than Tyrfing, forged for the hand of a King!*

They came out of the deep woods, onto a spot where the trail turned downward in a switchback; it had been roughly reinforced with logs and rocks to prevent the soil from washing in the winter rains, and those in turn worn by boots and the odd hoof. From here you were a hundred feet above the funnel shape of the little valley running out into the broader stretches of the Willamette and could see it all with a sweep of the eyes.

A winding strip of forest followed Artemis Creek; the rest of the vale was divided into small fields by neatly trimmed hawthorn hedges studded with lines of poplars and oaks, well grown but usually no older than Edain. Some of the fields were the pale brown-blond of reaped wheat, or the gold-shot green of standing barley a month or two from harvest. The vivid grass of cropped pasture lay dreaming beneath the warmth of a sun that brought out the rich smell of earth and sap; white-coated sheep and red cattle grazed there, and beneath orchards. Plots of potatoes and vegetables were grouped closer to the walls of the Dun. Beeches lined the white-surfaced dirt road that followed the tumbling water, and dust smoked away behind an ox-wagon that moved there, small as a child's toy with distance.

"And isn't this a brave bright sight," Edain said, his voice soft with love. "I can remember the time my father took me to this spot, after the first harvest I recall clear, and pointed out our fields and our neighbors', where I'd worked carrying water to the binders and myself so proud to be part of it. Often and often I thought of this on the journey there and back again."

Asgerd tried to see it as he did; tried and failed.

Oh, it was beautiful enough, she thought; beautiful with an alien comeliness. *And rich, richer than Norrheim.*

Some of the crops were the same; her folk grew wheat and barley and oats and spuds too. But here they planted wheat in the fall and harvested it in the summer, instead of putting seed down in spring and making prayer and blót to Frey and Freya and Thor that the weather held long enough to get it in come fall. Norrheimers reaped with one eye on the sky, dreading clouds and cold driving rain to make the grain sprout and rot in the stack, hail that could beat it flat, and even early snow. Here it was one fine warm day after another for the ripening.

So in the Mackenzie *dùthchas* barley went mostly to beer and oats to horses and they didn't bother with rye.

Everyone ate fine feast-time white bread made from wheat flour every day if they pleased, like a great chief. There were fruits here she'd only heard about in tales, apricots and cherries, pears and peaches and nectarines, even grapes for wine. You could graze stock outside ten or eleven months of the year, too; she'd never seen such a wealth of strong fat beasts. Winters here were chilly and wet, not the endless gray iron cold and driving blizzards she'd grown up with, and there were near a hundred days more between the last killing frost and the first.

Rich land well farmed and plenty of it, she thought. *The only wealth that's really real. Never a hungry spring for my children, when they come; a place for them to grow straight and strong and carry our blood down the years in our children's children.*

But for a moment she was possessed by a bitter longing for the hard pine scent of the homeland winds, the pale light of the short midsummer nights gleaming on the silver bark of the birches, and even the bright chill of a winter morning when the land seemed crusted with diamond and the air crackled in your nose. There was no point in talking of any of that. She had made her decision, for reasons which still seemed good, and she would abide what came of it. Edain best of all, and where he was she would make her home.

"The harvest was fine," she said instead, the surefire conversational gambit; she couldn't imagine anyone not being interested in that. "The heads in the sheaves were thick and heavy."

"Fifty bushels the acre if it's one, despite pushing it just a wee bit early for the war's sake and letting the grain dry in the stooks," Edain agreed. "Nor any sign of the rust. As good as any can remember since the Change."

He cocked an eye at her. "And you pitched in very

well, with not a word said. Everyone was pleased, and more than one told me so."

Asgerd flushed, happy and a little angry at the same time that anyone could have doubted her. She'd seen lands where a few rich lorded it over all others and despised toil and sweat, but she was glad that among Mackenzies everyone worked, and fought when needful. Back in Norrheim she'd often seen King Bjarni with his hands on the handles of a plow or the haft of an ax, and Queen Harberga busy with loom and churn or helping get in the hay.

"Who but a nithing would do otherwise?" she said. "When there's real work to be done, you do it with all you have. The wights give no luck to the lazy, nor would Frey and Freya if I lacked respect for Their gifts."

Edain chuckled. "I know you, acushla, and have for a year now; and I know your folk a little, so I know why your back's up and bristling like an angry cat. There's no harm making a good impression on those who *don't* know you or them, though, eh? We Mackenzies think well of a hard worker too, and you're the new wolf in the pack here."

She nodded. *I haven't met many Norrheimer men who are as good at following a woman's thoughts,* she mused. *He's a troll-killing terror in a fight, my Edain, and a stallion in the blankets, and he can hunt anything that flies or runs, but in some ways he's as sensitive as another girl.*

The thought gave her a flush of pleasure. She hid it by cocking her head to one side and considering Dun Fairfax itself, seen as a bird or a God might view it and away from the confusing thronging closeness that had blurred her vision of it before. There was nothing quite like a *Dun* of Clan Mackenzie in Norrheim. The thorp of a *godhi*, the home-place of a ring-giving drighten chief, would come closest; but that would be dominated by the Hall, and none held quite so many dwellers. Most Norrheimers lived each family of yeoman *bondar* by itself in the center of its allodal family land, the way her own parents and siblings did, with perhaps a few dependents' homes to make a hamlet for the most prosperous.

Dun Fairfax was a rectangle surrounded by a palisade of logs set in concrete and bound together with steel cable. There were blockhouses at the corners and flanking the gate made from squared baulks of timber; the whole was built from *big* logs, as thick as her body and many man-lengths high, for the trees grew tall and great here. They'd been stripped of bark, too, and varnished and oiled and polished, and bands across them had been carved with low-relief patterns of twining leaves and vines and serpents and elongated beasts, colorfully painted and inlaid with glass and stone from which whimsical faces peered, human and demi-human, bestial and divine.

Mackenzies were fond of that effect, but it always made her feel as if something was *looking* at her, just out of sight at the corners of her eyes. Here you always felt that the Otherworld was only a half step away.

A clear space of close-cropped pasture was kept outside the walls. Within were the homes and workshops along cobbled lanes, the tall steep-pitched covenstead that served for ceremony and gatherings and school for the children, and a communal barn and grain elevator and warehouse where things like the reaping machines were kept; there was a pond like a blue eye near the center where ducks and geese swam, surrounded by willows and oaks and a stretch of grass. Smoke drifted blue from brick chimneys in roofs that might be mossy shingle or flower-starred green turf, and very faintly she could hear the *tink-tank-clang* of a smith at work. The largest house was a pre-Change frame structure not at all unlike some she'd seen as a girl, but it was much altered and painted in a pale blue. The corners and windows and door lintels had all been set with bands of carved planking picked out in gold-yellow and scarlet and green.

Beautiful, but different . . . very strange . . . witchy, she thought.

"Too crowded," she said aloud, and then again had that disconcerting feeling that Edain was following her real thoughts. "All those households within one wall."

"Ah, well, it was bad in Norrheim after the Change but worse for us," he said blandly. "For ten years war hung over us like a thundercloud of threats and raids before it burst; I remember the wars against the Association, though I was naught but a nipper when Rudi was taken prisoner, and the northerners besieged Sutterdown, and I recall Da leading our archers out to the Field of Gold. And bad bandit troubles before and after and during that, gangs of the spalpeens, so it wasn't safe for families to live apart on their own as your folk do. We got into the habit of dwelling close, so."

"It's still as packed with folk as an egg is with meat," she grumbled.

"Forbye it's a bit crowded now, yes, what with the easterners we've given refuge and our own numbers growing. Perhaps after the war, we'll get together with Dun Carson and some others and found a new settlement."

Unspoken went: *if too many don't die in the battles to come.*

There was quiet pride in his voice: "We've done it before and more than twice; this is the oldest Dun in the Clan's territory, after Dun Juniper. And Dun Juniper's . . . different. This was the first of our farming Duns, and the pattern for the others, so."

The bigger house was the Aylward household, where her man's family dwelt. Her marriage-kin now. She took a deep breath. No task grew easier and no danger grew less because you flinched from it. Just as she did they both heard soft quiet steps coming from below. Hands went to weapons, and Edain made a *brzzzzzlll* sound between his teeth, the buzzing trill of some local bird she didn't know. The like answered it, and they relaxed; then a man and three dogs came into sight.

"Dickie," Edain said, slipping the arrow back into his quiver.

His younger brother was just eighteen and hence a little younger than Asgerd herself, in a kilt but barefoot, with only a sleeveless shirt below his quiver and a bow in his hand and a dirk at his belt. He had a kin-look of Edain, but his long queue of hair was a brown ruddy with the tint of old rust, his face half-covered with freckles where it wasn't pale, and his build more lanky. Two of the dogs were just out of pup-hood, two years or so with heads and feet still a little large for their frames; the other was a gray-brown bitch of six or seven. All three were enormous, mastiff-Dane crosses with a strong trace of timber wolf.

"Stay, Garbh," Edain said.

The bitch came over to him, sniffed politely at Asgerd's hand, accepted a ruffling of the ears, then sat down by her master with a thump of tail against packed dirt and leaned her massive barrel-wide head into his thigh. A slight lift of the lip to show fang kept the younger dogs well mannered when they showed an impulse to leap about. They were the get of a sister from Garbh's litter, and had accepted her authority instantly.

"Edain," the younger man replied, and: "Sister," to Asgerd with a casual nod.

And he's *always just taken me as I am,* Asgerd thought gratefully. *Neither too friendly or hiding behind formal manners, more as if he'd known me from a baby and remembered me sitting on the porch sucking my thumb. Right now I think he wants to talk to his brother, though.*

"I'll go down," she said. "Your mother may need some help, with the feast preparing."

"See you in a bit then, *mo chroi*," Edain said.

The Aylward brothers squatted side by side with their bows across their knees, looking down at the Dun that was the home where they'd been born.

"That is a fine, fine figure of a woman you've found yourself there," Dick said after an instant, nodding down the trail after Asgerd.

"Or she found me."

"Stubborn and close-mouthed, though."

"Ah, you just noticed! Not that any Aylward has ever been such before, *cough* our da *cough*."

"And when she does talk, it's always as if she were chanting a tale."

"She thinks we Mackenzies gabble too much and too quick," Edain said with a grin. "All her folk talk like that. Something to do with their Gods, d'ye see."

Dick snorted. "Well, the father always says we talk like . . . like the *stage Irish*. What that means perhaps Ogma of the honey tongue knows, but I do not."

"I've heard Lady Juniper say something of the sort," Edain said, and shrugged.

Their generation was used to finding those who'd been adults before the Change odd, even the most beloved or respected. Then he went on: "How else should Mackenzies talk? We're Gaels and that's how we speak.

I've no complaints about Asgerd; when she *does* speak, it's usually something worth the hearing and not just clack for the sake of it. No complaints in general; let Lady Aeval who rules the marriage bed bear witness."

Dick nodded: "She's clever and hardworking, too, and not so bad a shot with a bow in her hands; you and she should make some fine comely bairns, which the Mother-of-All grant. But can she *cook*, brother?"

Edain laughed. "Over a campfire, yes, but we've not had our own hearth yet! Her folk do well enough; plain good cooking the most of it, not as subtle as ours, and they've less to work with in that grim shiversome icebox they inhabit. Their beer is sad beyond description—no hops—but they make a fine mead and good whiskey and cider and applejack. And they liven up considerable at a feast; no lack of the craic."

Dick reached into his sporran and pulled out a scone wrapped in a broad dock leaf, breaking it and offering Edain half. He took it, biting into it with relish. It was still faintly warm, with a brown crisp crust on the bottom and a soft steaming interior thickly studded with Bing cherries and hazelnuts, the whole sweet with honey.

"Ah, and on the quest I missed the mother's cooking something fierce," he said through the crumbs.

"I don't hold with foreign food myself," Dick agreed. "Now, what's this I hear about an *Óenach Mór*?"

Edain nodded. "On the fly, so to speak. There will be business to do for the Clan, and it can't wait, so the levy will be the assembly too, so to say. And sure, they're collecting the proxies so there'll be a quorum with the marching host; it's a war we're going to, not a cèilidh. Lady Juniper's been busy with that, Rudi having other things to put his hand to the now."

Dick's brows went up. "We've already voted for war, and that some time ago."

"It's that Rudi . . . the High King . . . can't be tanist anymore."

His younger brother sat bolt upright and sprayed crumbs; Edain pounded him helpfully on the back. "And why not, by Anwyn's hounds?"

The Chief always had a tanist, a designated successor in training; it had been Rudi Mackenzie for six years now.

"Because he's the *High King*, y'daft *burraidh*!"

"A blockhead, am I? And why shouldn't he be Chief in his time, as well as *Ard Rí*?"

"Because he's to be High King of all Montival, of which the Clan is only a part, and not the largest part at that. Which means he belongs to all the peoples, not just us. And it would be just a bit of a slap in the face to all the rest if he were to be Chief, the Mackenzie Himself, wouldn't it now? He's to be King over them, but that doesn't put *us* over them, so."

"Oh," Dick said, knotting his rusty brows. "Well, since you put it that way. But who's to be tanist, then? May the Gods grant the Chief a long life, but . . ."

"But we all of us pass the Western Gate someday. Well, in strict law we could choose anyone. If I were a betting man, I'd say that Lady Juniper's middle daughter would be the one to back. A good deal of quiet talk's been going on with the notable folk in each Dun to that effect, and in Sutterdown. And not just since Rudi returned. The Chief saw the necessity of it as soon as the news that Rudi was to be King came back, and folk took to it so enthusiastic and all."

"Ah," Dick said. "Well, I wouldn't want to choose any outside the Chief's line anyway, given a choice. There's

Lady Eilir, but she's with the Rangers. Fiorbhinn's a likely lass, though."

Edain shook his head. "She'd do at a pinch; but she's very young yet, not under the Moon, and besides she's more for the music and the magic. Maude's near as old as Rudi was when we hailed him tanist, and she's clever and good-hearted. She'll be a steady hand on the reins."

"The Chief's a bard, and a priestess of power, and a good Chief too."

"That she is, but a child can get some of the gifts and not others. Forbye Fiorbhinn doesn't want it, and does say so with great enthusiasm and determination. Mentions that her first decree would be that everyone must speak in rhyme at all times, and the second that all dishes but ice cream and apple pie be banned. And she's only half in jest. Maude will do what duty says, regardless."

"Which is what's wanted, true enough," Dick said, and finished his half of the scone.

They both took a swig from Edain's canteen, poured a little water on the ground and dusted their hands beside the trail. Each dropped a small piece broken off from the scone for the purpose as well.

"Let the spirit of the place take her due. All the rest is yours, little brothers," Edain murmured, welcoming the insects and birds, then went on: "We had some fine eating in those foreign parts when we guested with great men, but nothing to compare with home to my reckoning. Well, except in Readstown, where Ingolf the Wanderer's kin dwell along the Kickapoo River; Wisconsin it was called, before the Change. His brother's wife Wanda is a hearthmistress there, and a brewmistress of note as her kin were before her, even before the Change."

"Good, she is?"

"Better than good, by the Blessing! Such beer as Lord

Gobniu brews in the Land of Summer. And her meat pies would make you weep. Also their sausages are good, and their cheese is very fine, as good as the mother's or the best from Tillamook."

"You always did take tender care of your stomach, Edain. You'll get all you can guzzle tonight," Dick said, with a smile that was half-sour. "I fair couldn't stand it the more. A fine fat yearling buck I brought in yesterday, and six rabbits—"

They both absently made the gesture of the Horns to Cernnunos, the Master of the Beasts, to acknowledge that their two-legged kind took of the bounty of the woods only when they walked with His power. Deer swarmed in the forests round about, and even more in the overgrown abandoned fields that still made up most of the Willamette country; not only were they good eating, but hunting helped protect the crops and gardens from their nibbling scourge. No fence or hedge made by man would keep a deer out, or a rabbit or a fox.

"— and that's as much as I propose to do. Running about waving their hands in the air, they all are, and screeching. Nerves on end, with the levy and the war and all."

Edain looked out, listening to his brother's voice with the ears of the mind.

"It's not just the womenkind who've driven you out on this fine day," he said. "You're not one to balk at peeling a few spuds."

"Well . . . mind, I'm happy to be in the High King's Archers. But it'll be a wee bit odd, not to march with the Dun's levy."

Edain laughed and slapped his brother on the shoulder, callused palm echoing on hard muscle.

"If you're afraid of being too safe . . . well, lad, we'll

74 S. M. STIRLING

be by the High King's side. Never a dull moment in battle, I promise you that. That's not all that's bothering
you, *mo bhràthair*!"

Dick sighed, a sound like the relaxing of a constraint.

"It's the father," he said after a moment, his voice
catching a little. "Fair worried I am. He *would* do too
much when we brought in the wheat, and I think he
pulled something in his back, though the barbs of the
Gáe Bolga itself couldn't drag a word of it out of him, you
know how he is."

"That I do, and I know *just* what you mean."

"I'm that afraid he'll kill himself when the spring-planted
barley comes ripe, we'll be gone to the war and the Dun'll
be shorthanded. If any man with Mackenzie on the end of
his name has earned the right to take a rest in the sun, then
by Lug Longhand and Ogma and Brigid and the threefold
Morrigú and all the Gods of our people, isn't it him? By
hard work and harder fighting both. But will he listen to
me, or you, or Tamar, or even the mother?"

"Not a bit will he. Though it hurts our honor as his
children that he won't let us take better care of him."

Edain closed his eyes for a moment, then opened them
and shook his head; Garbh looked up and whined slightly
at his tone as he went on: "Aye, it's bitter hard to see the
old man fail. You don't remember him as well as I from
when he was in his prime, First Armsman of the Clan for
all those years."

Dick nodded. "And the new little ones, they probably
won't remember him at all."

Edain's breath hissed between his teeth; it was all too
likely. Seventy years was *old*; three-score and ten were the
years of a man, as the Christians said.

"It karks at his pride that he can't go with the war-levy,
of course. So he does too much else."

Dick sighed again, in resignation this time.

"Well, at least the mother will have him to fuss at while we're gone, and her babes and Tamar's. It's luck Tamar has one at the breast and can't answer the levy-call herself, for she'll be company for them both and keep an eye on him."

The air of Dun Fairfax was warm and drowsy, heavy with the good cooking smells of baking and roasting and simmering. But the scents subtly differed from what she was used to; more spices and pungent herbs, a broader range than her folk had, and the cooking done more often with sunflower oil or canola and less with butter or lard. Despite her good intentions, Asgerd ducked into the Aylward house through what had once been its double-car garage.

That had been modified to make it a workshop, though rolled bedding was strapped to the walls as well right now; the outer side had a trellis trained with roses, a blaze of color and sweet heavy scent. She had expected it to be empty and give her a spell to nerve herself to plunge into a hard-working crowd who all knew each other from the inside out and she the white crow in the flock. Instead Sam Aylward was sitting at the workbench near the big double doors, before the clamps and spokeshaves, the vices and drawknives and drills.

Run from your fate and you run towards it, she thought to herself.

The old man was fingering the tools neatly racked there, below the bundles of yew staves and hardwood burls. He wore only a kilt, and you could see that he'd been a powerful man once, built much like Edain, but the flesh was gaunt and thinner on the heavy bones now. You could also see the marks of every weapon known to man; knife and sword, spear and arrow and ax, even the round puckered scars left by bullets before the Change—Erik the Strong, King Bjarni's father, had had some of those that she had seen while her family was visiting at Eriksgarth over the festivals.

Asgerd felt a little awed; hers were a warrior folk who honored courage as the first of the Nine Virtues. And someone, sometime, had used red-hot iron to write in an odd curling script on Sam Aylward's belly, but the letters trailed off. He looked up sharply when she cleared her throat, his gray eyes searching beneath the white tufted eyebrows.

"Ah, Asgerd. Come on in, my girl."

His accent was nothing like the usual Mackenzie burble and lilt; it was slower and deeper, sonorous, in a way Edain had told her was from the English lands where he'd grown: he pronounced the last two words as *moi guurl*.

He saw where her glance had gone. "Yus, that were interrupted. By Sir Nigel, 'im who's Lady Juniper's 'usband now, long ago, when I were Edain's age and he was captain of my SAS company. Glad Oi was of it, and that's a fact."

"Hello, good father," she said, a little formally.

"And 'ello to you too. All's well up to Dun Juniper?"

She nodded. "The King commanded us to go home." A ghost of a smile. "Said Edain could throw himself in front of danger later, but for now he'd put his face in the midden and hold it there if he didn't come down and have the parting feast with his kin."

Sam Aylward laughed. "Good man, Rudi. Good officer, too, come to that. Sir Nigel taught him well."

So did you, old man, and you taught Edain well too. But

you are the sort who will praise another's deeds before his own, I think.

Then he turned to the workbench. "Oi've summat for you," the old man said. "Bit of a gift loik. I was meanin' to wait until the levy left, but per'aps it's better now."

"Ah!" Asgerd said as he pulled back a cloth.

The bow was beautiful, a long shallow double curve in and out with the polished yew limbs, orange heartwood and pale sapwood gleaming under varnish and oil. The riser-grip in the center was from a maple burl, its curling grain promising hard rigid strength. The nocks at the ends were elk-antler, translucent as amber, and they were carved with gripping beasts in the style of her own people. He must have gone looking for that, consulting some book or Lady Juniper.

Sam grinned as she took it up and held it out, feeling the sweet balance.

"Six foot two, reflex-deflex, and near eighty-five pound even on the tillering frame for the draw. Oi don't think that'll overbow you, you've bin practicing 'ard. That hickory bow Edain made you out east is a foine piece o' work, but you'll be needing two at least, for a long campaign, and mountain-grown yew is best at the last."

Asgerd swallowed. "Thank you, good father," she said. "This is lovely work, and a real battle-tool. I will not dishonor it."

"Oi can still make 'em, just slower loik," the old man said, and waved away her thanks.

Then he winced and halted the motion.

"Don't you fuss at me too, girl," he said sharply as she came forward with a frown on her face.

"I'm not fussing, I'm finding out what's wrong!" she said sharply, and pressed down on his shoulder.

He winced again, but was silent long enough for her to probe the muscles along the ridges of his spine with ruthless fingers.

"All right, good father," she said briskly. "On your face. This bench will do."

"Thank you, girl, but—"

"But nothing. I grew up on a farm too, old man; do you think I've never seen a man who's pulled his back before? And I know what to do. I've done it often enough for my father and my brothers!"

The glare turned to a wry nod. "Oi wonder if my boy knows what 'e's gotten 'isself into," he said, and obeyed. "Damned if Oi don't loik you, girl. You go straight at things."

"See if you like me so well after I'm finished; this is going to hurt," she said.

Asgerd looked along the bottles and jars racked behind the workbench. There would be oil, and . . .

Her nose led her to a small vial. "Wintergreen, good," she said. "Too strong, though. I'll mix it with some oil. Now let's get to work."

She rolled up the sleeves of her shirt and did. Her father-in-law's breath caught once or twice, but he made no other sound. When she was finished he sat up cautiously and worked his shoulders while she cleaned her hands on a rag.

"Believe that's eased it," he said.

"Now go and rest for a few hours," she said; when he bridled, she shook a finger in his face. "You wouldn't overburden a piece of wood, why do you think your spine is any different? Do just as you please, good father, but if you don't rest now you'll be stiff as driftwood tomorrow again, *and* as brittle."

He laughed softly. "Yes, ma'am," he said, and got up.

The door from the inner house opened, and a faded woman in her fifties with yellow-brown hair liberally streaked with gray came in. She was not in the usual Mackenzie kilt, but in the shift and tartan arsaid that older woman often preferred—an arsaid wrapped around the waist to make a long skirt under a belt, and then one end was thrown over the shoulder and pinned. She was taking off the apron she'd worn over that, and dabbing at a flush of sweat on her face with a corner of it that wasn't stained or flour-coated.

"Sam?" she said. "Are you all right the now?"

"Better than Oi was, luv," he said.

His expression made the leathery weathered surface of his face crinkle into a web of wrinkles, but also made it seem younger too as he smiled at his wife. His daughter-in-law could feel the love there, not much spoken but as comfortable as a low fire of coals on a cold day.

"Asgerd 'ere gave me back a bit of a rub, where it were stiff this last while. Now I'll 'ave a nap, if you can spare me. Be fresh for the big dinner, eh?"

The woman blinked. "That's a fine idea, we'll be eating about sundown. Nola and Nigel are in their truckle beds there too, be careful not to wake them, now. It was hard enough to get them asleep and out from underfoot."

"Oi will, luv. They sleep 'ard as they play, at that age, eh?"

She looked after him and shook her head, then looked at Asgerd. Blue eyes met blue.

"Well, and how did you manage *that*? Without clouting him hard enough to crack the thick stubborn skull of him, to be sure."

Asgerd ducked her head. Edain's mother was mistress of this household, and she knew her manners.

"Good mother, I . . . I just told him I'd been raised on a farm and knew what to do when a man pulled his back, and not to be foolish but to lie down so I could fix it."

She indicated the bench. Melissa Aylward came over and looked at the dish of improvised liniment, sniffing at it.

"Essence of meadowsweet and sunflower oil. That would do nicely. I add a little mint-water when I make up a batch for the stillroom."

"My mother does too," Asgerd said. "But there wasn't any to hand."

Melissa nodded. "So it isn't all swords with you, then, girl?"

"Oh, no," Asgerd said, surprised; though they hadn't had much time to talk, or she thought much inclination on the older woman's part. "I trained to arms, we all do in Norrheim just as you do here, but I wasn't a shield-maid until my man Sigurd . . . the one I was to marry . . . was killed. By the Bekwa savages, led by a red-robe, a *trollkjerring* of the CUT. I heard that the night I first saw Edain."

Quick sympathy lit the other woman's face, and Asgerd turned her head aside slightly.

"That is a good loom," she went on determinedly, walking over to where it stood tall at the other end of the big room. "My mother has one much like it—a bit higher, a little narrower."

"Sam made it for me . . . sweet Brigid, twenty-three years ago last Imbolc," Melissa said.

Asgerd touched the satiny finish of the wood, pegged and glued together from oak and ash, beech wood and maple, and carved with running vines at the joinings. Just now it was set up to weave a stretch of blue cloth with yellow flowers at the corners, half done but already lovely.

One of the good things about weaving was that it could be interrupted for something more urgent and taken up again an hour or a day later; she supposed that was why it was usually woman's work, though she'd known men who did it well. If there was anything that made for interruptions more urgent and more often than a small child, she'd never heard of it.

Melissa went on: "He copied it from Lady Juniper's that she had from before the Change—she taught me to weave, like many another. We like to work here together in the winter afternoons, Sam and I; he'll be at the bench, and I at the loom."

Asgerd looked more closely, whistled under her breath, and traced one of the joints with her thumbnail. It was so close-set there was hardly even a catch when she ran it across the surface; the whole of it was like that, mortise-and-tenon joins pegged together with almost invisible smoothness. Even the king-bolts that could be taken down to disassemble the whole thing for storage were countersunk to be out of the way yet instantly accessible.

"This is beautifully made, so light and yet so strong!" she said.

Every ounce of unnecessary weight in a loom's moving parts was something you felt in your shoulders and back after a day spent weaving; any half-competent carpenter could knock together something that relied on sheer bulk, but paring weight to a minimum without losing strength or rigidity took real art at every stage from selecting the materials on.

"Like fine cabinetwork," she went on. "I've never seen better."

Melissa swallowed. "Sam always has been proud of his carpentry and joinery, though, sure, he doesn't talk about it much," she said. "People came from all over to learn it from him, those first years. Bows yes, but not just those, and he made . . . oh, looms and churns and a dozen other things, getting ideas from books and old things from museums and then figuring out how to do them properly. And they came to learn farming from him, too, the old ways of doing it, he'd go 'round giving a hand to all and showing the way of it. There's many alive and well today on the ridge of the world with children and grandchildren of their own, who would have starved half to death or outright died without my Sam!"

Asgerd nodded. After courage and loyalty, a man's pride was in the strength and skill of his hands, the work that fed his children and made strong his house and kindred. She knew that love of craft as well, and the kindred pride in keeping going uncomplaining when your bones groaned with weariness and all you wanted in the world was food and bed.

"Lovely," she said again, and sat at the weaver's bench.

When Melissa nodded permission at her inquiring glance she ran her hands over the heddle and beater, touched her feet to the paddles that would shift the warp and weft and the cord and lever that would throw the shuttle, looked at the little wheeled baskets that held supplies out of the way and yet to hand.

"This would be a pleasure to work at," she said. "I can feel how everything's *just* where you want it."

"That cloak you brought, was that your mother's work? It's well done," Melissa said. "Only a little worn, and you must have used it fair hard on a journey like that."

"She taught me but it's my work, good mother," Asgerd said, letting a little of her own pride of craft show. "That journey cloak, I sheared the sheep and cleaned and spun the wool and wove it; it's a twin to one I made for Sigurd to use when he went in Viking to the dead cities. Just plain weaving, of course, nothing fancy like this, but it *has* worn well, and it's kept me warm and dry many a time."

"It must be nearly waterproof, done with the grease in that way," Melissa said.

Then she sighed and sat on the bench before the loom, beside the girl.

"I'm . . . I know I've been less welcoming than I might. Than I should have been. I've been . . . anxious about things, sure and I have, and more things than one. And the Lady is taking me out from under the dominion of the Moon now, into the Wise One's hands and near to my croning."

That puzzled Asgerd for an instant; her people didn't have a formal ceremony for that, as they did for coming of age. Then she nodded understanding.

"All of which I offer as some poor excuse," Melissa said.

"Good mother, I didn't expect a dance of joy when your son came home with a stranger, a foreign bride. You don't know me or my kin or my very folk. I could have been an ill sort, one who did him no credit. I'm not like that, but I expected to have to prove . . . Well, if a man of my kindred, say one of my brothers, had come back with a Mackenzie maid for handfasting, it wouldn't have been all hot mead and kisses at first from the women of my kindred either!"

"It's been hard, with Edain away, hearing nothing but the odd letter, and those often of some battle or peril he'd been in and me not even knowing," Melissa said softly, her eyes seeming to look beyond the wall.

"I can see that. I've been frightened for him more

than once myself, even there with him! Though it was a comfort to have Artos King on hand."

Melissa nodded. "Rudi . . . Artos . . . is a great hero, one whose song will live forever. Yet it's perilous to stand too close to a hero in a tale! He's been in and out of this house all his life, and I love him too; Lady Juniper was my sponsor in the Craft, and . . . But Edain is *mine*, my first son, the babe I bore beneath my heart and carried in my arms, new life in those years when it seemed death had swallowed all the world."

"And he always will be your son," Asgerd said. "You and the good father raised him to be a fine man, strong and kind both. My man, the one I will walk beside all my days, shipmates through life, and who will be the father of my children. The grandchildren I will lay in your arms, good mother."

"I would like that, sure and I will like it very much indeed," Melissa said.

Then, unexpectedly, she chuckled. "Though with twins only two years old myself . . . I hadn't expected that, after twelve years without a hint and not for want of trying. There's a good many infants around this house the now!"

"The twins are fine children!" Asgerd said, with genuine enthusiasm. "So strong already, like little Ratatoskr-squirrels for dashing and climbing, so bold and fearless!"

"So hard to keep out of everything that might burn, cut, drown, crush or poison them!" Melissa said. "The great thing with *grandchildren* is that you can hand them *back* to their parents and get a moment's rest now and then!"

Then she extended a hand. "Shall we start again, and see what comes of it, Asgerd Karlsdottir? Asgerd Aylward Mackenzie, too?"

Asgerd took it in both of hers. "I would like that. And

now let me help with the rest of this feast. I can chop and mince and peel a potato and knead bread and roll pastry and baste meat, even if I don't have all the kitchen arts you do." With a wry smile. "Of which I have heard the praises sung near every evening for full three thousand miles of campfire meals, let me tell you!"

Melissa laughed again, carefree this time. "Girl, with that in your ears day and night, it's surprised and astonished I am you didn't hate me already by the time you arrived!"

They stood and made for the door, arm in arm.

CHAPTER FOUR

Ritva Havel blinked. "I thought I was fully recovered from the concussion," she said, stepping back and lowering the point of her wooden blade.

"Aren't you?" Ian Kovalevsky said anxiously, doing likewise and letting his shield down.

Neither of them went entirely out of stance until they were three paces backward. He was barely limping anymore, and neither was she, though they were still being careful. Not as careful as Dr. Nirasha would have liked; but they were both in their early twenties, in robust good health and in a profession where a fairly casual attitude towards risk was part of the package and wounds just a cost of doing business. Ritva doubted the doctor would have approved of the padded practice gear, or the cloth-wrapped wooden swords in their hands. The hot, bronze, hay-smelling distances of the shortgrass prairie stretched around them, with the white walled mass of the Anchor Bar Seven homeplace tiny in the distance, and the blue eye of the little lake and the green-and-yellow streak of the irrigated land. An eagle cruised not far away, looking over a flock of ewes and lambs, but respectful of the mounted shepherdess' bow.

"I thought so, but I could *swear* that's—"

She went over to her saddle by the picnic basket; their mounts were grazing free, both being too well trained to need hobbles. The binoculars were securely cased; she freed them and trained them to the northwest.

"Ah, the *palantír en-crûm*," Ian said; he'd been picking up a little of the Noble Tongue. Then he blinked. "That isn't a bunch of cowboys or militiamen, is it?"

"No," she said, without taking the glasses from her eyes; her voice bubbled with delight and curiosity. "I'm afraid not."

Kovalevsky looked down at the picnic basket with its earthenware jug of beer, roast-beef sandwiches and pickles and salad and Babushka pirozhki, sweet pastries stuffed with sour cherries and nuts. His vanishing hopes were in his sigh. Ritva began stripping off the practice gear. The redcoat did the same.

"Who is it?" he asked in a resigned tone, absently rubbing at the still-sore point on his right buttock where the arrow had struck.

A series of liquid trills answered, and then she shook her head and dropped back into English: "Sorry, forgot."

Poor boy. You actually had a pretty good chance of getting lucky, she thought. *You're sweet, which is a welcome change from Hrolf.*

"I think it's my aunt," she went on. "My mother's younger sister. The *Hiril Dúnedain*. A party of my people."

By the time the party reached her it was obvious. A dozen Rangers, all of them known to her—the Dúnedain weren't so many yet that she couldn't remember them, especially the ones based out of Mithrilwood. She waved and called greetings to the green-clad riders. They had a couple of Anchor Bar Seven riders with them, probably from the patrols; one peeled off and galloped for the homeplace.

Lots of remounts and they've been pushing hard, she thought.

You could go nearly as fast as a rail-borne pedal car if you had three or four horses and switched off several times a day. For a while, at least, and if you didn't mind your backside getting thoroughly tenderized. There was a very old joke about a book titled *Thirty Years in the Saddle,* by Major Assburns.

And in front of them all were Aunt Astrid with her disturbing eyes of silver-rimmed, silver-threaded blue, Uncle Alleyne blondly handsome, Uncle John bulking huge under a red-brown thatch just showing some gray with his greatsword slung over his back, and raven-headed Aunt Eilir beside him grinning. The whole ruling quadrumvirate of the Folk of the West; it must be something important to bring them all out here in the middle of a war when they'd be badly needed closer to home. Everyone dismounted, and Ritva went to one knee, put hand to heart and bowed: "Well-met, my liege-lady and kinswoman; and all of you, my kin, my brethren."

Astrid smiled and advanced, holding out her hands. Ritva placed hers between them. Close-to you could see that she'd spent many days in the saddle moving fast, but she showed the strain little as yet, though there were small lines beside those odd compelling eyes.

"Ritva Havelion, you have brought honor to the People of the West. You have helped to bring our King, your kinsman, back once more to his people. You have helped to lay the very foundations of the Kingdom of the West, of Montival. *Mae coren!* Very well done!"

Ritva felt herself blushing, and astonished at it. Off by yourself, you could think of Astrid Loring-Larsson as something of a figure of fun, however formidable. In her presence, the sheer burning power of *belief* caught you up again. Looking into the moon-rimmed eyes, you saw yourself as something else again from the light of common day.

I don't think I have it in me to believe in anything *quite that strongly. Does that mean I'm more sane, or something less than she is?*

Then, rebelliously: *But I probably have more fun!*

"Did you see Rudi . . . Artos, Aunt Astrid?"

A brilliant smile answered her. "We did, at Castle Corbec, for the handfasting with Princess Mathilda."

Neithan! she cursed silently. *Bad luck to be laid up healing.*

She didn't resent it . . . much. There simply had been no time to waste waiting for her, and she hadn't been in any condition to be moved. War was like that; she might have been crippled or killed, with only a little less blind luck.

"And we saw the Sword of the Lady. Marvelous, a wonder, like Glamdring or Orcrist or even Andúril Flame of the West!"

I hope you didn't tell *him that,* she thought. *Mary and I tried to convince him to name it Andúril and he didn't react well* at all.

"Through it the light of the Elder Days is brought to Middle Earth once more. And we are on a mission of our own at the High King's command," she went on. "One which will bring the Rangers glory and undying fame!"

Uh-oh.

"The code name is Operation Lúthien."

We are so fucked! she thought.

"We'll need fresh horses, Ritva," Alleyne said; he dropped into English for that, looking at the redcoat. "I understand they're available here?"

"Yes, sir," Ian Kovalevsky said. "This ranch raises them and sells saddle-broke four-year-olds, and the Force and the Militia regiments have brought in more."

Ritva introduced him, adding: "A very brave man, and he fought extremely well against the Easterlings . . . the Cutters. The Force are the local equivalents of the Rangers."

A party was riding out from the tented camp beside the homeplace. They cantered up the rise and drew rein, a dozen men in light-cavalry gear over plain gray-green uniforms of linsey-woolsey. Their leader was a tough-looking bandy-legged little man of about forty with a face like an intelligent rat and sergeant's chevrons riveted to the short sleeve of his mail shirt. He took off his helmet as he dismounted, scratching vigorously at his cropped graying brown hair, and then his eyes went wide in astonishment.

"Little John? John 'ordle? Fuck me sideways! You're alive?" he blurted in a thick clotted accent.

"Was last toime Oi looked!" Then the big Ranger did a double take himself. "Geoff? Geoff Bainbridge? What the 'ell are you doin' 'ere, Geoff? You were on Salisbury Plain, last toime Oi saw you, drivin' a Challenger. Oi got over 'ere from Blighty about fifteen year ago. Thought *you* were a gonner these twenty-five years."

"Ah were on a trainin' course at CFB Suffield, me and two thousand others, just before the Change. Lucky as fuck that were an' all!"

"You don't know the 'alf of it, mate!" Hordle said feelingly.

"Aye, Ah do. An RN ship docked at Churchill three

year back and dropped off a packet o' English newspapers. Sounds laak it were raaght bad back 'ome for a while. Expected Leeds were totally fooked any road—seems Ah were raaght. Raaght bad all round, sounds laak."

"Bad? Fuckin' 'ell, worse than bad, mate. Worse than bad . . . but over quick, for most of 'em at least. How'd things go over 'ere?"

"It were raaght rough the first couple o' years 'ere too; fuckin' Calgary and Edmonton near dragged us down wi' 'em an' buggered t'lot o' us. Would've, if hadn't been so fuckin' cold, that got most who walked out. Then we got things sorted out, laak. Ah've got a wife an' kids and a bit o' a farm goin' a ways north o' 'ere now. Till Ah got called oop fer this lot, any road."

"We need some 'orses, Geoff. Quiet loik, away from pryin' eyes. Paperwork'll all be done roit later."

"Ah think sommat can be dun," the little man grinned. "If that there redcoat lends an 'and."

"Good. 'Ave a sandwich, mate," he added, taking one out of the basket in each hand and starting his own with an enormous bite. "S'goof," he added through a mouthful.

"My picnic!" Ian said . . . but quietly.

"You Rangers can *move*," Ian Kovalevsky said a week later. "Even by the standards of the Force."

"They sold us good horses back at the Anchor Bar Seven," Ritva said; they both had the habit of talking without looking at each other as they rode, which was useful—her eyes were moving ceaselessly and so were his. This was potentially hostile country. "And we have well-callused backsides."

Ian grinned. "After the way you got wounded bringing the alarm about the Cutters and your brother Artos saved everyone's bacon by showing up in the nick of time it's not surprising. You guys could have had the horses for free, if you'd asked. With me thrown in."

The Rangers—plus one member of the Force sent on *special detached service* by an amused and agreeable captain—were riding under a bright cloudless summer sky. Around them lay bunchgrass and bluestem turning from green to gold, whispering in long ripples to the end of sight and standing high on the horses' fetlocks. Land crept by to the steady walk-trot-canter-walk pace, changing from flat grassland to occasional steep wooded hills, or cut by deep ravines and then subsiding to open level ground again. This high plateau that had been known as the Eye of Idaho once; white-topped mountains showed west and east, with the deceptive look of the big-sky country that fooled you into thinking something three days' ride away was only a few hours' distance.

The air was warm with summer, but not hot; they were four or five thousand feet up here. Small blue flowers starred the tawny-green grass in swales where the dark basalt soil was damper, and insects burst out of it before their hooves, or now and then grouse or partridge. Ahead, the party's spare two-score remounts—the remuda, which despite the sound was a Spanish word, not Sindarin—grouped together in a well-trained knot, requiring only an occasional canter by the pair assigned to rearguard to keep them bunched. She was glad of that; leading reins were a trial, especially when you had three or four horses each. A big remuda was the way to travel fast, though. With enough remounts you could make a hundred miles a day or more in summertime, especially if there was good grazing or feed available along the way.

"Beautiful beasts," he said.

Ritva nodded, watching with pleasure their glossy hides move. These weren't the ones they'd taken south over the Drumheller border, through the lands where the Dominion, the PPA, the US of Boise and the Prophet's domains met over hundreds of miles in a tangle of wilderness they all claimed but mostly didn't control. They'd given the garrisoned fortress-city of Moscow a wide berth, and then Nez Perce supporters had supplied remounts at the northern edge of their territory; the nascent Bearkillers had made friends there and elsewhere in this district when passing through Idaho right after the Change, and *Hiril* Astrid had been with them then. She'd returned last spring, as well, and had renewed those ties with locals who didn't care for President-General Martin Thurston and his wars.

These glossy Appaloosa-spotted beasts were still quite fresh, and they'd brought the Ranger party far and fast. Now it was time to meet the next set of helpers here in enemy territory.

Though I should remember Idaho *and its people aren't the enemy. The usurper Martin Thurston is the enemy, and his ally the Prophet of the Church Universal and Triumphant.*

They swung westward a little to skirt a marsh where water glinted amid stands of reeds and patches of open water; the Rangers were in a loose diamond formation, carefully irregular so as not to attract attention from a distance by hanging up a *we are military* sign.

Ducks lifted thousandfold from the swamp, and white herons waded around its edges, probing for frogs; a line of old fence posts stood disconsolately in the shallow water, tilted and blackened, gaps showing like missing teeth and with a few strands of rusty barbed wire still clinging to them here and there. There was a dense fringe of youngish willows and cottonwoods and other water-loving trees tangled with undergrowth along its edges, and the horses snorted and shied as the party approached.

The Dúnedain leaders had probably veered that way to keep the timber between them and prying eyes on the higher, drier ground eastward beyond the wetland. Ahead someone stood in their stirrups and raised a hand, then swung it leftward: *investigate.*

Ritva swung her horse into a lope with a shift of balance and the grip of her thighs, an arrow ready on the string of her recurve saddlebow. Her mount was usually a well-behaved beast, but laid its ears back as they approached the woods, and now and then snorted in a fashion that plainly said in Horse: *Smells bad, boss. Are you sure you want to go there?*

When its hooves started to squelch a little and the ground gave off a rich muddy smell she leaned far over, left knee bent and right heel hooked around the saddle horn as the horse walked slowly along the edge of the firm ground. The marks in the bare mud between two clumps of grass were unmistakable, cat-pugs about as broad as she could have spanned if she stretched thumb and little finger apart as far as they would go. Bigger and squarer than the more common cougar, and mountain lion didn't like this sort of ground anyway. Tigers, on the other hand . . .

They do like a swamp, the stripe-kitties, when they can get it. Big snowshoe feet and they swim well too. Is it my imagination I can smell him? No, it's there, like a tomcat, but even more rank. A male then, and big, warning off his brothers. The wind's in my face, right from the woods, so he can't be too close or the horses would be acting up more than they are. I wish we had Edain and Garbh along, she's the best tracking dog I ever met.

The lead party had halted. They'd be looking at her with Astrid's Zeiss binoculars, an heirloom from her father Kenneth Larsson. Ritva remembered her grandfather with affection—he'd died in a boating accident when she was about fourteen—and he'd loved gadgets, having been an engineer as well as a very wealthy man before the Change. The 20x60 S-type monstrosity was typical of the sort of thing he'd collected, with an utterly ingenious mechanical stabilization system that hadn't been in the least affected by the Change, and it would make nothing of a thousand yards. She pulled herself back into the saddle with a flex of the leg, then slipped her bow back into the scabbard at her left knee and the arrow into her quiver, stood in the stirrups and brought her hands before her face, palms in.

Then she made claws of the fingers and raked them outward sharply, twice, making the gesture broad and obvious. That was Sign for *tiger*, and her honorary Aunt Eilir had made the visual language part of the Dúnedain curriculum, back when she refounded the Rangers together with Astrid in the years after the Change. That was probably because she'd been deaf since birth, but also because it was extremely useful to be able to exchange complex information silently.

Two more of the party trotted back on the other side of the remuda, pushing the beasts towards the marsh and its fringe of woodland despite their unease. The commanders came up; *Hiril* Astrid was casing her binoculars in their padded-steel case.

"That was good scouting, Ritva," she said with a nod.

"Thank you, my lady," Ritva acknowledged.

Which was a bit formal, but they *were* in the field, not sitting over wine in Stardell Hall listening to a song or a reading from the Histories. The four older Rangers looked a little more worn than their followers; not that they were anywhere near their limits, merely that there was more discomfort behind their hard-held faces.

"Scout net," Astrid said, and two more of the Rangers trotted away.

Alleyne brought out a map, and everyone else squatted around it with their reins looped through their belts and their horses occasionally taking a nuzzle at their hair.

"This marsh isn't mapped, but I think it's *here*," he said, tapping a spot. "The wetland's probably recent. Within the last twenty years from the trees, though cottonwoods grow bally fast."

"And this St. Hilda's place should be about six to eight miles south and west," John Hordle rumbled, his finger moving over the waxed linen like a sausage with auburn fuzz.

Astrid sighed. "This all looks so different from when Signe and Mike and Dad and I came through in the first Change Year," she said, gesturing at their surroundings. "Most of this was plowed land, winter wheat and black fallow, with gravel roads every mile. See where the dimpled lines run, with more sagebrush and less grass? That's the old roadbeds."

"The ironic thing," Alleyne said, his eyes still on the map, "is that there are probably more people living here now than then. There wasn't any famine here, and this Lewiston place over a bit west was a substantial city and the ranchers here must have taken in some of them. And of course everyone's been breeding like rabbits since."

That's an odd thing for him to say, Ritva thought absently. *Uncle Alleyne and Aunt Astrid only have three themselves. That's not many at all.*

"There was black plague in Lewiston," Astrid said, her weirdly beautiful face looking stark for an instant. "Pneumonic form. It came in with refugees from Spokane; we heard about it, and Mike turned us back when we saw the smoke from where they burned the bodies. Saw it. And . . . we could smell it. But I know what you mean."

It took a moment for Ritva to follow the thought; she was distracted by the casual mention of a journey that had become a legend in itself, and hearing her father—whom she barely remembered herself—referred to so humanly as *Mike*. It had been Astrid who coined the great title of Bear Lord for him, much against Michael Havel's liking, from what she'd heard.

But I've been on a longer trip, and one that will be more of a tale! she thought suddenly. *All the way to Nantucket and . . . well, not quite back, for me, not yet. Dad would have been so proud!*

Ian nodded agreement.

"It's the same where I come from, sir, ma'am," he said, in English—he'd been following the Sindarin conversation fairly well after a spell of total immersion and a lot of saddle-time studying a borrowed phrasebook. "We have more people now than before the Change in the Peace River country too, but there are abandoned fields and big grain elevators and such all over. We only need . . . oh, about one twentieth the tilled land. Less, maybe. I guess it must be like that in a lot of places."

"Lot o' people fed from these fields," Hordle said. Unspoken: *And they all died when food couldn't travel far anymore.* "No need to farm most of it now, loik the lad says."

Eilir Signed: *But we know St. Hilda's still there. Sheriff Woburn said it's thriving, in fact. And it's friendly; it should be, the way you guys rescued them from those awful bandits back in the day. He said he'd have the Abbess . . . Reverend Mother Dominica . . . warned to expect us. We need local help approaching Woburn at his own ranch. There's sure to be some sort of government surveillance.*

Ritva winced slightly at the reminder of what was fairly ancient history to her, because the tendrils of it came down to her own time. The bandits' leader, the self-proclaimed Duke Iron Rod, had turned out to be working with Norman Arminger, who'd tried to push the PPA's borders this far in the early days—Lewiston was the head of navigation on the Columbia-Snake system. Eddie Liu, the first Baron Gervais, had been his liaison with them, supplying weapons and advice; he'd been the Lord Protector's right hand in any number of malicious plans. But his son had been Odard Liu, and *he'd* been one of the nine questers who'd gone to Nantucket. He'd saved Mathilda's life in battle at least once on the journey, and might well have saved them all in Iowa by the way he'd kept the mad tyrant Anthony Heasleroad amused and distracted.

And he'd died just short of the goal on the shores of the Atlantic, in a last stand that left him lying like some paladin from a *Chanson* with a broken sword in his hand and dead Moorish corsairs in a ring around him. She'd watched him die, making his last farewells calmly despite the bone-spears in his lungs and smiling as he felt the breeze of Azrael's wings.

Not fair to blame us in the younger generation for our parents' sins. You have to keep that in mind a lot with the PPA. Odard could be a pain in the ass, especially all that time when he was trying to get into our pants just so he could notch the Havel Twins on his belt, but he really shaped up on the Quest and got over himself. That last part of it he was like an obnoxious brother you love anyway.

"We should approach them carefully, even with the password from Woburn," Astrid said. "The probability of running into enemy agents goes up very sharply from now on, and nothing attracts the eye like group movement. This here would be a good place to keep the horses; there's cover, water, and grazing. And the tiger's scared off a lot of the game, so hunters are less likely to stumble across us."

Hmmm, Ritva thought. *You know, she's right. I haven't seen any elk or black-tails or buffalo or antelope for the last hour or so. And there should have been sign of muskrat and beaver around here, it's prime for them.*

"Kitty might 'ave a go at the 'orses," Hordle mused.

"Not too likely with, say, four guards," Alleyne said and nodded thoughtfully. "This is rich land in high summer, and a tiger would have to be very hungry indeed to try for something guarded by that many humans. Easier to go out where it usually hunts, and cats don't go looking for fights."

Eilir nodded. *Unlike humans. We should do a sneak. Here, west of the monastery, through these wooded hills. Then we can send one or two people down to make contact.*

"Let's do it," Astrid said. "Time presses, the armies are already moving toward battle in the West, and Operation Lúthien *must* succeed in time. Coneth, you're in charge here."

A short, olive-skinned young woman silently bowed with hand on heart.

"I'm leaving . . . Hírvegil, Tarachanar and Ýridhrenith with you. Hold and keep close concealment for three days, and then use your initiative if we haven't returned."

Ritva felt a moment's sympathy as Coneth gulped slightly and bowed again.

"N'i lû e-govaded ' wîn, Hiril," she said, which meant *Until we meet again, Lady,* roughly.

Rangers had discipline; within fifteen minutes a rope

corral had been made on a dry spot shielded by half a dozen willows for the remuda, the pack-beasts offsaddled and the gear and supplies covered by camouflage nets, and the stay-behind party were busy building a concealed blind—what Dúnedain called a *flet*—in the limbs of the biggest cottonwood. The rest of the band switched to fresh horses and remounted.

"By pairs, at ten-minute intervals, and be careful not to cross each other's paths. *Gwaenc*—we go!" Astrid said.

Why did I have to be the one person *sent down to make contact?* Ritva thought a little sourly underneath the pine trees. *I'm not really a diplomatic type. Oh, well, it's part of the job.*

Most of the Rangers were farther back, keeping watch in all directions. Eilir looked at her and smiled a little impishly; you could see her mother Juniper Mackenzie in her then, though her face was longer.

Then the world seemed to shift a little. With a tiny shock Ritva noticed that there were more small lines beside her eyes, and not just weariness and the weathered look of those who were often outdoors regardless of rain or season. Eilir Mackenzie-Hordle was growing older.

Whoa. It's just being away two years. She looks fine and I'm older too—not a teenager anymore.

Eilir was a mother and near to middle age now, though it would be a trim handsome middle age. It was natural, the Doom of Men . . . but somehow it felt as if the ground had stirred.

Mary and I went to join the Rangers because Mom *seemed like a prematurely old fuddy and granddad was dead and the Rangers were all young like us . . . and because the Histories spoke to our souls, of course. And Aunt*

Astrid was family, and Eilir was for all practical purposes except Mom never really liked Lady Juniper but come on, Rudi's my half brother, get over it, Mom. Mithrilwood was like an endless game that never had to stop. But it's not a game, it's life. I'm grown up now.

Eilir's grin got wider; a lifetime spent lipreading had also made her uncannily acute at following expressions.

You're growing up, niece of my anamchara, she Signed. *Even Astrid and I did that, you know, eventually. Mithrilwood isn't Neverland, nor yet Aman the Blessed. It's just home and the place my children were born, which is fine enough and more.*

Ritva replied in Sign herself, which was policy where even low voices might be overheard: *Ah . . . sorry . . . I was just wondering, Why me? really. For this contact mission.*

Really?

When you were used to it, Sign could convey dry pawky irony as well as any tone of voice.

Eilir went on briskly: *Well, we picked you because you're the most experienced Ranger we have here who's not well known yet. We four are. I'm deaf, my beloved little John's freaking fee-fi-fo-fum huge, Alleyne looks like, well, Alleyne, and Astrid is . . . Astrid,* she Signed. *And because you're younger and people pay less attention to the young. Because you're a woman and people feel less threatened by women—Manwë and Varda alone know why. Plus tall fair people fit in even more here than most places. Take a look, familiarize yourself with the layout.*

She handed over the precious Zeiss glasses and Ritva leveled them across a low-cut stump; the woods on the hill above the settlement were obviously carefully managed and healthy. St. Hilda's Monastery lay below them, the shadows just beginning to lengthen. From the look, most of it had been there before the Change, but there had been a great many alterations and more than a few additions. The core building was built of bluish-gray stone, twin-towered, as much like a castle as a church, and surprisingly modern in appearance; the lower windows had been sealed. There was a brick wing that had the alien boxy look of late pre-Change work, and a stretch of buildings off to the north.

Farther out were truck gardens, fairly substantial orchards, and a big neatly laid-out farm with fields of varied crops separated by board fences and rows of poplars; a few hundred acres of wheat and barley rippled, yellow streaks showing amid the light green. More recent construction surrounded by fenced paddocks was probably barns, storehouses and workshops; the tall arms of a timber-framed windmill were unmistakable, though the sails were feathered and bare right now. Several well-kept dirt roads led away, east and north and south; they were fairly busy, wheeled traffic and bicyclists and folk on foot.

All in all it looked like a prosperous town, or perhaps a great noble's estate, except that there were no obvious defenses. Though the twin-towered church could easily be turned into a fort: the chronicle Astrid had written of the Bearkiller journey westward, *The Red Book of Larsdalen*, said that the bandit lord Iron Rod had done exactly that.

They all gathered at the back of the hillock to see her off, except for the lookouts, of course. Most of that was to take turns examining her from head to toe; you always did that when you could, before a clandestine insertion. Nobody caught everything, and a different pair of eyes was always welcome.

I'll look less conspicuous without this sword, Ritva Signed, though she'd feel naked without it, too. *Straight long swords aren't much used here, from what we've heard.*

Ian hadn't learned the finger-tongue yet, but he understood when she undid her weapons belt, and silently held out his own with the stirrup-hilted curved saber and bowie. Sabers were the second-most-common long weapon in Idaho, after the wider-bladed cutting sword known as a shete. She slipped it out of the sheath and tried the balance; somewhat heavy for her wrist, but the weight wasn't thrown as far forward as she expected. You could thrust with this, though not as well as with the double-edged blade the Dúnedain usually carried.

She buckled the belt, drawing it in to the last notch and working the leather there to make it look used before tucking the tongue in and out, and checked herself over.

Ian was helpful again: "That braid is sort of distinctive too."

Eilir clucked her tongue in agreement, and Ritva sighed and turned, kneeling and letting her quick fingers undo their own work.

The Ranger fighting braid did what it was supposed to do—keep your hair out of your eyes when you were moving quickly—and it was ornamental, running from brow to nape in a series of intricate tucks and plaits. Unfortunately, nobody else but the Folk of the West used it, as far as she knew. Also it was impossible to keep up all by yourself.

And Mary and I aren't always together anymore. Good luck with Ingolf, sis, and I still wish I'd won the toss for him. Though Ian is refreshingly nice, I think. I have got to stop being attracted to Bad Boys like Hrolf. They don't change.

Eilir tapped her on the crown of her head to show it was done; now her wheat-colored hair fell halfway down her back in a single simple braid, tied off with a plain rawhide thong at the end.

None of them were in the special Dúnedain field kit right now; they'd packed that away and picked up bits and pieces of local gear to give the right mixed look and plausible little details of craftsmanship and style. Only the wealthy or their close retainers dressed in new or nearly new matched outfits, now that the last reserves of pre-Change salvage had worn out or rotted. Standing out from the patchwork masses was one of the main reasons the upper classes spent lavishly on that look.

Ritva wore stout nondescript boots and doeskin pants and a long pullover linsey-woolsey shirt, a broad-brimmed low-crowned hat and a kerchief around the neck drawn through a leather ring, all none too clean after their long journey. A sheepskin coat worn bald in places was rolled and strapped to the blanket behind her saddle; her re-curve in its scabbard by her knee would pass as the type anyone might use, and a quiver and round shield were as much part of outdoor wear as shoes. She had laced leather arm-guards and steerhide gauntlets, though armor would have been going too far.

All in all, she looked like many another thousand cow-girls here in the mountain and range country.

Except where the Cutters run things, she thought with a scowl. *They think women in pants are an abomination. But then, they think pretty well* everything *is an abomina-tion. From the way most of them smell, soap included.*

Here in notoriously well-policed Idaho it wasn't even so very odd that a comely young woman would come into a town by herself. She'd still be noticed; strangers were always noticed. The only places she'd ever been where that wasn't so were a handful of large cities. And there weren't more than a handful of large cities *in* the world a generation after the Change, a world where the overwhelming majority lived in places the size of St. Hilda's or smaller.

"I'm off to Bree," she said, and Aunt Astrid chuckled.

"Let's hope there aren't any alarming and unexpected delays with your contact."

St. Hilda's wasn't *entirely* without defenses. A quartet watching some black-coated Angus in a meadow noticed as she cantered along with a packhorse on a leading string, and three set arrows to their bows as they legged their horses closer while another drew a shete.

Closer, and she could see that the archers were women, and the man with the shete was a hard-worn thirty and with only two fingers on his mutilated left hand. That could have been an accident in half a dozen trades, but she would bet on a sword-cut. He rode close and checked her over, noting the rolled pup tent, duffel bag and camping gear on her spare horse.

"Your name?" he said, sheathing the blade.

"Jane Cross," she said, falling into a ranch-country rasp.

It was actually the accent of the Bend country just across the Cascades from the Willamette and Mithrilwood, but it would pass anywhere in the interior in a casual conversation with people expecting a stranger. Local ways of speech had diverged widely in the last generation now that twenty miles was a good day's journey again and everyone from farther than that a de facto foreigner.

"What're you doing in these parts?"

"Lookin' for respectable work and a bunk, before summer's past, sir. Maybe some place to settle."

"You don't look hungry."

A shrug. "Rabbits ain't hard to come by, but . . ."

He nodded understanding. Anyone with the right tools and skills could feed themselves for a while in the wilds in the warm season, though even then it was risky to travel alone. A simple sprain or fall could kill you with nobody there to help. Winter would be deadly. Plus even if there was much empty game-rich land between settlements all of it anywhere near civilization was claimed by *somebody*, who'd eventually run off a vagrant hanging around the fringes. You had to; neglecting that was how bandit gangs got started.

"How come you're wanderin' loose?"

"My Rancher up in the Panhandle country had to let some hands go, what with the war and the taxes. Got no kin there now, my folks is dead and they were from Spokane way back. Don't know how they'll manage without us, but—"

She shrugged. The man nodded, a little sympathy softening his hard scarred face.

"You're not the only one on the road. The good Sisters do what they can, but times is hard hereabouts too. All the younger menfolk gone with the call-up, and fewer hands to do the work and taxes higher than ever so the Ranchers have trouble payin' the ones they do have."

She looked at the wounded hand; it was healed, but the mutilation must have been fairly recent from the purple flush still around it. He shrugged. "Damn Protectorate shellbacks got me at Pendleton last year, the knight-boys. Anyway, tell 'em up at the convent that Seven-Finger Jack passed you through."

She nodded respectfully, and walked her horse forward as he reined aside.

Rudi would have left Idaho alone if Martin Thurston

hadn't allied with the CUT and attacked us, she thought. *He is a wicked man, a parricide and a bad ruler and he must be put down, but I wish we didn't have to kill and maim honest farmers and herdsmen to do it. If we can bring all these lands into the new High Kingdom and under the King's Peace, people can live safely by their own firesides and reap what they sow. Now* that's *worth fighting for!*

"Even worth dying for," she murmured very quietly to herself. "Though I'd rather not. It's a fine summer's day and I'm young yet."

She rode past a gate. There were tents up in what was usually a pasture, and more in the orchard beyond; their occupants seemed to be mostly women and children. Closer to the main buildings of the abbey several long sheds were under construction, with work-crews pounding earth down between the moveable frames and trimmed logs and shingles waiting to make rafters and roof.

One of the workers looked up and then climbed down the ladder to walk over towards her; Ritva politely dismounted and even more politely hung her saber from the saddle over the bow-scabbard. The greeter was a nun, not much older than Ritva and with her dark robe kirted up to her knees, showing practical denim pants and boots beneath. Her sleeves were rolled back from hands thick with mud, and more splashed on her cheeks and her off-white headdress.

"Seven-Finger Jack said to tell you he'd passed me through," Ritva said, and gave her cover story again.

"I'm Sister Regina," the nun said. "Welcome to St. Hilda's! I'd shake hands, but—"

A laugh, and a wave of a capable-looking muddy paw.

"What can we do to help you, child of God?"

"Ah . . . I'm looking for a place I can sleep safe and

not be bothered 'cause I'm female while I look for work," she said. "I'm more than willing to pitch in with anything here, too. I can rope and brand, do any sort of ranch job with stock or crops, milk and churn, spin and weave. I'm not afraid of sweat and I'm not picky." She put on a scowl. "I tried the army, but they've got this fool new regulation against women, even if they can pass the tests and volunteer. Didn't used to be like that in the old General's time! Not for the cavalry, at least."

Sister Regina smoothed a scowl of her own with what was obviously an effort of will.

"We live by the Rule of St. Benedict here," she said, pointedly looking at the worn, sweat-stained hilt of Ritva's borrowed saber. "We insist on peacefulness. There is no room for quarrels here."

"I'm peaceful as all get-out, sister, as long as others are peaceful around me. I don't belong to your Church, though."

"That makes no difference; you belong to God, as do we all."

She pointed up the graveled dirt track. "You're welcome to stable your horses there, and your gear will be safe—you can deposit any money or valuables with the Bursar for safekeeping. We're crowded, but there will be a place to sleep, and food for you and your beasts."

"I can pay a little, sister."

The nun smiled. "We ask nothing, not even many questions. Our houses are the Inns of God, the last refuge of the weak. Help in whatever way you wish or can, when you can. God bless you."

Ritva pushed on; the place had a hospital, and a big school—apparently one for girls, who all wore an odd archaic pinaforelike uniform. On top of that, it looked to be taking care of a lot of displaced people, cripples and the sick and just plain desperate, the detritus and back-wash of war and of a government harsh in its demands and merciless with any sign of dissent.

It took a while to get the attention of the harried sisters in charge without being obtrusive, and all of them looked too junior to trust with her message to the Mother Superior. For that matter, many of the nuns and all of the gray-robed postulants looked younger than her own early twenties.

Supper was served in a long refectory that had been hastily converted from some sort of storehouse, clean but very plain and very crowded indeed, mostly with people who looked as if they had stories worse than the one she was using for cover. It was dim, as well, lit only by pine-splints clamped in metal holders to the walls; that probably meant they were economizing on the fats usually used for lamps, keeping it to cook with or make soap instead.

The food was dark bread, butter and cheese and chipped plastic bowls ladled full of a thick soup of barley and potatoes and other vegetables that tasted as if it had some passing acquaintance with meat-bones on the stock side of its ancestry. There was enough if no more, but the meal would have been more appetizing if it hadn't been clear that the bathing facilities were being worked in shifts too, and if there had been fewer unhappy children, some of whom needed changing.

When her group was finished eating she helped load bowls and plates and carry them to the kitchens, and volunteered to help wash. That ended up meaning mostly carrying wood to feed the hot-water boiler. There were many hands, but she was taller and stronger than most here. Patience finally got her close to the middle-aged Sister supervising the whole process.

"Hot work, sister," she said, grinning and wiping her forehead with one sleeve; it was still warm in the building, though cooling rapidly into the clear night air outside. "Hope there's water enough for a bath?"

"Cold water, I am afraid, child," the nun said.

"That'll do fine, in summer," Ritva said cheerfully. "Like to shake your hand in thanks for you folks' kindness. Makes me think well of your religion, so to say."

The nun beamed at her in a tired sort of way. Then her eyes widened very slightly as she felt the scrap of paper in Ritva's palm. The corner was dark; she seized the Ranger's hand for a moment, turning it over and examining the calluses before dropping it and casually tucking the folded note into a pocket in her habit. If you knew what you were looking for a person's hands were one of the best indicators of what they were. Most people had calluses; even clerks usually developed one on their pen finger. The patterns were very distinctive, though.

You got a very particular set from drilling with the sword for hours a day nine days in ten from the time you were six or so. That was one of the things even a really skillful disguise couldn't completely hide; Ritva had the *swordsman's ring* of hardened skin running all the way from the tip of her right index finger around the web of her hand and up to the top of the thumb.

"Sleep well, my child," the nun said smoothly. "May only good visions visit you."

Ritva was tired, but she thought she might not have slept all that well even if she hadn't been waiting. There had been a stress on the *visit* part of that.

Waiting for arrest, perhaps, she thought mordantly. *I'd certainly be more comfortable out under the stars. Praise to the Valar I got the outside place!*

The long tent was so old that it smelled of a pre-

Change synthetic canvas, much patched over the years with this and that. It was also very crowded and too warm for blankets; all women, or older girls, but no children. Someone not far away had an alarmingly persistent cough, too. She found being confined with that rather more frightening than most straightforward dangers; you couldn't shoot a germ with arrows or cut it with a sword.

A glimmer of starlight and lighter air, and a hand touched her shoulder.

"Come, my child," the figure said very softly.

The dark habit disappeared in the moonless light, but the coif gave the face an eerie detached frame. It was the same nun she'd seen in the kitchens. She was glad that the Sisters weren't so otherworldly that they let more people than absolutely must know a secret.

"I come," Ritva replied as quietly.

She picked up her boots and followed that beckoning, walking a dozen paces with dew-wet grass soaking through her socks before she could stamp them in to the welcoming leather. The night smelled of green growing things and wetted dust, intensely clean and welcome.

"There's someone back there with a very bad cough," she said quietly.

"We know. It's a chronic pulmonary disease, not tu-berculosis. Probably caused by smoke. Unfortunately we can do nothing for her but pray and give morphine when the pain is bad. Beds in the hospital are needed for the treatable sick or the infectious and those closer to death."

They walked together beneath the rustling fruit trees of the orchard, the pruned branches just over their heads with green apples showing like the fists of babies. Most of the settlement was dark as well, with only a few lanterns glowing, but the high rose window of the church shone.

As they approached down a narrow lane flanked by

poplars, Ritva heard slow solemn music and voices singing. A swelling chorus of women's voices, rising and then sinking to a background as a single high clear alto rose with an almost unbearable intensity:

> *"Ave Maria, gratia plena*
> *Dominus tecum, virgo serena;*
> *Benedicta tu in mulieribus*
> *Que peperisti pacem hominibus*
> *Et angelis gloria*
> *Et angelis gloria—"*

For an instant she shivered with a feeling that was chill down her spine, yet without the slightest hint of threat or malice. It was not her faith, nor was this a way of life that had the slightest attraction for her, but there was a power and clarity in it that could not be denied.

Many paths, she thought. *Trite but true.*

They came to a small door; the nun unlocked it before them and then secured it behind again. Up a narrow staircase, feeling her way along with one hand on the worn pine of the handrail. Then the kindly glow of lamplight from under a door. The nun made a gesture to stay her and slipped through the door; a moment later after a murmur of voices she returned, beckoned, and then left with a smile.

That's a little odd, Ritva thought an instant later as she returned the nod. *We didn't exchange more than a few words, but I actually feel as if I knew her.*

The chamber within was an office, but there was a neatly made cot in one corner, and a window that probably gave on the interior courtyard when it wasn't tightly shuttered as it was now. The walls were unplastered brick, and the battered pre-Change metal desk and shelves bore books and account-books and sheaves of indexed letters arranged very neatly. The only touches of color were a portrait of a robed woman with *St. Hilda of Whitby* beneath it, a Madonna and Child, a beautifully carved modern crucifix and a portrait of the current Pope, Pius XIII, that looked like a woodblock done from a photograph.

Ritva made the gesture of reverence that the Dúnedain shared with the Old Religion towards the holy images, clapping her palms twice, softly, and then bowing with them pressed together and fingers beneath her chin. *Her* people were courteous towards the fanes of others, whether it was reciprocated or not. Then she stood easily, waiting a moment for the lady of the plain clean chamber to speak first if she would.

It wasn't a bleak room, though; the austerity was of a friendly sort, the bareness chosen because it sufficed and didn't distract from things thought more important. The stern-faced woman behind the desk probably looked friendly often enough too, judging by the way the lines around her mouth and eyes lay. Right now she looked very tired, and not just because she'd probably been up all night, and extremely serious. Her face was rather horselike, and Ritva judged she'd been about the Ranger's age at the time of the Change.

No point in a who-can-wait-longest match, and I'm the guest here asking for a favor, Ritva thought.

Then she put her hand on her heart and bowed. *"Ni veren an gi ngovaned, naneth aen,"* she said. "In the Common Speech, I am very pleased to meet you, Reverend Mother."

"Sit, my child," she replied, with a wry quirking smile. "I have been expecting this visit for some time, since my last talk with Rancher Woburn."

Ritva pulled a small knife from her boot-top first, slit

open a seam on her belt, and produced a set of thin onionskin paper documents. The abbess took them in worn fingers, fished spectacles out of a pocket, turned up the lamp and read. At one point she looked up sharply. "The *leaders* of the Dúnedain?"

Ritva spread her hands, and the Abbess nodded.

"Yes, there is no need for me to know more about that."

At last she sat back and sighed, then crossed herself and bent her head over clasped hands for several long moments, in prayer or meditation.

"You come highly recommended," she said when she looked up again. "Not least by Abbot-Bishop Dmwoski and Father Ignatius. I know of the Order of the Shield of St. Benedict, and news of the good father's vision of the Virgin in the Valley of the Sun—"

She paused to bow her head to the Madonna.

"— has spread widely to us of the Church."

"I was with him on that journey, Reverend Mother," Ritva said. "I'm not of your faith, but he is a very holy man. And a very clever one as well; clever, brave, a faithful friend. The High King has appointed him Lord Chancellor of Montival."

The eyes of the Abbess were a cool blue-gray. They studied her for a moment before the religious spoke herself: "But his is a militant order, and necessarily involved in politics and war. We . . . are not. We have our life here according to our Rule, here and in the daughter-houses we have established since the Change. We work, we teach, we heal, we help God's poor, and for our joy and our rest we have prayer. All this I would endanger, if I help you and you fail. Possibly even if you *succeed*, in the end."

Ritva nodded gravely. All that was perfectly true. Reverend Mother Dominica *had* to think of it. She was responsible for her followers, after all; and for all those who depended on her Order.

"Everything you are and do is endangered if we lose, Reverend Mother. As it was in the days of Duke Iron Rod, but more so."

The older woman flinched; very slightly, but Ritva was sensitive to such things. *Oops,* she thought. *She must have been a member back then too. Or one of Iron Rod's prisoners, or both.*

"I have tried to forgive," the nun whispered after a moment. "But to forgive evil men is not to submit to the evil they do. You are right that we owe your family a debt from those days."

She sighed. "I've also heard of this Sword of the Lady. A pagan thing, and a pagan King wields it."

I'm a pagan thing *myself,* Ritva thought; she restrained herself from arguing: *It's all different avatars of the same Lady, right?*

Christians could be irritatingly rigid about that. She'd had two years of Father Ignatius' implacably polite certainty to drive home the lesson.

"I'm the High King's half sister," she pointed out instead. "And I've known him all my life and besides, it's the same with us Dúnedain as it is with the Mackenzies: it's a point of *our* faith that everyone finds their own path to the Divine. We're in more danger from you than you from us. There will be a lot more Christians in Montival than anyone else, and your type of Christian is the commonest. Matti . . . the High Queen Mathilda . . . is one of you. Whereas the Church Universal and Triumphant . . ."

"They are evil and they serve evil," the Abbess whispered. "I don't say that idly or simply because their theology, the public version, is absurd. There must be freedom—even for error." She smiled a little. "Even for taking the stories of a long-dead Englishman who was a good Catholic with appalling literal-mindedness, for example, my child."

Ritva suppressed an impulse to stick out her tongue. She suspected that the Abbess read it anyway.

"But while that may be *wrong*, it is not *evil*," the Abbess continued earnestly. "And General-President Thurston has . . . changed since he came back from his meeting with the false Prophet Sethaz in Bend last year. He was always a very hard man, very ambitious, but . . . the new decrees are ominous."

"They're straight out of the CUT's book," Ritva said; she'd been reading the briefing papers the leaders had brought along during the ride south. "And they're just a start."

"Can you tell me what *use* you will put our aid to, if we give it?"

"No, of course not, Mother Superior. You don't need to know. That's *need to know* in the technical sense. You know we'll use it to fight the CUT and the parricide Martin Thurston and I can't give details."

A long silence, during which the older woman's gaze turned inward. Then: "Yes. Tell me what you need us to do."

"No more questions?" Ritva asked.

The Mother Superior smiled. "If it is to be done at all, it should be done well. When you make a decision, think carefully, pray, consult where appropriate, and then *make* it. Half measures give you all the drawbacks of each alternative and none of their advantages."

Ritva rose and bowed a salute, hand to heart, as she would have done for her own superiors.

"So also says the Lady of the Rangers, and the other

leaders of our people, my kinsfolk," she said. "And my brother Rudi . . . Artos . . . as well. Are you sure you were never a soldier, Reverend Mother?"

She smiled and shook her head. "Only a foot soldier of Christ, my child. But in this office I have had to make decisions in plenty. Your aunt is a wise lady, if she grasps that, because it is not an easy thing to do. And your High King doubly so, because he is still a young man."

A slight wince. "It is no easier when lives ride on it."

Ritva listed the aid that Operation Lúthien would need. The Reverend Mother sighed, pushed herself back slightly from the desk, and opened a drawer that proved to hold a typewriter.

"What you need, then, is primarily information and recommendations," she said, as she inserted a sheet of paper in the roll. "Between us, St. Hilda's and Rancher Woburn will be able to furnish those."

Then she smiled; it made her face much younger for a moment, reminding Ritva of Mary's—which was to say, herself—when they were thinking up some prank.

"In fact, we may be able to furnish unexpected help *from above*, so to say."

Ritva nodded. *I wish I could be as carefree about this as Mary and I used to be on missions,* she thought. *But this time it's not just my life. It's the life of my home . . . not just the Dúnedain, either. All of Montival.*

CHAPTER FIVE

CASTLE ODELL, COUNTY OF ODELL
(FORMERLY NORTHERN OREGON)
PORTLAND PROTECTIVE ASSOCIATION
HIGH KINGDOM OF MONTIVAL
(FORMERLY WESTERN NORTH AMERICA)
JULY 31, CHANGE YEAR 25/2023 AD

C astle Odell was small compared to the great fortress-palace of Todenangst, but substantial compared to anything else built in the PPA's territories since the Change; towers and curtain-walls and rearing central keep beneath bright banners. Conrad Renfrew had started it in the second Change Year, right after he was granted the fief to hold as tenant-in-chief, direct vassal of the Crown.

After he'd conquered it for the Association, Sandra Arminger thought.

The carriage of the Lady Regent of the PPA rolled past the tents of the levy's encampment and men gaped or gathered to cheer as the black-and-gold coach and its escort of men-at-arms and mounted crossbowmen of the Protector's Guard swept by. More bowed and then waved and called greetings in the town.

Though considering who was in charge before, it's no wonder he's always been popular here. Not something that you could say about all our new lords. Mind you, Lady Val-

entinne had a good deal to do with it, starting with being native to the place. Tina mellowed him, which caused problems with Norman if not with me. He was still angry about the accident and the scars in those days, and she helped him deal with that.

His engineers had used Lenz Butte as the base, rising nearly two hundred feet over the rolling surface of the valley; the little red-tiled town of Odell clung to its base to the east by the road and railway, dwarfed by the castle and the newly completed Cypriot-Gothic cathedral. The slopes below the white-stuccoed ferroconcrete ramparts were terraced gardens. Just now they were a blaze of roses, the scent full and sweet in the warm drowsy summer air through the open windows of the carriage. The clatter of her escorts' hooves came through as well, then the hollow drumming on the drawbridge; trumpets rang from the gatehouse, and they passed into its gloom beneath the arched ceiling that held the murder-holes and portcullis and out into light once more.

"This is a bit private, Jehane," she said to her amanuensis as the driver pulled up with a *whoa*. "It'll be easier to tell the Lord High Chancellor to act his age and stop being an idiot if it's all in the family. Keep going on the précis of those reports."

"Yes, my lady. The Castellan here is currently Lord Ramón Gómez González, Baron de Mosier, his family are vassals to House Renfrew. Arms, Gules, a castle of three towers argent, in base a key fessways the ward to the sinister or. His wife is Lady Gussalen of House O'Brian, and they just had their first boy. Named Bertrand. He's taking the field with the rest of the *arrière-ban*, and Lord Akers, Baron de Parkdale succeeds him as Castellan then."

"Lord Akers the elder?"

"Yes, Sir Buzz is down on the southern border with

the forces of the Three Tribes and his own *menie*. They're screening against the enemy concentrated in the Bend area."

"Thank you," Sandra said warmly.

She had most of the same facts at her fingertips, but it was nice to see that Lady Jehane had made such progress. She smiled again, a closed secret curve of her lips.

"My lady?"

"Just remembering how much raiding there was back and forth across that area during the Protector's War. Castle Parkdale was built to guard *against* the Three Tribes. Time, politics and war make strange bedfellows."

A varlet leapt down from behind the carriage to open the door and fold down the step. Sandra gathered the pearl-gray silk skirts of her cote-hardie and let Tiphaine d'Ath hand her and Jehane down. The courtyard was bright, and she blinked for a moment amid the stamp and clatter of destriers and coursers and rouncys, the rattle and gleam of armor. The interior walls all glowed with color as well, climbing roses twined through light lath trellises, until they seemed to flame and shimmer in green and crimson and white and pale pink. There was another clank and thump as the soldiers present all brought their right fists to their chests and bowed, which was protocol for fighting-men under arms in a public venue.

The roses are Tina's work, Sandra thought. *And she does it very well. She hasn't much head for politics but she's not stupid at all.*

"Baron de Mosier," she said to the dark-faced nobleman who saluted Tiphaine and bowed Sandra through into the gate of the keep.

He had a neatly trimmed black mustache and goatee. *Which makes him look like Evil Spock from the Mirror Uni-*

verse. And nobody here but Conrad and possibly Tina would have the least idea of what I was talking about if I said that.

"How pleasant to see you again," she went on. "I trust that Lady Gussalen is well, and young Lord Bertrand?"

"She is very well, God be praised, and thanks be to my patron St. James, to whom I have lit many candles," the man said, trying to hide his flush of pleasure as he crossed himself. "My son is also well, my lady Regent."

"The Grand Constable and I wish to see my lord Count Renfrew. We're expected, you needn't have us announced."

"He and the Countess and their children are in the solar, my lady Regent," the baron said, looking a little dubious at the informality but obedient nonetheless. "We were expecting them down momentarily. This way—"

"I'm sure you're extremely busy with getting the garrison ready to march, Lord Ramón," she said with a smile.

"That is so, my lady," he said as he took the hint.

"Though if you could show my lady-in-waiting Lady Jehane to the reception chamber?"

"I'll see to it at once, my lady Regent. God give you good day."

The escort from the Protector's Guard fell back as well, when Tiphaine raised one pale brow at their commander.

"I think I can take care of the Lady Regent, Sir Tancred," she said dryly at his hesitation.

The Baroness of d'Ath was like a slender silver statue in a full suit of plate, and her fingers rested on the pommel of her long sword. The grip had scales of dimpled black bone; they were cut with twelve small notches, and each had a tiny piece of silver wire hammered in for emphasis. Those represented only the noble Associates she'd killed in formal duels, of course. Mostly on Sandra's clan-destine orders; a few had just been people she thought needed to be dead.

"Certainly, my lady Grand Constable," he said, salut-ing stiffly.

Though you can feel their paranoia burning, convinced that Cutter assassins with curved knives are lurking behind the tapestries, Sandra thought. *Or possibly that the Lord High Chancellor and his family will strangle me and the Grand Constable. Then again, you don't want* much *of a sense of humor or proportion in your bodyguards.*

A solar was always on the higher levels of a keep's tow-ers; that was the only place where it was safe to have larger windows. Castle Odell didn't run to elevators, ei-ther. She lifted her skirts slightly and toiled upward, re-minded of the loathed but conscientious hours she put in on the Steppercizer back home. The floral motif contin-ued in tile and wall-paintings as they climbed—a castle had to be strong, but that didn't necessarily mean bare concrete. Her soft shoes scuffed upward through the nar-row bands of light cast by the arrow-slits, beneath the ring and clang of the Grand Constable's steel sabatons— Tiphaine could walk like a cat in anything else, and didn't apparently feel the fifty pounds of armor at all.

They were as alone as possible; in fact, she couldn't recall being more alone anytime recently, and spent a mo-ment enjoying the unfamiliar sensation. Then she halted at a landing, as if for breath, and spoke quietly.

"What do you think of Operation Lúthien? From your own experience doing special operations for me back in the day."

"I was your assassin, my lady."

"Same thing, and answer the question."

"It's insane, my lady," d'Ath replied. Grudgingly:

"That doesn't mean it won't *work*, necessarily. The Rangers are good at what they do, and they've pulled off stunts nearly as weird. It's just . . . I'd prefer fewer trappings out of myth and legend. Astrid Loring is always the starring lead in her own production of *Middle-Earth: the Fifth Age and the Rebirth of Glory*, playing on the inside of her eyelids."

Sandra laughed, a gurgling sound. "Baroness d'Ath, where are we? At this moment, I mean."

"Castle Odell . . . oh."

Sandra saw a rare moment of confusion on the Grand Constable's impassive, regular-featured face. She was a borderline Changeling, old enough to remember the world before that March day in 1998, but young enough that she usually didn't unless reminded.

"Point taken, my lady. This . . . well, it's not what I expected as the rising gymnastics star of Binnsmeade Middle School, let's put it that way. But unlike the Third Age, the Middle Ages actually *did* exist, once."

"Not like this, they didn't," Sandra said.

"As they should have been," Tiphaine quoted sourly.

"Exactly. I *have* studied history, and believe me I know. And I made sure you did, too."

"I wonder what a real fourteenth-century European would make of the Association?"

"Fascination and horror, I should imagine. He'd probably think he'd been carried off to Faerie or Avalon by Morgan le Fay."

"Or gone to heaven, if it was a woman."

"A good point. Now, Operation Lúthien might work?"

"Yes. With Astrid and her merry band doing it in person."

"Could *you* pull it off?"

"Not now. I'm still better than she is with a sword—in my own opinion—but I've been playing general for years; I'm a little rusty at the ninjitsu. Of course, there are probably plenty of very able up-and-comers, but while they might be a hair better physically none of them would have had as much practice in planning and execution. Both of us are just about to reach the point where increased experience no longer fully compensates for the reflexes slowing down. And even back in the day I wouldn't have recommended anything so risky . . . though the upside if it does work is large?"

"Huge," Sandra said flatly; that was a political question more than a military one.

"And if it fails"—Tiphaine said, and a slightly anticipatory note crept into her normally expressionless voice—"if it fails, all we've lost is one deranged fangirl and a few adults who are still obsessed with tree houses."

"Tsk, tsk, I believe you're letting your personal dislikes influence your judgment, Tiph. Besides which, the Dúnedain Rangers may be very useful to the dynasty in the long run."

"I can see that. A self-financing, independent clandestine operations unit that doesn't have to account to anyone for what it does . . . or for its budget."

Sandra smiled and turned one hand palm up: "Useful, that could be. Convinced, I am."

"My lady?"

"Classical reference. Sorry."

Tiphaine blinked and went on: "But it doesn't need *her* running it."

"It would be better if she did for a while yet. Her own obsessions will make her extremely loyal to the bearer of the *Sword*, you see. Which is to say, to the father of Mathilda's children, and therefore loyal to his heirs, who will be *Mathilda's* heirs and hence *my* heirs and *Norman's* heirs; and with a little luck she'll plant that deep in the Dúnedain cultural memory bank. And in her own children. After that it will be Mathilda's worry, or that of her descendants, but they won't be able to complain I didn't do *my* job."

Tiphaine's lips curled upward very slightly. "As always you see farther than any of us, my lady."

"It's a moot point if we don't win the next campaign, which Operation Lúthien might help with. And now let's try to talk some sense into Conrad about strapping on a sword again at his age."

"Not much chance, my lady."

"Around five percent, if that, but one has to try." A frown. "It's annoying. I *need* Conrad as Chancellor. There's nobody else who has the same precise combination of abilities and contacts and reputation, and who's also absolutely reliable. His sons are too young to fill his shoes yet."

And besides that, I would actually miss him, she thought but did not say.

The solar's inner room opened off the stairwell, and it had a lived-in look of scattered books and pictures, a big embroidery frame for tapestries, a spinet and harp and lute, comfortable sofas and armchairs, a bowl of nuts on a table before the empty swept hearth with its bouquets of roses and dahlias. And it was full of the younger Renfrews. The Count of Odell's elder sons were both in their twenties and blue-eyed like their father, one with light-streaked brown hair and one with dark. They were taller than their father's middling inches, but both were taking after his solid muscular build, which their suits of plate emphasized; the armor clattered as they took one knee before her on the glowing rug. Their younger brother Ogier was taller and lanky and just on the dark side of blond, green-eyed, and seventeen, with an unfortunate spray of acne across his cheeks. The age meant he still probably had a few years of squirehood to go, and also that he was growing restive with it.

He knelt gracefully in his half armor and thigh boots, sweeping off a roll-circled hat with a dangling liripipe tail. That involved transferring the two visored sallets he was carrying to the crook of his left arm. Sandra Arminger extended her hand for the kiss of homage, and to touch the proffered sword-hilts. She had to suppress a smile as Ogier provided a moment of unintended comedy, juggling the helmets and the blade to free a hand and blushing at the noise.

"My lord viscount Érard, Sir Thierry," she said to the older boys.

They're men *now,* she thought. *Do keep up with the times, Sandra! But it does seem only yesterday they were playing hide-and-seek with Mathilda.*

"And young Ogier, ready to win your spurs, I see."

That was more than a metaphor, these days; the older sons had the golden rowels of knighthood on their heels and he didn't. He perked up at the thought, since wars were the fastest way to do so, though he was rather young for it.

The girls were in a cluster of their own; Deonisia, raven-haired, pale and striking at nineteen, with a twin-peak headdress; Genovifa, sixteen, with red-brown hair flowing out of her maiden's plain wimple and freckles and a figure already lush, which even under modern conditions would grow plump before thirty if she didn't watch it, and Melisant who was black-haired like her elder sister and just eight though destined to be tall judging from her hands and feet, solemn in a young girl's long tunics, and already with a reputation for being scholarly.

I must keep my eye on her. The others are loyal and no fools, but she has real potential. She's clever. It would be a shame to waste her on the Church. I'll suggest that she be enrolled as a lady-in-waiting when Mathilda sets up her own household.

"And my ladies of House Renfrew," she said to them, repeating the gesture.

They sank into deep curtsies and then kissed her hand and murmured: "My lady Regent!"

More bows and curtsies for Tiphaine d'Ath, part of the complicated dance of precedence; she was their superior by official rank, and a tenant-in-chief, but not their overlord in the chain of vassalage and of lower title than their parents.

How solemn the younger generation are about it all! They live it. Tiph and I have known these children since they were crawling and dribbling, but the ritual is part of being grown-up to them.

"Is your father still determined to take the field himself?" Sandra asked.

"Of course, my lady Regent," Érard said, looking slightly astonished. "Where else would the Count of Odell be at this hour of peril, unless it was sword in hand at the head of his men, foremost in your host?"

"He has always been House Arminger's greatest support, my strong right arm," Sandra said with a sigh. "Where else indeed?"

Because at seventh and last, he's a male idiot, after all, she thought, as the whole family fairly beamed with pride. *They never really grow up, even the smartest ones. Even poor Norman could be led around by his pride. Led to his death, at the last.*

The young viscount hesitated, then asked, presuming a little on long friendship: "Your Grace, is it true that the High King and the Princess Mathilda have returned and are wed, with a great army at their back?"

The Prophet and President-General Thurston undoubtedly know the strength of the League of Des Moines to the last man and pike, she thought. *There's no harm in encouraging people here by telling them the same things. Don't make things secret just for secrecy's sake, Sandra! That way lies madness.*

She paused for a second, then decided and spoke: "It's true that the High King is in Montival once more; and the former Princess Mathilda is now Her Highness, Mathilda, High Queen of Montival. Though of course we haven't had the coronation yet, that will have to wait a little."

That brought exclamations of delight, and she went on: "They're hurrying south with a substantial force of troops, from our allies to the east and from the Okanogan baronies. And their diplomacy has secured a very much larger army to attack the enemy on their eastern border; over eighty thousand men are marching on Corwin, according to our latest news."

We can fight wars across continents again instead of merely with our immediate neighbors, Sandra thought. *Oh, hurrah for the light of returning civilization!*

"And the Sword?" Deonisia asked breathlessly. "My lady?"

And there's no point in pretending that the Sword isn't what it undoubtedly is.

"The Sword of the Lady is . . ."

Terrifying, she thought. *Like a myth, something out of the Chansons de Geste or Wagner, but actually* there *to be seen and touched. Putting me at serious risk of terminal worldview collapse.*

Aloud she completed the sentence: ". . . all that rumor spoke of, and more. Forged in Heaven for the hand of our High King Artos, like Durendal and Curtana and Joyeuse."

The siblings all smiled and glanced at each other. "That's very good hearing, Your Grace," Érard said. "God be praised, and Holy Mary who watches over the Association . . . I mean, Montival . . . and the Princess . . . High Queen . . . Mathilda!"

"God be praised indeed. And His mother and all the bright company of the saints," she said, and joined in crossing herself.

With perhaps a sliver less sheer pleasure at her own hypocrisy than the gesture usually gave her, since it turned out from all the evidence that there really *was* something to it. It was hard, to be stripped of the cold comforts of her simple atheistic faith in middle-age. The more so as the evidence seemed to lead to the conclusion that *all* the religions were true, including the ones that flatly contradicted each other.

My head hurts when I try to reconcile that with . . . with anything! It's one thing to be an atheist, and another to be a flat earth atheist. But whatever else is true, it's also true that human beings can no more live without politics than they can without air. Politics I can handle.

"Now if you'll excuse me . . ."

She walked through the vestibule; there were no ushers or ladies-in-waiting or other such vermin around at present. This would be a family matter; she and Tiphaine counted more-or-less in that category. As she paused under the open pointed-arch doorway of the solar's light-filled outer room she heard two voices singing: Conrad's growling bass, and Valentinne's light wavering soprano under the tinkling of a lute. Sandra recognized the music and words instantly: it was an old minstrel's tune from the Society days before the Change, but seldom sung as wholeheartedly back then as she heard it now.

It's The Old Duke, she thought. *Well, I knew this was a forlorn hope.*

She paused for an instant, looking through and seeing Conrad's shaven dome beside Valentinne's silver-streaked light brown:

> *"I laugh at those who call me old*
> *Who think my age their best defense;*
> *For often fall the young and bold*
> *Who fail to laud experience.*
> *My sword and I are much the same:*
> *Our actions swift and sure . . .*
> *Each scar I wear, each graying hair*
> *The life I gave to her."*

Sandra felt a slight pang at the sight. There had been no one for her, not since Norman died . . . the politics were impossible . . . and they'd never had quite *that* sort of relationship anyway. The pair went on:

> *"Throughout my life I've led my men*
> *Where Crown and Prince command*
> *And always does my Lady tend*
> *To children, hearth and land.*
> *My wife and I are much the same:*
> *Our actions swift and sure . . .*
> *A husband fair, a home to share*
> *The life I gave to her."*

They started a little as she came into the room. She inclined her head, then gestured Valentinne to continue playing. She did, and Sandra sang the next verse by herself, with a few modifications: she was a contralto, and her voice was larger than you'd expect from someone several inches below average height:

> "To those who thought our lack of sons
> Would end my Norman's line
> I laugh and toast my daughter
> Who upon her throne shall shine.
> My child and I are much the same:
> Our actions swift and sure . . .
> A privilege rare, a crown to bear
> The life I gave to her."

Conrad grinned at her, the hideous old white scars knotting on his face, and all three finished together:

> "So every passing year preserves
> Familiar rhythms and the new
> And through it all I lead and serve
> With joy—as I was born to do.
> My land and I are much the same:
> Our spirits swift and sure . . .
> Each oath I swear, each shouldered care
> The life I give to her."

"It's good to see you again, old friend," she said to Conrad, taking both his hands for an instant.

"And you too, Tina," she went on, exchanging a kiss on both cheeks.

Valentinne was in her early forties, twelve years younger than Conrad. The Countess of Odell was of average height, with the beginnings of a double chin and warm green-flecked brown eyes that were usually happy and a little distracted; there were faint paint-stains on her fingers, from the art whose results hung on walls and stood on the big easel beneath the eastern window of the solar: it was a redoing of her classic *Raoul of Ger and the Easterlings*.

"You haven't been able to talk him out of this folly, and convince him he'd be more useful here?" Sandra said. "He's my Chancellor, after all!"

Valentinne looked as if she'd been crying last night, and she was in the formal cote-hardie that she usually managed to avoid, a pale blue-and-gold affair.

"No, Sandra," she said, a determined smile on her face. "I knew it wouldn't work, anyway."

"Didn't keep you from trying," her husband observed.

"And good to see you, Lady d'Ath," the Countess said; though in fact Tiphaine's cold coiled violence had always made her a little nervous. "How's Lady Delia? She's six months along now, isn't she?"

Tiphaine smiled slightly; the Countess of Odell and the Châtelaine of Barony Ath were good friends.

"Delia's well, but growing huge, and sends her regards. And she'd like you to be there for the accouchement, Lady Odell, particularly since neither I nor Lord Rigobert are likely to be able to take the time."

"Of course, if . . ."

If we're not all under siege in our castles by then, Sandra filled in. *Or dead.*

". . . if circumstances allow," Valentinne finished.

"No reason they shouldn't," Conrad said. "You could take the girls. This campaign's going to start a long way east of here."

The Count of Odell was already in full armor except

for the helmet, which showed his fireplug build; he'd put on some flesh since he resigned as Grand Constable to be Chancellor full-time a decade ago. Now he snorted and rose with a slight grunt and clank, tucking his helmet upside down under his left arm with the gauntlets thrown in the bowl; the bevoir hid his chin and neck, giving his cannonball head an oddly detached look.

"I'm still stronger than a lot of the men I'll meet," he said, slapping the hilt of his rather old-fashioned, Norman-style chopping broadsword. "And age and treachery beat youth and gallantry most times."

Tiphaine d'Ath raised both eyebrows. "Still stronger, yes, Conrad," she said. "Also stiffer, fatter and slower these days. I'd hate to lose the man who helped shape me into the murderous, evil bitch I am."

"Blame Sandra for that," he laughed.

And he's looking positively carefree, Sandra thought. *Men and their games!*

"Besides, I'm planning on directing the levy of County Odell, not fighting with my own hands," he pointed out. "Not unless I have to. Worry about Érard and Thierry more, they'll be at the head of their men-at-arms. And Ogier is at the reckless age."

From the haunted look in her eyes, Lady Valentinne had been thinking along the same lines. Conrad paused to glance out the west-facing windows in their Gothic tracery; he'd be looking down on the rolling orchards and fields of the Hood River Valley, off to Mt. Hood's snow peak, towering dreamlike and huge and distant.

What's he thinking? Sandra mused. *Of how we fought and worked to build this new world? Of what we were, and are, and what we might have been if the Change hadn't come? Or just that it's a beautiful day?*

Then he bowed them out into the other room, and

extended a hand; his wife rested her fingers on the back of his, and they followed. He smiled at his children, as they gravely bowed or curtsied.

"Kiss your sisters and make your devoir to your lady mother, boys," he said, thumping their shoulders as they straightened and grinned back at him. "We have a war to fight. And you girls give me a kiss as well, eh?"

They did, and then the whole assemblage trooped down to the courtyard. The Castellan was there, with an older nobleman—

Lord Akers, Baron de Parkdale, Sandra's mind supplied. *Lamed in the Count's service back when we were doing the first salvage run on Seattle. Son down with the Three Tribes, helping patrol against the enemy occupation forces in the CORA territories. I should mention that.*

There was some ceremony; Lord Ramón passed over the white baton of his office to Lord Akers, who would command the skeleton garrison of oldsters, the halt, the lame and those *really* too young to take the field; the castle chaplain blessed everyone, though doubtless they'd already had morning Mass; and Lady Valentinne bound a favor on her husband's arm, a ribbon she'd woven from flax grown in her herb garden, prepared with her own hands. Her daughters did the same, and for their brothers as well, except for young Melisant, who shyly showed them a book-sized triptych of St. Michael she'd painted in a stiff, glowingly sincere style. She'd dedicate that for them in the Cathedral and burn candles before it until they returned.

At last Conrad stood pulling on his gauntlets, ready to hand her up into the carriage and swing into the saddle of his own traveling rouncy. He chuckled as he slapped fist into opposite hand on each side to settle the leather-palmed metal gloves.

"What's the joke?" she asked.

"That even if . . . that *whatever* happens now, I'm a lucky man. Lucky in my wife, my children . . . lucky in my whole life. Thanks, Sandra."

"Thank *you*, old friend, and take care of yourself. I need you still, your loyalty and your wits and the fact that you were never afraid to tell us when we'd made a mistake. Mathilda will need you, too."

"I'll do my best. I haven't seen my grandchildren yet, though Érard's little Alaiz is expecting! To tell you the truth, I don't know how much the kids need any of us fogies anymore, Sandra. It's their world now, and they're more at home in it than we can ever be. Let's give it to them in good condition."

CHAPTER SIX

SUTTERDOWN
DÙTHCHAS OF THE CLAN MACKENZIE
(FORMERLY THE EAST-CENTRAL WILLAMETTE VALLEY,
OREGON)
HIGH KINGDOM OF MONTIVAL
(FORMERLY WESTERN NORTH AMERICA)
AUGUST 1, CHANGE YEAR 25/2023 AD

F rederick Thurston was the second son of the founding General-President of the new United States—the country everyone else called the United States of Boise. He wasn't in its green uniform, though. He'd insisted on that, wearing a nondescript outfit of coarse-cloth shirt and trousers and brown boots instead, and he was unarmed except for the belt-knife that virtually everyone carried as an all-purpose tool. He took a deep breath, and drew calmness on himself like a cloak; this wasn't going to be any easier if he waited.

I've made my decision. Now I've got to do *it.*

"You should be fancied up a bit," his wife said. "Your uniform, or somethin' to show you're someone."

There was a Powder River rasp in her voice; Virginia Thurston (née Kane) had been born and raised there in the grassland country of what had once been eastern Wyoming, until the Church Universal and Triumphant and its local allies killed her father and seized her family's

Sweetwater Ranch and she'd stumbled into Rudi Mac-kenzie's camp on the edge of the Sioux country on a blown horse. The two of them were nearly of an age, not quite twenty-one, but their looks were very different. Virginia was middling-tall for a woman, slender but whipcord-tough and tanned, with long brown hair worn in a braid, a narrow straight-nosed face and blue eyes.

Fred was a lithe, long-limbed broad-shouldered young man a little over six feet, with bluntly handsome features; his skin was a light toast-brown color, and his short black hair curled naturally. He grinned at his wife; they'd been together just over a year, and married for less than half of that—a handfasting ceremony in Norrheim, on the borders of the Atlantic.

"You look good enough for both of us, honey," he said.

She snorted. Her costume was full-fig formal for a prosperous Powder River rancher's daughter in this twenty-fifth year of the Change, acquired here since they got back to Montival and at some trouble and expense. Linen blue jeans with copper rivets, heeled riding boots of tooled and colored leather, a buckskin jacket worked with colored quillwork and fringed along the seams, a colorful bandana about her neck and a broad-brimmed black Stetson on her head. Her belt was covered in worked silver conchos, and a smaller strip of the same went around her hat; the hilts of her shete and bowie knife were jeweled, if also perfectly functional. More silver and tooling made the saddle and bow case and tack on her gray Arab match the arch-necked mettlesome horse itself, with ribbons woven into its mane. He'd noticed that when it came to horseflesh she was cheerfully rapacious in a way that was probably influenced by the close contact her family had had with the Sioux to the east of them. Or possibly just the obsessive focus on horses natural in a place where they were the difference between life and death.

"You made me drop the chaps, *honey*," she pointed out. "Those were *good* chaps."

"You look like there's a sheep in your family tree with those things on. And anyway, this is the best way to approach them, believe me. They're going to be sensitive as a singed wildcat, seeing me on the other side."

"OK, darlin', you know your own folks best."

They mounted outside the front gate of Brannigan's Inn, where they were staying like most visitors to the Clan's only large town, and rode through the crowded streets and out from Sutterdown's west-facing gate. Fred looked up at the walls; Sutterdown wasn't very large, no more than five or six thousand people, but the defenses were strong. There were still scars beneath the stucco, where cast-iron shot and steel darts had struck in sieges long ago, in the wars against the Association.

Beside the gate on either side were two great statues twice man-height, wrought from the trunks of whole black walnut trees and cunningly carved in the likeness of a woman with long golden hair standing on a seashell on the left, and a naked man holding a bow and crowned with the sun on the right.

He'd been with Rudi and Edain on the Quest all the way from Idaho to Norrheim on the Atlantic and back; he understood something of the theology of the Old Religion, the faith nearly all Mackenzies followed. Sutterdown worshipped the Lord and Lady in the form of Apollo and Aphrodite; that didn't stop them from being just as obsessed with Celtic paraphernalia as the rest, but then the Clan regarded consistency of that sort as small-minded. The smile died on his lips as he looked up at those forms.

Even in the bright warm sunlight of a summer morning there was something disquieting about the face of the Lady of the Doves. At first glance a welcoming beauty as of a woman grown, a mother and lover, but underneath it a childlike wonder, and behind them all a sternness—something not evil or wicked, but as implacable as a winter storm or a glacier grinding its way down a mountaintop. And the face of the God was clear and bright as the sun-rays above it, but in the eyes was a darkness and a mystery, something that you could meet alone in a nighted wood.

"Man, but the fellah who carved that knew somethin' about his business," Virginia said soberly. "I like the Mackenzies well enough, but they're sorta spooky sometimes. You think you've got 'em pegged . . . and then you don't."

"I know what you mean," Fred said, touching the Valknut around his neck.

"Now, *that* was spooky, too," Virginia said. "OK, the Old Man likes you. But him showin' up and saying so, that was just a mite scary, you ask me. Methodists don't have that problem and I like it that way."

Fred nodded. He'd acquired the sign of Odin in Norrheim, when the *seidhkona* sat on the Chair of Magic in the hall of Bjarni Eriksson and the spirit of the High One had possessed her.

Before then, I was looking for a faith. That's when I really found it. Not the most reassuring one, but . . .

Then he grinned. "Remember what Father Ignatius went through? So Methodists don't have that problem . . . not *yet*."

Virginia laughed too, and then suddenly her face went serious. "Well, dang, that would be funnier if it was funny, you know?"

They crossed the bridge beyond the gate, where the Sutter river curled around two-thirds of the town named for it, in a natural moat. Rudi Mackenzie and his guard were waiting for him at the edge of the tented encampment east of town; a dozen had sprung up around the little city as the Clan's levies mustered and moved northward, amid the orchards and reaped fields. Most of the High King's Archers were with him, their racked bicycles behind them, leaning on their unstrung bows or against the trunks of the cherry trees.

Their commander Edain was playing a long side-blown wooden flute bound with silver bands, what the Mackenzies called a Patten, a slow wild smoky sound. His wife Asgerd and Mathilda were standing as Rudi sang to the tune, looking halfway between abashed and laughing-happy:

> "From far away I'm coveting
> Your white violet skin
> And missing the fall of your hair
> Worlds away I'm courting your everything
> And giving you all that I dare
> The wild foxes danced
> When you laughed in your cradle
> The magpies fell silent
> When you learned to sing
> Imagine my luck
> To be part of your fable
> Where you hold my heart
> Like the fruit in your hand . . ."

Fred wasn't much surprised. Most people sang or played; it was the only way to have music, unless you were able to hire specialists or acquire the fabulous rarity of a windup phonograph. Mackenzies made more music, and better, than any group he'd run across in very extensive travels; they'd been founded by a musician, after all, and they associated it with both holiness and leadership.

The song ended, and Edain wiped down the flute and tucked it away in a boiled leather tube.

"Merry met, Fred, Virginia," Rudi said, seriousness dropping over him like a veil.

He was in plain Mackenzie gear, kilt, plaid over one shoulder, knee-hose and green-dyed shirt and flat bonnet with a spray of raven feathers in its silver clasp. And at his right hip, the Sword of the Lady. Fred found his eyes skipping aside from that, and made them steady. After all, if there was one phrase which summed up *his* faith, it was "don't flinch."

"Let's be going, then. Do I need guards for this?"

"No," Fred said.

"Yes," Edain said, simultaneously.

They looked at each other, Fred glaring in frustration; Edain folded his arms over his barrel chest and the green-leather surface of his brigantine armor.

Rudi looked at his follower. "I need to persuade them, Edain," he said mildly. "They're fighting men, and you know how such react if you point an arrow at them."

"That's your job, *Ard Rí*. My job's to be in a position to kill any evil bastard who might take it into his head to win the war at a stroke by killing *you*. And that, by the Dagda, I will do if I have to knock it into your head with His club."

"All right. A score, no more; there are the camp guards, and the prisoners aren't armed."

"No, they're not *supposed* to be armed. And by your own word, they're fighting men. The only time such aren't armed is when they're dead."

Edain turned and barked an order; twenty archers fell in, and strung their bows with the left tip against one boot and the leg over the risers to bend the heavy staves. The High King's Archers were the hundred-odd best in the Clan and the pick of the followers the quest had acquired along the way, and Fred doubted that the fabled weapons of the old world could have done much better than their bows at a pinch.

"I'd better not come at all," Mathilda said thoughtfully. "There was a lot of tension between the Association and Boise, even if we never fought, and Fred's father used us as a boogeyman. Feudal isn't a word with, mmmm, positive connotations over there."

Fred shot her a look. Before he could speak Rudi did, grinning: "*Mo bòidheach*, back then you . . . collectively speaking . . . *really were* the boogeyman."

"Hmmmf. Well, anyway, they don't have any history with Mackenzies, except recently. And you and Edain saved Fred's father's life during that brush with the Cutters, right after we met them out east over the mountains."

"Right you are, acushla. It's not as if you had nothing to do, sure!"

Fred blinked and took a deep breath. His father's death still *hit* him, occasionally. He remembered that occasion just after Rudi and the others had showed up in Boise territory vividly; it was barely two years ago. The last time the world was *right*, before what he thought had been solid dissolved beneath him into a morass of treachery. The desert road in the bright sunlight, the taste of dust, the steady tramp of the troops, his father a grimly competent tower of strength, and still the man who'd been there all his life, the private man the iron reputation didn't know. Then the sudden paralyzing horror as he realized there were assassins hiding in the guard detail itself, and the cloth yard shafts going by with a *whippt* and driving into armor with hard ringing impacts . . .

Before Martin was a traitor. But he was, even then: I just didn't know it. Rudi and Edain killed those Cutter infil-trators, but his own son killed Dad later at Wendell. I didn't think I could hate anyone in all the Nine Worlds as much as I hate Martin now, but he's still my big brother. Even when he was an asshole I loved him, but now . . . I guess you hate someone who's turned on you worse than someone who's just an enemy.

He took a deep breath. *Duty first.* That was something his father's training and that of his new faith agreed on utterly.

"Let's go, Your Majesty," he said formally.

A little to the north was the canal that supplied the town's water and powered its mills; they could hear a grumbling sound through the screen of trees, as grain was ground and wood sawn and flax pounded. Then they turned south and crossed the Sutter river itself and its band of oaks and firs, willows and shaggy meadows; that was Clan land, sacred to Cernunnos and Flidais, barred to heavy use by humankind and the tame animals that lived with men. Its edges were marked at intervals by tall stakes carved with a stag-headed man or a white deer, and the Mackenzies made a reverence as they passed. Several had small offerings of flowers at their feet.

Or it's a State park, he thought dryly. *And protecting stream banks from trampling and erosion makes excellent sense. Though . . . I do remember Dad complaining about how hard it was to enforce regulations like that. Maybe it's easier for people to defer to a Lady who drives a chariot pulled by snow-white deer through their dreams than to bend their necks to a rule in a book written by a bureaucrat far away.*

*Of course, you can just kill anyone who breaks your rules.
I know someone who thinks like that . . .*

"Somethin' on your mind, Fred?" Virginia said softly,
under the clop of hooves and creak of saddle leather.

"I was thinking about home, honey," he said. "My
mother and sisters, trapped there with . . . him."

"We'll see to that," she said stoutly.

He took a deep breath. *Don't flinch*, he told himself.
And in the meantime it was a fair day in pretty country,
riding a good horse past orchards and fields, with the fir-
sap smell of the mountains that reared westward coming
on the warm breeze. And he was young, and the woman
he loved rode at his side, and he was going to set his
people free.

The prisoner-of-war camp was a mile south across flat
open land; close enough to the town to be convenient,
but beyond the ring of crofts worked by people living
within the walls and equally far from the nearest farming
dun. It was shaggy rough pasture and clumps of bur-
geoning young forest in normal times, with low wooded
hills beyond. The camp was rows of tents, or rough barracks built of poles, wattle-and-daub, and salvage goods
from nearby ruins. A board trestle brought in water from
a spring, and a few more substantial buildings had been
run up to serve as an infirmary, cookhouse and bathhouse; there were piles of boards from the sawmills near
Sutterdown, ready to be turned into weather-tight winter
quarters. Neatly tilled vegetable gardens surrounded it
all, and he could smell that it was well policed, just turned
earth and woodsmoke and the warm scents of vegetation
with no reek of unwashed bodies or overfull latrines.

Rudi reined in, and gave a slight sideways inclination
of the head to indicate that Fred and Virginia should ride
in first. There was a fence around the camp, but no wall;

it was a marker rather than a barrier, and the twoscore of Clan warriors with spear and bow looked relaxed enough, like the pack of big shaggy hunting dogs at their feet. A parade ground was already crowded; most of the seven hundred men here had been taken near Dayton, back in March.

Frederick shivered a little. He'd heard about that. A CUT Seeker had been with them. And Juniper Mackenzie had been there too . . .

"Ten-*hut*!" a sergeant barked as they rode up.

The High King's guardsmen put their bicycles on their kickstands and stood at parade rest behind Rudi Mackenzie—or behind High King Artos, probably. They didn't have shafts nocked, but that could be changed very quickly indeed with the bows strung. Fred dismounted and walked forward. The men were braced at attention, but quite properly they were looking at Rudi. A quick glance showed him they were mostly in good health. Well fed, certainly, and only a few showed healing wounds. Their olive-green uniforms were the field model, meant to be worn under armor and optimized for endurance and protection rather than comfort. The rough cloth was clean but worn and patched, and a few had been eked out with civilian gear.

The High King leaned forward on the pommel of his saddle and waved a hand towards Fred.

"I'm not the center of this occasion, to be sure," he said in a clear carrying voice. "Stand your men at ease, if you would."

Fred took a long breath and stepped forward. A rising murmur started to turn into shouts as dozens recognized him. One of the officers drawn up to the right of the block of enlisted men shouted: "Sir!"

That was aimed at Artos, *not* at him; the man was ostentatiously ignoring Frederick Thurston. He was in his thirties and gaunt-looking, with an empty left sleeve pinned to his olive-green jacket. The other hand pointed at Fred, who recognized him; he'd been tight with Martin.

"Sir, this is . . . is unacceptable."

Rudi smiled. "Captain Hargood, isn't it?"

"Ah . . . yes, sir. Centurion Hargood, under the new regulations, technically."

"Well, Captain Hargood, there's naught in the rules or customs of honorable war, from before the Change or since, which says prisoners can't be *talked* at. I can't make you pay attention and I certainly can't make you believe what you hear—wouldn't if I could, unlike some people I could name—but I can and *do* insist that you stand quietly. Now go do it, man, and stop wasting our time."

A pause, then his voice went hard and cracked out: *"Back in ranks!"*

Hargood blinked and recoiled half a pace, then obeyed. Fred took one more step forward and flung up a hand.

"Nobody has to listen to me," he said, pitching his voice to carry as he'd been trained. "Anyone who doesn't want to hear what I have to say can leave right now. No names, no punishments."

The buzz rose and then fell, as the ranks rippled. A good many left; he estimated that it was more than a tenth but less than a fifth. Hargood hesitated, since he was more than smart enough to realize that the exodus was lowering the hostility quotient Fred had to face, but then decided he had to join it for form's sake.

I do like putting an enemy where all his choices are bad, Fred thought grimly.

Not all the looks he got from the rest were friendly, but they seemed willing to listen, at least.

"You're mainly the Third Battalion, right?" Fred said. "That correct, Sergeant Saunders?"

He was looking at a platoon sergeant he'd met on maneuvers when he was in the ROTC. The man licked his lips, looked to either side and then cleared his throat and spoke:

"Yes . . . sir. We got . . . captured in March, up north and east of here."

"That would be near Dayton? Castle Campscapell? Stand easy all, by the way."

"Yessir, big concrete fort, castle, whatever." He paused to lick his lips. "We took it last year, after this CUT guy opened the door, is how I heard it. You know what happened there when we were taken, sir?"

"I heard about that when we got back, yes. I've talked to Lady Juniper about it. She tried to explain and she was using English, mostly, but it didn't mean Thing One to me. Something about casting trouble in your dreams. And she said that she could only do it . . . do it without some sort of heavy blowback . . . because the CUT had one of their Seekers there and *he* was doing things."

The sergeant nodded vigorously. "He . . . he'd talk to you and it was like flies buzzing inside your head, I'm not shitting you, sir. Like the world was twisting into a bad dream, and maybe if it went on long enough you wouldn't wake up. And we're *still* trying to figure out what the hell happened that night; we just . . . had some real strange dreams and then woke up and there were a bunch of Mackenzies standing over us. And that Seeker dude was lying with his body in one place and his head about a yard away and the biggest badass I've ever seen with the biggest Godammed sword was standing over him grinning like a cat."

"Little John Hordle. He is sort of impressive."

"That was how the Third got here. Some of the rest came in just lately, from the Tenth and Fifth and some cavalry pukes, but a lot of those were wounded, and they were all captured in the usual way."

Fred nodded. "Have you men been treated all right?" he asked.

The noncom shrugged, looking a little less nervous; he was a snub-nosed young man about Fred's own age, with close-cropped blond hair and a healing scar across the side of his face.

"Yessir," he said. "It's not a beer-bash being a prisoner, but we got good medical care and plenty of plain food. Better than field rations, a bit. Work details for the enlisted men but nothing too hard and no direct help to the enemy war effort, farm work and lumberjacking mainly, just about enough to earn our keep."

There were nods from many at that. The majority were from farm families themselves, doing their compulsory three years of military service, which became *for the duration* in time of war. They knew that food might grow on trees, but that it didn't prune or water or pick or pack itself, and they'd all been doing hard work since they were old enough to scare birds out of a grain field or carry water to their parents during harvest.

"The guards haven't been rough on anyone who didn't try to escape, either; some've made breaks for it and they got shot or mauled by those fucking dogs when they were chased down and recaptured, but that's by the book if you take a chance on it. Mostly it's just sort of boring. We play a lot of baseball and football and that thing the Mackenzies play, hurley they call it in English, sometimes our team against the guards. They'll even let parties go hunting, if we give our word to come back by sundown, and we get to keep the meat."

"Nobody did that and then ran?"

"Nossir. We, ummm, sort of made sure of that. A promise is a promise and anyway it would screw things up for everybody. Someone wants to try to escape, fine, but no breaking the rules."

"Good to hear it," Fred said sincerely, and asked no more; there were times when an officer was well-advised not to pry. "OK, you're off the hot spot, Sergeant."

Rudi had told him that his mother had strongly suggested that the Boise prisoners be kept in the Clan's territories. There were fewer grudges, and Mackenzies were simply less likely to do harm than some of the rougher barons up in the PPA lands. His eyes went along the line of faces, some angry, a few smiling, more wary and neutral. They all knew who he was; most of the ones who hadn't met him would have seen him at a distance at one time or another. The US of Boise was a very big country, over a million people and that outnumbered even the PPA, but he'd still gotten around. For that matter, he took after his father though he wasn't as dark, and people who were visibly of part-African descent weren't all that common in what had once been Idaho.

He stood at what wasn't quite parade rest and went on: "All right, I'm not a damned fool. There's only one real question: that's who killed my father. Killed the President. My brother Martin says it was me. I say it's him; and I saw it. OK, what about proof? I can't give you any. The nitty-gritty is that you're going to have to decide who you believe. But here's a couple of things to think over."

He squared his shoulders. "Martin wanted to be President. That was something everyone knew. And now he's running things back home. Dad was getting ready to call elections, and since then . . . well, Martin says he may regularize things *when the emergency's over*. Want to bet that's going to be about the Fourth of Never?"

There were some nods at that, but it wasn't all that important to these men. They were all Changelings. They could read and write, his father had been insistent on keeping the schools going even in the terrible early years, but the old world wasn't really real to them. Few of them had the visceral commitment to the old ways his father had had; he didn't himself, though he was closer to it. They'd grown up in a benevolent despotism, thinking of General Thurston as the one who'd saved their families' lives, the stern wise father figure who brought order out of chaos and let every man reap what he sowed. And not least, the one who'd put down the pretensions of budding land-rich would-be patricians.

Not that Dad wanted to be a despot. But at first it was just a struggle for survival and doing what he had to do day by day, and then he thought he could put enough of the country back together first so he could have real elections that would give him legitimacy as something more than a local warlord, and it turned out to be a lot tougher proposition than he thought. By the time he admitted that, a lot of water had gone under the bridge; Dad was stubborn as a granite butte. Martin could probably have won real elections if he'd been old enough to be a candidate under the old system, but he didn't want that anyway. He wanted to be Emperor or something like it, and hand it down to his son. And that was before he started getting involved with the CUT.

"OK, Martin's behind this alliance with the Church Universal and Triumphant. Does *anyone* here like the idea of that? Those people have *slaves*, and they don't even bother calling them *Registered and assigned Refugees* like Pendleton . . . which Martin also allied us with. Dad declared war on the CUT when they trashed New Deseret and he fought his last battle against them at Wendell. Fought them and beat them, I was there. Now they're supposed to be allies working for national reunification alongside the United States. Does *anyone* here really believe that? Is there one single man here who'll get up and say it with a straight face?"

This time the silence was deeper.

Fred went on: "Dad broke up some of the big ranches so guys like you could have their own farms after the Change."

A youngish ranker spoke: "Seems like the Mackenzies did that too."

Fred nodded. *I wish I'd thought of making that comparison, but these men have been around the Clan longer than I have. The Clan at home earning a living, that is, and not just Rudi and Edain traveling through the wilds.*

"Yes, they did."

"They're pretty good folks," another said judiciously. "They remind me of my neighbors back home—except they're so fucking weird, sorry, sir, but they are, and I don't mean just that Juniper Lady who is deeply *scary* weird. They're all weird, putting out milk for the fairies at the bottom of the garden and stuff and talking to trees and animals and going dancing through the woods bucknaked with antlers on their heads and I don't know what else. But pretty damn friendly to us, considering everything, though."

"Some of the girls are *real* friendly sometimes," a man said dreamily, and that brought a general laugh.

"Right," Fred agreed. "But back home, instead of keeping public land in reserve for new farms, Martin is handing out vacant tracts in great big chunks to his cronies and supporters. Not just grazing land like Dad let the ranchers keep, but good land that could support dozens of families. *Your* families, someday, if you're not in line to inherit a farm from your parents."

"Cronies and supporters like Hardass Hargood's family," someone muttered. "I actually heard the son of a bitch say they *deserved* it because of all they sacrificed to serve the Republic, like I'm here 'cause it's so much fun? What the fuck are we, leftover mutton hash?"

He subsided at an elbow in his ribs, but there were nods at that too.

Fred struck the argument home: "And he's assigning the Deseret refugees to work it for them. Temporarily . . . until the Fifth of Never, right? And there are these new laws about what women can do—that's CUT stuff, and no mistake. He's not using them, they're using *him*. Right, now put all that together, and who is it who's really likely to have killed Dad . . . the General?"

Another silence, deep and prolonged; men were exchanging looks, squads unconsciously drawing together. *Squad deep* was Boise slang for *people you can trust*. Another man spoke:

"Right, sir, what do *you* want?"

"I think I'd make a good President," Fred said.

I really think I would. And I know for a fact that Virginia would dance on my face in her cowboy boots if I said otherwise. But I think I would . . . Dad was a great man but his head was stuck in the old world. This one's a different place. Without the machinery, the people *are different, and that's not counting stuff like the CUT and the Sword of the Lady.*

"But I'm not going to just take it. If we—Montival— win this war, I promise here and now, and I'll repeat it whenever anyone asks, that there *will* be real elections within six months. Not 'if circumstances permit' or 'when the emergency is over' because circumstances are never right and life is one fucking emergency after another. Six months, come flood, war or forest fire. And everyone can pick whoever the hell they please, every four or six years or whatever we decide. If it's me, fine. And we can work out a real constitution, because the old one wasn't made with this world in mind and most of the old States don't exist anymore. Folks changed when the world Changed, too."

"And if they tell you and your new friends to take a hike?"

Fred smiled grimly. "If the people—which includes women and refugees—want someone else, well, Hell, I can live with it. I won't starve and I'm not afraid of working for a living, and neither is my wife . . . this is her, Virginia Thurston, by the way. She comes from southeast of us, east of the Rockies on the High Plains. The CUT ran her out of her home; they're doing their job there too, and their job is being evil sons of bitches."

Rudi cut in: "And sure, I'll give Fred a job like that if you don't want him." He snapped his fingers. "There aren't so many good men who are true to their word about that I'd want to waste one. Carry on; just making that clear."

The speaker nodded at him and turned back to Fred: "But you want us to be part of a *kingdom*?"

Fred nodded crisply in turn. "Yes. The High Kingdom of Montival. My dad wanted to put America back together. He was a great man, he made a country out of chaos and plague and people terrified they were going to die. A lot of you wouldn't be here today if he hadn't been that sort of man. Hell, *I* wouldn't. He went back into Seattle to get my mom out when he came back from the scouting mission to Idaho and found things had gone to shit. But by the end of his life, he hadn't even put all of

Idaho back together. Part of Idaho, and a few chunks of what used to be Washington State and Nevada. He didn't want to make war on ordinary people to do it, either. I know Rudi Mackenzie . . . High King Artos, the redhead on the horse over there. We went all the way to the Atlantic together. Some real strange shit came down."

"*Tell* us!" someone said. "The way that witch . . . she's his mom, right? The way she put us all to sleep . . . and held off that Seeker asshole . . ."

"It's a new world. The rules changed at the Change. But the High King can do some of what Dad wanted done—put a big chunk of the country back together. In a different way, sure. But it's one that a whole lot of people have already *agreed* to. So the names are different, big fat fucking hairy deal. It'll mean no more wars among ourselves, no more marching around and burning farms and getting your head knocked in because . . . someone . . . wants to be first in line at the Parade of the Assholes. He's promised, and I believe it, that we'll be able to run our own affairs the way we please. We'll have our own laws, and our own army to back it up. All we have to do is admit that everyone else gets the same privilege, and if they want to dance naked in the woods with antlers on their heads"—there was a general laugh at that—"that's between them and the mosquitoes. We'll put joining the High Kingdom to a vote too. I'm for it."

"I'm for getting back home, Goddammit," someone called. "I want to get back to my girl and the farm and anyone else can call themselves kings or barons or Chiefs or bossmen or the fucking Wizard of Oz as far as I'm concerned. They leave me alone, I'll leave them alone."

"Right," Fred said, nodding vigorously at the roar of assent. "Are there any crazy bastards here who *want* a war? We're all soldiers. We know what fighting really means. Sometimes you have to do it, but that doesn't mean anyone who doesn't have his head up his ass goes *looking* for one. Not just because it sucks for us, but because of the risks to everyone else back home too. Martin's not only got us into a war *here*, he's got the Dominions and the Midwesterners into the fight. The Canuks and the Iowans and their friends are marching right now. Marching towards our *homes* while we're dicking around on other people's ground."

"Is that really true? And do they mean it?" a soldier asked anxiously.

"People, *believe* it. Do you think all these Mackenzies could get together and put a story over on you?"

"Hell, no," the sergeant said thoughtfully. "A lot of the time they can't agree on the time of day. They argue for the fun of it, like it was a poker game. Sometimes they argue and then switch sides and argue the other way 'round just for something to do. Someone would have talked to us. It's true, or at least they all believe it is, and they're not stupid."

"Right. I saw the Midwesterners forming up outside Des Moines with my own eyes, and people, there are a hell of a lot of them and they're not stopping for shit. The CUT killed their Bossman and tried to kill his whole family; his widow's running the show there now and she's out for blood, and the rest of them are baying on that track like hounds after a cougar."

"*We* didn't kill her man," someone pointed out.

"Sure, the Prophet's boys are first on the menu . . . but they and Martin are joined at the hip. He's already pulled troops out of this theatre to go east, you must have heard about that before you got captured. Are you all that hot and bothered to go get killed to defend *Cor-*

win? Or seeing your neighbors and cousins marched off to do it?"

A brabble started to break out, and Fred held up a hand. "I'm not telling you to make up your minds right away. Go think it over. Anyone who wants to come with me . . . that'll be a hard row to hoe. It'll be dangerous and in more ways than one. You can stay here and be safe and get three squares and a place to flop whatever happens and whoever wins, if that's what you want to do. Like I said, think it over. You're free men; make your own decision."

He stood, looking at them steadily. The gathering had turned from a drill-parade formation to a circle of interested men. Now it began to break up into groups arguing or talking, softly at first and then more loudly as they walked away. And some *weren't* leaving, around a hundred.

Fred waited impassively until it was plain who was doing what. Sergeant Saunders, the man he'd talked to first, was the highest-ranking.

I'm not surprised. Martin's made all the officers from company-grade up swear an oath to him personally. It'll take something heavy to shift them. They've got more to lose, too; it would be easier to retaliate against their families than against a lot of anonymous rankers.

He looked at the sergeant and raised an eyebrow; that was a habit of his father's he'd picked up.

"Sir, I don't know about anyone else here, but I'm volunteering to follow you. I believe you and that makes Martin a murderer and a traitor who's sold us to the CUT. Word about that's been going round . . . and I don't like the way a couple of people who got too loud about it disappeared, either. Shit, that's a big fat fucking load of proof that it's true right there. I want to be able to speak my mind without looking over my shoulder and wondering who I can trust! That's no way for free men to live."

"Good man," Fred said, keeping the smile off his face; the last thing he needed was to look like a grinning kid.

Then he raised his voice a little more. "That what the rest of you think?"

Murmurs, and then a chorus of *Yessirs*.

"OK, think about this a little more, people. If Martin gets his hands on you, he'll have you executed as traitors to *him*, sure as God, sure as fate. It's win or die if you enlist with me. And I have the High King's word he'll *try* to avoid having us fighting our own people, use us against the CUT's men . . . but there's no guarantee there."

Heads turned to Rudi; he shrugged and turned both hands up. "I do promise I'll try. I don't give oath I'll always succeed because I don't promise what I know I can't do. That comes back to bite you on the arse, sure and it does, and you end up paying when you can least afford it. As your commander here said, there are no guarantees in war. If you enlist with him, you enlist with *me*, and soldiers under my command do what they're told whether they like it or not, and it will be *not* quite a lot of the time."

Saunders laughed. "That sounds familiar, sir. I'm in. This needs doing. I don't expect to like it. I don't expect an egg in my beer."

A few edged out from the back, but that left over ninety; about as many as had refused to even listen to him.

"Get the men organized by squads, Sergeant," Fred said.

"They mostly are already, sir. I can shift the others 'round."

"Do it. And collect any personal possessions from barracks right away. I don't want a battle here. Oh, and one last thing. All of you remember, if you sign up, you don't get to change your mind while this war's on. Anyone who tries is a deserter and gets what deserters usually do. Understood?"

"Yes, sir!"

"He can't *hear* you!" Sergeant Saunders said.

"Sir, yes, sir!"

"Get them moving, Sergeant."

Several hours later the tents were going up much nearer Sutterdown. They were standard US (of Boise) issue; so was the hoop armor and curved oval shields with the thunderbolt and eagle, the short swords and daggers, the heavy throwing spears stacked while the men worked. It had all been captured with them, and there was more than enough. They'd even been able to match individuals to their own gear for the most part, though Boise soldiers were taught how to modify equipment to fit. Fred smiled as one of them patted the worn, sweat-stained bone hilt of a short stabbing sword in passing, like someone greeting a favorite hound. They hadn't looked beaten-down in the POW camp, but they were walking noticeably taller now, with no fence around them and weapons to hand.

"One thing," he said to Rudi.

The High King of Montival was busy; a messenger handed him sheaves of papers, and he flipped through them in a way that looked casual but wasn't. Every so often he'd drop his hand to the Sword and close his eyes for an instant.

"Fred?" Rudi said without looking up.

"You said you couldn't make them believe anything . . . but you *could*, couldn't you?"

"Ah," Rudi said, handing over the sheaf of reports.

His right hand went to the crystal pommel of the
Sword, moving his palm on it with a caressing motion.
The blue-gray eyes went blank for a moment, as if he was
looking at something within and taking the weight and
heft of it.

"Now that, my friend, is an interesting question. Perhaps not, with so many. Perhaps yes, because what you
said *is* the truth, and the Sword of the Lady reveals truth
as surely as it cuts bone. But I *will* not use the Sword so.
That is my choice, and let that be my responsibility, for
good or ill."

Fred was conscious of a feeling of relief; when Virginia
blew out her cheeks it was an audible mark of the same
emotion.

Rudi laughed. "It's exactly the way I feel about the
matter, do you see? For it shows that I am still . . .
myself."

"I doubt you're as reassured as the rest of us, Rudi.
Oh, and I think it would be a good idea, once I get the
men in order, to let them go back and talk to their friends
in the POW camp, individually or in small groups. Walking ambassadors, right?"

"And to be sure, you're more than a pretty face, Fred."

Fred frowned. "It's not enough, though. I need something to convince the waverers, the ones in the middle
who're of two minds and who just don't *want* to believe
something so skanky could have put Martin in charge.
And more officers would help. We need a *lot* of defections
to even the odds."

Rudi grinned at him. "*Air mo chùram.* Which is to say,
it's on my mind, Fred. Now as to where to use these men

of yours when they're ready . . . I was thinking of adding them to my Royal Guard, so I was."

Fred nodded slowly. "They'll appreciate the gesture, Rudi."

"Not that it means following at my arse all the time, mind you. More a matter of stiffening the battle line at crucial points and being the ones who rush around to the hottest fires."

"Sounds like . . . useful work."

"Sure and if you'd said *fun* I'd have called for the healers of souls."

As he turned away, Virginia slapped her husband on the shoulder. "Turns out you were right about how to handle your folks," she said. "Just don't let it go to your head, you hear?"

Fred laughed shortly. "One platoon? I don't think that's too likely."

CHAPTER SEVEN

General-President Martin Thurston looked down from the gatehouse. His aides glanced at each other; one was annoyed, the other sweating in a terror he could not have named even to himself. Martin knew it.

I know everything, some corner of his mind thought. The joy was unbearable yet detached. *I am knowing. I need not do, only be.* The detachment was the joy.

Existence spiraled downward. Beyond matter, beyond the decay of the last particle, there was only information. All that had ever known, all that had ever been, all that had ever thought. Falling inward towards nothing. It was gross material *things* no more; in some unimaginable future of cycle upon cycle it would *never have been* made of mere things. Only thought, from the flash as the high-dimensional membranes met at the beginning of a universe to the cold death of proton decay at its end and the cycle commenced again, a universe not merely permeated by mind but one that *was* Mind. Thought that was thought about thought, endless repetitions spiraling into—

"Sir."

The vision crashed away in a stab of unbearable sorrow. Thurston turned with a snarl, his eyes locking with the officer's. The man stumbled backward with a scream, the reek of his sweat harshly, hideously *material* in a way that made the ruler's stomach knot; yet even vomiting was itself foul, contaminating. How could you vomit away the gross stuff of your *self*? One of the guards jumped forward in a clatter of armor and put his big curved shield between the man's back and the top of the stone stairs at his heel, grunting as the officer's weight came on the semicylinder of plywood and sheet metal and leather.

He staggered. A hand gripped his arm, and he shook his head, suddenly conscious of the looks of the others.

"What's the problem, gentlemen?" he asked.

"Sir, you looked, ah, odd."

He waved it away, slapping the vine-stock swagger stick in his right hand into the palm of his left. "We were discussing the logistics," he said.

"Sir, with forty battalions that's going to be very tight."

We must move quickly. But we cannot see. The enemy fogs our vision, and above fly hungry birds, ready to eat the seeds we plant.

"Nevertheless, it has to be done. The enemy isn't idle and we have to hit them before—"

You will not die, birds. You will never have been; yes, you and Those who sent you!

HASTY CREEK RANCH
GRANGEVILLE COUNTY,
CAMAS MILITARY DISTRICT
(FORMERLY NORTH-CENTRAL IDAHO)
JUNE 28, CHANGE YEAR 25/2023 AD

The Sheriff's property was not far south of the little town of Craigswood; Ritva thought the core of it had been an inn—what the old world had called a motel—and probably picked because there was good water and a place for a mill at a nearby stream that ran down from high wooded hills to the open prairie. That part was far from the center now, used as housing for bachelor ranch hands. The rest was buildings of rammed earth or notched logs squared on top and bottom or mortared fieldstone, or combinations. Law in the United States of Boise had always frowned on private fortifications, but the layout of the ranch had a foursquare strength and the lower windows could all be quickly closed with loopholed steel shutters.

The Dúnedain party arrived just as the purple faded in the west and the warm butter-yellow of lamps started to make stars of windows where the homeplace lay scattered below them. They rode down a gully through pine forest, out of the strong sappy smell and into the open; a wind from the east brought the homey odors of cooking and woodsmoke and manure. The grim-faced and silent older men and younger women who took their horses away and showed them to the quarters where they could stow their packs and wash before walking over to the main house asked no questions.

Sheriff Robert Woburn greeted them in the vestibule, where they swapped their boots for slippers and hung up their weapons; no doubt in wintertime it also served to keep too much warm air from escaping. He was a lean man in his sixties, his white hair still thick, eyes a snapping blue and face craggy and seamed. His hand was strong but knobby, and rough as raw horsehide.

"I hope we're unobserved," Alleyne said.

"Less traffic here than at St. Hilda's," he said. "The Reverend Mother got me the message and I've arranged to get everyone I'm doubtful of off the place."

"It will still leak," Astrid said. "Just more slowly, hopefully."

"No help for that. And this here is Major Hanks."

"The man with the airship!" Ritva blurted; she remembered it vividly.

Not least because it saved all our lives. Though it's a haywired sort of thing.

"The sort-of airship," the soldier said; he was in plain civilian denim and linen, with a bristle-cut of graying brown hair. "I see you remember our little meeting in Boise and points east."

"Considering how you saved us all, yes, I do," she said, shaking his hand enthusiastically.

"How's Father Ignatius? There was a man who appreciated good engineering!"

"He's helping build a kingdom now, sir," Ritva said. "Artos, the High King, he was Rudi Mackenzie when you met him, has appointed him Chancellor of the Realm."

"Dang, a politician who does sensible things. I may die of shock," he replied, with bitterness behind the smile.

The main hall of the ranch house reminded Ritva a little of Stardell in Mithrilwood. The decoration was entirely different, but the tight-fitting logs squared on top and bottom on a fieldstone base were similar, and so were the exposed rafters above. There was a big stone fireplace in one wall, empty and swept on this warm summer's night, and a trio of tile stoves in corners that probably did more in blizzards even if they lacked the cheery crackle. The walls held hunting trophies, elk and bear, cougar and wolf and tiger. And against the far wall was a skeleton, with the door to the kitchen beneath the place where its belly would have been . . .

"Valar bless!" she blurted. "What's *that*?"

Woburn laughed, and his soldier guest from Boise chuckled. *That* was the bones of an animal that must have been twelve feet at the shoulder, with a massive skull and two long curling tusks.

"An Oliphant!" Astrid said in fascination.

"Mammoth, actually," Woburn said, grinning.

"Same thing," she said with conviction. "Third Age, you see. Where did you *get* it! It's magnificent!"

"Someone found it over at Tolo Lake not far from here a few years before the Change. Nobody wanted it anymore, so I sent a few wagons over to Craigswood when we built this place and brought it back."

"It takes up a lot of room," a daughter-in-law said; she was evidently the lady of the household, black-haired and much younger, only a little older than Ritva herself. "Please sit."

They all did; the Dúnedain, Ian, Woburn and his daughter-in-law, Hanks and a taciturn leathery man in his fifties who was evidently the ranch's top hand. A trio of middle-aged women in housedresses brought out food; platters of grilled pork chops crusted with chili-flavored breading, mashed potatoes with chives and butter, green salads of lettuce and spinach, celery and tomatoes and onions, glazed carrots, orecchiette pasta and broccoli baked with pine nuts and cheese, onion-and-cabbage pancakes with sour cream, hot biscuits and fresh bread, pitchers of cold spring water and several bottles of red wine from down around the Boise area.

"You folks enjoy," one of them said as the rancher nodded thanks.

Despite his friendship with St. Hilda's, Woburn said grace in some different Christian fashion. Ian used the Catholic form, which would be convenient if things went well; after all, the Historian had been a Catholic, and a minority of Dúnedain were too. Ritva tried to imagine one of the more austere varieties of Protestant living as a Ranger, boggled instead and abandoned the effort. Instead she signed her plate, invoked the Valar, and fell to with a will. They'd been on trail food for quite a while, not pausing to hunt or caring to risk a fire; St. Hilda's had been rather Spartan as well.

Nobody's more than three days from being very hungry indeed, she thought. *Which means no lord or ruler is more than three days from very bad trouble.*

She took another chop; the fat at the edge was just as she liked it, slightly crisp.

Dad said that was something rulers should keep in mind, I was young but I do remember that. People get really cranky when they don't have enough to eat.

At last Astrid leaned back in her chair, turning a glass of wine in her long-fingered hands. "You're prepared to take the risk?" she said.

"I'm not taking a risk, I'm trying to avoid it," Woburn said. "I've got two sons with the army. I want this damned war stopped before too many mothers' sons die in it. And Martin Thurston . . . Yeah, I was angry with his father for taking land from us ranchers, but at least he had a real reason. Not just to keep his supporters happy. He's not fit to rule."

"No, he isn't," Hanks said. "He killed his father."

A mirthless smile. "That's why I'm in hiding. Eventually it got back to the National Police that I was one of the ones telling the truth. Sorry, spreading subversive slanders and libels."

Alleyne leaned forward, his hunter's face keenly interested: "How would you estimate the numbers who believe each version?"

"Hard to say. Nobody's conducting public opinion polls these days."

What— Ritva thought. Then: *Oh, going around asking people what they think. I wonder how they did that without getting chopped up or shot?*

Hanks went on: "Assuming I'm controlling my confirmation bias, in Boise city it's maybe half and half. Outside it, patchy. But nobody's talking about it much, either. There's no proof either way and Martin still has a lot of supporters who aren't shy about suppressing slanders, as they put it."

The Dúnedain leaders looked at each other. "So it's evenly balanced," Astrid said. "The High King was right."

"What is it exactly that you want to do?" Woburn asked.

"We want to rescue the captive and tell the world the truth," Astrid said.

"Well," Woburn drawled, "to do that you'll have to pull the wool over their eyes first."

A week later, Ritva Havel restrained an impulse to rub at her buttocks. When you'd been riding as hard and as long as they had, your tailbone kept trying to burst into sight and wave itself.

"Christ, I'm sore," Ian said, and stood in the stirrups and rubbed himself vigorously.

So much for self-restraint, she thought sourly.

They were by themselves, unless you counted two remount-packhorses each and a pair of collies and a flock. The horses were well trained, though they had them on leading reins here on this crowded road near the city. The dogs were *extremely* well trained, enough to make her feel awkward; she could swear they gave her disgusted looks sometimes. The worst of it was the sheep. Two hundred and sixty of Rancher Woburn's animals, driven all the way from the Camas Prairie.

Two hundred and fifteen now, as they approached the capital city. The rest had died in ways that often displayed a certain strain of idiot genius; eaten by wolves or coyotes or cougar was the simplest, ranging up from there to one that had managed to crawl into a culvert just before some rain, get stuck, and drowned. Though the runner-up had strangled itself reaching for a leaf by sticking its head into the fork of a young aspen and struggling until it choked.

The grilled ribs and chops had been *some* compensation. Now they had to keep them from spilling off the road; the suburbs and buildings on the west side of the Boise river had been torn down, like many such around still-inhabited cities and towns, but they had been torn down much more *thoroughly*, including tearing up foundations. Right now they were a dense network of tidy little truck-garden patches, irrigated by canals and windpumps and green with a dozen varieties of fruit and vegetables and small pastures for milch cattle. She didn't want to think of the legal complications of letting the sheep stray, in this rule-obsessed land.

"How on Arda do sheep ever live long enough to breed?" she said rhetorically, after they had headed off a mass break towards rows of carrots whose tops showed green against the dark soil. "Why doesn't someone kill them, for that matter? Not to eat, just because they're so *stupid* and *annoying*?"

They were moving very slowly behind a convoy of wagons, big ones drawn by oxen and loaded with— ironically enough—bales of raw wool. The greasy lanolin-rich smell was unpleasant, but not impossibly so. The road was mostly pre-Change, with holes in the pale aged asphalt neatly patched or filled with pounded crushed rock; they kept up the old custom of traffic taking the right here, and the left was fairly densely packed, which meant they couldn't take the flock around the great vehicles and their crawl.

"I don't know how sheep *do* live long enough to make little sheep," Ian Kovalevsky said. "My family didn't raise 'em. Cattle, yes; beefalo, yes; horses, yes. Even some pigs. But not sheep. It's too cold for them in the Peace River country, and a bit too wet; we trade south for our wool, they have big flocks down around where we met in the Triangle country, the dry prairie. And I thought cattle were dumb!"

"Why couldn't he have sent us with a herd of cattle? You're used to them and I've done a little droving now and then."

Ian shook his head. "Not if we wanted to travel in pairs. You need at least four, maybe six people to push even a small herd of cattle any real distance, and a wagon. To tell you the truth, Ritva, apart from horses . . . well, it's not an accident I left the farm!"

Just then a cry came from up ahead, from someone on the stretch of roadway just this side of the bridge over the Boise river.

"Way! Make way! Clear that lane for westbound military traffic!"

The harsh shout was backed up by a bray of trumpets,

the deep-toned tubae, along with a dunting snarl she recognized as an oxhorn. Her brows went up; Boiseans didn't use those, although many other peoples did.

"Now, do it now or get ridden down! *Make way!*"

Everyone on the left crowded over. The two sheepdogs were nearly as hysterical as their charges, as the influx squeezed them into a solid bleating block of rolling eyes and exposed tongues. They did their duty, though, keeping the sheep together with nips and barks, sometimes running over their heaving backs to do it.

Ritva's stomach clenched when the column rode out. Horsemen in three-quarter armor of lacquered leather plates edged in steel, its liquid sheen a dull red the color of dried blood, armed with bow and shete and nine-foot lances. Every breastplate bore the golden-rayed sun of the Church Universal and Triumphant, and so did the round shields slung over their backs.

Their spiked helmets were slung to their saddlebows; the heads were cropped close enough to be like plush fur, even shorter than Boise regulars, or shaved altogether, in odd contrast to tufts of chin-beard. Their faces were things of slabs and angles, all with a slightly starved look. She'd met men like that before, more often than not over a blade or in a shower of arrows, though once at closer range.

Not just Cutters. Not rancher levies. That's the Sword of the Prophet.

The savage training of the House of the Prophet in Corwin bit deep, and it marked a man more than the scars of fire. She let herself look alarmed and curious, with a bit of a gape; it was a mark of the discipline of the riders that not one of them turned his head aside to glance at a good-looking young woman. When the last of them rode by and the short train of two-wheel carts that carried their minimal bagged had passed she blew out her cheeks.

"Those guys look serious," Ian said quietly.

"*Tell* me. We had a bunch of them chase us from not far east of here *all the way to Nantucket*. Nothing stopped them except killing."

"That frightened off the others?"

"No, I mean nothing stopped them except killing them all. All except the last five."

"Determined."

"*Ai*, you have no idea. There were over five hundred to begin with."

"*Very* determined. So five gave up?"

"That was after my big brother had the Sword of the Lady. That can . . . do things . . . even to *them*."

"Oh."

"Note that the Sword of the Lady is a long way away from us, right now. But the Sword of the Prophet is right here, and so are some of the Seekers."

"Yeah, that had occurred to me now and then."

Traffic took a while to unsnarl, but eventually it started moving again and they crossed, over the tree-lined river and to the high steel portals of the gate-complex, then through its tunnel darkness and into the city. The city wall was high, about the same as Portland's, but they hadn't bothered coating it in stucco—old Lawrence Thurston had been an inhumanly businesslike man. She didn't know if Boise really smelled a little worse than it had last time, or that was her imagination; it certainly wasn't *bad* compared to some she'd sniffed, and positively fragrant next to the coal-smoke reek of giant Des Moines. There was no way to cram tens of thousands of human beings and their fires and forges and animals inside a wall and not have it smell bad to country-bred noses.

"Ah, the smell of civilization," Ritva said.

Ian snorted, then said: "I think we drop off the sheep here inside the gate. Isn't that the sign Woburn told us about? And I'd better become mute, it's what it says on my draft exemption papers."

A broad avenue led eastward from the river gate to a golden-domed building that had been the State capitol; the walled citadel that held the General-President's residence was south of it.

Last time here I was an honored guest, when we were heading east to the Sunrise Lands. Now I'm a spy and I'll be tortured and killed if they catch me. It's an up-and-down life in the Dúnedain Rangers!

Like most walled cities there had been a lot of infilling since the Change, second stories added to houses and new workshops built. Like the more closely regulated cities, Boise also had a stretch of cleared land just inside the fortifications, letting troops move quickly in an emergency. It also served as holding pens for livestock; each dealer had a sign with his name and license number. It was all very orderly, as far as anything concerned with sheep and other beasts with wills of their own could be. They turned the flock in between the wattle hurdles and into the corral. They quieted quickly; sheep weren't intelligent enough to figure out what humans had in mind for them. Unlike pigs. Pigs were *dangerous* in large numbers, for exactly that reason.

The contractor who'd bought Woburn's sheep was a weathered middle-aged man; he took a look at the flock with an experienced flick of the eyes, scanning for sickness or scrawny individuals. Then he went through and checked a few at random to make sure they were what they appeared. The sheep were mostly overage ewes, sold off when their best wool and lambing days were done. The hides would bring nearly as much as their tough stringy meat, with leather in such demand for the war, but soldiers weren't picky eaters either.

He had an assistant, a youngster in his late teens with stained working clothes and a shepherd's crook. He was staring at Ritva, which wasn't unusual, but there was as much hostility as jittery adolescent lust in it. He was silent until she handed over the invoice with Woburn's signature.

"What are you doing with that?" he said. "Why isn't the man handling it?"

"I'm giving it to your boss, stranger," she said mildly. "And you should mind your own business."

"*You've* no business handling that, girl," he said. "You should be home, and dressed decent. Let men do men's business. The day is coming—"

Ritva stuck a finger in the young man's face, the point almost touching his nose, and he jarred to a halt in astonishment.

"Who *is* this asshole?" she asked the dealer.

"He badgers the flocks for me around the town pens," the man said. "And he's my cousin's kid, for my sins. That side of the family has been listening to the new preachers."

"He pisses off the people you do business with," she said; Ian was keeping quiet, in case anyone was struck by his accent. "And my brother here is mute, or *he'd* be pissed off."

Which accounts for why he isn't in the army, she thought.

"The little dick ain't me," the dealer pointed out. "And the sheep don't mind his disposition."

He signed the spare copy, and took out a checkbook with the grizzly bear logo of the First National Bank of Boise on its cover. Ritva had just turned to untie her horse string when the sheep-badger spat on her foot.

"Sorry," he said with a sneer. "Aiming for the dirt."

Very slowly, she turned around again and smiled at him. The grab and twist that followed were almost too swift to see; the young man had just enough time to clutch himself and screech before he folded up and fell to the ground, with his tongue waving in his speechless mouth like an undersea weed.

Ritva waited for an instant, then kicked the fallen man twice with cold deliberation, hard enough that the steel-reinforced toe of her boot made thudding sounds with a very satisfying undertone of *crunch* but not hard enough to kill. He began to whimper, and then vomit in helpless choking, gasping heaves. Blood and bits of tooth came along with the contents of his stomach, a sour bite under the warmer musky smells of sheep and sheep-dung and straw.

"Any problems?" she said to the contractor, using the fallen man's hat to wipe her boot and then throwing it into the puddle of puke.

He grinned. "Wanted to do that all this year myself, but he *is* family. Let's get you gone before the Natpols"—he meant the National Police, who were Boise's constabulary—"show up. Here's the check and give my regards to Rancher Woburn. I'll take care of the dogs the usual way."

She folded it and tucked it into a pocket; she'd cash it if possible. *Woburn's* cover story was that she and Ian were bandits who'd jumped the legitimate drovers and run off the flock and stolen the documentation, and he had cowboys of his own ready to swear to it. Whether that would help if the current regime in Boise decided he was guilty was another matter, but he was ready to take the chance. When they were far enough away not to cause any curiosity about a mute speaking, Ian muttered: "Wasn't that a bit conspicuous?"

"Only in the *right* way. Judging from the people we met on our way here, that was a perfectly credible reaction. People in Boise the city think of cowboys . . . and cowgirls . . . as the type who take offense. And he did spit on my foot, sweetie."

"Remind me never to spit on you. Of course, I doubt I'd be inclined to. You play rough, don't you?"

Ritva shrugged and made a slight moue of distaste. "The little *orch* was a Cutter. I've hardly ever met a Cutter I didn't want to kick to death, and I've met quite a few. And my father had a saying . . . I'm not old enough to remember him saying it but Aunt Astrid is . . . that you should always kick a man when he's down. It's much easier then."

"You don't think he'll come after you?"

"Probably not. He might have if I'd left it at the playful little tweak to the crotch. But as Dad said, if you leave the mark of your boot-leather on a man's face, he's going to remember who won the fight every single day."

She added parenthetically: "Men are sort of silly that way. You have to . . . to . . . be *firm* with them sometimes. Not sensible ones like you, of course."

Ian nodded, giving her an odd look. Then he said: "Should we be looking around ourselves so much? I mean, it's a big city but we're supposed to be natives."

"No, we're supposed to be hicks from the backlands," Ritva said. "Believe me, we'd stand out if we *didn't* gawk."

"It *is* big, bigger than Lethbridge. I've never seen anything this size. Amazing! It reminds me of my parents' stories about Edmonton. They lived there before the Change, then they got out early and went to join my uncle on the farm up in the Peace River country. Is Portland this big?"

"Boise's even bigger than Portland. By about a quarter, say seventy thousand people. Only half the size of Des Moines, but that's just *ridiculously* big, like everything there. Iowa gave me hives."

It had been only two years since the Quest passed through Boise, and much remained the same; people still moved with a brisk purposefulness, there was less noise than you'd expect, and squads swept up even the horse dung almost as soon as it fell.

But some things have changed, oh, yes.

The big, vividly tinted posters on four-sided hoardings still marked every crossroad within, color lithographs of the type you might see advertising a merchant venturer's ship fitting out in Newport or an upcoming tournament or guild festival in Portland. But the emphasis was very different. Before, they'd mostly been of implausibly square-jawed men and women doing various tasks; soldiers, of course, but also nurses, farmers, smiths, weavers, potters, scholars, mothers, all looking forward with set purpose and some patriotic slogan below to complement the industriously patriotic things they were doing above.

Now they came in only two varieties. One showed the faces of President-General Martin Thurston and the starved-wolf, shaven-headed countenance of the Prophet Sethaz, both looking off into a distance of blue sky and white clouds and glowing sunlight. Beneath the picture was printed:

TOGETHER WE ASCEND in great block capitals.

The rest were of a soldier in Boise's hoop-armor and big shield, advancing forward with only his eyes showing over the rim and his sword held down for the thrusting stroke; behind him were a stolid-looking farmer or laborer hoeing, and a woman carrying a child and wearing an ankle-length skirt with her eyes cast down beneath a kerchief. The words read:

FIGHT! WORK! BELIEVE! OBEY!

"Now, tell me. Is this the viewpoint of the *good* side or the *bad* side?" Ritva murmured very quietly.

"Well, it's not so different from what the PPA puts out, sometimes."

"Oh . . . well, they're not that bad. Not anymore."

They turned into a side street, past a mouthwatering display of fruit and vegetable shops that extended back into the low buildings like Aladdin's cave of treasures: baskets of blackberries glistening like dark jewels, raspberries red as blood with cherries a darker color, golden apricots and orange pumpkins and red-yellow blushing peaches and nectarines, vividly colored peppers and aubergines, lettuces and radishes and more. Boise ate well from the intensively worked small farms in the rich irrigated country round about. That gave way to a stretch of leatherworkers specializing in saddles—everyone there seemed grimly busy on government contracts—and then a series of two-, three-, and four-story buildings that had been linked together and reworked with more chimneys and other modern improvements, including automatic-valve watering troughs along the pavement outside. A new-built wall surrounded what had been a big parking lot, now courtyard and stables, and wrought-iron letters above the gate proclaimed:

DROVER'S DELIGHT INN
COWBOYS WELCOME
FIGHTS ARE NOT
CLEAN FACILITIES FOR ALL BUDGETS
MEALS REASONABLE
HOT WATER FREE

"This is where we stay. Or get arrested for torture and death, if anyone blabbed," Ritva said cheerfully.

Privately she was prickly aware of all her weapons; she *didn't* intend to be taken alive.

Am I getting more nervous as I get older? Or is it just getting more real *to me. I remember how Mary and I used to go whooping in having a high old time and being excited and everything . . . says the crone of twenty-two. Oh, well.*

Everything looked normal enough. In particular there was no ominous quietness; in fact everyone was dashing around with the normal quotient of quarreling and laughing and the odd drunk snoozing in corners. As they watched, an active one was ejected by three of the staff, one on each arm and one holding his legs. They gave a concerted heave-ho, and he landed in a trough with a tremendous splash and a volley of screamed curses. A nearby Natpol trooper in leather armor and green uniform laughed and strolled over. His crossbow was slung over one shoulder, and his dagger and short sword at his waist, but he had a yard of nightstick in his hand, made from dark heavy iron-hard mountain mahogany. He twirled it around by the thong above the handle, then stood tapping the business end into his left palm as the inn's staff led out a saddled horse and followed it with a hide sack that probably contained the drunk's worldly goods.

The drunk sobered rapidly, between the cold water and the grinning policeman; he swung into the saddle with a wet slap of soaked denim against leather and walked his horse into the traffic.

"You save me a lot of trouble, Charlie," the Natpol said to the man who'd been on the legs. "Sometimes I think I should split my pay with you, damned if I don't."

"Damn cowpokes get sand in their throats and think they can wash it out with whiskey," Charlie grumbled. Then he nodded to Ritva and Ian: "Help you?"

"We just got in and dropped off a flock from Hasty Creek ranch up in the Camas prairie country, with an army contractor name of Wadley," Ritva said. "My brother and I need the usual for a couple of days. Got some business to do before we head back."

"Hasty Creek?" Charlie said; he was in his late thirties, a heavyset man with glossy brown muttonchop whiskers, light eyes and muscle under fat, and a white apron over his clothes. "Your credit's good, then. Settle up the day before you leave, but just to be sure you pay for a full day if you're not out by noon that day."

"That's fine."

The Natpol was about Charlie's age, but trimmer; he walked with a slight limp, probably from his army service. She remembered from her last time here that the police were a reserved occupation for veterans, with those who had non-disabling injuries getting special preference. Lawrence Thurston had always taken good care of his followers, though Ritva disliked the whole concept of a single police force.

Well, you could call the Dúnedain a police force in peacetime, I suppose, but nobody has to use us and we don't patrol streets and look for petty thieves, we chase real bandits and things like that. And Ian's people, the Force, the redcoats, got their start about the same way. This National Police thing with one of them in every village still seems unnatural and I don't like it.

"Your papers, miss, sir?" the policeman said courteously. "Just in?"

"Just in this morning," Ritva said; it was around noon. "My brother can't talk. Never could, nobody can tell why."

She handed over the passportlike folders. The trooper checked through them rapidly, looking up to confirm the photographs; duplicating those quickly without attracting attention had been the most difficult part of the help

Woburn and St. Hilda's had given them. Luckily Woburn was a district magistrate, and the monastery had a photographic section as part of its high school. There was a central record, and . . .

We're fucked if he goes to the trouble of checking it, but that would take a while anyway, she thought, as she smiled sweetly at the man.

He read them conscientiously. They stated that Jane and Jacob Conway had been adopted by a couple of Woburn's retainers after being found wandering emaciated and alone in the winter of the second Change Year. That was towards the tail end of the utter chaos, when such things were still common even in areas of high survival like Iowa. It would account for Ian's muteness too. People scarred by their experiences in the terrible years were common enough, and would be for another generation.

"This is all in order. Please remember that the rules have to be tighter in a city with so many people living together."

"See you, Charlie," he added to the innkeeper.

"See you, Johnny," the man replied.

Ian and Ritva dismounted, and Charlie casually went on: "Impressive, those bones, aren't they?"

"Mammoth, Mr. Gleam," Ritva said.

That was the primitive sign-countersign they'd arranged; besides being a business partner of Woburn's, Charlie Gleam had a sister who was a member of St. Hilda's, and Woburn had foreseen the need for a quiet channel into the capital years ago.

Gleam bustled them into the courtyard, with just enough care for the retainers of an important man but not enough to make anyone wonder why two nondescript—

Well, unusually and strikingly good-looking but otherwise *nondescript.*

—drovers were getting special treatment. The staff hurried off with their horses, Gleam handed over a key and told them their room number, and they both made a beeline for the bathhouse. That was pointedly encouraged by several signs and heavy hints from the staff, too. If an inn wanted to keep the bedding free of miniature freeloaders that was essential. From what she'd heard people in the business say, the Brannigans in Sutterdown for instance, it was a never-ending struggle anyway, an insectile version of the way the Rangers had to keep whacking down bandits in the outlands with strong soap and hot water the equivalents of blade, bow and noose.

The facilities were segregated by gender, as was common almost everywhere in traveler's inns, even in those run by peoples like Mackenzies or Dúnedain who didn't bother among themselves. She grinned at the attendant, grinned even more at the sight of the boiler and buckets, and turned her clothes and the replacements in the saddlebags over to be washed. The locked trunk on one of the packhorses would be deposited in their room safely enough; the worst possible thing she could do would be to hover over it like a mother hen.

It's even good luck that that detachment of the Sword of the Prophet was leaving when we came in. It made it less likely the gate-guards would search everything. That might have been awkward.

Instead she stood naked on the concrete floor and poured the first, the most delicious bucket of the hot water over her head. Even in summer, washing with a cloth and basin, or even diving into a stream, just wasn't the *same*. As she cleaned herself she chatted with half a dozen other women who were using the same big brick-walled room with its small high windows and drifting wisps of vapor, and smell of soap and steam and hot metal and rock. Outside the palaces of rulers and manors of great nobles she'd never been in a place where there were bathing facilities meant for individual use; it was simply too costly in terms of fuel and laid-on water and labor. The better class of inns had places like this, and analogues were common in villages and steadings and estates.

Then she lathered up with the strong soap, suds all over and working it into her itchy scalp with vigorous fingertips, then another bucket and a scrub with a woven equivalent of a loofah and a rough washcloth, and more soap and water and then a blissful soak in one of a row of tubs under a sign that read *clean out your own bath or pay fifty cents extra*. Money wasn't a problem, but staying in her role was, and she dutifully applied the brush and turned the tin tub over to drain and dry.

When she had toweled herself she felt that a good part of the long hard drive down from Drumheller had gone down the wastewater drain too, flowing out to water and irrigate the city's surroundings.

I'll bet the oldsters will feel even better, she thought with a slight smile.

They and the rest of the Dúnedain commando would all be arriving at intervals, by twos and threes—lone travelers were rare enough to attract attention, if they came from any distance, even more than large groups. You had to let any suspicion that *was* aroused die down between parties, too. Infiltration was like hunting; patience was the first necessity.

In the meantime . . .

She pulled on the plain linen robe provided for five cents, pushed her feet into the cord sandals, left a few other orders with the attendant, who promised to pass them on. Then she asked directions, which ended with the dread phrase *you can't miss it*, and got thoroughly lost.

The set of buildings was a maze, and many of the corridors had no windows and hadn't been modernized with skylights, which left them very dim indeed. She would have been much more at home in an unfamiliar benighted forest or mountain canyon, since she'd been a country dweller all her life and a rover of the wilderness nearly as long; in the end she used her nose, moving away from the distinctive slightly musty-dusty scent that marked areas kept weathertight but not much used, and heading back into the occupied portions.

"Four thirty-two?" a woman carrying two baskets said. "Hey, I'm headed that way. Follow me."

Ritva thought that the part of the complex they ended up in had probably been an office building before the Change; it had a dropped ceiling with acoustic tiles, some of which had been replaced over the years with neat squares of polished wood. She noted the fact absently, with the part of her mind that was always concerned with potential escape routes and avenues of attack, and made a note to check the old ducting. There were times it was big enough for people to crawl through, though fortunately or deplorably noisy.

"Hi!" she said, as she opened the door.

Ian looked up, but kept to his disguise of being mute and just nodded. Ritva felt a glow of approval; he'd picked up tradecraft very quickly indeed. The Force—it had *Royal* in its formal title, oddly since none of the Dominions were monarchies—was like the Rangers in that it patrolled against bandits, protected trade routes and put down the messier sorts of crime. Its military role in time of war was more conventional, though, probably because the Dominions had taken less of a beating after the

Change than her part of the world. Drumheller and Moose Jaw and Minnedosa were all big, the same order of size as the PPA, they all had strong central governments, and they'd had less in the way of conflict and internal squabbling than the lands of Montival-to-be. The Dúnedain did a lot more in the way of clandestine operations.

Which means we're a lot better at sneaking.

When the inn servant had put the baskets on the table, told them where the jakes were (without telling them they couldn't miss it) and left, he did speak.

"You must be *clean*," he said, a little teasing. "I know that it takes women longer to wash than men—"

"That's because we actually wash, and have a better sense of smell," Ritva said loftily.

"But forty-five minutes?"

"I went . . . exploring."

"Ah, you got lost too!"

They both laughed. Ritva admired the way he did it, wholeheartedly but gracefully, with a hint of shyness.

Maybe I'm getting over my Big Bad Boys fixation, she thought. *By Ever-Young Vána of the Blossoms, I hope so. The bad boys can be a lot of fun, but they wear. Oh, how they wear! I grant Ingolf was big and bad but not a bad boy, but Mary won him. I will never, never let her use her own special lucky coin for something important again.*

Meanwhile Ian was unloading the baskets. "Nice picnic, eh?" he said.

There was crusty bread, half a dozen types of cured meat, several of cheese, a double-walled crock that kept a savory-smelling ham and bean soup warm, a salad, and a bowl of fruit, along with various accompaniments, a jug of apple juice, and two bottles of a very decent red wine she remembered from her previous trip through.

"But why not go down . . . oh, ah?"

"This *is* the first time we've had any privacy in weeks, and not been exhausted and smelly to boot, right? I thought we should . . . use it to get better acquainted. The others could start getting in as early as tonight."

"Right. Absolutely right. Who wants a crowded common hall anyway?"

Ritva gave a long slow smile. "And you've never done it until you've done it in Elvish, believe me."

CHAPTER EIGHT

County of Aurea
Portland Protective Association
(Formerly central Washington)
High Kingdom of Montival
(Formerly western North America)
August 5, Change Year 25/2023 AD

Bjarni Eriksson, King in Norrheim and often called *Ironrede* by his people, laughed with delight as he put his new horse through its paces in the warm late-afternoon sunlight. It was dry in this part of Montival, in the rain-shadow of the Cascades, and dust puffed up around its high-stepping feet with a peppery scent that mingled with horse and man sweat. The mount was a six-year-old stallion, seventeen hands high and glossy black, long-legged, deep-chested, arched of neck, with nostrils like red-rimmed pits. He *almost* expected it to breathe fire.

Bjarni had ridden as far back as his memories stretched, and he'd been six at the Change. He could just barely recall bits and pieces of his father's trek with his followers from Springfield to Aroostook in northern Maine, and the founding of Norrheim, and sitting before his father in the saddle with one powerful arm around him. After that he'd been the son of a great chieftain with a big farm and scot paid by his followers besides, and able to keep a number of horses. He had thought he knew what there was to know, apart from a few specialist tricks.

He'd never in all his life put foot to stirrup on anything like this, though. Riding the superbly trained animal was as much like dancing as anything he'd experienced before.

He leaned his weight slightly to the front and clamped his thighs tighter, and the horse started forward as if sensing his very thought. Then there was a rushing speed, and it seemed to float upward over the white board fence. The landing was without breaking stride, and it was scarcely necessary to touch the reins to bring a halt once more.

It made nothing of his weight, though he was a broad-shouldered, barrel-chested, thick-armed man of medium height, near two hundred pounds of tough muscle and heavy bones, with the large strong hands of a swordsman and woodsman and farmer. The brick-colored hair bound back from his face with a headband stuck to the sweat on his neck, and more ran into his short beard; his skin was reddened too, by long exposure to wind and weather and now by the fierce sun of cloudless summer in this part of Montival. The little blue eyes in his snub-nosed, high-cheeked face were calm and steady, a net of wrinkles at their corners even though he had just thirty-one years.

He looked at the beast's ears and grinned. It was sweating freely, but an hour spent at everything from galloping to jumping had barely scratched the surface of its energy.

"You want to run, don't you, boy?" he said. "Ayuh, you do! Soon, soon."

He swung down from the saddle, and ran a hand down its neck; then he reached into a pocket of his breeks and pulled out an apple. The horse plucked it from his palm and crunched it with slobbering pleasure. One of his followers who was horse-wise came to remove the tooled, silver-studded saddle and lead it away for grooming and watering.

Bjarni was shaking his head as he turned away to the waiting knot of folk at the gate of the paddock. A rolling plain stretched away in all directions. Reaped grain was straw-blond, alfalfa a dusty green, with here and there the darker shade trees and orchards and vineyards around a village, the church steeples and whirling wind-pumps rising above. The fields still under harvest were bright burnished gold that shone with an almost metallic luster as horses or mules hauled the turning creels of the reaping machines through, laying the cut grain in bands lighter-colored than the stubble. Workers followed binding the sheaves and stooking them into pyramids.

It is a golden land hereabout this time of the year, he thought. *Perhaps that's why they named this shire so.*

Looking at it in August you wouldn't think there was enough rain to produce a crop, but the ears were heavy in the fields of wheat and barley; for a moment he simply smiled at the comforting beauty of the sight. It made him itch a little too; it seemed unnatural not to pitch in. Many of his men had, from the same feeling and because it was a chance to meet the local women, but he was too busy with the mustering.

There were pine-clad hills to the north, just visible beyond the walls and towers of Goldendale town and castle. To the north and west a great white peak floated in the distance. Mount Adams, they called it; another like it lay south and west, Mt. Hood, the two framing that side of the world. Even after the long journey from Norrheim in what the old world had called northern Maine he still found his breath taken away sometimes by the *scale* of the landscapes here in the High West. You'd hardly credit that many days' travel separated this spot from those high snowfields, or that Hood was on the other shore of the great Columbia itself, in green rainy forest country. Behind Adams was another, even greater.

The world is wider and more full of wonders than I knew before Artos Mikesson and his questers rode into my garth last Yule, he thought. *More dangerous, much stranger, and more beautiful. Yet I would give it all to sit by my own fire again, with Hallberga beside me and our son in my lap while we watched our daughter play.*

He picked a towel off the fence and wiped his face and neck; it was also *hot* here, though the dryness made it easier to tolerate than a like day back home.

Not that we have many days like this! And we could use some, come harvesttime.

"That horse puts my horsemanship to shame. What shall I do with him, Lady Signe?" he asked the woman who'd given it to him. "We Norrheimers aren't fighters on horseback, like you Bearkillers. We plant our feet with Earth, Thor's mother, when we make the shield-wall."

"Take him home with you after the war, and put him to your mares, Bjarni King," she said. "And when you see the foals he gets, remember us here. Your folk may need warhorses, someday."

She was a tall fair woman a little more than a decade older than him, with the Valknut of Odin around her neck and a set of rough dark clothing; man's boots and breeches and jacket, though there was certainly a good-looking woman beneath them, and her face was still handsome. He judged that she could use the long single-edged, basket-hilted sword at her belt with some skill.

This one is a she-wolf, he thought. *Shrewd, brave, loyal to her own, but very hard and used to rule, I would say; her man fell and she has striven to take his place while her sons grew. Still, she's guested and gifted us well, and her people . . . or some of them . . . are true folk who follow the Aesir as we do. Well, not* exactly *as we do, but close enough. And they have many arts I want for Norrheim, and they're fell fighters, as dangerous as any I've seen.*

"I shall name him *Vakr*," he said.

She smiled. "Ah, *Hawk*, for the horse of Morn who rides out to bring the dawn," she said. "A good choice."

He inclined his head. "You know the ancient tales well, *gythja*," he said, giving her the title of Godwoman.

That could mean either chieftainess or priestess, since either made sacrifice to the Mighty Ones. He had been a *godhi* himself, when he was merely chief of the Bjornings, his own tribe, and before he became the first king of Norrheim. A chief made offerings; just as he led his folk in war and presided over the folk-moot, the thing, so he stood before the Mighty Ones for them. A king most of all, who must be father to all the land.

"I'll breed Vakr to my mares and the colts will be the envy of Norrheim. *And* others will think it a favor indeed if I let them do likewise."

Her nod told him she'd thought of that too; the network of favor and obligation was one a leader had to know how to weave and tug on at need.

"Those of my folk who are true to the Aesir will hold a *blót* soon," she said. "We will give cattle to the Gods for luck and victory in this war, and feast, and drink sumbel to hail the Gods, remember the dead and make boast and oath. You and yours are welcome to share the rite. And the beef!"

"Many thanks, if you will let me send cattle we find ourselves to be given with yours. It is fitting that you

Bearkillers should lead the rite; this is your land, and you know the holy wights who ward it under the high Gods."

She smiled, looking much younger for a moment. "This here"—she tapped a boot on the sparse grass beneath them, and a little dust puffed up—"is not ours, exactly. For various values of *us* and *ours*."

"Ah, yes," Bjarni said. "Your pardon if this hard head of mine hasn't gotten all the details of this realm hammered into it yet."

Signe's smile grew into a grin, a remarkably predatory expression. "The details of who owned what resulted in a lot of skulls getting hammered in my youth, the years after the Change," she said. "And we've yet to pound home the lesson these boundaries are not for our enemies to rearrange now, either."

Bjarni gave her the same wolf-grin back, and so did several of his countrymen. The play on words appealed to their sense of humor and his. The world was a place of strife; no less than a wolf pack, a tribe or kingdom had to be ready to fight for its hunting grounds, or to take what its people needed from others, though no man could guarantee triumph in every fight.

Though my old friend Thor has lent me his might. And the All-Father can give victory where he pleases.

But even the Gods would go down in wreck at the end, when the horn of Heimdalr blew for the final battle. Then Asa-Loki and the Jotun lords would ride against them to Vigrid plain, on the last morning of the world, when the stars fell from the sky and sea overwhelmed the land. It was for that fight that the High One gathered the spirits of fallen heroes in his hall. A man *could* strive with all the craft and might and main that was in him, though, and face death undaunted. And so could a woman.

Signe's son Mike Mikesson—Mike Havel, using the

old system that was still popular here—touched his own backsword.

"We've made a start on showing Boise and the CUT the point of our arguments in this lawsuit," he said solemnly, though with a twinkle in his sky-colored eyes. "But we'll still need some cutting remarks to finally convince them our case is stronger."

Bjarni laughed aloud. "This cub's growing fangs, by almighty Thor!"

Mike Jr. was just on the cusp of young manhood, perhaps a little short of eighteen years; already tall and broad-shouldered, with a shock of corn-colored hair, and already with a few scars on hands and face to show his words weren't just an untried youngster's air and wind. He'd be stronger when he got his full growth, there was still a bit of adolescent lankiness to him, but he was more than strong enough to be dangerous already, and Bjarni judged by the way he moved that he'd been very well taught. Between his brows was a small round mark made by a hot iron; his mother had the same. That was a mark the Bearkillers reserved for their best, what they called the A-list, and it was never granted for anything but proved courage and skill in the arts of war.

Bjarni turned to Mike's mother again. "I was near the Bearkiller land, but pressed for time, when I visited Artos Mikesson's garth at Dun Juniper. When the war is over, I will come guest you awhile at your Larsdalen, if you wish it."

Her lips thinned a little, but she answered in friendly wise: "Yes, that would be good. Ours is much like the Mackenzie land, but on the other side of the Willamette. Save that the mountains to our west between us and the sea are not as grand as the High Cascades to the east of theirs. My father's family, the Larssons, held a farm there for long and long, generations before the Change. They did more, but that was the first they took, long ago, when they came west-over-sea from the ancient homelands."

"Fine fat soil, then, good pasture and plenty of forest and the Gods of weather are kind to you," he said. "You are lucky. The valley of the Willamette is some of the best farming land I've seen, and I've traveled far. Better than Norrheim, and especially better weather."

Though not much *better than some of the land I saw lying near empty as we journeyed,* some corner of his mind thought. *In what the old world called Quebec and Ontario. With Artos Mikesson's help we beat the Bekwa. Not just beat them but wrecked and crushed them, at the Seven Hills fight. Which opens the way there; Norrheim is a small kingdom now, but it needn't always be so. Our numbers grow, and there's room there to make safe our folk and feed our children's children's children.*

She nodded. "All that my husband Mike, the first Bear Lord, won for us with his craft and drighten might, and died defending."

Bjarni's eyes went to the white peaks again, and he thought of the canyons of the Columbia he'd passed, towering above like the walls of Valhöll above a river to rival the Mississippi itself, with the waterfalls cataracting down the cliffs.

"Yet all this land of Montival is a fit home for our Gods," he said. "A giant's country, made to breed heroes! I have my own land, but I honor yours."

"For the which I thank you," another voice said, in a musical lilt. "And it breeds fine horses too, of which it seems you have acquired one of the best."

Bjarni started a little. Artos Mikesson was a big man, but so graceful and light of step that it was eerie sometimes. And any man who carried the Sword forged by

Weyland the Smith beyond the bounds of Midgard had something of that about him anyway. Bjarni had heard the High One confer kingship on Artos himself, through the seeress his spirit possessed.

"Your Majesty," Signe said, bowing.

"Lady Signe," Rudi said in turn, returning the bow and hiding his slight amusement. "I've just come from reviewing your Bearkiller encampment. May the Dagda club me dead if I could find anything not in perfect order. *And* you were prompt. Mike Havel would be proud. Corvallis, on the other hand . . ."

The big fair man beside him snorted. "*We're* all here, ten thousand of us. Fourteen hundred A-listers, eight thousand pikemen and crossbowmen, fifty field catapults. Plus the garrisons we've got over in the Cascade forts backing up the Clan's troops. Corvallis was always a day late and a dollar short in the wars against the Association and they're keeping up the batting average."

The war-leader of the Bearkillers had the snarling red bear's-head of the outfit Mike Havel had founded on the shoulder of his brown cord jacket; in that as in other ways Eric Larsson looked very much like a male version of Signe, which wasn't surprising, since they were fraternal twins. The sign on a silver chain around his neck was a cross, though. His left arm ended at the wrist, to continue in an artificial hand of metal, which accounted— partly—for his nickname: *Steel-fist*.

"That's not diplomatic," Rudi said, slightly chiding. "And I have good friends in Corvallis. They're just . . . a little slow, taken as a whole."

"Not diplomatic, but it's true though," another voice said. "They surprised us in the Association unpleasantly a few times during the old wars. Turning up late can be effective if you're so late you're not expected to turn up at all."

Rudi could see Bjarni blinking at that cool soprano, with its sound like water running over polished stones in some mountain stream. Then his eyes narrowed.

Yes, he's a shrewd one, Rudi thought. *Enough to take in something unfamiliar and not just stick to his first thought.*

"Bjarni Eriksson, called Bjarni Iron Counsel, King in Norrheim," he said in introduction. "Lady Tiphaine, Baroness d'Ath and Grand Constable of the Portland Protective Association. Which is to say, war-leader of their host."

Tiphaine d'Ath was in full plate, from steel sabatons on her feet bearing the golden spurs of knighthood to the bevoir that protected neck and chin; a mounted squire carried her helmet and gauntlets, and another her lance and her shield with its arms of *sable, a delta or over a V argent.* Her eyes were the color of glacier ice, level and almost expressionless.

"Your Majesty," she said to Bjarni, with a thump of right fist on the lames of her articulated breastplate, and a bow; as a noble to a sovereign, but not her own ruler.

Bjarni extended his hand. They exchanged the Norrheimer wrist-to-wrist grip; his eyes widened a little as he did.

Then she turned back to Rudi. He went on with the orders: "I'm sending you and fifteen thousand troops to Walla Walla, to take overall command in the County Palatine of the Eastermark. A thousand of the light horse will be refugees from the Bend country south of the Columbia, CORA ranchers and their retainers, horse-archers. Also the Lakota contingent, and Colonel Ingolf Vogeler's Richlanders, another eight hundred together."

She nodded. "The CORA-boys will be useful and they're certainly well motivated. The Sioux and the Richlanders are to demonstrate the support we . . . Montival . . . have from the east, I suppose?"

"Yes. The Richlanders are good horse-soldiers, and highly disciplined."

"The Sioux aren't well disciplined, I take it, Your Majesty?"

"Not disciplined either well or badly; they're splendid warriors, but not soldiers in our sense of the word at all, at all. And treating them with a heavy hand is as futile as pushing on a rope. Only ropes don't bite when pushed, and they do . . . so perhaps pushing on a rattlesnake would be a better metaphor? Also they have a rooted conviction that all the horses in the world belong to them alone. I suggest you deal with them through Ingolf, as much as possible."

"They'll take his orders?"

"No. They may well *listen* to him, though. And he knows the Lakota well."

"He should," Eric said with grim amusement. "From what he's said, he learned his trade fighting them back east."

"He did. And he and *intancan* Rick Mat'o Yamni, Rick Three Bears, their war chief, are friends. All of us on the Sword-Quest spent some time with the Seven Council Fires last year, and fought by their sides. You'll find that Ingolf is a very good light cavalry commander; competent in other things as well, some of which will be relevant and some not. A steady man and sure of himself, but adaptable, and vastly experienced; there's few tricks of that sort of fighting he does not know. And my half sister Mary . . . Mary Vogeler, now . . . will be with him, along with two dozen Dúnedain Rangers."

"Your Majesty," Tiphaine said, nodding in the manner of someone thinking hard. "Yes, I can work with the Sioux. Or around them, needs must."

"And I'm giving you two thousand PPA men-at-arms, the rest bicycle-born foot troops and field artillery," Rudi went on. "Among them seven regiments of pike and crossbow infantry from the Yakima. They'll have their own field batteries in support."

Tiphaine's pale brows rose slightly, the more visible against her tanned skin.

"The Free Cities of the Yakima League and the Association have an, ah, unfortunate mutual history," she said.

Rudi grinned. "Meaning, you and they fought hammer and tongs for years, to be sure, when the Association tried to overrun them and divide their land into fiefs," he said. "You did exactly that with the Tri-Cities, which they thought of as theirs. Yet we're all part of the High Kingdom now, and must learn to work together. Also the Yakima Valley will be at your back, hence their homes, hence excellent motivation. Forbye they'll see Associates fighting to *help* defend their homes, the satisfaction and wonderment of the world it will be to them, to see you."

"Politically astute, my liege," she said.

"Hopefully; and more of the same will be required in the Eastermark, dealing with the local lords."

"That," she said, with a small, chilling smile, "I think I can do."

He nodded, not altogether in agreement. "Not just putting them in fear. We won't be able to hold the enemy in that area. Your job is to slow them, sure, and bloody them, and keep them pinned until they've exhausted their supplies, and lead them by the nose to where I want them; but don't get caught in any action you can't withdraw from. I leave that to your judgment; just let you bear in mind that you can use the army I've given you, but you cannot lose it."

A faraway looked came into her eyes; the look of someone considering a difficult but interesting challenge.

He nodded. "But that's not enough. The castles and especially Walla Walla *must* hold, and hold strongly even when the enemy occupy the open plains. The nobles there must do their best, not every man for himself and fighting just enough to satisfy honor. Starting with the Count Palatine himself they must be resolved to tie down every enemy soldier they can and do the foe every harm they're able, despite the risks. I rely on you to see to that, as well; I've more than enough to do here."

"Let the flies conquer the flypaper," she said, with what he thought was a very faint hint of amusement. "We were on the other side of that often enough. I've seen your plans, Your Majesty. Persuading the County's nobility to go along with them may take a little work. The equipment we're bringing ought to make a start on that."

"Which shrewdness is why I'm sending you, my lady Grand Constable. This is a task both political and military, and it will take nice judgment and hard fighting both."

She nodded, briskly this time. "The Yakima regiments can bicycle down their valley and then barge down from the Three Cities to the Wallula Gap and meet me at Castle Dorion; we can draw on the supply magazines there. The main force from here can travel up the Columbia to the Gap, and then we'll put our supplies and the heavy gear on the rail line to Walla Walla and march. I'll have the movement orders drafted by tomorrow morning and the lead elements moving by dawn of the day after."

She frowned and looked southward. "I'd like to send

the Richlanders and the Sioux on ahead. They can use railcars along the river gorge and move a lot faster, then push on and join the screening force that's covering the enemy garrison in Castle Campscapell."

The Montivalans winced slightly; something flickered even in the Grand Constable's pale eyes. Campscapell had fallen last year, and in mysterious circumstances. Losing it had been a strategic disaster for which they'd paid heavily since.

"It'll improve morale in County Palatine, to see our allies passing through towards the enemy," she continued. "That will whet their appetite for hope, and the main field force will give them something more substantial. Also it will get the Sioux out in the boondocks. With an enemy force they can expend their energy on killing and robbing, and accompanied by someone they trust."

"The screening force is under Lord Forest Grove?" Rudi said.

He'd have remembered that himself, he thought; but with his palm on the hilt of the Sword there was no need to struggle with memory or call for files from his staff. It flowed in currents like the deep strong movements of the ocean, any knowledge he'd ever so much as glimpsed just *there* in any form he wanted it. He no longer feared the sensation.

I'm . . . resigned, he thought. *It's even coming to seem natural. And sure, it's as convenient as an ever-filled stock of firewood in winter. I'll have to watch that I don't make the Kingdom too dependent on it in the long run, to be sure.*

"Lord Rigobert de Stafford, Baron of Forest Grove, yes, Your Majesty," the Grand Constable said. "With local forces of the County called out under the *arrière-ban*, mostly, besides his own *menie*, and a thousand or so from County Chehalis who he's been hammering into shape for eight months now. A very capable man; aggressive, but not reckless."

Unexpectedly Signe spoke, with her brother nodding agreement: "He's the PPA Marchwarden of the South, so we Bearkillers have a border with his bailiwick. I've dealt with him myself. A hard bargainer but honorable."

"Very well, I defer to your wishes, Grand Constable; send those units immediately."

She bowed again. "I'll get things moving then, Your Majesty."

A polite nod to the others, and one of her squires led her courser forward. She put one hand on the cantle of the high knight's saddle and made a skipping leap. Her left foot caught the stirrup, and she swung onto the horse with a light clatter of gray steel. The party of Associates reined around and cantered off. Bjarni watched consideringly.

"How effective is that armor?" he asked; his own folk used knee-length tunics of mail or scale, and simple conical helms with a strip riveted to the front as a noseguard.

"Very," Rudi said; then he touched the Sword that hung at his right hip. "This could cut it, but an ordinary slash with an ordinary sword, no, it's about like trying to chop through an anvil. Even if you're very strong, the most you could do would be to *dent* it quite a bit, knock the wearer down and bruise him badly. You have to thrust, *so*"—he indicated face, armpits, groin, the backs of the knees—"and even then you'd best be lucky. You need a two-handed weapon like a long ax or a greatsword to pierce plate. Or something that concentrates impact, like a war-pick, or a war hammer. Or a lance with a charging horse behind it, or a hard-driven bodkin-tipped arrow or bolt hitting just right."

"It doesn't seem too heavy," the Norrheimer said meditatively.

His concern was more or less abstract, a warrior's curiosity about his craft. All the people who wore plate in this war were on his side.

"Fifty pounds or a bit less for a suit in her size," Rudi agreed. "More than mail, but not so very much more. And it's nearly as flexible as one of your hauberks. The weight's well distributed by tying and buckling it to the point strings on the arming doublet and breeches instead of hanging everything from the shoulders. And it's much better protection from arrows and bolts than mail. The way it traps heat is the worst drawback; you get tired faster, and you can sweat yourself into a faint if you're not careful. That's why she was wearing it, probably. You have to keep yourself accustomed to the heat and constriction. Forbye it's good exercise."

"Still, wearing it and moving quickly needs strength. You have many strong shield-maids here."

Bjarni looked surprised when the others chuckled.

"Everyone else here does, except the PPA," Rudi explained. "Tiphaine and . . . perhaps fifty or sixty others all told. Including my Matti! Their custom doesn't hold with it. Nor their God, or at least so say many of their priests; it takes great skill and even more strength of will to break those barriers. She's an exception. I told you how we Mackenzies captured Mathilda on a raid during the War of the Eye, when we were both around ten?"

Bjarni nodded, and Rudi continued: "Well, Tiphaine—she was knighted and ennobled for it and granted the fief of Ath—snatched her back that spring, with a small picked band. *And* myself, the both of us being not twice bowshot from the gates of Dun Juniper when she struck, the which was ingenious and bold. She got us back out of the Mackenzie dùthchas to Castle Todenangst with cloth yard arrows raining about her ears, too, which was not merely bold but skill of a miraculous degree—even on foot the Clan's warriors can push a pursuit like wolves on the track of an elk and run horses to death. Lady Sandra stashed the both of us at Castle Ath for some time . . . which is where I began learning swordplay from her."

"She's good with a blade?" Bjarni said, his own hand dropping unconsciously to the hilt of his broadsword. "I thought she might be, from the grip she gave and the pattern of calluses on her hand."

"I first beat her sparring when I was twenty-one, and didn't again for some time," he said soberly. "I've never crossed blades with anyone faster in all my travels. As swift as I, and more nimble. I have more reach and I'm much stronger, of course, but her blade-art is complete."

The others all nodded, Signe a little unwillingly. A speculative look came into Bjarni's blue gaze; to a warrior, everything that wasn't a prize to be seized was a potential challenge to be overcome.

"Don't even think it," Rudi said, and Eric nodded vigorously.

Signe smiled grimly. "Did you see the hilt of her sword, my friend?"

Bjarni nodded, obviously puzzled. "A very good weapon, if narrower than we like in Norrheim, I suppose for thrusting strokes against the joints in plate. And well-adorned, the silver setting off the back horn."

"Those twelve silver bands aren't adornment, Bjarni King. They're a death-tally and public warning," she said.

"Holmgangs?" Bjarni said, using his folk's word for a duel.

"Technically," Eric laughed, but this time it was utterly without humor. "I saw a few of those . . . you couldn't really call them fights, though the victims were experienced swordsmen. They were executions. *Slow* executions. It was more like a cat playing with a mouse than combat. And one of the few occasions I've seen her really smile."

"Brrr!" Bjarni said. Then, with blunt practicality: "And what's my part in this plan you make, my blood brother?"

"Never fear, you'll hear it soon." He turned to Eric and Signe. "I brought two thousand Drumheller cavalry with me when we crossed the Rockies at Castle Corbec," he said. "Medium horse, lance and saber and bow, mail hauberks and plate for the arms and legs."

"About what we Bearkillers were using ten, fifteen years ago," Eric said thoughtfully. "I liked what I saw of them there. Trained in cataphract tactics like ours, too?"

"Precisely; well trained and drilled. Also Drumheller is *not* part of Montival and will not be, and they *did* fight the Association, when they tried to take back that western part of the Peace River country the Lord Protector grabbed off in their despite, the spalpeen. County Dawson, it is now; about which they are still bitter, so. So I'll be brigading them with your Bearkiller A-listers, giving out it's the best tactical fit—the which is true—and to avoid unnecessary memories of a painful and awkward sort."

"That ought to work," Eric said thoughtfully. "We're more mobile than the Association knights, we don't need a light cavalry screen as badly, and we have a lot more punch in a charge with the lance than pure horse-archers."

"It's fair pleased I'll be if it does work," Rudi said frankly. "Fitting this collection of puzzle pieces, not to mention the odds and sods trickling in from everywhere between Dawson and Ashland, into an army I can use without it coming to pieces on a battlefield like a soggy biscuit in hot tea is a nightmare of purest black, and we've little time."

Sober nods, and he continued: "Well, you'll be receiving them in the next day or two. And I'm off. This High King position needs about six men to fill it."

"You won't be disappointed in us Bearkillers, Your Majesty," Mike Jr. blurted. Then he quoted: *"Always faithful."*

That was the motto of a band of warriors their common father had fought with, before the Change.

"Mike, *mo bhràthair*, you were at my wedding!" Rudi said. "And saw me pale and wan with terror until your uncle slipped me some brandy. It's a little too formal that was, brother, for an everyday occasion like this."

"My liege, then," Mike said.

"That will do. Feel free to add embellishments when you're convinced I've gone lunatic; I've yet to see a battlefield where men didn't feel that way about the high command, at times."

The tall young man's face split in an answering grin, and the High King went on: "Every time we meet you favor our father more; you've more of his cast of face than I do, I'm thinking. Perhaps by the end of this war you'll be wearing the Bear Helm, eh?"

Mike's face flushed; he met Rudi's eyes for a long moment, then gave a slight nod. Eric's brows went up. Signe went pale.

After a long moment she bowed to Rudi. "Hail, Artos King," she said; there was a slight choking in her voice. "I wished that. I hadn't thought you'd aid me in it."

Rudi smiled. *I know it's a charming smile,* some corner of him thought. *Matti's told me it is often enough, and sometimes with a deal of exasperation in her voice. Still, if the Gods gave it me, I should use it, and I'm not putting it on, either. I've always liked Signe better than she did me, Eric is a man you're glad to have at your back, and of young Mike I'm fond in truth.*

"The Bearkillers will be a stout pillar of the High Kingdom," Rudi said. "The more so with the bond of blood between my House and the line of the Bear Lords."

"We will be your sword and shield!" Mike blurted, then blushed as his mother and uncle shot him quelling looks. "Well, we *will*."

Rudi made his farewells and turned to Bjarni. "Walk with me, blood brother."

The Norrheimer did, squinting westward for a moment past his own people's encampment; the lines of tall slim poplars on the plain were casting long shadows. They were alone. Except for Edain and the score of the High King's Archers behind them, of course, and a half dozen of Bjarni's *hirdmen*, walking with mail byrnie clinking and conical nose-guarded helmets on their heads, round shields on their left arms and spears or great long-hafted axes over their right shoulders. All of the guardsmen were out of earshot, if they spoke quietly.

"Bad blood there, eh?" Bjarni said shrewdly, inclining his head slightly back towards the Bearkillers. "Or there was."

Rudi shrugged. "My blood father rescued my mother from some Eaters—mad cannibals—"

"What we called troll-men," Bjarni nodded.

Such bands had been common throughout the more heavily peopled places in the year after the Change, as the desperate millions ate the storehouses bare to the last hidden scrap and then turned on each other amid chaos, fire and plague. Where the cities had been most dense, their savage descendants were the only human thing left, save scorched bones split for the marrow.

"—not long after the Change. They were both of them on scouting missions, you see. And . . . well, that night was when I was begotten. Mike Havel wasn't handfasted to Lady Signe then; they weren't even betrothed, really, though they were thinking of it from what I've heard."

"Ah," Bjarni said. "And there's the rub, eh?"

Rudi nodded: "She always held it against mother, and me. Less so as the years have gone by, but it's also a bitterness to her that *her* son will be a chief in my kingdom, and not the other way about, you see. Mike himself doesn't mind; we've always gotten along well and he's a likely and good-natured lad. Also just the now he's at the age when he needs a hero to worship, or an elder brother. Whether he'll still feel that way ten or fifteen years from now . . . we'll see."

"I do see," Bjarni said. "My folk have their own rivalries. It's the nature of the sons and daughters of Ash and Embla. So that's why you said your half brother has more of a look of your father."

"Sure, and it's the truth . . . though not by much, we're both his image in body and face, though we're taller than he was by a few inches. And the neither of us have his coloring; he was black-haired, perhaps because he had an Anishinabe grandmother, one of the First People, though for the rest he was mostly Suomi with a dash of Svenska and Norski. But young Mike *does* have a bit more of his face, I'd be saying. He was a handsome fellow, my father, among much else."

"He must have been a man of strong main"—which meant soul-strength, in the Norrheimer dialect—"and a fighting man of note and able to steer matters wisely,"

Bjarni said thoughtfully. "From what I've heard, Gods aside, he puts me in mind of my father, Erik the Strong."

"A fair comparison. I remember him only a little, but he left a great mark on the world passing through it, and from that you can see the shape of the man who made it."

The land wrinkled up before them a little, scored and gashed and littered with rocks ranging from loaf-sized to real boulders; as you went south here you met spots that had been cut by water into gullies long ago. Three sentries rose out of nowhere, with arrows on the half-drawn strings of their longbows, Mackenzies in ghillie cloaks; those were hooded lengths of camouflaged cloth sewn all over with loops. The loops were thrust through with bits of grass and sagebrush or whatever else fit the landscape, and if the wearers knew what they were doing they could be nearly invisible even in open ground. Rudi had spotted them, but Bjarni gave a slight start.

The leader of the trio tossed back his gauze-masked hood as he took the draw off his string. He was painted for war in the Clan's style, patterns of scarlet and black swirling over his face to give it the look of his sept totem, a fox-mask in this case. The moon-and-antlers of the Mackenzies was blazoned on the green leather surface of his brigantine, and there was a tuft of the reddish fur dangling from a silver ring he wore in one ear.

There was something a little foxlike about his eyes too, despite his dark hair and olive skin, darting and quick and cunning. Doubtless that kinship of spirit was why he'd dreamed of Fox on his vision journey as a youngster; that was part of the Clan's coming-of-age ceremonies.

"*Chomh gilc ie sionnach,*" Rudi said gravely; *clever as a fox* in the old tongue, and the motto of the man's sept.

"That we are, High King. Pass you may, lord, and those with you," he said, tapping his bow stave against the brow of his open-faced sallet helm in salute.

Then he turned, waved to someone farther down the slope, and made a slight chittering sound with tongue and teeth. It might have passed unnoticed anywhere insects formed the background of life. The sentries took different positions, sank down . . . and were once more nearly invisible, even if you'd seen them do it.

Bjarni looked behind him as they walked on. "Your folk take war seriously," he said approvingly.

"That we do, or we'd be long dead," Rudi said, hiding a grin. "We have no Fluffy Bunny sept . . . sorry, an old joke among us, I'll explain another time if you wish."

And you Norrheimers find us deplorably flighty and light-minded and long-winded and fanciful about all else, he thought but did not say. *While the most of my clansfolk who meet them find your people a staid and stark and solemn-dull lot who find little mirth in anything but hitting folk with axes. It would be a drabber and less interesting world if everyone were the same, would it not?*

The Norrheimer gave a slight grunt of surprise when they came over the slope and saw the Mackenzie camp below. The plain around Goldendale was really a plateau at the foot of the hills behind the town, and its southern edge was valleys where water had cut back long ago; the ground became rougher as you went south to the Columbia at Maryhill and less of it was farmed. This was a broad open swale, the bottom perhaps twenty or thirty feet lower than the higher plowed fields. The bulk of it was in grass turning gold in the sunset light, with thick-scattered clumps of oak and pine in the lower parts. In time of peace it was a preserve for the hunting and hawking of the Associate lord who held these lands, and in war a fine campground that didn't interfere with what remained of workaday life.

Scattered almost as thickly through it were the small tents of the Mackenzie host, grouped in threes and those in circles for each Dun; Sutterdown's contingent had four circles, they being the Clan's only approach to a city, grouped around their banner of sea-blue and sky-blue blazoned with a scalloped shell and lyre and bow. Little efficient cook fires cast a trickle of smoke into the air, just enough to let you get a whiff of the wood burning and a bit of the food. The other camp odors weren't too bad; Mackenzies were as cleanly a people as they could be, and this group hadn't been here long yet. Rudi walked down the track at an easy swing, taking off his flat Scots bonnet now and then to wave back greetings.

A different set of tents caught his eye as well, about a score and in rigidly regular lines; the flag that flew over them was the ancient Stars and Stripes.

"Ah, Fred Thurston's here," Rudi said. "And by the looks of it, his little force has grown. More prisoners going over to him, and we've had a few deserters as well."

Bjarni made a skeptical sound. "Fred Lawrencesson I know and like," he said. "He's a good fighter and no fool, and the High One did claim him in my own hall—a great honor, though it's a dangerous one. He's one of the true folk. Yet I'm not altogether sure of his followers, men who'd turn on their lord."

"Martin Thurston isn't their rightful lord," Rudi pointed out, then thought a moment to put it into terms his friend would grasp at once and with his gut as well as his head. "He killed their father by stealth and treachery."

"True, true."

"And then he lied about it, got his men's oaths under

false pretense. His oath was false, and he made theirs false too."

"Also true. The Gods hate an oath-breaking man, they send him bad luck and bad luck is catching, like a flu. But . . . well, it's all a tangle as bad as Sigurd and the Rhinegold."

"That it is. We'll cut that knot, though."

The Mackenzies were mostly readying their dinners, practicing archery at targets of rolled straw matting or working on gear or just lolling about passing the time at games or songs or storytelling or lively arguments. War was mostly boredom, when it wasn't terror. The Boise men were drilling, moving with a smooth machine-discipline that was almost eerie to watch as they cast their heavy javelins, formed and re-formed and changed front, then suddenly clumped together into a walking fortress that had shields on all sides and overhead as well.

"Pretty," Bjarni admitted. "We do something like that, but not as smooth."

He looked around at the clansfolk. "Those thin gold collars mean the handfasted, don't they?" he said after a moment.

When Rudi nodded, and touched the torc around his own neck, the Norrheimer continued: "You're putting everything you have into this, aren't you?"

"Yes," Rudi said. "As you did with your folk at the Seven Hills battle, Bjarni King. You couldn't hedge your bet and neither can I. We have to win the campaign coming up or be ruined, and to win it we have to load a rock in our fist before we hit them, so to say."

This wasn't just a group of wild youngsters. Many of these folk were solid householders with crofts and work-steads and children back at their Duns. And there were stacks of boxes and sacks, wagons parked in long ranks, even longer ones of bicycles, horses grazing under watch-ful eyes. And great man-high banks of stacked wicker cyl-inders full of bundled arrows, more than all the other supplies together.

They came to his goal, a series of larger tents where a brace of guards stood, tall men leaning on Lochaber axes—gruesome weapons with hafts five feet long and a yard of chopping blade that tapered to a wicked point, with a hook behind. The Clan Mackenzie's standard flew above, a silver crescent moon cradled between black ant-lers on a green field. The sides of the tents were brailed up to let the breeze in, and he could see folding tables and chairs, racks for records and account-books and maps, and men and women busy at the paperwork that any army seemed to accumulate. They were winding it up, though, as the light died. That came earlier down here, with the higher ground to cut off the sunlight.

As the red sun dropped the clansfolk put aside any work or play that could be halted—he saw cards, dice, baseball and a whooping impromptu *Iománaíoch* game with the ball flying up amid a waving of ax-shaped hurly sticks—and turned to face the fiery glow that turned the western horizon crimson and light the sky above pale green. Voices took up a long wordless note, more and more until you realized that there were many thou-sands scattered down the valley. Singing well was as much a part of being a Mackenzie as shooting with the bow. Rudi turned westward with the rest and raised his voice, his arms spread above his head, palm-upward in the Old Religion's gesture of prayer. Then the song began:

> *"We know the Sun was Her lover*
> *As They danced the worlds awake;*

And She lay with His brilliance
For all Their children's sake.
Where Her fingers touched the sky
Silver starfire sprang from nothing!
And She held Her children fast in Her dreams."

Bjarni and the Norrheimers stood aside, inclining their heads to show a guest's respect for customs and Gods not their own. The massed voices rolled on, bidding farewell to the day in a hymn that Rudi's own mother had composed:

"There was a glory in that forest
As the moonlight glittered down;
And stars shone in the wildwood
When the dew fell to the ground—
Every branch and every blossom;
Every root and every leaf
Drank the tears of the Goddess in the gloaming!
There came steel, there came cities
Wonders terrible and strange,
But the light from the first-wood
Flickered down until the Change.
And every field, every farmhouse,
Every quiet village street
Knew the tears of the Goddess in the gloaming!
Now the Sun comes to kiss Her
And She rises from Her bed
They are young—and old—and ageless
Joy that paints the mountains red.
We shall dance in Their twilight
As the forests fall to sleep,
And She whispers in our ears the word remember!"

The silence held for a long moment afterwards, as the sunlight faded. Rudi dropped his hands, still feeling the peace of it plucking at his heart, like a bard's hands on the strings. Then he shook his head slightly. There was little enough peace he'd have in the next few years.

Well, the more reason to grab what moments I can, he thought.

He strode forward towards the area in front of the command tent. There was a fair-sized fire there, down to red-and-yellow coals now, and a bustle of cooking. A big man dressed only in a kilt was crouched over a young sheep, no longer quite a lamb—a yearling wether, he thought—holding its shoulders pressed between his knees and its head in his hands.

"So, little brother, we are sorry," he said, in a soothing, crooning voice as he stroked its head until it quieted. "But we are hungry and must eat. We thank you for your gift of life. To us also the hour of the Hunter will come, for Earth must be fed. Go swiftly and without pain to the green clover-meads of the Land of Summer where no evil comes, and be reborn through Her who is Mother-of-All."

The big hands clamped and he twisted with a sudden violent swiftness. Muscle moved and then stood out on his bare shoulders and arms like a swelling wave. There was a crackling snap like a green branch breaking, and the animal gave one single kick and died before it had time to bleat. A boy and girl in their mid-teens stepped forward, took the carcass away and began bleeding and butchering it efficiently, the sort of task helpers of their age did in any Mackenzie force, learning the routine of war before they were old enough to stand in the bow-line. A collection of big shaggy dogs gathered to watch intently, tails wagging as they waited for their treat of blood and offal but too disciplined to do more than whine softly and lick their chops.

"Merry met, Oak," Rudi said to the man as he straightened.

Oak Barstow Mackenzie nodded back; they clasped hands for a brisk shake. The First Armsman of Clan Mackenzie was about Rudi's height and not unlike in build, though eight years older and a trifle heavier; his long queue of hair was the color of summer-faded meadow grass, and so were his long mustaches. He'd been an orphan of the Change, one of a busload of schoolchildren on tour left stranded by the roadside and lucky enough to meet the bulk of the Singing Moon coven on its flight from Eugene to what eventually became Dun Juniper. The fledgling Clan had continued to adopt such foundlings as often as they could without actually starving all through those early years, and it had paid in a manner which showed the truth of the Law of Threefold Return.

"Merry met, *Ard Rí*," Oak said, using the old tongue's term for a High King. "And to you too, Bjarni Ironrede. Join us; there's plenty for all. And Mother sent along some of her BBQ sauce."

"That's an offer I'll accept gladly," Rudi said. "Aunt Judy's herb-lore is of the best, for healing and cooking both. And merry met to you as well, Fred, Virginia. How are your men shaping? More in?"

"Two hundred thirty altogether, sir," Fred said. "And they're shaping very well indeed. A lot of squads decided to come over together and they're glad to be in the field instead of in a camp."

Rudi sat on one of the rocks that had been rolled around the fire. Absently, he noticed Edain detailing units of the Archers to eat by turns while the others stood watch; Bjarni's guard-chief was doing something similar.

I'll just be learning to live with that unsleeping vigilance, for I think it's my fate, he thought.

Darkness was falling now, as the long summer twilight faded; the coals underlit the faces around him, giving them an odd bony look with the lanterns in the tents throwing contrasting shadows. The meat had gone on the fire, mostly on wooden skewers, sending up fragrant smoke and making the coals flare where drops of fat landed. There was a bubbling pot of beans stewed with onions and dried tomatoes and chunks of bacon, another of greens, and one of the helpers was frying sliced potatoes in a pan.

"This is more like a hunting trip than a war, so far," Oak said as plates were handed around. Grudgingly, as he took a loaf of rough maslin bread from a basket and tore off a piece: "The PPA has done all they promised in the way of supplies. We're even getting these from the city bakeries by the wagonload every day. And they've assigned us enough wells, though only just."

Rudi understood the scowl. Oak's sister Aoife and his foster brother Sanjay had all died in the wars against the Association. But his foster father had been killed by the CUT in the battle at Pendleton last year. Chuck had been First Armsman after Sam Aylward resigned the position, but Oak hadn't inherited it because of anything but proved ability. He'd been his father's right hand for years anyway, as Chuck had been Sam Aylward's before him. The Clan had an informal approach to such matters.

"It'll be dog biscuit and jerky soon enough," Rudi said.

He pulled the eating tool out of the little sheath on his dirk scabbard, with a spoon on one end and a fork on the other.

"You're ready?" he went on, catching the chunk of

bread Oak tossed him out of the air and sticking the fork-end in it.

"The last three thousand from the southernmost Duns are just here the now," Oak said. "All together, twelve thousand one hundred fifty-two archers fit to stand in the bow-line. Not counting healers, pipers and *eòghann*."

Seeing Bjarni's puzzlement, Rudi spoke aside to him, nodding to indicate the teenagers: "*Eòghann*. Youths and maidens not yet old enough to fight, to 'take valor,' as we say. In a stand-up battle they mainly carry arrows forward to the bow-line from the reserve stocks. It's important work."

Someone handed him a plate loaded with fried potatoes, boiled kale and skewers of grilled mutton. He made the Invoking pentagram over it and murmured a quick thanks to the Mother, and Her Consort who died to give the grain life and rose again each year. The Norrheimers and Fred Thurston hammer-signed theirs, and spoke their own blessing: *Hail, all-giving Earth*.

Oak nodded as he ladled out beans: "The test for the First Levy is shooting twelve arrows to the measured minute and keeping it up for ten minutes, from a bow of eighty pounds pull or better, and putting nine of each twelve into a man-sized target a hundred yards away. That's the minimum, you understand, not the average. Against massed targets we usually start shooting at about three hundred long paces' distance."

Bjarni's brows went up. "Twelve thousand archers . . . twelve arrows a minute . . ."

"That's twenty-four hundred a second," Rudi said, touching the Sword. "Or just under a hundred and fifty thousand in one minute. It is," he added gently, "a great whacking lot of arrows, the which is why we call it an arrowstorm. Nor are most battles only a minute long.

Hence the *eòghann* scurry about a good deal, the darlings."

Bjarni pursed his lips. Behind him Edain chuckled very quietly; he'd been the first to show the Norrheimers what the Mackenzie yew longbow could do, in their own distant homeland. Now their king was contemplating what twelve thousand such bows could do to a force trying to close with them. Rudi knew that wasn't entirely fair; Edain was known as Aylward *the* Archer for a reason. Nor was the great armor-smashing stave he carried typical. *That* bow drew over half again the minimum allowed.

But it's mostly fair if not entirely, Rudi thought. *A fifty-pound draw on a hunting bow will put a broadhead through a bull elk's body, breaking ribs going in and coming out; I've seen it done. Eighty pounds on a warbow will do for a man, sure, often enough even if he's wearing a tin shirt.*

"That *is* a great whacking lot of arrows," Bjarni said. "How many do you lug about with you?"

Oak grinned. "You ask the right questions, Bjarni King," he said. "And the answer is *as many as we can*. Also the *eòghann* run out to scavenge as many spent ones as they can from the field, when it's safe. Food can be foraged at a pinch and you can fight barefoot or even bare-arsed if you must, but a cloth yard arrow needs well-seasoned straight-grained wood for the shaft, good flight feathers from a goose and glue and thread for fletching, horn for the nock and fine hard steel for the bodkin, and all put together with skill in the making. Fashioning arrows is one of the tasks we do in the Black Months, when the farm work is less. It's part of the Chief's Portion."

"The scot, you'd say," Rudi amplified. "The tax."

"And nobody skimps the work, when their lives and families might rest on it," Oak said. He turned his face to Rudi. "And another four thousand archers in the forts in the Cascades, the ones who can fight but aren't up to much hard marching for one reason or another. The enemy's withdrawn some men from overmountain and the Bend country, but not all of them."

Soberly, he met Rudi's eyes. "This is all we have, High King. If we lose it the Clan dies."

Rudi nodded, equally grave; all that was a fifth of the Clan's total population, and a much higher share of its adults.

"I know. It's still our best chance. Our archers and the Association's knights are the biggest edges that we have, and sure, I intend to wring every scrap of advantage from both that I can."

Then he took up a skewer of the wether's flesh, biting off a chunk. The tender meat was juicy-pink in the center and Judy Barstow's sauce, tangy with garlic and sage and peppers, was crusted on the seared outer surface. It would have been finer still for marinating awhile, but it was better than ample for a war-camp.

"See you, Oak," he said, gesturing with the remainder of the kebab, "I've read your reports on the fighting you did in the mountains west of Bend while I was gone on the Quest. You beat them handily, but don't judge all that they can do by what happened when they had no choice but to charge you on your own ground in the passes. *Or* by the poor and pitiful performance of hungry frightened plainsmen clumping in high-heeled rawhide boots through a strange snowbound forest."

Oak nodded. "From first to last the CUT's horse-archers were a pain in the arse at Pendleton," he said. "Much more so when we were forced to retreat, and *they* had room to maneuver fast. They're hard trouble in any sort of open country, and that is a fact. That's how my father died."

And you took a spectacular vow of vengeance at Chuck's passing ceremony, Rudi thought. *Will it cloud your judgment?*

He didn't think so, and he wasn't sure whether that was the long knowledge of growing up in the same Dun as this man, or something the Sword of the Lady gave him. He'd always been fair to excellent at reading folk, but with the Sword at his side no man could lie to him, even if the words deceived the speaker himself. He found himself fighting to keep that from souring his view of humankind, sometimes.

"We had a lot of trouble with them in the battle at Wendell," Fred observed. "And that's how they beat Deseret—more cavalry and moving faster. You can fight them with infantry but you need *some* horse-archers yourself, and a shitload of field artillery really helps, since it outranges their bows. Then if they thin out their formations to cut down their casualties they drop the intensity of their firepower a lot."

"We needed the cavalry and catapults badly to hold them off so that we could break contact," Oak agreed. "We'd have been surrounded and whittled down to nothing, else, instead of just hurt."

"Just so, and Lugh of the Many Skills knows the Boise infantry are a bad lot in a fight too. Very disciplined, very well drilled in their maneuvers and it's an annoyingly persistent set of *omadhauns* they are to boot."

Fred grinned. "Yup. If they try charging us, well, we'll give them as much trouble as they want."

"Exactly. It's uncomfortably good at combined-arms work Boise's army is, and *they* have no religious scruples about making catapults of their own, unlike the CUT. I'm doing what I can about that stubbornness, breaking their heads from the inside, you might say, and Fred's been a help. But in the meantime I think you're going to need a reaction squad of head-bashers in the more usual sense of the word, more than Fred's band can provide, and I've just the men for the core of that."

Bjarni was mopping up beans with a chunk of the bread. He nodded, still chewing, drank from the mug of watered wine beside him, and spoke: "That we can do. We're not wizards with the bow like you Mackenzies, but handstrokes are our sport and our delight. And my five hundred are picked men, the best fighters of all the tribes of Norrheim. Well used to fighting side by side by now too."

Rudi slapped him on the shoulder. "That they are, Oak. For planting their feet in the dirt and locking shields to conquer or die where they stand, I've seen that there's none like the warriors of Norrheim. Pitiless fighters, fell and grim. Also they're the truest of men to their oaths, and fear does not enter into their actions."

There was a slight happy growl from the armored *hirdmen* behind their king; he couldn't have picked a compliment from all the world's tongues that would have pleased them more, as long as it came from someone they respected.

The which they do, after the Seven Hills fight, at which all these men shed sweat and many let their blood on the ground from their wounds. And for their pledged oaths many of them will die very far from home, meeting their end on foreign ground with their last sight the faces of angry strangers. I will do what I must, for the kingdom's sake and the world's. And for my children yet unborn. The praise will also go a way to reconciling them to being brigaded with Fred's not-really-turncoats. It's an acrobat a High King must be!

"Now, when is this battle where we Norrheimers will

do our head-bashing to be?" Bjarni said, belching contentedly and handing his plate to the youth. "And where?"

More of the watered wine went around, and a small sack filled with dried fruit and nuts. Oak leaned forward eagerly as well, and Fred's face had a wolf's keenness.

"It'll be as late as I can manage," Rudi said. "Around Samhain, if I can harry and delay until then. Yule would be too much to hope for."

He turned aside to Bjarni for a moment: "Samhain's our festival of the dead and the Otherworld, that ends the sacred Wheel of the Year. The Quarter Day at the end of October. Lughnasadh is the summer festival, just past."

Oak hissed between his teeth. "Samhain? That long?" he said, obviously thinking of the autumn planting and a hungry year to follow if it was skimped.

"Everyone planted more last fall than normal, I hear, and we can put in more spring grain next year needs must. Time fights for us, remember; time, and the land itself," Rudi said. "The enemy outnumber us three to two; or they will at the beginning of things."

"It would have been two to one, if you hadn't gotten us allies," Oak acknowledged.

Rudi nodded; it was true. "I'll make them leave their base of supply far behind, draw them in, with each step making them weaker as they must detach forces to guard their lines of supply and invest the strongholds. Then I'll bring them to battle at the time and place I choose."

"Where?" Oak said.

"The Horse Heaven Hills," he said, nodding eastward.

Bjarni frowned, and Rudi drew in the dirt with a twig, showing how those lay between the valley of the Yakima river and the Columbia, a little east of where they were now.

"Or at least Horse Heaven is my choice," Rudi said, seeing the lay of those long swells in his mind. "The enemy, the dirty dogs, will have a plan of their own, the which is a reason why we call them *the enemy*. It's nicely varied terrain, not too closed in to maneuver freely or use our heavy cavalry, and not so open there's no element of surprise or choice of ground. They might try to go north of there, up the Yakima, but that would trap them in a cul-de-sac and the Free Cities are too strong to storm with an army still on their flank."

"It's rich land, if they're hungry," Oak said. To Bjarni: "A great valley, closely tilled—watered by channels from the river, one fortified village and walled town after another, field after field. Densely peopled with strong yeomen, and they good farmers and stubborn fighters both."

"Rich land but with all that's edible behind walls," Rudi said. "Or it will be after my orders are carried out. Taking the Yakima would only make sense in a slow campaign aimed at steady conquest of one bit at a time, but now that the League of Des Moines and the Dominions are marching up their backsides they don't have that luxury."

"You think that will make them give you a fight where and when you want it?" Bjarni said. "Letting your enemy set the terms of battle is halfway to a battle lost. If they have good war-captains, they'll know that."

Rudi nodded. "They'll go for our main field army, the beating of which is their only hope of any real victory now. Castles and walled cities can slow and frustrate an invader, but it's only in concert with an army that they can defeat him. That's the bait I'll dangle before them, snatching it away again and again by taking positions too strong to attack as I fall back."

He smiled. There was something he'd read once . . . and the Sword prompted him. He said something in another language. When the two men looked at him questioningly, he went on:

"In our tongue . . . *Those skilled at making the enemy move do so by creating a situation to which he must conform; they entice him with something he is certain to take, and with lures of ostensible profit they await him in strength.*"

"That's sensible," Bjarni said.

"Sun Tzu generally is, the wit and keen insight of the man."

"I've read him, Dad was big on his *Art of War*," Fred noted soberly. "The thing is, Martin read him too. He's an evil treacherous shit but he's not stupid."

"You're thinking of the man as you knew him," Rudi said. "I have grounds to suspect he's much changed. Also knowing what you should do and overriding impulse are two quite different things; and he'll be much concerned with things at home, and even the most absolute ruler must take the opinions and feelings of his war-captains into account. By Samhain they'll be mad with rage and fear and hunger and want nothing so much in all the world as to *finish* it. Then I'll offer battle in a position that looks just a little more doable from their side than it really is, and—"

Bjarni drew a thumb across his throat below the dark red beard and made a horribly realistic gurgling sound, like a man drowning in his own blood, rolling his eyes upward; the coal-glow from the fire added an unpleasant touch to the pantomime. He and Oak barked laughter together. Fred looked grim; any victory would mean the death of a good many of his people.

"Or so we hope." Rudi nodded.

They discussed options and details, munching on the raisins and slices of dried peach and apricot and apple, the walnuts and hazelnuts in the bag and calling over a couple of those with clerk's skills to take notes. After an hour or so a stir came from the northward.

"Ah, and yet another detail to squeeze into the capacious folds of the dying day," Rudi said. His head turned to look down the valley. "Twelve thousand . . . not a quorum by itself."

Oak nodded. "Counting proxies, yes, though. They're all duly registered, so we have the *Óenach Mór* here with us, that we do."

A helper brought round water and a well-used cloth, and they washed their hands.

"*Óenach . . . Mór?*" Bjarni asked.

"A . . . folkmoot," Rudi said. "Each Dun in the Mackenzie dùthchas has its *óenach*, its assembly of adult members. And *Mór* means *Great* in the old tongue of our ancestors. The Great Moot, you might say, where the Chief presides and decisions are made for the Clan as a whole. The votes must represent the majority for the decision to be lawful, by pledged proxy if they can't be there themselves. In ordinary times it's a great holiday, with games and contests and plays and such, held yearly after the harvest festival. Lughnasadh, about this time, in fact."

Bjarni's eyes lit. "Why, that's like the *things* for our tribes, and the *all-thing* for Norrheim!" he said. "The town meetings, as the old folk called them."

"Mmmm, ours are more noisy than yours, I'm thinking," Rudi said judiciously. "They certainly last longer, as a general rule; though I'd say this one may be mercifully brief. You're welcome to watch."

"I'll bring my men and they'll sit on the edge," Fred said, nodding. "It'll impress them. In more ways than one."

A stirring came through the darkness, and then the keening, droning wail of the pipes with a thuttering roar of drums beneath it. Rudi grinned to himself; his mother had composed that tune, too, when someone insisted. He thought it had been Dennie, a friend of hers who'd had a big role in establishing Clan customs in the early days.

Officially the title was *It's a Clan We Must Be*, from the first speech she'd given to the little band of fugitives meeting at the old hunting lodge that had become the core of Dun Juniper. She herself had been known to refer to it as *Hail to the Chief*, which oldsters considered a great joke; some obscure reference to the ancient world.

His eyes sought her eagerly. *After Matti, the one I love most in all the world,* he thought. *And Sir Nigel. I need their wisdom. And Maude and Fiorbhinn, so grown while I was away!*

Juniper Mackenzie listened to the pipers and the hammering rattle of the Lambegs and the dunting snarl of war-horns calling the assembly and smiled to herself. Beside her Nigel Loring, her man, leaned his head towards her.

"That's your *ironic* smile, my dear," he said.

The smooth cultured drawl of the grandmother who'd raised him was still strong in his voice. His parents had both died within a few years of his birth, and his grandfather Eustace had stood too close to a German howitzer shell during the retreat from Mons in 1914, leaving a young widow and a posthumous son. He'd been in middle age when he arrived a fugitive from Mad King Charles in England, fifteen years ago, during the War of the Eye. Now he was unambiguously old, his head egg-bald, the last yellow gone from the clipped white mustache. He was still slim and erect in the Clan's formal garb of tight green jacket with lace at throat and cuffs and double row of silver buttons, badger-skin sporran, kilt and plaid, flat Scots bonnet with silver clasp.

"I was thinking that I should never have let Dennis at my Gaelic dictionary and *Myths and Customs of the Ancient Celts*, the illustrated one, at that. The glee the man had in him when he persuaded people to take up some bit of Victorian-fantasy folderol that drove me wild, back in the early years! In the end the only way to stop him tormenting me with it was to go along, so . . . and I couldn't bear to quash folk when they needed something to catch their fancy when all else was so bleak. And he thought it the cream of the jest that he was nine-tenths English by blood himself, and the rest everything under the sun *but* Irish, or even Scots. Whereas I had my mother speaking the Gaelic to me in my cradle."

"Ah, well, old girl, remember the definition of an Anglo-Saxon: *a German who's forgotten his grandmother was Welsh.* Back in the old days I did always note that it wasn't the people from the Gaeltacht who went barking mad for the Celtic-Twilight, Deirdre-of-the-Sorrows bit."

"No," Juniper said shortly. "They were too poor and too sensible, both. What my mother would think of this festival of deranged romanticism run amuck I shudder to imagine. It was hard enough on her when I went over to the Old Religion."

"She might note that it was an Englishman by the name of Rawlinson who invented the kilt."

"He probably just stole the credit for it," she said loftily, and saw the glint of amusement in his rather watery blue eyes—they'd been injured in some distant land in battle before the Change.

Oman, it was called, she recalled. *Odd, to remember a time when places halfway around the world were more than distant rumor, when it really* mattered *what happened there. Nigel isn't the only one who's old. I'm spending more and more time remembering, and less than I should focusing on the future. It's well that Rudi is High King now, a Changeling King for the Changeling world. Time for oldsters to take another step back.*

They'd had practice talking quietly for each other's ears only, but Juniper thought that Fiorbhinn caught a little of it. The girl had inherited the music from her side of the family along with a very keen set of ears, and her mother's bright leaf-green eyes, though her hair was white-blond with summer. The eyes sparkled now, and she carried the case with her small harp proudly, with the gravity only eleven years was capable of.

Maude was fifteen, coltish and slim and slightly awkward with it, brown-haired and grave. She was also swallowing a little now and then behind her calm face. Maude had always been the good one, steady and sensible and clever and kindhearted but not foolishly so, without the tang of wildwood magic that rang in Fiorbhinn's blood and out through her music. This wasn't something she had anticipated.

Which just goes to show the limits of being sensible, my girl, Juniper thought sympathetically. *For this is a matter of the Chieftainship, and truly that has something beyond the schemes and thoughts and reasons of humankind. There is a true magic to it, a thing that lifts us beyond the veils of the everyday. There always was.*

Rudi stood waiting for her; he removed his bonnet and bowed, smiling. Their eyes met as if in complicity, sharers in some solemn game, and her heart twisted with love and the sorrow that was its shadow.

I loved him so as a baby, and a child, and now a man. I protected him from all I could, but in the end love means letting them go.

The procession led to the edge of a slight rise; the valley fell away downslope and southward from there. It was packed now, a sea of upturned painted faces that stretched into a firelit darkness where clumps of leaves glittered amid the rising sparks of the torches. A rolling cheer started as she stopped and raised her hands; it built rapidly into a war-yell, the racking banshee shriek surging back and forth as blades and bows were thrust into the air. Juniper shivered a little. Mackenzies weren't exactly warlike; at least, they didn't go out and start wars as a group. On the other hand, when someone provoked them . . .

O Powers, she thought, not for the first time. *What have we brought back, to run wild once more upon the ridge of the world?*

Quiet fell as she brought her staff up to make the Invocation, the silver Triple Moon on its top glittering. The throng raised their hands as she spoke, her strong trained voice ringing out: "I am Juniper, the Mackenzie of the Clan Mackenzie, Chief and Bard and Ollam, trained and consecrated to this my task. I am called here, by you and the Gods to hear, to judge, and to speak. Does any deny my right or my calling? Speak now or hold your tongue thereafter, for this place and time is consecrated by our gathering. All we do here is holy."

A long silence and she continued, face raised: "Let us be blessed!"

"Let us be blessed!" the great crowd murmured, following her line by line.

"Manawyddan—Restless Sea, wash over me."

A green branch sprinkled seawater, and she tasted the salt on her lips like tears.

"Manawyddan—Restless Sea, wash over me."

"Cleanse and purify me! That I may make of myself a vessel; to listen and to *hear*."

"Cleanse and purify me! That I may make of myself a vessel; to listen and to hear."

"Rhiannon—White Mare, stand by me, run with me, carry me that the land and I can be one, with Earth's wisdom."

She bent and took a clod of the dry friable earth, touching it to her lips. There was a long ripple as the Mackenzies did the same.

"Rhiannon—White Mare, stand by me, run with me, carry me that the land and I can be one, with Earth's wisdom."

"Arianrhod—Star-tressed Lady; as you light the firmament above us, dance in the light of this world of ours, dance through our hearts and through our eyes, bring Your light to our minds."

She took a torch from her daughter Maud and lit it; the resinous wood flared up, and more lit all across the valley as her people called the response. The chanting rolled on:

"Sea and Land and Sky, I call on you:
Hear and hold and witness thus,
All that we say
All that we agree

All that we together do.
Honor to our Gods! May they hold
Our oaths
Our truths."

Then she spoke formally: "Let all here act with truth, with honor and with duty, that justice, safety and protection all be served for this our Clan, and may Ogma of the Honey Tongue lend us His eloquence in pursuit of Truth," she said. "This *Óenach Mór* is begun! By what we decide, we are bound, each soul and our people together."

A tension went out of the air in a long sigh. She put aside something of the ritual voice and went on: "I yield to my son, Rudi Mackenzie, called Artos in the craft, and tanist of this Clan."

She stepped back. Rudi stood tall for a moment, his arms crossed over his plaid and the tall raven feathers in the clasp of his bonnet flickering slightly, like a wing of shadow. When he spoke it seemed almost quiet, yet rolled out through the sough of night wind and the slight tearing ripple of flame: "My people, what were the words spoken by my mother over the altar at my Wiccaning? That day in the first year of the Change, in the depths of the winter when the Sun turned towards the light once more?"

A long moment of rustling silence, and then many thousand voices took it up, Juniper's among them. It was almost as if that *voice* spoke through her again, as the babe stirred in her arms and reached out one chubby hand to grasp the ritual sword in the *nemed*, the sacred wood above her home. But this time it was not through her alone; through many and many, as if some great rough beast spoke as its moment came at last:

"Sad Winter's child in this leafless shaw—
Yet be Son, and Lover, and Hornéd Lord!
Guardian of My sacred Wood, and Law—"

His people's strength—and the Lady's sword!

Rudi was silent again when the voices died away. Then he put his left hand to the hilt of the Sword and drew it slowly, raising it above his head.

There was a gasp. Juniper felt the same slight involuntary *huh!* escape her own lips. She wasn't sure that she *saw* anything at all, save a gleam of starlight and moonlight and firelight, but it seemed to blaze until all her eyes were filled with it.

"Artos!" someone called; and that name had been given him by her on the same day.

Then the name over and over again, until he suddenly sheathed the Sword. *That* cut it off, as he had swung that supernal edge against the sound.

"My people," he said into the silence. "A Mackenzie I was born, and among the very first begotten and born in this new time after the Change. A Mackenzie I shall be until I die. But Chief of the Clan, the Mackenzie Himself, I can never be."

Another roar, this one of protest. Rudi waited it out.

"I am the Lady's sword!"

That brought ringing silence, and he went on: "I am called by the Powers to be *Ard Rí* in Montival. The High King must be King of all his peoples and give good lordship and fair judgment to all; yes, and be *seen* to do that. I see men and women of our Clan from Sutterdown here, which is under the patronage of Apollo, the God who loves above all justice and due proportion in men and realms. Nor, by the Mare and the Raven and the Moon, does Rhiannon love it less."

He shook his head. "Your Chief I cannot be. And therefore I cannot be tanist, the successor. You must choose another, while my mother can yet train your choice."

He stepped back, and ostentatiously crossed his arms again. Juniper quirked a smile as she took up the words: "Long ago, at our first *Óenach Mór*—and it's considerably smaller that was!—"

That produced a startled laugh.

"I swore that I would be Chief only of a free folk. You may choose the Chief you will, and you may choose the Chief's tanist."

A low murmuring went through the throng, and then Oak Barstow stepped forward into the semicircle of firelight before the natural dais. His voice was more of a battle-shout than a bard's, but it carried well enough. "I say that we should have none but the blood of Lady Juniper to be Chief of the Clan; this by our free choice. Who says *aye*?"

A roar, one loud enough to make her almost take a step backward; it took a moment for quiet to fall again, and she felt a prickle of tears. Partly of joy—that love and offered devotion made all the years of work and worry seem less hard. And partly a mother's love of her children, for they would bear that burden after her.

"Lady Eilir has pledges to the Dúnedain," Oak went on, in a fine carrying roar; bards with the outer Duns relayed his words. "The Rangers are our friends and kindred, but they are another folk with their own laws and ways. Lady Fiorbhinn is too young—"

"And would be better suited to run crowing through the treetops and fly to the Moon, than to be Chief of three children in a bathtub, let alone a great roynish Clan!"

Her clear young voice cut through effortlessly. There

was a swelling ripple of laughter out to the edges of the great assembly. Oak's booming laugh was loudest of all. The smile was still in his voice as he went on:

"That leaves only one of Lady Juniper's children; and well she is suited to the task, as we all know. I call on the *Óenach Mór* to hail Maude Loring Mackenzie as Tanist of the Clan, to follow the Chief and learn from her and to be the Mackenzie in her turn. All for?"

"*AYE!*"

Juniper could see her daughter blink, as the force of the giant shout hit like a huge padded club at her chest.

"All against?"

There was a long silence; a few individuals stirred, began to rise, looked around the circle of those from their own Duns and sank down again. Oak's laughter was loud again. "Well, that's a first, just as this is the first Great Assembly not in the dùthchas of the Clan! But we should start the counting now, or it's very tired we'll be by tomorrow!"

CHAPTER NINE

CHARTERED CITY OF GOLDENDALE
COUNTY OF AUREA
PORTLAND PROTECTIVE ASSOCIATION
(FORMERLY CENTRAL WASHINGTON)
HIGH KINGDOM OF MONTIVAL
(FORMERLY WESTERN NORTH AMERICA)
AUGUST 5, CHANGE YEAR 25/2023 AD

Mathilda Arminger, now High Queen of Montival save for a few details concerning coronation ceremonies, groaned slightly as the ladies-in-waiting and the maids started to remove her surcote and the long tight dress and the not-quite-crown with its silk veil. She'd been *slightly* daring, going back to the books—which was where the Association's fashions had come from in the first place, really, before they took on a life of their own—and was wearing a formfitting kirtle of fourteenth-century style. The buttoned sleeves were normal, but *these* buttons were a full two inches apart, carved from golden tiger eyes into the Lidless Eye sigil of her house, leaving the cloth to stretch and show inch-wide medallions of her own flesh all the way up to three fingers below the shoulder, where her chemise started. The fabric was a peacock-patterned green silk, a precious rarity available only since a little trade with East Asia started up again in the last few years.

It was low cut from the very edge of her shoulders down to the middle of her breastbone, covering all but the very highest beginning swell of her breasts. There were drawbacks; she couldn't lift her elbows above breast level, and it had required tight lacing, but there was less sheer bulk of fabric than with most court cote-hardies, which meant something in this weather. The overrobe was a very loose surcote, open at the sides from under her arms to hip level, of chocolate jacquard brocade with silver and gold flames broidered along the edges.

The ladies lifted off the surcote, unlaced the kirtle down her back and unbuttoned the arms, which felt as if she'd suddenly been released from a set of prisoner's irons. Then they coaxed the three inches of tight sleeve down her arms and swept the whole affair away, which left her with the chemise—cotton thickened to double layers in places to make sure sweat didn't stain the silk. Nimble fingers took care of the buttons and hooks and removed the fabric, and she felt almost *cool* as the air hit her skin.

Thankfully the day's heat was fading anyway now that the stars were out and she could escape the interminable banquet in the Great Hall below.

Where eyes bugged at this outfit, for various reasons. I suspect a lot of the women were taking careful notes!

The solar of Castle Goldendale was most of the way up the dojon tower of the keep and four sets of high arched windows marked the center of each wall, all open now and letting in a very pleasant cooling breeze. One corner of the big square room had a fireplace, empty and swept and garnished with bouquets of roses and dahlias and geraniums now; the other held the spiral staircase. The walls were pale plaster carved in spiderwork Gothic low-relief patterns and the floor was mosaic tile, light blue with a border of green and yellow flowering vines. A few colorful modern rugs were scattered across it.

Westward the new-risen moon shone on distant snow peaks, like a dream of cool peace in the purple night. Below the lights of the little town were coming on, the warm glow of lanterns and candles, the evening bells from the cathedral and the other churches—there were six, in a town of four thousand, plus a chapel that the other varieties of Christian used in rotation, a small synagogue and a once-clandestine and now merely inconspicuous covenstead.

Outside the walls with their pacing sentries were the tented camps of the gathering armies. They were there to protect the town, of course, but she couldn't blame the citizens and the local fief-holders from feeling nervous at having so many armed men around, and right in the middle of harvest at that.

"Hose and houppelande, please, mesdames," she said, when they'd gotten her down to her underwear.

Another chemise, plain this time, then the tight hose of bias-cut linen; she'd gotten used to pants on the Quest, and she'd always been able to get away with practical dress more than most noblewomen, because of her birth and training. Right now she had a reasonable excuse, too. A plain set of shirt, jerkin and loose houppelande coat was a lot more comfortable than anything else respectable for someone of her rank, and she would be on campaign soon.

Though an arming doublet and suit of plate is actually more uncomfortable *than a cote-hardie, hard though that would be to believe if I hadn't experienced both. Which is something not many people have done.*

At least she didn't have to feel morally uncomfortable about kicking someone out of their quarters. County Aurea was Crown demesne land, and Castle Goldendale was held by an appointed seneschal rather than as an autonomous fief; it had been built as a headquarters and strongpoint during the wars against the Free Cities of the Yakima League to the north.

A man-at-arms of the Protector's Guard came trotting and clanking up the stairs, thumped his fist to his breastplate and bowed as the staff set out a collation and left.

"Grand Constable d'Ath, Your Highness."

"Admit her, thank you," Mathilda said.

Good old Tiph, she thought warmly, as the familiar light quick steps sounded on the stone risers.

Then: *And there are probably tens of thousands of people who wouldn't* believe *that* anyone *could think of Lady Death that way.*

They hadn't had her around all their lives, of course; hadn't been her pupil in matters warlike. And those were also people who hadn't realized at about the age of eleven that quite a lot of people wanted to kill everyone named Arminger, and that a major reason they *couldn't* was that Tiphaine d'Ath induced extremely well-merited soiled-breeches fear in the enemies of her family and House.

In theory I don't really approve *of Tiph,* Mathilda thought, as she smiled in greeting. *She's an unrepentant sinner in a lot of ways. In practice I'm extremely glad to have her around and besides that I* like *her and Delia. I hope my children will have the chance to be glad of it as well; a dynasty can't have too many loyal, able supporters. Or friends. Swords about a throne.*

"Your Majesty," Tiphaine said, making a leg-bow and sweeping off her hat.

"My lady Grand Constable," Mathilda said. "Or as some dare call you . . . *Tiph.*"

That startled a rare snort of laughter out of her. Mathilda went on: "Sit down and have a drink, Tiph. You look as if you could use one."

Tiphaine was in boots and trews and padded arming doublet with mail grommets under the arms. All were black; that was part of her image, and also better for not showing stains. She looked dubiously at the furniture— one of Mother's salvage teams had furnished the domestic parts of this castle from a raid on a Gustav Stickley exhibit in a Seattle museum—and then decided her wargear wasn't going to do any harm to the Craftsman- school solidity. She poured herself a glass of wine from the delicate Venetian-style glass decanter turned out recently in a Portland workshop and sat back, easy as a cat—though a tired cat pushing forty now.

"And no formality in private, Tiph. We don't have time."

"I've been jumping around like a Tinerant tambourine dancer," the Grand Constable admitted. "You look a bit frazzled too, Matti. Are the local nobility and burghers adequately soothed and stroked about having armies assembling in their fields? Better you than me for that, frankly."

"You could do it."

"Yes, but I don't *want* to do it. What sort of reaction did you get?"

"I subtly pointed out that the manor-lords and their tenants would make a lot of money by having so many hungry wage-packets walking around, and that the city was creaming off a lot of gold," Mathilda said. "They're nervous, but reassured. It was worth sitting through one banquet. Rudi managed to escape because it was all Associates and they needed to be reassured by one of their own. Or at least that was his excuse! Plus he had some

Mackenzie politics to take care of after the military stuff, and he really *did* have to handle that himself."

Tiphaine sipped at the wine. "His Majesty just gave me my marching orders; I'm off tomorrow. Well, the *army* he just gave me is off tomorrow, I'm probably going to have to arrive first *and* last to chivvy everyone along, particularly the Yakima contingents who aren't used to working with the Association. Including them is a good move in about four separate ways, but I'm going to have to sweat to make it work the way he wants."

Mathilda tried to imagine Tiphaine doing anything else with a mission, and failed.

"Rudi's brilliant about that sort of thing," she said instead, with a glow of pride. "Not just a pretty face! Young for it, but he's a first-rate general."

"I've observed that," Tiphaine said dryly; she *had* been one of his trainers, during his months every year in Association territory since the Protector's War.

Then with something that might have been the barest hint of a wink: "He's even sort of cute . . . for a guy."

"You're impossible!" Mathilda said.

"No, just improbable. Fortunately only stories have to be plausible; real life just has to exist. Otherwise I'd simply refuse to believe the Sword of the Lady was there at all, for example. Now, what's on your regal mind?"

"First, let Delia know that I'm sorry you two—and Rigobert—couldn't be there for the wedding up at Castle Corbec. We're going to have a commemoration ceremony after the war in the Cardinal-Archbishop's cathedral in Portland, and I want Delia as one of the Matrons of Honor."

"Thanks, she'll love that. We'll come and she can be matron enough for both of us," Tiphaine said, refilling her glass. "What's the serious business?"

"Ah, there's some information I need. Chancellor Ignatius has his old boss Abbot-Bishop Dmwoski working on getting an overall view of the CUT's espionage and infiltration operations in our territory."

"Good choice, Matti," Tiphaine said judiciously. "He was uncomfortably smart when he was fighting against us, and he's still plenty sharp even if he is semiretired. Plus he has extensive contacts. We need *some* people who aren't rushing around being too busy to see the big picture."

Mathilda nodded agreement. "And the CUT's going to be a long-term problem even if we manage to decapitate them. Right now he's getting down to the bottom of the House Liu matter. Incidentally I'm going to swear Huon Liu as one of my squires tomorrow and take his sister Yseult into the household as a lady-in-waiting later; if she's got the smarts, and I think she does, I'll have work for her."

Tiphaine frowned into her glass. "Are you sure that's wise? Speaking of decapitation I *did* do in several of their relatives, one way or another . . . chopped their mother into dog-meat scraps personally and with my own hands, for starters. Had a nasty turn with the rabid bitch *infecting* me somehow, like a bite from a mad dog."

Mathilda sighed. "Those were necessary measures. I think their personal experiences will make them know, not just know but really *understand*, that it was necessary. That's also why I'm having Dmwoski brief them fully, not just pump them for their perspective. They're smart kids, and besides I owe a rather large debt in that direction for what Odard did. Right now I want you to give me your own impression of what happened with Guelf Mortimer and that agent right after the Battle of Pendleton." She quirked one corner of her mouth up. "Or the *Cluster-Fuck of Pendleton*, as I understand you christened it."

Tiphaine shrugged. "I'm actually rather proud of how I handled that. A fighting retreat may not get the bards and troubadours excited, but it's technically the most difficult battlefield maneuver, especially with an army made up of contingents from all over, none of whom love each other that much . . . good practice for the opening phases of this campaign, in fact. Oddly enough, Guelf Mortimer helped a good deal while we were breaking contact, him and Sir Constantine 'Raging Bull' Stavarov. Stavarov's just an obnoxious idiot, of course."

"But a good Anvil," Mathilda said with a chuckle, pouring herself a glass of the wine.

It was a local vintage from the Columbia gorge, a red Malbec with a taste of plums and herbs in its inky purple depths.

Anvil was a phrase Tiphaine had taught her, originally coined by Conrad Renfrew back when he was Grand Constable; someone solid iron from ear to ear whether he had a helmet on or not, useful primarily for dropping on or throwing at the enemy like a large hard heavy weight. And if the anvil broke . . . you got another anvil.

"If you can imagine an Anvil with a really bad temper and testosterone poisoning," Tiphaine said. "Guelf, besides being a traitor, had delusions of intelligence . . . and if he'd been twice as smart as he thought he was, he'd have been a half-wit. I *did* submit a full report on the business, though."

"You don't have to hint if you think I'm wasting your time, Tiph. I've read the report and Ignatius forwarded it to Dmwoski; it's got all the *facts* but nothing more. What I want is the rest of it, all the details, how it *felt* at the time. I need to get what Mom calls the *gestalt* of the whole business. Also I have to know how much to tell Huon and Yseult. I'm not going to hide the essentials but there may be personal details they *don't* need to know. They're going to be here in a while, they're fighting traffic on the rail line from Portland, but we'll have time."

Tiphaine sighed; the younger woman knew that talking about her own emotional states was something her Grand Constable didn't like, as in *would rather juggle live squid in a confessional booth.* She also knew that likes and dislikes weren't all that important to Tiphaine d'Ath when business was involved.

"Well," Tiphaine said, letting her head fall back against the sofa and closing her eyes. "We finally managed to shake the CUT light cavalry off and consolidate around Hermiston, right on the old border we got after the Protector's War."

"Just a strip along the south bank of the river there, though."

"Right, I spent my last day or so there securing the south flank with the CORA levies, who had all the organized cohesion of a bucket of snot. I left the rearguard there and headed back to Portland to get my finger on the pulse and start getting ready for the next enemy offensive because them getting Pendleton really screwed our position, especially south of the Columbia. Nothing between them and the Cascades except the CORA, barring Odell, though we had the castles along the river at the dams and bridges. The first thing *I* knew about what was going on was—"

TOWN RESIDENCE OF THE BARONS OF FOREST GROVE
878 SOUTHWEST GREEN AVENUE
SUBURBS, CROWN CITY OF PORTLAND
(FORMERLY PORTLAND, OREGON)
PORTLAND PROTECTIVE ASSOCIATION
HIGH KINGDOM OF MONTIVAL
(FORMERLY WESTERN NORTH AMERICA)
SEPTEMBER 21, CHANGE YEAR 23/2021 AD

Tiphaine d'Ath woke to the sound of a little bell tinkling, and made the hand on the hilt of the sheathed dagger under her pillow relax. It was a little dangerous to wake her up directly when she'd been in the field, though even unconscious she knew Delia's touch. She could tell Delia was not in the bed, though. At seven months gone she was a significant weight, dipping even a really good pre-Change mattress like this one.

She sighed, rubbing one hand over her eyes. Candles and two alcohol lanterns lit the room and she couldn't tell what time it was, or for a moment where she really was. Her eyelids were a little crusted with sleep, but they didn't burn as badly as they had when she'd collapsed into bed whenever-it-was before. She'd had a vicious migraine yesterday too, the usual one you got if you wore a helm all day with the inside padding tight around your head and were clouted a couple of times to boot, but by now it was down to a slight throb. She could still feel every overstretched tendon, bruise, wrench and minor abrasion and nick.

Long dismal experience told her that getting up and moving would warm the injured muscles and make her feel a little better. The rest needed willow extract and time; more time than it used to, at that. Her sword hand and wrist in particular felt as if someone had driven a laden wagon over them. Her page Lioncel de Stafford was standing by the bed, muffling the little bell he'd rung and looking disgustingly young—which he couldn't help, at twelve—and fresh and blond and rested.

She sat up, running her fingers through her own tangle of pale hair and then spreading her hands out and looking at them:

God, did I go to bed without even washing? Yes, apparently I did, that's dried blood under my nails. Delia is a saint. At least this nightshirt is clean, or was before someone put it on me.

"I'm awake, brat, you can put the bell away. Are your mother and father here? What time is it?"

"Yes, my lady. No, my lady. Six fifteen in the morning, my lady. A train arrived with a number of badly wounded men from Hermiston at four a.m. Dowager Molalla and the train master sent for help."

Tiphaine frowned. *Shit, what went wrong now? Did they take a slap at Hermiston? The way I had it set up we should have fed them their livers if they did and the Viscount knows his business.*

She tossed the covers back. *I usually wake up when Delia gets out of bed; I must have been really wiped this time, as well as getting older.*

This was Delia's room, and she could have told that at a glance even if she hadn't woken up here often enough before; pale pastel colors, controlled and elegant froufrou around the canopy of the four-poster, a spectacular tapestry on one wall showing a mountain scene that looked as if it were taken from a Maxfield Parrish poster and probably had been. Some books, a dressing table that looked as if you needed a seven-year apprenticeship and an examination before a panel of guildmasters to handle all the stuff, an embroidery frame, a fretwork door leading to a clothes closet nearly as large as the bedroom.

There was a gentle scent of sachets and bouquets of roses and rhododendrons, and—

"Oh, God, coffee," she said.

About one ship a year came in from the Big Island of Hawaii to Astoria or Newport, with coffee as part of its cargo. There were definite perks to being a baron and Grand Constable.

Lioncel brought it from a wheeled tray; it already had the cream and two spoons of sugar she liked. She drank, yawned, swallowed the paper of bitter powdered willow bark extract he handed her, drank more of the coffee and thought as her brain lurched back into motion. Barony d'Ath's town house was smaller and several blocks away.

Right, memory working now. I got in well after dark last night and there was still blood drying in places all over my armor. I was punch-drunk, thirty hours in the saddle and skirmishes and no sleep.

Lord Rigobert de Stafford, Baron Forest Grove and Marchwarden of the South, had been waiting at Union station. He'd slapped her on the back, told her that everything was in hand and bundled her exhausted form into his pedicab and sent her to his town house and his wife: her lover, Delia. Who had poured several glasses of something sweet down her throat and gotten her into this room, nightshirt and bed, and then darkness had walked up and clubbed her unconscious when she was halfway to the pillow.

Yes, the bathroom was the door to the left. She glanced back at the bed, shaking her head minutely in surprise. Getting the seven-month pregnant Delia out of bed usually involved her bouncing and squirming around. They had made a game of it for all of her pregnancies. Today Delia had managed to get herself up and out of the room without waking her.

If I was that dead asleep, I really did need Rigobert to take over last night, she thought as she ran the water into the basin, washing her hands. *Well, that is one of the things a second-in-command is for.*

Bits of brown flake circled around the marble of the sink as she scrubbed at her hands; her shield-hand knuckles were badly skinned, which meant she'd lost the shield and hit someone or something very hard with her gauntleted fist. Someone; a glimpse returned to her, near-darkness, a bearded snarling face and the crumble of bone under the steel and leather as she struck again and again. Hand-to-hand combat usually ended up as a plain old-fashioned beat-down at some point, and plate armor was surprisingly useful for that, too.

She called through the slightly ajar door: "Lioncel, have any messages come for me?"

"Yes, my lady. Five or six dispatch wallets. But my Lord my father said that he was taking them back to Customs House for your staff and Dame Lilianth to sort and you could deal with them later when, ah, when you were *firing on all cylinders* again, whatever that means. No more have come since."

"*Officious.* Your father is *officious*, Lioncel. Where's Diomede?"

"Yes, my lady. Sleeping, my lady. He'll be up soon. We switch off at noon, today. And you really should take a shower."

"You're *officious*, too, Lioncel."

Tiphaine suppressed a small smile. Lioncel had been well trained by her previous pages when they were promoted to squire. But he was still her son in all ways that mattered; it occasionally showed up in little details and matters of attitude and tricks of speech. And she did need the shower which the gravity-fed water system allowed here. She was becoming aware of how *badly* she needed it; whatever washing she'd done last night had been fairly sketchy.

"What will my lady wear, today?" asked Lioncel beyond the door.

"Working clothes, Lioncel; trews and T-tunic. Court garb is suspended until further notice."

The bathroom was large too; in some ways Delia enjoyed being a noble more than she did. Tiphaine did an abbreviated stretching routine, then ducked into the etched-glass enclosure, turned on the hot water to just short of scalding and stretched some more, grabbing the flower-scented soap. Delia no longer made the stuff with her own hands as she'd done when it was an experiment; the little factory she had established in Forest Grove four years ago was in full production, along with the lavender plantings and rose-plantation. Both baronies made a fair sum off selling it; everyone grew wheat and a lot of manors had a winery, but really first-class soap was getting harder to find. Demand for this had been brisk once the pre-Change stockpiles ran out and it became obvious how much better it was than the sandpaper most amateur soap-boilers were turning out. Managing things like that came under a Châtelaine's duties, which was one reason why it was a demanding job.

Stiff muscles relaxed and some of the soreness washed out with the massage of the pounding hot water, and the sting as scabs came loose reminded her of where to dab iodine when she got out. Her scalp especially felt much better with accumulated battle filth scrubbed out and the last of the nagging headache gave up the ghost as the neck-muscles unclenched.

She toweled off and pulled on the modern underbriefs and linen . . . bra. As usual, she grimaced at that. The death of the last elastic sports bra had been an occasion for genuine mourning. No matter how brief or what fancy name they were given, or whether they laced up the front like these or not, it was still stays, basically. You did *not* want things to bounce and swing when you were fighting.

Lioncel had her clothes laid out. Black trews in a soft linen twill, plain white shirt with a keyhole neck; black chamois jerkin with an inconspicuous mesh-mail lining; a T-tunic in a dark charcoal with silver and black embroidery at the collar and hem, and her arms quartered with the Lidless Eye on the chest. The thin kidskin gloves stung as she eased them on, since the insides had been dusted with disinfectant powder. Plain black suede half-boots with the symbolic golden prick-spurs and a black leather belt, and then a chaperon hat completed the outfit.

"And the number two sword, my lady?" Lioncel asked.

"Yes, number two," she said.

She had six nearly identical ones besides the Grand Constable's sword of state for formal occasions—which had an equally functional blade, despite the jeweled pommel and ivory-and-silver-wire hilt. The one she'd come in with last night would be off to the armorer for repairs and sharpening and disassembly to make sure none of the blood was still under the cross-hilt guard or down the tang starting rust. She touched the double-lobed hilt and the dimpled bone and bindings were smoothly firm; when she half drew it the edge was just right, knife-sharp but not honed so razor-thin it would turn easily the first time it hit bone or armor. The metal was layer-forged alloy steel, the wavy patterns of its surface gleaming under a very light coating of neatsfoot oil, and it slid back into the sheath with precisely the right very slight resistance.

She would have been shocked if it *hadn't* been perfect, but you always checked your own weapons.

"What's the motto, Lioncel?"

"Take care of your gear, and your gear will take care of you, my lady. The one time you're careless is the time it will kill you."

She tossed the sword on the bed and sat, and Lioncel finished drying her hair with warm fluffy towels and then carefully brushed it out. Tiphaine would have rather gone down with wet hair, or done it herself. It was the job of her page. That Lioncel took pride in it argued well for his character.

When he approved, they went down to the breakfast nook where Rigobert's staff had laid out bread, butter, cheese, jam, platters of sausages and bacon and scrambled eggs and more coffee, plus a large bowl of oatmeal cooked with apples for Lioncel to start with. Tiphaine let Lioncel pour her coffee; an Associate learned to command by learning to serve.

First Armand and Radomar, teaching me how to accept service; now Lioncel and Diomede. And I can't steal one tittle of what they consider their job without them raising a very, very polite ruckus.

"Thank you, Lioncel. Please sit and eat, yourself."

This was her usual command when eating alone and her pages had learned to eat with her; however, they always sat *after* they had served her. Tiphaine shook her head in private amusement at the size of the portions she *had* to eat these days. A Bearkiller doctor she'd enjoyed talking with a few times had worked out that a knight actually burned off nearly half again as many calories as a peasant on average.

Government by pro athlete, had been the way he'd defined the PPA's neofeudalism.

And the last few weeks in camp had been short enough rations that she ate with gusto.

"Aunt?"

Tiphaine nodded; the keyword told her this was Lioncel to Tiphaine, not a page to his knight.

"Yes, Lioncel?"

"Aunt, how bad is the situation?"

Tiphaine sighed as she met the serious pale blue eyes.

Looking more and more like Rigobert every day . . . and me, since Rigobert and I have similar coloring and builds. He's going to be tall, too . . . which both of us also are.

"It's bad, Lioncel."

She bit off a piece of bread and Tillamook cheese and stared at the ticking grandfather clock against the far wall of the room for a moment, composing her thoughts. He was old enough to be a squire soon; nearly old enough to be treated like an embryonic adult, by modern standards. Certainly old enough to get the unvarnished truth.

"The expression I like to use is *cluster-fuck*. It's very rude and describes the situation to a T. It also means that more than one thing went wrong at once, and the things that went wrong each made the other things worse than they would have been by themselves. We did very well to get out of it without being wrecked beyond recovery."

"What's it called when *everything* goes wrong at once?"

"Dead and defeated."

A flash of fear shadowed the boy's eyes for an instant. His jaw clenched. "That means really bad things to Mom and Diomede and the baby she's going to have, doesn't it?"

Tiphaine nodded. *Not fear for himself. Lioncel would have been considered insanely courageous, or pathologically fearless in the old days. Today, the rest of the pages at court know better than to tease or harass him. It's not just that I'm known to kill anybody threatening my family. Lioncel is shaping up to be a really solid, mean fighter himself and there's no backing down in him.*

"Lioncel de Stafford."

He looked up at her, blue eyes meeting gray.

"This is what we're *for*, boy. We put ourselves in the front line between danger and those we love, those who look to us for protection. There will always be some danger or threat, because that's the way human beings work. This is why we have the lands and the castles and power and deference from the commons. It's the price we pay, not just the danger but the responsibility and worry and the knowledge that everything turns on our making the right decisions, and it's what being an Associate and a noble means."

Also it means we were a very successful gang of strong-arm artists back when, right after the Change, but it's not just a protection racket anymore. Things change. Kings start as lucky pirates, and wolves graduate into guard-dogs. The myths they used to tie everything together were stronger than Norman or even Sandra suspected and the stories speeded up the process quite a bit.

The boy looked down at his plate and visibly put the worry aside.

"Will you be going to the War Office this morning, my lady Grand Constable?"

"Yes, boy. Order the pedicab when you're done with breakfast, please. You'll come with me. Tell Diomede that he'll come down with my lunch, your lunch, and his lunch from the kitchens here."

Because I swear I've lost seven or eight pounds in the last two weeks and I was lean to start with; anything I lose is muscle and I need it all. Grandmother told me once when I was about six that her *father used to eat sandwiches with lard for filling and I just thought it was gross. But he was a lumberjack. He needed them.*

"We'll share it and he will stay. You go home then, and study. I heard something about geometry difficulties."

"Yes, my lady. Why do I have to study geometry? It's boring; all those lines and arcs and sines and cosines and problems."

Tiphaine gave him a hard look. "That's an important skill. Numbers are how you analyze the world; they're how you do siegecraft for war, construction and surveying for peace; fight legal battles; aim a catapult . . . If you can't do it, or at least understand it, you're helpless in the hands of those who can, like lacking a hand or a foot or an eye. Hasn't your tutor explained the applications to you, boy?"

He shook his head, brightening up quite a bit. "It's good for things? Like sword training?"

Tiphaine growled. "I'll talk to the man tonight; remind me. Right now, finish your breakfast."

She sipped her cup of coffee, pausing to admire the delicate rose flower pattern on the cup. She knew Delia had picked it out from the large warehouses the PPA kept for Associates when she'd married Rigobert, and she'd been working with a group of noblewomen and guildsmen here who were trying to get a bone-china works going in Portland for when the plunder ran out. This porcelain had blue roses. The set at Montinore Manor had yellow roses.

And my town house has plain brown dishes because I picked them before I wangled Delia into the office of Châtelaine of Ath and she dove with headfirst glee into Patronness of the Arts and Leader of Fashion mode.

The proprieties required Delia to stay in the Forest

Grove town house when visiting Portland, mostly; and it was large enough for the nursery. The d'Ath town house on Cedar Street had been picked out before she realized she would turn into a family woman with a spouse who entertained during the Court season in the city, so it was comfortable enough but rather small and out of the way. All three used it for flying visits when they didn't have time for the panoply of service and state.

I suppose I could request another town house, there are plenty on minimal-maintenance, there's still less than forty thousand people inside the walls of Portland and only a few hundred in this neighborhood, but I'll let Diomede do that when he's married and old enough to need it. Probably we should get a residence in Newberg, as well. Assuming we win the war, of course.

She put the cup down, stood and slid the scabbarded sword into the frow-sling that hung from her belt and walked briskly out to the porch, nodding as servants curtsied or bowed. Outside she returned the fist-to-chest salute of the squire in half-armor commanding a squad of six crossbowmen on guard outside.

"Will you require an escort, my lady Grand Constable?" he said.

"No, I think I can survive in Portland, Jeffries," she said.

Lioncel was just coming around the corner of the street, perched on the back of the pedicab Rigobert kept for town work, with the de Stafford arms displayed on the side: *Gules a domed Tower Argent surmounted by a Pennon Or in base a Lion passant guardant of the last.*

That was a heraldic joke, if you knew how to read it, rather like her own but a bit less blatant and, she had to admit, more witty.

She glanced up at the white-pillared portico of the

residence, then looked east towards the heart of present Portland, squinting a little into the sunrise. This was an extramural suburb, literally so these days—better than half a mile outside the city walls. Behind her rose the densely wooded West Hills, green and purple shadows in the light of dawn. Those had been parks and exclusive residential neighborhoods before the Change, and it was all part of the New Forest now; you could smell the fresh greenness of it, and the sky was thick with birdsong. That was Crown demesne under special forest law, and permission to hunt there or an invitation to parties at the royal retreat in the Japanese Gardens was a mark of great favor.

This neighborhood at their foot was reserved for the town house complexes of noble families, prestigious because of the greenery and open space but not too far from the City Palace downtown and the social-political whirl of Court. Each had a central residence, and several other structures taken over and modified for the trail of servants and followers. Their retainers made sure the hoi polloi didn't intrude, so the usual urban chorus of street vendors and would-be troubadours and the roar of hooves and wheels were lacking, only pedicabs and an occasional rider or horse carriage moving along the curving, tree-lined streets.

It was all very pleasant, and by no coincidence at all kept the nobility's household troops outside the walls of the Crown City. She swung up into the cab and Lioncel got in beside her.

"Customs House," she said to the man on the pedals. Then: "Odd," to Lioncel.

The driver-rider pedaled hard down Vista to Everett through the brightening day, then turned east on the thoroughfare, sounding an imperious bell with his thumb and occasionally shouting for way. Most of the passersby scattered at the sight of the arms on the pedicab or simply because it certainly held someone influential.

"Odd, my lady?"

"The word *cab* used to mean a public vehicle for hire. They were everywhere and people flagged them down and were taken to where they needed to go. There was enough business that several hundred could work all day long. In the downtown and on docksides, where the streets were really narrow, pedicabs like this were used. We still call these things *cabs* but they're private vehicles and only nobles and a few guildmasters and such have them."

The boy nodded, polite but slightly baffled, and Tiphaine stifled a sigh.

They just don't have the background. Best to live in the present as much as you can, Tiphaine, like a Changeling which you almost *are anyway. The oldsters get tiresome when they go on about the old world and I don't want to end up like that. Of course, everybody thinks about the past more as they get older. I'm just starting to realize that's because you've* got *more past as you get older. And Portland sets me off because I was born here. Forget it. That Portland died at the Change, this place just has the same name and some of the geography. It's like a new person wearing a dead man's shoes.*

The trip from the de Stafford residence to the South Park blocks and the old Customs House was quick, less than a mile and a half. Most of the buildings outside the city wall had been systematically torn down to leave clear fields of fire for the monstrous throwing-engines on Portland's walls, except for the Civic Stadium to the south of Everett, still used for soccer, baseball and jousting tournaments. Tented camps with troops from all over the Protectorate and the other realms of the Meeting sprawled over the open space usually used for turnout pasture and truck gardens and livery stables, and there was a thick mist of woodsmoke as cooks started their morning fires.

As always, she felt a prickle of unease as she approached the city wall.

You do, if you remember how Norman used the labor camps as a horrible example of what could *happen to you. People sobbed with joy when they got picked to be peasants on the manors instead. That's a long time ago now, but the memory sticks.*

The defenses ran along the eastern edge of what had been Interstate 405, which neatly enclosed the old core of Portland, the original city along the west bank of the Willamette before the twentieth century and sprawl. The broad roadway was sunken well below the surface most of the way too, which had made it a perfect dry moat; apart from narrow laneways left for workmen it was a continuous bristle of outward-slanting angle iron posts now, set deep and then ground to vicious points and edges like a forest of swords.

The wall itself was poured mass concrete sixty feet high and thirty thick, around a frame of steel girders ripped out of old skyscrapers. Round towers stood at hundred-yard intervals, rearing twice as high and thick enough to seem squat, each a miniature fortress in its own right that could be cut off from the outside by raising footways and slamming thick steel doors. The towers had steep metal roofs like witches' hats, steel plated with copper; a hoarding of the same material made a sloping roof over the crenellations of the wall. Wall and towers both were machicolated, the fighting platforms on top protruding over the walls on arches so that trapdoors could be opened to drop things straight down.

"Say what you like about Norman, he didn't think small," Tiphaine said, looking at the curiously graceful massiveness of it, glistening in the dawn light with the white stucco that covered the whole surface.

"My lady?"

"Nothing, boy."

Most of the bridges that had crossed Interstate 405 had been destroyed. The others had been fortified with Norman Arminger's usual combination of brutal functionalism, paranoid thoroughness and deliberately soul-crushing use of intimidation-architecture. Everett Street Gate was typical. They crossed a drawbridge that could be raised instantly by giant counterweights, then a great squat castle of four towers on the western bank of the 405, with the roadway running past massive gates of solid steel and under a high arched ceiling pierced with murder-holes and slots for portcullis after portcullis to drop, more gates, the bridge with sections that could be dropped at the pull of levers or flooded with burning napalm or both, then another castle as strong as the first in the city wall proper.

The guard commander gave her a swift but genuine once-over before passing her through; despite the early hour the traffic was heavy, but the crossbowmen were still searching wagons and pulling random or suspicious travelers aside for more thorough searches. Tiphaine nodded sober approval; she'd signed off on those orders herself, and damn the inconvenience. Being dead was more inconvenient still.

Lioncel looked at the fortifications with innocent pride; they'd been finished before he was born.

"They say Des Moines in Iowa is bigger, my lady, but I doubt there's a city anywhere that's stronger!"

"Probably not," Tiphaine said, and the page rested silently; he knew better than to try to chat.

She swung down from the pedicab outside the building that housed the War Ministry, across from a small square of greenery and trees. Other pedicabs came and went along Park, and horses clip-clopped; churls and varlets pulled handcarts, led long teams of oxen that dragged heavy wagons, hurried about errands. A streetcar rumbled by behind its six-mule hitch down tracks completed just last year, and there was a scattering of private carriages as well.

Farther north and closer to the river-wall the Main Post Office building was serving as a hospital and relocation depot, since it was amply large and was conveniently across the street from Union train station. A trickle of ambulances passed, taking the recovering elsewhere, and everyone tried to make way for them.

"Lioncel," she said. "Go down to the hospital and make sure your lady mother isn't overdoing it. If she is tired or *looks* tired, tell her I said to go get some rest and to remind her she's seven months pregnant. If she won't, go find the Dowager Molalla and get Phillipa to help you chase her home. Don't take no for an answer. Once you've done that, get one of the housemaids to sit with her while she rests and come back to my office."

"Yes, my lady!"

He smiled, ducked his bright head with its black brimless page's hat, and dashed away.

The guards in front of the five-arched granite loggia of the War Ministry were a platoon in three-quarter armor with glaives, seven-foot pole arms topped with a wicked head like a giant single-edged butcher's knife with a thick hook on the reverse. They were at parade rest—feet apart, left hand tucked behind the back, extended right hand holding the weapon with the butt against the right foot and the rest slanted out. As she came up they went to attention and rapped the steel-shod butts of the glaives against the pavement, and Tiphaine returned the salute gravely.

Their gear was not quite the kind the Association used, and the sigil on their breastplates was the snarling red bear's-head of the Bearkillers. They weren't A-listers, the Bearkiller equivalent of knights; things were too fraught to waste elite troops on duty like this, though even Bearkiller militia had a precise snap to the way they did things.

But they're doing something useful here, not just propping up their glaives. They're showing for everyone to see that this is an alliance and we're all in the war together. Armed Bearkillers in Portland, the people founded by Mike Havel, the man who killed Norman Arminger. Now if we had more than a talking-shop to coordinate things at the top, we'd be . . . not fine, you can't be fine when you're outnumbered two to one . . . we'd be a lot better off. The problem is none of the existing rulers will bow to one of their own.

The legend along the top of the loggia had been switched from *US Customs House* to *War Ministry of the Portland Protective Association* long ago. Now that was tactfully obscured by staffs bearing a dozen flags, covering all the more important realms of the Meeting. The Lidless Eye in gold and crimson on black wasn't even in the center.

Sandra really *knows how to handle this sort of thing,* Tiphaine thought. *Considering that this is where we plotted and planned and schemed to conquer everyone and divide their land up into fiefs. What a magnificent bitch that woman is!*

The building was a block-square pile in the Victorian era's idea of Italian Renaissance style right down to the terra-cotta up on the fourth-floor roofs and the Doric columns. The nineteenth-century stone-and-brick construction was why it had been a natural for post-Change conversion once Portland settled down, with a hundred thousand square feet of office space that *didn't* absolutely depend on powered ventilation to remain habitable. She flung up a hand to halt a rush of paper-waving bureaucrats trying to get her attention as she came through the doors and into the marble splendors of the lobby, grunting thankfully when a pair of her military secretaries showed up and started running interference.

The situation room on the left occupied one of the flanking tower chambers with an overhead skylight; it was in purposeful movement when she stuck her head in, under the management of Lord Rigobert, Baron Forest Grove, Marchwarden of the South and currently her number two.

He gave her a quick nod that said: *under control.* Tiphaine could see several Bearkillers and some Corvallans with him, all gesturing at the same great square map table. Aides moved unit markers with rods like pool cues, and the technical conversation stopped now and then for quick lessons in various groups' military terminology.

We're trying to keep a lid on the news of the Great Pendleton Cluster-Fuck; a panic would be a bad thing. But it'll break soon. News still moves.

She'd never been able to really understand the impulse to run in circles and squeal when faced with a problem; she knew it *existed* and had to be dealt with, but she couldn't imagine how it *felt.* Even as a child she'd always been able to put danger out of mind with a simple effort of will and go on with what needed doing. Otherwise she couldn't have been a gymnast and spent hours every day stressing her body to ten-tenths of capacity.

Fortunately the heliograph net is the fastest way to move

information and we control it, so we can get ahead of the curve, if we're sharp, and Sandra most certainly is. She'll have a version that's spun our way and have it out so widely and thoroughly that it'll be the one most people accept, the more so as it'll be true enough that the actual news reinforces our subsidized troubadours and newsletters and Sunday sermons.

Up through arched doorways, marble-clad piers, beams with classical plaster moldings, murals and groined vaults, a grand cast-iron stairway extended from the center of the first floor to the fourth floor, with marble treads, double balusters with spiral and acanthus ornamentation. Tiphaine took the stairs three at a time, dodging the steady stream of pages who charged up and down with a sublime disregard for any obstacles and packets of messages in their hands.

It's a minor miracle this didn't end up as the Lord Protector's City Palace, she thought. *Though the Central Library's about as good.*

She strode through her outer office, where what she privately dubbed the *widow brigade* was busily keeping up with the constant flow of paper reports; male nobles dodged this sort of job when they could, and the clerics who swarmed over the ordinary civil administration of the PPA weren't considered suitable. Typewriters clacked, adding machines clattered and rang their bells; abacuses made rattling sounds and pages ran back and forth on soft-soled shoes, yelping:

"Excuse me—"

"My lady!"

"Not *there*, you nit!"

While carrying completed reports, paper and ink supplies, food, and drinks . . .

Maps flapped back and forth on swinging panel poster

display racks as the clerks pushed in pins updating troop positions, enemy sightings and resource allocation.

Color-coded file bins crowded the aisle to her office; more hung around inside, packed with information, sorted in any order she might need. Carefully stacked piles of dockets, folders and accordion files covered the long tables that ran around the outer wall of the ante-chamber. As she entered her own office and racked her sword she could see a neat pile of dispatch wallets on the desk sorted into levels of urgency as indicated by the knot codes, right beside the Seal and the tray of red wax disks.

Rigobert brought six packets in, according to Lioncel; that's nine there. They breed the way coat hangers used to do in closets. I'd better process them.

A map table, much smaller than Rigobert's down-stairs, tried to make sense of troop dispositions and the strategic situation.

What a cluster-fuck, she repeated to herself after a quick look to check for major developments.

"They have humbugged me, by God," as Wellington put it. *At least we had contingency plans in place. And thank heavens for Sandra's habit of collecting valuable people!*

Meticulous notes on her desk flagged the most urgent files in order of priority. Which important task was done by . . .

"Dame Lilianth, if you would," Tiphaine called, rais-ing her voice slightly.

Dame Lilianth of Kalama did not look like a spy as she came in and firmly closed the glass door behind her; she hardly even looked like an office manager. Five foot four, plump going on fat, rosy cheeks, her silvering hair hidden under a light blue wimple that picked up the lighter color on her brocaded cote-hardie. She *looked* like a happy ma-tronly woman whose primary concern was spoiling her grandchildren and perhaps puttering around her garden bossing the workmen.

Tiphaine suddenly grinned sardonically at her and Dame Lilianth matched her expression with an equal savagery.

I look pretty much like what I am. She doesn't. Both useful, Tiphaine thought.

Lilianth Oppenhier had been an Office Administrator in the days when light traveled along wires rather than coming from oil-soaked wicks, and a member of the Society. Sandra had taken her and her three daughters into the household when her husband was killed in the opening moves of the Protector's War and her lack of a male heir lost her a land claim in a legal mud-wrestling match with House Gutierrez. Since then she'd been extremely useful and had prospered accordingly. Sandra Arminger knew how to reward good service, and in more ways than simple largesse.

"There's a little nuisance to get out of the way first, my lady Grand Constable," Lilianth said. "Herluin Smith's widow is asking for a page placement for their son, Henriot. This is the third letter in three months, she's using the squeaky-wheel principle, but she does have a claim."

"That's Mary Smith we're talking about . . . why is every other woman in the Association named *Mary*?"

Lilianth grinned at her. "Including me. Mary Oppenhier. Sandra was very firm that I needed to use my Society name forevermore . . . for the reason you just stated."

"She renamed *me* out of a book, when I made Associate, and I never even liked the character—a pathetic little dweeb. *I* should have gotten Yolande or Heuradys."

"Oh, *those* books. What *were* you called, my lady? I've never heard."

"Collette. Collette Rutherston; strange, I haven't thought of that in years. At Binnsmeade Middle School they used to call me *Collie* and go *woof-woof* at me in the corridors."

Back before we reinstated the Code Duello. Nothing like the prospect of dying with six inches of steel through the brisket to keep people polite.

"The mind boggles. Do you want me to hint that Mary Smith should remember that squeaky wheels make good firewood?" Lilianth said.

"No, no. We're feudalists."

Which means you can't separate the personal and the political and everything is family and patronage.

"Have a polite letter sent to her saying that after the crisis is past, meaning if we're still alive, say between Michaelmas and Christmas, I will find a place for the boy. By the way, how's Ysolde? I see that she's going to pop, probably a month after Delia?"

Lilianth turned her head towards the door for a moment. Her eldest daughter was outside, updating some of the graphs posted on the far wall. She'd made an extremely advantageous marriage with the Betancourt family's eldest, not least because Sandra worked the network behind the scenes. As a bonus the two young people liked each other.

"That's all working out very well, my lady," she said, with satisfaction in her voice.

Tiphaine nodded and looked at her desk. "Where shall I begin, Mistress Lilianth?"

"The Lady Regent sent a very urgent and confidential dispatch box yesterday, quite late. I have it under lock and key."

Right, Sandra doesn't joggle my elbow for trivia, Tiphaine thought.

One of the nicer things about working for the Spider of the Silver Tower was that she gave you a job and the resources and information you needed and then left you to get on with it.

Though God have mercy if you screw the pooch, for she won't.

"I'd suggest that you start your day with that. You can continue with the dispatches from the hospital and the death letters."

She plucked two wallets out of the pile. Tiphaine took them and waited for Lilianth to bring Sandra's dispatch.

No need to guess what it's about. Mathilda's letter is quite clear; Alex Vinton finked her out to the Cutters off there in the wilds of Idaho, and did it with Mary Liu's knowledge and approbation. The only upside is that Odard Liu wasn't involved; he got screwed over too, and saved Matti's life. And he's Baron Gervais now, so since the head of the family is loyal and can be shown to be loyal we needn't proscribe the lot of them and attaint the estates. That would drop the horse apple in the bobbing bucket right along with the Golden Delicious just now, the way the nobility are antsy about things in general.

But Mary Liu would have to go, one way or another. Which probably meant her brother Guelf Mortimer had to go, too, he was a notorious grudge bearer and was almost certainly involved in anything she was. Her other brother Sir Jason had been a serious loose cannon, and Tiphaine had had to deal with him back fifteen years ago. There wouldn't be any need to cook a trial for Mary, the evidence was right there, but Guelf might be awkward if he didn't fuck up in dramatic fashion or show what a skank he was politically.

The problem was that so far he'd been performing far better than she'd expected. Killing a competent leader *just because* had a serious potential for blowback down the road these days. It wasn't like Norman's time, when nobody knew in the morning if their head would be attached to a spike over the gate at sundown.

Will the Lady Regent prefer a large public trial for the Dowager Baroness Liu or a nice private referral to the Court of Star-Chamber, which is to say, herself? A large, very emotionally charged trial, against a woman who has proclaimed her ill-usage since before the Field of the Cloth of Gold will not go over well with the Associates with this war getting going and so far not going well at all. On the other hand, just having her mysteriously drop dead . . . we've been trying to cut back on stuff that raw, getting ready for the transition when Mathilda turns twenty-six and becomes Lady Protector. On the third hand, Mathilda ran away with Rudi and they're off looking for a magic sword in the Death Zones of the east, and along the way she just handed us this can of worms. Damn it, I love the girl like a kid sister but smart as she is she's a pain in the ass sometimes.

She was still thinking hard when Lilianth came back with a small steel box. It had the Lady Regent's personal sigil on it, an etching of the Virgin subduing the Dragon of Sin, which was one of Sandra's private jokes. The same was stamped onto a paper-and-wax seal over the lock.

"I witness that the seal is unbroken," Tiphaine said, then flicked it off with the point of her dagger.

"I witness that you have broken the seal and unlocked the dispatch box," Lilianth said as Tiphaine turned the key.

The Grand Constable gestured to the door. Lilianth closed it as she left. The carrick bend knot wound with copper wire was one used only by Sandra Arminger and only to Tiphaine or Conrad Renfrew. She drummed her fingers on the disk, still turning over the implications of Mary's treason and the way the Associates would react to any public news of her complicity. Then she neatly snipped the copper coils and undid the knot and unfolded her instructions.

Hmmm, she wrote this with her own hand; and she was upset. Unusual for Sandra, but then Mathilda is the focus of everything for her. Her latest amanuensis . . . Lady Jehane, of House Jones . . . is what, seventeen? Why didn't she entrust it to her? She's old enough and she'll have to deal with the grittier aspects of life, soon enough.

Tiphaine read the directions again.

Oh! Tricky, very tricky. How are we going to do this? Glad I stuck Guelf with Viscount Chenoweth at Hermiston, he's nicely out of the way for now and young Renfrew can keep an eye on him.

Tiphaine closed her eyes, used a mnemonic trick to make sure she'd memorized the Regent's missive and then set it alight in the room's empty fireplace. A few strokes of the poker made sure that nobody could reconstruct anything from the ashes as well.

She sat for a moment in silence, then looked up as the door opened.

"The condolence letters, my lady," Lilianth said.

An unpleasantly long casualty list was attached, and the allies had suffered badly while breaking loose too. Tiphaine took the letters and began to sign them carefully; it was her job to take care of the noblemen, just as each lord would do the same by letter or in person for his subordinates. No dashing off her signature in the pre-Change fashion. Each one was a work of art, and much treasured by many of the recipients.

They gave their lives for the Association, the least the Association can give them back is a duly formal letter of thanks. And for once it's not the most unpleasant duty in prospect.

She shook her hand out when she'd finished and

plunged into the data in the rest of the files and reports. It was even soothing, in a way; when you were in the thick of things any battle felt like a defeat and an actual defeat felt like unmitigated disaster.

But according to this it's more of a mitigated *disaster.*

Meanwhile she could feel her subconscious chewing over Sandra's orders and the information she had and coming up with a way to reach the desired outcome. A page came in with a list of provisional unit movement orders from Rigobert de Stafford; she glanced at it, went over to the map, thought for a moment and scribbled *approved, d'Ath* on the bottom and set him running back to the situation room. The door opened at ten, just as she was about to call for a stenographer, and Lioncel came in with a cup of hot coffee. She gave a slight jerk of her head towards the desk.

"Good, I'll have an errand for you soon. Put it there. Did you get Delia home?"

"Yes, my lady, at your orders, my lady. Lady Phillipa had to help me, but we sent her home an hour ago. Lady Phillipa asked me to help with the records and said she'd make it good with you."

Tiphaine nodded. "I'm fine with that. Does she need any more help? I can probably send over a few of the widow brigade."

Lioncel grinned. "She says *no.* I say *yes,* my lady. She doesn't want to interfere with the war ministry's needs."

Tiphaine scribbled some names on a scrap of paper and waved her hand in dismissal. "Notify these that they're seconded. And send Dame Lilianth in on your way," she said as she took a quick swallow of the acrid brew.

Better watch it or I'll be peeing all afternoon, she thought. *And remember what the headaches were like the last time you had to cold-turkey, the stuff's too expensive and the supply's too unreliable to get really dependent on it.*

"Sit, Dame Lilianth. I am going to make you the pos-sessor of a secret and part of a conspiracy. I have instruc-tions from the Lady Regent and wide latitude on how to carry them out."

The older woman sat, her plain brown eyes deliberately and annoyingly bland. "By your word," she said, an ironic twist to her voice. "What can I do for my lady the Spider?"

Tiphaine leaned back in her swivel chair and put her hands behind her head, staring thoughtfully at the cof-fered ceiling.

"It's complicated and it will need us to be very quiet and sneaky. As a start, I want you to have a fainting fit— people actually believe in those again, so useful—and call for your son-in-law's brother's help. He's on garrison duty with the city castellan, isn't he?"

"Garrick? Certainly . . . what next?"

"It's enough like my special-ops days to make me feel nostalgic. We—"

As the door closed on Dame Lilianth, Tiphaine broke open the next dispatch. *My head hurts again . . . but not as much as Astrid's does!*

Alone, she let a sudden sharp grin split her face. She relished the second of pure, unadulterated joy contem-plating Astrid Loring's concussion gave her. The thought of how the fact that Tiphaine had rescued her from the wreck of her covert ops mission gave a more subtle plea-sure; it would be grit under the Hiril Dúnedain's eyelids for the rest of her life.

Or it would be for me, in her position, and I can hope *we're enough alike for that to be so for her as well.*

She worked her way through the day's stack of wallets and made a good start on the stack of allocation files. The

Association's military system was largely self-financing, but only as long as you didn't need to use it for anything but routine. Once vassals had done more than their regulation forty days of service in the field, they had to be paid. And of course all the allied contingents were trying to shift as much of *their* costs as possible onto the Portland treasury.

Lioncel brought her lunch. And his brother, two years younger and as dark as Lioncel was fair, but otherwise much like his brother. The three made their usual quick meal in the office on the pork-loin sandwiches and potato salad and fruit. Dame Lilianth scolded as Diomede tried to avoid getting a huge yellow mustard blot on his hose—and succeeded in getting it all over the floor. After he had cleaned it up, she sent him out with Dame Lilianth and Ysolde to work on organizing the kitchens to cope with the influx of temporary workers; that was good training in logistics.

She was deep into a plan submitted by the Count Palatine of Walla Walla to reinforce Castle Campscapell and wondering if it could, just possibly, be a scheme to get his own troops inside that Crown fortress when a quick tap on the door broke into her concentration.

"Come."

Her senior squire Armand Georges poked his head in.

"Urgent dispatch, my lady Grand Constable."

"Another?"

She managed to keep most of the sound of resentment out of her voice; this sort of thing went with the job.

"What is it *this* time?"

"Sir Guelf Mortimer of Loiston . . . did a bunk."

"Shit! A bunk?"

"Fled. Scarpered. Twinkle-toed into the wild blue distance. Absent without leave . . ."

"All right."

Tiphaine snapped her mouth shut, and squeezed her

eyes shut for an instant. She'd parked him out at Hermiston to keep him on ice while the Gervais problem was dealt with. On the other hand . . .

"Tell me how Guelf pulled it off."

He shrugged. "From what we've managed to piece together, he conned each of the back-scouting parties into believing he was with the other one. Unfortunately for him, Sir Thierry Renfrew ran into a CUT probe down the Columbia. He fought and called for reinforcements. That's the train that arrived at four this morning with the wounded. Chenoweth called up Mortimer's picket. They had some trouble finding them. He finally tracked them down late yesterday. Guelf left early on the nineteenth."

"Days! He could be anywhere by now."

"But there's not much doubt where he's headed. Gervais."

"Yes." She frowned. "That getaway was a lot more subtle than Guelf's usual level. But heading for Gervais is putting his head on the block and even he should have been able to see *that*. Uncharacteristically smart, then bone-stupid even beyond his usual."

"Offhand, I'd say that means he's being used as a puppet, and by someone who doesn't care about the consequences for him."

"Good analysis."

She smiled then, and even Armand blinked, though he'd been one of her operatives for years.

"I was hoping to keep the Gervais problems on hold, but the operation's ready to go. And Guelf has just delivered himself into my hand. Desertion in the face of the enemy!"

She held her right hand out, palm-up, and then slowly closed the long fingers into a fist. Then she reached out for Chenoweth's dispatch.

"Go find Sir Garrick Betancourt. He'll be down with the Marchwarden of the South in the situation room. Tell him *drop the hammer*. Verbal orders only, of course."

Armand nodded and left at a brisk walk; running would attract the eye and arouse curiosity.

Tiphaine leaned back from the crowded desk and let her fingers trace the pommel of the misericord dagger at her belt.

Thirty miles, give or take, and the rail runs right through Gervais. Betancourt should be there by midafternoon if he pushes it.

Mistress Douglas came in with a new sheaf of papers and searched for the correct docket to file them in.

Tiphaine followed her out to talk to one of the typists.

"Mistress Romero, write and send a message to the Regent. It can go in the clear, as fast as possible. Guelf Mortimer of Loiston has drawn the dotted line."

Puzzlement, and then she could see everyone assuming that it was some private code. It was; the rest of the phrase was *on the back of his neck*, which was where the headsman's ax went—Guelf wouldn't rate the two-handed sword, not being a tenant-in-chief.

CHARTERED CITY OF GOLDENDALE
COUNTY OF AUREA
PORTLAND PROTECTIVE ASSOCIATION
(FORMERLY CENTRAL WASHINGTON)
HIGH KINGDOM OF MONTIVAL
(FORMERLY WESTERN NORTH AMERICA)
AUGUST 5, CHANGE YEAR 25/2023 AD

Mathilda grimaced slightly as Tiphaine halted her narrative.

"There weren't any palatable choices right there, were there, Tiph?"

"That's war for you, Matti. Particularly this type; we just couldn't take any chances on the politics of it. Fortunately I'm not at the ultimate policy-making level. I'm more like a crossbow. You point me and pull the trigger."

"And I *am* doing the aiming now, and the only ones I can blame things on if it goes wrong are Rudi and God, which wouldn't be a good idea. Well, the Liu siblings need to know *some* of that. That way of dealing with Mary Liu was *so* Mom, though. Just trying to follow her logic makes my brain hurt, sometimes. It's always there but it's . . . twisty."

"At least you *can* follow it. Thousands couldn't, and a lot of them came down with a case of the deads. Not least the late unlamented Dowager Baroness Liu, in the end."

The man-at-arms came back up the stairs.

"His Reverence Abbot-Bishop Dmwoski, Your Majesty," he said. "The Honorable Huon Liu, heir to Barony Gervais; the Honorable Yseult Liu."

Tiphaine looked at her, and Mathilda nodded slightly. Then she smiled and rose as they entered and made their bow and curtsy; she advanced and kissed Dmwoski's ring respectfully, then extended her hands to the youngsters. She'd known them socially, of course—Odard had been a frequent companion of hers for years before the Quest. But they'd both been teenagers and then young adults, and at that age you tended to ignore younger siblings who were still children. Neither had been presented at court.

And their mother tended to keep them very close, she thought. *Even before she went to the bad.*

"Lord Huon, Lady Yseult," she said gently. "I am so sorry about Odard. I miss him terribly, but you can be very proud of him. It was an honor to be his friend and liege."

She liked the way Huon reacted, dignified but reserved; for a fifteen-year-old it was rather impressive. He moved well, too, and looked as if he'd have something of Odard's wiry strength. Yseult was more reserved still, and . . .

Tiphaine gives her the willies, though she hides it well. Of course, looked at objectively Tiph is scary as hell; she doesn't scare me *because I grew up around her. She did* kill *Yseult's mother. So I don't expect more than courtesy, but if the girl is going to be around Court, she just has to get used to it.*

"And you all know Baroness d'Ath."

Another round of polite bows. Mathilda could tell that Dmwoski was being a bit chilly, and Tiphaine was secretly amused by it; she respected Dmwoski despite his faith, not for it.

I don't think the Lius noticed. They're smart enough, but young yet.

The cleric and the Grand Constable were both far too self-controlled to make it obvious. Or to let personal dislikes interfere with the job, for that matter.

"Please sit, and help yourselves," Mathilda said. "I understand you've been on the train all day, and it can't have been much fun."

"Crowded and slow, Your Majesty," Dmwoski said. "But that's only to be expected in wartime."

Mathilda chatted a little to relax them; Huon grew enthusiastic about the gear and horses he'd picked up in Portland, and the prospect of going on his first real campaign after training to war all his life, and his swearing ceremony as a squire. That was natural enough, since it was a big step and one that was overdue. After a few minutes he was also wolfing down the chicken empanadas. Yseult nibbled on one and agreed that she was up to transferring to a forward field hospital of the type the Sisters were setting up here in Goldendale.

"Ah . . . do you want to take my oath now, Your Majesty?" Huon said.

Mathilda shook her head. "Tomorrow, and publicly," she said decisively. "That will be better, if you think about it."

She watched them carefully; Yseult grasped the point first, but Huon was only a second behind. A public oath would be a public statement: *I trust Huon Liu at my back*, or more specifically *I trust Huon Liu at my back with a dagger, twenty-four/seven*. Neither was obvious about it either, which was good.

People might, *would*, still talk, but they'd do it in a whisper and not where he could hear. More important, they wouldn't do it where the High Queen or anyone close to her could hear it either.

"I understand that you've been eager to hear the results of the Most Reverend Father's investigations," she said after a moment's quiet contemplation. "Besides being most helpful."

"Ah . . . not exactly *eager*, Your Majesty," Huon said.

He and his sister exchanged a glance.

Those two are allies against the world, Mathilda thought. A little wistfully, since she'd been an only child. And necessarily a little isolated from others her own age by her birth, except for Rudi.

Though that only child thing may have been for the best. Still, I'm glad my children will have lots of brothers and sisters. Kinship is . . . not everything, but close.

"But we do want to know," Yseult said. "It's, ummm, hit us so often and so badly, but a lot of it was just bewildering, especially at the time. We only knew the bits that happened *to* us, Your Majesty, and then it was like . . . we had to realize that all this had been going on around us without our knowing."

Mathilda nodded. "That's part of growing up, but this is a pretty extreme case. You've earned the right to know," she said. "I'm going to tell you what happened immediately after Pendleton. That was when my letter arrived back home, about how Alex Vinson betrayed us . . . betrayed me *and* Odard to the Cutters. Unfortunately, that was also when the CUT decided to activate your uncle Guelf. Whether he liked it or not. They probably knew the news would get back, after Odard and I were rescued."

Dmwoski nodded. "As I've said before, there is no spoon long enough to sup safely with them. I heard a little of this from a Mackenzie who was involved."

"I debriefed the Renfrews," Tiphaine said. "And handled a lot of stuff later that revealed what had been going on at Hermiston. Chime in if I'm missing anything, Most Reverend Father. What apparently happened is that Guelf got desperate because—"

HERMISTON, COUNTY HERMISTON
(FORMERLY UMATILLA COUNTY)
PORTLAND PROTECTIVE ASSOCIATION
(FORMERLY NORTH-CENTRAL OREGON)
SEPTEMBER 17, CHANGE YEAR 23/2021 AD

Sir Guelf Mortimer felt he was doing a good imitation of a brooding falcon as the pedal car rumbled into the Hermiston station and orderlies rushed forward to take the badly wounded away. The brooding was keeping his chatty squires away from him, at least. He hoped they were still smarting from his tongue-lashing.

"Off and down, off and down, clear the line!" someone shouted.

No word from the Ascended Masters, he thought. *Was it*

because I was always with the Odell crowd, or that they don't have any word for me?

Odo was clinging to him as they jumped off the pedal cab. The boy was shaking and had bruises under his eyes, emphasized by the light of the flaring torches that supplemented the alcohol lanterns; the sun was nearly down, though the western horizon was still eye-hurting crimson. As soon as the Gervais men were clear a party came running up with loaded stretchers.

On another siding, reinforcements were jumping down off a train of eastbound horse-drawn rail wagons and falling into ranks, their three-quarter armor incongruously clean and their eyes wide as they stared about at the filthy blood-splashed scarecrow figures, the limping walking wounded and the grisly shapes on the stretchers. Corvallans, from the Benny the Beaver image on their breastplates; their knockdown pikes or crossbows were still slung over their backs as they formed up and marched away.

"OK, Odo. Tonight you will camp with us. But tomorrow you and Father Stanyon are taking Terry home for burial. I don't want you slipping out of that."

And in this heat, we'll have to get a well-sealed coffin.

His heart ached for the boy as he shook his head, dark greasy hair clinging to his skin, tear tracks down the dirty cheeks, mouth gaping as he yawned so wide Guelf wondered if he'd crack the jaw joint. And while disobedience couldn't be tolerated, at least he'd done it from an excess of spirit.

"Let's go find Father Stanyon," he said firmly, suppressing his own wide yawn.

"Charlmain! You and Brandon get the men bivouacked and set up sentries. I don't care how safe you feel; we've left a lot of angry enemies behind. They thought they were going to swallow us down and they didn't and they'll be feeling cheated."

The squires knuckled their foreheads and went in search of Sir Thierry's provosts and directions to the campgrounds. Guelf found Stanyon a block away, after pushing his way through streets that were a mass of troops and horses and vehicles almost to the edge of the castle moat; the little town was so insignificant it didn't even have a wall, and the few locals were like chips on a torrent. One of the warehouses was being used as a field hospital. As he walked into its lantern-lit dimness there was a heavy smell of spoiled blood from the bandages heaped in corners, heat, sweat, pain and disinfectant. Healers from half a dozen of the allied powers were sorting and doing emergency surgery on a set of bloodstained tables. A line of volunteers stood ready to lie down next to the injured and provide transfusions.

Odo slitted his eyes to keep out as much as he could. Even Guelf gulped a little. He was well used to the butcher-shop horrors that happened when men hacked and stabbed with edged weapons, but there was something chilling about this in an entirely different way. Moans and shrieks sounded every now and then, not often enough to be disregarded, so that every new one hit you fresh.

The seven wounded from Gervais who'd survived and three bodies of those who'd died here were laid together. Father Stanyon and a Mackenzie medic were standing toe to toe over one unconscious figure. The kilted clanswoman was slight but bristling, her brown braid swinging as she shook her head emphatically.

"And what part of *no* is it that's too complicated for you to be understanding the now, you cowan blockhead?" she shouted in a Mackenzie lilt, arms windmilling the way they did.

"Here's my Lord, talk to *him*, pagan bitch!" the priest shouted back.

Guelf grunted; he felt as if his eyes had been taken out and the backs sanded, then the sockets dusted with hot ash before they were replaced. He glared, but neither quailed.

"Out," he snarled, and turned on his heel. "Now!"

Outside, Father Stanyon spoke in an angry, even tone. "She dosed that man we picked up with laudanum. Dosed him heavily, forced it suddenly down his throat."

Guelf frowned. "So?" he asked.

Even he knew that was standard if you didn't want to inject a wounded man with morphine, which was expensive even for military use and had to be saved for the most urgent cases. Ones who were unconscious or who couldn't keep an oral medication down.

The Mackenzie medic nodded at him. "Not going to apologize, my Lord. Both the Father and I agree, the spalpeen isn't actually one of your Gervais men."

Baffled, Guelf's stubbled face swung back and forth. "He isn't?"

"No." Father Stanyon hesitated. "He's dressed in the bloodstained clothing of one of ours, however. Blood all over the right kidney."

Guelf growled. That was the mark of an assassin; a knife in the kidney was the fastest and quietest way to kill quickly. There was a whole knot of big blood vessels there, and if you stuck the blade deep, in just the right place, and twisted sharply, unconsciousness followed almost instantly. It was a lot easier and less obviously messy than slitting a throat too, if you left the knife in for a moment.

"Killed one of ours to sneak in one of their spies?" he grated.

The Mackenzie nodded briskly, removing the surgical mask that had fallen around her neck over the thin golden torc.

"Yes. 'Twould be my guess, do you see, that he threw himself down looking all wounded and hurt to be carried in, planning to get up when nobody was looking in the hurry and chaos. Blood on clothing is not the most uncommon of things about here, I'm observing. It's the Mother's own luck that I happened to do a quick triage check; and there the spalpeen's back was, not sliced or cut or stabbed at all. So I grabbed the creature's nose and poured the dose down his throat."

Now what?

Guelf felt like a parrot lived in his brain; or that an ax had cut it in half. One side of it was reacting with an instinctive rage. The other . . .

Was he sent to contact me? I can't tell. And the man is unconscious and going to stay that way . . . damned officious Mackenzie. Better send him on to the Grand Constable. The Witch-Queen might easily learn too much. I can't kill him or keep him, that would make people suspicious right away!

"Right. Father Stanyon, my thanks for defending our interests and referring this decision to me. I'll take the advice of our ally. Who should take charge of the prisoner, witch?"

The Mackenzie gestured to the men standing by. Both of them were notably hard-faced, and the clothes under their armor were a uniform brown. Scratches and dings and a spray of something reddish-brown dried across one didn't disguise the snarling face-on bear's head.

"Those are a couple of Larsdalen men; they came with us. They'll get the prisoner to the Grand Constable or Lady Juniper, if I ask. Lady d'Ath is with Odell west of here, at Biggs Junction; our Chief is at Dun Juniper. *Mac an donais!* Just get the creature out of here, and fast would be best. He *smells*, and in more ways than one."

Guelf bowed, a short gesture. "He's all yours, gentlemen; take him to the Grand Constable and report all you've heard. Just give me back the clothes; I hope to identify the man he killed. One more notch on the blade."

"Come, Odo, we need to say good-bye to Terry and check on Chezzy."

Guelf sighed gently as he turned away. If the man had been his contact, it was a good thing the Mackenzie had intervened. Good in the short term, at least. A bubble of fear was starting to burn down under his breastbone; fear worse than a spear point coming for his face.

The Mackenzie nodded. "I want him out and harmless. We've been warned that the Cutters sometimes possess powers dangerous to ordinary folk, so."

Father Stanyon crossed himself and murmured a prayer.

The Mackenzie gave him a sardonic look. "We'll hogtie him and send him on to the Grand Constable . . . but he goes drugged. I know more about magic than you do. By definition. And the first and the last and the heart of it is paying attention."

Guelf looked at Father Stanyon.

He was one of Pope Leo's men. Very strict, but very brave, and honest . . . Well, so am I! I just know more. Now what? I want to say good-bye to Terry, check up on Chezzy and go to sleep. God, I must sleep!

"Sir Guelf . . ."

Guelf Mortimer began to start up from his bedroll and

draw his sword where it lay near him across his saddle, but forced himself to be still instead.

Am I dreaming? Did I hear that?

It was very dark, but the steel might be seen. He knew that voice: Alex Vinton, Odard's manservant. But there was nobody here, nobody at all.

God. I keep waiting for provosts with a warrant for arrest. Or to turn around and it's that bitch d'Ath, smiling. Or one of her pupils. Or I just don't wake up. Did the man talk? It's days now . . . of course he'd talk! Everyone talks when you hold their head under water the fiftieth time! Did he know my name, that's the question.

There was just a hint of light on the rolling ground around him, starlight teasing with almost-sight.

Or maybe . . . maybe they don't talk. The Ascended Masters . . .

The whisper hung in the star-spangled dark. The moon hung low in the west, this late in the night; a few days past full. Guelf turned, thrashed a second, kicking off his blanket, and staggered up to his feet and away from the sleeping men, past the one sentry.

"Back in a minute," he mumbled, fumbling with his trews.

"Aye, my lord," murmured the sentry back.

The latrine was ten paces farther on and a new dark shadow was lying on the far side of the little ditch where the excess dirt had been piled up. The bright moonlight distorted expected shapes and humps.

"Sir Guelf?"

"Vinton?"

"Yes, my lord."

Guelf controlled his anger. Yelling at the man was not going to help right now and would wake the men behind them. They were all Loiston Manor men, but you never could tell. Chenoweth had had words with all of them before they'd left.

"What news?"

"The Ascended Masters say you are to return to Gervais as fast as possible. A spy has found you and the Lady Mary out and we couldn't intercept either the spy or the dispatches. They've been in the hands of the Regency for several days now."

"What's happened with my damned nephew?"

An odd sound came from across the ditch. "Captured with the Princess by the CUT. I freed him; the fellowship freed her. The little nephilite whore sent the news to her bitch of a mother."

"Does my nephew *know*?"

"Good question. You've been standing here too long. I'll meet you on the Woodburn Road after you've helped your sister burn the papers. That's the most important thing; those documents would tell the enemy too much."

Strange, he thought, letting a stream go into the stinking trench. *I'm really going to do that. I can't really tell why I'm going to do it, though.*

The thought floated away. There was a rustle and Vinton was gone. Guelf shrugged before making his way back to the men. He didn't lie down, but paced quietly near the sentry instead.

His mind was moving, thinking, planning, but the forepart of his brain refused to analyze it. Now and then he'd feel another surge of fear, as if he were floating over one of the waterfalls in gorge of the Columbia, weightless, rushing out into space and turning and turning with the rocks below, and then it would slip away again.

I must get back to Gervais, Guelf thought and spat reflexively. *No, the longer but more sure route is my best bet.*

Dawn came soon, touching the eastern horizon with a

paler color. He grabbed one of the bicycles and spoke quietly to the sentry.

"I'm uneasy about our railroad team. *Something* woke me up. Tell Sergeant Gavin to carry on as planned and I'll rejoin you late tomorrow."

"Sir Guelf, do you think you should? Alone?"

If anything was lacking to convince him that his cover had been ripped, this questioning of his orders was it.

"I'm not losing seven good men just because I'm too timid to follow up my instincts. Carry on."

He wanted to snap, to yell, to roar at the impertinence of the man . . . But he didn't want to wake up Sergeant Gavin.

Let the interfering old relic sleep. If I'm gone, he'll wait for me to return. Besides which, he really needs to get the scouting done, not waste time chasing a wild hare called Guelf!

CHAPTER TEN

ARMY HQ
THE HIGH KING'S HOST
HORSE HEAVEN HILLS
(FORMERLY SOUTH-CENTRAL WASHINGTON)
HIGH KINGDOM OF MONTIVAL
(FORMERLY WESTERN NORTH AMERICA)
AUGUST 8, CHANGE YEAR 25/2023 AD

Crack.

C   Huon Liu grunted as the shield buffeted into his, taking him at a wicked angle that threw the stress across his leg rather than punching straight back into his fighting crouch. He snarled and switched stance as fast as he could, trying not to stagger, giving ground and bringing the shield up. The armored figure rushed at him with a movement as smooth as oil, nothing to see above the shield save the long vision slit in the curved visor. He was wearing an open-faced sallet himself, but he'd been maneuvered until the lowering sun was making him squint.

Perhaps if he tried a looping flourish cut and—

Crack and his sword struck against the shield, jarring his right hand and arm. It pushed in, binding and hampering his sword-arm.

The other sword lunged towards his face. He brought his shield up and around and ducked his head, desperately trying not to block his own vision. The other's shield twitched out to block his cut at the leg then darted in to lock its edge under the rim of his and lever it aside.

Another quick pivot, and the blunt tip of the wooden practice sword struck the back of his thigh with paralyzing force. Huon gave an involuntary grunt of pain and went down on one knee, desperately propping the point of his shield on the ground and against his shoulder, whipping his padded oak sword back.

The High Queen stepped back and used the edge of her shield to knock her visor up. Her face was red and streaming with sweat, but she grinned at Huon.

"Not bad, youngster. And you don't give up, which is the essential thing. If they cut off your arms and your legs, your last words should be: *Come back, you coward, I'll* bite *you to death!* But you're still thinking too much while you're doing. Just throw the lever and let it *happen.* Disarm me, you two."

Huon levered himself back to his feet and racked the battered practice weapons with the others; nobody in the Household slacked off. Even the Queen spent at least two hours a day at it, and she had enough other work to choke a horse. There was no choice; if you lost your edge you were easy meat in a fight.

Though with armies this big—St. Michael witness, tens of thousands!—commanders may not fight with their own hands as much or as often. But it'll still happen, and it only takes once to die.

He was wearing the gear he'd picked up in Portland; a brigantine of small steel plates riveted between two layers of leather on his torso, plate vambraces and greaves, a mail camail for neck and shoulders and rows of steel splints on leather for his thighs and upper arms. It was good protection by skilled armorers, and even with the letter of credit he hadn't *quite* dared to order a suit of plate that he'd outgrow in a year or less with the prospect of doing it all again several times before he reached his full height. He wasn't going to be towering, but his hands and feet indicated he'd be adding inches yet.

Right now the armor seemed to be squeezing at him, and he made himself control his breathing. Ogier de Odell was the other Royal Squire now. He was in a suit of plate—he was also a year older—and he'd already relieved Mathilda of the shield and drill sword. Huon lifted the helm and padded cap off her coiled brown hair, transferred them to the armor stand outside the door-flap of the tent and began on the buckles and straps and the slip-knots in the laces of the arming doublet as the High Queen stood or moved to ease their task.

Ogier grinned at him as they worked; he was a good sort, and didn't presume too much either on his years or his birth; of course, he was very much a younger son of the Count of Odell, not his Viscount-heir. With two sets of trained hands at the task it went quickly. He still felt a little reverence as he handled the suit. It was made from arcane pre-Change alloys that were usually too refractory to work, matchlessly light and strong, the sort of thing only a monarch could afford because it involved a team of highly paid specialists for a year or more using technology right at the limit of the possible.

"You're in my position right now," she went on to him as the plates came off.

A page came with a T-tunic to replace the doublet, and Huon handed her the sword belt with the live steel. In the field you wore it even when you were sitting down to eat.

"Your Majesty?" he said, as he knelt and cinched the tooled leather.

"You're fighting opponents with more weight and bulk. There are ways around that, and it's a good idea to know them. You'll be bigger than me soon, but you're never going to have the High King's inches, or even Ogier's."

"Odard wasn't a very tall man either, my lady," Huon observed.

About your height, in fact, he thought; Mathilda Arminger was very tall for a woman, maybe a thumb's-width over average height for a man. *Odard was medium-sized, but he was quick as a weasel.*

"No, but he was very bad news in a fight," Mathilda said. "I saw him kill a lot of bigger men. Including a Moorish corsair in his last fight who, and the Virgin witness that I'm telling you the truth, was the size of Lord John Hordle and had at least as much muscle. He used a brassbound club I could barely lift one-handed."

Huon blinked; the Dúnedain leader had beheaded an enemy's warhorse with a single stroke of his greatsword once, and taken off the knight's head with the next, chopping right through the bevoir plate. It wasn't the only legendary feat that hung around his name. The thought of his brother's end brought a familiar rush of mingled pride and grief; also a twinge of doubt that he'd ever be able to live up to the legend.

Mathilda grinned. "Don't worry, you've got years to do that."

He bowed, and flushed at her good-natured chuckle.

"Now disarm and come join me at table."

Ogier helped him, though the squire's kit he wore was a lot easier to shed than a knight's outfit. He suppressed a groan of relief as the armor and padding came off and the hot dry air dried the sweat. This area had plenty of heat and dust, and only just enough water for drinking. The smell wasn't too bad; everyone went down to the

Columbia and washed once or twice a week and you got used to rankness in the field.

We wash once a week whether we need it or not, as the saying goes, Huon thought.

"Perceptive, our liege-lady, isn't she?" Ogier murmured. "Sometimes you suddenly remember who her mother is."

"She's kindhearted, though," Huon said, also quietly, since the implication was that the Lady Regent was *not.* "*And* she's good with a sword, too. I thought maybe it was troubadour's spin, but it wasn't, was it?"

"Nope. She's no d'Ath or Astrid Loring, but she's pretty good, definitely better than the average man-at-arms, the speed and skill makes up for the bulk. Especially in *this* armor. They're thinking of marrying me off to Anne of Tillamook, you know?"

"I've met her. She's very nice," Huon said, wondering at the segue. "My sister spent some time there and she says Anne's a good mistress."

Yes, I'd heard about that match. It's logical; she inherits. Tillamook isn't exactly rich, but a Countess isn't going to wear wooden shoes even if a lot of her subjects do! He's a third son, but his father is a Count. And the families are allies, so it makes sense to link them.

"She's very *smart,*" Ogier said. "And pretty, too; and our children would be heirs to a County, even if it's a bit of a damp, remote one. But I won't have to worry about my wife knocking me off my horse at a tourney, if you know what I mean."

"Neither will the High King," Huon pointed out. "Sweet St. Michael, have you ever seen the man spar? I did just a couple of days ago. He makes the Protector's Guard knights take him on two or three at a time so he'll have to really work."

Ogier nodded and gave a grunt of agreement. "And he deals with them like he was stropping a razor," he said. "He may be a pagan, but by *God* he's a fighting man!"

Then he clanked off to take up his duties; he was in charge of the inner guard this watch. A bell rang from somewhere nearby, and was echoed across the encampment. The royal pavilion wasn't very large, but it had a tall flag post with the banner of Montival at its peak; now that was lowered, and respectfully folded by a detail. From here you could see a dozen separate encampments, the contingents of the gathering host. It was six—just time for the Angelus—and a haze of woodsmoke lay over the rolling hills and their coat of golden sun-dried grass, with here and there a patch of reaped wheat.

The bell rang again, and the household all knelt except the guards on duty. Chancellor Ignatius had come in today with a wagonload of paperwork, and he led the Angelus. Huon sank to his knees with the others, his crucifix in his hands, and let the comforting familiarity of the words roll over him:

> *"Angelus Domini, nuntiavit Mariae;*
> *Et concepit de Spiritu Sancto.*
> *Ave Maria, gratia plena, Dominus tecum . . ."*

To the final *Amen*.

Varlets set up the folding tables and chairs. Mathilda looked up suddenly at the beat of hooves. Her face was no more than ordinarily pretty with youth and health. But as she smiled she suddenly looked beautiful for a moment.

That's what the troubadours sing about, Huon thought; and suddenly felt a little ashamed about fumblings with servant girls. *Will I love someone like that someday?*

The High King and his escort reined in; Huon hurried over with the others to hold the horses. He was in Associate-style tunic and trews, and he leapt down with a foot-over style that kept his back to the horse. Then he caught Mathilda up and whirled her around, despite a laughing protest.

"There'll be time enough for state and pomp, sure and there will," he said, and kissed her. "In the meantime, I've brought guests to the bounteous epicurean feast we're laying out this eve."

Huon had already seen Yseult, riding beside the old warrior Abbot. At her he *did* grin, and then made a little game of handing her down high-courteous-wise.

"Fine manners you're picking up at court," she said.

He snorted. "Bruises black and blue are what I'm picking up," he said pridefully. "Her Majesty beat me up and down the exercise yard, and when it isn't her it's Ogier. They're merciless."

A shadow of concern flickered through the tilted blue eyes, and he smiled and shook his head slightly, giving her his hand to the table. The camp cook served out bowls of the evening's variation on what the army spread through the western fringes of the Horse Heaven Hills seemed to eat every day about this time.

"Ah, yes, the old soldier's superstition," Dmwoski said.

Everyone looked at him, and he went on: "The stubborn belief if the sun rises in the east it is an omen predicting stew for supper."

"And that would be funny, if only it were funny," the High King said, without looking up from a stack of papers he was editing with quick flicks of a pencil; *no* or *yes* or *investigate this*.

Huon helped to hand the bowls around—page-work,

but Mathilda hadn't had time enough for any squeakers yet, appointments like that were delicate political balancing acts anyway—and sat. The stew was mostly beans and peas, and chunks of an extremely salty dried sausage that had probably been mostly pork at some point, and whatever vegetables were available, fresh or starting in a sun-dried state. There was a stack of flat wheat cakes fresh from the griddle as well, and a rock-hard Sbrinz-type cheese to grate on the stew, and a bowl of raisins for dessert.

Yseult was eating hers willingly enough, but she raised her brows at the way Huon shoveled down his bowlful and went back for seconds before she said, "It just occurred to me that Odard probably ate like this all the way to the lands of Sunrise, on the quest for the Sword. And, well, he was sort of picky about food and clothes and keeping state. If I'm remembering him properly."

Rudi Mackenzie . . .

Or should I just think of him as High King Artos or simply Artos or what? Huon thought.

. . . snorted and handed the papers off to an assistant who seized them as if they were a precious relic and dashed off virtually dancing with glee. Huon jumped slightly; Mathilda was acute, but the way the High King could concentrate on several different things at once was *disturbing.*

"Your recollection is entirely correct and true," Artos said to Yseult. "He would haul that set of court dress for himself and Matti all the way to Iowa despite all our mockery—and it's well that turned out. It helped him charm the Bossman there."

"And my cote-hardie did the same for the Bossman's wife."

"Yes, and whose idea was it to bring *that*? His. The which was worth hearing him swear he'd run wild and chew on trees if he had to have scorched stew of stringy venison one more time. Though he did say *I told you so* about it after Iowa more than was comfortable or right. He could have a tongue like a needle. Sometimes he'd stick the needle in just to make the person in question screech and jump."

Mathilda looked off, a rolled-up wheat cake in one hand. "When we didn't have *anything* to eat he'd joke about that, too. Laugh that it was the first thing we'd had in weeks not fried in grease."

She smiled at Yseult. "He was the worst camp cook! Sometimes he'd trade off and do the scouring and washing instead just to avoid eating food he'd prepared himself."

"Or desecrated himself," Rudi agreed. "I swear by Brigid that the raw materials were usually more tasteful than the end product, uncooked meat included."

His face had changed, becoming more approachable somehow as he reached for a flask of wine covered in woven straw.

"Now you, *a ghràidh*, got to be quite good at making whatever we had edible. Better than this, to be sure."

"Oh, this stew is savory enough," Mathilda said, wiping her bowl with a piece of the flatbread.

"By *savory* you'd be meaning *thick, brown and salty*, no doubt."

Huon blinked. It was a little difficult to imagine the fastidious brother he remembered slaving over a campfire. Much less the *High Queen*, not to mention the heir to the Protector's position, scrubbing out pots and dishes with sand and ashes.

"And here we are, already hashing over the past like withered elders sitting in the sun and dwelling on their youth," Rudi said.

"Sometimes the past is key to the present," Dmwoski said. "This mission of mine has proven that once again."

Mathilda used her eyes in a quick commanding flick, and most of those present withdrew; the trestle tables were taken down. Lamps were coming on throughout the sprawling tent-city, but most would go to sleep with the sun sinking westward.

"Go on, Most Reverend Father," Rudi said to Dmwoski.

"I will; some of this I learned from the Grand Constable, and some from Lord Huon and Lady Yseult, and other parts from the records. I think I have put it together accurately, but let them correct me if I err."

He looked down at his hands, his strong-boned furrowed face underlit by the coals of the fire.

"The Lady Regent and the Grand Constable acted quickly when the news of the enemy prisoner and Sir Guelf's defection reached Portland. The Grand Constable had alerted Sir Garrick Betancourt to hold himself in instant readiness . . ."

CASTLE GERVAIS, BARONY OF GERVAIS
PORTLAND PROTECTIVE ASSOCIATION
(FORMERLY WESTERN OREGON)
SEPTEMBER 22, CHANGE YEAR 23/2021 AD

The solar was quiet, quiet enough that the *tick* of a needle piercing cloth was loud. Yseult was curled up in the window seat, restlessly staring out the eastern window of the tower, across the Five Great Fields of the home manor, sunlight glinting on the almost glassy stems of the reaped wheat and the nearly motionless leaves of the Lombardy poplars in the rows separating the fields. The air was warm and drowsy, smelling of slow-flowing water in the moat beneath the pads and blossoms of the lilies, and of the warm stuccoed concrete of the castle walls themselves. It was much better than winter, when they soaked up the dank chill and released it again to keep you in the right mood for the Black Months.

She'd pulled her fair braid over her shoulder and was nibbling on the end. Huon was out east, serving at Pendleton as a page in the fighting train of Sir Chaka Jones, Baron of Mollala. Odard was even farther east, in Boise, Idaho, the guest of President pro-tem Lawrence Thurston, according to his last letter. Which was dated a long time ago, so he might be anywhere now.

Odard didn't always have time for Huon and me, but he was nice *when he did.*

She sniffled quietly, and winced. *Here it comes,* she thought, *wait for it . . . wait . . . five, four, three, two . . .* Mary Liu reached for her scissors, silk sleeve rustling. A quiet snip and a quick snap.

"Ysi! Daydreaming again! What have you done so far?"

Yseult swung around and lifted the heavy weight of the altar cloth she had been embroidering before it slid to the gleaming wood floor. She brought it over to her mother, sitting between two south-facing windows. As she gave it over she snuck a quick look at the narrow face under the widow's wimple. They were alike in some ways; her mother had fair hair too, though graying now, and blue eyes. But the bones of her face were much sharper, and Yseult *hoped* she would never have that look of settled discontent.

Her heart sank. *Mama's been on edge since the letters arrived from Boise.*

Yseult watched nervously as her mother slid the embroidered cloth through her fingers. Mary's moods had been unpredictable since Odard left; it paid to bet on the side of strictness, especially for her only daughter.

Yseult swallowed as Mary's fingers stopped at the section she'd been working on so desultorily this morning and yesterday.

"This is as bad as your stitches when you were five! You need to pay attention, Yseult. You *are* fifteen. I was a married lady by the time I was sixteen! And *much* better with my needle. A *King's* daughter had to set an example, back when we were in the Society."

If you were a King's *daughter, why aren't you a Princess?*

Yseult gulped back the words, surprised that she'd dared to think them in her mother's face.

Lady Phillipa told me that was just a fantasy of yours. That it didn't mean the same thing in the Society and you weren't a King's daughter, anyway.

She clenched her teeth as her mother pushed the heavy cloth onto the table with a quick nervous gesture and walked a few steps towards the fireplace and back.

"Hand!" she demanded.

Yseult gasped, but held out her right hand, palm up. No good ever came of whining or trying to get out of her punishments. Her left hand grasped her parting gift from Brother Odard. A two-sided medal with St. Bernadette of Lourdes on one side and the Immaculate Conception on the other that hung on a fine gold chain around her neck.

Her right hand trembled and she couldn't stop two tears sliding down her cheeks as she waited for the ruler to snap against her tender palm.

"Crying!" exclaimed Mary, contempt and dismissal in her voice. "Here."

She thrust the heavy linen back into Yseult's arms. "Pick it out, from here to here. Then put it away for now.

I won't have slovenly work on the altar of the Lord. You can . . ."

A scratch on the solar door interrupted her tirade. She turned and Yseult drew in a quick, shuddering breath of relief, rapidly and neatly folding the cloth.

"Romarec, what is it?"

"My lady, your brother begs an audience."

Yseult looked at the matronly housekeeper in some surprise. The last she'd heard, Uncle Guelf was leading the Gervais *menie* in battle out in Pendleton.

What's he *doing back in Gervais?*

She began to sidle towards the servants' door; strict, hard-handed Uncle Guelf ranked low on her list of people to welcome.

"Certainly. Send him up and do you take this child of mine with you," said Mary, a tight smile on her face. "She is to work on her sewing with you until the altar cloth embroidery is good enough for me."

"Yes, my lady."

Goodwife Romarec bobbed a curtsy, met Yseult's eyes and made a very small hand gesture to her and held the door open. As she shut the door behind them, Yseult sighed, her palm tingling where the ruler had not hit. Romarec instructed the waiting page to bring Lord Guelf up and waved Yseult towards the door to the servants' hall.

"Come, young Mistress," she said. "What's amiss?"

Yseult gave the housekeeper a rather watery smile. "Mama's so annoyed and angry all the time, these days. I know the Regent said we all have to do our part in this war, but I wish I could do my part staying with Aedelia Kozlow or Jehane Smitts."

Romarec led her down the servants' corridor, frowning.

"You wouldn't be allowed. Not with the Regent as angry as she is with your mother over the Sutterdown assassins. It took some months for the news to percolate down, but that's why each family has withdrawn their maidens and none have offered you a spot."

She eyed Yseult, but Yseult shook her head. "Mama never said what happened with the Re . . . *Wait!* The Lady Regent was mad at *Mama* because brother Odard saved the life of the Mackenzie and the Wanderer? I mean, I mean, mostly he was trying to keep the Princess safe . . . She's not very easy to keep safe."

Romarec shot a quick glance up and down the length of the hall before saying softly: "Little Mistress, your mother does you no favors by keeping you ignorant."

Yseult sniffed and pushed the heavy white cloth into the housekeeper's hands. She pulled out her hankie and wiped her eyes and blew her nose defiantly.

"Sorry, I was afraid I'd drip on that pure cloth. Mama would have had kittens—more kittens. Mama—Mama and Uncle did something, and Odard came back really angry, but I didn't hear what he said to her. She wouldn't tell me, anyway. Sometimes the other maids-in-waiting would tell me things."

Yseult felt her lip pout out and sucked it back in. Lady Mary had a habit of pinching it if she pouted in front of her. The housekeeper shook her head and hesitated, before opening the door to the large bright room that was the servants' sewing room. Five peasant girls were sitting by the north-facing windows. They looked up and smiled before continuing their work. Romarec spread the altar cloth with its white on white counted cross-stitch over a table in the back. She lowered her voice.

"It's not something I should talk to you about; it's not safe. The Lady Regent was so furious your mother nearly lost her head. Those assassins were sent by a kingdom to the east; Cutters they call them. Your mother and your Uncle Guelf snuck them in, hid them, and gave them money and information. Your mother's goal, as she told me, was the death of the Mackenzie tanist. Rudi Mackenzie, their Chief's son. But it all went wrong, and the Princess Mathilda and Lord Odard were put in mortal peril as well."

Yseult froze, the room going dark around her. Sparks of light starred the blackness and she swayed, clumsily thrusting a hand out for balance. Romarec's scolding sounded distant through the sea-surf roaring in her ears. Something hit the back of her legs and she sat abruptly on a hard chair. A glass was thrust in her hands and that distant voice ordered her: "Sip!"

Yseult felt her teeth begin to chatter and clenched her jaw. *I won't be weak!* She sipped, nearly coughed at the fiery-sweet taste of the herbed apricot brandy in the flask and looked up, her sight clearing. Romarec's concerned eyes met hers. She nodded and sipped again.

"My mother endangered the *Princess*?" she whispered, incredulous. "That would be *treason*, and not petty treason either! Why are any of us still alive?" Her mind made a leap. "Odard! Odard fought for her. She must have begged his life of the Lady Regent."

Then she waved her hand as Romarec glanced to either side again. "No! No, you are right. Not now. Some other day. Now, I should do what Mama says."

A frisson of fear ran down her back, a physical sensation like the edge of nausea, and she shuddered. Her appalled understanding of her mother's idiocy made her stomach twist as if she'd eaten green apples, a knowledge as much of the gut as the brain. Fear for herself warred with fear for the whole family; high treason could see them all executed and the lands attainted. And treason was tried before the Court of Star-Chamber, not a jury of your peers. The Lady Regent was not known for being forgiving about anything, much less the life of her only child and heir. Having that child and heir run off—the rumors were plain it had been without permission, and there had been a rare public loss of temper by the Lady Regent—wouldn't have made her any sweeter about it.

Goodwife Romarec nodded and straightened up, speaking in a normal voice: "Well, my little Mistress, seeing that you have been assigned to sew with me, I'll tell you that I can really use the help. These are five new maids, each as clumsy as a cow with her needle and each one worse than the last, but they're all I have, now the maids-in-waiting are gone, to sew all the clothes that we must provide for the castle. We need to make sure the Christmas distribution is done, and we only have a few months to get through the tasks."

Yseult smiled. She wished she could hug so lowly a person as the housekeeper. But Lady Mary frowned on what she called Yseult's *familiarity with the lower classes.* That was old-fashioned thinking, of course. Nowadays nobles *knew* who they were. Instead she nodded.

"Yes, Romarec, I think that will help me become more disciplined. What times do you think I should work for you?"

"I . . ." Romarec studied the altar cloth, running it through her hands. "What are these symbols?" she asked.

Yseult shook her head. "Mama tells me what to embroider, by the count. She'll give me a starting point, but she won't explain. She told me that it would make me concentrate more, that I was getting distracted and letting the colors and shapes guide my hands and not the pattern, itself."

Romarec shook her head. The last foot of cloth she frowned at. "*This?* She thinks *this* must be taken out? Child, your mother never could decide from which side of her mouth she should blow! *I* can see the difference, with my eyes six inches from the cloth, but on an altar at five yards, white on white, it's not going to show at all. Howsoever, your Lady Mother is sure to ask and inspect. So, come meet my new girls, pick this out and I will expect you here from nine in the morning every day. You will have elevenses with us and eat dinner with the castle staff and work until three in the afternoon."

"And then?"

"Thusly, Master Johannsen will still see you at four for your riding lesson, and we will inform Mistress Virgilia that your tutoring will be in the evening."

Yseult nodded, relieved to be free of the hot, boring solar and out of her mother's sole company.

How awful! I never felt like this about Mama, before. But there were always maids with us!

She picked out the slightly sloppy stitches, wondering why Guelf was in Gervais and what the war news from Pendleton was.

Maybe Guelf brought a letter from Huon? Or one from Odard! Dispatches? Or mischief? Mischief! What a word for high treason. What will happen to us?

She tried to settle the gnawing worm of anxiety in her stomach by ignoring it, forcing her hands not to twitch. She wasn't very successful. Some time later as she carefully taught Martha how to do a stretch stitch so the cuffs would stand up to rough handling she suddenly wondered:

Jesus' wounds! Should I tell the Regent my uncle is here? What if he ran away? No, he'd never run from a fight . . . But, what is *he doing here? What should I do? Odard! Huon! Where are you? I need your help!*

At three, her dilemma still unresolved, she raced up the stairs and back corridors to her own apartment, two rooms in the west tower's third story; the light was always a little dim here, because this low the windows were all narrow slits, but space was always at a premium in a castle. The passageways seemed very empty and bare without the men who'd marched east with the host to Pendleton; it made you realize how the vassals and their *menies* doing garrison duty made up so much of its usual population. With only the families of the permanent staff and the remnant of older men and boys too young to take the field she felt like one of a handful of dried peas dropped into a drum.

Her maidservant helped her out of the soft violet cotehardie and rose linen chemise, then hesitated.

"Is there news from the war, my lady?"

Yseult blinked, and then remembered that the girl had a sweetheart who was a spearman; her previous maid had been her first, and had just left to marry a blacksmith in town.

"No, Hathvisa, there isn't. I'll tell you if I hear anything, though."

"Thank you, my lady. The riding habit?"

"Yes, please."

She pulled on a riding tunic, then the heavy brown pleated wool split skirt, and shrugged into the short tight jacket. She rejoiced in the relative freedom of movement the riding habit gave her as she stamped into her boots and snatched up the hard leather riding hat. Racing down the stairs, she was tempted to stop at the little prie-dieu just inside the door of the castle chapel her mother had set up to the Immaculate Conception and St. Bernadette.

Later, when I get back! That's what I'll do! I'll ask my saint and see if she can help me figure out what to do!

Master Johannsen was waiting for her in the court-yard, holding the reins of her spirited little bay palfrey, Iomedea. Yseult shook her head at his offer of a leg up, swung into the saddle and then followed him out into the pasture north of the town that the castle also used as a training and tilting ground. That was empty too, none of the tall coursers or destriers whose hoofprints still marked the green turf, the stands that were put up for a tourney gone except for the anchor-points.

The lesson concentrated on defensive and aggressive moves that an unarmed woman, mounted, could use when under attack. With her new understanding of her danger from her mother's actions, Yseult wondered at the content of her lesson since January. They finished with his usual command.

"Ride now, for an hour, practicing your canter and trot."

Another hour of freedom from the solar was precious to her.

I might not be horse-mad like some girls, she thought. *But I'll take a horse over alone with Mama right now, any day! And I don't even have to take an escort, with men so short.*

She finished off her workout by taking the bridle path northeast along 99E, up to the tangle of vines and quick-growing sumac, poplar and hemlock and sapling oak that was rapidly obliterating the burned-out site of old Wood-burn. Her father and later her mother had supervised the stripping and destruction of the deserted town. She could just remember watching the foresters fire the controlled burn when she was five, and the quick-growing trees planted for fuel and coppice were already fifteen or twenty feet tall in this moist mild climate.

She circled north on the edge of the raw young forest.

Only the castle folk used South Boones Ferry Road, so she shook the reins and galloped over the familiar winding path, spurring Iomedea around the bend into Parr. A man stepped into the path and snatched at the bay's bridle. Yseult gasped but there was no time to be afraid, or to think. Horsemaster Johannsen's voice rang in her head.

"Wait for it, wait . . . four, three, two . . ."

Iomedea reared and crow-hopped, obedient to the signals she sent. She raised her quirt . . .

Thee may not need it, little Mistress, she heard Johannsen say in her mind. *But nonetheless, I'll be teaching thee a few maneuvers. The mare's a nice girl and will learn well, and it never hurts to know.*

Even as she brought the quirt down, cutting at the ragged man, her eyes met his. He started, dodged the whip and jumped back into the trees. Yseult gasped and set Iomedea forward at a hard gallop, her heart pounding.

I didn't think I would need a groom here! On my own land! Who was that? she wondered. *I thought I knew him, just for an instant . . . I'd better tell the guard captain right away.*

Anxiety and fear rode with her as she hurried back to town at a trot. She pulled up at the edge of the built-up area; Gervais wasn't big enough to rate a city wall. A Tinerant caravan was setting up as she did, their barrel-shaped house-wagons grouped in a square and a wild music of violins and guitars sounding; the ragged, gaudy figures made extravagant bows . . . one of them still juggling cups and daggers and apples while he did. A storyteller was declaiming to an audience of village youngsters and youths: *"Know, O Prince, that between the years when the oceans drank Atlantis and the gleaming cities, and the rise of the Sons of Aryas, there was an Age undreamed of, when shining kingdoms lay spread across the world like blue mantles beneath the stars . . ."*

She threaded her way through the crowds, not presuming too much on deference; she was a lady, but a very young one. Early evening, just as the sun set, was her favorite time in Gervais; everybody was in a good mood and thronging the streets between the shingled brick and half-timber houses and workshops, calling greetings and laughing. Hooves clattered on brick or asphalt paving.

Then a chill. A detachment of men-at-arms in the black armor of the Protector's Guard lounged in front of the Chinese Hand Inn, drinking beer and munching on bread and bowls of sweet-and-sour chicken. They whistled and wolf-called as she rode by, laughing at her glare and elevated nose. An under-officer came out of the inn with a wineglass in one hand and a chicken leg in the other to snarl at them: "Show some manners there, you dogs! Can't you see that's a lady?"

Doubtless they were the escort for some courier. Yseult arrived back at the castle with her cheeks flushed by more than good exercise.

As she dismounted in the stables, her uncle Guelf Mortimer strode in, calling for his groom. He saw her.

"Where've you been, *brat*? Your mother's that worried about you! Go to her *right now*!"

Yseult ducked around him and ran. Guelf was rough spoken and known to slap people who displeased him. Her other uncle, Jason, many years dead, had been rough mannered, too. Yseult rushed into the castle.

Why's he so mean? I might as well stay *downstairs with the cow-handed sewing maids,* she thought resentfully. *At least they are polite to me! Of course, they have to be.*

In the great hall she hesitated, torn between conflict-

ing desires. The chapel and prayer called; Guelf had ordered her to go to Mary, and she really needed to change.

Chapel can wait until after dinner, she decided. *I'll be
calmer then and won't hurry things. I must listen for the
voice of the saint or the Immaculata with calm or I won't
hear it. So, what to do now? It's a toss-up. Will Mama be
angrier with me for coming to see her in all my dirt or if I
come in later and make her wait? I'd better go see her first.*

She scratched at the door and slipped in when her
mother called.

"Back?" asked Mary.

Yseult eyed her warily. She stood by the fireplace stirring the coals with an iron poker. There was a sheet of
paper in her hand and the grate was adrift in ashes. Ashes
sullied the expensive rug from Oregon City that Mary
stood on. More papers littered the large worktable by the
southern windows.

"Yes, Mama."

"Well, how do you like spending the day with the sewing maids?"

There was a small sneer in Mary's voice. *What is she
sneering about? Me liking the maids? Or did Uncle Guelf
upset her? He's always telling her what to do and it makes
her mad.*

She answered the question with a question. Father
Haggerty got annoyed when she lied to her mother.
"Working with five cow-handed seamstress apprentices?
How do you think I like it?"

*Ooops, that sounded really impertinent, and my voice
sneered too.*

Mary giggled, a sound Yseult had never heard her
make before, and tossed the paper into the fire. "Well,
indulge your taste for the lower orders. I think . . . it's
September . . . October, November, December, January,

February, March . . . Yes, my fool of a daughter can leave
the company of hicks and fools on April Fool's Day. That
works out nicely. You may have your supper and lessons
with Virgilia in the evening and break your fast with me
in the morning, here in the solar."

Yseult gaped and then snapped her mouth shut. *What
will happen on April Fool's Day?* she wondered. *And why
is she giggling? Usually she's mad after Uncle is here!*

She watched Mary pick up another piece of paper and
suddenly wondered. *Where is her rosary? I haven't seen it
dangling from her belt in months. She used to make such
a point about it, about being Catholic* originally *not a
change-Christian . . . but I haven't seen it . . . in forever.*

Mary turned towards her, raising the very fine, fair,
plucked brows. "Did you need anything before you sit
down to lessons?" she asked.

"No, Mama."

Yseult swallowed and shook her head. She edged her
way to the servants' door in the west wall, intent on getting out of her mother's presence.

*I have to think! Why am I just noticing things now?
What do they mean?*

The rosary was gone from her mother's belt and so
was the lovely enameled locket of the Annunciation she
had always worn; a gift from her father. Mary giggled
again and turned back to the fire.

The main door to the room crashed open. "I arrest you,
Mary Liu, Dowager Baroness of Barony Gervais, on the
charge of High Treason. Do not resist your arrest or you
may be put to the Question, or executed out of hand!"

Yseult froze, breathless. Her mind went blank as the
Lady Regent's men tramped into the room in full armor,
swords drawn. It was as if her mind was an eye, and it had
looked into the sun.

Mary reacted instantly. She whirled from the fire, her green silk cote-hardie swirling and flaring into the hot coals as she grabbed the poker like a club and ran. She managed to get two steps from the fireplace, running towards the paper-loaded table, her burning train scattering glowing embers across the carpet. The sergeant behind the captain was faster; two strides brought him within reach of Mary and he swung an armored fist to her stomach with a dull *thud*.

Mary's small body rose until the tips of her satin slippers left the rug, then folded around the point of impact as if bending in. The poker fell with a muffled thud. The servants' door slammed open into Yseult's back, throwing her face down, left cheek skinning across the precious rug and grinding into the hot embers.

"We've got possession of the Castle, Sir Garrick," said the man at arms standing by her head.

Yseult gasped and choked and sneezed on the fine paper ashes. She lay dazed, unable to move; to understand what was happening; to see anything but the man's steel sabatons and the point of the long sword in his hand; to hear anything but the harsh voices and the creak and clatter of armor as they moved around the infinitely familiar room now made strange. She could see her mother's small body heaving.

The sergeant beat out the flames in Mary's silk skirts with his gauntleted hands. She fought madly as soon as she managed to whoop in a breath; struggling and screeching, clawing at the armored man as though her soft nails could rake through an Associate's panoply. Two more men at arms, men Yseult recognized as part of the group who'd teased her earlier, trotted in with a bundle of white cloth.

Mary was yanked upright, her arms forced into sleeves

much too long for her, the tunic buckled in back and then the arms crossed over, wrapped around and the sleeves brought forward to buckle in front. Yseult shuddered, gasping, almost glad she was lying on the ground in case she fainted.

Mama's eyes! she thought. *They're* black. *No, they can't be. The pupils must have gotten so big I can't see the color . . . I think I'm going to be sick.*

A second cloth was wrapped and strapped around her waist and legs. Mary's headdress fell off, her graying blond braid flopping free, coming loose in wild tangles, her body still heaving and twisting in the soldiers' hands. Yseult propped herself up with her right hand, her left cheek throbbing, her left arm a mass of throbbing pain from shoulder to wrist. Three clerks were helping the man called Captain Garrick sort through the papers on the table; he was a tallish brown-haired man with a neat pointed chin-beard and mustache, in full armor except for the gauntlets and helm. Two more were smothering the fire and carefully pulling out the charred scraps.

"How much did she burn?" asked Sir Garrick.

"Hmmm," said one of the clerks. "I make it ten pages by the surviving edges and corners. She didn't do the best job. What are they?"

"Probably drafts of their letters." Sir Garrick frowned down at the bound woman struggling and screaming at his feet.

"Adolphus!" he snapped. "Quiet her down. I can't hear myself think."

A slender unarmed young man wearing a white tabard with a red cross on the shoulder came forward. After frowning for a few minutes he pulled a small brown bottle out of his leather satchel.

"Laudanum," he said briefly. "I hate to use drugs, but

I don't have too many options. I could try to gag her, but the danger of her choking or aspirating is very high. The danger of overdosing her on opium is lower, but still significant. Especially with a case of hysteria like this."

Sir Garrick grumbled under his breath. "She'll do herself an injury anyway if we don't quiet her, and we need her alive." Louder he said: "Drugs. I take the responsibility."

Mary struggled and thrashed like a salmon in a net, but Adolphus was very good; he dribbled the drops in one by one. Yseult blinked, trying to sit. An ungentle hand, gauntleted and armored, pushed her back down.

"Bide where you are, girl," said the rough voice. "Bide quiet, that's best."

She lay watching her mother try to spit out the drops and Adolphus pour small amounts of water in her mouth and rub her throat. Gradually her struggles eased and she lay still, breathing heavily. Sir Garrick turned towards Yseult and smiled thinly. She cowered, feeling much like a rabbit confronted by a coyote. Or a wolf.

"Vulture and her chick, all in one net. Neat. Ah, Goodwife Romarec, attend."

Yseult's teeth chattered; her skin wrinkled as if it were freezing cold, not a warm early evening. Romarec was frog-marched into the room and shot one quick glance at Yseult before bobbing her curtsy to the knight. With her came all the higher staff; one of the men had a bleeding bruise across his cheek and was being assisted by two of the Protector's Guardsmen.

"Sir?" the housekeeper said; there was a slight beading of sweat on her brow, but her voice was quietly respectful.

"Attend, all of you."

He pulled a leather tube from his belt, twisted off the cap that closed it and shook out a roll of heavy paper, the kind used for official documents. It was sealed with a blob of red wax and ribbon; he held it up, then showed it to his own second-in-command.

"Fulk, witness that this is the Lady Regent's personal seal, and unbroken."

"I witness it, Sir Garrick."

The man went on in a loud official voice: "I am Sir Garrick Betancourt, belted knight and second son of the Baron of Bethany, Captain of Lancers in the Protector's Guard under the Grand Constable of the Association, Baroness d'Ath. I will now break the seal and read this warrant."

He flicked off the wax with a thumbnail, undid the ribbon, and opened it.

"*The bearer has done what has been done by my authority, and for the good of the State*. Signed, Sandra Arminger, Lady Regent of the Portland Protective Association, holder of the Crown's rights in ward for the Princess Mathilda Arminger."

Yseult's breath caught again. He could have them all *killed*, right now, with that backing him up. With a warrant like that you could do *anything*.

"Fulk, witness that this is the Lady Regent's signature."

"I witness it, Sir Garrick."

"By this warrant I am empowered to take possession of Gervais and arrest the Liu family as instructed."

He turned to Romarec. "Pack for her ladyship: two sets of underclothes, two dresses, two surcoats, a cloak. They should be old clothes, linen and wool only, shoes and warm boots, socks. Bed linen, a blanket, the silly things a woman needs to primp with and whatever sewing project she has in hand. My squire Kai will accompany you. Make sure you put nothing dangerous in the bundles."

"Scissors, sir?"

"Bring them to me. They will be delivered to Fen House."

Romarec bobbed again, turned and turned back. "Fen House? Where is that?"

"That is none of your concern. Mary Liu is being arrested for treason. She will be kept under wraps there until such a time as the Lady Regent believes she can move forward in this matter."

"Is House Liu proscribed or attaindered?" she asked.

"That is none of your concern either," answered the captain.

Romarec drew herself up. "I have served House Liu for more than twenty years, my lord. I believe it is my concern."

He gave her a nod of grudging respect. "No. For now the demesne is going to be under my guardianship until the Lady Regent has tried the Dowager Baroness. All her children need to be present for that. At the very least you can expect her to be kept under arrest in Fen House until Lord Odard returns."

Tears leaked down Yseult's cheeks at the thought of her brother, stinging in the burns.

He's so far away! He's our lord but he can't protect us now!

Then she remembered Huon, her other brother, waiting for battle in Pendleton. *What has happened to him?* she wondered. *Chaka likes Huon; he should be protected, but the Lady Regent . . . How could Mama put us at such a risk!*

Romarec left and returned after a time with three large duffel bags; the kind soldiers used to cart their kit to battle. Not the fine wooden trunks that opened into a traveling wardrobe her mother used to travel and visit in

Association territories or to visit Court. Romarec picked a pair of tiny scissors—thread nippers—out of the work box and tied the basket up in a large napkin and stuffed it into the third duffel. The scissors she handed to Sir Garrick.

"Good," said the captain. "Now, attend. Do you know Alex Vinton?"

The housekeeper bobbed a curtsy for a: "Yes, my lord Odar's valet and manservant."

"Have you seen him in the last month or so, or even since he left?"

The housekeeper shook her head, but Yseult gasped and burst out, "S-s-s-so tha-tha-that's who tha-that was!"

Sir Garrick turned and swiftly knelt by her. "Who, when?" he asked urgently.

The hand was still pressing her down and her teeth were chattering as she said: "The man, I, I, I—I—"

Sir Garrick frowned and said, "Let her up, soldier. A glass of water, please, Adolphus."

The chirurgeon brought the water as Sir Garrick helped her sit. She was trembling now, huge shudders traveling up and down her body as if powerful hands were shaking her. Her teeth chattered against the glass. Adolphus frowned and tilted her head, pulled at her eyelids and pressed her fingernails.

"Shock," he said. "It's hot in here, but is there a blanket?"

Romarec pulled one out of the cupboard and brought it over.

"Open the windows. I want air in here, as long as we don't shock her further with a sudden temperature drop."

The men silently moved aside and allowed the housekeeper to wrap up Yseult in the blanket. The windows all banged open. Yseult saw relief on the faces of many of the men crowding the stuffy room. The brisk evening air stirred, bringing a medley of scents; cook fires, jasmine from the garden, the stables, and an odd thick iron smell.

She saw Sir Garrick nod to an unspoken question from Romarec. The woman settled behind Yseult and hugged her.

Adolphus put the glass to her mouth. "Sips," he ordered. "Very, very small sips. You are in shock. If you try to gulp, you will choke."

Yseult sipped, and sipped again. Slowly the shudders settled down. But her tears still ran, stinging her left cheek as they slid over the burns. She saw Sir Garrick's face, annoyed, but resigned.

"Let her cry," he said to the medic. "I'll get nothing out of her until that's over."

He knelt with a clank and put his hand under Yseult's chin, the harsh calluses on his fingers like human sandpaper. It felt like her father's hand or Odard's.

"I need the information, soonest, daughter of Gervais! Control yourself like a noblewoman. Quickly!"

Yseult nodded and gulped . . . which started hiccups. Romarec chaffed her hands and rubbed her back. More handkerchiefs appeared at her gesture and Yseult breathed deeply. Her breath kept catching on her hiccups, but they faded away as she kept breathing and sipping from the glass Romarec held.

Twice today, some distant part of her thought wryly. *It's turning out to be a real black letter day.*

Romarec gave her the glass, but her left hand wasn't working and Adolphus had to catch it. "Saints Cosmas and Damien! What happened? How did you injure your wrist?" he asked, probing.

"Doo . . . doo . . . door . . . hit me . . ."

"Where?"

"Back."

Quick competent hands probed up and down her spine and shoulder blades. She twisted away as he touched where the door had hit her. He took her face again and tilted it.

"Burns, rug and embers. Ah! From your mother's gown. You must stop crying, you've washed them with enough salt water to clean them, that's for sure, but it's getting inflamed. I think you'll have a few scars.

He turned to Romarec: "Goodwife, get some soft cloths, soak them in water as cold as you can get it and dab at her face. Get the swelling under control. No arnica or witch hazel; this one's too close to her eye. Just cool water."

Adolphus wrapped her wrist in a tight bandage and pinned it to the front of her riding jacket. She concentrated on sipping, holding the glass in her right hand.

"I . . . I can talk, Sir, Sir Garrick," she said.

"Good girl! Ten minutes to control a hysterical fit, all on your own. You've got steel somewhere, Gervais."

She shook her head, tears still trickling down her cheeks. The left one stung and throbbed.

"I—I went riding over the east bridle path today. I left the castle about five, five thirty. Master Johannsen might know exactly when."

"Were you just getting back when we saw you?" asked Garrick.

She nodded. "I was going to find Jubal, the Captain of the watch, and tell him. But my uncle yelled at me and I went to find Mama and forgot. A—a man, a—a beggar, I thought—tried to grab Iomedea's reins from me about halfway along Parr Road, where it bends south. He looked at me, and I thought he looked familiar, but I couldn't think of anyone . . . I hit him with my quirt and he jumped back behind the tall oak tree. I thought it was because I hit him, but maybe it was because I wasn't who he thought would come?"

"And once I asked about Alex Vinton you remembered who it was?"

Yseult flushed at the skeptical tone in his voice. "It was his eyes . . . That's all that he couldn't disguise. He was hunchbacked, dirty and had dreadlocks . . . Alex was always well dressed and clean and he taught us dance, and he was always very upright and picky about posture."

Yseult leaned back against Romarec, suddenly very tired.

What an awful day! she thought, and then had to control the hysterical giggles that threatened to set off the hiccups again at the utter banality of *that.*

Sir Garrick stood back up and ordered a manhunt along the path.

"Find that landmark and comb—fine-tooth comb—the entire area. We *have* to find him. Alive and able to talk if at all possible, but don't let him escape even if you have to shoot."

She pressed the burning cheekbone into the soft, cool cloth, wiping her face with a sigh.

"I guess that's really bad? He must have come to talk to Mama?"

Garrick looked down at her. "I wonder just how much you know and don't know?" he asked thoughtfully.

Yseult shuddered again and sipped more water. *Breathe,* she ordered herself. *Sip. We are in so much trouble. I'd better not ask anything else.*

The wrapped, now still body of Lady Mary was carried out, along with the three duffel bags; diligently searched by Sir Garrick before being sent on. Yseult kept an unexpected smile off her face as the much detested white on white altar cloth popped out of the third bag. Yseult heard a thump. Sir Garrick leaned out of the window and waved her over. Romarec helped her up and over to the window. Her mother lay in an oxcart, the duffels holding her in place.

"She's off to Fen House, where she'll stay until Lord Gervais returns. You'll go to Todenangst, yourself. The Lady Regent summons you and your younger brother to await her pleasure. She told me to reassure you that Lady Mary will not be killed out of hand. Once Lord Odard is back she must stand trial for high treason and he must defend himself from the charges of accomplice . . . as must you and Huon."

Yseult gulped. The cart moved forward and she gasped, the gulp turning awry and she choked and coughed and wheezed desperately. Lying on the cobbles in a pool of blood was the hapless, headless body of her much disliked Uncle Guelf.

"Oh, poor Layella; lost her babe and now a widow," exclaimed Romarec. She crossed herself and then grabbed Yseult as she swayed.

"Where's his head?" asked Yseult.

Her voice sounded distant, beyond the heavy surf roaring in her ears. *That makes three,* spoke an unruly voice in the back of her mind.

"Taken to be displayed on the traitor's wall at Todenangst."

She decided that must have been Adolphus speaking, for Betancourt spoke right afterwards.

"Sit her down. Romarec, pack for the girl. Include a set of court clothes, but mostly what I told you for her mother. She will need an attendant in Todenangst; not you, who?"

Sparks danced before Yseult's eyes and she concentrated on not throwing up. "Mistress Virgilia, the Lady Governess," she heard. "Or the old nurse, Carmen Barrios. Her own maid is inexperienced."

"Not the nurse. I remember her; she's very old. Virgilia . . . Would that be Virgilia Santos? A collateral of Baron Jacinto Gutierrez?"

"Yes," breathed Yseult.

"She'll do. Where is she?"

Romarec patted Yseult on the shoulder. "I'll bring her with the bags. Will you take Yseult away in a tumbrel as well?"

"No; she'll ride. She has two horses, I believe. I'll send them with her, and one of the undergrooms."

"Goodwife," said Yseult.

Romarec stopped and looked back, "Yes, little one?"

"If the captain allows, pack the books on my nightstand. There are several and they are my special favorites."

Sir Garrick gave a quick nod and Yseult wondered why none of the other men had taken off their helmets or gauntlets. She caught his eye.

"What happens to my Aunt Layella, and her sister, poor Aunt Theresa, who was supposed to marry Uncle Jason? What will they do now? Can they stay at Loiston Manor? All the house of Gervais is gone or under arrest; we can't protect them. Will you protect them? And where are Odo and Terry Reddings? And Sir Chezzy?"

Sir Garrick grimaced. "All good questions. I don't have answers for every one. Sir Harold Czarnecki was wounded on September fifteenth during the retreat from Pendleton."

She gasped and he frowned at her. "Yes, I suppose everybody will soon know. We broke our teeth on Pendleton. Boise and the CUT were there. With force much greater than we had expected. Czarnecki's squire was killed in action. Young Odo Reddings was shipped out with Czarnecki and Terry's body. They're all at McKee Manor, as of this morning. And under guard. I am appointed steward for this land. My job is to determine how deep the rot has penetrated. Was it just your mother and uncle? Or are the rest of the adults in on it? We can't risk them being Guelf's agents or dupes."

Yseult shuddered. Sad Aunt Theresa, who had lost the child her Uncle Jason had left her pregnant with when he was captured and murdered on a mission for Gervais, was unthinkable as an agent of evil; much less gentle Aunt Layella who had lost her babe just six weeks ago. And this man, the Regent's agent, would have to question them hard and long. She shuddered again and blotted quick tears as a sudden thought obtruded . . .

Terry! Dead? How much more *death will I see today?*

The papers were sorted, docketed and bundled up, along with the charred fragments from the grate. Yseult could hear Sir Garrick's men tramping through the castle, scaring the servants as they searched, their voices loud and echoing down the corridors. A few times she heard crashes.

Sir Garrick cursed under his breath and strode to the entranceway.

"This isn't a sack! Have a care, there! Fulk, go see that they stay under control."

Yseult felt a glassy calm descending on her, and a huge weariness. The housekeeper brought three packed duffel bags in for her and her fleece-lined cloak. She huddled Yseult into it as she whispered, "Courage, dear heart. I'll be waiting to hear good news of you."

For once Yseult didn't care about the strictures on her conduct. With a sob she turned and hugged her, one armed.

"Take care, take care!" she whispered. "I will pray for you."

"And I for you, chick."

"Will you give your oath to stay with your escort and not try to escape?" asked Sir Garrick.

Yseult looked up at the knight with swimming eyes. "Yes," she whispered. "Parole. I will cast myself on the mercy of the Lady Regent. I swear by God the Father, God the Son and the Holy Spirit, Amen."

She crossed herself and hesitated as the armored man gestured to the door.

"But, please, can I take my Bernadette and my Immaculate Conception from the chapel? I—I was going to go there to pray this evening"—a short hysterical laugh escaped her—"but matters seem to have overtaken me! I promised."

Sir Garrick sighed and nodded. "I'll take you there. Let me first check your bags." He pulled everything out, shook each piece and repacked the bags. Just as neatly as Goodwife Romarec had done in the first place, she noted. Yseult sighed with relief to see her Bible, her first book on St. Bernadette, *Our Lady's Little Servant*, the Werfel novel, *Song of Bernadette*, and Trochu's serious work on her as well as the collected writings of Bernadette edited by Laurentin.

At least I'll have those, she thought, only briefly regretting the seven novels on her bookshelf.

"Everything is in order here. Let's go to the chapel. I'll have to check everything you wish to bring."

He stood and turned to his men. "Ranulf, Digory, take four men-at-arms. Mount the girl on her own horse; make sure you bring her other one. Get some pack mules for these; pick ones that can keep up. Each of you take a remount as well from our string. Master Johannsen will help you. It's twenty miles, give or take, to Todenangst. I expect you to arrive around midnight. You'll take care of the girl; she'll not be able to mount on her own with her arm injured. See that she's treated with the proper respect due a young Association noblewoman or I'll have someone's ears."

He escorted her down the stairs and to the pretty chapel off the great reception room. It was late and the stained-glass window was dark, only the wavering light of the votives dancing over the nave. Garrick snapped his fingers and Yseult stifled an improper giggle as two oil lanterns appeared like genies. He placed them on the altar. She picked up her rosary from next to the saint's votive; a confirmation gift from her mother—pink quartz beads carved in the shape of roses, with an amethyst cross carved with doves dangling from it.

Suddenly timid, she pushed it into her pocket as she shot a look at the knight, and then knelt on the rose velvet cushion before her special prie-dieu. She looked up into the tapestry she had worked years before when she decided to give her devotion to the Saint and Virgin. The compassionate face of the Immaculata and her saint, kneeling below, steadied her.

"I don't know what to ask for, Lady, Saint. Help me find the strength to walk down this valley of fear, I guess."

She stood, pillow in hand. Garrick had one of the bags opened and stuffed the pillow in. He gestured to the rest of the setup.

"All of this?" he asked, a slightly ironical note in his voice.

She sighed and shook her head. "No, just this porcelain of the Saint and the picture of the Virgin and her Basilica."

She passed them to the knight and he carefully packed

them in the duffels, muffling them in layers of cloth and padding. He finished fastening the bags and stood.

"Does all your family give their devotion to Bernadette and the Immaculata?" he asked, standing.

She looked up, startled, and shook her head, thinking his eyes were a surprisingly light sage green next to his dark skin.

"Just me. Dowager Phillipa gave me the child's book. And I've been on the lookout for older books about her ever since. Years ago, Mama set up my own oratorio here so I could have all my things just so. I learned tapestry stitch making that arras."

The man nodded. "My family has a special devotion to these two, and to the healing arts. Adolphus is my cousin. Well, time to go. Come, young Gervais, your horse awaits."

He took her out to the courtyard. The callused hand took her chin and tilted her face up.

"I can give you no hope, daughter of Gervais. I will pray to God and do you pray to Lady Sandra as well as the Virgin. You are caught deep in this coil. Hope, faith, humility, *might* bring you free, if you are innocent. I will do my best for your people here."

Then she was walking down the steps, glad of the warm wool riding skirt, the heavy jacket and the cloak draped over her. Torches flared in the courtyard but she didn't see her uncle's body, though the stink of sudden death lay heavy.

Yseult looked up as she finished the tale. There was warmth in Mathilda's brown eyes as she pressed a hand on the younger woman's shoulder.

"That was very hard," she said.

Yseult nodded thanks, then burst out: "My mother and uncle, they were so *stupid*!"

The High King snorted. "That they were. It was stupidity and no more ambition than many another has shown before them, at first, before the . . . enemy . . . took advantage of the door they'd opened. But stupidity is often punished more heavily than mere wickedness, the world being what it is. I don't suppose it's any consolation, but many another has made the same mistake. In this war, they usually pay heavily for it."

CHAPTER ELEVEN

The leaders of the Dúnedain sat around the table and stared glumly at the map of Boise city. John Hordle ate another bite of his roast-beef sandwich, but with a gloomy air as if he were going through the motions, his huge body hunched over and his mop of reddish-brown hair tousled from having his sausage-like fingers run through it once too often. Ritva stayed back a little, standing easily and keeping a discreet silence.

The room was fairly big and dusty-disused, set in a far corner of the Drover's Delight. With only one alcohol lantern on the table there was a puddle of light and faces in a surround of gloom. Alleyne was carefully measuring distances on the map with a pair of compass needles; he'd always been a detail man. Eilir was lying back in her chair, her arms crossed on her chest and eyes closed, either thinking very hard about the rounds of fruitless discussion or asleep.

"Sod this for a game o' soldiers," John said, finishing his sandwich and wiping his hands on the red-and-white checked cloth it had been wrapped in. "Woburn promised us she went *out*, 'er and the kiddies. Without that, it's not just 'ard, it's bloody impossible."

"Old information," Charlie Gleam said, rubbing an exasperated hand over his pate. "Last three weeks, Mrs. Thurston doesn't go out except by day, and always without her daughters Shawonda and Janie."

Charming youngsters, Ritva remembered. *And I liked their mother Cecile too.*

"*They* go out without *her*. Always heavy guards, all from the Sixth Battalion, which is not only Martin's pet but a lot of the men have become Cutters just lately."

Eilir opened her eyes and Ritva filled her in. *Is it a leak?* she Signed when the younger Dúnedain was finished. *About us, that is.*

Ritva said the words aloud; she was officially in the inner circle because she was translator between Eilir and the locals, and Ian was here because he was the Drumheller representative. The other eight Rangers were on guard in strategic places. Being inside a walled city made everyone nervous. You could lose yourself in a crowd here, but actually getting *out* would be hard.

"No," Gleam said. "No, I don't think so. I think it's just that they've been getting less ready to put up with Martin. He's *really* antsy about anything they might say that could get spread around. So now they don't talk at all when they go out. The word from my contact in the Presidential Compound is that it's gone beyond quarrels. Now there's just this icy silence, they tell me. Even Martin's given up talking, though he insists on having dinner with them every Friday. Martin's wife Juliet is the only one who still tries and she's been drinking a lot lately. Mrs. Thurston . . . Cecile Thurston, sorry . . . talks to *her* a little, about young Lawrence Jr. Only to be expected since he's her grandson."

"Wait," Astrid said, holding up a finger.

She had been sitting silent with her elbows on the table and her chin on her paired fists, her silver-rimmed eyes looking at the map from under heavy lids.

"Alleyne?" she said after a long moment. "Possibilities? What can we do without getting the targets out of the compound? Is any form of direct assault possible?"

"Even if we infiltrate, there aren't enough of us to try anything resembling a face-to-face fight, even for a few moments. We could go *in* on the airship," he said thoughtfully. "Rappel down from the gondola, and then—"

John Hordle made a sound like a hippo with a stomachache.

"Are you bloody barking mad? Rappel down into the courtyard of a bloody fortress, with the buggering blimp on a level with the towers, which will be shooting bloody flaming bolts at an 'ydrogen-filled bag, then fight our way through a couple of 'undred guards, all sodding sixteen of us, and then fight our way back and climb up the ropes? But before we try this lark we all bend over and kiss our arse good-bye, roit?"

"Sorry, old boy. Just taking a shot into the blue sky. It wouldn't do, would it?"

Astrid nodded. "I'm afraid so, *bar melindo*. If we get Mrs. Thurston and Janie and Shawonda onto the airship, they almost certainly won't shoot at it. But before then . . . very big target. If we do it at all, it has to be a lightning strike. Even so, we would need more swords than we have now. There would probably have to be a sacrificial rearguard, now that I've looked at the ground myself."

Major Hanks was there too, still looking worn from his own swift journey south, though he'd done some of it on the rails.

"I'm afraid Lady Astrid is right. The hydrogen isn't quite as inflammable as you might think; it has to be mixed with air to burn quickly, and when it leaks it leaks *up*. But an incendiary bolt or a spray from a flame-thrower . . . sorry. And it's only really dirigible, steerable, in a dead calm. But about the rearguard, ah, that might be done."

"Let's concentrate on how we're going to get the people we want out of the compound first. And we can't take just Cecile or just her daughters," Eilir said through Ritva. "That wouldn't do at all. Almost better to do nothing."

"Wait," Astrid said again. "Wait . . . what was that you said about Juliet Thurston drinking a good deal?"

Gleam nodded. "That's the rumor. Well, the complete rumor is that she and Martin had some hellacious fights. Then he beat her, and she stopped fighting and started drinking."

"Wait a minute," Ritva blurted. "He *beat* her?"

She obviously wasn't translating and the leaders stared at her.

"*Hiril*, I was here, remember," she said. "I have relevant observations."

Astrid nodded and raised a hand in permission, and her niece went on: "Two years ago, they were very close. The rumor *then* was that Martin was ambitious, and that she was right behind him pushing with all her weight and fitting herself for a consort's crown. I only met her in passing, but she was . . . impressive. Hard, very intelligent, I thought probably quite ruthless too, though maybe not cruel for the sake of it. *Not* the I-deserve-it type."

Gleam nodded. "Yeah, that's how it was then."

Astrid rested her chin on her hands again, something stirring in her moon-shot eyes.

"And when was this change? When she had her child?"

"No, a good long while after that. Just lately, since he got back from Bend in May. That's where he had his conference with Sethaz. He'd done that before, but this time . . . there was something different about him. A lot of people noticed it, and apparently the First Lady did more than most. Which makes sense."

"Let me think."

Astrid closed her eyes; there was silence except for the tapping of a venetian blind against the frame of an open window in the cool night breeze. The street outside was quiet too, and then the tapping of a Natpol's truncheon against the walls rattled through the silence as he walked his rounds.

"It's risky," she said at last. "But it's our best chance. We have to get someone into the compound and get more information about this. It's that or go home, and the fate of the High Kingdom may depend on this."

Everyone turned and looked at Ritva.

Dulu! Ritva thought. *Help!*

Ritva had her hair hidden under a kerchief, and she wore a longish brown wool skirt, brown because it hadn't been dyed. Keep your eyes down, slump a little, don't swing your legs, hesitate a bit before you move your hands. Those minor things added up; they changed the gestalt that people recognized as much or more than they did faces, especially faces they weren't very familiar with. The best protection was to look *bored*, though. Boredom was like a magical force pushing people's attention away.

"Delivery from Ayers for the President's mother at the Brick House," she said to the guards in a singsong monotone.

The soldiers at the entrance to the Presidential Compound were standing to attention; she watched a fly crawl over the face of one of them, and he didn't move even when it reached his eyeball, merely blinked. There was a Natpol doing the actual examination of documents. Ritva smiled nervously through an impulse to sweat. *These* documents weren't even improvised fakery; they were just someone else's, quickly stolen by a Dúnedain team who'd snatched the bearer and had her tied up in a warehouse. The black-and-white picture was of a tallish blond woman of about her age, and there was about the degree of general resemblance Ritva bore to half the young women in Boise. But she wouldn't have been fooled herself if she made an effort to compare picture to features, not even briefly. Luckily not even Boise's obsessive devotion to order and regulation extended to using *color* pictures. And it was natural to be nervous around a document check outside the dwelling of a ruler.

Act like a peasant who's bringing something to Regent Sandra at Castle Todenangst, Ritva thought. *You've watched the poor devils sweat there, often enough.*

"Pass," the Natpol said in a tone as bored as the expression on Ritva's face. "Next!"

The Presidential Compound bore the marks of haste in its construction. This had been the citadel from which Lawrence Thurston extended his realm, in the chaos of the first Change Years; there had been chaos and fighting in Boise, and then typhoid and cholera and the Black Death, until he came and gave men a name and a flag to rally around.

The walls were high and thick, but they'd been roughcast and smoothed only enough to give no easy handholds. They followed the lines of a block across from the State capitol, with what had been the Williams Office

Building as their core; it was the Citadel now, bulking high with cranes and machicolations above. Other buildings had been incorporated into the outer wall, sometimes simply used as forms into which concrete was poured. It gave the fortifications a weird angular look, jagged and irregular. Most of the interior was a concrete-floored parade ground, where soldiers and bureaucrats and their various hybrid offspring clattered back and forth to the offices around the periphery amid the odd horse or mule-drawn cart.

It is a castle, just a strange-looking one, Ritva told herself. *It does all the things a castle does.*

The General-President was *not* at home right now. They'd checked that carefully.

I am brave. I am very brave, in fact. But I am not stupid and I don't want to die, she thought.

She walked to the Brick House; it was an ordinary two-story dwelling of red brick with a shingle roof, substantial but not really large, disassembled in some wrecked suburb and rebuilt here. The *current* General-President had a much more extensive suite in the Citadel, and another in a fortress south of town. A pair of soldiers stood at the steps that led up to the verandah, big concave oval shield on shoulder and six-foot javelins braced to the side, armor and the brass eagles and thunderbolts on the shields polished blazing-bright. Their eyes followed her, but neither moved until she reached the steps.

Then they both turned in, and the spears moved out to make an X in front of her.

"Name and business," one of them said crisply.

"Wanda Meeker," Ritva said. *I've got more names than the Lady these days!* "Delivery from Ayers Produce."

They looked her over, checked the basket with its two dozen eggs in straw and bricks of butter wrapped in coarse paper on a lump of ice in a clay cup, and one of them said: "Pass."

Then they turned back, with a crisp stamp of hobnails and a toss that sent their spears turning and then slapping back into the callused hands. It was discipline for discipline's sake, but oddly impressive. Ritva remembered how she'd walked up these steps the last time—in Dúnedain formal blacks with the crowned silver Tree and Seven Stars on her jerkin, Mary and the other questers at her side. *Then* she'd been Lawrence Thurston's honored guest after Rudi and Edain saved his life, about to set out on a path that led to the battle at Wendell and the ruler's own death.

Now . . . she pulled the bell-handle. The string attached to it yielded with a feeling of weight on the end that ran through a copper tube into the house. Bells tinkled, and she heard slow footsteps and a shadow behind the beveled glass panels of the door before it opened.

"Did I order this?" Cecile Thurston said. "I suppose I did. Come in, come in."

Ritva blinked, shocked. She remembered Lawrence Thurston's wife as a quiet woman who'd radiated both strength and warmth and showed a flash of cutting wit now and then; she'd been educated in some profession that the Ranger didn't remember, before the Change. Now there was little of the light brown left in her hair as she stood in the door of the Brick House, and the gray that had spread to most of it seemed dull. So did her own blue eyes.

Lawrence Thurston helped build this house with his own hands—she told me that, and he shrugged and laughed and they looked at each other. Hard enough to lose your man like that, but to have him killed by one of your sons would make it altogether worse. It's probably a good thing she has daughters to worry about.

And there was little energy in the way she walked. In the kitchen her two daughters were sitting at the table busy at what looked like schoolwork; one of them jumped up to take the basket and transfer its contents to a big icebox, made from a cut-down refrigerator in the usual way. They didn't look much different from what she remembered, skins of dark-olive shade and tightly curled hair, the elder round-faced and the younger thinner. Their faces were drawn with worry, though, and there was a wariness to their eyes that hadn't been there before. The kitchen smelled pleasantly of soap and wax and the roses and dahlias which stood in vases on the window-ledges, and faintly of cooking.

And there was a pregnant blond woman sitting at the table too, with a two-year-old boy squatting on the tile floor by her side and a cup of chicory non-coffee before her. She was extremely pretty, but slightly puffy around the eyes, which were a little bloodshot too.

Juliet Thurston! Ritva thought, keeping her face bovine-calm and uninterested. *Rhaich, Rhaich! Siniath faeg!*

She mentally added a phrase which translated literally into the Common Tongue as: *An individual excessively attached to their mother in a carnal manner who is also the offspring of a female Warg.*

The tired eyes scanned across her listlessly, then came back. The wife of the ruler of Boise yawned and said: "Lawrence, go play in the living room."

"No!" the boy said.

Lawrence Jr. was a handsome-looking lad, and he grinned with a gap in his white teeth as he used a two-year-old's favorite word; both his parents were well made, with the long-limbed build he showed promise of. His eyes were a brightly alert dark blue, and his hair curly and brown with light streaks from the summer sun. He was clad in a miniature version of Boise's army uniform, complete with small boots.

"Lawrence, do I have to tell you twice? The third time comes with a spank."

"'Kay, Mom," he said.

His air was cheerful, just a child whose attention had been gotten, and he picked up the painted wooden cavalrymen he had been marshaling and gallumphed out of the kitchen making horse-noises. The living room was visible from here, but far enough away that a soft-voiced conversation couldn't be heard.

Ritva wasn't openly armed; the little knife on her belt was the universal tool nearly everyone carried. The blade was only four inches long, but it was honed shaving-sharp, and it was good steel. A step, a blow, a slash . . .

No, she thought. *I can't kill cut a mother's throat in front of her toddler, and her with child. Better to use it on myself.*

That was illogical, she knew. In war she'd be perfectly ready to pull the lanyard on a trebuchet and send a five-hundred-pound boulder over a city wall to strike whom it would, and this *was* war. Some things went deeper than logic, though, or beyond it. Everyone was looking at her; the listless, slightly slumped body language was gone and her body was quivering with alertness, her weight up slightly on the balls of her feet and everything flowing smoothly.

Juliet's face had firmed too. "Mary Havel, isn't it? Or the other one?"

Three slight gasps, and then she saw recognition dawn on the others, too. Very carefully she spread her hands and kept her own voice level and light.

"*Mae govannen,* my ladies," she said. "I am here to see if you need our help. I am Ritva Havel, yes."

The fog seemed to clear from Cecile Thurston's eyes as she peered and then slowly recognized the Dúnedain too; it had been only the one meeting, several eventful years ago, after all. Her daughters sat bolt-upright, and the eldest said: *"Elvellon!"* she said: *The elf-friend!*

Ritva held up a soothing hand at the clumsy Sindarin that followed. She remembered that Shawonda had been entranced by the Histories even when they first met; she guessed shrewdly that she'd fled into them since as a refuge from her troubles, and as a source of strength and hope in a world whose foundations had crumbled beneath her in a welter of treachery and blood. The Rangers got a fair number of recruits from exactly that pattern of thought and feeling.

"In the Common Tongue, *nethig*," she said; that meant *little sister*, and brought a tremulous smile.

Juliet's reaction surprised Ritva most of all; she buried her face in her hands for a moment and started to cry. Not what she would have expected given their previous acquaintance, at all. Doubly so before a stranger.

"I take it," she said carefully, "that you want to leave too, ah, Mrs. Thurston? Leave your husband?"

"Oh, God, yes, please, he's not Martin anymore! Since he came back from Bend . . . he, he, he *hit* me. And then he said if I argued with him again he'd cut out my *tongue*, that I didn't need that to *breed*."

Cecile Thurston gave a grimace of distaste, and the two girls stared at their sister-in-law with shock and dawning horror; evidently she hadn't said that in front of them before.

"I can't . . . I can't bear the thought of him *touching* me again!"

Well, that settles that, Ritva thought. *This can't be a put-on to set me up. Cunning elaborate plans like that only happen on the spur of the moment in stories. She'd just yell for the guards, and I can't get out of here. And I've hardly ever seen anyone so frightened . . .*

She remembered fighting the Seeker who'd cut out Mary's eye; his own gaze, like a spiral downward into a depth that wasn't even black, was *nothing*, un-being where even meaning was no more. Then she tried to imagine waking up and seeing that on the pillow next to her, and felt a rash of sweat break out under her arms and around her neck, along with a twist in the stomach.

"Euuuu," she murmured to herself.

Juliet scrubbed at her face, and called mastery back to herself with a series of deep breaths. "How . . . what can you do?" she went on steadily.

Ritva shook her head. "This change in your husband, it happened after he came back from meeting the Prophet, Sethaz, in Bend?"

"Yes. Before then, he was . . . he was *Martin*. Now it's as if there's two people in his head, or another one that can put Martin on like a *mask*."

Like one of those grubs that eats out an insect from the inside, Ritva thought. *Only with the soul as the host. I won't say that, though.*

Cecile was glaring at her daughter-in-law; Ritva could fill in that too. As long as it had merely been a matter of parricide and usurpation, Juliet had been all for it. Only once the whole web of betrayal had turned on her had it become *bad*. The older woman took a deep breath and obviously pushed the matter aside for later. She did say: "It wasn't Fred, was it."

The inflection didn't have a question in it. Ritva replied gently but firmly: "No. It wasn't."

Then: "Do you have a map of the city?" she said. And to Juliet: "When is your . . . when is Martin due back?"

"The day after tomorrow," she said. "There's a report of some sort of force moving through Nevada . . . but there are always Rovers and bandits down there."

And we went through that way for a while, Ritva thought; it was the path that avoided Boise's all-too-active patrols.

"Can you get out of the Compound?" Ritva asked. "Taking all here with you?"

Juliet cast a quick glance at the others. Ritva caught it and went on: "The mission is to rescue Lady Cecile and Janie and Shawonda . . . Fred's kin. To them we have a debt of honor. You were no part of our plan and it's an added risk."

The bloodshot eyes were shrewd. "And you need them to undermine Martin's position."

"Yes. Will you, too, denounce him?"

Juliet took a deep breath. "Yes. Yes. I can't stay, I *can't*."

"Then we have little time. Ah, thank you, Shawonda."

The girl spread a map of the city out on the kitchen table; it was a modern one, showing the walls. "Now, *can* you get all these outside the Compound walls?"

Juliet nodded, her fists clenching. "I . . . I think so. Yes. As long as Martin isn't here. For a little while at least. But there will be guards, at least two platoons of the Sixth."

"*That* I think we can take care of. Show me where it's credible you'd go . . ."

When they had finished Ritva nodded briskly. "Here, then." She tapped a building. "This shopping expedition is credible?"

"The commander will be pleased. He'll think it means I've persuaded Cecile and the girls to be, uh, cooperative."

Juliet frowned. "But how does just getting us out of the Compound help? There's the city wall, and the Compound's in continuous touch with the defenses there by semaphore and heliograph!"

Ritva smiled thinly. "Trust me," she said. "I've gotten all the way from Montival to the Sunrise Lands and back."

Though that didn't involve something like this, she thought behind her confident expression. *Dulu! I hope Aunt Astrid likes this idea!*

CHAPTER TWELVE

COUNTY OF THE EASTERMARK
CHARTERED CITY OF WALLA WALLA
PORTLAND PROTECTIVE ASSOCIATION
(FORMERLY EASTERN WASHINGTON)
HIGH KINGDOM OF MONTIVAL
(FORMERLY WESTERN NORTH AMERICA)
AUGUST 23, CHANGE YEAR 25/2023 AD

"That's that," Grand Constable Tiphaine d'Ath said, tasting sweat on her lips.

It must still be well over ninety degrees, though the temperature was falling a bit with the sun. She slapped her leather riding gauntlets into the palm of her left hand in a slight puff of dust. The omnipresent grit was one of the things she disliked about the eastern fiefs; her own estates were in the northern Willamette valley, which had a decently moderate climate where things stayed green year-round. Then she stifled a yawn, brought on by the sultry stillness as much as real fatigue. The sun was low in the west, turning the thin clouds there crimson, and the sky was darkening towards night eastward behind the distant line of the Blue Mountains. At least it would drop to decent sleeping weather later. The air here was too dry to hold the heat long.

The end of a long summer day, and she'd been the first to get off the train an hour before dawn after a short

THE TEARS OF THE SUN   339

period of semisleep on the pitching, clanking vehicle. Since then she'd been supervising while the army she'd brought pitched camp outside Walla Walla's northern gate and unloaded supplies for the campaign.

Ah, the glory of knightly combat.

"Right, that's the last of them, my lady," the commander of the Protector's Guard said, mentally checking off a list. "The signals chain says the line's clear as far west as the Wallula Gap. We're holding the rest of the empty rolling stock just east of the city ready to come back through."

"Get that started now, Sir Tancred. I want them out of the way and the line and stock ready for military use."

A final load of boxes came off a railcar and onto a wagon, and a clerk stepped forward and ran a paintbrush over a stencil on their sides while another made a tick on a ledger. The team of sixteen big mules had been led away and replaced by fresh beasts, hitched to what had been the rear of the train and hitched up to pull it back westbound; they leaned into their traces to get the six empty flatbed cars away from the platform. It halted again where the refugees waited to embark.

A crowd of a hundred or so civilians surged forward under the direction of a file of infantry; mostly peasants by their shapeless undyed linsey-woolsey clothing and floppy homemade straw hats, and more than half women with youngsters.

"No, no!" the sergeant in charge screamed. "All you strong ones, hand up your bundles and brats! Then you push to get it started, and *then* you climb on. You, you, you—"

The butt of his spear flicked out and tapped to conscript volunteers.

"—just grab the handles . . . oh, St. Dismas have

mercy, the fucking *handles*, the . . . these things, these things! Just wait until I tell you, then push, then get on!"

They handed up bundles and baskets and swaddled infants, then settled with dumb patience, half a dozen ready to push each car. They were silent save for the wailing babes and toddlers, their eyes wide and bewildered as they stared around at city and army. Most of them were Changelings, and probably hadn't been more than a day's walk from their villages since they were born. Or at least had been toddlers themselves when their parents were resettled.

Tiphaine nodded to Sir Tancred. "Warn Sir Varocher at Castle Dorian that five or six thousand civilians are heading their way, mostly sick or children and their mothers. He has authority to draw on the other castles and the stores in Wallula Town as necessary. They'll need to be fed and checked over by the physicians before they're loaded on the barges."

She paused for a moment and then added in the same flat tone, "Emphasize that I and the Lady Regent will be *extremely displeased* if they're not treated in a humane and chivalrous manner, peasants or no."

He scribbled a note on a clipboard and shouted for a messenger. The warning would be taken seriously; when the Lady Regent Sandra was *extremely displeased* the headsman's ax or the two-handed sword reserved for noble Associates tended to become involved. Or people just mysteriously dropped dead with no apparent cause or had perfectly plausible accidents and wise living people carefully didn't comment. A page dashed up, bowed, took the note and ran for a tall metal framework not far away, scampering up the rungs of the ladder built into it as agile as a monkey. Moments later the heliograph atop it began to blink.

"What's the condition of the railroad draught teams?" she asked.

"Not bad, my lady. We've replaced the worst tired ones from the town and the Count's herds, one-for-one, on your authority. There's plenty of alfalfa and sweet clover hay by the watering points and we've been baiting them on that and milled barley and oats and bean-mash as they came in. The first in are already rested and well fed and ready for another run. The Count's men have been very cooperative and pretty well organized. Not to mention his veterinary officers."

"They'd better be, Sir Tancred," Tiphaine said. "We don't have time for pissing matches or screwups. Not if we're going to make the enemy react to us, rather than the other way 'round."

Walla Walla hadn't been a large city before the Change as they reckoned things then; a bit under thirty thousand, and reasonably compact, with less sprawl at the edges than most urban settlements of the time. It had also contained the fortresslike State Penitentiary, with over two thousand hardened cons, who'd broken out on Change Day Five and taken the city over. When the Lord Protector's troops arrived later that year, there had been a mass uprising of what was left of the population in their favor.

"All aboard!" the train driver said. "Loose brakes—"

The brakemen spun their wheels, and the stronger passengers-to-be the sergeant had selected set their hands to the grips and pushed to get the cars rolling; the mules knew the drill, and started to lean into their collars even before the long whip snapped over their backs. The crowded cars began to move along the rusted steel, to a chorus of shrieks and wailing children. Inching at first, slowing again for an instant as the pushers clambered aboard, and then rumbling up to a fast walk; an animal could pull a *lot* more on rail than on even the best road.

Tiphaine nodded in satisfaction. One of the first things

she'd learned back fifteen years ago when she moved
from small-unit black ops into the conventional military
was just how hard it was to keep a major troop movement
from seizing up into a series of ungovernable traffic jams.

*Conrad and his staff taught me that; and how hard it
was to get everything in the right place at the right time so
people don't get hopelessly lost, starve, get sick, or run out of
crossbow bolts or horseshoes at a crucial moment. Sandra
always was good at finding her people mentors.*

Conrad Renfrew had also been in charge of that first
expedition of conquest up the Columbia to Walla Walla;
from what Tiphaine had read in the records, he'd killed a
couple of hundred of the convicts, recruited about
seventy-five for service elsewhere, and put the rest to
forced labor for the rest of their short miserable lives,
mostly getting in the harvest round about and then making a beginning on the fortifications and helping make
things habitable for the refugees from Spokane and the
western cities and the Columbia plateau selected for re-
settlement on the new manors. Then he'd installed the
present Count's father, who'd been his second-in-
command and to whom Norman Arminger owed multi-
ple favors, and departed for the next urgent job. Of which
there had been an infinite number then.

A nice workmanlike job, Tiphaine thought judiciously.
Solid, like Conrad.

She'd been fourteen then, training with Katrina in
Lady Sandra's household, initially for clandestine work.
Young females made extremely efficient assassins, if they
had the right attitudes, training and native talent. They
just didn't attract the eye of wary suspicion the way your
average hulking macho brute did, particularly if the target
was a hulking macho brute, which most had been. Pro-
found surprise had been the last expression on a lot of

faces she and Katrina had dispatched to their putative rewards via stiletto, crossbow, piano-wire garrote, poison-filled hypodermic and various other unpleasantnesses.

It was very like Sandra to see the possibilities instantly when two vicious, intelligent, hungry, traumatized and extremely athletic barely teenaged girls managed to infiltrate her heavily guarded private quarters and demand a job on Change Day Forty. Norman Arminger had just laughed himself sick and told her to go ahead with the Sailor Moon Squad if she thought it was worthwhile. They'd both agreed that the rough and ragged material they were trying to forge into an elite needed a lot of culling, particularly the non-Society elements.

People don't realize how much of what Norman did was possible because he had people like Conrad carrying water for him and Sandra to handle the Deep Thought. What's that old saying, you can accomplish almost anything if you're willing to let someone else get the credit? And now it's my job to see that this place doesn't fall and plays its part in the campaign, and I don't care a damn if the chroniclers all go on about Rudi and Mathilda and don't give me more than a footnote.

Walla Walla's defenses stood in a stout irregular rectangle now, ferroconcrete and rubble walls forty feet high faced with hard granite; round towers reared half that again at intervals, with conical roofs of witch-hat shape on top sheathed in lead or copper, the whole surrounded by a deep moat. The wartime hoardings were up over the crenellations of the wall, sloping metal-faced timber roofs that protected the fighting platform from arrow fire and let defenders shoot and drop things straight down from under cover.

The old penitentiary had been the foundation for the big castle that made the northwestern corner of the new walled city; she could see its massive machicolated towers silhouetted against the blazing colors of the western sky. A blimp-shaped observation balloon at three thousand feet up stood black against the dark blue vault of heaven, the long curve of its tethering cable hardly visible at all.

As she watched a signal light began to snap from its basket, aimed east in a rapid flicker of coded Morse, probably sending to one of the castles in the foothills of the mountains there.

There were still around fifteen thousand people here in peacetime, half what Portland had and nearly as much as Corvallis. The rich farmlands, pastures, orchards and vineyards of the Walla Walla valley and the timber of the Blue Mountains to the east brought it wealth, as did trade in peacetime; in war it was an outpost against the city-state of Pendleton to the south and the United States of Boise to the north and east. Or against both and the Prophet's hordes from Montana now.

Banners flew from the peaks of tower and gatehouse. Besides the scarlet-yellow-black Lidless Eye of the PPA, there were the arms of the Aguirre family who were Counts Palatine of the Eastermark and Barons of Walla Walla—*Or, a tree vert with a wolf passant sable, on a tree brun*—and now the crowned mountain and sword of the High Kingdom of Montival flying above them all. Sandra had seen to that throughout the Association territories and encouraged it elsewhere, even before the putative High King got back.

Well, I helped train Rudi . . . Artos . . . all those years since I first kidnapped him. He's certainly very capable; a little sentimental, but hard enough when he has to be, and extremely smart. Deadly dangerous with any weapon, too. I wouldn't have believed a man over six feet could move that fast, if I hadn't seen it myself. The only man I've ever met as fast as I am.

Her thoughts shied away from the Sword of the Lady. Not that she didn't believe in it; it was so real that your belief became utterly irrelevant. *Too* real. You got the feeling that it could tear through the fabric of things at any moment, like a heavy weight through damp paper. Meaning itself crumbled around it.

She went on aloud: "All right, get them moving in relays, Sir Tancred," she said, as an empty train rumbled in from the east. "It's important that their kinfolk inside the walls know they're safe. See all those watchers on the parapet? Seeing vulnerable dependents heading out will help morale a great deal. They can fight to defend their families while the families are out of immediate danger."

Tancred nodded, looking thoughtful for a second; he was an extremely capable young man or he wouldn't be commanding the Protector's Guard regiment, but he needed to gain a broader perspective if he was going to rise further. Another thing Sandra and Conrad had drummed into her hard long ago was that a big part of commanding was finding which of your subordinates could learn and then keeping them at it.

A second throng of civilians waiting a hundred yards farther down rose to their feet. This clump was more feisty, or just more frightened, and tried to stumble forward in a rush. The infantry sweating in their harness cursed wearily as they locked their big kite-shaped shields together into a wall to keep the frightened peasants from cluttering the track too soon. The train screeched to a halt as the brakemen wrestled with the horizontal wheels between each car.

She heard the sergeant shouting again: "Get back there, you dimwit churls, wait your turn—*wait your Saints-forsaken turn*—push them back, men, *push* them, *Turchil, you weeping pustle on Satan's dick, put your shoulder into that shield and* push, *man!*"

"They'll be loading the noncombatants and refugees and sending them west all night, then, Grand Constable," Tancred went on. "If we push, we should be able to get it done by the time the army's ready to march, which will leave the line clear and the rolling stock and teams on hand at our supply base on the navigable Columbia. There's an intact line all the way northeast to Dayton we could use as we advance."

"Very good, Sir Tancred," Tiphaine d'Ath replied. "We should get out of the way, then. You're camp commandant until I get back from consulting with the Count. I'll probably be staying the night at the City Palace; it would raise questions if I didn't."

She'd have to wait for the local overlord to come out; it would be within her rights but a political *faux pas* to enter the city before an invitation and ideally himself to welcome her in person, and she'd sent word she'd be busy all day. On the other hand, it would also be impolite not to be here near the gate waiting to be greeted at the hour she'd specified. Tiphaine d'Ath tried very hard never to be *unintentionally* offensive.

"Don't take any nonsense," she went on. "You speak with my authority, and the Lady Regent's, and that of the High King. And send me Lord Forest Grove soon as he's ready. Tell him the Count should be here fairly soon, and I'll need him then to report on the situation up near the front."

Lord Rigobert Gironda de Stafford, Baron Forest Grove, was in charge of the allied . . .

Montivalan. We're all part of Montival now, not just allies. Completely and utterly forget how we spent the first ten Change Years fighting each other, Tiph, and the next ten watching each other with gimlet-eyed suspicion and thinking about fighting each other again someday. Down the memory hole, as Sandra puts it. You've got seven regiments of Yakima foot from the Free Cities in this army and glad to have them, the stubborn bastards fought us to a standstill, after all. Montivalans.

. . . Montivalan screening force to the northeast.

His men were buying time for this army to form up. Buying it with blood, and now he had to come back for a *conference*.

There was no avoiding it, but Tiphaine d'Ath looked in that direction, towards the distant line of mountains, and suppressed a fierce desire to be *there*.

And to know what the hell's been going on up there. Reports just aren't the same.

COUNTY OF THE EASTERMARK
BARONY OF TUCANNON
(FORMERLY SOUTHEASTERN WASHINGTON STATE)
PORTLAND PROTECTIVE ASSOCIATION
HIGH KINGDOM OF MONTIVAL
(FORMERLY WESTERN NORTH AMERICA)
AUGUST 18, CHANGE YEAR 25/2023 AD

Make a mistake, you sons of bitches. You're out there. I can feel it, I can smell it. Come on, screw up.

Ingolf Vogeler carefully leveled the binoculars from where he lay just below the crest of the ridge, using a hand to shade the lenses so they would give no betraying flash in the noonday sunlight. This whole country on the fringe of the Blue Mountains was smooth ridge and slope-making valleys, sometimes with a bit of a creek running down the vale between, sometimes dry, getting steeper as you went east.

Send me a nice cocksure kid, Lord, he thought. *Or Manwë or Varda or whatever. Nineteen, a hard-on with legs, he's invincible, he's immortal, he knows it all. Give me something to work with.*

There was a thin stand of tall straight ponderosa pine along the top here, smelling like butterscotch and vanilla as sap oozed out of cracks in their orange bark; the trees got thicker behind him too, up into the heights. Downslope were scattered thickets of shrubby mountain mahogany, and then grass rolling away in billowing folds that rose up the slope on the other side. Very faint marks in it along the contour indicated that it had been culti-vated before the Change, but now it was in bunchgrass again, bleached almost white by summer but still good fodder. A herd of several hundred sheep and a few alpacas grazed it, and drank from the little summer-sunken trickle through the cottonwoods at the base.

"Good woolies," he murmured very softly to himself. "Just eat the grass, drink the water, crap wherever the hell you please, look appealing and vulnerable. *Good* woolies."

Though in fact they were still looking spindly with the late-spring shearing; you forgot how leggy sheep actually were if you only saw them with twelve pounds of fleece wrapped around them. A couple of mounted girls in leather pants and thin shirts and broad-brimmed Stetson hats watched over them, directing their dogs and keeping an arrow on the string for predators. That probably made both the humans and the sheep down there a lot more comfort-able than his light mail shirt and the padded gambeson underneath it left him. He was used to sweating, though, and it was more bearable in this dry Western climate than in the humid Midwest summers he'd grown up with.

Minutes crawled by, the smell of sap grew stronger, and small pale grasshoppers went by his nose in ticking leaps. Ants trooped through the pine needles and sparse grass bearing a beetle aloft in bloodthirsty triumph, and somewhere a ground squirrel whistled, sounding a little like a woodchuck but with more of a chitter to it. Occasionally a little of the light powdery loess soil would blow into his face with a gust of the wind that soughed through the branches of the tall straight pines, and the dirt stuck to the sweat.

A golden eagle soared down the little valley, and several collies ran around barking hysterically in protective reflex as its broad-winged shadow fell on the flock. It sheered off at an upraised bow, evidently thinking the lambs not worth the risk of an arrow; in his considerable experience most predators knew the range of human weapons to a foot. A big golden eagle could carry off a lamb. Some folk trained and used them for hunting deer and wolves, which Ingolf considered more trouble than it was worth. Pronghorn antelope trooped by out in the rolling country northwestward, raising a thin cloud of dust as they moved from north to south and occasionally breaking into a leaping frenzy for no perceptible reason except that they liked to jump and run.

His eyes kept up their steady, methodical scan. His attention was carefully general, waiting for the break in the pattern that would leap out because it didn't belong. Then something tickled at the edge of his sight. He turned the glasses that way, and it became a tiny horseman with two remounts on a leading rein coming up out of a swale. That might be a scout, prepared to ride fast and far to escape pursuit if he was spotted. There was a quick blink of light as the distant man stood in the stirrups and raised something to his face. Ingolf put down his own binoculars and saw the same flicker of light again, and then once more. Without the glasses nothing was visible except the flash, but that could be seen for miles. And binoculars meant . . .

"Gotcha, you stupid careless fuck," Ingolf murmured, with a surge of savage satisfaction mixed with professional disapproval. "Now go back and tell your dumb careless friends that a mutton dinner's just waiting for them. Grilled lamb chops too, you betcha, real tempting after a while on hardtack and beans."

The problem with sending out scouts was that the scouts could be seen themselves . . . and when you ran into a scout screen, seeing them told you a lot right there.

Plus he'd never yet met cavalry who could resist stealing livestock, *or* burning stuff down, and a good many of his thirty-one years had been spent as a horse-soldier himself, after he'd left home in a hurry, that or as a salvager working the dead cities. All the way across the continent, from his home along the Kickapoo river in what had once been Wisconsin (and was now part of the Free Republic of Richland) to the Pacific, with a side trip through the Wild Lands of the east to Nantucket, and he'd done it more than once. He doubted anyone since the Change had bounced around as much as he had.

And a lot of them are calling me Ingolf the Wanderer now. I'd be flattered, except that I'm damned sick of wandering. And I'm a married man now. I want to settle down, put my legs under my own table and my head under my own roof on my own land every day. OK, Ingolf, let's win this war so we can.

Ten minutes, and the man disappeared, even his dust-trail invisible through the binoculars. Ingolf waited another ten, then cased the precious instrument and wormed his way backward on hands and knees to where he'd left his round shield, quiver of arrows and four-foot recurve horseman's bow. He shrugged the archer's baldric over his shoulder; the strung bow was pushed through loops on the outside of the quiver. Then he crawled a bit more. Not until he was a good ten yards back did he rise to one knee, turn and wave his hand in a signal.

A horse and rider lay at the base of the slope. The man slapped his mount's neck; the horse rose, and the man was in the saddle as it did, and trotting west a heartbeat after. His own men were out there, and the Sioux contingent under Rick Three Bears, and Ingolf's wife Mary, and *her* followers—Dúnedain Rangers. Of which he supposed he was one too.

Sorta. Kinda.

"Go let 'em know, Mark," Ingolf muttered. "I've got to see the local panjandrum."

He walked down the slope, a big broad-shouldered man with a bear's strength in his long limbs and thick shoulders. But he moved lightly, with a sort of lazy precision; his shaggy ear-length hair was sun-faded brown, his eyes dark blue in a weathered face that had been better looking before a broken nose and a fair assortment of scars, some showing as white hairs in his close-cropped beard. There was a sword by his side, the heavy horseman's chopping blade known as a shete, and a bowie on the other hip, with the handle of a tomahawk tucked through a loop at the back.

None of the weapons clattered as he scooped up his helmet—a locally made sallet with a neck-flare—and trotted across the open grassland with the scabbard of the shete in his left hand. The black cottonwoods here were thicker than in the next valley over with the sheep, up to forty or fifty feet tall, with a dense understory along their edge. He slowed down as he approached them and waved his sword-hand to show it was empty.

Because there are a bunch of local yokels with crossbows there; I'm not coming back to the same spot I slipped out of.

*I don't think some of them really grasp the distinction be-
tween* stranger *and* enemy *all that well. Christ . . .
Manwë . . . but a lot of the peasants on these Association
manors are more like turnips than people. And I thought we
Readstowners were hicks!*

"Come ahead!" someone said from ahead of him.
"Slowly!"

He came ahead . . . slowly. Sure enough, two crossbows
were pointed at him, and a bunch of spears with unpleasant foot-long heads sharpened until the naked metal
gleamed. The men behind them were bearded if they were
old enough for it, with fairly close-cropped hair; short hair
was a lower-class marker here, like their shapeless linsey-
woolsey shirt-tunics and wool pants and moccasinlike
shoes tied at the ankle with thongs. Ingolf spread his arms.

"Ingolf Vogeler. Your ally. Remember?" he said.

The powerful smell they gave off was just summer and
not much opportunity to wash in the last little while.
They didn't have the crusted, scabrous appearance or the
hard stink people did in areas where the habit of washing
at all had died out. And the weapons were pointed up
once they recognized him as one of the newfound allies
helping them fight Boise and the Prophet. A couple of
them even smiled.

Better than I expected.

"Take me to your leader," he said.

"The lord baron has arrived with his *menie*, my lord,"
one of them said.

His full-time soldiers, Ingolf mentally translated. *What
we'd call his deputies back home, or National Guardsmen.*

"Girars, you show him," the oldest of the men said; he
might have been anything from a work-gnarled thirty to
fifty.

The militiaman delegated for the job was pathetically

young, not more than seventeen and a bit scrawny with a growth spurt, with only a little yellow peach-fuzz on his acne-scarred cheeks. The steel-strapped leather breast-plate and simple bullet-shaped conical helmet he wore both seemed too big for him; he left the four-foot kite-shaped shield propped against a stump, which was a bad sign. Ingolf's own went on his back on a leather strap, where he could swing it forward with a quick duck of his left shoulder and pull.

Yeah, those big shields weigh fifteen pounds, the way they make them here. But if you suddenly need a shield, you need it bad. *I'd roast his ass for leaving it just 'cause it's heavy and awkward if he were in my outfit. Better years of a sore arm than one minute of an arrow in the gut. I'm tempted to do it anyway, but I don't know the baron well enough to interfere in his chain of command.*

The militiaman led Ingolf forward and down the bank of the dry river to the sandy bottom, an arroyo they called it hereabouts. The branches of the cottonwoods mingled overhead, turning the creek bed into a tunnel of green that sparkled with moving golden flickers.

It was cooler here, too, and easy walking. No water showed, but the sandy bottom was damp in spots, and insects buzzed and clicked. This was a fair-sized river in the winter rains, to judge from the height of the banks; it might flow at night even in August, when the cotton-woods weren't sucking water and pumping it into the air. It was a convenient place to be safely out of sight in day-time right now, but it would be dangerous a little later in the year; he'd spent enough time in arid areas to under-stand what a flash flood meant.

"My lord . . . is there going to be a fight?" the boy asked after they were out of sight and hearing of his friends and neighbors.

Ingolf stopped himself from barking: *I'm not a lord!*

He *was* a Sheriff's son back home—his father had been the one who organized his remote rural district after the Change and led the effort to deal with the failure of the machines and the wave of city folk fleeing chaos and starvation. He'd become a powerful landowner in the process, a giver of judgments and leader of the local Farmers and their dependent Refugees in war and peace. Now Ingolf's elder brother Edward held the position.

And actually does a pretty decent job at it. I . . . well, I can't wish we hadn't quarreled when Dad died. If I hadn't stormed out, I wouldn't be where I am now, which is not such a bad place. I'm glad we made it up when the Quest passed through, though. Glad I got to see Wanda again and my nieces and nephews even if young Mark is a pain in the butt sometimes.

Being a Sheriff didn't mean quite as much back in Richland as a title of nobility did around here and they were a *lot* less formal about it, but he was roughly equivalent to the younger son of a baron in Association terms.

The whole feudal folderol is pretty damned silly to my way of thinking, names from books and all, but they take it very seriously indeed here in this part of Montival. And they outnumber me about six, seven hundred thousand to one and I have to stay here for now, so they can call themselves whatever the fuck they please, right.

"Probably there's going to be more than one fight, kid," he said instead. "Those bastards aren't invading your land 'cause they love you."

"I'm not scared, my lord," the boy said, lying transparently. "It's just . . . my family's not far. My mom and my brothers and sisters and all."

"Then don't let them get past you, that's all I can say. Kill the other bastard before he can kill you and your home and family are safe. Running from a fight just means it follows you. It's as simple as that."

The boy's grimy knuckles tightened and went white on the spear shaft; he'd probably take the advice to heart. Ingolf had long since seen that it was a rare and lousy specimen of a man who couldn't show willing with his back to his home and kin.

And probably he'll get himself killed and die still a virgin, poor brave little clod. I've also seen how much willing counts for when amateurs go up against real soldiers with real gear, who know what they're doing when the amateurs don't.

Another set of sentries stopped and identified them, and then they began to pass horses picketed on either side of the arroyo, tethered to ropes strung from pegs driven into the sandy soil. Most simply stood hipshot, their tails swishing regularly; others were being watered, with buckets filled at holes dug in the lower parts of the sandy bed of the seasonal watercourse. The homey, familiar smell of horse-piss, horse-sweat and manure added to the odors of damp sand and sun-baked earth and grass and sagebrush.

Lord Maugis de Grimmond, Baron Tucannon and enfeoffed vassal of the Counts Palatine of Walla Walla, was a year or two younger than Ingolf, which meant he'd been four or so at the time of the Change. His parents had both been SCA members in Oregon who threw their lot in with Norman Arminger and ended up with a barony here.

Mathilda is a fine person, but her dad was one heap big bad badass, from all I've been able to gather, Ingolf thought. *Still, needs must. Those were hard times. Mary's father, Rudi's dad Mike Havel,* killed *Arminger.*

Though he'd only survived it by about forty minutes before dying of the wounds Arminger inflicted; and now

Rudi was married to Norman Arminger's only child. The family politics here got twisty, and he was still learning his way around them. For one thing, Rudi's mother Juniper Mackenzie hadn't been married to Mike Havel, either. Mary's mother, Signe, *had* married him. She still wasn't what you'd call overenthusiastic about Rudi or Juniper, though she and the outfit Havel had founded and she ran, the Bearkillers, had accepted High King Artos grace-fully over around Larsdalen on the other side of the Willamette from Clan Mackenzie. Mary and her twin Ritva had moved out from there in their teens to live in the woods with their Aunt Astrid, who was . . . strange. Even by comparison with other people who'd had a rough time in the first Change Year.

Like most Changelings his age Ingolf had elastic stan-dards when it came to what was or wasn't outright bark-ing madness, having grown up among an adult population many of whose members had been strained beyond the breaking point by what they'd seen, suffered and done to survive. They were functional most of the time or they'd have been bones in a ditch somewhere, but screaming sweating nightmares or people who suddenly burst into tears or rages at odd moments were pretty common, and every year brought a trickle of suicides done one way or another. His own father had just taken a bottle out to a barn and drunk himself unconscious now and then; you could see it coming on in his eyes, when he got to re-membering.

And Mike Havel wasn't nasty like Arminger, or crazy like Arminger, but he was a hard man and no mistake. Dad did what was necessary back then too, so I'm not going to be too snippy about this baron guy's parents. They lived, and so did their kids. And if it helped to plaster everything with names out of old books, so be it.

Their son had coarse, curly bowl-cut red hair of a dark copper color like an old penny, pale skin of the sort that turned ruddy rather than tanning, slightly buck teeth, a big nose and ears like the handles of a jug. He also wore a full set of Western plate armor except for the helmet and the gauntlets, which lay beside him, and while he wasn't particularly large he moved as if the weight and heat and constriction didn't bother him more than day-clothes.

He was busily engaged in cutting bread and cheese, using a painted shield as a platter. Ingolf dredged up newly acquired heraldic knowledge to read it: *Argent, a fess Gules, in chief two greyhounds courant proper* while the nobleman stopped and glanced up at the pair. The peasant spearman bowed low in a complicated gesture with something like a curtsy involved. Maugis returned it with a nod that was . . . literally . . . lordly.

Mind you, he could have just ignored the kid.

"Thank you, Girars . . . Bero, get some of this, take it back to the rest at your post, boy . . . and tell your father I'm glad he's keeping a sharp lookout," he said.

"Thank you, my lord!" the youngster said, louting low again as he accepted the loaves and cheese and meat wrapped in a length of coarse sacking.

"And Girars, next time you leave your post, take your shield with you as well as your spear, or you'll be very sorry."

"Yes, my lord!"

The nobleman turned to Ingolf, and bowed respectfully with the gesture between equals.

"Colonel Ingolf! Welcome, my lord of Readstown. What news of the enemy?"

Of course, when it comes to people here being polite to me it sure as shoot doesn't hurt that I went with Rudi all the

358 S. M. STIRLING

way to Nantucket and back and am officially now one of the
Nine Companions of the Sword-Quest in song and story. Or
that I married his half sister on the way, Mary being a big
wheel among the Dúnedain Rangers and now a princess,
more or less. Since Rudi is High King Artos these days. I
didn't realize quite how important she was, and it wasn't
why I married her, but since it's a fact . . . well, use the mojo
where you can get it, Ingolf old son. Sure as shit beats being
a wandering paid soldier the local Farmers wouldn't let in
the front door and the Bossmen treated like something nasty
you scrape off your shoe on a hot day.

"Looks like we'll have company the way I thought, my
lord Tucannon," he said aloud.

"You saw them?" the nobleman said eagerly.

"Saw one of them, and *he* saw the sheep. It was an
enemy scout, all right; I caught the sun-blink off his binoculars. I sent my aide back to alert our own scouts and
they should be reporting in . . . an hour to three."

The baron nodded. Binoculars were an expensive specialty tool and among the most prized of salvage from the
old world; the modern replacements just starting to appear were bulkier, not nearly as good, and almost as expensive. Field glasses ended up in the hands of those
whose missions really demanded them, or those of extremely high status.

Ingolf went on: "And you can bet he's part of the
screen for a cavalry outfit. One gets you ten they take the
bait."

That brought a general rustle. About forty of the men
sitting with their backs against the bank upstream of him
munching on sausage and bread and cheese were
equipped in articulated steel plate much like their lord;
some of them de Grimmond's household knights and
men-at-arms, and the rest his vassal knights called up

from their manors and *their* men-at-arms. They were the ones who fought as heavy cavalry; the twelve-foot lances they'd carry were stacked neatly in pyramids of ash wood and steel.

Very bad news if you can't get out of the way, dodge around and pepper them with arrows, Ingolf thought. *If you can . . . not so much.*

He had a suit of plate complete too, the gift of Sandra Arminger, but he preferred lighter gear for work like this.

You have to use great big horses with that ironmongery, and even bigger ones if they're wearing armor too. They're fast in a charge, but not what you'd call nimble, and they get tired out quick.

Rather more men wore light armor of leather and mail like Ingolf's; they also had tight horseman's breeches, swords and powerful recurve bows of horn and sinew and wood. This far east the PPA bred its own cowboys and hence horse-archers. There were also foot spearmen with the same big kite-shaped shields as the knights and crossbowmen with small round bucklers and their specialist missile weapons; both carried swords as well and they wore what they called three-quarter armor here, which was like a man-at-arms' but with some of the pieces left off. Spearmen and crossbowmen and men-at-arms were the three types of soldier that Association military tenure required landholders here to maintain and furnish at need.

All those looked at least unbothered by the prospect of bloodshed, working on their gear or talking quietly and joking as they ate, a few praying with their rosaries in their hands, a couple even sleeping; but then it was their trade, more or less, even if the infantry did farming on the side and the horse-archers stared up the ass-end of a lot of livestock. The rest of the force were dispersed up and down the arroyo in spots where water was available and the cover good, several hundreds strong; they were peasant militia not unlike the unfortunate Girars, a few callow-eager, most grimly determined. Ingolf suspected that their main military purpose would be to absorb arrows that might otherwise hit a real fighter.

"If they do come, we're ready," said the baron.

Ingolf looked back over his shoulder, juggling distances and the lie of the land.

"You sure you can take heavy horse down that slope?" he said, a little dubious. "Looked mighty steep to take fast, much less a flat-out charge in all that gear."

The baron laughed and handed Ingolf a length of dried and smoked mutton sausage, salty and greasy and pungent with garlic and sage and hot peppers, balanced on a thick chunk of maslin wheat-and-barley bread with a slab of strong-smelling cheese a little runny with the heat. There was a helmet full of onions not far away, another full of raisins and dried apricots, and someone was handing around a skin bottle of water cut with a rough red wine. Ingolf sat with one foot drawn up—which let you get back on your feet in a hurry, a fixed habit he'd picked up long ago—and set to the food, using his own helmet to hold things he wasn't chewing on at the moment.

It was all reasonably undecayed, and far, far better than some things he'd eaten in the field. Nearly raw foundered mule three days dead, eaten in a weeping late-autumn rainstorm that kept smothering the fire, for instance.

"Lord Vogeler," de Grimmond said patiently. "This is not only my barony of Tucannon, it's Grimmond manor, the place I was raised as far back as I can remember and where I've spent nine-tenths of my life. I've ridden and hunted and hawked and walked and strolled and camped out and searched for strayed stock and led my men-at-arms practice and occasionally fought bandits or raiders over every inch of it starting when I could walk three steps. Yes, it's steep right there, but we can do it."

"Point taken, my lord," Ingolf said. "I'd laugh at you if you gave me advice on using terrain back in Readstown. We'll need confirmation on how many of them there are before we settle the details of the plan, of course."

He finished the food, extracted some gristle from between his teeth and went to check on his horses, including his favorite, a big brown gelding named Boy he'd picked up in Nebraska years ago. He made a point of feeding them some of the apricots. A horse wasn't like a water mill where you pulled a lever and got a given result. It was *important* that it liked and trusted you as well as knowing you were boss.

Then he went back and waited, thumbing through a copy of *The Silmarillion* from his saddlebags, which was more or less essential if you were going to be part of the Dúnedain Rangers, into which he'd married. This edition was from the Mithrilwood Press. The cover was gilt-stamped tooled leather over board, and it had annotations by her aunt Astrid Loring-Larsson, the Lady of the Rangers, along with her *Helpful Hints on Modern Spoken Sindarin* at the end. She had started the Rangers a few years after the Change, she and her *anamchara* Eilir, Juniper Mackenzie's daughter. They and their husbands still ran the outfit.

That priest I met in Fargo said Christians and Jews are People of the Book. Well, so are the Dúnedain Rangers! Or Books, plural.

He'd actually read some of the other stories by this guy when he was younger . . .

OK, hold that thought. According to Astrid Loring, the

Hiril Dúnedain, those aren't stories, they're the Histories and the Englishman was The Historian, inspired by the Valar demigods even if he didn't know it and every word is goddamned gospel true. I don't know if all the Rangers actually buy that . . . I'm not really sure how seriously Mary takes it . . . but on brief acquaintance with her aunt I think that living in the woods with Astrid for a couple of years would convince pretty well anyone, much less a bunch of impressionable teenagers who wanted to believe in the first place . . . It's the official line anyway, sure as shit stinks. What the hell, it works. And it's no sillier than all these Protectorate guys ready to draw swords over who gets to paint what stuff on their shield. All your perspective, I guess.

When you considered what the Cutters believed about their Ascended Masters and the Nine Rays and whatnot, it wasn't even very strange. Nor was the Church Universal and Triumphant just imagining things. There was something there, it just wasn't what they thought it was.

A soft call came from one of the sentries and he stuffed the book away. A few minutes later two figures came up leading their horses.

The one in the lead was Mark Vogeler, his nephew and aide-de-camp. The boy would be eighteen about Christmas, but he was tall and well built for his age; still gawky but when and if he got his full growth he'd look a lot like his uncle, except that his hair was the color of corn tassels and that his snub-nosed face was considerably less battered. The mail shirt and helmet he wore, his shete, tomahawk, the quiver over his back and the laminated recurve bow in its saddle scabbard on his horse, were all of the highest quality and they'd been new that spring.

But they'd seen use since. The long trip from Readstown and several stiff fights had knocked a lot of the puppylike piss and vinegar out of the eldest son of Edward

Vogeler; he was no longer quite the brash youngster who'd virtually blackmailed his kin into letting him come along to the war. The grin was still wide and white in his dark-tanned face below the mop of summer-faded hair.

"Reporting, Colonel Vogeler," he said, saluting and handing over a folded sheaf of papers. With a bow that showed how quickly he'd picked up local custom: "My lord Tucannon."

The other newcomer was in worn buckskins deliberately stained and mottled in shades of brown and sage-green to make them better camouflage. He was a short brown-skinned man in his thirties with black braided hair and high cheekbones, definitely Indian or mostly so. He bowed as well but remained silent afterwards, squatting with his reins tucked through his belt and munching on a handful of the apricots someone passed him.

"Ah," Ingolf said, flipping quickly through the papers covered in small, neat handwriting and hand-drawn maps. "Yup, Lady Mary's report. About three hundred fifty men, Boise light cavalry, regulars, all horse-archers, with a battery of four springalds along with them. Damn, horse artillery. I hate those things."

Everyone in hearing nodded, including the men-at-arms. Plate would turn most arrows, unless they came from a powerful bow and hit just right. Springalds were like giant crossbows on wheeled carriages, but they threw four-foot bolts powered by an entire set of leaf-springs from the rear suspension of a light truck. They had three times the range of a bow and they'd punch through knight's armor as if it were made from old tin cans. A good crew could fire nearly as fast as a crossbow, with two men heaving on the cocking levers from behind the steel shield that protected them from arrows.

"They're advancing in squadron columns—"

Which meant forty or fifty men each.

"—with a good screen out. A remuda of a couple of hundred horses bringing up the rear. A reconnaissance in strength, the lead element of a powerful raiding party out to disrupt your harvest and seize or destroy what they can, or both. Likely both. And they're definitely turning east towards that valley, so it looks as if they're going to go for the sheep. Confirmed by Rick Three Bears."

Ingolf grinned. "He adds that they're well mounted. *Those horses are plain wasted on white-eyes*, quote unquote."

De Grimmond looked encouraged. And also, Ingolf thought, the tiniest bit uncertain. That was natural; he knew Ingolf and his Richlanders and the Dúnedain only by reputation, and the Lakota contingent led by Three Bears barely even by legend. The leather-clad man who'd come in behind Mark Vogeler spoke.

"My lord, I can confirm that."

De Grimmond nodded. "Go on. Tom Yallup, isn't it? You saw it?"

The man was a Yakima, from a tribe farther west who'd lost heavily in the Change and then in the long brutal wars between the Free Cities of the Yakima League and the Association; they'd ended up tributary to the PPA on what was left of their land. The tribute included horses, and in time of war scouts. Both had a high reputation.

"Tom Yallup, that's me, my lord," the man said, looking pleased at being recognized. "Yeah, I saw it. Their commander had this sideways red crest on his helmet."

"Definitely Boise," de Grimmond said. "A Centurion's crest. Old General Thurston had an odd obsession with Ancient Rome and his son's worse."

Ingolf coughed frantically. "Sorry," he gasped. "Swallowed wrong."

The Indian scout went on, shaking his head ruefully: "It was hard keeping up. Those Rangers, they're like ghosts. Real smooth scouting, real smooth, they've got an eye for the way the land lies. And the Lakota . . . they're some serious 'skins, my lord."

"Right. Let's proceed, then."

Ingolf nodded. "We come in behind them; my Richlanders first, to hit their rearguard, and the Sioux behind as reserve, to make sure none of them escape. The enemy will try to disengage and break contact when they realize they're outnumbered, the valley side on the south isn't impassable for mounted men and they'll think they can get around us that way, hit us on the flank or escape and get back to their main body. You ram into them right then when they're not expecting it and the impact ought to break them. And, my lord, the High King instructed me to say that he wants prisoners, if they're willing to surrender. Particularly if they're US of Boise men."

De Grimmond nodded. "It's in accordance with the laws of chivalry anyway," he said. "But thank you for the reminder, Lord Vogeler; it'll help keep that in my vassals' minds. God go with you."

"Good luck to you too, Lord de Grimmond."

"It is a good day to die," Rick Mat'o Yamni—Three Bears—said solemnly, in a deep sonorous voice, with a broad gesture of one hand.

Rick was a young man, about Rudi Mackenzie's age, with a hawk-nosed high-cheeked face and a complexion a little darker than a deep tan; his fur-bound braids were a very dark brown, and there were green flecks in his dark eyes. His mother's name was *Fox Woman*, from the color of her hair; she'd been one of the many *volunteers* who'd ended up joining the Lakota nation, as it re-emerged from the Change. By now the Seven Council Fires dominated much of the northern High Plains; since last May they'd also been formally part of Montival, in exchange for complete internal autonomy and a pledge of help in defending their borders.

Rick's father John *Whapa Sa*, Red Leaf, had negotiated it. He'd also sent his son and three hundred warriors along when Rudi came home to Montival, as a symbol.

"It is a day when the sun shines on the Hawk and on the quarry," Rick went on, raising both hands in a hieratic gesture. "We shall take many horses, many scalps!"

Three Bears had white and black bars painted across his face, the eagle feathers that marked his deeds in his braids, and his steel helmet was topped by buffalo hair and horns. There was an ornamental vest of white bone tubes across his entirely functional shirt of riveted mail, and a string of perfectly genuine tufts of scalp-hair down the leather seams of his buffalo-calf breeches. Tom Yallup was staring at him and his followers—some of whom were in full fig of eagle-feather bonnet—with a look halfway between fascination and suspicion.

Suddenly Rick grinned at him and burst into laughter, leaning his hands on the pommel of his saddle.

"Nah, I'm just fuckin' with your head, dude."

He turned to Ingolf. "OK, cousin, give us until"—his arm pointed accurately to where the sun would be at about three—"to get into position and start playing Cowboys and Indians. We want to make sure we get 'em all. Otherwise we're blown and whoever's following on will know where we are."

"Right," Ingolf said. "That would be a *bad* thing. Hey, *tahunsa*, remember we're supposed to take 'em alive if we can."

"Sure thing, Iron Bear," he said, which was mildly impolite; his people didn't use personal names when it could be avoided. "*Shee!* How could you possibly think we'd do anything else? Gentle as kittens, that's us."

Then he stood in the stirrups and waved his bow overhead. "*Hokahe!* Let's go, Lakota!"

The Sioux poured away in a torrent, their horses moving like a wave of flowing water up the slope to the west and disappearing as if they were the passing of a dream.

Mary Vogeler, née Havel, laughed beside him. "What do you think the odds are they'll take any prisoners?"

"Fucking zip, honey," he said. "But they'll collect every single horse, you betcha."

"Ah . . . Colonel . . . Iron Bear?" the Yakima scout asked.

Mary answered him. "We spent some time with the Oglala last year. A good deal happened. I'm *Zintkazawin*, for example. *Yellow Bird*."

She touched the wheat-blond hair that rested in a tight, complex fighting braid at the back of her neck below her light helmet; the ribbon that ran through it helped secure the patch over her missing eye. The other was a bright cornflower blue, in a face that was smoothly regular in a chiseled Nordic way.

"Rudi . . . High King Artos . . . is Strong Raven. It's a considerable honor to be taken in by the Lakota," she added sincerely.

Tom Yallup looked after the Sioux war party. "They really are some *serious* 'skins," he said again.

"Tell me," Ingolf said. "I spent the first four years after I left home fighting them, and I never, *ever* want to have to do that again. It's a lot more fun having them on my side."

He turned and beckoned. Major Will Kohler came up beside him and drew rein.

"Yah hey, Colonel?" he said, in a heavier version of Ingolf's rasping, singsong Richlander accent.

"Let's get our Cheeseheads ready," he said. "We'll be moving out in about twenty minutes."

There were still three hundred and sixty of the First Richland Volunteer Cavalry alive and fit for duty, after the long trip from the Kickapoo through the Midwest and the Dominions with Rudi and the rest of them. Their round shields were painted brown, with an orange wedge, the national colors of the Free Republic of Richland.

Like the Sioux contingent they were a symbol, in this case of the alliance against the Prophet between Montival and the League of Des Moines that encompassed the Midwest realms and their various Bossmen. They were also all volunteers, wild young men of the Farmer and Sheriff classes for the most part. Major Kohler had been the chief arms instructor for the Vogeler family Sheriff-dom in Readstown; he was the oldest man in the regiment at forty, and he was a big part of why they'd shaken down very well. The other was the educational value of hard experience.

Educational for the ones that lived, Ingolf thought grimly. *There were four hundred thirty of them when we left. But they're not complaining.*

Instead they were finishing off baiting the horses, feeding them cracked barley from nose bags. These were fairly tall beasts, not as muscular as the destriers, but not cow ponies either. More like what they called coursers here, and they benefited from some grain before really hard work. Then each squadron led theirs away from the water hole and put on their tack. If you could, you always rested your horses and unsaddled whenever possible, letting them roll and graze; every moment of that added to their endurance and speed when you desperately needed it. Horses were curiously fragile beasts, despite their size and strength. Dead ones had littered the trail of every big army he'd ever seen.

The orders were passed, blankets and saddles went on quickly, and each squadron mustered under its banner. Ingolf looked them over with a pang. They were him, minus a decade in most cases, big fair muscular young men born and fed from the same soil and folk that had bred him, and when they were gone back home—or dead—he'd probably never see their like again.

The Dúnedain were something else, wearing mail-lined leather tunics in sage-green and elegantly practical clothing of similar shades, chests blazoned with the Tree and Seven Stars and Crown and riding some of the prettiest horses he'd ever seen, mostly Arab by breed. They bowed in the saddle to him, with a massed murmur of *"Ve thorthol."*

Which meant *at your command*, pretty much. He was getting good at conversations in pseudo-Elvish as long as they were mostly commonplaces and clichés. Though the first time Mary had started yelling in it during a clinch he'd nearly been thrown off his stride.

"No dirweg," he replied: *take care*, or *stay alert*.

Polite youngsters, superb scouts in open country and even better in forests, very respectful of him as Mary's husband and increasingly for his own abilities . . . and all of them at least a bit weird, in his opinion. He supposed they were his future, rather than his past.

"I'll keep the enemy in sight . . . in our sight, out of theirs," Mary said cheerfully, swinging up into the saddle of her dappled Arab mare as gracefully as an otter climbing onto a rock. "And let you know if they turn away from our muttonish bait."

They reached out and touched hands for an instant;

then she turned the horse with a motion of balance and thighs, and cried: *"Garo chúr an dagororo! Noro lim, Rochael, noro lim!"*

He suppressed his anxiety with a practiced effort of will. Mary was very, very good with her weapons; most of the few professional fighting women he'd met were. Male soldiers could get by with being average, more or less, because most of the opposition would be too. You had to be way out on the right edge of the curve if you were going to risk your life over and over again fighting people on average bigger and thicker-boned and stronger than you were. His wife wasn't petite; she was a big strapping young woman taller than the average man, heavy as some and as strong as many. Sparring with her was like trying to nail a ghost to a wall, she was fast as a cat and sneaky as a fox, an even better rider than he was and a dead shot with the recurve . . .

Of course, you can still just get unlucky, especially if there's artillery involved . . . back to business!

"Ensign Vogeler!" he said as they bore away northwest.

Mark brought up the trumpet he wore on a baldric.

"Sound *advance in column of twos.*"

This was all supposed to buy time. He hoped someone was using it.

CHAPTER THIRTEEN

COUNTY OF THE EASTERMARK
CHARTERED CITY OF WALLA WALLA
PORTLAND PROTECTIVE ASSOCIATION
(FORMERLY SOUTHEASTERN WASHINGTON STATE)
HIGH KINGDOM OF MONTIVAL
(FORMERLY WESTERN NORTH AMERICA)
AUGUST 23, CHANGE YEAR 25/2023 AD

Tiphaine nodded as Sir Tancred saluted with fist to breastplate, whistled for his squire and horse, and detached a *conroi* of lancers and two of mounted crossbowmen to stay with her. Only a few of her own *menie* were with her now and they all had real work to do; if you were a retainer of d'Ath you usually had more urgent things to do than dance attendance and lend her credence.

Then he swung easily into the saddle despite a full set of plate and cantered off to the army camp that had sprung up outside Walla Walla's northern wall in the course of the long day now ending. She looked after the Guard commander with a slight envy; *he* had a straight-forward job to do.

Whereas I have to spend the evening herding barons and bucking up justifiably terrified townsmen and reassuring a Count. Still, that's a big part of higher command.

The force she'd brought was off the trains and camped

on what was usually common-pasture for the chartered city's horses and mules, with a few spilling over into stubble-fields. A low constant rumble came from it; rows of tents, dust smoking from under wheels and hooves and boots, picket lines, neatly racked bicycles and pyramidal stacks of twelve-foot lances and seven-foot infantry spears, lines of field artillery parked next to their limbers. Grooms and squires were leading strings of horses down to the water of the little Walla Walla River, or to irrigation ditches; files on work detail made the light loess soil fly in a chorus of spades and dirt and muttered curses as they dug sanitary trenches. Light blinked fiercely from metal, and here and there the heraldic banners and shields of baron and knight were splashes of color, but most of it was variations on the color of the soil.

A little farther off the landscape still looked peaceful and prosperous despite its aridity, surprisingly so to someone reared west of the Cascades. Here it was two months before the winter rains were due and it seemed dubious that it had ever rained at all. Reaped grain fields stood sere and yellow-brown, shedding ochre dust to the occasional whirling wind-devil, with the odd remaining wheat-stack like a giant round thatched hut of deeper gold. Poplar trees made vertical accents along a canal, more conspicuous for the general lack of trees, with here or there the intense green of vines or fruit trees or alfalfa and sweet clover in blocks startling against the dun landscape. Rippling distant hills quivering with heat haze were the brown of summer-sere bunchgrass. The creaking sails of tall frame windmills circled, grinding grain or pumping water, and villages of rammed-earth cottages stood each with its church steeple, clustered around the gardens and groves of manor houses often based on pre-Change farms.

You couldn't see how few folk remained, or how the ones who did worked at a frantic pace with spears close to hand, under the protection of mounted guards. The smell right here made it obvious that peace had flown, though. She took a deep breath through her nose. War did have a set of smells all its own, like the varied bouquets of wine. She liked wine well enough; Sandra had put her through an informal course in telling the various types apart. But she was a connoisseur of the bouquet of lethal conflicts.

Even when you weren't fighting in a miasma of copper-iron blood and the unique scent of cut-open stomach, or marching past the week-old bloated bodies of dead livestock and smoldering burnt-out houses. Mostly war smelled of old stale sweat soaked into wool, unwashed feet and armpits and crotches, horses, and canola oil smeared on metal and leather and long since gone rancid. A big camp like this added the woodsmoke of campfires, salt pork and beans and tortillas cooking, the charcoal and scorched metal of the little wheeled forges the field farriers used, and latrine trenches. It was all the smell of her trade, the way manure was to a groom or dye-vats to a clothier or incense to a cleric.

Getting the expeditionary force detrained and ready to march had gone fairly smoothly, but she'd been at it all day. Too often dealing with various noble scions who insisted on quarreling over precedence and citing cases right back to the day Norman Arminger proclaimed himself Lord Protector, and who considered themselves too important to listen to anyone but the Grand Constable in person.

That was the drawback of calling out the *arrière-ban*, the full levy of the Association; you got everyone who had military obligations to the Crown, which meant mobilizing a lot of contumacious, well-and-high-born pricks who hated taking orders from *anyone*, even if their lives depended on it. Some of the great families had followed their medieval models all too seriously.

I haven't had to kill any of them. Yet. Which is almost disappointing. Though it's fun bringing home that the rules in the Schedule of Ranks really, really, really do apply to the ones who think they can't possibly be expected to go on campaign without three pavilions, a chef and hot and cold running mistresses.

A very small bleak smile turned her lips; she had a long straight-nosed regular face, but at that moment it looked very like a predatory bird. She'd had any baggage found over the established maximum for a man's status pitched off the barges on the Columbia or the railcars as they turned up later and left for the fish, the coyotes, the camp followers and anyone who had a use for a down mattress or six sets of court dress or a knock-down bathtub or a crate of Domaine Meriwether Cuvée Prestige '15 with bottles of pickled oysters on the side. Excess servants had been shed with a little more ceremony, but not much.

The fingers of her left hand touched the twelve silver-inlaid notches on the hilt of her long sword, the metal smooth and cool against the callused skin. Nobody had argued much, however purple their faces turned.

A party rode up from the camp. A nobleman in gear that looked to have seen hard use in the last few days led them, and over their heads a fork-tailed baron's pennant flew from a lance. A squire behind him carried a shield that had been recently and roughly field-repaired after being hit repeatedly with things sharp and hard and heavy.

"My lady Grand Constable," Rigobert Gironda de Stafford said, thumping his breastplate with his right fist in salute before he dismounted.

"My lord Marchwarden," she replied, returning the

gesture. "Your horses look hard-used. I suppose screening us up there required a lot of riding."

She turned and gestured for a squire. "Get my lord de Stafford and his party fresh coursers, and have these seen to. Bring water for his men, and bread and cheese and raisins if they want it."

The nobleman nodded his thanks. "We've been busy, my lady. Just got in, in fact. It's quieted down up towards Castle Campscapell a bit now or I wouldn't have been able to make this meeting, but it's the stillness before the storm. I'm extremely glad to see you've brought us a substantial force."

He cocked his head and looked at her. "You were smiling a most evil little smile just now, my lady."

Tiphaine let it grow . . . just a little. This particular campaign would probably be a preliminary to the main event, and she was going to use it to toughen up some of the feudal levies who hadn't seen the elephant in this war yet. Toughen them up or kill them off; either would do.

"I know that expression, Grand Constable," the lord of Forest Grove said with a grin of his own, offering his canteen. "Someone who deserved it suffered, eh, my lady d'Ath?"

"Suffered the loss of oversize tents and silk sheets and overweight private rations, my lord Forest Grove," she said, putting the canteen to her mouth and tilting it. "And the services of various doe-eyed beauties."

It was field-purified water, cut one-to-six with harsh coarse brandy to cover the chemical taste and kill any bacteria the chlorine missed. The mixture cut the gummy saliva and dust in her mouth quite nicely; she swilled it around, spat and drank.

"But they can't say I didn't warn them," she finished, handing it back.

"Thirty lashes with an acerbic tongue and an icy stare, too," Rigobert said. "The novel experience of having to bow their heads and stand silent while their arses are roasted in public will be good for them. It'll rectify their humors, though not as much as a good bleeding and purge would."

They were both in half-armor, the articulated lames of the back-and-breasts covering their torsos, pauldrons and faulds on shoulders and thighs; with their junior squires standing by, the rest of the gear could be donned in less than two minutes. Sweat and dust clung to their faces beneath the peaked Montero hats—the type she'd always thought of as a Robin Hood hat, from an old movie she'd watched on TV before the Change. Nobody put their head in a steel bucket if they didn't have to right that moment. She could feel more sweat trickling down her neck and flanks and between her breasts, itching and chafing in the padded arming doublet and her underwear as it baked to a rime of salt in the hot dry air and then more dripped in, long-familiar and still irritating. The interior was *hot* this time of year, and its mountain-fringed geography made the Walla Walla valley warmer still.

"Is the Count due?" de Stafford asked.

He was seven years older than she, in his mid-forties, a tall broad-shouldered man with pale blond hair like hers worn in the usual nobleman's bowl-cut, eyes of a blue that was startling against his tanned face, and an unfashionable short-cropped beard that emphasized his square chin and ruggedly masculine good looks.

In fact, we look enough alike to be brother and sister. Rigobert might actually have been a tolerable sibling, unless he was a lot less bearable as a teenager.

The thought was oddly wistful; she'd been an only child.

A few of the less experienced or more naive staff officers and messengers in the group around her looked surprised that he dared to bandy words with the Grand Constable, who had a reputation for a cold, distant masterfulness. Tiphaine's mouth quirked a little more as she jerked her head slightly and the circle around them widened to allow more privacy.

Or to put it differently, I have a reputation for being a murderous evil reptilian unnatural bitch who's inhumanly good with a sword and under the Lady Regent's protection, she thought. *Rigobert's a special case, though.*

She looked at her watch, a self-winding mechanical model from the old world.

"Not for about another fifteen or twenty minutes, my lord, assuming he's punctual. We got the encampment settled just a bit faster than I anticipated and told him we would."

"Any news from Delia?" he asked.

"A letter just in," she said, fishing it out from where she'd tucked it into her thigh boot. "She's well, Diomede sends his love and wishes he were here and not in Tillamook, where incidentally he's going to stay if I have to tell Baron de Netarts to chain him to a dungeon wall, Heuradys has learned to say 'no,' and our beloved Delia herself feels like an overripe watermelon about to split, she says. Also she sends *greetings to my beloved beard*."

"I'm her beard, she's mine," de Stafford laughed as he took it and read it eagerly.

Her Châtelaine and lover of fifteen years, Delia de Stafford, was married to Lord Rigobert. The Barony of Forest Grove was the next tenant-in-chief holding north of her manors, and its lord had about as much erotic interest in women as Lady Delia de Stafford did in men, which was even less than Tiphaine did. Fathering Delia's children had involved what passed for high-tech medicine these days, namely a pre-Change turkey baster.

"Ah, I see Countess Odell has arrived for the accouchement, with her girls. That will be a comfort," he said happily. "To them both. Valentinne will worry less about Conrad and her sons with something else to occupy her time and Delia will feel better with company and mothering, she's always been a social sort and makes friends easily."

So do you, Rigobert, she thought. *Including people like me, who really aren't easy to be friendly with.*

"I hope it's a daughter," he went on. "Delia does so want a matched set of four, Lioncel, Diomede, Heuradys and . . ."

He glanced at her with a raised eyebrow.

"Yolande if it's a girl, Rigobert for a boy, we thought," Tiphaine said.

The Lady Regent had arranged the marriage a little after the War of the Eye and not long after Tiphaine was given the title and estates of Ath as grounding for a rising succession of military commands. It was one of Sandra's classic kill-three-ducks-with-one-bolt political rim shot maneuvers, at one swell foop turning Delia from Tiphaine's plebeian and clandestine girlfriend into a noblewoman eligible for a post such as Châtelaine of a baron's household, giving public cover to Tiphaine, Delia and Rigobert all three against sheet-sniffing clerics and similar vermin, and giving Sandra a valuable two-way source on the distaff side of the nobility's gossip-and-intrigue pipeline.

She'd sized Delia up quickly, and foreseen that her spectacular looks, fashion sense, personality and organizing skills would make her a star of the castle and manor house feast, hunt dinner, ball and masque circuit in jig time with a little discreet patronage. The social order hadn't jelled as hard then, either; it would have been a bit more difficult to bring off in the increasingly Changeling-dominated present, the time of the second generation's flowering.

"You'd name the boy Rigobert? Why thank you!" Delia's husband replied sincerely, with a winning smile. "I'm flattered."

But the Baron of Forest Grove genuinely *liked* Delia; they had become close friends, and he had been a good if slightly long-distance father to the children she insisted on. He was also extremely capable, and not only in the straightforward head-bashing style of most Association nobles; he'd been a junior spook of some sort for some agency that didn't officially exist before the Change, as well as an SCA fighter, and valuable enough that Norman Arminger had put aside his—literally—medieval prejudices on the subject of gay people to make use of him.

Odd. In retrospect as an adult rather than a creeped-out and perpetually seething-angry teenager, I don't think Norman really hated us, not in the visceral loathing sense.

Rigobert folded the letter, handed it back, and then raised a brow at her expression.

"Just thinking of Norman," she explained.

"My sympathies, my lady. I hope you recover quickly and don't lose lunch."

He raised the canteen in another toast. "May his bigoted, sadistic, rotten soul roast in Hell to the cheers of his innumerable victims," he went on—quietly—and drank.

She took the canteen and sipped herself. "Though to be fair, as far as the bigotry goes I think he just *thought* he should hate queers because he was such a fucking Period Nazi purist Society geek, killer psychopath academic subdivision. Sort of like wearing hose and houppelande.

He was playing a role twenty-four/seven. And he scared me, frankly."

"Me too. Not much of a difference on the receiving end whether he was sincere or not," he said a little sourly. "What was that ancient Greek saying? *The boys throw stones at the frogs in sport, but the frogs die in earnest?* When Norman cut someone dead, he didn't do it metaphorically. Usually it involved him laughing hard with blood up to his elbows. I've never met a man who enjoyed killing more and I've known some ripe evil throat-cutting bastards in my time. Been one myself, at need."

"True. But you have to grant that at least he didn't have any *racial* prejudices. Gender yes. Us, yes. Race, no."

Which was true; about one in five of the Association's nobility were what the old world would have called members of a *visible minority*, as opposed to about one in twenty-five of the general population. Not that anyone gave a damn about that sort of thing anymore; things like class, kin and religion were vastly more important now.

"That's probably only because William the Bastard and King Roger II of the Two Sicilies didn't have racial prejudices either," Rigobert said sardonically. "Hanging around Sandra so long has made you inhumanly rational, my lady."

"It is catching, my lord Forest Grove," she admitted. "Though as far as excess rationality goes, remember that Sandra truly *loved* Norman."

To herself: *And he had it in for gay men much more than women, which makes it easier for me to be objective. But that's standard. It's even authentically medieval, from what I've read; without a dick involved somehow it wasn't* real sex, *or not real enough to be a serious sin, even a perverted variety, back during the Reign of the Penis.*

"Oh, well, I got a happy marriage out of it in the

end," Rigobert said lightly. More seriously: "And the kids, which I find in retrospect I wouldn't want to have missed."

"Me too. And I was never a rug-rat fan either; as usual when Delia insists on something, she turns out to be right."

She sighed slightly. "How long are we going to be haunted by Norman's ghost?"

"Up until about the time Rudi and Mathilda's eldest takes the throne," Rigobert said. "And he or she will be Norman's grandchild."

He drained the canteen and tossed it to a page. "So may the Lord Protector get an occasional day off from the furnace. He did some good too, even if unintentionally."

The arrangement had started as pure and rather resented protective coloration as far as she was concerned, but it had eventually made Tiphaine and Rigobert . . .

I think you could say friends, she thought. *Though I don't have many, never did, except for Sandra and Conrad and that's a liege-vassal thing too. Certainly we're colleagues and close allies. He's fun to go hunting and hawking with, too, and I've had some very pleasant times just hanging out with him and Delia and the children and sometimes his current boyfriend. It's only taken fifteen years for us to reach the stage of exchanging BFF confidences. Delia must be mellowing me at last.*

"Which reminds me," she said to him. "There's something I've been meaning to do for a while, when there was time. There won't be any unless I *make* the time, so . . . Rigobert, stand witness for me, would you? Since we're waiting for the Count anyway."

"At your command, my lady," he said, doffing his Montero and bowing slightly; they were of roughly equal status as nobles, but her appointed Crown office as Grand Constable was higher than his as Marchwarden of the peaceful southern flank of the Association.

She glanced around and called sharply: "Armand! Rodard! Attend me!"

The most senior of her squires looked up from the papers in their hands, handed them over to clerks and then hurried over, bowing formally and standing at the Association equivalent of parade rest, with their left hands on their sword-hilts and their right tucked behind their backs. Both were dark-haired boldly handsome young men in their twenties, with slightly hooded blue eyes . . . and nephews of Katrina Georges, Tiphaine's first lover, who'd been killed in the run-up to the Protector's War fifteen years ago. The parents hadn't long survived the Change, but thanks to Katrina and Tiphaine their children had. She'd handled their training as pages and squires since her own knighting.

"Kneel!" Tiphaine said.

They did, going down on one knee with their eyes wide. Tiphaine drew her long sword and tossed it a little to settle the grip. The gesture attracted more attention; as a baron and as commander of the Association's armies she had the right of the High Justice twice over. There were probably some people here who knew her only by reputation and thought she was going to start beheading with her own hands. Though that sort of thing wasn't done as much these days.

When she spoke, it was pitched to carry beyond her bubble of privacy. "Esquires, knights, and all gentles of the Association who are within hearing of my voice. Know that these men are of good birth and Associates of the PPA. For some years they have served me as esquires, and have proven valiant in battle, faithful in service—"

And extremely efficient in some covert ops work, but let's not break the flow.

"—and skillful and courteous in those arts and graces which become gentlefolk. I am therefore minded to dub them knights, which is my right as their liege-lady, as baron and tenant-in-chief, as Grand Constable of the Association and as myself one who wears the golden spurs and belt of knighthood. Do any here dispute my right or know of an impediment in these men? If so speak now, or hold your peace thereafter, for you may be called to court under oath as witnesses of this ceremony."

Silence fell in a circle of the busy, bustling scene. Tiphaine looked around, her pale gray eyes cool and considering. Then she turned to the two men, facing Armand first; he was the elder, after all.

"I dub thee knight," she said, and the flat of the blade rang on his armored shoulder. "I dub thee knight," as she flipped it to strike the other side and then sheathed it.

Then: "Receive the *collée.*"

That was a slap on both cheeks, delivered forehand and backhand; it was supposed to cement the moment in your mind, and she gave it in the traditional style, a hard smacking buffet both ways. Knighting in the field was traditional too, and if anything, more prestigious. Armand was fighting down a grin as he drew his own sword and presented it across his palms. Tiphaine held it up and kissed the cross the hilt made before returning it.

"Take this sword, Sir Armand de Georges, knight of the Association . . . and the High Kingdom of Montival. Draw it to uphold the Crown, Holy Church, your own honor and your oaths to your liege, and to protect the weak as chivalry demands."

"I will, my lady and liege. Before God and the Virgin I swear."

"Then rise a knight! And I welcome you to the worshipful company of that most honorable estate."

She repeated it for Rodard; when they were both on their feet she waved aside their thanks.

"It was overdue. The spurs and the vigil and the calligraphy on parchment can wait. Style yourselves household knights of Barony Ath and your stipends are doubled. We can discuss fiefs and manors after the war."

That made their ears prick a little, beneath very well-schooled calm; they were loyal, but naturally ambitious. All noblemen lusted after land, herself included. She added, "Not to mention the marriages Lady Delia has been thinking of arranging for you, *in loco parentis*. Dismissed."

There was a little alarm on their faces as well, when they turned away. Then she nodded to Rigobert.

"One more thing. Lioncel de Stafford! Attend me!"

The page dashed up; he was one of a brace of six she had running messages, all about as old as pages got and by modern standards eligible to be taken on campaign; his younger brother Diomede was eleven, and still serving in an ally's castle on the far-off Pacific coast. Delia's oldest child took after his father in looks, fair and blue-eyed, tall already at fourteen and from his hands and feet going to be even taller. He was wearing a light mail shirt, a steel cap, a sword and a buckler, with a crossbow slung over his back. Pages weren't expected to fight, but you couldn't rely on the enemy to observe the niceties, especially when fighting the Church Universal and Triumphant. Who were either bugfuck crazy, possessed by demons, or both.

Probably both, when it comes to their leadership. And I thought the Change was the weirdest thing that could ever happen. Never say ever.

"Lioncel de Stafford," Tiphaine said formally; she usually called him *Lioncel* or *you* or *boy!*

He bowed deeply with the standard graceful sweep of right hand, uncovered and drew himself up in sudden conjecture, visibly suppressing an impulse to give his hair an emergency comb; it was in what was once more literally a pageboy bob and considerably tousled by a day of wind and dust and hard scrambling work. She wore her hair that way herself, since going the full monty to a bowl-cut would be more of a thumb in the eye to the clergy than was wise, even for her.

"Let this company witness your words," she said.

Everyone in her *menie*, her fighting-tail of personal retainers, knew the answers, and of course the boy's father and his following did too, but it had to be spoken aloud for the record.

"What are your years?"

Lioncel swallowed, going a little pale as what was happening sank in. "I will be fourteen years come the Feast of Saints Crispus and Gaius, my lady."

Which was October fourth; she remembered it herself because it was Lioncel's birthday, but the Church calendar was the natural set of references to his generation of Associate. He was conventionally pious, despite his mother being a secret witch and Tiphaine having been, until recently, an even more secret atheist.

"Fourteen would do, and October's close enough in wartime. What is your birth?"

"Ah . . . I am the son of a belted knight, born in wedlock to a gentlewoman Associate of noble blood, my lady."

"What is your service?"

"I, ah, I have served as page in your household, and for a year in that of the Baron de Netarts who is Marchwarden of the Coast, before returning to you this summer, my lady. I have been under instruction as a page since I was six years old, learning courtesy and good service."

"Is it your will to take service with me as squire, your parents having given their consent?"

"Y-*yes*, my lady!"

She ignored the sudden crack in his voice that had him blushing crimson, and spoke to carry again: "On this day, I have chosen to take Lioncel de Stafford as my squire, deeming him of good character and sufficiently instructed in the knowledge suitable to his years. Does any here know of an impediment to this oath?"

Silence, and she went on: "Kneel!"

She drew her sword and planted it point-down. Lioncel hesitated for an instant, then set his hands on the quillions; she clasped hers around his and looked down into his eyes. The fingers felt a little chill beneath hers despite the hot day; he hadn't been expecting this.

"The path of chivalry is a long one, and the honor of knighthood not easily won. Are you willing to devote yourself to this cause?"

"I am." The boy's voice rang, strong and steady now.

"Then repeat after me: *Here I do swear—*"

"Here do I swear—"

"*—by mouth and by hand*"

"*—it is my intent to become a knight*"

"*—to learn by service*"

"*—to act always with honor*"

"*—and as the guardian of the honor*"

"*—of the knight I serve*"

"*—to obey my knight and my knight's teaching*"

"*—that I may learn skill and courtesy*"

"*—to follow always the virtues*"

"—of faith and hope"

"—charity and justice"

"—of prudence, temperance and strength."

"So I swear."

The boy's face was shining as he finished. Tiphaine replied, "In return for your service, and your devotion to chivalry, I swear to teach you what I can, and to find instruction for you in what I cannot. I will furnish you with arms, horse and gear as needful and see to your honorable maintenance as befits your station. You shall be my vassal in arms and my pupil, and your service is not menial or infamous. As my honor reflects upon you, so does your honor reflect upon me. Whoso deals ill with you deals also ill with me, and at their peril."

She released his hands, wiped the point of her sword carefully on one sleeve before sheathing it and pulled a badge with her arms out of a pouch. Then she pinned it to his cap before she drew him up by his shoulders and exchanged the ritual kiss on both cheeks.

"By wearing my badge, you declare your service to me, and my sponsorship of you."

Rigobert was beaming with fond pride; Tiphaine drew him and the broadly grinning Lioncel aside, and the other baron hugged his son. Lioncel returned the gesture, then faced Tiphaine proudly; now he was forcing himself not to finger the badge in his cap that marked his acknowledged exit from childhood and into the intermediate status of a youth.

"Lioncel, do you know why I took your oath as squire today?"

"Ah . . . no, my lady."

"First, you deserve it. In peacetime, I'd have waited another year, but we're at war. That leads to the second reason. You are your father's heir, but your younger brother Diomede is my son and heir by adoption, and the Barony of Ath, title and lands, go to him and the heirs of his body."

Lioncel nodded; he'd already started his study of feudal law—the Association's system was based on twelfth-century England under the Anglo-Norman kings, as modified by the peace treaty at the end of the Protector's War and more subtly by Sandra Arminger in her term as Regent since. A nobleman needed some acquaintance with it, if he weren't to be helpless in the hands of his advisers.

"Nothing is certain in war. Your father and I may both fall in battle. I don't expect it, but it could happen."

Lioncel nodded gravely; even as a youngster the son of a knightly house did not hide from the facts of life and death. He had been raised with the knowledge that war was the nobility's trade and avocation, and death by the sword their accepted fate. One that might come calling at any moment to exact the price of their privileges.

"If we did, your mother would take seisin of Barony Forest Grove by dower right until you came of age, in trust for you and your sister, and would have a third of the mesne tithes as widow's portion for her lifetime after you came of age and took seisin in your own right; that's settled law. But Diomede's position would be . . . ambiguous, and so would Delia's with regard to Ath and its revenues. Your lady mother would need your support because she has no formal right to Ath from me *except* through Diomede and that's uncertain. Technically Diomede is *my* son, but of course I'm not married to her so she can't claim seisin by dower right if I die or the widow's portion of the revenues. Dower descends from the husband, it doesn't rise from the child."

Dammit, she thought. *Norman and his obsessions! Not*

to mention the Thomas à Becket fixation a lot of the clergy have developed. Why on earth couldn't Delia and I get married? We have been for all practical purposes for a decade and a half!

Aloud she continued: "It's a nice point of law and some Chancellery clerk or worse still some Churchman might start a suit alleging Diomede was an orphan in need of wardship and that she had no standing to claim ward over him since a child can't have two legal mothers. The thing could be tied up in the courts for years with the land going to ruin. A page is a child; being a squire doesn't mean you're of age but it does give you a foot on the bottom rung of the ladder. It proves that you're old enough to take a legally binding oath of vassalage, so you can't be completely ignored. And as elder brother, you *do* then have certain rights where a minor sibling and the sibling's inheritance is concerned, and your mother through *you* since you'd be automatically under her ward as a widowed mother of a minor heir. Understand?"

He frowned, pale brows knotting in his tanned young face. "Yes, my lady, I think so. God and your patron saints protect you and my lord my father, but if the worst should happen, I will be my mother's strong right arm and my brother's shield and prove their rights against any who deny them. I swear it before God and the Virgin and my patron saint, St. Michael of the Lance."

He crossed himself and she nodded.

"Good. In the meantime, you're the most junior of my squires instead of the oldest page in the household. And you're not going to be old enough to fight as a man-at-arms for another five years or so, is that clear?"

A nod, and she went on: "Sir Rodard will find you enough work to do, esquire of House Ath. *Hop!*"

"Thanks, my lady," Rigobert said as the boy raced off.

"I should have thought of something like that. I still find myself thinking like an uncle rather than a father sometimes, and as for being a husband . . . And there are other times I have to remind myself I really *am* a feudal lord, not just playing at it."

Tiphaine gave a faint snort; she was a crucial near-decade younger and that sort of feeling hit her less often, but . . .

"Tell me. My highest ambition in Middle School was going to the Olympics as a gymnast. Until the world ended, when *not starving to death*, and *not getting raped, butchered and eaten by cannibals* or *not catching the Black Death* soon came to the fore."

"I knew you were a complete jockette, but I'll bet you wore black and red flannel shirts, too," Rigobert said with a grin. "Flannel shirts and a white A-shirt underneath, and skate shoes?"

"Oh, incessantly; with a trucker's hat, no less. I think the thirteen-year-old boys hated me because I looked more like a thirteen-year-old boy than they did."

"Not a mullet. Please, *God*, tell me you didn't have a mullet."

"Mother wouldn't let me, but that would have come in a couple of years. And when I turned twelve I realized I was desperately in love with Melissa Etheridge and put a great big poster of her on the inside of my locker door and played her music twenty-four/seven on my Walkman."

Rigobert laughed, and Tiphaine smiled thinly. She'd never lost herself in laughter easily, not when she was sober at least, and for her being thoroughly disinhibited was usually a bad idea. She envied him that easy laugh a little. It was odd to realize she couldn't have had this conversation with Delia either; not because they didn't share everything, but because the younger woman simply didn't have the referents to understand it without a lot of backing and filling. She'd grown up a miller's daughter on Montinore Manor and hadn't even learned to read until her late teens. Tiphaine shook her head as memories opened like the door to a dusty cupboard.

"I was a complete caricature of a baby-dyke-in-training and didn't even realize it until I caught myself in the middle of a daydream of rescuing Melissa from a stalker and then smooching her passionately . . . my family didn't talk about things like that so I didn't even really understand the names my beloved classmates were calling me. I did know they weren't well meant, you bet I did."

"Was it *possible* to be that naive in 1998?"

"For a while, if you were a lonely introspective only child of a single mother who was extremely religious, with no friends except your gymnastics coach. And she was terrified of being hit with 'inappropriate conduct' accusations by a hysterical parent. Everyone knew before I did, except my mother and she was deep in denial."

"Wasn't as much of a problem for me," Rigobert said, with a reminiscent smile. "It might have been hellish if I were swish, but—"

"Yeah, you're even more butch than I am," Tiphaine said sardonically. "Football star, right?"

"Not dumb enough for football. Basketball, track and field, karate, and fencing club. I was such a model of blazing macho hotness even the straight guys wanted me," Rigobert said. "Ah, high school, the amount of action I—"

"Now you're boasting . . . wait a minute, do you realize our speech patterns just lost twenty-five years?"

The other baron shook his head. "You're right. Best

not to dwell on the past . . . it was just seeing Lioncel looking so damned *young*. And looking so much the way I did at that age . . . though I'm pretty sure he's straight, come to that."

"He is," Tiphaine said definitely.

A conversation about stumbling upon him and a servant girl in a linen closet back at Montinore Manor came to mind; Delia had found it hilarious and she'd thought it rather embarrassing.

"Lioncel's greatest ambition is to be a gallant knight and a good baron, and I think he's going to achieve it," she said instead.

"He's a fine boy, all three of us can be proud of him, but . . . they scare me, sometimes, the Changelings. No offense."

"None taken. I'm a borderline case anyway. I can remember the old world, bits and pieces, particularly the last couple of years before the Change. I simply don't, usually, unless it comes up the way it did just now. The last twenty-three years or so have been a lot more fun than my childhood anyway, on the whole."

"It's Changelings raised by Changelings who really give me that odd feeling, and Delia's seven years younger than you; she *is* a Changeling and no mistake. From time to time I look back on the way we set things up in the early years and think . . . *what have we done?*"

Tiphaine's expression went colder than usual. "We all did what we had to do, in those days," she said, very softly. "All of us. *Everybody* did what they had to, or they died, like ninety-five percent of the human race."

Rigobert inclined his head in silent agreement, memories of his own moving behind his eyes. Anyone old enough to really remember the first Change Years and the great dying knew that expression, from the inside as well as from their mirror; it would die only when the last of them were gone.

"Not quite what I meant. I was thinking of the Association's trappings in particular," he said more lightly after a moment. "We all went along with it and now . . . now it's just the way people around here live."

"Norman did *that*," Tiphaine observed. "God help us if he'd been obsessed with first-century Rome or Chin Dynasty China or the Old South. Or been an old-fashioned Red with a man-crush on Stalin."

"And if Norman hadn't existed, we'd probably all three have been dead these twenty-five years now and the children wouldn't have been born, so done is done and probably for the best." Rigobert sighed. "*We* can't complain, seeing we not only made it into the small minority who survived but came out very much on top of the heap. I try to do right by the peasants on my manors, but being a baron is *much* more pleasant."

"Except when we're doing the hard parts."

Rigobert smiled. "No, sometimes then too, don't you find? Sometimes *especially* then."

COUNTY OF THE EASTERMARK
BARONY OF TUCANNON
PORTLAND PROTECTIVE ASSOCIATION
(FORMERLY SOUTHEASTERN WASHINGTON)
HIGH KINGDOM OF MONTIVAL
(FORMERLY WESTERN NORTH AMERICA)
AUGUST 18, CHANGE YEAR 25/2023 AD

"Gotcha!" Ingolf said as his force came in out of the westering sun.

From here, several miles out on the high plains leading from the mountains down to Dayton, the valley with the sheep looked different; the rugged peaks in the background seemed closer, and the whole thing more closed off. And you could see most of it was rolling, not a steep V down to the little creek. The shepherdesses had fled in well-simulated terror, scattering their sheep artfully as they went, and the Boise cavalry had spread out to get the flock under control.

Almost all of them would be cowboys from the ranching parts of Idaho originally anyway; you nearly had to be born at it to make a good horse-archer. They'd know how to gather a mob of woolies. It was probably a homelike interval in the war for them . . . until the moment they felt the hook inside the delectable bait. He looked behind. Most of his men would still be hidden by the folds he'd been diligently following, but they were getting too close for caution.

"Sound *advance in file order*," Ingolf called, and legged his horse up to a canter.

The sweet notes of Mark's bugle rang. The columns opened out like fans; a few moments later the First Richland was strung out in a great line two men deep, rippling and twisting as it moved over the swells of the ground. Ingolf looked left and right and over his shoulder; the Sioux were closing in from the rear, their formations more like the flocking of birds than regular lines, but keeping up easily. Three Bears slanted through the Richlander files to ride beside him, his quarter horse matching the longer strides of Boy.

"Got 'em all!" he called, over the growing, growling thunder of hooves; there were fresh scalps at his saddle. "And the remuda. Good horses."

Horse-theft was the Lakota national sport; you just had to accept that they were obsessed.

"Any prisoners?"

"Nah, they all fought to the death. Brave as shit. Look, cousin, I've got a bad feeling about this. They may not have been alone, you know? Yellow Bird and her tree huggers and some of my boys are sweeping back west of here."

"Good. Let's get this part done quickly."

He chopped his hand left, to the north, where the little creek ran down from the hills and came closer to that steeper edge of the valley.

"Keep them from getting across that, will you? It's fordable everywhere but it'll slow them if they try to cross and you can shoot the shit out of them. We need them bunched and I don't want to extend that far. Your call on when you get stuck in."

"Right, cousin. *Ki-yi-yip-ki!*"

He angled away again, and the Lakota veered in that direction, pulling ahead at a gallop. A growing pillar of dust was rising from the pounding hooves, fortunately mostly swept behind them by the wind and the speed of their own passage. The spicy scent of crushed grass mixed with Ingolf's own sweat and Boy's and the oily metallic smell of his mail and the muskier stink of leather. Ahead the Boise formation was reacting with commendable speed now that they'd realized . . .

They're about to be corncobbed, Ingolf thought with a taut grin, reaching over his shoulder for an arrow.

The wind in his face would give the other side a slight advantage in a horse-archery duel. You had to be careful about that sort of thing, and remember always that mounted men could only shoot ahead, behind and to a half-circle arc on their left. Even worse, the enemy had a battery of four springalds. *Spitters*, they were called sometimes. Not as bad as scorpions or twenty-four pounders throwing dart-bundles, but bad enough and very mobile.

A four-horse team could drag them almost anywhere cavalry could go, and about as fast.

The Boise cavalry were back in formation already, four blocks three men deep—risky, but it would add firepower and weight to any charge. Now they were rocking forward, but between the blocks of the enemy formation loomed squat wheeled shapes behind angled arrow-shields . . .

"For what we are about to receive, may the Lord make us truly thankful," Ingolf muttered, then louder: "Mark! Drop behind me!"

Reluctantly the boy obeyed; Major Kohler was over on the left flank of the formation with the other guidon banner so that a lucky spray of shafts couldn't decapitate the regiment, but being a commander meant you got shot at more, and that was that. You were completely useless if your men couldn't see you, and if they could the enemy could too.

Up to a hand gallop now, the knotted reins dropped on the saddlebow, guiding the horse with weight and thighs alone. It took almost as long to train a cavalry mount as it did the rider, longer in proportion to life span, ordinary horses were useless for this . . .

TUNG! A great metallic bass throb of a sound, like the world's biggest untuned lute, and instantly the *crack* as the springald's slide hit its stops and the dart flashed free.

Something arched out from behind the onrushing body of horsemen. It seemed to go faster as it approached, a blur in a long shallow curve traveling too fast to really see. Then *shunk!* as it struck the dirt fifty feet ahead of him and buried half its length in the ground. He was past it immediately, close enough to see the malignant quiver of the sheet-metal fins that fletched it. Then another went by, and he could hear the *whipppt* of cloven air as it passed his left shoulder. Death missed by six inches; it would have torn his arm off at the shoulder if it had struck. And there was a huge scream from behind him, just an instant before it stopped sharp as an ax-cut.

Mark! he thought, then ruthlessly suppressed the wave of anger and grief.

More three-pound darts traveling hundreds of feet per second; one made a brutal wet cracking sound as it passed entirely through a trooper not far to his right in a spray of blood and broken mail-links and killed the man behind him too. Another skewered a horse, punching into its chest and disappearing entirely into its body cavity. The beast went down between one stride and another, limp as a banker's charity, tangling the feet of the mount behind as it tried to leap the sudden obstacle. The second horse went over in a tumble of limbs and crackle of bone, the rider flying free to strike with crushing force. And they were close now, close, four hundred yards, three hundred . . .

"Shoot!" he bellowed.

Few of the men could hear him. They could all see and the commanders would relay the order; he rose in the stirrups, twisting his torso as he drew against the recurve's hundred-pound resistance with the thick muscle of arms and shoulders, chest and gut. The arrow slid through the centerline cutout in the bow's riser, and the smooth curved limbs bent back into a deep C-shape, sinew stretching and horn compressing on either side of the central layer of hickory.

He let the string roll off his draw-fingers.

Whap!

Three hundred and fifty shafts followed within a second, arching into the sky like slivers of incarnate motion, seeming to pause for an instant and then plunging downward. The enemy shot in almost the same instant, and in the passing of a fractional second Ingolf fought and won the usual battle of will not to duck and hunch his head forward. You got hit or you didn't; he'd had both. Instead he was flicking out more arrows, shooting as fast as he could draw and adjusting the angle as the forces came together. More men and horses went down on both sides, falling out with iron in their bodies, going limp or thrashing out of the saddle, horses suddenly uncontrollable with the pain of sharp steel and wood in their flesh. Not much to choose between his men and the enemy in speed or accuracy of shooting, but there were more of his and the Sioux were into it now too, at extreme range.

Six arrows, seven, eight—

He thrust the bow into the boiled-leather scabbard at his knee. The same motion helped slide the yard-wide round shield off his back and onto his left arm, and an instant later the shete was in his right hand, moves practiced for decades. That switch needed careful timing; too soon and you got shot at without being able to reply, too late and you were fumbling with things while the guy on the other side cut you out of the saddle like a side of pork. Juggling your weapons like that, fast but without dropping anything, was a big part of cavalry training. It was even worse if you had a lance to worry about too.

The enemy's trumpets sounded, a harsher deeper blatting tone than the ones his people used. The Boise horsemen responded to the order with beautiful precise discipline, reining in from their gallop and turning; their whole formation was racing away back up the valley in a brace of seconds, with the troopers turning and firing backward. The Parthian shot, and his men couldn't shoot back. He thrust his shete skyward to keep them from uncasing their bows again, and heard officers and noncoms taking it along the line:

"Blades! Blades!"

They'd be wondering why he gave that order, but they obeyed, hunching with their shields up under their eyes as they rode. The enemy were thirty yards away, edging to the right as the Lakota shot at them from across the little creek or began to cross themselves in fountains of spray from the plunging hooves of their horses, holding their bows high over their heads to keep them out of the wet, their yelping, yipping war cries splitting the air.

Thock!

An arrow thudded home in his shield, slamming through the sheet metal and leather and plywood, the point appearing as if by magic with four inches of shaft behind it. He grunted with the impact as it rocked him back in the saddle; sheer dumb luck it hadn't gone through his left arm. He'd fought an action with an arrow there once and didn't remember it fondly. Also he'd lost that skirmish and barely gotten away with his life.

Tock!

Another; he used the hilt of his shete to break them off with two sharp blows. One of the oddities of command was that you had to keep *thinking* when things like this were happening.

The Boise troops were bunching closer together; their commander was aiming at the gentlest, or least steep slope—up ahead to the right. If he could get his men across that he had options. If he stayed to fight, he didn't. The numbers were against him. Being outnumbered two to one didn't mean you were half as strong as the other side; the ratio of combat power was more like four or five to one, other things being equal.

But I know something you don't, you son of a bitch! It's even worse than you think it is right now.

The onrushing Richlander line overran the springalds and a few sections stayed to deal with them. The battery commander had wasted time trying to hitch his weapons up to their teams, and they all paid for it. There was a brief flurry as the gunners swung cocking-levers and bill-hooks, the cavalry shetes rising and falling in lethal chopping arcs, bright and then throwing arcs of red drops. It ended soon; artillerymen rarely got a chance to surrender when those they'd been shooting at from out of bow range got within arm's reach of them for payback time.

Then . . .

Perfect timing, Ingolf thought vengefully.

The line of the crest above suddenly bristled steel and the Boise formation halted in a ragged stutter with yells of dismay. Steel lance heads glinted above bright pennants flapping in the wind, the steel of armor on man and destrier glinted, a glow of color shone from the heraldic arms on their shields. Another trumpet sang, this time the high harsh sweetness of a Portlander oliphant.

A cry rang out from forty throats, muffled by the visors that turned their faces into blank steel curves with only the vision slit showing dark, but still deep and hard:

"Haro! St. Joan for Tucannon! *Haro!*"

The lance-points of the men-at-arms came down in a long falling ripple, and their followings came up behind them, ready to run in their wake through the hole they'd punch in the enemy formation.

"Haro! Chevaliers, à l'outrance—*charge!"*

Nine minutes later Ingolf stopped his shete in midswing; the jarring mental effort left him weak and gasping for an instant. The Boise trooper who'd dropped his saber and cried for quarter had his hands crossed over his face and his eyes screwed shut. When he didn't die he opened them again.

"Down!" Ingolf barked. "Down and hands on your head!"

The man scrambled out of the saddle to obey, kneeling with his palms on top of his helmet, and his horse galloped off with its stirrups flapping. The will to fight ran out of the Boisean formation with an almost audible rush that spread throughout the milling chaos of the melee battle in instants; their commander put his cross-crested helmet on the end of his sword and pushed it high.

"We surrender! Quarter, comrades, we call for quarter! Throw down, men! It's useless! Throw down!"

They did. It didn't always save them. Most human beings found it hard to kill; once rage and fear had pushed them into that state of un-mind, it was even harder to stop. Officers and sergeants and corporals in the Richlander force grabbed men and held them in bear grips until the killing madness ran out of them, sometimes stunning with a blow from the flat or knocking them out of the saddle with the edge of a shield. The knights dealt with their subordinates a bit more roughly, clubbing more than a few militiamen down with broken lances or skull-shaking kicks from armored feet and stirrup-irons.

The Sioux weren't even trying; he heard the savage guttural blood shout of *Hoon! Hoon!* as the steel drove home. More and more of them were crossing the river, too.

"Kohler!" he shouted.

"He's dead, sir. Arrow through the throat."

Damn, he was a good man. Just bad luck. Later!

"Then you, Captain Jaeger! Get your men behind me, *now*! Shields up, shetes down."

They followed as he booted Boy back into motion, and he wheeled them between the Lakota and the bulk of the Boiseans, holding up their shields but not the threatening steel. Violence wavered on the brink of reality for an instant, and then Three Bears rode up to Ingolf's side, reining in stirrup to stirrup. He rose in the saddle and shook his dripping shete at his own folk, shouting something in the fast-rising, slow-falling syllables of their language—which was mostly used for ceremony and important public announcements these days, something that probably redoubled the impact. They stopped, looked at each other sheepishly, shrugged, and pulled back.

"Thanks, cousin," Ingolf said, looking down at his sword-hand.

It was glistening with thick red liquid, and so was the whole yard-long shete and more was spattered across his thigh and torso and some on his face, and his gauntlet was greasy where it had run down under the cuff and soaked into the leather. The harsh iron-coppery stink was everywhere, and he felt the weary disgust, the sense of let-down-ness that he always did after a fight. For a while you were just an armor-clad set of reflexes that shouted and struck, and then you had to be yourself again.

"Colonel!"

He whipped around. Mark was on a horse that was obviously not his own, and his bugle was bent nearly in half where it rested on its sling across his chest.

"You OK?" Ingolf barked.

Christ, Varda, whatever, thank You I don't have to write that letter to Ed and Wanda. Not this time, at least!

"Nothing hurt but my bugle and my pride, Unc . . . Colonel. A springald bolt went right through Dancer's neck and cut the saddle-girths and the next thing I knew I was lying flat on my ass. Took me a while to catch a loose horse. Where's Major Kohler?"

"Dead," Ingolf said, and the boy's face struggled with shock for an instant.

"We've got work to do," Ingolf said grimly. "We made the mess and now we need to clean it up."

Mary rode up laughing a couple of hours later, cantering past the rows of Boise prisoners sitting with their hands still on their heads. Ingolf looked up at her with relief; just beyond the prisoners were the rows of wounded, and he'd been consulting with the doctors, his own and the Boisean medic squad. The dead were a little farther out, their shields over their faces and a couple of walking injured to keep the birds away.

His wife had a bright scratch across the matte green paint on her helmet, just the sort an arrowhead would make when it banged off the steel. Two inches lower and it would have punched through her face and into the brain.

I've been in this business too long, Ingolf thought. *I've seen too many of the people I care about die. It's starting to get to me more and more.*

He shook his head and looked at the Portlander beside her in the dented and scuffed suit of plate. The man had a tower and a lion on his shield, still discernible beneath a couple of arrow-stubs despite a lot of recent dings and nicks and one lopsided corner looking like someone had hit it with an ax, very very hard. A war hammer in his right hand rested with its shaft across the high steel-plated cantle of his knight's saddle; the end of it was caked gruesomely, with drying bits of hair and bone and skin caught in the serrations on the blunt side and bits of sticky gray goo as well.

Sometime in the last hour, hour and a half from the state of that. And he didn't stop to smell the roses afterwards, his horse is foaming its lungs out. Big courser and not a barded destrier, must have been a mobile fight.

The face below the raised curved visor was older than Ingolf by about a decade or a bit more though not as banged up, running with sweat and red with exertion—fighting in armor was like that, especially in that sort of armor in this sort of heat, and you didn't get over it quick—but it looked coolly amused and totally in command of everything around, starting with his breath. Also it had the sort of sculpted but slightly harsh good looks that would make women coo; the short golden beard added to the impression.

"You've done a nice little job of work here, Colonel Vogeler, Lord de Grimmond," he said, his voice deep but smooth. "I don't believe we've met in person before, Colonel. Marchwarden Rigobert de Stafford, Lord Forest Grove, currently in charge of the Crown's forces in this area. I'd offer to shake hands but I'm a bit messy right now. I've met your charming and capable spouse, Princess Mary."

He handed off the war hammer to another man, probably his squire. "Well-met again, *Maugis*," he said to de Grimmond; they exchanged a knuckle-tap, a clunk of armor on armor. "And thank you for your aid, *intancan* Rick Mat'o Yamni."

"What happened out there?" Ingolf said bluntly, jerking his head to the west a little.

He couldn't look there now, because the sun was only a couple of hours from setting, but he needed to know. His mind filed away the fact that this Portlander had gone to the trouble to learn the Lakota for *war chief*. It was an extremely tactful thing to do, when you had one under your command. When it came to bloody-minded touchy pride the Sioux and the PPA's nobility were surprisingly similar.

"There were more of them," Mary said. "Heading

towards Dayton originally, but they probably saw your dust when you mousetrapped their cavalry, and they veered this way. Quite a lot of them. We got cut off and fell back south to try to get around them, and then ran into Lord Forest Grove's outriders. Which was a very considerable relief. And he acted very quickly."

"You supplied us with just the information we needed," de Stafford said, with a savage grin and an inclination of his head.

Then he took a moment to unfasten the straps of his visored sallet helm and take it off, shaking his sweat-darkened hair out with a grunt of relief, leaving his head looking rather odd above the *bevoir* that buckled to the upper part of the breastplate and protected his chin.

"They had about four battalions of infantry and a couple of cavalry regiments," he went on. "A raid in force and enough to invest Castle Dayton and do much damage if we didn't hit them hard. We had a stiff brush with them, and then their infantry pulled back on bicycles with their cavalry screening them. It might have been much worse if we hadn't been forewarned, but there didn't seem much point in following. They could get back to Castle Campscapell faster than we could pursue, and it's useless to attack a castle that strong if the garrison is alert. Without the sort of special help they had taking it last year."

Ingolf nodded wearily. Given a few miles start and on some sort of road, men on bicycles could run to death any horses ever foaled. There simply wasn't any return in trying to catch them.

"Thank you, my lord," he said. "That might have been awkward, if they'd showed up here."

"You're entirely welcome, but they'll be back . . . and this is a close relative of yours, from the good bones?" he added curiously, looking at Mark and smiling. "Not your son, my lord? Too old, I should think."

That's sharp, Ingolf thought. Aloud: "My nephew, Ensign Mark Vogeler."

"Off to a good start in his career, I see. Well, Maugis, Colonel, we need to talk. Can your wounded be moved?"

A doctor looked up from one body resting atop the folding table he was using and threw aside the broken shaft he'd just extracted from the muscle of a thigh. He was an older man, gray-bearded, with blood splashed on his gloves and apron. The one shuddering through the leather strap clenched in his teeth was young Girars, but the peasant boy looked as if he'd make it. They were saving the ether for the really serious cases; two men picked up the stretcher he lay on and carried it off.

"They'd better be, my lords. I need to get them under cover by nightfall, though fortunately it won't be too chilly," the doctor said. "Moving will hurt some but help more."

Then, absently under his breath as he returned to work, "Christ, I never thought when I got out of Johns Hopkins I'd end up sewing up sword-cuts and pulling out arrows in godforsaken Walla Walla County."

"We have plenty of wagons and carts, my lord de Stafford. It's not far to Castle Tucannon and the Grimmond-on-the-Wold manor," the local baron said. "My people should be arriving with the transport any moment."

"Then let's get moving."

De Grimmond fell behind for a moment to whisper into Ingolf's ear as the Marchwarden rode on with his lancers at his heels.

"Ah . . . about my lord de Stafford . . . just a word to the wise . . ." he began.

Ingolf blinked in surprise as he listened; Mary snorted

from his other side as the baron heeled his horse forward again.

"You mean you couldn't *tell?*" she said.

"No," Ingolf said shortly.

"Tell what, Unc . . . Colonel?" Mark said.

Ingolf thought for a moment, then told him. The young man goggled for a moment. "*Him?* But . . . but . . ."

Mary laughed, which added to his confusion; he had what he probably thought was a well-concealed burning crush on his uncle's wife. Who was only five years older than he was, after all.

And good-looking if I do say so myself, Ingolf thought a little smugly. *If you like 'em tall and blond and with an eye patch, which I do.*

She reached over and tweaked the young man's ear. "Welcome to the club of those who've had their butts looked on with the eyes of desire, Mark," she said. "*I've* been a member since I was much younger than you, and it's always a hoot when guys complain about it. That's what I noticed about Lord Rigobert; he *didn't.* Look lecherously, that is; not even a glance."

"Lord de Grimmond said he's a perfect gentleman, though. Knows how to take no for an answer," Ingolf said. Then he grinned. "It probably isn't relevant, Mark. I never did make a try for every pretty girl who caught my eye, either."

"You'd better not," Mary said, amused; Mark sputtered a little more.

"You look like a landed carp," Ingolf said; teasing the boy was probably unkind but irresistible. "And you're turning the color of a ripe tomato. What's the problem?"

"Because he looks like, well, like a fighting man!"

This time Ingolf laughed out loud; Mary chortled too, not unkindly.

"Son," he said, "what did I tell you *assume* does?"

"Makes an Ass Out of You and Me," Mark answered automatically. Then: "Oh."

"Yeah. *Oh.*"

Mary rolled her eye skyward. "If you knew the number of times people up here in the PPA have just taken it for granted I like girls because I wear pants and I'm not the flounces and furbelows type . . . since we got back and there's this starry-eyed *Companions of the Sword-Quest* thing going around I've had to *literally* kick them out of my bed at least once . . ."

Ingolf started to laugh helplessly; it wasn't the first time he'd done that on a battlefield with the stink of death in his nose, or Mary either. That was where and when you needed a laugh most. Worry aside, there was a lot to be said for having a wife who was in his line of work. They could share things that most couples couldn't.

Mary pointed an accusing finger at him. "You didn't help! You stood there and brayed like a laughing jackass, just like you're doing now. And then she *cried.*"

"Welcome to the club of them as has been cried at by girls, honey. I've been a member of that one a long time, too, and it's sort of a hoot to hear a woman complaining about it."

She snorted, and turned back to Mark, who was crimson to the ears. Ingolf sympathized, abstractly. The kid was probably also longing to be able to adjust his jock-cup.

I remember what it was like to be a hard-on with legs at that age. Thinking about gargling vinegar would give me one, much less imagining that *situation!*

"It's just *so* annoying!" she said. "And it's true about 'assume,' Mark."

Ingolf reached over to tousle his nephew's hair. "I

couldn't tell everything about de Stafford there, but I *could* tell he *is* a fighting man to be careful of, and I'd still say he's exactly that. The guy whose brains were decorating that war hammer would say just the same, only he's doing it sitting on a rock in hell . . . or the Halls of Mandos . . . cursing him as the world's most dangerous killer faggot. Don't assume about that. Don't assume about anything, Mark. It can get you killed."

CHAPTER FOURTEEN

"Are you sure, Colonel Nystrup?" Astrid asked conscientiously.

It wasn't that she wouldn't send people on a suicide mission, Ritva knew. It was just that she wouldn't *lie* to them about it first. She wanted them to know what they were getting into without a shadow of a doubt.

The warehouse belonged to a Mormon merchant who'd traded widely in alum, soda ash and other valuable minerals, and had been built by stripping out everything but the load-bearing concrete members from an office building. The trade had declined in the long destructive war between the CUT and New Deseret, and nearly halted altogether since the Battle of Wendell. He'd turned it over to other uses without a murmur, or any questions, then packed his family and portable wealth and left town in a hurry. The huge first floor stretched empty around them, dusty, smelling of chemicals, with spears of light from the high small windows.

"Lady Astrid, we are *extremely* sure," Nystrup said.

He'd gotten a little thinner than she remembered him,

from the time the questers passed through the CUT-occupied parts of New Deseret east of here and helped his band of partisan fighters; a leanly fit man in his thirties, fair and with a snub-nose that had been made more snubby sometime in the recent past with a blow. The sixty Mormon guerillas grouped behind him all looked as if they knew their business. Judging from the scars and what she saw in their eyes, Ritva judged that they meant what their leader said. Years spent fighting the CUT forces occupying their homeland had winnowed them with fire.

"We are not engaging in suicide," he went on earnestly. "That is damnable sin. We are taking on a dangerous mission that we know carries a very high risk of death, for our homes and land and people, and for the Church of Latter-day Saints, and for God, and against the servants of the Adversary. This war must be won, or our families will know only death or slavery. Part of Deseret holds out yet, but more than half is occupied by the false Prophet's troops, and our refugees here in Boise are treated more and more badly. This . . . this Montival is our only hope. I have met Rudi Mackenzie, and we know that he has been sent as our deliverer."

Astrid nodded. "Come, then," she said gently. "Now is the time. Operation Lúthien is a go."

Above them a rope shook. John Hordle came sliding down it with a rattle of equipment, in Dúnedain battle gear with his greatsword slung over his back along with a longbow and quiver. Eilir followed him, similarly clad but carrying the recurve of horn and sinew that most Rangers preferred.

The wind is from the north and rising, she Signed. *I don't like the taste of it, either. I'm afraid that the blimp may go faster than Major Hanks calculated.*

Ritva winced slightly. If the rendezvous didn't go as planned, they died; it was as simple as that.

Alleyne signed from the door: *Street empty. Go!*

The four wagons were standard US of Boise army-issue, rated to carry a ton and a half of cargo beneath their canvas tilts. Half of the guerillas were already in Boise's uniforms and hoop-armor as well; now they put on the helmets, low-crowned affairs with a flared neck-guard and folding cheek-pieces. When they tied the cords to those beneath their chins little could be seen of their faces, and they took the shields and javelins from the vehicles and fell in with a creditable imitation of the smooth precision to be expected.

Ritva pitched in with harnessing the six-mule teams; the familiar task helped her calm herself, long slow breaths easing the knot in her belly until she felt loose and relaxed. She pulled on her close-fitting steel cap of blackened steel, climbed into the wagon and lay down, checking that all her weapons were ready once more, and that her eye was near one of the knotholes in the planks which made up its side so that she could look out. The Ponderosa pine wood was new, and she could smell the sap. It was a little thin, too, flexing where she pressed against it.

Some contractor is padding his accounts using unseasoned wood that's not of the right grade. Tsk!

The thought almost made her laugh, but you couldn't let your emotions loose at a time like this, even positive ones were a risk. In a way, a sudden surprise was easier than methodical waiting; you just reacted by trained reflex. She let her mind drift instead, mainly going back over the day she'd spent at the Drover's Delight before the stretched-out arrival of the others.

Ian really is sweet, she thought happily. *And smart and*

*funny and good with his hands . . . in more ways than one.
But I'm definitely not going to go live on a farm in northern Drumheller, ever, ever, ever. If you shout there at Yule
the sound doesn't thaw out enough to hear until Ostara!
Shudder! Oh, well, the war's likely to last a while. We'll see.*

The object of her meditation crawled into the wagon
and wiggled through the other Dúnedain until he was
snuggled behind her; mainly symbolic, when you were
wearing a mail shirt.

"Not very private," he murmured. "In the Peace
River, we have sleigh rides for courting. A nice buffalo
robe can conceal a multitude of sins."

"Shhh!" she said affectionately.

A set of sacks filled with wheat husks was tossed in to
cover the layer of fighters in the bed of the wagon; unless
they were examined closely they'd look just like full sacks
of actual grain, but they were light enough that they
could be pushed off instantly. She could smell the redcoats' sweat, and it wasn't just wearing a mail shirt and
padding on a warm day. They weren't simply going to a
fight, they were going to a fight that was certain death
unless everything went right, including actions by strangers they didn't know beyond brief acquaintance.

*Poor Ian is even worse off. He doesn't know us, or Aunt
Astrid and Uncle Alleyne or anyone but me . . . and we've
only known each other a couple of months, though it's been
intense.*

There was a special rankness to the sweat of fear.

She didn't mind; courage wasn't a matter of whether
you were afraid, it was a matter of what you *did*. Nearly
everyone was afraid before a fight if they had time to
think about it, especially if they'd seen and felt and
smelled the results and knew bone-deep how easily it
could happen to them. Even if the surge of rage and ef-

fort burned it out during the actual face-to-face killing, the waiting was hard.

Which is why you want the waiting to be over. Sorta.

People who were never frightened were *scary.*

Aunt Astrid is scary, for example, Ritva thought, as the wagon creaked out of the big doors of the warehouse.

The day outside was much brighter, though there were plenty of clouds and it was well after dinnertime in the long summer evening. Her sandwich and cup of bean soup wasn't lying too heavily on her stomach, and they'd all eaten several handfuls of dried fruit with honey for the quick energy, along with one small shot of brandy.

Aunt Astrid is scary because she doesn't control the fear, she just doesn't feel *it. I think something must have happened to her after the Change that burned it out though she never talks about it. I don't think she sees what the rest of us see. I love her as my kinswoman and liege, almost a second mother, but I'm afraid of her too.*

This might not be the riskiest thing Ritva had ever done. Probably the flight from the Sword of the Prophet in the Sioux country last year was that, where they'd dodged behind a herd of stampeding buffalo to escape just a hair ahead of being trampled into mush, or the fight on the rooftops in Des Moines when the Seeker had made the assassins into puppets of meat with the same not-mind looking out from each pair of eyes—

Manwë! The things I do! And it always seems like a good idea at the time!

—but this was right up there with the worst things she could remember doing deliberately and in cold blood. The feeling that they were completely dependent on someone else for a chance at escape wasn't very pleasant either.

Breathe in. Breathe out. Work the muscles, don't get stiff,

*keep centered. Just do your best and let other people do theirs
and afterwards you can tell stories about it.*

And Martin Thurston had threatened, sincerely, to cut
out his wife's *tongue*. Even though she detested the
woman, that . . .

*Was exactly what you expect from Cutters. I don't know
what it is, Rudi tried to explain but I got the feeling he really didn't understand it himself after we came out of . . .
wherever we were on Nantucket. But whatever is doing
things to the Cutters' spirits, that whatever-it-is hates us for*
existing. *We really, really need to do this.*

Noise built; they were into the populated part of the
city, and she could see narrow glimpses of horses and
bicycles and pedestrians and pedicabs and wagons and a
handcart full of very fresh green onions that made her
eyes water for an instant until she had to bite her lip to
smother a sneeze. The steel wheels of the wagons grated
and rattled and banged on the pavement, and the bed of
the vehicle punched at her side as it hit little ridges and
dips; nobody wasted leaf springs on a mass-produced
freight carrier like this. Then the traffic thinned.

"Roit," a deep bass voice said, cheerfully. John Hordle
was a bit scary too. " 'ang 'ard, all. Time for the kiddies
to play the *fall down and bleed you evil buggers* game."

Let your mind flow. Don't think, just be, just do.

A stretch of pavement, the gravel-and-concrete patches
light even against sun-faded asphalt a generation old. A
stretch of roadway, with a sheet-metal watering trough
and an automatic nose-operated dispenser. Another one
of those a little farther down, and an extremely fancy
black carriage, with the Presidential seal on its doors, and
a driver and groom watering an equally fancy set of
matched black horses; she hoped with some distant corner of her mind they wouldn't get hurt in the contentions

of men. And a line of soldiers standing in a double file at parade rest against the plate-glass windows of the jewelry store.

At least I'll have these sacks of chaff off me in a second. It's filtering down through the burlap and it itches. *And I'll be smelling something besides scared excited soldier.*

It would probably, almost certainly, be blood instead, and the smells you got when bodies were cut open. Until then she had more light and air than the rest of the dense-packed crowd in the wagon.

No thought. Be. Do.

Her bow was between her and the side of the wagon-box. She reached slowly over her shoulder and pulled four arrows out of her quiver; goose-fletched shafts of dense Port Orford cedar with horn nocks and wicked bodkin points of hard alloy steel. At this point-blank range she could put them through plate, even, if they hit square on. A flicker of memory told her how little protection the light mail under her jerkin would be, but that faded away. She tucked the arrows between her left forefinger and the riser of the bow. Ready, ready . . .

"Platoooon . . . *halt*! Right face!"

The guerillas in Boise army gear came to a stop, crash-stamping in unison and turning to face the escort guarding the General-President's family. A man jumped down from each wagon seat, hitting the quick-release catches in the military harness of the teams and making as if to take them to the troughs.

The Decurion in charge of the detail was wearing sunglasses as well as his helmet with its stiff upright brush of scarlet-dyed hair from a horse's mane. They were probably for effect, given the way the day was turning overcast.

"What are you Fifteenth Battalion pukes doing here?" he asked, flourishing the swagger stick he wasn't strictly entitled to. "This is an interdicted spot, so get your weevil-wagons and glue-bait mules and your own sorry Reservist asses out of—"

Nystrup was leading the guerillas playing escort. He didn't waste time on talking. One hand flashed out and took the platoon-leader by the back of the neck under the flare of his helmet. The other drew and struck with his dagger, driving the point up through the gap in the jaw-bone and the palate and into the Boise soldier's brain. The man toppled back

"NOW!" roared Hordle's bull-bellow.

White fire erupted in Ritva's mind, like glowing ice. The light sacks flew in every direction from the wagons as they spouted warriors. She came up to one knee in a smooth roll, stripping an arrow out of the bundle she held against her bow and onto the string and throwing arms and shoulders and gut into the draw. The arrow slid through the cutout in the riser as the lead kiss-ring brushed between her lips, and she let the string fall off the fingers. Less than a second and a half had passed, and the arrow drove over a snatched-up shield and into a man's face with a solid moist crunching *whack* sound that might come back to her in the night sometime. Again, again, a torrent of whispering death from forty bows—

The guerillas on foot had all thrown their *pila*. They weren't experts, but the distance was ten feet and there were thirty of them with strong arms and they were full of desperate hate. Some of the big javelins missed and smashed into the glass window. Others thudded into shields as the Sixth Battalion guard detail reacted with trained speed. Many found flesh.

The survivors crowded back towards the tall worked-bronze doors of the shop; not running, but backing with their shields up and putting their bodies between the unknown enemy and their ruler's kin, slightly crouched with their blades out ready for the stabbing stroke. Whistles trilled, calling the alarm.

More arrows punched into the heavy plywood and sheet metal, *crack-crack-crack*, and more men fell or dropped the shields as the points gouged through into arms. Soldiers were pushing out through the doors to join them, the other half of the guard detail, and the formation was shaken for a moment.

That instant's gap was enough. A great high silvery shout: *"Lacho calad! Drego morn!"*

The Dúnedain war-shout, alive again in the Fifth Age: *Flame light! Flee night!*

And Astrid Loring-Larsson's voice. She was moving, long sword and dagger in hand, like a human blade of black and silver, spired helm and elf-boots, a soaring leap from the wagon to the trough and then another that sent her spinning in midair in a three-quarter tumble right over a man's head and landing with the blades already moving.

In Dúnedain training a move like that was called a *Jakie*, for some reason, and they did a lot of them. Many involved running up trees and going *across* buildings and leaping from rock to rock through the hills. Eilir was half a pace behind; she hit the wall running and went straight up it and spun-flipped and landed beside her *anamchara*.

Astrid killed the man over whose head she'd jumped before he could make himself believe what she'd done, a thrust to the back of the neck that flicked out and back like a frog's tongue after a fly and he dropped as limp as a puppet with the strings cut, in a sprawling crash of armor.

"Lacho calad! Drego morn!" Ritva shrieked as she dropped her bow.

She leapt, landed in a crouch, spun in a circle on one

heel as her sword came out, blade a silver flash as it went snicking through a booted ankle and hamstring in a drawing cut, stripped her buckler off its clip on her belt. Ian was beside her a quick breath later, saber working in a frantic X as he guarded her back with steel and round shield. The Rangers poured forward in a leaping shouting glitter of steel. The four-foot blade of John Hordle's greatsword swung in three quarters of a circle and broke a shield and the arm under it and gouged into a face hard enough to shatter it in a spray of teeth and blood. Alleyne was beside Astrid too, lunging and cutting and striking like a big golden cat.

"Arise, ye Saints!"

The Mormons poured after them, nearly as quick. A dozen of them locked shields and smashed into the display window, where the glass had already been weakened by the punching bodkin points of the arrows and javelins. It turned into a glittering wave of fragments, and then their hobnailed boots were trampling the mannequins and sending sprays of gold and platinum, diamonds and rubies and tanzanite into the body of the store.

The Dúnedain followed, on their heels and then past them with a dreadful bounding agility, accompanied by one swearing, scrambling member of the Force.

Ritva vaulted a display rack, rolled under a thrust from a *pila* and cut backhand and upward into a groin; the man screamed astonishingly loud and thrashed, and blood sprayed across her torso. Another was beyond him, swearing as the dying man tangled his feet and display cases on either side pinned him in place; she charged, shoulder-checking him in his shield as he staggered. That was like ramming her shoulder full tilt into a brick wall, but he went over backward and two Mormons jumped on him, their sword-arms pumping like pistons.

It was obvious where the two Mrs. Thurstons and their children were; as agreed they were clutching at pillars and cabinets and screaming at the top of their lungs as their guards tried to drag them to what they thought was safety, adding one more element of chaos to the scene. The spot they'd picked to linger was cluttered, too; big leather sofas, discreet and heavy display cases with marble bases, and the desks and counters of the shop staff.

That left no room for the soldiers who hadn't gone to hold the door to form a shield-wall. In an open field they would have been more than able to hold the Rangers and the Mormons both until help arrived, even outnumbered; they were strong, picked men, beautifully trained and equipped. The problem was that they were trained and equipped for one type of fighting and only that, each man a part in a single many-legged machine. This brawl-mêlée left them in isolated ones and twos facing Dúnedain, whose war-style brought a malignant perfection to a tumbling slashing stabbing scramble from ambush.

The Mormons simply swarmed those facing *them* under, showing a reckless disregard for consequences. The Thurstons kept screaming, a needle-edge of distraction, and those trying to drag them away snatched up their shields as the swarming fight staggered near. Ritva forward-rolled around her sword-hand under the thrust of a *gladius* and came to a knee, hammered the edge of her little steel buckler down into the man's foot in a grisly crunch of small bones breaking, then thrust upward into his throat and killed him as he bent over in swift involuntary reflex.

A leap forward, across a tile floor already slippery with blood, and she found herself facing the last soldier of the Sixth still standing. He'd lost his helmet and was flicking his head to get the blood out of his eyes from a cut on the forehead. He was a young man, younger than she, with bristle-cut red hair and a freckled face whose skin was tight over the bones and wet with sweat and blood. The green eyes were utterly steady as he set himself to die.

A flickering long-lunge towards a foot brought the shield down; Ritva knew somewhere far from the present all-consuming moment that she was moving to ten-tenths capacity in an impossible blur of speed, almost as fast as Astrid. She turned the lunge into a feint with a skip and a beat, and drove the sharp point of her long sword into the upper part of his arm, just below the spot where the leaves of the *lorica segmentata* stopped. The point ripped into meat and glanced off bone, and the soldier gave a muffled cry of despair and pain as the shield dropped out of his hand; the Boise type were held by a central grip, not loops with a forearm thrust through.

Two more lunges drove him back towards the Thurston family as the point flickered in faster than thought. He still had his short sword, but the *gladius* was not meant for fencing. As he felt the family at his back the soldier suddenly threw the sword at her and turned, grabbing Shawonda Thurston in his arms and wrestling her around by main force, putting his back between her and the blades of the attackers he thought menaced them for one last sacrificial moment.

Ritva ducked and batted the blade aside with her buckler, a hard bang and ring of metal; a whirling two-pound Frisbee of edged metal thrown by a strong man was not something to be taken lightly. Her body was already moving forward, feet positioning for the lunge that would slam her point into the back of the soldier's neck above the edge of his *lorica*. A sweet inevitability of motion, truth in bone and nerve and metal—

Shawonda Thurston's desperate face was looking over his metal-clad shoulder, eyes enormous. She wrapped her arms around his neck in a convulsive movement, her head jammed into his shoulder.

"No!" she screamed. "Don't! Don't!"

Ritva's battle-trance broke at the desperate appeal. She diverted the killing lunge upward with a wrenching effort, and her body slammed into the young man's back and bounced off it; he was hard-braced, and the combined weight of him and his armor and the girl were twice her mass. The soldier and Shawonda stumbled backward without falling, but they were close to it.

Ritva moved again, but this time she reversed the weapon. The fishtail pommel of her long sword had an outer rim like the edge of a blunt chisel. She struck with it against the young man's head, behind the ear. He didn't go absolutely limp; you couldn't hit someone in the head that hard in a combat situation and be sure you weren't killing them. He did lose all interest in everything but lying still and hurting as the shock rattled his brain in its fluid casing. Shawonda released him and stared at his body lying at her feet.

"He'll live," Ritva said, and shook her with a push of buckler on shoulder. "Pull yourself together, girl!"

Shawonda did; she took a couple of sobbing breaths and then crouched to pull the wound pack from the soldier's belt. She ripped the pad open with her teeth and strapped it against the wound in his left arm with a swiftness that showed she'd taken first-aid courses.

"He was nice," she said, with tears tracking down her face and diluting the red spatters that flecked it. "He talked to me when his sergeant wasn't there."

Then she stumbled back to her mother, wiping her hands on her skirt. The older woman put an arm around her and hugged both her daughters to her body, nodding over them at the Dúnedain.

Ritva spared time for one sharp nod back, then looked down at the soldier for an instant. Her lips quirked, and she dropped back into *Edhellen*: "You are one *lucky* son of a bitch. You really got a triple return tripled on chatting her up like that!"

The screams had cut off, except for young Lawrence Jr.'s, and his mother was soothing him; you could hear the sharp hoarse panting breaths of the survivors, and moaning and whimpering from the hurt. The rest of the raiding party came up. She did a quick scan; ten of the Mormons were dead, three of the Rangers, and others were having wounds dressed. The soldiers of the Sixth hadn't gone down easily, surprise and numbers and bad ground or no.

One of the Dúnedain was carried between two guerillas, and another was applying pressure to a pad. There wasn't much point from the look of it; that deep a stab wound up under the short ribs made with enough force to penetrate mail would probably be fatal even if it hadn't nicked a lung, and there was blood on her lips as well. It was Condis, whom Ritva had known a little and rather liked, even if she was very earnest. Now the knowledge of death was in her dark eyes, and her face was rigid with the strain of not screaming.

Astrid came over as they set her down, looked at the wound and up at the Mormon holding the bandage. He shook his head very slightly.

"Hiril," Condis mumbled, struggling not to cough. "Lady. Send . . . me to Mandos. Please, you."

"Are you sure, brave one?"

A nod, then a grimace and: *"Nidh, naneth, nidh!"*

Ritva swallowed. That was: *It hurts, mother, it hurts!* Sometimes there was only one last gift to give a friend.

Astrid went quickly to one knee. Her left hand cradled the girl's head to position it, and she bent to kiss her gently on the forehead despite the spray of blood coughed into her face. The motion hid the sweep of her hand as she drew a long slender knife from her right boot, and it moved in a swift precise thrust. Then she kissed the still form's forehead again, closed the staring eyes and stood, wiping a sleeve over her face to clear her eyes and sliding her knife and sword carefully through the crook of her elbow to clean them before she sheathed the steel. A friend laid Condis' sword on her body and folded her hands on the hilt.

"Go in peace, Bride of Valor," Astrid said; that was what *Con* and *dis* meant. "Wait for us, in the silent halls of the Uttermost West. It will not be long."

Then she raised her head. Members of the raiding party were already rushing past her towards the stairs, with bundles of arrows and glass globes full of clingfire. A dull ringing sounded where a padlock was being pounded off a door by a sledge; the upper stories of this building were kept locked as storage. Immediately afterwards there was a rushing thunder of boots on metal treads.

Ritva's eyes went up too. The flat roof above would be either the platform for escape, or the last place she would ever see.

"Tolo a nin," Astrid said. *"Gwaenc!"*

Ritva translated. "Come with me. Let's go!"

Martin Thurston looked up as he rode through Boise's gate. The signal heliograph on the northwesternmost of the four towers was snapping, repeating a message as a request for clarification. The gathering clouds made it dim, thunderheads towering from black bases up to cream-white and then turned crimson by the westering sun. Something within him would have noticed the beauty of it once, if only in passing.

Nothing is nothing nothing now. Bits and bits that flake off and spin down and down and nothing is nothing and that is very good.

The signal was faint, not enough sunlight striking the mirrors, but then someone touched off the limelight. High above, hydrogen and oxygen and wood alcohol sprayed out of nozzles onto a stick of pure quicklime. A few seconds, and the light blinked brightly again. Martin frowned. He knew Morse as well as he read English, and the message was being sent in the clear; the identification number was a relay station well north of the city. And . . .

"Blimp?" someone said. "There *aren't* any blimps."

"There is the *Curtis LeMay*," Martin said.

"But that flying white elephant and all its gear were decommissioned and broken up and sold for scrap after Wendell!"

"Perhaps not," Thurston said.

He could feel things *moving* in his mind. Like fish under water, or worms in earth. Some part of him was astonished at the detached curiosity of the other part as it considered the sensation.

"Things were confused just then. Paperwork could have been misfiled by traitors within our ranks. Message, maximum priority, all weapons emplacements on wall and citadel. Fire on the blimp. Incendiary rounds authorized. Category A mission rules of engagement, execute immediately."

Another man grunted. *Category A* meant *ignore collateral damage*.

A panting messenger approached, letting his bicycle

426   S. M. STIRLING

fall. A Natpol, wheezing and red faced. Shields blocked his way as he bent over, holding himself and gasping.

"Sir!" he shouted, over the ten yards. "Sir, we have a situation!"

"Let him through," Martin said.

They did, though two *pila*-points touched the back of his neck. By then he had his breath back, a little.

"Mr. President, there's an incident at Aladdin's Emporium. Sir, your wife was . . . is there, with your son and mother and sisters. Sir, it's enemy spec-ops forces and Mormon terrorists. They appear to have hostages, sir. Your family."

Part of the sweat on the man's face was sheer terror. Martin could feel the rage that *would* have flowed through him, even taste it, something like sucking on rusty iron. But the emotion chased itself around in a circle, like a hamster on a wheel at the other end of a reversed telescope. There if he needed it, but not really part of him.

"Nothing," he said.

Everyone was looking at him. He could *use* the responses that might-have-been.

"Nothing can be gained by panic," he went on; it was what he *would* have said.

"Centurion Leiston, another maximum priority message. Launch gliders from all fields within reach."

The man was in his late twenties, one of Martin's inner circle; he looked up at the weather, calculated the risks, and nodded brusquely before dictating quickly to messengers who dashed off at the run. The ruler of Boise went on: "That blimp is not to escape under any circumstances. Category A rules of engagement. *Do it.*"

He turned his head. "Legate Koburg. The first auxilia of light infantry, I want some missile troops. And the rest of the Sixth."

Martin drew his saber. "Sixth Battalion. *Follow me!*"

The men had heard the Natpol's news. They roared their anger as they swung in behind his horse and began to double-time down the pavement in a slamming unison. Thunder flickered across the northern horizon, no louder than their feet.

"We'll hold them as long as we can," Nystrup said. "They can't get at us more than two or three at a time in the stairwells. As man is, God was; as God is, so we shall be. Get going! Use what we've done. Make it count."

Astrid raised her sword into a salute, and turned. The Rangers followed her, each giving an instant to the same gesture. Ritva leaned against the stairwell wall for a moment after they had trotted upward for a while, wheezing. Even the light armor of her mail-lined jerkin felt like iron bands around her chest for a moment. There was nothing on Arda that drained you like fighting. Not practice, not the hardest labor, nothing. After the clear madness was past you paid for what you'd done to yourself.

"You OK?" Ian asked in a throaty rasp, the sort of voice you got when you'd been screaming war cries for a while.

His had been: *Maintain the Right!*

"Sure," she said, taking another deep breath. "Just reaction. I've got my friends with me, what more do I need?"

They pushed up the last stretch of stairwell and out onto the flat roof with its rusted ventilators. The air was colder than she'd expected on an August evening, cold and with a feeling of chill beneath that. Black clouds were piling up above. Dúnedain *ohtar* had lit green smoke flares at each corner of the roof and then those of them still hale knelt behind the low coping at the edge, bundles of arrows at hand. Ritva and Ian did likewise; he looked down and murmured: "High enough."

They looked at each other gravely; that meant high enough for a final leap, if worse came to worst. Then motion caught her eye.

"Troops here!" she shouted, and it was echoed moments later from all four sides of the building.

The Boise soldiers were moderate-sized dolls from four tall stories up; she could hear voices and make out words when someone shouted. They seemed to be crossbowmen in mail shirts mostly, arriving first on bicycles and then stacking them and taking up firing positions; then regular infantry, hundreds of them, tramping at the double. *That* drowned out the voices, until they came to a halt with an earthquake stamp.

An officer stood forth, and raised a speaking-trumpet to his mouth.

"Terrorists!" the amplified voice blared. "You are surrounded by overwhelming force! There is no escape! Surrender!"

Ritva grinned. Ian chuckled. "There's a flaw in his logic," the man from Drumheller said.

She raised her face and shouted back to point it out: "If you're so overwhelming, *yrch*, come up and *make* us surrender!"

From the stir and growl along the serried ranks of eagle-and-thunderbolt shields, they wanted to do just that. Astrid came up behind the pair, with the Thurstons. The growl grew louder.

"There's blood on the face of the President's sister!" the officer shouted, and there was genuine rage in his voice. "We demand she be given medical attention immediately, or you'll be a week dying!"

Astrid had a speaking-trumpet of her own; it had been a good bet that they'd need one at some point in this mission.

"It isn't her blood, good sir," she said, loud but not shouting. "Fighting is messy."

She handed her canteen to Cecile Thurston, who poured water on a handkerchief and wiped her daughter's face; that had the added virtue of getting rid of the drying tear-tracks.

"I'm fine, see?" the girl called. "We're all OK, Mom and Janie and little Lawrence. And Juliet," she added as an afterthought.

Ritva and Ian grinned at each other; there wasn't much love lost there. The girl looked as if she would go on, but Astrid murmured softly to her: "No, not yet. Too risky."

Ritva felt a chill. That was the measure of Martin Thurston's damnation; he'd staged his coup to make his son heir to power, and now there was a real risk he would order his family silenced to *protect* that power.

And there was Martin Thurston himself, standing impassively with his red-white-and-blue crested helmet under one arm and his strong handsome dark face turned upward. Ritva's string-fingers itched; it was so tempting to try to pick him off . . . win half the war at a stroke . . .

No. The Cutters have their luck too. Those men by him could put their shields over him in half a second.

He stretched out a hand and the officer put the speaking-trumpet into it. The sky was mostly overcast now; Ritva smelled damp dust, and felt a single cold drop flick her cheekbone. That made her suddenly aware of her own thirst. While she was drinking the tepid but infinitely delicious water from her own canteen, Eilir came up and Signed, cautiously turning her back so that nobody below could see. ASL was fairly common among Mackenzies and all Dúnedain knew it, but that wasn't to say someone down there might not have some knowledge of the visual language.

The blimp should have launched some time ago. We have forty-five minutes until rendezvous, but that was the conservative still-air estimate, before the wind picked up so much. It'll be earlier now. No way of knowing exactly how much.

Astrid nodded and turned her eyes back to the street. Martin Thurston spoke; there was something about his voice that put Ritva's teeth on edge, unless that was just her own knowledge of the man coloring perception.

"What do you demand for the return of my family unharmed?" he said, iron in his tone.

"Nothing!" Astrid called back, joy bubbling in hers but sternly controlled.

Yup, this is definitely a high point for Aunt Astrid. She really lives for this stuff. It is *scary, I mean, I'm getting a rush about it now and then but I'm only doing it because it really needs to be done and you might as well enjoy an adventure if you're going to do it anyway, being glum doesn't help anything. Hunting's as much rush as I really want, or riding a fast horse, or a glider or a sailboat, or sparring, or sex and wine and listening to poetry. But with Auntie, it's like she's reading it in the Histories* at the same time *that she's doing it and we're Lúthien going into Angbad to rescue Beren. She'll make a really cranky old lady someday.*

Astrid went on: "We are here to rescue these ladies and their children, not to harm them. We will not threaten or hurt them, nor shield behind them, under any circumstances whatsoever, though it cost our lives."

Ritva shivered. There was a mad splendor to Astrid Loring-Larsson at that moment, as wisps of her pale hair floated around her blood-spattered face and her moon-shot eyes looked at something beyond the world of common day. Something that frightened you and made you long for it at the same time. It was the feeling you got when the sun went down and for a moment the clouds turned into a golden unknown archipelago of islands in the sky, along a glittering sea road to the infinite.

"How do you intend to keep them, then?" Martin asked.

"By our swords, our courage, and our luck," Astrid said. *"Artos and Montival!"*

The General-President handed the trumpet back to his retainer, turned on his heel and walked towards the building. Men followed him, and then Ritva couldn't see them at all.

Martin looked around the sidewalk, shattered glass crunching under his boots, then walked into the room. Someone had put up a couple of bright lanterns, and the light flickered over bodies and blood and jewels; the air was rank with the coppery stink that happened when men bled out. The darker dung heap stinks weren't as strong; when armored men fought you didn't often get cut-open bellies. The killing wounds were usually to the head and neck and limbs, or deep narrow stabs. He looked at the arrows scattered around or standing in the dead; men were loading the fallen and a few living wounded onto stretchers.

"About sixty of the enemy, give or take half a dozen," he said, an intent look on his brown face. "And they're down about a quarter of that, counting the badly wounded they'll have."

The Natpol on the scene shot him a glance of respect for the quick analysis.

"Yes, Mr. President, that's my estimate. We caught one of the staff—the others are scattered, we're contacting them as we can—and she said *dozens and dozens.* You know how civilians are, I thought she might be exaggerating."

He nodded his head to a sobbing older woman who was sitting in a chair, talking and wiping at her eyes and nose with a handkerchief while two of the police took notes.

Martin went on absently: "Sixty or so from the wagons, and the size of the escort of fake infantry that others mentioned, and the way they overran eighty men of the Sixth so quickly, even with the advantage of surprise. Having surprise is a force multiplier but there are limits."

"I've got the men who tried to rush the staircase, sir. It, ah, didn't turn out well."

Another stretcher; the Natpol on it had an arrow in one shoulder, and a bandage around it. The bleeding wasn't very bad, and it made more sense to get him to a hospital here in the city than to try to extract it in the field. The policeman stopped cursing the enemy and the pain when he saw who was standing over him.

"Report," Martin said.

"Sir, as soon as they evacuated the ground floor my patrol tried to push up the stairs. It's a stairwell built around a solid rectangular core and they're barricading the stairs two times per flight, at least. They've got bows and lots of arrows and *pila* as well. You have to go uphill at them . . . sir, we tried."

"Carry on," Martin said to the stretcher-bearers.

The Natpol officer began an apology. Martin cut off the useless blather with a motion of his hand.

"Your men are lightly equipped and mostly past prime fighting age," he said. "Don't waste my time. Now, you got at least one of the staff, that woman there, and she was here all through the attack, correct?"

"Yes sir. But she's not very coherent. Shock, I think."

Martin walked over to the witness. "Ma'am," he said. *Something* crept into his voice. Her tears stopped, and she stared at him with her mouth a little open, the pupils of her eyes expanding as they met his.

"How many staircases?" he asked.

"One, Mr. President. There was another one but it was salvaged and the floors sealed. The one we use, it's over there."

She pointed. He nodded and went on: "The elevator shaft?"

Another pointing gesture. "It was sealed off."

"You think there were how many of the terrorists?"

"It seemed like a lot but"—her face went blank for a moment, as if her brain was accessing information without the personality getting in the way—"fifty or sixty or a few more."

"Some of them were Mormons?"

"Most of them, sir. I think. The ones in American uniforms. They were shouting *Arise, ye Saints,* I know Mormons do that. It was . . . it was all so fast, and there was so much noise and then the blood, blood everywhere, and the ladies were screaming and I didn't know what to do—"

"Thank you."

He turned to Koburn, the legate of the Sixth, as she began to sob again.

"Get the elevator shaft open."

"Sir, the cables will be gone, it'll be bare."

Wire cable was prime salvage, with a dozen high-priority uses. It was absolutely certain that they would have been stripped from a building inside the city wall decades ago.

"And it would be a deathtrap if they caught on."

"It might be useful anyway, if they don't think of it or don't have enough men to guard against low-probability risks. The stairs are going to be a deathtrap for sure. Do it, the auxiliaries have the gear needed. Fall the men in."

More and more files of the Sixth had been coming in behind him. Some of them had been roughly shoving things out of the way to clear space, including the bodies of the enemy. Martin walked over to one, a woman, young and dark, and slighter than he'd have thought passable for rough work. The pommel of her sword rested at the base of her throat, with her hands crossed on the hilt and the blade point-down along her body, like the sculpted image of a Crusader on an ancient tomb. The outfit was all matte black, except for the silver tree and stars and crown on the front of a leather jerkin whose rivets showed it was lined with mail; they'd evidently switched to full uniform for this, bravado or some sense of the rules or both. The wound in her side would have killed her, but someone had hurried the process along. Someone with a good eye, a strong wrist and a knowledge of anatomy.

"Dúnedain, definitely," he said, using a toe to point to the symbol.

"The woot-woots who think they're elves?"

"They think they're Numenoreans, in fact. Friends of the elves."

"Ah, the Arrowshirt son of Arrowroot bunch with the invisible companions. Totally fucking insane."

"It makes as much sense as most myths and they don't have to come up with an explanation of why they're not immortal. And consider what they just pulled off right under our noses."

He turned to the ranked mass filling the great room. "Men of the Sixth Battalion!" he called.

They braced to attention; there was a thunder-crack sound as they all rammed the butts of their *pila* down on the stone floor.

"My family's held hostage on the roof, and we can't assault the roof directly because we can't use fire support. The only other way up is the staircase and it's held by fanatical terrorists. Clearing it's going to be ugly, and I can't lead you in person, that would be dereliction of duty. I won't order anyone to go where I'm not going. All volunteers, take a step forward."

There was a second for men to sense the comrades on either side, and the entire unit paced to the front and snapped to a halt again. Again emotion stirred; it would have been an iron pride, a few months ago. Now it flopped somewhere in the emptiness of his skull, nothing in nothing in nothing, like a dying fish in the vacuum of the Moon.

"And I wish I *could* come with you."

That was even true; some part of him wanted very much to die. That was out of the question just now if it could be avoided.

"Attack by files. Rotate every five minutes; the enemy can't face relays of fresh men. Legate, lead your troops!"

"We're going to make it," Ian said.

"I mean, probably! If nothing goes wrong!" he added frantically, as Ritva and several Dúnedain spat or made the sign of the Horns or other gestures against ill luck.

The rattle-bang-thump sound of combat was continuous from the doors of the stairwell; they'd barricaded the exit with everything they could find, but the sound of sword-blades and the flat snap of bowstrings sound, the battle cries and the screams of pain . . . they were all getting closer. Ritva didn't like to think of what it must be like in there, fighting in the near dark.

And out of the north, a long orca-shape was coming. Still a tiny dot, but unmistakable; in this Fifth Age of the world, what else flew like that?

Well, Windlords and dragons. But we don't have those. At least not yet, I suppose anything's possible. I wouldn't have believed the Sword of the Lady if I hadn't seen it or what happened on Nantucket if I hadn't been there.

She pulled a monocular out of its case on her belt and looked. The ship of the air was just as she remembered it, three hundred feet of blunt-pointed teardrop with cruciform stabilizer fins, and an aluminum-truss keel along the bottom anchoring a spiderweb net of light cables that distributed its weight over the great gasbag. The gondola was slung beneath like a stylized Viking longboat sans dragon's head; it was taut fabric over an aluminum frame as well, with the captain's post and wheel at the front and a propeller and rudder at the rear. You couldn't see it from here, but the slender hull held twelve units made from recliner cycles on each side of the central walkway to power the propeller shaft.

That was the power source. Unfortunately it was a rather feeble one, and the stiff wind was far more than it could handle. That was why Lawrence Thurston hadn't built more of them. *Curtis LeMay* was extremely useful in a dead calm, and nearly helpless as an ordinary balloon in anything else. Gliders had far lower payload and endurance, but you really *could* steer them in most weathers.

"One pass," she said. "And that's *it*. They can't turn back against the wind, just steer a little across it . . . yes, they've spotted our smoke flares."

The great shape became more nearly circular as the nose turned towards this building.

"Why are they coming in so low?" Ian asked.

"Something . . . about conserving ballast and gas, Hanks said," Ritva said; she wasn't sure what those meant. "I didn't follow it but evidently if they go up and down they eventually run out and wouldn't be able to go up and down anymore . . . oh, *trastad*!"

The towers on the northern wall were shooting at the blimp. Smoke and yellow flame trailed from some of the catapults; globes of napalm wrapped in burning cord fuse. One struck . . . and then bounced away from the soft resilient surface of the gasbag, to trail down into the city and splash into a spot of scarlet. She thought she saw someone crawling up the netting and spraying something; then the airship pitched sideways for a moment and headed back towards them.

"Eyes on the streets!" John Hordle shouted in his Hampshire-yokel version of Sindarin, as everyone turned to look. "You dim thick gits *want* a scaling ladder up yor bum?"

Ritva was *supposed* to be looking north, but she did a quick check to make sure that no storming parties were forming up. The enemy couldn't shoot up at them; that would endanger their leader's family. And if the Dúnedain were alert, they could shoot *down* and throw globes of fire. But the other side might think it worthwhile, if they were pushed.

"They're a little west of where they should be," Ian said quietly.

The shark shape of the *Curtis LeMay* grew closer; probably they were only pedaling to keep steerage on her. Suddenly a dozen cords dropped down, whipping in the wind.

"*Rhaich,*" Ritva said dully.

Will anyone remember our heroic last stand? Or will we be just a footnote in a report on terrorist attacks?

The airship came on, rushing, suddenly huge. It would recede just as quickly, and just a bit too far to the westward despite the rudder and the frantic pedaling that drove the propeller. The wind was blowing harder . . .

John Hordle was up and across, running with a speed astonishing in a man seven inches over six feet and broad enough to seem squat. One of the tethering ropes was blowing beyond the northwest corner of the building, just out of reach. John reached the corner and *leapt* out into space.

He disappeared bellowing beyond the edge of the roof. Ritva felt her mouth drop open and her eyes go wide; Ian was goggling too, and a couple of other people looked just the same. The huge bulk of the airship bobbled in flight, its tail starting to pivot inward a little; it made you realize how light and fragile it was, not the solid sky-filling thing it seemed—

"Rhaaaaich!" she screamed.

What John Hordle was trying to do suddenly flashed into her mind, not a chain of logic but something you saw in an instant blaze of light. And what *she* had to do was equally obvious.

It involved jumping off a four-story building.

She was up and running before Ian's question had time to get started. The thought of dropping her sword belt or quiver was rejected as she went, building speed; the heavier she was for this the better and there was not a fractional second to spare.

Unless a couple of extra pounds makes me miss and go crunch! *Rhaich! Rhaich! Tulkas the Mighty, give John strength! Nessa, Dancer of Stars, give my feet wings! Dulu! Help, help! Mom!*

Her feet hit the coping and she was soaring out over emptiness, only the thin-thread line ahead of her. Her gloved hands reached, grabbed for knotted rope, touched, slipped, she was scrabbling downward, falling . . .

An ape-long arm snagged at her and caught in her sword belt for an instant. That gave her time to clamp on with arms and legs, and a crazed memory of scrambling up his form as a child and swinging on his arms as if they were the tree limbs they resembled went through the memory that remained in muscle and nerve. A ham-broad hand boosted her up, and she stood on his shoulders and clamped her hands on the rough surface of the rope. A shock went through it, and she looked up to see Astrid clinging above her, legs neatly wrapped around the cable and one hand waving back at the roof.

"Show-off!" Ritva screamed. "Sometimes I just *hate* you, Auntie!"

The nose of the *Curtis LeMay* was down at a thirty-degree angle. It was still moving southward at a brisk clip, but it was also pivoting around the weight attached to the prow of the gondola, and the gondola was under the forward quarter of the gasbag. A three-hundred-foot length covered a lot of ground when it pivoted; the dangling lines swept across the roof, and frantic hands made them fast to old rusted stanchions and framework even as they were dragged across the gravel and crumbling asphalt. The blimp heeled far over as its broadside caught the wind, but the line to which Ritva clung swung back towards the building.

"—innocent!" Martin heard, in his mother's voice. "Frederick is innocent! Martin killed his father to seize power! Frederick sent these people to rescue us, and we're going willingly. Martin is a traitor who betrayed

America and killed my husband. Cast him off, cast him down!"

The scaling ladders up the inside of the elevator shaft had chain sides and light metal batons for rungs. They'd fastened them to whatever projected, or in a couple of instances driven pitons into the concrete; the light infantry unit had mountaineering equipment in their packs. They'd simply ignored his attempts to lead them up the dark vertical rectangle.

Now he ignored them, kicking free of a clutching hand to swing across and clamp a hand on the ledge of the uppermost opening, then two, then chin himself and climb up. The first troops through had pried the rust-bound elevator doors open with swords and boots; a broken *gladius* rested there. He pushed his way through the little antechamber, and out on the roof where a double file of crossbowmen waited, kneeling and standing with their weapons leveled.

The *Curtis LeMay* was tethered at nose and tail to the eastern side of the building, shuddering in the wind. The gusts of rain made a tattoo on its fabric, unfortunately not enough to drown the speaking-trumpet from the gondola.

"It's true!"

That was his wife's voice. Rage flowed through him, cold as treacle, like living clouds drifting in a universe without stars.

"I heard him confess it. He threatened to kill me if I talked!"

The shouts were directed down at the street, but they were perfectly audible on the rooftop as well. The men were *listening*. And they were intimidated by the huge bulk that towered over them, paralyzed into a perfectly receptive frame of mind. Calculations of the least-bad course of action flowed through him, pinning inevitability.

"Shoot," he said, loud but not forced. "Both ranks, fire at the gondola. *Now!*"

Silence stretched for a moment. Heads turned to look at him, eyes wide with horror under the rims of their helmets.

A centurion spoke, his voice shaking: "Sir, it's your *family*. Your *son* is on board there!"

"I said shoot! I'll have anyone who refuses executed for cowardice in the face of the enemy!"

He grabbed a crossbow and backhanded the man away when he tried to cling to it. Snuggle the weapon into his shoulder, breath in, breath out, hold it halfway and squeeze at the trigger, with the shouting face and the blowing blond hair in the aperture of the sights—

Tung.

The butt punched at him and the bolt whipped out. Even as it did, something covered Juliet, taking her out of the sights. Instants later the cables were released. Weights fell from the keel of the gondola, the emergency ballast, plummeting down into the street. The airship jerked upward as if wrenched by an invisible hand, dwindling southward under a sky dark with thunder. A few bolts fell back, and Martin stood impassive, with the rain sluicing down his face like tears.

CHAPTER FIFTEEN

COUNTY OF THE EASTERMARK
CHARTERED CITY OF WALLA WALLA
PORTLAND PROTECTIVE ASSOCIATION
(FORMERLY EASTERN WASHINGTON)
HIGH KINGDOM OF MONTIVAL
(FORMERLY WESTERN NORTH AMERICA)
AUGUST 23, CHANGE YEAR 25/2023 AD

G rand Constable Tiphaine d'Ath nodded and looked at her watch once more, eyes narrowing with calculation as her mind returned to business after the brief family digressions:

"Now he *is* due. Let's see if we can get this crowd of cow-country yokels organized. The Count should be—"

A harsh chorus of trumpets from the city's gate-towers made her look up.

"Speak of the Devil and—" Rigobert murmured.

The north gate of the city was open, though heavily guarded. Wagons were pouring in over the patched, faded asphalt, mostly loaded with grain and produce; livestock on the hoof added its own pungencies. The crossbowmen were diverting refugees who couldn't work or fight or who had young children in tow, off to holding camps where they'd be shuttled east, and sometimes that required explanations. Occasionally of the sort that you administered via a smack with the metal-shod butt of the weapon, but not too many. Even the peasants knew how highly relative the safety of Walla Walla was and were unwillingly willing to see their most vulnerable moved farther from the path of the invasion.

"—and de Aguirre appears," Tiphaine finished.

The brassy scream came again from the gatehouse, and a file of foot soldiers double-timed out to make a lane by holding their pole arms horizontally and pushing. Everyone who could moved off the double-lane roadway. The lord of Walla Walla rode out from under the teeth of the portcullis and across the drawbridge in a rumbling drumbeat of hooves, threading his way through with a mercifully small entourage of household men-at-arms and hangers-on. They spurred over to the command group by the railway siding at a round canter and reined in a respectful fifteen paces away before they dismounted.

Spraying dust and gravel on someone afoot was bad manners.

Felipe de Aguirre Smith, the current Baron Walla Walla and Count Palatine of the Eastermark, was in his early twenties. His father had been one of Norman Arminger's recruits from the rougher side of society. A gangbanger, in fact, what the euphemistic family histories churned out by tame troubadours and the College of Heralds called a *freelance man-at-arms*—but he'd adjusted well.

It had helped that he was more than intelligent enough to realize that when you *were* the government you sheared the sheep rather than skinning it; Norman hadn't promoted many *stupid* hard cases to high positions and those few hadn't lived long enough to breed for the most part, given the high turnover in those days. And he'd married a prominent local woman too, named Smith of course, which had eased matters considerably. Like others in their position they'd both taken up Society customs, at first to curry Norman's favor and then with a convert's zeal. The world right after the Change had been gruesome enough that pretending the previous eight hundred years hadn't happened or didn't matter had real and broad-based appeal.

The first Count had also died in the early stages of this war, during the battle of Pendleton nearly two years ago. She had known his son slightly for years on a social basis, since the Association's higher nobility wasn't all that large, and dealt with him fairly often since in her professional capacity. Tiphaine's private judgment was that he was quite good as a knight, and at least competent as a commander. But a bit of a worrywart and inclined to dither while trying to cover every possible contingency, when the weight of overall responsibility came crashing down on his shoulders. Which was unfortunate, since even a bad decision was usually better than no decision at all.

So don't put him in situations where he has to make strategic decisions at the quickstep, she thought. *He's fine at tactics and has plenty of experienced advisers on his staff. Just point him in the right direction and tell him what to do and he'll keep trying his best until the ax hits where the chicken gets it. And his vassals respect him, which is the important thing.*

Count Felipe swung down from his courser, a fine sixteen-hand black. He was in civilian dress but the daywear version of it, what a nobleman wore when he was out hunting or traveling in warm weather; turned-down thigh boots with the golden spurs of knighthood on the heels, tight doeskin riding breeches, baggy-sleeved linen shirt beneath long T-tunic with his arms on an embroidered shield, cinched by a broad sword belt of studded and tooled leather and a round chaperon hat. A little taller than Tiphaine, and with something of the same leopard build, male version. His square face was clean-shaven but with pale olive skin and the blue jowl of a man who needed the razor often, his eyes dark brown with green flecks, his thick bowl-cut hair a black so complete it had blue highlights.

"My lady Grand Constable," he said, sweeping off his hat and making a bow.

That was tactful. As a Count, he greatly outranked her status as a mere baron, albeit she was a tenant-in-chief like him rather than the vassal of some higher nobleman; but as Grand Constable she had the pull on *him*, particularly since the *arrière-ban* had been called and martial law declared.

"My lord Count," she said, matching the gesture with a microscopically lesser bow, which was tactful but firm; then they shook hands.

"And my lord de Stafford," de Aguirre said.

This time the bows exchanged matched; a Marchwarden and the Count Palatine of the Eastermark were precisely equivalent, though one title was hereditary and the other wasn't.

"It's extremely good to see you here, my lady . . . and the army you brought, frankly. If you and my lord the Marchwarden could accompany me to the City Palace, we've arranged a dinner."

At her expression he smiled, looking tired and dogged. "A working dinner, not a banquet, my lady. No jugglers or musicians. We've been . . . very busy. I've invited those most crucial to the defense of the city and County."

She nodded. "By all means, my lord. That would save considerable time, in fact; I'd planned on calling you and your chief vassals together for something similar tomorrow."

He turned to de Stafford. "Baron Tucannon arrived yesterday and has been giving me a lively account of your doings, my lord."

"The regard is mutual, my lord. A fine commander and true knight."

De Aguirre turned back to Tiphaine: "And if it won't offend your well-known martial hardihood, my lady, one night in a place with hot water and soft beds might provide a pleasant memory in the coming campaign."

This time she smiled, at least with her eyes. "By all means, my lord Count. Hardship when necessary, but not necessarily hardship."

That startled a laugh out of him, as squires brought up their horses; also coursers, not the precious destriers they rode into a formal battle.

The only thing lacking will be Delia. But I have to set an example and she's not mobile right now anyway. And she is at least far, far west of here and right next to a castle.

She turned her head to Rigobert as they rode under the gate, after the usual glance most people made at the barred fangs of the welded-steel portcullis above. The groin-arched tunnel stretched ahead, loud with the metallic echo of horseshoes on asphalt; overhead just beyond the reach of a mounted man's lance the grillwork of the murder-holes gleamed, where men waited with cocked crossbows and cauldrons of hot oil and hoses that could spray napalm.

"Barony Tucannon," Tiphaine said, calling up the files in her head, mostly from last year's edition of:

Fiefs of the Portland Protective Association: Tenants In Chief, Vassals, Vavasours and Fiefs-minor in Sergeantry.

After a moment she went on: "Tucannon . . . That's Maugis de Grimmond, isn't it? Youngish, red hair, ears like a bat. Vassal of the Count, rights of Low, Middle and

High Justice, thirty-six thousand acres, twelve manors, held on standard service terms for fifty men-at-arms, fifty light cavalry, spearmen and crossbowmen in proportion and the mesne dues and public service things, and the usual forest rights in the Blue Mountains . . . and he has that beautifully placed castle. He's not much at Court though he did the Battle Staff course at the University in your bailiwick, I've only met him a few times in passing. Is he capable?"

"Very," de Stafford said. "Wasted rusticating in that arse-end of nowhere barony, I'd say, but he likes it there. That and his family are all he really cares about. He's been a great help so far, though. And could be more of one, if things turn out as badly as we expect. Quite crucial, in fact."

COUNTY OF THE EASTERMARK
BARONY OF TUCANNON
MANOR OF GRIMMOND-ON-THE-WOLD
(FORMERLY SOUTHEASTERN WASHINGTON STATE)
PORTLAND PROTECTIVE ASSOCIATION
HIGH KINGDOM OF MONTIVAL
(FORMERLY WESTERN NORTH AMERICA)
AUGUST 19, CHANGE YEAR 25/2023 AD

Ingolf Vogeler woke, yawned, stretched comfortably and for a moment just enjoyed feeling clean and reasonably well rested between linen sheets and snuggled close to his wife. Then another knock came on the door and he realized the first one had woken him up.

He was wearing drawers and Mary was in a long shirt that would do for a shift. From what he'd seen, the Association folk were about as modest about skin as his own people . . . which wasn't something you could just assume when you traveled far. Places had started out different before the Change and gotten more so, fast, when the world closed in again and each area was isolated from the other's ideas and customs. And some were left to stew in whatever lunacy had bubbled to the top when a charismatic madman took charge. He'd seen places where you'd get attacked for taking off your shirt—men would.

"Come in," he said.

The door opened and a servant girl came through with a tray that held a steaming pot of something aromatic. Probably not coffee or real tea this far from the coast, and not chicory either from the smell; after a moment he identified it as peppermint tea. A moment after that he really looked at the shadows cast through the window.

"Holy . . . holy things, what time is it?"

The servant girl smiled. "It's eleven of the clock, my lord," she said. "Lord de Grimmond said that we should let you sleep, you'd been fighting for us and then working hard with the troops and the wounded late into the night."

She was unremarkable in every respect, and dressed in a plain good outfit of a short knee-length tunic over a long ankle-length one, with a shirtlike shift underneath and a kerchief on her head and stout shoes. The smile was welcome, though; late though it had been, everyone in the little town of Grimmond-on-the-Wold had turned out to help with the wounded by torch and lantern light, and they'd pitched in for the Richlanders and Sioux just as hard as they had for their own folk. It was nice to be a valued ally, even if it was mainly because they were scared spitless at what was coming at them.

I would be too. Hell, I am scared. I was a prisoner in Corwin, even if I don't remember all of it—and don't want to. I know what the Cutters are, and Boise's in bed with them. Not so sure about God being the way Mom thought, but the Devil? You betcha.

"Thank you," he said, accepting the polished wooden tray.

Mary sat up and murmured thanks as well, reaching for a cup.

"Luncheon will be in an hour, my lord, my lady; *en famille*, in the gazebo court. Lord de Grimmond said to tell you that everyone you want to contact immediately will be there."

"Lord de Stafford?"

"He's gone, my lord. He left his regards and said he had to get back to his main force to make sure everything was ready. He didn't say ready for what, my lord."

She bobbed a curtsy and left, with the quick step of someone who has important work waiting.

"What time did we get to bed?" he said, rubbing his face, doing it carefully because of a couple of bruises. "I feel indecent, lying up this late. There's a lot to do."

Mary made an indelicate slurping sound as she sipped the hot tea; he followed suit. The acrid-sweet liquid seemed to clear the cobwebs from his mind, enough for him to notice that there was a bandage on his right forearm, and from the dull ache underneath a couple of stitches, not quite sharp enough to be real pain. It was a familiar feeling, and a familiar place—that was the most vulnerable part of a swordsman's anatomy and he had the white scar lines on his skin to prove it, this would just be one more. You could wear a vambrace, but he'd always thought the minute loss of speed wasn't worth it most of the time.

He worked the fingers, testing the feeling in his arm and the degree of play; nothing serious, and he could use it hard at a pinch, though ideally he'd wait a few days before putting any strain on it.

"When did we go to bed or when did we get to sleep?" Mary asked, working her eyebrows and grinning. "As I recall, you weren't *that* tired. At first."

"Well, a soldier learns to—"

"Sleep and eat and whatever, whenever he can. I *am* a Ranger, darling. Same saying. C'mon, they've got *showers* here. Solar heating system, all the hot water we want on tap."

"Didn't we shower last night?"

"How often do you get the chance? Without waiting for the water to heat, even?"

"Point," he said. "Very definite point. Have to keep this bandage dry somehow, though."

"I'll soap and rinse and dry you again. Thoroughly, very thoroughly. And whatever."

When they came out again, dressed for the day in a clean set of the rough clothing you used when traveling or fighting, the bedding had been stripped from the four-poster and their own kit was on the bare frame, neatly strapped up into their saddle-rolls. Ingolf looked around the room again, this time by daylight. An experienced eye told him that nothing except the double-glazed sash windows was pre-Change; he'd worked for years running a salvager outfit making trips deep into the wildlands to loot the dead cities. It hadn't been that different from his previous job as head of a troop of paid soldiers; in fact, they'd included a lot of the same people.

That lack of old-world goods was a little rare; most places had a mixture, with more new-made as the years went on. The rest of the room was just a big rectangle with pleasantly shaped wooden furniture in the rather twisty PPA Gothic style, armor-stands for their harness and weapons, exposed but smoothly planed and attractively carved beams above, a floor of polished western larch, and a couple of alpaca rugs patterned in vivid geo-metric patterns of black and red and off-white. A fireplace was built into one wall, a closed model with a metal door in its tiled face, empty now with summer. The only fancy touch was a Catholic prie-dieu in a corner, with an image of an armored woman with a halo in the central panel of the triptych facing it.

"St. Joan," Mary said, making a reverence with hands pressed together before her face. "She's their patron here, and a powerful one when you're fighting invaders."

He was still figuring out the Dúnedain attitude to-wards religion. It seemed to include cheerfully stealing everything from anyone; sort of like the Old Religion of Rudi's bunch but with different names. He'd been brought up a conventional but not very intense Catholic himself, and gotten careless about it in his wandering years. Since Nantucket, he'd become increasingly unwill-ing to be skeptical about *anyone's* approach to the super-natural, which caused its own difficulties. He didn't feel comfortable with treating faith as a buffet lunch, either.

He also noticed the windows were deep-seated, confirm-ing his initial impression that the manor was built by ram-ming moist earth down hard between frames and then letting it air-cure, what some called *pisé*. The natural texture of well-made rammed-earth *pisé* was like a coarse porous stone, often with the impress of the framing still visible, but the interior here was smoothly plastered and the outside whitewashed. One of the advantages of the material was that it was no great trouble to make it as thick as you wanted; at this second-story level it was over a yard through. They had fittings for steel shutters, too, and the wall surround on the window wasn't square, it was beveled in. That would let you step up to a slit in the shutter and shoot an arrow or cross-bow bolt through it easily at any angle under full protection.

Uh-huh, he noted. *Wall all around the manor gardens, too. Nothing to a siege train or field catapults, say twelve-pounders, or even just regular troops with assault ladders, but you could put the whole village in here for a while and stand off bandits or a casual raid easy. Rammed earth's not quite as strong as concrete, but it's more than halfway there once it's had time to cure and it's a lot cheaper and easier to come by. Good stuff, as long as you can keep too much water off it.*

They passed more people stripping and bundling and crating things outside, turning what had been a big rambling comfortable house into an empty shell, and dodged a string of eight men with a long rolled-up rug or major tapestry. He found the sight oddly melancholy. One of the crew working at removal was the girl who'd brought them their tea.

"Taking stuff up to the castle?" he said, as she passed with a big basket full of linens.

"Oh, no, my lord. The castle's much too crowded with more important things. This is all going up into the mountains."

The gazebo court turned out to be part of the gardens at the rear of the house, which covered several acres. The gazebo part was a long arched wooden trellis, overgrown with a great sheet of green vine thickly starred with trumpet-shaped crimson flowers; the table was underneath. The rest of the gardens were a spectacular blaze of flower beds and blue oaks, copper beeches and poplars, with the odd stretch of lawn. Terraces and wandering paths paved with basalt blocks stepped down from the higher terrace the house was built on, with water channels running down stone-lined troughs to a swimming pool not far away. The leaves of espaliered fruit trees shimmered green against the whitewashed surface of the perimeter walls, alternating with fragrant deep blue Chinese clematis twined through trellises.

The warm air was heavy with sweet scents, drowsy with humming bees; a flock of birds with light gray bodies and bright yellow bellies and underwings went by, swooping after insects. A terra-cotta fountain of descending bowls tinkled nearby, welcome in this arid heat. Baron Maugis was already at the table, along with an older woman in a dark green cote-hardie and white wimple and lace shoulder-veil who was probably his mother, and a younger one with pale tilted eyes and a slim build, dressed in a riding habit with a divided skirt, who was certainly his wife. She was just handing an infant to a nanny and setting aside a broad hat. Her hair tumbled like a black torrent down her back through a light wimple, hardly more elaborate than a kerchief but bound with silk cords. Two other children were there, a boy of about six guiltily wiping his face with a napkin and a girl half that age sitting on her father's lap.

Mary sighed, and Ingolf nodded. "You know, I could get used to having a place like this," he murmured to her. "They do look all-'round comfy, don't they?"

His wife gave a slight rueful chuckle. "I think you could get the land out of brother Rudi after the war, lover, but I doubt he'd hand you a few thousand people to develop it with, the way the Lord Protector did our host's father. For that matter, there *aren't* big bunches of people around . . . loose . . . anymore. Arminger just culled them out of the ones running from the cities and they were glad to get the chance."

"Well, we can have the kids on our own, when we finally get the time and quiet, and our own homeplace somewhere. Anywhere but a city, eh?"

She nodded agreement with a shudder; both of them

had seen the great cities of the world, Portland and Boise and even distant, mammoth Des Moines. They were country folk to the core and the thought of living all their lives in one of those ant-heaps—Des Moines had over a *hundred thousand* people—was loathsome.

The baron and his lady looked up and rose to make them welcome as the servants led the children away. Mary put hand to heart and bowed.

"Mae govannen," she said. "Well-met, my lord, my ladies."

"Uh . . . hi," Ingolf added. "My lord, my ladies."

"My wife, Lady Helissent de Grimmond, my lord, Your Highness," Maugis said.

Ingolf knew enough to bow and kiss the ladies' hands when they were extended to him palm-down, taking them gently in his. They both started to curtsy to Mary; as the new High King's half sister her status had to be stratospheric, not to mention that her father and mother had been and were respectively the sovereigns of the Bearkillers and her aunt led the Dúnedain.

"Please," Mary said, with a graceful gesture. "I'm just a commander of Dúnedain Rangers for now."

Maugis nodded acknowledgment of the courtesy as she exchanged kisses on the cheek with the women of his family, and bowed over her hand.

"And my lady mother, the dowager Baroness, Lady Roehis de Grimmond."

"Originally Jenny Fassbinder," the older woman said; she was in her sixties but looking very healthy for it, with a worn gentle-looking face but an ironic quirk to her mouth. "A long long time ago."

Helissent gave her a look of fond exasperation and gestured towards a buffet laid out on the side table. "We're not keeping any state today, Lord Vogeler, Lady

Mary. The staff are far too busy, I'm sure you understand."

"Uff da, of course! There's a war on, no need to apologize, my lady."

"Do help yourself. The others will be here soon."

He did, feeling sharp-set as he lifted the anti-fly gauze over the various dishes; he'd done hard work all day yesterday and as far as he could recall dinner had made lunch out of his helmet look like a banquet. There was a ham, and what they called a mutton-ham here, which was a leg of mutton pickled and cured the same way as ordinary ham and surprisingly good; cold fried chicken; some salads; half a dozen types of bread and rolls. And all the fixings, rather like a very good picnic. Mary constructed herself several large sandwiches and filled a plate with the green salad; she had a passion for those.

To his pleasure there was also a decent *potato* salad, creamy with well-made mayonnaise and with flecks of peppers and onion, something which he'd had trouble getting on this side of the continent. Few people outside Richland and its neighbors really seemed to understand what could be done with potatoes.

"Delicious," he said sincerely, when he was back at the table.

There was also a crock of beer; only moderately cold, but quite good, well hopped and nutty. He didn't like the prospect of wine in this heat even if he was sitting in pleasant shade, or this early in the day for that matter. Mary and the Association nobles sipped very slowly at small glasses of it, between draughts of fruit juices.

"Dang, but this is good!" he said. "You've got a good cook!"

"He was chef in a restaurant in Seattle and my husband Lord Amauri found him in a group of refugees,"

Lady Roehis said. "Quite able, but given to tempera-
ments. And he drinks, sometimes. His children are just as
good and they don't, not that way."

Maugis rolled his eyes slightly in an agreement that
hinted at crises over the years.

His wife went on: "Aleaume—our eldest son—was
complaining about there being no French fries. For the
last month, they are all he wants to eat."

Mary laughed. "My aunt Astrid's daughters Hinluin
and Fimalen are five, and they were like that for a while,
only with them it was noodles. Nothing would do but
noodles. And nothing *on* the noodles but butter. I love
them but they drove me and my sister crazy while we
were living in Stardell Hall."

"You have to be crazy to be a parent," Lady Roehis
said confidently. "But it's a rewarding insanity, in its way."

Everyone chuckled, but Ingolf thought after an instant that it was a rather odd way to talk about it, though
it *was* funny. But strange, as if having kids were a hobby
you could choose not to have. As far as he knew it was
just something you did, like growing up. Unless you
couldn't, which would be like being born with a club-
foot, a terrible and pitiful calamity.

He searched for something to say, not wanting to
leave the whole burden to Mary; he'd left home at nineteen, and at that age you ignored younger kids just as
hard as you could, being falsely convinced you were a
man now. His life afterwards hadn't been very domestic.
But he *did* like flowers.

"Ah, these are lovely gardens, Lady Helissent."

Helissent nodded towards her mother-in-law. "Lady
Roehis did those, starting from *nothing*. This was bare pasture when she arrived in the second Change Year, and thin
pasture at that! I wouldn't have believed it possible until I

saw it, and you're right, it's lovely. I'm from Barony Skagit originally, myself—my elder brother, Sir Adhémar de Sego, is a knight there, and holds Sego Manor as vassal of House Delby as my father did while he lived. Flowers are easy in Skagit. I was used to things being green *naturally*."

"Including the people," Maugis said with a smile. "Skagit's on Puget Sound, my lord Vogeler. Where they think it's a drought if the moss on their north side dies."

"As opposed to places where the rabbits starve to death if they don't *run* between blades of grass," she said tartly, and they both laughed.

Mary's hand stole into his beneath the table and squeezed. *It's true, when you're in love you see it everywhere,* he thought.

"My father picked this land when this county was shared out among the conquerors, and his comrades in arms thought he was crazy," Maugis said. "My lady wife is quite right; there was no settlement here; we have photographs. Nothing for miles but a few farmhouses, and thirty miles north to the nearest rail spur. But *he* saw the possibilities, and so did my lady mother."

"We wanted to get as far from Norman Arminger as we could," his mother said suddenly; she'd been looking a little abstracted. "Somewhere he'd never think of visiting. That was worth living in tents for a year, and dugouts for another, and the castle until this place was ready. *Anything* was worth getting out from under his eye. Court was a cesspit then. Dreadful man, absolutely dreadful. When I knew him in the Society I thought he was just an asshole, as we said then, but after the Change he blossomed into a *monster*."

The other two nobles stiffened in alarm, looking around reflexively. Lady Roehis nibbled on a biscuit and smiled at them, irony and affection mixed.

"He's dead," the older woman said. "He's *long* dead. Good riddance. And nothing would delight his evil heart more than knowing that fifteen years later he could still frighten people, ones who'd been children when he died. I think I'll take a nap before we go up to the keep, dear."

"Ah—" Ingolf said, as she nodded politely and left.

Mary spoke: "Lord Maugis, she's perfectly right. I say it, and my husband and I are good friends of Princess . . . High Queen Mathilda. And here's the others."

Ingolf breathed a well-concealed sigh of relief; at least he thought it was, until he caught Mary's sideways glance and smile.

"Captain Jaeger," Maugis said.

Mark was with the other Richlander, but looking a bit shaken, almost certainly from memories of the fight surfacing. That happened after the insulating rage and fear burned out of your blood. It was worse when it happened at night when you were half asleep.

And the captured Boise commander. "And Captain Woburn . . . Rancher Woburn, I believe, too; your father is a Sheriff as well, isn't he?" Maugis went on. "Please join me and my family for luncheon. As a Montivalan I say, let us put aside the war for a little; as a soldier, I say, welcome, comrade."

Woburn looked as if he'd been having those night-thoughts too. It was worst of all when you'd lost, and were lying alone blaming yourself for it.

Jaeger filled half his plate with the potato salad and took a tankard of the beer; evidently Richland's foodways bit deep. The Boisean ate as well, but kept silent; he was limping and had a couple of bandages and his left arm was in a sling, and no doubt he was hurting for his men. Ingolf sympathized, but he had business to do. Fortunately it was all stuff the Boisean already knew, or which he wouldn't at all mind the enemy knowing if by some unlikely chance he got loose.

"I'm promoting you to Major, Jaeger."

That got a blink and a smile, but not a big one; which said that Jaeger's priorities were good.

Kohler thought he was sound, and Kohler was a good judge of men.

"Pick your own replacement for your command and run the name by me. What's the state of the regiment?"

Since I'm now going to have to be more hands-on. Dammit, Kohler, I needed you! I've got half a dozen jobs to juggle! I only took the Colonel's post because you needed someone whose father was a Sheriff as a figurehead!

He'd led them to victory more than once, led from the front, and his latest plan had let them give the enemy a lot more of a world of hurt than they received. That had probably kept the men reasonably happy with him, even though he was busier than he liked with other things half the time. It wasn't that he *couldn't* run a light cavalry regiment; he'd done it before, and pretty well. Time, time . . .

Jaeger flicked his eyes aside at Woburn while he chewed hastily; Ingolf nodded very slightly. *Let him know how light we got off; can't hurt, might help.*

"Three more of the wounded died overnight, Colonel," Jaeger said when he'd swallowed.

He had medium-brown hair and was whippet-thin despite the way he was shoveling in the potato salad and mutton-ham and something very like kielbasa, and tomatoes and onions dressed with oil and vinegar and crusty rolls and butter, and eyeing the pastries. He'd eaten that way every time Ingolf saw him have an opportunity, but he wasn't surprised at the man's looks. From what older people said now and then, fatties had been common before the Change even among farmworkers, though that was difficult to imagine. You certainly weren't going to get that way doing what a horse-soldier did these days.

"Richter and Smith died of internal bleeding, the doctor tried, but too much was sliced up. They had to stop transfusing them, there were men who might recover who needed it and only so many donors."

Ingolf sighed. There were places that could store refrigerated blood for a while, but they were few and far between. Triage was an ugly fact of a fighting-man's life, but it *was* a fact. You weren't doing anyone a favor if you let a man who had some chance to live die just to keep someone who *didn't* have a chance going another half hour. There were times when the only favor you could do a comrade was a quick knife-thrust; at least they'd been spared that.

"The third?" he said.

Can't recall anyone else who looked that bad and it's too early for infection to show up.

"Sir, Olson got hit on the head hard enough to dent his helmet in, but he was doing fine and then . . . he just started breathing funny and died, real quiet."

Ingolf nodded. Head wounds were tricky that way; there was no way to see inside a head, of course, and nothing much the doctors could have done if you *could* see inside. They could pick fragments out of a depressed fracture or trepan for pressure on the brain if you were lucky, but that was about it. He'd been knocked out once and had had blinding headaches at intervals for six months afterwards; sometimes men never did entirely recover from a clout to the skull; and sometimes they just died, like Olson.

Three more dead made ten too many, but fewer than he'd expected. Ten dead altogether and thirty non-walking-wounded of whom only half a dozen would be crippled for life was a light butcher's bill for an engagement that size, but then winning always made for a lighter payment. The Boiseans had taken five times that. Still, you died just as dead either way.

"The rest seem to be doing well. The doctors here are excellent, that's what our Doc Jennings says. One of them went to the same school his own teacher did. And uh, Lord Rigobert left some of his medics too, and more medical supplies, so we've got enough morphine for the bad cases. He pulled out at dawn, couldn't have slept more than a couple of hours, that's one busy man. The Tithe Barn thing we've got all the wounded in is as comfortable as you could expect, sir, it was just used for a grain store, pretty clean."

"I'll drop in on them again today," Ingolf said. *And it won't be quite as bad this time.* "The rest?"

"Camp's pitched in the reaped fields about a half mile out of town. Still putting up the tents."

Which wasn't urgent; in weather like this it was probably more comfortable to just roll in your blankets than sleep in a stuffy tent. Most men preferred them if they had a choice, though. Probably because they gave an illusion of permanence, of home, in the enforced nomadism of a soldier's life. They were a shell you could take with you.

"There's a good well of clean water we can drink straight, plenty of it and a wind-pump, and the distance might, ah . . ."

"Make it harder for bored troopers to come into town and get drunk and cause too many problems," Ingolf said.

The younger Richlander nodded. "Yessir. And maybe we should provide working parties to our hosts, sweat some of the devilment out of them once they get over the fight and start feeling bored and randy again. Uff da, this officer's job, it's like being a nanny, isn't it, sometimes! I figure that's why Three Bears put the Sioux even farther out."

Says the graybeard of twenty-four, Ingolf thought.

"That, and they don't like being crowded; and he's scouting out to the north right now. Supplies?"

"Plenty, sir, we don't have to touch the reserves. Lots of firewood ready-cut. Lord Maugis here gave us a bunch of the sheep."

Maugis shrugged and spread his hands. "Sheep and battles go ill together, and the meat won't keep in this heat. That was my demesne herd, too."

The Richlander nodded. "And all the vegetables and fresh bread and fruit we can use, which is making the men happy, and some pretty good beer, I'm having that carefully rationed. We paid, of course."

"Of course," Ingolf said gravely.

He and Mary glanced at each other. They had permission to draw on the Crown accounts through Sandra Arminger, but Rudi was still fairly heavy with gold—the friendly new government of Iowa had given them a substantial going-away present to mark the alliance. As it turned out, gold was relatively more valuable here in Montival. Ingolf knew why. There were more ruins in the east, particularly more big ones, and the big ones were where most of the precious metals could be found. You had to have a grasp on the economics of the trade to succeed as a salvager. The difference in purchasing power was about two-to-one for gold, a little less for silver.

But it's going to run out someday not too far away. Wars are really expensive, and then Rudi's going to be dependent on his mom-in-law for an allowance. Which will make everyone else unhappy or even get them thinking she's taking over using him and Matti as a false front, and I've noticed other people in this neck of the woods aren't too fond of the PPA. Or he's got to get them all to pay him taxes so he can be independent, which will also make them unhappy, and he'll probably have to borrow a lot from the bankers too. The Destined Prince with the Magic Sword is wonderful, but less wonderful when he asks you to cough up every tenth bushel and piglet and takes out a mortgage on your farm.

Maugis smiled. "Cash is always useful, Esquire," he said; Jaeger blinked a little at the unfamiliar title. "But note that my bailiff is selling you *fresh* produce."

It took a moment for Jaeger to get the implications; Mary snorted a little under her breath, but Ingolf thought the man wasn't slow, just deliberate.

I'm not selling anything that would be useful in case of a siege, in other words.

The captured Boise officer had been eating with concentrated attention; probably they'd been on thin rations for a while. The enemy army was so big it was straining their logistics just by being all in one place, and they'd also probably looked forward to getting somewhere they could forage from the enemy. Ingolf waited for him to slow down and make a second trip for dark red Shuksan strawberries and cream. He could ease himself by thinking of it as plunder.

"Have your wounded been treated properly, Captain Woburn?" Ingolf asked, a formal note in his voice.

The man nodded, equally *correct* as the saying went.

"Yes, Colonel Vogeler. I wouldn't be here, otherwise. My medical officer survived, he's been working with yours, and he tells me that they received the same care as your men. I've visited them and they're as comfortable as possible. The rest of us have been well treated and well fed, and the guards are no rougher than necessary."

He swallowed; he was an unremarkable-looking young man, medium-brown hair and blue eyes, with a rather long bony face and weathered skin, not big or small but hard-looking and very fit, with large hands and wrists. He forced those eyes back to Ingolf.

"Thank you, sir. It's . . . not exactly what I'd expected."

"You're welcome, though technically you're Lord Maugis' prisoners."

"Thank you as well, then . . . my lord," the Boise officer said.

Maugis nodded gravely. "You are welcome, Rancher Woburn. It's an obligation of chivalry to care for the defeated."

That brought an odd look; he wondered what sort of propaganda Boise pumped out about the PPA. Boise went in for propaganda a lot, posters slathered all over the place, he'd seen that traveling through its territory on the way to tell Rudi about the Sword, and then again when they all came back heading east; they'd returned by the northern route, through the Dominions. He doubted General-President Martin Thurston had stopped the practice when he took over from—after killing—his father Lawrence. He'd certainly put out enough lies about his brother Fred being responsible for their father's death; Fred had been one of the Companions of the Quest, and Rudi intended to see him in charge in Boise when things were settled.

Assuming we win, of course. And "assume". . .

Boise's posters never said much that was good about this part of the world, and probably a lot of it was deserved, though not as much these days as in the past. There were still barons who would have been a lot rougher than de Grimmond, though, even with the High King issuing orders.

Ingolf spoke again: "Your men fought hard against odds when we surprised you, no panic. And they're very well drilled. When you reversed front on us after that arrow-exchange it was like one man moving; it's a difficult maneuver and I've never seen it better done. If we hadn't had an ace you'd have gotten away and hurt us badly in the process."

"Ah . . . thank you again." Bitterly. "Those sheep were a trap, weren't they? Bait."

"Yup," Ingolf said, and ate a bite of honey cake with whipped cream.

"And I led us into it and lost half my command," the younger man said with soft bitterness, looking down at his bowl. "Lost all of it and me, too. It'd be easier all around if I'd taken an arrow in the eye. And I'm supposed to be a trained officer!"

"Son, if something looks too good to be true, like a nice tasty flock of sheep just begging to get put on the grill, it usually is. If it's any consolation I got sucker punched pretty much the same way back . . . when I was younger than you are now and had a command I deserved a lot less that you did yours. Training does only so much. Experience you have to get the hard way. You pay for it, and your men pay for it, and that's just the way it is in this screwed-up world."

Woburn looked up, eyes narrowed in thought. "You're not from around here, are you, sir? I can't place your accent."

"Nope. I'm from the Free Republic of Richland . . . the Richland in Wisconsin, not the Richland over near Kennewick on the Columbia."

The other man's eyes widened. "The Midwest? Then—"

He shut up quickly. Ingolf ate another forkful, before

he said judiciously: "Yup. It really is true that Iowa and the others are marching. On Corwin, for starters, but they're going to keep right on going as far as Boise and they're not likely to be in a real good mood by then. Hell, after the way the Cutters killed their Bossman on his own ground, the Iowans aren't in a good mood *now*. Iowa's run by his widow these days, you know. I was there when they mustered outside Des Moines. Must have been seventy, eighty thousand men—and that wasn't counting the ones who were joining 'em later. They've got more if they need 'em."

"That's a large force," Woburn said, a little white about the lips. "Still, numbers aren't everything."

"They're mostly pretty green, except for a few from Fargo and Marshall who were in the Sioux War," he added honestly. "But there are a hell of a lot of them and their gear and logistics are good. The Sioux are coming west too, and they've got blood in their eyes and scores to pay off. You had some experience with them yesterday."

Woburn was silent for an instant, then doggedly returned to his food. "And thank you for . . . stopping those . . . Sioux." He'd probably been about to say *savages*. "They'd have killed us all."

Ingolf nodded. "They're not what you'd call fond of the CUT," he said mildly. "They've got good reason, and there weren't a lot of rules when they fought 'em the last time, out there on the High Plains east of the Rockies."

That brought the other man's head up. "We're soldiers of the United States, not that f- . . . not the Prophet!"

What everyone else called the United States of Boise called itself the United States of America, and some of them actually meant it. Ingolf chuckled slightly. "Captain Woburn, have you ever been out of Idaho before?"

He opened his mouth, closed it, then said with stubborn honesty: "No. Never even as far as Boise until I did the Officer Candidate School course."

"Well, I've been all the way from Nantucket to the Willamette. More than once. And young feller, the United States is deader than . . . than Rome. Than f-. . . freaking Babylon, come to that, or those other places in the Bible, Nineveh and Egypt and whatnot."

"All the way . . . are you *that* Ingolf Vogeler?" Woburn blurted, his eyes going a little wide.

"Yup." Ingolf nodded towards Mary. "And that's *the* Mary Vogeler, formerly Mary Havel. Rudi's sister. High King Artos' sister, Mike and Signe Havel's daughter, Astrid Loring's niece."

She smiled charmingly. "My mother and father met your father a long time ago, in Idaho. The Camas Prairie, isn't it? Just after the Change."

Woburn took a deep breath. "Well, that's, ah, startling. Yes, I remember Father telling me about that."

"I'm sure he told you about the fight against Iron Rod," Mary added.

Yeah. Mike Havel saved Woburn the elder's bacon back then. We won't mention the fact that Arminger was backing Iron Rod by proxy.

"And Captain Woburn?" Ingolf went on calmly. "Just for your information, I was at the Battle of Wendell, when old general Thurston died. He was wounded by the Prophet's men, but his son Martin killed him, your current ruler and the one who came up with this alliance with the Prophet and the CUT. I know Fred Thurston didn't do it, Martin did. I was there."

"So was I," Mary said crisply.

"Is that the truth?" Woburn said quietly.

Ingolf shrugged. "Either my word's good, or it isn't,

and you'll have to be the judge of that for yourself." He held up a hand. "Just think about it."

Woburn gave a jerky nod. "May I ask what's to be done with my men?"

Maugis nodded in turn, smiling politely and slipping in a small needle: "The High King's orders are that all Boise prisoners are to be kept separate from the Prophet's men . . . I trust that's satisfactory?"

Woburn flushed, and the nobleman went on: "You'll be taken to Walla Walla and then on the rail line to Wallula, and down the Columbia by barge to join the others; we've got over three battalions' worth of your comrades by now. The High King has also commanded that Boisean prisoners are to be treated strictly according to the laws of war. Enlisted men may be required to work, but nothing excessive, officers to keep their sidearms and be allowed to give parole, prisoners will get the same rations our men eat, and no degrading punishments. Perhaps he'll talk to you himself."

The Boisean was silent for a moment. "I should return to my men, my lord."

"By all means. If you have any needs, please inform my guards and they'll relay the message to me. We're rather busy and stretched thin here, defending our homes, but I'll consider anything within reason."

Then he went on to Ingolf: "Come walk with me, Lord Vogeler."

Mary caught his eyes and nodded very slightly; Mark gave a slight yelp as if someone had kicked him under the table and subsided, and he didn't think Lady Helissent missed any of it. Captain Jaeger stood and gave him a salute and then headed back to the buffet one more time before he'd have to get back to the regiment.

The two men strolled out through the busyness of the

manor, down the front steps and toward the heavy steel-strapped timber gates.

"Getting your stuff out while the going's good?" Ingolf asked.

Maugis shrugged. "Yes. Though in the end, things can be replaced."

He gestured at the big house. "This is earth and stone and timber; I love it because of the memories it holds for me of my childhood, and because my own children were born here, but it's not . . . not something that can really die. We can rebuild if the enemy wreck it, though losing the labor that went into it will hurt. But it's the people that are the core of it."

They walked out the front gate of the manor gardens. The outer wall of the great house grounds formed one side of a town square paved with squared blocks of basalt, with a big fountain in the center, one of several where the folk could fill their buckets as they pleased.

Trees ringed it, maples and oaks, and other buildings; the tall church, a bathhouse-cum-laundry, a tavern with a creaking sign that read *The Hawk and Bear* showing a very large eagle fighting a very small grizzly and right now doing a land-office business. There was a potter's shop too; a wheelwright's long sheds; and several stores selling things, rather than relying on peddler's carts or passing Tinerant caravans. This was a baron's seat as well as the village of a manor.

Everything was built of the same materials as the great house, tile roofs over whitewashed *pisé* walls on knee-high foundations of mortared basalt stone. The square was thick with activity, some of it preparation for a big public feast; there were a row of fire pits with whole carcasses of pig and sheep and ox roasting over them and giving off clouds of savory smoke as grease dripped on the coals, and women were setting up trestle tables and a series of stands that would hold barrels.

"I will be giving an address to my people tonight," Lord Maugis said. "One way or another."

Ingolf's eyes were shaped by a lifetime's campaigning; they rose to the heights eastward, the first time he'd done that here in daytime. He stopped still for an instant and whistled. He'd known that Castle Tucannon was on a hill over the town. And it was, but that was like saying that the ruins of Chicago were *large* or that Iowa had *a hell of a lot of people*.

This whole range of low mountains had obviously been a plateau once, and then been cut up by water action far in the past into a maze of ridges, peaks and canyons that got steeper as you went farther in. This looked like a lot of the ridges on the edge of the high country. Only the end of the ridge had fallen off somehow, leaving better than a hundred feet of nearly sheer basalt in a horseshoe shape with a tangle of huge rocks at the base.

The castle had been built atop that; it was the usual basic Association design, doubled as they sometimes were to enlarge it—what they called a *mirror keep*. But the outer walls were at the edge of those cliffs, and the builders had improved them by chopping out any projecting spurs. Mounted on one of the towers was a tall Ponderosa pine trunk, about a hundred feet tall with a ladder up its side and a small platform on the top. He tried to imagine what sort of a vantage it would give you, and failed. And it probably put Castle Tucannon in connection with the heliograph net all the way to Walla Walla, which would mean all the way to Portland and beyond.

Say what you like about this Arminger guy, he knew how to get things built, not just how to kill people.

"There was a solid path in from the other side; my

father's builders used that, then cut it away afterwards and put in a bridge that could be brought down quickly, as well as the drawbridge," Maugis said, as they resumed their walk. "My sire always did have a good eye for ground."

"Water?" Ingolf asked, and Maugis nodded respectfully.

"You do see the essentials, my lord Vogeler. The rock is basalt, but there's limestone under it. Water drains down from the mountains through the strata and breaks out as springs there, at the base, plenty even in high summer like this. We run the town's water in from there through pipes, and there are deep tube wells and reservoirs under the keep. And we use chambers in the rock for bulk storage after the harvest . . . a bit cumbersome, but it means there's a four-year supply there at any one time."

Maugis smiled, a hard expression. "And besides getting away from the Lord Protector—quite true, by the way—*that* is a reason why my father picked this place for his stronghold. A major one. He told me he was looking carefully all the time the Association was pacifying these lands. Most of the poor harried starved wretches welcomed overlords with real weapons who could give them peace to plow and plant."

Light wagons and packtrains were heading upslope; the jagged peaks of the Blue Mountains lay dreaming and purple there to the eastward. Some of them bore the goods he'd seen coming out of the manor, others bundles of weaponry or farm tools or things less readily identifiable, still others household furnishings more humble than the baron's.

"Not all going to the castle," Ingolf said; it wasn't a question.

He estimated that the tall stronghold could be held securely by about two hundred men at a pinch, and three or four hundred would be ample. If they had their families along, it would be pretty tight quarters. Build small and high was a good rule for a fort, and that one was high and no mistake. Ingolf couldn't think of any way to storm it at all, offhand, as long as the garrison stayed alert. Even getting close to it would be dangerous, given the vantage it provided for catapult fire, and shooting back would be a joke with that elevation.

"No, not even most is going to the castle. The mountains were another reason my father took seisin of this grant, and not just for the water and timber, though that's why my manors are all in the foothills. There are caves up there, and old buildings from before the Change—ranger cabins, and so forth."

"Hmmm." Ingolf scratched at his beard. "And you've been working at them since your father's day?"

Maugis nodded. "For the last twenty years, and there are hidden storehouses underground we've been filling since the war started last year. Good grazing, too; it's not all forest and rock, there are flat areas with plenty of grass, and there's the devil's own lot of game, boar and bear and deer and elk. Not to mention tiger and wolf and cougar. We use the high country in dry years for summer grazing; my folk *know* those mountains. I'm not sending any to Walla Walla to be shipped down the Columbia . . . and possibly never come back."

Ingolf nodded understanding. The baron was being forethoughtful for his people, and for his own family's interests as well. There wasn't any serfdom anywhere in Montival, or slavery. Fifteen years ago the treaty at the end of what everyone but the PPA folks called the War of the Eye, what they termed the Protector's War here, forbade any law that limited the right to emigrate. Anyone who wanted to leave could, debts or no. But that meant leaving the only home they had, with nothing more than the clothes they stood up in, and no skills but one particular type of farming.

Few would face that if they weren't impossibly badly treated at home. However, if you'd been shipped to a distant city *anyway*, with the government footing the bill, heading home away from the bright lights might not seem very attractive at all. Or at least some would stop on a manor where a holding was available from a lord greedy for workers; there was more good land everywhere than there were hands to till it.

"That castle could be held by a corporal's guard, my lord," Ingolf said thoughtfully. "Well, them and some catapult crews."

"And I *could* do it that way," Maugis agreed. "Keep a minimal garrison and the most vulnerable noncombatants in the castle. Everyone else in the hills, and then raid out of them with the barony's fighting men when the enemy occupy the lowlands . . . which they will."

"Yup, they will," Ingolf said; he wasn't going to lie to this man. "Hopefully, not for all that long, but for a while, yeah."

"Tell me, Lord Vogeler, how many men would you need to comb these mountains against me and my neighbors if we took refuge there? How long would it take?"

Ingolf's professional reflexes kicked in. He looked up at the peaks to the east—one of them still had a little snow on it and must be around seven thousand feet—and ran what he knew of the terrain through his mind.

"At least five thousand men and a lot of equipment, if you gave me a year," he said. "Not counting the ones you'd need to besiege the castles around here, or at least solidly invest them. Maybe two years to do a thorough job. Ten, twenty thousand and even more gear if you wanted it done quick and dirty. You'd need good troops you could trust to get out there in small units and get stuck in whenever they could, not just go through the motions when someone higher up was looking. And some engineers to build roads and fortified posts, plus labor. And it'd cost you, money and blood both. That's natural ambush country, looks like."

Maugis nodded quietly. They walked on through the town, the baron nodding response to bows and curtsies and salutes; nobody was going to interrupt him, of course. Grimmond-on-the-Wold had something like eight hundred folk in peacetime and many more now. That was big for a village, but not a place that had wholly made up its mind to be a town either, and certainly not even the smallest city.

"I could raid from those hills and tie down that many troops or more," Maugis said. "I could make trying to move supplies through this country . . . anywhere between here and the Snake River . . . a nightmare of endless harassment. Ambush convoys, kill foraging parties, cut off patrols, burn outposts."

He turned and gestured to the town and the lands beyond. "I know that this doesn't look like much to a traveled man," he said.

"Actually it looks pretty good," Ingolf said sincerely. "Mary and I were just now saying that we envied you. Well, would envy you if it were peacetime."

Maugis smiled; it was an oddly charming expression, and made his rather ugly face handsome for a moment.

"Thank you," he said. "This is my . . . my world, if you know what I mean. My own particular world."

Ingolf dredged his memory for a word he'd heard; his

family were mostly Deutsch if you went back far enough, along with a slew of other things including a lot of Nor-ski. They had preserved a few bits and pieces of that her-itage, and not just recipes for bratwurst.

"Heimat," he said. "An old word. Your heimat is . . . your little country, the first homeland of the heart. The place where your roots are."

Maugis nodded quickly. "Exactly. I've enjoyed my times at Court in Todenangst and Portland, the univer-sity in Forest Grove, visits to Walla Walla, tournaments and meetings of the Peers, theatre and concerts, but this place is my *home*. All of it, and the people are my people."

Most of the folk of Grimmond-on-the-Wold were peasants, who tilled the little garden tofts around their three-room-and-a-loft cottages that gave off the tree-shaded streets. They had their strips in the big open fields of wheat and barley, canola and sunflowers and clover westward, their stock in the common flocks and herds. From that they paid a share to the lord, and worked two or three days a week on his demesne land; that included a long south-facing slope of goblet-trained vineyards green and bushy with summer and the orchards around the irrigation furrow beneath. Some of the little houses were neatly kept, with flowers planted around their door-ways. Others had patches flaking from their whitewash and chickens walking in the door.

None of them looked truly miserable; the people in them certainly weren't underfed, or very ragged, or too smelly. The toft gardens all had abundant vegetables and a few fruit trees; there were chicken coops and the odd pigsty or shed for a milch cow down at their far fence. There were refugees in Richland who lived worse. The upper part of the town held larger houses as well, from the reeve's and the bailiff's up to those of the household knights.

"Heimat," Maugis repeated, rolling the word around his mouth to taste it. "I like that. It . . . fits."

Since this was a baron's seat, it also had two or three of the things the ordinary manorial village had one of, bakeries and blacksmith's shops and some full-time weavers. The blacksmiths had the usual piles of bundled scrap metal around their doors, and they were working too hard to notice their overlord walking by; metal hissed viciously with a vinegary smell and a spearhead was quenched, with a grinding chorus of metal shoved against spinning honing wheels beneath. Most of the other craftsfolk looked about as busy.

"War wears things out," Maugis said, nodding at them. "Things and people."

"God knows it's worn holes in me," Ingolf said ruefully, touching the dent where his nose had been broken.

Down at the end of the single street were a set of huge barns, long work sheds, a tall windmill and a tangle of corrals. Those were swarmingly busy too.

"I could turn these mountains into a running sore when the enemy come . . . as they will. Or I could put up a single fight on the plains for honor's sake, and then just defend the heights, giving a bloody nose to anyone who pokes it in and hoping to deal as best I can with whoever has the victory in the end."

"You could do that, my lord," Ingolf said carefully, as he might to a horse he wasn't sure might bolt. "But you'd be making it that much less likely we win the war."

"Yes," Maugis said calmly. "And I have obligations to the Count, whose vassal I am. He's a good man who does his best, and even his father—who was a jumped-up thug with a veneer of courtesy, as *my* father said—gave us good lordship, mostly, which is as much as a vassal can rightly demand. The question is, can the Count protect me and mine in return for my service if I throw everything into the scales for him? I'm not a household knight who can fight with no thought but to die at his lord's side. There are more than four thousand people living in this Barony, Lord Vogeler, commons, clerics and gentles alike. They're *my* vassals; they look to me for protection in return for their service and obedience, and I have sworn to provide it. For that oath I must account before the very Throne of God."

He crossed himself. "Most of the time being a baron is a fine thing, the wealth and power and glory of it. There comes a time to pay for everything, though, if a man's to be a man indeed and not just a wolf that walks on two legs with his sword for fangs. And only the lesser debts can be paid in cash. These decisions are mine to make here, and *that* is my burden."

"There's more involved than the Count Palatine," Ingolf said. "Or Walla Walla and the County of the Eastermark in general."

"Yes; there's *his* overlord the Lady Regent, and the new Kingdom. Lady Sandra I know a little, and she is very able, she's led the Association well. But she's colder than the dark side of the Moon. A ruler must make sacrifices, and balance this loss against that, sometimes ruthlessly; I know that from watching and listening to my father work, and my own experience. But she would sacrifice my barony and its folk without even a moment's hesitation if it served her aims, as if it were an entry in a ledger or a cutting bar in a hay-reaper. I cannot give fealty to a machine or a mere form of written laws. It must be to a *person*, someone who respects my honor, who loves it, even if he sends me to death and condemns my lands to the fire for a greater duty's sake."

"She's not the big boss anymore, Lord Maugis."

He stopped and looked at Ingolf Vogeler. "I don't know Rudi Mackenzie," he said. "Or Artos the High King. But I do know *you*, a little, Lord Vogeler. We've fought together side by side, and I've seen you at work with your own troops. And I flatter myself that though I'm young yet, I'm a fair judge of men. So tell me about Artos. Tell me if he's a King worth risking all this"—he moved his arm about—"for. Is he a man who loves his vassals' honor as much as his own? Is he worthy of true fealty, that I can ask my followers to lay down their lives and risk their homes for him?"

Ingolf stood rooted to the spot. *Hell, how do I answer that?* he thought desperately. *OK, I know Rudi pretty damned good. We were together through two really stressful years and a lot of . . . wait a minute.*

"Lord Maugis," he said. "I could tell you what I think of Rudi . . . the High King . . . but that would just be words. My opinion at most. Let me tell you what I've *seen* him do, these last two years and more, since I rode into Sutterdown with the Prophet's men on my tracks. Words are cheap, but a man is what he does."

When Ingolf finished, he found his throat unexpectedly dry. And the sun was much lower, low enough to make him blink in surprise. They were sitting on a stone horse-trough with a spigot above it. He turned it on, and drank a double handful of the cold mineral-tasting water, shaking out his hands afterwards. The air sucked the moisture out of his beard in moments, but it was a little cooler now.

Lord Maugis stood looking westward for a long moment, his left hand on his sword-hilt. When he turned he bowed.

"My lord de Stafford said that all the barons of the

County Palatine were summoned to a conference in Walla Walla by the Count, to consider our strategy in this war. If we could be spared from our domains. I think that I can be, now."

A bell began ringing; the big one in the church, going a slow deep: *bong . . . bong . . . bong . . .* a dozen times.

"And it is time to return to the square," he said.

They did. The bustle there was still going on, by the light of steel baskets of burning pinewood that lofted trails of sparks like little scarlet-yellow stars. The fire in the clouds westward was dying down, and the sky over the mountains was dark blue, a few first true stars showing. The moon was nearly full, shedding a silvery light almost as bright as the fires. And a timber podium had been set up in front of the manor gates, a simple thing that would raise a few people to about head-height over the pavement. The ground sloped away from there; it would give everyone in the square a view.

More and more people summoned by the bells were pouring in, until the area was packed. Lady Helissent and her mother came out, and her children. Her glance crossed that of her husband; he nodded to her. Ingolf could see something pass between them, knowledge and decision; Helissent's eyes closed for an instant, and then she took a deep breath and opened them and smiled bravely at the father of her children.

"If you would accompany me, Lord Vogeler, and your good lady?" Maugis chuckled at the look on the older man's face. "No, I'm not asking you to speak, just to . . . be present."

The local priest went up the stairs first in his vestments, and intoned a prayer. Nearly everyone crossed themselves and kissed their crucifixes, then joined in the last part of it:

"*. . . Dignum et iustum est. Amen.*"

Then the lord of Tucannon and his family and guests climbed up. Looking down, Ingolf saw a sea of faces, and at first was conscious mainly of the eyes. The gaudy haughtiness of the knights and their families and households was in the first row, shading backward into the shaggy dun mass of the commons, straw hats and kerchiefs and shock-headed children. There were a scattering of Richlanders and Sioux; even a few of the Boiseans were there, officers who'd given their paroles. Captain Woburn was one of them, his face impassive. The crackle of the fire-baskets ran beneath the sough of breathing.

Almost-silence fell as Lord Maugis stepped forward; then a bow swept through the crowd. The soldiers behind the podium came to attention, thumping their spearbutts and the metal-edged points of their four-foot shields down on the paving blocks. Maugis doffed his hat with a flutter of liripipe and returned the bow, not so deeply but a definite gesture.

"My people," he said. "My brothers and sisters—for any who fights beside me for this our home I call my brother—we are here tonight to celebrate and to mourn. We fought and beat those who threatened our land, our homes and our families—"

The crowd burst into a long rolling cheer, calling the baron's name. Maugis stopped for an instant; Ingolf could see him blinking in surprise. Beside him Mary murmured very quietly, but pitching it to carry to his ear: "I sort of like our host."

Ingolf nodded; he saw her point.

"—and that we celebrate. We mourn the loss of fathers, brothers, husbands. We pray that God will receive their souls, who died bravely fighting for the right."

He crossed himself. "Holy Mary—"

The crowd murmured with him, like wind through trees: "—mother of God, pray for us, now and at the hour of our deaths."

Maugis waited again. "I wish that I could say that this was the last battle we must fight. But it was not. The enemy is numerous and strong. He will come again, and we must fight, for he comes to kill our loved ones, to take the land that feeds our children, and to destroy our holy faith. The way will be hard, and many of us may fall. Pray to God and to our patron St. Joan for the strength to endure all that we must suffer and do."

Well, that's telling it straight, Ingolf thought. *Hope he knows his audience.*

Into the silence Maugis continued: "But we do not fight this fight alone! Not only all the Association, but all of the High Kingdom of Montival is fighting this war with us. Our High King, Artos, leads them; and he bears the Sword that was forged in Heaven and given to him by the Lady of Stars, the Queen of Heaven herself! If God is with us, who can prevail against us? *Artos and Montival!*"

The cry was unfamiliar, but the crowd took it up willingly; stories of Artos and the Sword had been circulating for a while now, even in out-of-the-way spots like this. Many of the faces looking up were exalted and rapt now.

"And we have strong allies. You see some of them among us now. More are marching against the enemy from north and east. A cheer, my people, for the allies come from far away to risk their lives beside us!"

Maugis laid a hand on Ingolf's shoulder for a moment, and the Richlander fought down an impulse to fidget and blush at the roar of acclaim.

"Already a great army gathers at Walla Walla, many thousands strong and led by the Grand Constable of the Association, and by our own Count Felipe, who is my overlord as I am yours. He has called me there to consult with him."

This time the silence had an edge to it. Maugis lifted his hands again.

"In the short time I shall be gone, I name my own good wife, the well-loved Lady Helissent, as deputy in my place. To assist her, our allies will remain here until I return in a few days. Give her your loyal service, your strong arms and wise counsel, as you have to me."

There were more cheers. Mary's lips moved close to his ear: "Pointing out his wife and children are staying right here," she said. "That was a smart move."

When the sound died down, Maugis' arm went to the trestle tables. "And now let us feast and dance, my brothers and sisters. Whatever storms come, let us remember this day, and that we are one, and that one with the strength of many. Here, and in lands we have never seen."

CHAPTER SIXTEEN

THE WILD LANDS
(FORMERLY HUMBOLDT-TOIYABE NATIONAL FOREST,
NORTHWESTERN NEVADA)
HIGH KINGDOM OF MONTIVAL
(FORMERLY WESTERN NORTH AMERICA)
AUGUST 14, CHANGE YEAR 25/2023 AD

R itva shivered.
Ian put an arm around her shoulder, and she
leaned into it gratefully as the dry wind flicked
around them, its hooting the only sound besides the spit-
ting crackle of the torch, its scent heavy with the smell of
the cut pine logs. Astrid Loring-Larsson looked inhumanly peaceful as she rested on the pyre, hands clasped
on the hilt of her sword. Though they were yards away,
the downslope put her on their eye-level.

The crossbow bolt was gone, and they'd found a
spring of good water here at the edge of the wooded
mountains that stretched north and west during their
day's labors. The body had been washed and dressed
again in the war-gear and then wrapped to the shoulders
in her dark cloak; the long white-gold hair lay over her
shoulders, stirring in the breeze beneath a thick wreath of
crimson columbine whose blossoms attracted a hum-
mingbird of iridescent green. There was a vulnerable look

to the moon-pale face that Ritva didn't recall seeing before, like a shy wild child lost in dreams.

She shivered again.

"What is it?" Ian repeated, whispering next to her ear.
She wasn't crying anymore; he knew it wasn't just grief.

"It was what she said at the end," Ritva said.

"I didn't understand it," Ian said.

And he'd been well back in the gondola when Astrid
died in her husband's arms, with Eilir's tears falling on
her face and John Hordle wringing great paws that suddenly looked so helpless. He didn't understand the Noble
Tongue all that well either yet, of course, and Astrid had
been gasping.

"It was . . ." Ritva thought. "She was hurting a lot and
she said good-bye to us all and told Alleyne to teach the
children she'd loved them and hadn't wanted to leave
while they were still so young, and then . . . I thought she
was gone and she opened her eyes and said: *Like silver
glass . . . green shores . . . the gulls . . . a white tower . . .
home, home, at last . . .*

"And then she died," Ritva whispered after a moment.
"One by one they go, the heroes, the legends."

The surviving crew folk of the dirigible were grouped
at a little distance, the ones not too badly injured to stand.
Major Hanks spoke a command and they came to attention, their hands following his to a salute. Behind them the
burnt wreckage of the *Curtis LeMay* was smeared across a
scrubby hillside, parts of the brush it had set afire still
smoldering though the tall plume had dispersed over the
course of the day. The Thurstons stood nearer, but Cecile
and her daughters were a little apart from Juliet; and they
stood on the side of her that put her son between them.
The boy was sobbing from the swirl of emotions around
them, but he was too tired to be loud about it.

The Dúnedain were closer still, and Ritva was near the leaders; she was Astrid's niece, after all. Alleyne had invited Juliet into the party, since it was to save her or perhaps her son that his wife had lunged forward, but there had been an icy politeness to it, and she had declined in a half-heard murmur.

"Farewell, beloved," Alleyne said, his eyes locked on the body. "Wait for me, until my work here is finished."

Farewell, anamchara, sister of my soul, Eilir's fingers said. *The threads of our lives are spun together forever.*

Together they stepped forward, their hands on the torch. The pine logs were stacked crisscross in six layers, and the gaps between them had been stuffed with branches and needles and bone-white fallen timber. The wind from the north was still brisk, even though the storm had blown itself out. The kindling caught with an eager *rick-rick-rick* sound, and then the whole pyre seemed to explode into a pillar of flame and smoke that rose and bent away from them towards the southwest. The summer-dry sap-rich wood burned with a dragon's hissing roar, almost instantly hot enough to turn bone to dust. Ritva felt her eyes water and brushed at them again.

Eilir was crying once more as they backed away, weeping quietly, her tears trickling down past a silent sorrow; she and Astrid had met in the first year of the Change, and sworn the *anamchara* oath not long after. They had spent a generation together. John Hordle wept as well, with the harsh jerky sound of a man unaccustomed to it. Alleyne's handsome face looked as if it were carved from ivory; his lips moved silently in words she couldn't make out for a moment, and then he bowed his head.

One thing's changed, Ritva knew suddenly.

Uncle Alleyne had never taken some things about the Rangers altogether seriously, though he'd been scrupulously polite and never made a fuss even as he gave all his considerable skill and ability to their affairs. The Dúnedain had already been refounded by Astrid and Eilir when he arrived fifteen years ago with his father and John, though not long before that. Now . . .

Now he'll live her dream, she realized. *And he'll do it perfectly. For her.*

They waited silently until the logs collapsed inward and the roar of the fire died down to a crackle that would last all night. Then he raised his head and gave the note. Ritva joined in on the beat, and every one of the Dúnedain as well. Eilir swayed to the rhythm, her hands dancing:

"A Elbereth Gilthoniel
silivren penna míriel . . ."

When they were finished, Ritva whispered again to herself: *"Thy starlight on the Western Seas."*

Then she shook herself. You had to be able to put things aside and go on. They were in a dangerous wilderness and there was a great deal to do. The ashes would be carried home in Astrid's helm, and by her long-standing will be scattered in Mithrilwood by the falls whose beauty she'd loved, but that was her husband's work and her *anamchara*'s. Caught in the storm's giant fist they had hopelessly overshot their rendezvous south of Boise, where helpers were supposed to be waiting.

They knew in a general sense where they were; it wasn't all that far from where the Quest had passed through going east two years ago, just before they ran into General-President Thurston the elder's column. They could locate themselves on a map as soon as they hit a marked roadway or abandoned town. What they weren't likely to find was people, or any of the things people would have with them.

Ian Kovalevsky looked around. "Looks a bit like the Rockies, only lower," he said.

Ritva snorted. "That's because it *is* the Rockies, more or less, sweetie," she said.

Sometimes she forgot that Ian had never been more than a few hundred miles from the place he'd been born. Most people traveled far less than that, of course, but you thought about them as the ones you rode by when you passed a farm or village. It had been all travel since they met. She'd never had the slightest impulse to farm, but she was beginning to feel that two years of rarely sleeping in the same spot for more than a day running was taking mobility too far.

The western horizon was jagged; the plain of sage-brush and yellow-brown grass heaved up into rocky heights, gray striped with red, and woods of aspen and bristlecone and lodgepole in sheltered spots. They had no food with them, but that wasn't the problem it would have been later in the year. They did have their bows and game looked to be available if not plentiful and Rangers learned how to forage for nuts and roots and edible greens. More serious was the lack of all camping gear; no tents, no bedding, no salt, nothing to cook with, only a few axes and hatchets. And . . .

"No horses," Ian said succinctly. "Plus we've got wounded and carrying them's going to slow us a *lot*. Not to mention a two-year-old."

Ritva sighed. "We've done what Operation Lúthien was supposed to do, more or less," she said. "All those people in Boise heard Cecile . . . and Juliet . . . and we've *got* them and Martin doesn't. That was *real* important, it's why this was such a high-priority mission. It would be a lot better if we could get them back to Montival quickly and completely out of his reach, of course. I suppose he'll have a cavalry brigade headed this way as fast as he can."

A long whistle split the air from the east, where the sentry was stationed. She read its modulations as she would speech or Sign: horsemen in sight.

The stillness dissolved in a rush for weapons and gear.

"No, I do not think it was an accident we met you," *Rimpoche* Tsewang Dorje said later that night, after the rising of the moon.

He leaned forward to pour himself a cup of the herb tea from the pot that rested by the campfire. More glowed across the rolling plain, hundreds of them. The folk of Chenrezi Monastery and the Valley of the Sun that looked to it for leadership and the ranches and tribes allied to it had sent their riders to war, across the wilderness to join the High King's host. That was partly because the questers had lived among them for a whole winter; and more because they trusted the Abbot when he told them it was necessary.

"But then, there are no accidents," Dorje went on. "We are all pilgrims on the Way; taking different paths, but eventually the paths will meet. Is it then a surprise that the pilgrims do likewise?"

The Abbot of Chenrezi Monastery looked exactly as Ritva remembered in her last sight of him when the questers left the Valley of the Sun in the spring of the previous year. The shabby wrapped orange robe might have been the same one. It left one shoulder bare, and the skinny knotted legs that ended in gnarled sandaled feet. His head needed no razor, and his face was a mass of wrinkles and yet somehow like a boy's, with a flicker of humor in the dark narrow eyes. The hard travel he must have gone through in the mountains and deserts had left no mark that she could see. You could feel the tough mountain peasant he'd been born beneath the bonze still.

Nor had the task of turning a panic-stricken resort community and a gaggle of quarrelsome Buddhists of a dozen different varieties thrown together by circumstance into a living community made him any softer in the years since the Change. She leaned back against her borrowed saddle and sighed with something that was not exactly pleasure . . .

More like relaxation, as if I were back at Stardell in one of the chairs by the fire and wine were mulling and snow falling against the windows. I don't know why, because we aren't *home and lot of what the Rimpoche says isn't exactly comforting.*

Lawrence Jr. scampered over, with his mother in pursuit; there had been wolf-howls in the distant hills, and it was not the sort of place you wanted a child to wander away from light and people. He took a look at the monk and then crawled into his lap. The man settled him comfortably, and then beckoned to his mother.

Ritva scowled slightly as she turned to her second bowl of stew; it had venison in it as well as dried vegetables and cracked barley and it had been quite tasty, for camp food. A lot of the folk from the Valley of the Sun didn't eat meat, but a lot did, and the ones who didn't weren't the sort who got in your face about it. It tasted less good with Juliet Thurston in the circle, and she wasn't the only one who felt like that.

"A fine boy," Dorje said, and smiled at the mother. "You are brave, to undertake the responsibility of raising him."

Juliet's face was usually hard and reserved, but the

lines of grief on it were visible now. She made a small sound and seemed to shrink into herself at the glares she would once have ignored.

The lama sighed and looked around at the others; the firelight picked out his wrinkles, like the hills and valleys of a mysterious country. Beyond gleamed the peaks of mountains where bear and cougar and tiger roamed, and men as savage as either.

"My friends," he said gently, "self-righteousness is the fumes of decomposing vanity; it is the means the Devil's Guard use to cloud the vision of those who truly love virtue. If someone is far along a journey to destruction, shall you hate them for waking to their situation, and turning about, and taking even a single halting half step back? Will that encourage them to take a second step, and a third? Or will it minister only to the darkness in our own souls?"

Ouch, Ritva thought, wincing; and again she thought she wasn't the only one. *Yup. He really does make you see things too clearly.*

Dorje went on to Juliet Thurston, his voice mild and implacable:

"He who puts his hand into the fire knows what he may expect. Nor may the fire be blamed. He who intrudes on a neighbor may receive what he does *not* expect. Nor may the neighbor be blamed. The fire will not be harmed; but the neighbor may be. And every deed of every kind bears corresponding consequences to the doer. You may spend a thousand lives repaying wrong done to a neighbor. Therefore, of the two indiscretions prefer thrusting your own hand into the fire. But there is a Middle Way, which avoids all trespassing."

"I . . ."

Whatever else she might be, Martin Thurston's wife

was no fool. Ritva could see her fair brows turn down in thought, and she believed there was a tinge of genuine gratitude there.

"What exactly do you mean, sir?" Juliet asked carefully.

"You have caused much harm, through vicious selfishness, and it turned on you."

"Yes," she said softly.

"You are fortunate it did so quickly; this is an opportunity. But do not fancy yourself uniquely guilty, a monster who is a wonder to the world; that too is vanity, and leads back to the same errors. You cannot undo the past by regret; nor can you avoid the painful consequences of your actions through fear. Both these things are equally impossible. Do not dwell on the past or deny it; do not fear the future."

"Regrets and fears are about all I have now," she said.

"No. You have a son; and you have amends to make to others. You have a task to do *now*, and virtue consists of doing it." Sternly. "So get to work, child!"

Ritva felt the force of that spear-sentence, even though she was not the target. Juliet blinked, gaping, and then nodded and sank down in a bit of a heap. Dorje inclined his head back to her and turned his glance away, in respect for privacy rather than dismissal. His hand continued to stroke the dark bronze of the boy's curls, and the child snuggled closer and dozed.

"You said that we'd meet again, guru," Ritva said.

Dorje grinned. "You and the others," he said. "I understand that you need to return quickly, not at the pace of this great mass of people?"

Alleyne nodded; he seemed to be a little less tight-wound now. "Yes, sir. Our mission was to rescue Mrs. Thurston . . . the elder Mrs. Thurston . . . and her children and reunite them with Frederick, who I understand you've met."

Dorje nodded. "A most earnest young man, for good and ill; but more for good."

Which is a great capsule description of Fred! Ritva thought.

Alleyne went on: "Partly because they were in danger; but also, frankly, because we need to get the truth of what happened out more widely. We've made a start on that in Boise, but it will be extremely helpful if we can get them . . . and the younger Mrs. Thurston and her son . . . back to Montival quickly. Living evidence, as it were."

Though technically we are *in Montival,* Ritva thought.

She knew what he meant, though; it was people that made a kingdom, not geography, and what few inhabitants there were in the wildlands probably hadn't heard that the current war was going on, or who the contending parties were. A fair number had survived the Change in this thinly populated wilderness, as numbers went in the modern world. But the reason it had been so empty back then was that there wasn't much in the way of water or good land. Almost all of the survivors had relocated afterwards, moving to where life was easier in places emptied by the great dying and where hands to work and fight were always welcome. There was a very thin scatter left, Rovers who lived by hunting more than herding. Most of them were people you wouldn't want to meet, especially if you were alone.

Still, it's sort of beautiful here. I like deserts, though I wouldn't want to live in one, she thought, looking up at the aching clarity of the sky, where sparks from the fires were scarcely brighter than the stars. *And it's certainly reassuring to see another twenty-five hundred good cavalry headed our way.*

"I will accompany you," Dorje said, and laughed at his

polite dismay. "My son, when I was five years old I walked four hundred miles across the Himalayas to reach Nepal. I know this scrawny old carcass of mine, and I do not delude myself as to what it can and cannot do. It will serve me as long as needed."

"*Ah, Hír i Dúnedain . . .*" Ritva said. "If he says he can do something, believe him. Really."

"I agree with you, *roquen,*" Alleyne said. To Dorje, in English: "Certainly you won't slow us down more than a two-year-old, sir."

Another of the Sun Valley folk leaned forward. He had an Eastern face too, but of a different stamp than Dorje's, smoother and the color of pale ivory, and he was about a generation younger, in a lean fit middle-age where every visible muscle showed like an anatomical diagram beneath the skin. He was clad in a set of lamellar armor linked with cords, a dao saber at his belt and a bowcase and quiver beside him.

"This is Master Hao," Dorje said. "He will make the practical arrangements. He is one of our brotherhood who has sought Enlightenment through the development of certain skills of mind and body."

Eilir Signed, and Ritva translated automatically: "You don't look much like my idea of a Buddhist monk, Master Hao."

She smiled when she Signed it. Hao didn't, but there was a knowledgeable respect in the glances he gave all the Dúnedain, and in the ones that returned. Ritva's muscles twinged as she recalled the months they'd spent in the Valley of the Sun; to let Mary and Rudi heal from their wounds, but they'd all trained under Master Hao and his acolytes as well. It had been . . .

Somewhat rigorous, she thought. *And the Pacific Ocean is somewhat large, rather wet and a bit salty.*

"Mine was a different path along the Way than the Rimpoche's," Hao said.

Dorje chuckled. "Many different schools came to that convention on *Buddhism on the World Wide Web*. This has made life more . . . interesting . . . since, after the Change converted our hotel into a monastery."

Hao snorted. "I must remain with the army, of course," he said.

Well, alae, duh, Ritva thought. *You're the commander, Mr. Shaolin.*

"However, we have a very large selection of horses and gear," he went on. "You may of course take your pick."

Ian gave an almost inaudible whimper, and she elbowed him discreetly.

Another relay race on horseback, she agreed. Then: *It's going to be hard on Cecile and the girls. And Juliet. Good thing we'll have liniment and some experienced field-masseurs, like me and Aunt Eilir. We can rig a carrier cradle for Lawrence Jr., but he's not going to be a happy camper after a while either, poor little guy.*

Alleyne brought out a map. "We're here," he said, pointing to a spot near Winnemucca. "We need to get here."

His finger came down on Ashland, in the Rogue River Valley south of the Willamette.

"The rail line was cleared and repaired that far three years ago, just before the war started. We can catch pedal cars from there, and then be anywhere on the rail net quickly, with a maximum priority to clear the track."

Hao looked, intent. "Your route?"

He traced it. "Dúnedain explorers have covered most of this area south of Ashland, from a bit west of here to the ocean and down into California, and this should be the least troublesome—the distance is about three hundred miles as the crow flies. About seventy to a hundred more as we'll be traveling, mostly along the old Route 140, but in summer and with plenty of horses, I wouldn't say it's too hard. A bit strenuous, perhaps. Seventy to a hundred miles a day."

Ian unconsciously rubbed at his buttocks. Ritva nodded, but then she looked at the face of the Lord of the Folk of the West. Something like this was *just* what he needed right now.

CHARTERED CITY OF GOLDENDALE
COUNTY OF AUREA
PORTLAND PROTECTIVE ASSOCIATION
(FORMERLY CENTRAL WASHINGTON)
HIGH KINGDOM OF MONTIVAL
(FORMERLY WESTERN NORTH AMERICA)
AUGUST 25, CHANGE YEAR 25/2023 AD

"Oh, by Saint Bernadette, that's awful!" Yseult Liu said, at the end of the story of the escape from Boise.

The Thurston girls looked at her solemnly, as they rolled the bandages and she contemplated their story of treachery and exile. They had a table to themselves in the city guildhall; apart from that, they were all doing pretty much the same work, making neat bundles of the clean linen. Nearly all the workers were women, but there was everything from gentlewomen to laborers' daughters here, supervised by the experts from the Sisters of Compassion. It was hot and stuffy despite the size of the room and the high ceiling and the tall open windows, and her hands felt a little sore from the frequent dips into disinfectant.

The bandages went onto wheeled trays that others pushed around, taken off to the ones who'd sterilize

them in autoclaves, seal and label them and then pack
them for shipment to the warehouses where they awaited
the need.

Soon, Yseult thought with a slight shiver. *The Grand
Constable is already fighting in the east. It's getting closer.
Huon will be there soon.*

"Uh . . . yeah," Shawonda said. "The Cutters *are* awful. They . . . they sort of *warp* things around them. Like
contagious miserable badness. It's scary!"

Yseult nodded vigorously, though she didn't add the
thoughts about demonic influences that naturally occurred to her. She wasn't under any illusions about why
it had been *suggested* that she take the Thurston daughters under her wing. It was a first installment on her future status as lady-in-waiting to the High Queen, even if
she still wore her oblate's robe and worked at a medical
task.

*Mathilda's feeling out what I can do and how well I can
do it. Which is exactly what she's supposed to do. And maybe
Shawonda and Janie will be ladies-in-waiting with me . . .
which would be fun, I think.*

A whistle sounded. "Shift change!" the guildmistress
of the weavers who was overseeing the whole affair called.

Everyone rose and filed out; Shawonda blew out her
cheeks in relief as they went into the courtyard. The walls
on either side gave shade, along with tall cottonwoods,
and there was a garden—at least, a fountain in the center
and several banks of flowers in raised beds between gravel
walkway. The building was new since the Change; there
hadn't been anything in the little town suitable for meetings of craft and merchant guilds and the Lord Mayor
and Council of Aldermen and the Confraternities.

The Crown had subsidized it, as part of the Regent's
Compassionate Feudalization program. She'd heard the

High Queen sigh over that term; then she'd acknowledged that it was perfectly sensible to give people positive incentives to act the way you wanted them to. Hence the three stories of stuccoed ferroconcrete gothic tracery around them, with the arched gateway that gave out onto the main square. They all drank from the cool water that sprang down in streams from the central spindle of the fountain and shook out their hands, laughing.

Yseult exchanged curtsies with others of those streaming out of the workroom; going first and sinking deeper to ladies of higher rank, returning those of her inferiors, and nodding and smiling instead when it was a non-Associate woman. The Thurstons looked on, a little puzzled at the ritual of precedence; she thought that Shawonda at least sensed that she was seeing the steps of a dance she didn't know.

Janie spoke as they walked back towards the castle; that took them along the town square, which was nearly packed, slowing their walk as they dodged around clumps of soldiers and clerks and clerics, craftsmen and peasants and laborers.

"You look a little like your brother," the younger Thurston girl said. "I liked him a lot. He made me laugh and he was so . . . so *elegant*."

The children's trousers attracted some eyes, but there were enough folk from outside the Association present that it would pass even in this little backland quasi-city—she could see three Mackenzie kilts and a couple of Bearkiller outfits at a glance, plus someone who was probably from Corvallis. There were political reasons for them not to wholly adopt Association ways.

Her oblate's robe was plain, but it got more deference and effort to let them through than an escort of crossbowmen might have, though she still had to navigate carefully around porters and the preoccupied. It took her a moment before she realized that Janie meant Odard, not Huon; time dulled grief, and it had been months now since she learned of his death.

"And he was so handsome." Shawonda nodded, her eyes looking a little dreamy for a moment. "Not as handsome as Rudi . . . I mean the High King . . . but really cool. He had such beautiful manners, he made you feel *special*."

The elder Thurston girl had a round face; she wasn't overweight, a little gaunt if anything, but that seemed to be the way her bones went. Her sister was much prettier and she thought always would be, though still a child rather than a maiden.

And they're the sisters of a ruler, of course, so it won't matter that much for them, Yseult thought. *They're both clever, which is more important.*

"Thank you," Yseult said. "He was a gallant knight and a good man and a wonderful brother . . . except when he was being a jerk; you know how brothers are sometimes."

They both nodded, and she went on: "He saved our family after . . . well, after what my mother did."

"Like our brother Martin," Shawonda said bitterly.

Janie took her hand consolingly. "It's good to see Fred again, though, isn't it?"

"Yes!"

They passed a knot of men-at-arms drinking outside a tavern that had spilled out to encroach on the way with trestle tables; they ignored the girls, sitting with their arming doublets half unlaced and intent on the tail end of a song:

"Now gracious God may save our King,
His people all well-willing,

Give his arms success at ending,
That we with mirth may safely sing"

And then the tune turned to a shout as fists pounded hard enough to make the tankards and baskets of bread jump:

"Deo gratias, Montivalia!
Redde pro victoria!"

The castle gate was even more crowded than the town; they barely crept in along the chained-off pedestrian edge of the drawbridge, but the squire who commanded the guard knew her face.

"My lady Liu," he said, thumping fist to breastplate and bowing his head. Then he turned and called, "Make way for the Lady Liu and her guests! In the High Queen's name!"

Nobody recognized the Thurstons yet, and it was uncertain how they fit into the Table of Ranks anyway; Yseult had decided that they were princesses, but wasn't going to insist on full state just now. The soldiers thumped the butts of their guisarmes as well, then used the shafts to open a lane for them, and Yseult nodded in reply. Another sign that she was being eased into her new status; and that she was shining in the light of Huon's reflected glory. It was certainly more agreeable than being a pariah under suspicion, but . . .

No, I must avoid bitterness. I have become cynical and reluctant to trust. My confessor is right; these are tasks I must work on. And these are nice girls who have suffered badly. My mother betrayed us, but at least she didn't kill our father, as their brother did. Take up your cross, Yseult Liu.

"It's good of you to volunteer to work so soon after

such a terrible journey," she said, as they climbed the spiral staircase of the donjon tower. "Everyone is putting state aside and doing what they can."

Their mother and sister-in-law were off making appearances where they told the truth about what Martin Thurston did, which was why she'd been set to shepherd and chaperone the girls. It had already started producing results that the High Queen was pleased with. None of them were getting much rest; the girls were still moving a bit stiffly, even after being able to rest on the railcars for the last two days of their headlong trip from the Wild Lands. The troubadours were already fitting it into the songs.

Shawonda groaned and made as if to rub herself rather indelicately. "Those Dúnedain are made of *iron*," she said.

"They're very hardy warriors," Yseult agreed; she didn't add anything about their morals or, for most of them, their religion.

"They're cool," Janie added. "I want to be one! Don't you, Shawonda?"

Shawonda looked a little troubled. "I've always loved the books, the Histories they call them. It was like being *in* the books to travel with the Dúnedain. But . . . and I don't know if I want to be a soldier. It was wonderful what the *Hiril* Astrid did, but . . ."

She shuddered. "The fight was so horrible. And I saw her die. It was awful, and she did it to save little Lawrence, or even *Juliet*, and it was so brave but . . . terrible."

Be fair about the Rangers, Yseult told herself. *Some of them are good Catholics. Besides which, that* was *a glorious and knightly deed that Lady Astrid did, the rescue and the way she put herself in the way of the bolt. We all die soon or late, but Lady Astrid's name will live while honor's praise is sung, and God loves those who imitate Christ by sacrifice, even if they don't know Him. I will pray for her; surely she's in Purgatory.*

"Well, they're not *all* knights-errant," Yseult said aloud.

She'd had a few romantic dreams about Mithrilwood herself; most girls did, for a little while at least, and some young noblemen. The old grudges had died away over her lifetime.

"There aren't any Ranger peasants," she went on. "But they have . . . oh, troubadours, bards they call them, and armorers, and healers, and craftsfolk. And they own ranches, and hunt and do forestry, and have houses in towns, and things like that, so some of them look after their properties."

They came to the chambers that had been turned over to the Thurston family; the set above were for Juliet Thurston and her son. She'd noticed how strained relations still were between Mrs. Thurston and her daughter-in-law, largely smoothed over by the grandson. That this suite was theirs alone was a mark of favor given how crowded Castle Goldendale was, even if it did mean the two girls were sleeping on truckle beds in this sitting room.

It was a pleasant enough chamber, shaped like a wedge of pie since it was in a circular tower, with plastered walls painted in hunting scenes. The location also made it easy to guard. There was no way in except through the outer gate, the keep gate, and then a guarded portal at the base. None of the windows were big enough for even a very *small* and lithe assassin to climb through.

The staff had set out a cold collation for them; regular dining in Hall had gone by the board, with everything upset by the mobilization. She'd heard someone grumble that they were all grazing like a herd, wherever they found a moment.

"Oh, good," Shawonda said. "I'm starved, but in weather like this a regular cooked meal makes you feel so logy and stuffed afterwards."

Yseult flipped off the white linen cloth. "Let's eat!" the sisters said in chorus, and took off the covers.

There was sliced ham, roast quail, potatoes done with garlic and herbs, a salad of roasted peppers and sweet Walla Walla onions and cauliflower dressed with oil and vinegar, another of greenstuffs, along with good manchet bread and a big apricot tart with cream. The girls waited while she said grace, then ate with what she recognized as good manners of a very old-fashioned sort, and enthusiasm.

Janie grinned and rubbed her hands after she'd loaded her plate. Yseult poured them all a glass of white wine. Janie paused and looked at hers a little dubiously.

"Am I allowed to drink wine?" she said.

"Well, some," Yseult said, surprised again.

Wine was what you drank with food, unless you had beer, which was slightly plebeian. This wasn't anything special, just ordinary drinkable wine decanted from a cask to a carafe and sent up from the kitchens.

I knew they were from a different country, but it's like they're from a different time. *I knew Boise clung to the old ways, but I didn't expect so much.*

"Why not?" she asked.

"Because I'm sort of young?" Janie said.

"You're what . . . eleven?" Yseult said.

"Since June."

"Well, I started drinking wine when I came out of the nursery . . . when I was six. Watered at first, of course. But don't worry, I won't let you get drunk!"

Janie nodded a little dubiously, sipped, made an interested sound but switched to the cool water instead.

"And it's exciting to be in a real *castle*," she said. "Pass the mustard, please . . . A castle with knights and everything! It looks just the way I imagined!"

Shawonda nodded and jointed one of the little birds, a little more restrained as befitted a maiden in her midteens.

"It's really interesting. But I don't want to have a banquet and everything *all* the time, not yet at least," she said.

Yseult blinked as she broke a piece of bread and buttered it.

What's odd or special about a castle? And castles are where knights live. Well, and manors. It's no more strange than finding a horse in a stable or a monk in an abbey.

"We don't have banquets all the time," she said instead. "Well, it's a little different at Court, naturally they keep more state than anyone else and entertain more, and this is a royal castle. But normally we . . . ordinary Associate nobles and our retainers . . . just eat in Hall, you know."

"What's that mean?" Janie asked.

Yseult blinked again, forced to think how to explain something she'd taken for granted all her life.

"Well, in *Hall* . . . you've seen the Hall here?"

Shawonda nodded. "The great big building with the dais at one end and that marvelous huge fireplace and the stained-glass windows down one side and the tapestries? And the lovely coffered ceiling."

Janie nodded. "Yes, we saw that when we came here. Mathilda . . . I mean, the High Queen . . . met us and gave a sort of speech, and there were a lot of people. But wouldn't that be for banquets? It's awful big for just a dining room."

"You don't have Halls?"

"Not like that," Shawonda said. "I mean, the capitol building in Boise has a big place where they have meetings, and sometimes special dinners. If you have dinner in a Hall, isn't that a banquet?"

"Well, no, it's used for banquets *too*, but those are special occasions. Banquets are different, it's mostly guests then, sometimes everyone's a noble. But a Great Hall has to be big because all the Castle people eat there, except some of the extra troops if there's a call-up, and it's where you have dances and things, and music and performers and maybe mystery plays, and a lord may sit in judgment there for his manor court or the Court Baron, and you play games in winter or sew there at times in the summer if the solar gets too stuffy. A Hall will be a bit smaller in a manor house than a castle but it's the same thing really."

"*Everybody* in a Castle or a manor eats in the hall?" Janie said.

"Most days. The family and any noble guests at the head table, and then the Associate retainers, and then the commons down below the salt, from the highest-ranking servants down to the stable hands and that sort. We don't all eat the same *food*, of course, or use the same tableware, but one reason common people want to serve in a castle is that they eat better than what they would get at home in their family's cottage."

Shawonda returned to the subject. "So you eat in this Great Hall place every day?"

"Not *every* day, especially not breakfast or luncheon, sometimes a lord will eat *en famille* with his wife and children or a few select guests in a solar or ladybower, but it's . . . well, people will think you're odd and, ummm, sort of . . . what was the old word . . . antisocial if you do that all the time. It's good lordship to sit at meat with your folk. Though it's nice to be private now and then, like this."

Shawonda looked down at her plate and realized it was empty except for a few clean-picked bones. Yseult thought she blushed, though it was a little difficult to tell for sure with the brown complexion.

"Go ahead," she laughed. "You've been on short rations, I know. Here, have some of the ham this time. The honey glaze is excellent."

"We were eating jerky and these hard biscuits and cheese and not much else while we rode so fast," Janie said. "We were so tired we didn't realize how hungry we were until we got to Ashland and we could sleep in a bed again!"

Her sister nodded. "Everything sort of blurred together after the first couple of days. I think there were bandits once and I didn't even *notice* because I was so tired and sore and half-asleep."

Silence fell for a few minutes; Yseult felt a bit amused at how the two made up for lost time, and restricted herself a little, passing over most of the red meat. Even if her time as an oblate was fading, it wasn't quite over yet, and the Rule of the Sisters called for moderation. Yseult poured them all more wine, red this time, and sliced the tart and handed round the honey-sweetened cream.

"You've heard all about us, Lady Yseult," Shawonda said.

"Please, let's be Yseult and Shawonda and Janie in private? You know, you're actually princesses, so I should be the one who goes after. I'm just a baron's daughter. Sister, now."

"We *are*?" Janie said. "Princesses? Really and truly?"

Her sister looked at her. "Remember what Mathilda

said back when they came to our place? I thought she was joking but now I think she really meant it. But don't start *calling* yourself a princess, Janie. It might cause trouble, people at home wouldn't like it."

She looked at Yseult. "But we don't know what happened with you, just that the CUT . . . got at . . . your mother the way they did at . . . Martin. Would you tell us? It . . . it would make us feel less alone."

"Like we're part of an army, not just people something bad happened to," Janie said.

She's no fool. Neither of them are, Yseult thought as she sipped her wine. *Maybe I should. We do have this in common. And . . . not to be cynical, but they are princesses. I like them, and it certainly can't hurt to be friends. You need friends in this world. Friends, and strong allies. And you can't have friends unless you're prepared to be one yourself.*

"Well, my mother was arrested, when the Lady Regent found out what she'd done," Yseult began slowly. "Everyone suspected Huon and me, too."

"That must have been awful," Shawonda said

"Were you locked up in a *dungeon*?" Janie said, with the ghoulishness of her age.

"Not quite! What happened was—"

CASTLE TODENANGST, CROWN DEMESNE
WILLAMETTE VALLEY NEAR NEWBURG
(FORMERLY WESTERN OREGON)
PORTLAND PROTECTIVE ASSOCIATION
SEPTEMBER 27, CHANGE YEAR 23/2021 AD

Her quarters at Todenangst were not quite a cell. There was a room that was small and whitewashed within and furnished with a plain bed with equally plain but adequate sheets and blankets, a small cupboard and a commode. There was a Spartan sitting room next to it, with a table and chairs and an étagère. The place smelled of soap and wax and, very slightly, of concrete still curing after all these years; a maid came through and cleaned thoroughly every day.

There was no need for her do to anything menial, no *dérogeance*, but it was very bleak.

She rose each morning when the sun came through the high slit windows, dressed in her riding habit, waited for the door to open and was escorted by an unspeaking squire with an equally taciturn middle-aged duenna to the stables and rode for two hours, in a walled tilt-yard of the Protector's Guard, under instruction and ward of the Master of the Stables, Sir Henri Gallardo.

Castle Todenangst was more than a castle; you could have lost Castle Gervais in it a dozen times over. It was a palace and a city in itself, the inner keep here alone a vast labyrinthine complex of towers and courtyards, little hidden gardens and terraces, armories and barracks, offices and halls and galleries, archives and libraries and chapels and quirking passageways. Some of it was bleakly plain like her rooms; some parts she traversed were stunningly beautiful and decorated with things new-made by the Protectorate's most skilled artists or plundered from half a continent. All of it had a faint air of menace that might be her imagination. After days she still felt she'd be hopelessly lost if she took one wrong turn, and almost grateful for the constant escort.

Sometimes late at night she thought of its building, twenty thousand men laboring through five years of hunger and brutal toil just for the main framework, some leaving their bones in its mass concrete bulk and most in the nearby graves. From the bed, if she stood, she could see the Black Tower glittering with the crystal inclusions in its dark granite sheathing. That had been the Lord

Protector's lair, and of him men still spoke with awe and dreadful fear.

After riding she went to confession—brief ones, where every day was the same—and Mass in an astonishing Lady Chapel that was like being inside a jewel, sitting between her guards of the day. Then the guards escorted her to the sitting room and a late breakfast, plain but adequate. After that she was free until her lessons and the escort to the baths where she was always the only occupant.

Free, she thought as she paced, after a time that seemed to stretch out forever and flick by in instants, both at the same time.

Free to do absolutely anything I can do in these two rooms! Free to pound my head on the walls!

Her books, brought from Gervais, she placed beside her bed; she arranged a little prie-dieu in her sitting room and spent hours trying to pray. A lute was brought at her request, and she was allowed to borrow, through Virgilia, any book she wanted out of the Todenangst libraries. That was one good thing, because they seemed to have all the books in the world. Virgilia gave her lessons from three to seven. The very first day the older woman told her bluntly that there were eavesdroppers, and her skin crawled at the thought that eyes might be on her at any moment of the day or night, and how the whole castle might be honeycombed by secret passages. The Spider had designed it, after all.

After that she kept her mind strictly on her lessons when Virgilia was there.

Each day she came back to the bare little room and tried to focus on a short list of tasks. She worked at making the hours pass by assigning to each one a different task. For the most part, she paced; unable to focus on any one task as raw worry gnawed at her balance.

Odard, she thought. *Where is he now, out in the barbarian lands? Huon . . . is he still a page at Mollala? Mother . . . Fen House . . . people whisper about it. Better than the dungeons, but . . . and will I ever leave here? What happens if I start to scream at the walls?*

She paced four quick steps one way and the seven at right angles, over and over as noon crept to one and Virgilia arrived to distract her. The fourth day as she sat and picked up a new piece of embroidery she'd started in hopes of focusing her attention once again, the door opened and Huon walked in.

The fine linen cloth with the pattern of yellow roses growing on it went flying as she sprang up. For one long second she stared at him and then they rushed together. Strong arms went around her and his tears fell on her shoulder. They swayed together, laughing and crying.

Huon had been a good three inches shorter than she when he left to go be Lord Chaka's page. Now he stood just slightly taller, and he even *smelled* different; clean, but with an overtone of smoke and leather and horse, and his hands were rougher with callus. When their spate of tears had passed she found herself sitting in the little window seat, still in his arms.

"Tell me," he said urgently, his rough voice breaking into a boyish treble. "Tell me what happened and how?"

"But I don't know!" she exclaimed, sliding her eyes towards the door and the wall she suspected of a spy hole.

Huon shook his head impatiently.

"Don't worry about them eavesdropping on us, Yseult. The Spider knows much more than we, and we cannot hurt ourselves any worse than Mama has already done. Our only hope is truth and mercy."

"Then . . . you know."

"Lord Chaka told me. What did you learn?"

"Goodwife Romarec said Mama and Uncle helped the men who came last year to Sutterdown and endangered the Princess."

"Tried to kill everyone in that building, *including* the Princess. And including Odard. He fought for her . . . fought *beside* her, and killed several of them at the risk of his life. I think that's why we were left alone for as long as we were. Mother was getting a second chance that he bought us with the sword and his blood. And look what she did with it!"

His voice had changed too, deeper and rougher, and there was a different look in his eyes. They said he looked more like their father than anyone else in the family, and suddenly she believed it. Her father had been a hard man; never unkind to her, and she remembered him affectionate with her mother, but a very hard man in very hard times. People had been frightened of him; commoners never talked much about him in her presence. The Lord Protector had used him like a dagger held up the sleeve.

"But before she could tell me any more, Sir Garrick arrived and took over the castle," Yseult said.

"Start at the beginning, then, Ysi. You and I are all of House Liu left here and we have only each other. You *must* tell me everything or I won't know what to do or say."

Yseult searched her brother's eyes. He was the only one of them to get ones of their father's dark blue, but with their mother's open lids.

He's only a boy! she thought, with a stab of remorse. *I should . . .*

She spoke aloud. "You're my little brother! I should be protecting *you*!"

Huon laughed suddenly. "And if we had a kitchen or a solar, you'd be bustling around doing all the womanly things, taking baskets to the poor and supervising the weaving and getting the winter supplies done and the herbs put up and the accounts balanced. And doing it right!"

"Listen to the bearded knight!" she said gaily, then hugged him again. "Oh, this is good. I thought I'd go crazy . . . how have you been, over there in Mollala?"

Enthusiasm glowed from him; he *was* still only thirteen. "It's great! Lord Chaka and the knights and their squires are strict, but they're fun too, and the other pages are mostly good guys. I thumped a couple and a couple thumped me and we all know where we stand."

Boys are weird *sometimes,* she thought, not for the first time. He went on:

"We train really hard and study, but there's lots of hunting, they're right on the edge of the Cascades there you know, and I've got a horse of my own and I've started again with the lance. And Lord Mollala says I've got a good seat and eye!"

"It *does* sound like fun," Yseult said enviously.

She should have been a lady-in-waiting; for a year or more now. Learning skill and courtesy and the ways of another great house, with a kindly noblewoman to oversee her, and parties and hawking and some carefully chaperoned flirting, and seeing new places and people and making friends among the girls who'd be close to her all her life and link the families together the way page service and being a squire did the boys.

Huon grinned at her obvious thought: "And if we were under siege you'd be counting chickens and eggs and firing those deadly little darts of yours at the invaders."

Yseult suddenly smiled. "I'm even better than Alex with the crossbow! Oh!"

"Alex? Vinton? He came back? I heard, but nothing definite."

"I think so . . ." Yseult thought carefully and then told Huon everything.

It took some time, but she didn't mind. *I want the Spider . . . the Lady Regent . . . to know the truth! The truth is I didn't know anything about treason! Neither did Huon!*

It might not make all that much difference. The law spread guilt for treason throughout the kin. More than an hour later Huon said, very softly:

"Par le bon Dieu!"

Yseult nodded, letting her head fall back onto his shoulder. In the keyhole opening of the neck of his shirt she could see the little medal of St. Valentine Huon had always worn. There was another medal next to it.

"What's that?" she asked.

Huon looked down and fingered the medallion. "Well, the Dowager Mollala gave it to me. It's a Michael; the archangel, you know. Grand Constable of the Heavenly Host. Said if I wanted to be a warrior I needed a saint that could do more than just be a target and end up a holy pincushion."

Yseult nodded. "Bernadette and Lourdes have been a great help to me."

"You always loved them."

She nodded again, suddenly tired. All the tension that had been holding her together for the last five days drained out of her body and surprisingly, she found herself very sleepy but content as she hugged her brother. It seemed like a long time later when a thought floated up in her exhausted brain.

"I . . . it's horrible, but I was . . . not *glad*, but, but, I wish I knew what words to use . . . when I saw Uncle Guelf's body in the courtyard, I wasn't angry he was dead. I felt like he'd deserved it and I was safer with him dead. How awful is that?"

Her brother sighed. "We probably *are* much safer with him dead and Mother under house arrest somewhere. They say to get out of a pit first you have to stop digging, and now he's buried himself and Mother can't do anything to make things *worse*. Where *is* Fen House? People just whisper about it when some noble *really* screws up and disappears."

"Sir Garrick said we didn't need to know. Do you know Sir Garrick?"

Huon looked down at her and shook his head. "The Protectorate is a big place, bigger than I realized. There's a lot more empty space between the baronies than I realized, too. The Betancourts live in Bethany, up near Portland, a little west. It's prime farmland, I think they have about a dozen manors, and vineyards in their demesne, too. A rich estate. But all the kids are a lot older than we are. Roderick and Garrick are the grandsons. I think old Lord Betancourt, the first of the line, is either dead or dying; though I might not have heard. They were Society people like Mother, but on both sides."

Huon was quiet for a time. Then: "I can understand your not being sad that he died. I'll bet the headless body gave you a shock, though."

Yseult shuddered. "I don't think it was the body. I've seen executions, after all. I think it was the unexpected sight, and *knowing* him. And he never used his head for anything but a helmet-rack anyway."

She knew that the words were just bravado, but Huon laughed in approval and hugged her and she relaxed.

I've missed him; missed being able to share my feelings and thoughts. Missed it so much.

Huon pulled her closer. "It could be. He just *knew* he was smarter and better than Mother was and that he was supposed to be the regent for Odard, even though he loved Mother. And Mama loved Guelf, but she hated it when he tried to tell her what to do. I went to Loiston to be his page, remember? It was just for three months and I was only seven. Mother made me come home when I swore at her. And she and Guelf had one of their fights over his teaching me bad language."

Yseult gave a watery chuckle. "The kind where we were scared they'd pull each other's hair out by the roots? I remember that fight!"

"I do, too. But I saw that he truly loved Layella and cared for Aunt Theresa. He was really hard on Terry and Odo, but then I realized that he was really stupid about *how* he showed how much he cared, but he really cared. So, I understand your not being unhappy he's dead. But I'm sorry; he did love us. I wish I knew what happened, that he abandoned his post."

"Did he? Did he really? He *ran away*?"

That shocked her to the very core. You could forgive an Associate most things except cowardice.

And treason, her mind added.

"Yes, but that's all I know. Walked out on all the men; just left them and headed back home . . . I don't think it was cowardice, really. He was a fighter, at least. Everyone agrees he fought like a lion at Pendleton! *Why?*"

"I was really sorry for Aunt Layella. I don't know if she cared for him, but she was a good aunt to us and Châtelaine for him."

She licked her lips; she was dancing around the most important question of all:

"Huon, why did Mama do this? What made her so mad all the time? She hates me. She's always after me, always irritated, always angry. And Uncle's . . . was . . . so much worse than he used to be, too."

Huon started, eyes focusing on her again. "But she didn't hate you!" he protested. "Mama loves you so very much. Don't you remember the silk violet dress with the eyelet surcoat she made for you that Easter you led all the girls into church? And the flowered drapes and hangings for your bed she embroidered . . . all your 'special' flowers?"

"Oh," breathed Yseult. "I'd forgotten."

Remembering Mary's tender hands dressing her and carefully braiding her hair in a complicated pattern. She'd been eight and so proud to be old enough to lead the girls with their baskets of flowers up to the altar.

"She did the white work herself. I still have it, carefully put away. Or, I did. She changed. She changed . . . when?" she asked, puzzled.

"Some when our father died, Lord Chaka says. I was just a baby. He told me she became obsessed with revenge. But it was the fortunes of war, for heaven's sake! He wasn't slain by treachery, that would be grounds for a feud. He died sword in hand with his face to the enemy. What better can you hope for? A *man* drops it once the war is over. But she was just a woman widowed and grieving."

"Hummmphf!" Yseult snorted, and Huon waved it aside. "Then, then Uncle Jason died in Corvallis and she had to struggle along with just Sir Richart Reddings to help her besides Guelf, and he kept thinking he should be in charge. And Sir Harold's father; but he was already old and sick. And he didn't like her very much."

"Was it then?"

"Later, I don't know. I know that she wouldn't let me leave to become a page, again. There were at least five offers that I heard of, good ones, Houses it would be smart to have links to, but she wouldn't even discuss them. That was three years ago, but I never knew why. I think, I think that was the start of a . . . a . . . worse change, but even Lord Chaka didn't know the true answer. He only had guesses."

Yseult pondered, picking at the crusty scabs on her cheek, before giving up on the conundrum.

"I wish I knew. It hurts to think of Mama being a traitor. It hurts the honor of House Liu and I don't know how we're going to make it clean."

Huon nodded. "Yes. But she never really accepted that the Lady Regent was her ruler. She felt . . . I've heard her say . . . that Gervais was an independent Barony, or should be, after the Lord Protector died."

"But that's nonsense! We're tenants in chief, we hold *directly* from the Crown, and that's an honor, it makes us equals of the Counts even if we're not rich. It was the Lord Protector himself who gave Gervais to Mama to hold in ward for Odard after Father was killed. We were there at court with Mother when he made the decree!"

Huon shook his head. "I would have been, what, under two? I don't remember it. We've been to court enough that it's all a blur that far back for me. But why couldn't Mother just be happy that the estates weren't put in Crown wardship until Odard came of age? What more did she want?"

"Oh, I know when that happened!" exclaimed Yseult. "It was a year or so after the war. Everybody'd lost a lot of peasants with the new law that they could move if they wanted to. And we hadn't. Somebody noticed and told on us. The Lady Regent sent a couple of spies. Mother and Guelf and Sir Czarnecki, the older one who died a couple of years later, had all blocked the 'tinerants from coming in and letting people know and they were keeping people against their will. And Mother was still running tolls on the highways and roads."

"She did *what*?" Huon pulled away from Yseult. "I am certainly learning a bit more dirty laundry than I thought was in the basket!" He shook his head in disbelief. "That was part of the peace treaty! And Gervais is really too close to Mount Angel and the Bearkillers and even the Mackenzies to risk any accusation of bad faith."

Yseult laughed, a catch in her voice. "Oh, Huon. I've never thought things out, just watched them happen and never questioned. Mama was called to court and given strict orders. Sir Czarnecki and Uncle Guelf were fined. So was Gervais, but the Lady Regent told Mama that she was fining *everybody who should have known better*. She never forgave it."

Huon sighed. A discreet tap at the main door panel announced their dinner.

"Two o'clock? I'm famished!" said Yseult. Huon nodded. The fare was very simple but filling and they ate quietly.

"I'd forgotten how happy we were once," Yseult said. "Before it changed. I feel sorry for Mother almost, but she . . . *made* it all go bad."

She picked at the crusty yellow scab again and Huon made a wordless sound of impatience and took her wrist.

"Leave your cheek alone! You'll scar if you pick at it! What happened?"

"I fell onto the embers. My wrist still hurts, too."

Huon scowled and released it at once. "Has the chirurgeon come?" he asked.

"No, why? I haven't asked for him. Do you think . . ."

The thirteen-year-old boy strode to the door and pounded on it.

"Ho-la!" he yelled, his voice deep and then cracking. "Guard, to me, to me, the Guard!"

The door jerked open and two feet of steel poised its point on Huon's breastbone.

"What?" asked the man-at-arms, gruffly, his face hidden behind the visored sallet helm.

"My sister was injured and nobody has bothered to send a chirurgeon to her. Her wrist and her face need attention! And put that blade down and your visor up! Don't you know better than to draw on a gentleman, and in the presence of a lady, you mannerless barking dog?"

Yseult held her breath as the barely visible eyes studied her brother and then her. Abruptly the steel was withdrawn and the man showed his face before the door slammed. There was no doubt that *Huon* was brave!

He turned, frowning. "Sister, tell me again about Mama and what they did to her when they took her prisoner."

When she was done he began to pace, frowning; some corner of her mind noticed that he took fewer strides to cross the strait confines of the room.

"Laudanum?" he said, half-incredulous. "A straitjacket? And she never used to have hysterical fits. I wonder . . ."

The chirurgeon came, a middle-aged man with a short grizzled beard. He clicked his tongue angrily when he saw the neglected burns and wrist.

"The wrist will need exercises. I'll talk with Gallardo; he can add it to your morning routine. I wish he'd told me, he's supposed to report on your condition."

"I didn't tell *him*, it's not his fault," said Yseult. "I didn't know it mattered."

The chirurgeon snorted. "Any injury that doesn't heal is a problem, and it gets worse if untended, young mistress. The face is a problem now. It's impetigo. Luckily we don't seem to have brought any serious diseases like MRSA through the Change but it's not good. I'm going to soak it, gently debride it and then paint it with Gentian violet. You will wear gloves all day, and keep your hands completely away from your face. Young Master Gervais, will you go to your chamber?"

Huon jerked out of his reverie. "Why?" he demanded imperiously; the man was a commoner.

"Because this will hurt your sister. I can't have you hit me because I hurt her," said the chirurgeon impatiently.

Huon glared at the chirurgeon and sat down next to Yseult and put his arms around her. "Hold on to me, sister, we'll weather this together."

"Oh, that *was* awful!" Shawonda Thurston said.

Yseult jerked a little, wrenched back across the years. She used an exercise one of the Sisters had taught her, thinking about a candle burning before the altar, to relax her mind; the muscles of her shoulders followed, and the pain in her knee faded.

"What happened after that?" Shawonda said.

"Do you want that last piece of the apricot tart?" Janie added.

Yseult laughed at her angelic expression. *I wish I'd had some sisters. We were always such a small family, just the three of us youngsters, and I was the only girl.* She realized that she was going to enjoy being a lady-in-waiting again, once things settled down. It had been the first time in her life she could be one of many of her own sex and age, and she wanted that again for a while.

"Go ahead," Shawonda said. "What happened?"

"Then . . . then I saw the Lady Regent, a few weeks later."

"*Weeks?*" Shawonda said indignantly. "How could she be so cruel to you, leaving you in that little hole? For weeks!"

"It wasn't so bad after Huon came. I knew *he* was all right. And I had my books and . . . well, the Lady Regent isn't cruel."

"She's kind?" Shawonda said ironically.

"No. She's, this is with ordinary people, you understand . . . she's neither. She's just . . . clever. Patient, and very very clever."

The elder Thurston girl shivered a little. "Sounds scary."

"*Oh* yes," Yseult said, her mind traveling back. "You have no idea."

CASTLE TODENANGST, CROWN DEMESNE
WILLAMETTE VALLEY NEAR NEWBURG
(FORMERLY WESTERN OREGON)
PORTLAND PROTECTIVE ASSOCIATION
OCTOBER 15, CHANGE YEAR 23/2021 AD

Yseult struggled with the cote-hardie. The voluminous folds kept getting hung up. Three weeks of physical therapy and exercises had helped her arm, shoulder and wrist. But she still didn't have the full range of motion back. With an annoyed exclamation she ducked her head down and bent her body, shaking herself and wishing for Carmen Barrios or Virgilia. The slubbed silk slowly slid off her arms and over her head.

Huon knocked on the door. "Ysi, Ysi, what's taking you so long? It's almost time!"

She looked at the pools of sunset orange silk on the floor, hesitated for the tenth time and then set her lips.

"Huon, please come help me. I can't get the dress on with my arm still injured."

"Help you!" Huon suddenly squeaked, a thirteen-year-old boy again, not a man impatient with female fripperies.

Yseult caught her breath on a sudden laugh. "Huon!" she chided. "I'm wearing the chemise and underclothes. I could get those on and laced up by myself. It's just the court cote-hardie. It's so tight and I can't lift my left arm enough. I'm perfectly decent."

She opened the door to the sitting room and looked at Huon and approved.

"You're going to be as much of a popinjay as Odard!" she said. "That looks really good on you. Now come help me keep up the reputation of House Liu!"

His cheeks were as red as the crimson shirt under his plain gray houppelande of fine merino wool. It was belted over parti-colored hosen in black and a darker crimson. The belt, with its empty dagger sheath, was one of Odard's; an elaborate affair of fifteen five-inch-wide black enameled plaques in a filigree pattern, set with lapis lazuli cabochons. It had a matching state chain over the shoulder that picked up the dark sea-blue of his eyes, like the Pacific off Astoria on a sunny day.

"I approve," she said. "Where are the shoes and hat?"

He waved a hand aimlessly at the window and said, "Shouldn't I send for a tirewoman?"

"We don't have enough time . . . and, Huon?"

He looked at her, inquiringly. She hesitated and shrugged.

"I think this is a test."

"Test?" he frowned. "Of what?"

"Resourcefulness and ability to think on our feet? Who knows; do you want to get into a who's-the-clever-one contest with the *Spider*?"

"St. Michael, no! I'm thirteen!"

"I don't either, and I won't when I'm thirty!"

A startled expression crossed his face. "I never thought of that! And, in that case, will you help fix *my* stuff, too?"

"Of course! I wouldn't have let you out of the room like that!"

"Why? What's wrong?"

She giggled, suddenly. "You might be heading towards brother Odard's dandyism, but you've got a long way to go yet! It's all in the details. I'll take care of it in a minute."

She picked up and shook out the sunset-colored cotehardie. "I'm going to crouch a bit and you throw it over my head and get my hands into the sleeves. Then you have to help coax the sleeves up each arm and make sure the skirts fall without getting tucked up at the waist."

Huon looked appropriately solemn as he carefully cast the many yards of raw silk slub over her head and they worked together on coaxing the tight sleeves into place.

"Your chemise is showing," he fussed.

She waved a hand at him. "No, it's supposed to show. I'm too young to be showing off my pitiful assets. It needs to be absolutely even all around, though."

She shrugged and lifted the collar of the complex dress while he walked around and around and carefully tucked and tugged at the delicate pink silk chemise. Then she reached under the skirts and deftly pulled the hem of the chemise. The wrinkles at the neckline slowly vanished. The chain and saint's medal were lightly outlined by the silk, but that was acceptable. She shook herself, making sure the gown moved freely, and moved into the sitting room and studied herself in the better light. Huon followed her out, carrying the rich caramel-colored sideless surcoat.

"Wouldn't it have been easier to just unbutton the buttons and then do it up?"

"The buttons are just for show," she said absently, carefully pulling the seams of her sleeves straight.

The obsidian buttons were burin-carved in a cloud

pattern, each one slightly different; they marched their way up to the elbow.

"And the front ones—if I did that it would button up all crooked. Some of the court ladies wear theirs so tight they actually have to sew themselves into them. Buttons would gap, do gap, these are for show, too . . . It looks very, very . . . ummm, when they do them too tight."

She felt her cheeks heat up. Huon laughed a small laugh that reminded her he was old enough to start looking at women *that* way.

"I've seen it. Like they painted themselves in silk, and nothing left to the imagination."

She nodded, still a little pink. Huon shook out the sideless surcoat, found the front and flung it over her head. It settled neatly around her and a few tweaks set it in place. The front and back had been cut out, too, and then lightly laced, to show off the cote-hardie itself.

"Where are your jewels?" asked Huon.

"Under the prie-dieu."

He brought out her belt and state necklace, pearl set copper, and helped her get them set just right. She swallowed a bit at the sight of the empty dagger sheath at her belt. She and Huon wore the sheaths as tokens that they were Associates; they were empty in token of the accusations against them.

She found the veil, gauzy wild pink that picked up the brilliant color of her dress. Huon carefully combed the disordered strands of her braided hair smooth and draped the veil. The copper and pearl diadem fixed it on her head.

"Doesn't this make your skin go green?"

"No. It would, but it has a lining of silver on the inside. That might make my skin go black. But it's a lot slower to tarnish than copper . . . Huon! I'm so scared!"

She saw his throat work and was sorry she'd spoken. "But, you're with me. We're House Liu! We can do this."

Huon's face firmed. "Right, Ysi. Our father came out of the Change a baron. There's strength in our blood."

"Come here and let me straighten out your houppe-lande and state chain . . . no, first put on your shoes and hat! Let me comb your hair . . ."

Fussing over Huon steadied her and she saw her brother relax and smile a bit and relaxed herself. The clash of spears thumping the hall warned her that it was time. She walked quickly but carefully back into her bedchamber, holding up her skirts. She gulped and touched the porcelain of Bernadette and the picture of the Virgin.

"Give me strength, but also, give me smarts. This is going to be very scary!"

She slipped the rosary under her belt and heard the door open. She walked out and gasped. Jehane stood there between the spearmen, Lord Chaka's youngest sister, and looking very grown-up now, her smooth brown face inscrutable.

Oh! I wish I could smile and dance up to her and hug her like I used to do. She was always so nice to me; but she looks . . . so, so . . . magnificent and so solemn! And she's the Lady Regent's amanuensis now. I have to be careful. Some days I wish I didn't have to grow up. Life was simpler back then.

Jehane nodded with regal calm. "Come then, young mistress, young master. The Lady Regent will examine you in this matter of the treason of House Liu."

Yseult shot a quick look at Huon and straightened her back. Her fingers pinched a small fold of the sideless sur-coat and the cote-hardie under it and lifted it, a scant inch from the floor. She glided forward and followed Jehane out of the room.

Two large men-at-arms in black armor stood at the door like the legendary metal men of the ancient world except for the faces under their raised visors, others beyond, in the corridor.

Things may have seemed *simpler in bygone days,* thought Yseult.

Even then she couldn't help admiring Jehane's magnificent pale green ermine-trimmed cote-hardie with the elaborate dagged sleeves faced in silver silk, black marks echoing the ermine. Either she had perfect taste, or the Lady Regent did and insisted on it for her immediate staff, or both. Probably both.

But they weren't, not really. I just never noticed what was going on over my head. Mother has been intriguing for years, and so has Uncle Guelf. What an inheritance!

Probably her father had as well, and her mother had helped. It was the play of great lords, the game of advantage.

The audience chamber to which they were escorted in the Dark Tower was an uncomfortable room despite the handsome stone of the floor and walls and the roof of carved plaster arabesques. Harsh light from the bare high windows fell in spears on the spot before a large desk of carved walnut on the slightly raised dais. The Lady Regent sat there, wrapped in a great cloak of priceless black-and-white ermine. Two Associates' daggers lay on the desk before her, points towards the accused, their bright edges glittering against the dark silky wood.

Yseult sank into a deep curtsy and held it, as Huon did his bow.

"Rise, and approach," the Regent said.

Yseult took a deep breath as they did, and let her eyes take in the room.

It was large and chilly, with a great medallion of the

Lidless Eye set in the wall behind the desk, jet and niello and obsidian and raw gold. Yseult looked for the hot-water radiators. They were there; bronze pipes running in through the classic cast-iron radiators.

So the Spider wants us to be cold and uncomfortable. Did she think I wouldn't notice and would just be frightened, or did she expect me to notice? Or is she testing to see if I do notice, and just caught that look at the radiators? Oh, yes, that's it.

Hard wooden chairs ranged in an arc before the dais, but Yseult and Huon were not offered a seat. Jehane sank in a deep curtsy to the Regent and sat quietly next to a girl about her age; she took up a little blond-wood writing desk on her lap and dipped a pen ready in the tiny bottle of ink built into it.

Standing beneath one of those glaring windows was the Grand Constable, Baroness Tiphaine d'Ath, in dark elaborate male court dress and an ostrich plume in the clasp of her chaperon hat. Yseult shuddered under the cold gray gaze.

Quietly Yseult identified some of the others. Chaka, Lord Mollala, young and burly and chocolate dark like his sister Jehane, with a frown on his scarred and bluntly handsome face. Sir Garrick Betancourt, and Lady Delia de Stafford, in subdued formal dress much less fanciful than what her reputation as a leader of fashion would make you expect.

Ranged along the back and sides were the faceless, black-armored men of the Protector's Guard. Two flanked the Lady Sandra, their naked long swords over their shoulders.

In the Lord Protector's day they would have been behind me and Huon. Ready to take off our heads. Lord Chaka's father stood like that once, after the Princess was kidnapped by the Mackenzies while she was visiting with him. He was pardoned, though.

The Regent studied them from behind the desk in a silence that stretched. Yseult looked up into the dark brown eyes under the cream-silk wimple with its platinum band. She'd heard of drowning in someone's eyes, usually in bad love songs, but never like this. Such an ordinary face, smooth and slightly plump and middle-aged . . .

For an endless time all was still. Then Sandra spoke, her contralto voice quiet and emotionless as water of rocks in an ornamental garden.

"This investigation is convened. Let it be noted that We—"

She used the royal pronoun, a sign that the business was very, very official. Jehane's pen scratched and scritched steadily on the paper. She wrote quickly and neatly in shorthand, a little silver clip holding her sleeve back from the ink.

"—are not sitting in Star-Chamber."

Yseult's eyes went up involuntarily. Star-Chamber *did* have stars on its arched ceiling, or so rumor said. Sessions of that court were strictly secret. Sometimes even the sentence was never announced, just carried out.

"Let Huon Liu and Yseult Liu be sworn."

A smooth-faced priest in a black robe brought out a great Bible in a tooled-leather cover, and a silver-gilt reliquary. Yseult put her hands on them and swore:

". . . by my hope of salvation and in the sight of God the Father, the Son and the Holy Spirit. Amen."

Everyone crossed themselves; she kissed her crucifix as well. *And I mean to tell the truth!*

The Lady Regent joined in the gesture. She was a petite woman in her fifties; a gray cote-hardie showed beneath the ermine robe, buttoned by steel-gray Madras pearls and silver.

All these powerful lords, Yseult thought. *And Lady Death, whose name is fear, and the Regent dominates the room as if she were a giant made of fire.*

She had wielded unquestioned power from the Willamette to the Yukon and inland to the Rockies for twenty-three years; fourteen of them all by herself, this little woman in silver and gray. The Lady Regent didn't blink for a long count of five.

Then: "We are gathered here to hear and ponder the matter of the children of the House of Liu. These are Yseult and Huon Liu, children of the late Eddie Liu, well loved by my late husband, and Mary Liu . . . not so well loved by myself."

Yseult swallowed. The brown eyes studied hers, moved to her brother, and a very small smile showed.

"I suspect that despite natural piety, you are not well pleased with her right now yourselves, children. She has been so *stupid.* Ambition can be dealt with; it's even useful. Against folly and self-deception, even gods contend in vain at times."

The very slight tinge of playfulness leached out of Sandra Arminger's voice. Something like the metal on the edge of a razor replaced it.

"Your mother is guilty of high treason. This is not in doubt. Her actions, her letters, the testimony of Castle Gervais staff; the actions of Guelf Mortimer, her brother, and Alex Vinton, who she made privy servant to your elder brother, all speak unambiguously for themselves. She intrigued with our enemy, the Church Universal and Triumphant and its Prophet Sethaz. She intrigued with them long before we became aware of their focus on our lands and people. She could have warned us; and we would have been much better prepared in September—but she didn't. Many good and loyal vassals have died because she didn't."

Yseult made herself breathe and forced her eyes to stay open. *She wouldn't have done all this just to kill us. We'd simply be dead.*

"Thus, the one hand. On the other"—one small, beautifully tended hand reached out and tapped a stack of letters on the desk, bound with a purple ribbon—"if these are to be believed, your brother is the pattern of a gallant and loyal knight. And they are from the Princess Mathilda, and Rudi Mackenzie, and Father Ignatius of the Order of the Shield of St. Benedict. My daughter is naturally of a more kindly nature than I, but she is nobody's fool and neither is Rudi Mackenzie or the knight-brother, and they all sing the praises of Sir Odard's courage, his skill at arms, his steadfastness, and his cleverness. Yes?"

Yseult took a deep breath. The praise for her brother and through him for her family and House made the blood rush back to her face and gave her strength; she could feel it curling up from her stomach into her heart and mind.

She blurted: "Odard . . . Odard is a true knight. And he truly loves the Princess Mathilda, my lady Regent. He would die for her."

"Absolutely true," Huon said with respectful firmness. She suspected he was also praying hard that his voice not break in midsentence. "He's deeply in love with her."

"Or in love with his expectations should he marry her," the Regent said. "That would provide a strong motive for his heroics, if true. Many men are brave in their own service. But more to the point, Rudi Mackenzie says quite bluntly that he and all the rest would have died if

Odard had betrayed them, which he had opportunity to do . . . and had opportunity to do in ways which would have been undetectable, and which would have furthered any ambitions he may have had with respect to my daughter. I have great respect for the Mackenzie tanist's judgment and long close experience with it. Nor is he such a friend of Odard's that he would shade the truth in such a matter."

Silence fell for a long time; the room grew a little darker, and she could hear rain beating down on the windows. The Black Months were at hand here in the Willamette, drizzle and slate-colored skies and short fugitive days. The Lady Regent moved one finger slightly, and the gaslights were turned on by the guards, each with a small *pop*. The mantels began to glow behind the frosted-glass fronts, and the mirrors behind cast the light.

Yseult struggled to read the Regent's smooth face and opaque eyes, and swallowed. Anything she said could kill her and Huon; but to stay silent was a hideous risk as well.

She's always been so closed. It's part of why she's so dangerous.

Yseult fought for balance. Huon's hand on her shoulder helped. *What does the Regent want?* she wondered. *Shall I grovel? Will it help? Or retire to a convent and make a vow of chastity?*

Then: *No. It wouldn't help. I can't guess what she's thinking but I can think clearly and use logic myself. And she'll respect that, respect boldness and clear thought.*

She nerved herself to speak evenly and quietly, her fear drying her mouth. "Lady; may we follow the pattern of our brother in courage and honesty. But also, *not* in the matter of frankness. Odard always played his cards close to his chest. I ask you openly, why are we a risk, two minor children?"

Another of those slight chilly smiles rewarded her, and a very small nod.

At least if we're killed, it will be after we've gotten a little respect!

Sandra gestured, turning her hand palm-down and then palm-up. "It is my policy always to punish treachery, and likewise always to reward good service. Which leaves me with something of a dilemma with respect to you twain; I can scarcely reward Lord Odard and then wipe out his family. Accordingly I will take no hasty or irrevocable actions; but neither will I take unnecessary risks. Ultimately this matter may well have to be settled by the Princess when she returns. I am, after all, Regent for her."

Yseult swallowed against the sudden tears. "Yes?" she heard the Lady Regent ask.

"Why are we a risk?" Huon said; it was the question she'd have asked again if she had dared.

The Regent turned both hands up. "At the very least, minor children may grow up into dangerous adults who have been secretly resentful for a very long time. Love for a mother is strong, even if she's an idiot. And there is more than politics at work here. Lord Betancourt, your report, please."

"My lady Regent."

The hard young captain she remembered in a suit of plate was dressed as a court dandy today, in shades of green and silver. His dark skin glowed against the silver rolled brim hat with the silver scarf trailing down. He came forward and made an elaborate leg to the Regent.

He was pretty scary that day at Gervais. He scared me,

anyway. But, thought Yseult, *I don't know if I like him looking so dandified. Odard dressed like that, but it distracted people from what he was really doing. Garrick is handsome, but, I think, too direct for the clothes to be a smoke screen. And his hair is wavy, but not as curly as Lord Chaka's.*

Yseult focused on his words, hearing his side of the day of her arrest. "Sir Guelf came out of the stables just as we arrived. He clearly knew what was forward and charged me with drawn blade and made no attempt to parley. It was suicide; and he was dead, very quickly."

Yseult controlled a shudder, remembering the body and the pool of blood among the straw and cobbles and horse dung.

"Around vespers, we finally ran the fox to his earth and Alex Vinton was arrested. He was sent to the Interlachen prison immediately."

"Thank you, Sir Garrick. How does the demesne under your stewardship?"

"Quietly, Lady, quietly. The people were not happy to hear of the arrest of the children. It is my sorrow to inform you that Lady Layella did die two days ago. The coroner's findings are attached to my written report."

Yseult gasped, a sad exhalation of woe escaping her. She fingered the beads on her rosary and promised to dedicate one hundred Hail Marys to her soul. Sir Garrick turned and bowed, a regretful expression on his face.

"I had sent for a midwife doctor from the Sisters of the Angels in Mount Angel. She cared for the lady, but her fate was written in the stars. She had a massive stroke; I understand a known, if not so common, risk of a difficult childbirth with a prolonged laying in afterward. Her sister, Theresa, was taken to McKee house to be with her surviving brother, Odo, under the guardianship of Sir

Czarnecki's mother. She has been helping to nurse the man."

He turned to the dais again. "The people of Gervais have taken heart from hearing that their Lord Odard protects the princess. And enjoys your full confidence. May I at this point request that I be returned to field duty?"

This time Sandra looked amused, though not in any way Yseult could have described. "No, my lord, you may not. Men combining competence and complete honesty in a situation where sticky fingers would be so easily deployed are not as common as one would like. Request denied."

Sandra looked at Yseult and Huon. "The 'full confidence' *is*, in fact, very true. He was injured, quite seriously, when the prisoners were liberated, protecting Mathilda."

Yseult curtsied again, trying to control her relief. *She wants us to be scared—and I am, at least!—but she's really not going to kill us or attaint the land. I will dedicate a candle the length of my arm to St. Bernadette and Huon will do likewise!*

"Now, Sir Stratson, how does it go with my prisoners?"

"My lady Regent," said a grizzled man, standing.

Yseult thought he looked like a tired old horse, with his long face and long yellow teeth and bulging dark eyes. His dark brown court clothes fostered the impression of an ancient, weary bay. He bounced slightly on his toes and chewed his drooping mustache, like a horse cribbing his bit.

"Prisoner, I fear, my lady."

Sandra's face hardened. "Not an escape, I presume."

"No, my lady. I'll explain. Lady Mary had recovered from the laudanum by the time she arrived. The instructions were quite explicit. We escorted her to her cell in the maximum-security block. I left the interrogation to the Baroness d'Ath, who arrived a few days later."

Maximum-security block? I thought Mama was under house arrest at Fen House!

Huon pressed her shoulder and Yseult snapped her mouth shut before she could blurt anything; once again she caught that indefinable sense of amusement. It was said the Regent doted on her Persian cats. Apparently they had something in common with her besides wearing long silky white fur coats.

Sir Stratson went on: "Vinton, however, I was instructed to break and given a series of questions to ask. This we did in the main block. We could not cross-check his answers later in the process. Vinton bit out his tongue about forty-five minutes into the questioning and aspirated his blood while his head was underwater, so that we didn't detect it until too late. He was dead in less than twenty minutes; we couldn't control the bleeding even with a cautery."

Yseult winced slightly, though the treatment was perfectly legal for a commoner in a treason investigation. Stratson bounced thoughtfully, and rocked a time or two on the balls of his feet in a gesture that was probably utterly unconscious.

"According to my chirurgeon, actually biting one's tongue out completely is an impossible deed."

"It is, unless the man is drugged," Tiphaine d'Ath said, in an interested tone. "I've seen it tried several times, and it never succeeds. Marvelous are the works of God. My lady," she concluded, bowing to the dais.

Stratson cleared his throat and continued:

"What answers Vinton gave us suggested that he was recruited by the Lady Mary or Lord Guelf sometime in the last two years and was their intermediary from the beginning of that recruitment. He gave us no information on who recruited them. However, his answers were not consistent with the evidence that was sent to me. Some of the letters were dated as much as five years ago and mentioned him as *our well-loved and trusted Alex.* We have the names of five Associate holders of fiefs-in-sergeantry in Gervais, Mollala, Hood River, Boring, and several farmers in Bend he claims constituted the chain of contacts. Rigobert Gironda de Stafford, Lord Forest Grove, is in charge of that part of the investigation. He told me that he felt nothing would turn up; that they were red herrings."

Sandra's eyes went to the Grand Constable. She nodded thoughtfully.

"Probably, my lady. A man determined enough to bite out his tongue would undoubtedly be coherent enough to lie under the water treatment, at least initially. You need to continue it for days or even weeks with these hard cases, and use very skillful interrogations to catch contradictions so that you can gradually break them down. I'm afraid much of what was gotten from this man will be worthless, and it will be very difficult to separate the pearls from the pig . . . dung quickly."

Sir Stratson rocked a few more times and then sat at the Regent's nod.

He must be a very stolid man, Yseult thought. *He just confessed failure in an important case to the Lady Regent.* She thought for a moment. *Though trying to fudge would be even worse, I think. You'd have to be very stupid to do that and I don't think she puts stupid men in important positions.*

D'Ath spoke from her spot by the window. Yseult frowned at the shiver that ran down her back. *What is it I sense? She's not an* evil *person; just odd and rare; but . . .*

"Lady d'Ath?" the Regent said.

"I got very little information from Lady Mary. She was her usual irritating self; complained about the accommodations, the food, the constant watching.

"She refused to say much about her work with the CUT. She did insist that she was only trying to improve the fortunes of House Liu. She was very clear that what she did was not, in her mind, treasonous."

"What passes for her mind," Sandra Arminger said dryly. "A world of its own, where every action of Mary Liu is wise and righteous."

Tiphaine inclined her head and continued. "She named her initial recruiter as Guelf and stated that Alex Vinton had recruited . . . she used the word 'converted' them; Guelf first and then herself. Vinton, she claimed, came to the castle some two or three years after the death of the late Baron Liu, with passwords Lady Mary recognized. He'd been one of Eddie's embedded spies in the lands where Eddie had tried to set up Duke Iron Rod for us, years ago. Out in northern Idaho."

"There's nothing in the records, but there wouldn't be, if he was running the operation personally," Sandra said. "We were a little scattershot in those days, scrambling to seize fleeting opportunities while things were fluid. Go on, Lady d'Ath."

"Lady Mary said that gave him the position of valet to Odard, who was just coming of an age to need a manservant. For his consequence, I suppose, and because this Vinton was a competent bodyguard. Odard would have been ten at the time."

Sandra's eyes went to the young Lius. Yseult nodded and confirmed it:

"I remember him first coming to Gervais. He became our dancing master, too."

Huon bowed. "I don't remember it, I'm afraid, my lady Regent. I was very young, he was a fixture as far back as I can think."

"Dancing master? What an odd profession for a spy," Lady Death said coolly. "Of particular interest to me was her stated ultimate reason for treachery. She blamed both the Lady Regent and myself personally for not rescuing her brother, Sir Jason, in Corvallis just before the Protector's War, and for the shaming Theresa Reddings received being pregnant at the time and betrothed to Jason, who was assassinated by parties unknown."

Yseult cringed slightly as d'Ath turned to look at her, and then forced herself to stand firmly erect.

"Is that true?" the Grand Constable asked.

"Yes. They were betrothed, but Theresa was very young and Sir Richart had imposed a long betrothal. Theresa delivered of a son that May. He died less than a month later of jaundice. She was ruined and could never marry."

D'Ath shook her head. "The things one learns. Beyond that, I am fairly sure Mary was lying; but about what and how is harder to determine and, as per your instructions, my lady, I did not use rigorous methods. Much of her motivation appears to have been an effort to balance the books as she saw fit."

"Spite is a luxury," the Regent said thoughtfully. "Like sweets, one should control one's indulgence for the sake of health."

The Grand Constable nodded. "I wish that Alex Vinton had not died under interrogation. I suspect he is . . . was the key to our twined two conundrums. Is this a religious conversion or an opportunistic using of tools to hand, and did they seek the CUT or did the CUT seek them?"

"It might well have *started* as opportunism and segued into something else," Sandra said. "That often happens; we wear a mask, and the mask becomes our face."

The Grand Constable fell silent and relaxed against the wall.

The Regent tapped her foot thoughtfully. A waiting silence fell over the chilly room. Yseult shifted her balance minutely and felt Huon's hand come to hold hers, hidden by the voluminous folds of her wool sideless surcoat.

"The problem," the Regent said suddenly, "is, as the Grand Constable says, twofold. While we have nominal freedom of religion in the land of the Association . . . since the Protector's War and the peace treaty . . . the Church is very much part of our identity and we tolerate the other religions not least because they remain inconspicuous and do not openly proselytize. What the CUT seems to have in mind here is invasion by conversion, followed by conversion after a successful invasion. It is possible. It has happened. Even if it fails of its main object, it is a formula for civil war, and that I will not tolerate."

She looked at Huon and Yseult. "Religion is as real as rocks, as a political factor. And yet . . . there is the little matter of the blown special operation last month in Pendleton. All the reports I've received suggest something more than simple logistics and superiority of forces were in play."

"Yes, my lady," Tiphaine said; she'd been in command of the Protectorate's contingent there. "And the Prophet Sethaz was *personally* present when the Dúnedain attacked the Bossman of Pendleton in his stronghold during that party. The reports indicate that the operation would have been completely successful except for his presence, and that he did some . . . quite remarkable things in his own person. We are still analyzing those aspects. I'd find them very difficult to believe except that Lord Alleyne Loring was the author of the report. And he's extremely realistic, usually."

The *as opposed to his spouse, who refers to her enemies as orcs and may very well see them that way* went unspoken.

The Regent tapped her fingers a few times on the desk; her equivalent of pacing and lashing a tail. When she spoke it was to Huon and Yseult:

"Your mother told the Grand Constable that Alex Vinton 'converted' them, she and Guelf. Did your mother *ever* speak in a way that made you think of another religion? Names of saints you'd never heard before, blessing that sounded different, preachers that looked or acted in ways you'd never seen?"

"My mother is a *good* daughter of the church! She was Catholic long before the Association existed!" Huon said, not shouting but very firmly.

Yseult was silent, remembering a missing rosary, a locket of the Annunciation that wasn't around Mary's neck and a gleaming white cloth with white on white counted cross-stitch embroidery. She raised her right hand to touch the medal that Odard had given her. It felt warm, and comforting to the touch.

"Daughter of Gervais?" Sandra said, the voice of implacable power.

"I, I . . . I was embroidering an altar cloth for Mama. The day we were arrested, she was very angry with me because I was sloppy and said she wouldn't have poor work placed on the . . . I can't remember just how she said it, but it sounded to me like the altar in Castle Gervais."

"So, you think your brother is right?"

"It's, it's . . . the design. There were symbols I've never seen on it. It was very complicated and all counted cross-stitch. Mother would tell me the pattern to embroider and I'd do that piece; but she never gave me the whole thing, or explained. Mother should still have it. Goodwife Romarec, the housekeeper, packed it in with Mother's stuff."

"Ah. That is information of some value, which must be looked into. But she didn't teach you anything, bless you, present you for baptism in an unorthodox cult?"

Yseult shook her head. "Nothing like that." She hesitated. "But that day . . . that day I noticed she didn't have her rosary hanging from her belt. I'd, I've spent hours trying to remember when was the last time I saw it . . . and it was the day my brother left. She took it off after leaving chapel and . . . sort of spilled it from one hand to the other before tucking it into her pocket. And I can't remember seeing it ever again. Or her locket of the Annunciation that Papa gave her, years and years ago."

Huon turned to Yseult. "Really?" he asked, his voice cracking. "Really? She wasn't a good daughter of Mother Church? She was so proud of being a true . . ."

His voice fell to a half sob. Yseult squeezed his hand, but shook her head sadly.

"And so," said the Regent. "I still do not know who sought out who. This is crucial. If CUT agents are actively recruiting, we must seek them out and take them in custody; and we may have a very serious problem with opportunistic treason. And winning battles will not win us the war. If, however, Mary sought them out, we probably have many fewer disaffected people to worry about. You children, then, are a problem. Are you hidden agents? What were called 'sleepers' in the language of my youth, or are you innocent children? Could Mary have placed some hold on you that will erupt through you at some point, will you—nill you? My decision on your destiny today rests on that question."

Yseult sighed and rubbed one hand over her forehead. It gave her a headache just trying to think like that.

Huon let go of her hand and stepped forward. "Madame, I am your loyal subject, and through you, that of the Princess my brother honors above all women. What oath would you require of me? I will swear whatever you wish with as many priests and witnesses as you feel necessary."

Yseult felt her heart swell with pride and love for her brother. "Yes, Madame, yes. What do you require of us?"

The Regent's face was smooth, bland; only her eyes, those dark chocolate eyes, held emotion. It was something cold and bitter and distant.

"The problem with that," she said dryly, "is that a traitor will, by definition, swear false oaths. A *capable* traitor will do so convincingly."

Yseult felt her mouth drop open slightly. *But . . . but if oaths have no power, the world would fall apart!* she thought, appalled. What was lordship and vassalage if not a network of oaths?

"I believe you are sincere *now*," Sandra said. "I flatter myself that I am something of a judge of people, and you two are vastly less experienced than I in the ways of the world. But should your mother come and beg of you to hide a ring, pass on a message or put powder in my soup or tea . . . what would you do then?"

Yseult opened her mouth and paused, hesitated and looked at her brother.

"Instruct us, my lady. Whatever you require of us, I

will swear to do. Do you require us to forswear our mother?"

Huon's voice was firm, but he paled. She trembled, reaching for Huon's hand. Bitter tears rose and pooled under her lids.

Mama! How could you? You have destroyed us! How can we make ourselves clean?

She gripped Huon's hand harder. He brought it out and patted it.

The Regent considered for a moment and moved a finger. The priest brought out the Bible and relics again, and Yseult put a trembling hand on the holy things.

"Do you swear on oath, on your soul and hope of salvation, that you believe your mother the Lady Mary Liu, Dowager Baroness Gervais, to be guilty of conspiracy against the Throne and hence of High Treason?"

"Y-" Yseult cleared her throat. "Yes."

Huon echoed her, misery in his tone.

"Do you swear on oath, on your soul and hope of salvation that for this your lady mother deserves death?"

A second, and then they both answered: "Yes." The word blurred as their voices overlapped.

"Very well," Sandra said. "That is unequivocal enough. Let it be so recorded."

The Grand Constable spoke: "You are taken in ward by the Lady Regent and will be assigned guardians who will stand in loco parentis to you."

Her voice was like winter water running over river stones. Yseult frowned at her again.

Cold, she's so cold. Brrr! I wonder how Lady d'Stafford can bear to be her Châtelaine? She's so pleasant, and such a good mother.

Huon asked, his voice suddenly deeper. "We understand. And I do see why you must doubt us, my lady Regent, my lords, my ladies. Do we stay here in cells?"

"No," said the Lady Regent, leaning back slightly in the high carved chair, and putting her hands under the cloak. "I need you out of the way, hard to find, and constantly watched. On the other hand, should this all be resolved and we defeat the CUT and Boise, then I wish you to be able to take your place in society without having to compensate for years imprisoned."

"Thank you!" Yseult blurted, and then hastily added, "My lady Regent. We thank you for your gracious courtesy and mercy to us."

The Regent smiled and shrugged. "If we are defeated, then I have no interest in what follows. I will be dead."

Yseult shivered. "Don't, my lady! *Don't!* We must trust the Princess and the Mackenzie to bring the Sword of the Lady to rescue us in time."

The Regent started to move her hand and then paused, looking as if she were struck by a sudden thought.

"You know, child, you may very well be right. Marvelous are the works of God. Very well. Mollala, will you and your mother harbor Huon, knowing that he might be a Trojan horse?"

The heavy-shouldered dark-skinned man stood and bowed.

"Yes, my lady Regent. I have grown fond of this boy, Gervais. I'll keep him in ward and teach him well, and watch his very deeds and words. My mother spoke with me before I came here. She also will swear to watch this boy. Right now, she's a little tied up with the hospital."

Huon stood straighter; it occurred to Yseult that he'd been nerving himself to be brave as he was led away to something like her own imprisonment, possibly for years.

Mollala is going to have one very loyal page. And one very loyal friend in years to come as Baron of Gervais, she thought. *That makes me feel warmer. That's how the world is supposed to work!*

The Regent turned to a quiet woman sitting next to Jehane. "Countess Anne, will you take the girl in ward?"

"Gladly. My sisters will be happy to have a companion close to their age. Yseult comes to us, moreover, with a reputation for fancy stitching. We will look to learn from her."

The Regent nodded to Yseult, who frantically scanned through her knowledge of the Protectorate's nobility.

Countess Anne? Tillamook! It's very remote . . . it's a poor county on the edge of nowhere, and there are raids from the Haida along the coast, but the Countess won't be wearing wooden shoes!

She bowed her head; then she met the Regent's eyes, seeing there a chilly approval.

I don't envy the Princess, she thought. *Not if she's always on trial like that! Or is it different with those two?*

Aloud she said, "Thank you, my lady Countess. I will try to be a good maid-in-waiting to you, and hopefully will learn of cheese making and preserves and perfumery."

"You must understand," said the Regent, "you are sent to Tillamook because I believe Countess Anne will detect treason very quickly, having had personal, close experience with one of the agents of CUT, previously."

Anne, Countess of Tillamook, coughed. "My lady Regent! I never said . . ."

This time Sandra smiled openly. "No, you didn't, my lady Countess, and I admire your discretion, but rest assured that I know a good many things people do *not* tell me."

D'Ath spoke from her place by the window. "You didn't say, but I did ask. I was ten days in your demesne . . . dealing . . . with that treasonous priest."

Dealing? Yseult asked herself. Priests were supposed to be judged by ecclesiastical courts under canon law. Then: *There are things I just don't want to know.*

"I had ample time to hear just what was happening and how you dealt with it."

"Which was very well," Sandra said graciously.

"Neat job," d'Ath confirmed. "Very professional."

Anne of Tillamook was looking slightly stunned.

Even a coastal castle, far from the center of civilization, was preferable to the bleak cell and silent treatment.

"My lady Countess, I understand and I submit myself to this. I also thank you, from the bottom of my heart, for accepting my service. Sharing a prison cell with my mother would not be my choice," Yseult said.

Sandra came down from the dais, a sign that the session was near its end.

Yseult looked at her. "And I can't absolutely swear that I *can't* be fooled into doing something foolish if my mother were to ask, my lady Regent." She curtsied and then knelt. "You are my Liege and I will obey you of faith and all earthly worship."

Huon knelt next to her. "Yes, my Liege. Gervais is yours and so are we."

They held their hands out, palms pressed together. Sandra Arminger took them between hers, and then raised each of them and presented her cheek for the ritual kiss. It was an acknowledgment of homage, and Yseult's heart leapt.

"Rise."

The Regent's smooth voice had a satisfied sound to it, and everyone else did.

"Take them, Jehane, Anne, Delia. Give them a meal in some pleasant but secluded place. They are not to speak with anybody else and must be returned to their cell."

She looked at Yseult. "But this is for the present in the interests of discretion, to keep the enemy as ill-informed as may be. Enjoy the rest of the day. Mollala, when you leave, take Master Gervais with you. Anne, you take Yseult. When do you plan to go?"

Yseult stood and then sank, trembling, onto one of the hard chairs she had not been allowed earlier. Action swirled around her. When Delia beckoned, she went without a murmur, only pausing to curtsy, once again, to the Regent.

CHAPTER SEVENTEEN

COUNTY OF THE EASTERMARK
CHARTERED CITY OF WALLA WALLA
PORTLAND PROTECTIVE ASSOCIATION
(FORMERLY SOUTHEASTERN WASHINGTON STATE)
HIGH KINGDOM OF MONTIVAL
(FORMERLY WESTERN NORTH AMERICA)
AUGUST 23, CHANGE YEAR 25/2023 AD

The streets of Walla Walla were crowded, as Tiphaine had expected. With soldiers, of course, for a beginning. The household troops of the Count, armored and steady. A bristle of pole arms and crossbows from parties of the city's own regiments, marching on foot behind standards blazoned with the images of the patron saints of their guilds and drummer boys wielding their sticks to a snarling rattle. The *menies* of those of his vassals serving here were much in evidence, from the plumed arrogance of knight and baron down to the spearmen trotting behind. And simply with people, swarms of them and their bicycles and pedicabs and horses and mules and oxcarts, and bewildered peasants with great bundles on their backs.

Even with the Count's trumpeters and outriders they made slow headway, the more so because loud cheers broke out after the ripple of bows at the sight of the Crown's banner, and those of Ath and Forest Grove on the pennants fluttering from the lances of their escorts. Now and then they passed a priest or friar haranguing the crowds; she caught *crusade* and *holy war* in their shouts. They broke off to lead the cheers for the Count and the Crown's officers.

Scared as hell and hoping this means they're saved, Tiphaine thought behind her impassive face; de Aguirre waved back cheerfully. *It may, people. Or it may mean you're fucked. Time will tell.*

Walla Walla had been low-built before the Change, most of the buildings one- or two-story brick and frame. Afterwards there had been a lot of infilling of vacant ground as was usual in walled towns and quite a few half-timber second stories, with workshops on the ground floor and families living over it. And far more churches and the little roadside shrines than you saw in most of the Association territories, and things like guild houses and public baths and so forth. Though they'd kept most of the tall shade trees and obviously the sewers and water supply were still working.

But the ambience would have warmed the cockles of Norman Arminger's black heart, she thought. *You have to hand it to him, his notions actually* worked *under modern conditions. Even he couldn't have pulled it all off if they didn't.*

Every smithy and carpenter's and leatherworker's and tailor's shop was spilling over with work as the city prepared to stand siege, masters and journeymen at their benches and anvils, apprentices dashing about playing fetch-and-carry knave; furnaces cast draughts of hotter air into the already warm streets; there was a sweet smell of cut wood and a musky one of glue and leather; seamstresses and tailors bent over their treadle-worked sewing machines amid a whining hum. Some workers paused to wave or bow, but she saw one man completely oblivious to the aristocrats' passing as he tapped hobnails into the sole of a marching boot.

"Now, *he's* got the right attitude," she said, and the Count and Forest Grove laughed agreement.

It wasn't all cheers for the banners of Ath and Stafford. Here and there a priest or layman scowled at Tiphaine; one friar actually turned his back. Tiphaine shrugged with a slight clatter of pauldron against breastplate.

Being universally loved was never my ambition, she thought. *Which is a good thing because I've never had a prayer of getting it. Delia and the kids love me; a few people like me; and everyone else respects, which is to say, fears me.*

Half the rooftops were spotted with cloths covered in turn with small objects, and small children sitting perched among them with switches to keep off birds and insects. There was a heavy sweetish smell she recognized, like a jam factory.

Drying fruit and preserves being put up inside, Tiphaine thought. *And tomatoes and whatnot drying too. And everyone with an oven making double-baked service biscuit.*

Though soldiers used unofficial names for the hardtack ration, *dog biscuit* was the least scatological. De Aguirre noted her glance as a child stood up and waved the switch he'd been using.

"Many of the country people have come in from the manors within three days walk," he said. "The castles . . ."

Would only have space for some of them even crammed to the gills, because we built them to hold down the folk of the countryside, not shelter them, Tiphaine thought mordantly.

A castle's perimeter had to be kept as small as practical; every foot of parapet that you needed to hold made it weaker, other things being equal. That was why a city like this required a huge garrison in comparison to even the largest keep, though its walls might be just as high and strong. She had some ideas about helping with that.

"So we're putting them to work," he said. "They welcome it. Everyone knows we have to pull together."

"You got in most of the harvest?" she said.

"Most of the fall-sown grain, and the garbanzos and field peas," he said. "We're threshing as fast as we can and getting it in sacks and under cover, but a lot's still in loose piles on the floors of churches and whatnot. Plenty of fodder, since we've sent so much livestock west, but it's bulky, we don't have enough presses for the loose hay that's normally kept in the fields or barn lofts. And a fair amount of vegetables for pickling and drying. The early fruit is coming in, cherries, apricots, peaches and pears— we're guarding the workers in the fields and risking enemy raiders, and preserving all of it we can, my lady wife and the other gentlewomen have organized supplies of extra jars and sugar and heating pans and are leading the effort. We're slaughtering everything but the breeding stock of our remaining beef herds and swine and drying, salting and smoking the meat wholesale."

Tiphaine nodded in sober approval. Food was *always* one of the most important factors in war; when you came right down to it, fighting was manual muscle-labor as hard as any in the fields, and like farming it also depended on the energy of huge numbers of draught animals who had to be fed as well. If an army didn't get enough to eat it mutinied or disappeared or just plain died, and hauling food from far away was a nightmare unless you had water transport or at least rails. A city or a castle under siege had to have rations too, and fruit and vegetables were important to prevent scurvy.

You could live a long time on bread and cheese, beans and a little dried fruit and pickled meat.

"But we're going to lose the rest of the fruit and the apples. Worse, the vintage," the Count said, wincing slightly. The local wines were famous and a major cash crop. "And it's not all that long before we have to plow and sow the fall grains."

"You probably won't be able to," Tiphaine said bluntly. "The Kingdom will see that your people don't starve, and you can plant more spring acreage next year. It'll be settled by then."

One way or another, she did not add aloud.

"If we have the seed grain and oxen and horses," de Aguirre said.

"The Kingdom will help there too," Tiphaine said firmly. "I have the High King's word on that, by the way. Everyone's going to contribute to help rebuild the damaged areas, my lord. If anyone suffers, then we're all going to do it together. Mutual help is what a Kingdom means."

The gloomy young nobleman perked up a little. "It's good to remember we're a kingdom now," he said. "And that we have a King. A High King!"

Then he crossed himself. "And the Sword we've heard of . . ."

"Quite real, and everything the tales say," Tiphaine said, copying the gesture. "Everything and more."

"Then with a Sword granted from the hand of the Queen of Heaven—I've heard of Father Ignatius' vision of her too—we have the certainty of God's favor! And with that, what need we fear?"

Rudi—Artos—has become our Lucky Rabbit's Foot, she thought. *Poor bastard, he doesn't dare lose anything substantial now. He's what's keeping our morale up, or at least his legend is. But it's a young legend, and still fragile. Well, no, it's not* just *a legend. The Sword is* real.

"We've been given a chance, and deliverance from the CUT's . . . magic, sorcery, Jedi mind-tricks, whatever they were. The rest we have to do ourselves, and be ready to sweat and bleed for it," Tiphaine said. "God expects us to work for His favor, my lord."

Or Someone does, she thought, conscious of the owl amulet around her neck beneath the breastplate and arming doublet.

Tiphaine's eyes narrowed as she looked at the City Palace of the Counts Palatine of the Eastermark. Someone who knew her very well would have read a detached amusement in the expression.

The Palace had been the Marcus Whitman Hotel before the Change; a three-stepped pile twelve stories tall at the highest point, built of brick-faced concrete in the 1920s' version of a vaguely Renaissance style. Education in Sandra Arminger's household had included a full course of actual history rather than the Society mythology turned from play into deadly seriousness which passed for it in the PPA territories most of the time. The Lady Regent herself had spent time seeing that her particular protégés really *understood* it, too.

Which added layers of ironic flavor to life. The people who'd built this hotel had had a great nobleman's town house as their model; in fact, back in France before the Revolution "nobleman's town house" was what the word *hôtel* had usually meant. It had acquired its modern meaning only after Madame la Guillotine resulted in an abrupt turnover and repurposing in Parisian real estate.

The joke was that now it *was* exactly what they'd dreamed, what a *hôtel* had originally been; and that it had been taken for that purpose simply because it looked suitable to men who were shrewd and practical and wouldn't have known the Italian Renaissance from an Olive Garden dinner special.

It had still needed a great many modifications over the last generation, and not merely because electric machines didn't work anymore. A palace wasn't just a place for a ruler to live comfortably, exhibit their stuff and hold parties, though those were essential parts of government. It had to be a barracks for troops and have dormitories for servants, workers, clerks, pages and squires; a clutch of offices and strong rooms; chapels and their attendant priests; armories and repair shops; an infirmary; schoolrooms; kitchens to feed all those as well as put on banquets; and court chambers to hear cases and settle disputes, with their records and law books and land-title registers; and stables and carriage houses and more, including dungeons.

Probably being in the middle of a chartered town full of skilled artisans and well-stocked merchant warehouses meant it didn't need the dairies and winepresses and weaving sheds and gristmills its rural equivalents would have, but it was still the center of a Great House with hundreds of residents and a ceaseless to-and-fro.

They rode through a low outer wall that closed off several blocks; it was mostly ornamental, which meant that the Counts didn't feel the need for a real fortification between them and the citizenry, though at need they could always retire to the castle. A small guard of halberdiers clashed the butts of their polished weapons down outside the gates; she was glad to see the Count wasn't wasting manpower. The cast-bronze lions there looked more recent than most of the decor.

"Made here in Walla Walla in my father's day, my lady,

may God receive his soul," de Aguirre said proudly as they dismounted and varlets ran to take their horses. "We have a fine foundry and good artists."

Tiphaine nodded; she was already running over what she would say to the assembled local magnates.

Not to mention I'm hungry. A hunk of bread and cheese in the saddle isn't much of a lunch, particularly when you had dog biscuit and jerky for breakfast.

The gilt-bronze and mahogany and marble splendors of the lobby had been carefully updated; the hiss of gas-lights overhead might almost have been Todenangst. Everyone parted with more bows. She thanked . . . whatever was Up There . . . inwardly that this was an emergency. The full panoply of courtly etiquette had always bored her like an auger, however necessary it was to keeping the wheels greased, and a painstaking provincial imitation was even worse.

The housekeeper showed her to a third-floor suite. Sir Rodard was at the door, with a towel over one armored arm.

"This isn't your job anymore," Tiphaine pointed out; then she sighed slightly as she used the hot damp cloth to wipe her face; the momentary coolness afterwards was even more welcome.

Rodard shrugged. "I'm still a household knight of yours, my lady," he said. "And it's a bit late to train an immediate replacement as body-squire."

He bowed her through. Lioncel was standing there directing a couple of pages and Walla Walla varlets with lordly insouciance as they unpacked and laid things out. He knelt, undid her sword belt and added it to the rest of her gear on an armor stand. The half-armor and her riding boots came off with equal efficiency, while she looked around and moved as necessary. The first Count's architects had probably knocked three or four suites together to make these guest quarters; excellent rugs that looked Indian of some sort, burnished furniture, chandeliers with their candles already lit in the gathering dusk, adding the scent of a lavish display of fine beeswax to the flowers in many vases. There was an ornamental but very practical set of wrought-steel bars set over all the windows, fine smithwork giving them the appearance of leafy grapevines.

Rodard had some of her papers already neatly set out on a half-acre desk, and her seal and a supply of colored wax to hand. There were even typewriters and adding machines in an alcove for anyone who had their accountants along. It hadn't been worth the trouble to bring in hers, since it was already so late and she was leaving in the morning. The last light was fading from the windows and glimmers of flame were showing across the city, gaslights and alcohol lanterns for the public buildings and homes of the rich; workaday tallow dips and canola oil for the rest. The city-glow was brighter than usual; mostly people went to bed with the sun, but the emergency meant they'd be working into the night.

"Quick work," she said to Rodard. "I wasn't sure you'd get here before I did, with the state the streets were in."

"Easier for a nameless knight and party to move through the streets than a Grand Constable, a Marchwarden and a Count, with three *conroi* of lancers behind them, my lady," Rodard said. "Incidentally it was Lioncel who suggested we just get the gear moving, trot the packhorses around to the east gate, and then ask for the details when we got here rather than trying to follow you. Saved a fair bit of time."

He winked as he said it; he'd have done exactly the

same thing, but it was an excellent sign that it had occurred to the youngest squire as well.

Lioncel bowed, blushing with pride. "Your bath is
drawn, my lady," he said. A quick grin: "This is the highest floor with running water and a boiler. I checked. The
top eight are all used for storage with cranes and tread-
mills for hauling things up the old elevator shafts. Family
quarters below us, staff housing and offices on the
fourth."

"Good work," she said, and restrained an impulse to
scoop a bound report off the desk as she passed. "Get me
a drink—beer, cold if possible."

He put it into her hand just as she threw the arming
doublet behind her; that had been a safe bet for anyone
who knew her. She walked into the bathing room through
a bead curtain. The marble tub not only held steaming
water but aromatically scented suds, and there was a
pleasant cross-breeze from windows on two sides of the
corner room. This *was* going to be a pleasant memory in
a few weeks; she'd always been fastidiously clean when
she could be, which in her line of work wasn't all the
time. The beer was icy-chilled and very good; some of the
best hops in the . . .

Montival, she thought. *Got to start thinking of it that
way. Not just the Association territories anymore.*

. . . High Kingdom were grown around here. That
and the hot water managed to relax her enough to almost
doze for a few minutes of soaking. At thirty-eight she
could still do nearly everything she'd been able to do at
twenty, but she found it took more and more effort plus
recuperation was slower, and the last weeks had been
hard. A sputtering jerk brought her head up as it slipped
below the surface.

There was even a genuine sponge to go with the

lavender-scented local soap, which was true luxury these days. Scrubbing briskly helped her back to alertness.

It beats washing *with a cloth and a helmet full of water all to hell,* she thought as she climbed out. *Damn, but I wish this war was over and won.*

The floor was some sort of slightly coarse-surfaced stone, easy under her feet and not slippery. She stood and looked at herself in the full-length mirror with a coldly objective eye, and at last nodded satisfaction. Naked she looked less slim than she did in clothes or armor, and the startling muscle definition was clearer. At just a hair under five-ten she weighed a solid hundred and fifty, and she'd never been more than a few pounds either side of that since she got her full growth. Of course, she'd spent a lot of that time doing very energetic things while wearing fifty pounds or more of steel strapped all over her body, besides conscientious training and recreations that included hunting boar, bear and tiger with spears.

"Conrad's right," she murmured; the conversation with Rigobert had reminded her of her youth, and so had the ceremonies that marked passages in the cycle of life. "I'm a big blond horse of a woman and I'd never, ever have made it to the Olympics as a gymnast. They were all little pixies and even at thirteen I was getting too tall. Pentathlon, maybe, if I'd switched to track and field in time. Still, I was *good.*"

She'd kept it up, too; on impulse she bent backward until her palms were on the floor behind her feet, brought one leg up and pointed the toe at the ceiling, then the other so that she was on both hands. Then a ninety-degree side-split, a scissors flip back upright onto the balls of her feet and a tucked back salto flip ending with her arms raised in that rather silly but obligatory ballerinalike posture you used to finish a floor routine—

That brought her face-to-face with the maid who'd just come through the doorway, with a pile of towels in her arms and a bulge-eyed expression at finding a naked and wetly glistening Grand Constable falling out of a midair somersault right in front of her. They were close enough that Tiphaine could feel the warmth of the heated fabric.

"Yes?" she said.

"MyladyIwassenttoattendyouasyouhavenomaid—" came out in a rush.

"Leave the towels," she said calmly.

"Yyyyyes, m'lady."

Tiphaine sighed inwardly as the girl set the heap of fluffy white fabric on a stone bench and knotted her fingers together.

I don't know what's more irritating, the usual goggling horror, or the occasional come-on.

"That will be all," she said patiently. "You may go. My body-squire and pages will attend me."

Hmmm. Bit of a pout along with the curtsy and swift withdrawal. Irritation Number Two, I think. Higamous hogamous, I am very *monogamous.*

Since she was alone, she allowed herself a very slight grin as she toweled down. Delia *was* fond of playing a game involving a lot of running and giggling she called "The Lustful Knight and the Innocent Country Maid" in honor of their first meeting at the feast when Tiphaine had taken seisin of Barony Ath during the Protector's War. It was always fun, especially when Tiphaine returned from a long absence.

"Now granted, I was a newly made knight, and I was both lustful and fairly thoroughly drunk by that point, but it was definitely Delia who murmured an invitation to inspect the fine embroidery on her underwear into my ear. Not that I needed to be asked twice in that state," she added to herself.

She tucked one of the towels around herself under the armpits as she walked out into the bedroom. Lioncel discreetly turned and looked out the window as she tossed it aside and pulled on the briefs, bias-cut linen sports bra and silver-gray silk shirt with a high mandarin collar and loose sleeves tied at the wrist. Then he whistled sharply for the pages over whom he now had authority—the general rule was that pages helped you put on clothes, and squires helped you don armor—and oversaw the younger boys as they helped her into semiformal dress. Assistance in dressing was something she'd finally gotten used to; it helped that this style really required it.

That started with the hose, also skintight and bias-cut; Sandra had told her once that it was amusing beyond words that the macho toughs of the warrior aristocracy had all ended up shaving their legs and wearing something quite close to pre-Change panty hose.

It is funny, if you think of it that way. I'd forgotten what panty hose were . . . and she didn't say, but I think part of the gleam in her eye was that it means I shave my legs and wear panty hose too, of course, which also wouldn't have happened without the end of the world.

Her hose were onyxine black, as was the sleeveless neck-to-thigh jerkin of butter-soft doeskin that went on next, fastened up the front with ties of braided black silk. Her shoes were black chamois as well, except for the gold buckles that secured them at each ankle, and the toes turned up—moderately, not the exaggerated length that high Court fashion decreed. The loose black knee-length houppelande overrobe had obsidian buttons and a collar open at the front and ear-high behind; the lower hem was dagged, and so were the turned-back sleeves that hung

almost as low, showing the rich dark forest-green jacquard lining.

She put her arms out horizontally while the pages fastened the belt of tooled black leather around her waist.
The purse on one side was largely ornamental, but the
dagger on the other was ten inches long and fully functional, for all the tooling and silver cutwork on the sheath.

Lioncel insisted on getting on a stool and combing her
hair, though strictly speaking that was no longer his duty,
and carefully placed the *chaperon* hat of the nobility on
her head. It was round and black, with a broad brim of
rolled cloth and a long flat green tail called a liripipe
down the back; he arranged the end over her right shoulder. Then he gave the livery badge above her brow a
quick buff; it was Sandra's arms quartered with her own.

Two pages brought a flat carrying case. Lioncel used a
key to open it, and drew out the gold chain of office he
placed around her neck; with similar reverence he pinned
the knot of ribbons that was Delia's favor on her upper
sword-arm.

"You can carry the sword, Lioncel," she said.

He started to grin and then composed his face gravely
though his blue eyes sparkled with excitement; he'd managed to make himself quite presentable, too, in a dark
brown outfit with a squire's brimless flowerpot hat.

You didn't wear a long sword to a formal meal; not
these days, when Eaters or enemies were less likely to
crawl down the chimney or burst through the door between the soup and the main course waving rusty kitchen
knives and lusting for your flesh or at least your dinner
and shoes. But a squire would carry hers behind her with
the belt wound around the scabbard, sign of the High
Justice and her jurisdiction throughout the Association
by right of office. It was a more practical reminder than a

gold chain with a heraldic medallion, since the hilt would be within reaching distance. And in the Association they didn't bother to deny that Justice carried a sword.

"Sir Rodard," she added as she signed the pages away and picked a rose out of a vase, trimming it and threading the stem through a buttonhole, leaving the great red bloom at her throat. "Did you send that girl in with the towels?"

"Yes, of course, my lady," he said, coming through the door and looking her over critically. "Splendid, my lady. Just the right touch of the sinister amid the dark elegance."

"Why did you do that, may I ask?"

"Modesty, my lady. It wouldn't be fitting for a man to carry the towels into your bathing chamber."

"Rodard, how many times have we ended up squatting over the same trench in the field?"

"This is the City Palace of the Counts of the Eastermark, my lady."

"Bullshit. I think it was your perverse sense of humor."

"I have been well trained in skill and courtesy, my lady."

Tiphaine's face was blank save for a very slight lift of the eyebrow at the unspoken, *by you.*

Rodard had changed out of the plain set of battle armor; he'd be sharing the watches outside her door, but right now he was in a modest, sober set of gentlemen's evening garments, a simpler version of what she was wearing. *With* a sword, though, and she knew that particular outfit had a lining of very fine mesh-mail in the houppelande. He and his brother were very good swordsmen; she'd trained them herself, passing on what Sandra's instructors had drilled into her along with a fund of lethal experience that spanned two decades now. Along with many other skills.

"Armand's on duty right now, isn't he?"

"Yes, my lady."

"Good. Get a crossbow; ordinary Armory pattern issue model. No quarrels, just the bow. Bundle it up and put it somewhere in the dining hall we'll be going to. Get it done right now, then tell Lioncel where it is before we go in."

"At once, my lady," he said and was gone.

"My lady?" Lioncel said.

"Was that a *question*, squire?"

"No, my lady."

There was a stamp and clash outside the door when she left; five crossbowmen in three-quarter armor came to attention, and three men-at-arms headed by Armand. She returned the salute and nodded aside slightly. The new-made knight stepped close enough not to be overheard.

"How would you get into those guest chambers, Sir Armand?"

Armand had the curved semicircular visor of his sallet helm up; it stuck out like the brim of a billed cap as he turned his head thoughtfully upward.

"Up the old elevator shafts to the storage levels," he said after a ten-second pause. "If they're anything like what I've seen in pre-Change buildings elsewhere they'll be very climbable."

Then another pause, and: "Hide until around three o'clock in the morning, then rappel down to one of the windows of the suite I wanted. A diamond-coated cutting cable would go through those grilles in a few minutes; they're just mild steel. I'd have used alloy there, myself, even if it's harder to work into pretty vines."

"How long?"

"The trip down and getting into the suite, fifteen minutes. Depending on how alert my lord the Count's guards are; but usually, men don't look up."

"My thoughts exactly. Your suggestion?"

"Four men awake at all times in our quarters, moving in pairs between the rooms in the guest suite, beside the guard on the door here."

"See to it. And would you have any difficulty in getting into the palace, given the perimeter wall and security arrangements you saw?"

"My lady, it's commendable that the Count feels no need of any great precautions against his people."

"Plain English, please, Sir Armand. Could you get in, and unobserved?"

"My lady, Rodard or I could do that at any time of day or night. Naked, while riding on a grizzly bear and playing a mandolin."

"My thoughts exactly, for the second time."

Lord Rigobert met her at the top of the main staircase. He was in much the same type of outfit as she, except that his houppelande and hose were parti-colored, scarlet on the right and pale gold on the left, and the liripipe was much longer, reaching to the level of his belt of gold links wrought in twining patterns with cabucon-cut garnets for the grapes. She had to admit that he could carry it off magnificently, and it went well with the arrogant jut of his short golden beard and large, shapely but scarred warrior hands. He bowed her forward, giving her a step's precedence.

"Lord Rigobert," she said quietly over her shoulder.

They walked downward past an honor guard on the landing where the staircase turned to the ground floor; that was the family quarters, and she was pleased to see strong grillwork doors on either side, evidently closed and guarded at night.

Not totally *trusting. Or his father wasn't, and established the routine.*

"Yes, my lady?"

"Does it strike you that this city is probably swarming with every possible variety of enemy agent?"

"Not a bit, Lady Tiphaine," Rigobert said. "The influx of refugees and troops from everywhere on our side and other strangers and general confusion would make it nearly impossible for anyone to slip in unnoticed."

"Ha ha big fucking ha, Rigobert, everyone's a court jester tonight."

"My guard captain is taking precautions, entirely serious ones."

"So is mine, but we need to talk to the Count after the dinner; I don't think he's considered the implications of us all being here for this one night."

As promised, the dinner was relatively small and select. The dining chamber was medium-sized, and windowless; the gaslights on their bright, expensive incandescent mantels showed murals of sporting scenes set in the Blue Mountains on the walls, with hounds coursing a stag on one side and a grizzly bear at bay before hunters with spears on the other. Those were far enough from the T-shaped table that she was fairly confident that nobody could eavesdrop through hidden grilles, even with a focusing horn behind it.

A herald blew a short note as Tiphaine entered, then announced her, without the annoying bellow some used:

"Lady Tiphaine d'Ath, Baroness of Ath and tenant-in-chief, Knight-Commander of the most noble order of the

Golden Horseshoe, Grand Constable of the armies of the Portland Protective Association! Lord Rigobert Gironda de Stafford, Baron Forest Grove and tenant-in-chief, Marchwarden of the South!"

The usher directed her to the seat on the Count's right; and there was a sudden tormenting smell of things grilled and boiled and simmered as the wheeled trays came in. The archbishop rose and said an elaborate grace; he was three seats to the left of the Count. The ceremonial jeweled saltcellar was at the junction of the upper and lower tables; the Count, his lady, principal landed vassals and noble officers like the city castellan were at the upper table. She noticed Baron Tucannon, both because of the distinctive red hair and because they'd been discussing him earlier. And if she was any judge, a number of the other vassal barons were listening to him very carefully.

Below the salt were the important commoners. Those included the Lord Mayor of the city, the guildmasters who headed their militia regiments, and a middle-aged abbess and a younger attendant in the dark blue habit and white wimple of the Sisters of Compassion, a medical order who'd spread widely in the last generation and who were apparently in charge of the hospital and clinics in the area.

And in a lot of places they're the only medical care the really poor see, the ones without a guild or confraternity or even a lord.

Tiphaine did more listening than speaking as the meal was served; the locals were talking business, and to the point, although they were also often taking up arguments and discussions they'd been at for months or years. Most of them seemed to be in good heart, and not just because of the Sword and the return of Rudi and Mathilda.

And I'm not one of the youngest present. I'm not even

below the average. That's happening more and more often. It's a Changeling world, or at least the world of the Changelings and their elder siblings. People like me, who've spent most of their lives in the modern world.

Meanwhile she ate; tiny venison sausages with candied apples, a green salad with goat cheese and the famous sweet onions of the area, a *frito misto* of seasonal vegetables, and . . .

She chewed a bite slowly and swallowed. "That is possibly the best steak I've ever tasted," she said. "And I *like* steak."

Tender, the firm marbled meat brushed with an oil infused with garlic and herbs before it was put on the grill, slightly seared at high heat on the outside and red in the center . . .

"We have sacrificed a good deal of our demesne herd of Aberdeen Angus," Countess Ermentrude said. "With the disturbed conditions it was necessary."

She was a pale willowy young woman in a chocolate-colored cote-hardie and twin-peaked headdress, about five months pregnant and with a round-voweled accent that Tiphaine took a moment to identify as from one of the very northernmost baronies.

Barony Dawson, up on our border with the Dominion of Drumheller. Not to mention our border with trackless wilderness stretching to the Arctic Circle. Yes, she met Felipe while she was a lady-in-waiting at court just before the war started. Her parents were locals who'd taken over Dawson before we arrived and decided getting a title and giving Norman a smooch on the hand were a better bargain than trying to fight us. They did well in that war with the Drumhellers.

Sandra had always encouraged marriages between distant fiefs and lordly families of different backgrounds, to keep the PPA's elite united. In fact, it was one reason why noble houses were strongly encouraged—required, practically speaking—to send some of their scions to Portland and Todenangst and the university at Forest Grove for a few years to mingle with their peers of the same ages.

The abbess spoke, unexpectedly; she'd been silent except when something relevant to her Order's area of operation had come up, and she and her attendant had been dining sparely on the salad and the excellent local bread, drinking water rather than the equally excellent local wines.

"The Lady Countess fails to note that most of those cattle were donated to our clinics and the public soup kitchens we and the regular clergy have established for the displaced," she said.

I don't think that's brown-nosing, she really likes her, Tiphaine decided. *Evidently Ermentrude takes her duties seriously.*

A lord's wife was supposed to be the one who organized welfare measures in the lord's fief; it was a real and demanding job, if done properly. Unofficially she was also supposed to be the voice whispering in his ear that tempered justice with mercy. Delia certainly worked hard at both in Ath and Forest Grove.

The plates were cleared, and then the servants set out platters of pastries and pots of monstrously expensive real coffee, moderately expensive sugar made from locally grown beets, and thick cream and decanters of brandy and discreetly retired. Tiphaine approved as she bit into an apricot tart. Far too many people assumed that servants didn't have ears, though Sandra had never made that mistake, and had any number of them on her clandestine payroll. Everyone looked up as she rapped a knife against a wineglass.

"All right, my lords and ladies, goodmen and good-women."

Public speaking had always been something that she loathed, but she was fairly good at it by now.

"I'm going to say a few words for all of you, and then I'm afraid there will be a private consultation with your lord and his barons and war-captains. I'm absolutely sure that all of you are loyal, but it's a simple fact that the more widely information is spread the more likely it is to leak."

She stood with her fingertips on the table and slowly looked them all in the eye. Most of their faces were neutral, politely attentive; everyone at this table was a politician, in their way.

Including me, she thought. *Dammit.*

"First, I bring you the greetings of our High King, Artos the First, and the High Queen Mathilda, our own Princess of House Arminger."

There was a murmur of pleasure, mostly genuine from the expressions. The Associates were generally happy that the grandchild of the Lord Protector would end up ruling the whole shebang, albeit by marriage rather than conquest. The dynasty was popular these days, far more so than it had been in Norman's time. For that matter, a lot of people still thought of him with gratitude. Commoners might be pleased for that reason—they were, after all, alive because of what he'd done—or because the next High King *wouldn't* wholly be the scion of House Arminger. Plenty still remembered just how heavy his hand could be, too.

"Next, I have intelligence to share with you concerning the larger course of this war. As of a month ago, the armies of the Lakota nation . . . now part of the High Kingdom . . . and our allies of the League of Des Moines and the three Dominions have crossed the borders of the territories held by the Church Universal and Triumphant. Those armies are more than ninety thousand men strong, horse, foot and artillery, and they are converging on Corwin, the Prophet's capital in the Valley of Paradise. They've already won several engagements. Taken together, we—the alliance against the Prophet and Boise—now have superior numbers. That changes our long-term prospects rather substantially."

This time the pleasure verged on delight. Tiphaine held up one long hand.

"And the CUT *has* withdrawn some of the troops they were massing in Boise's territories to attack us, taken them back across the Rockies to the Bitterroot country and the High Plains while the passes are still open. We think that shifting forces around to compensate for the new eastern front is the reason we haven't seen a full-scale attack yet this summer. However, that attack *will* come, and very soon. The Prophet has *not* taken all his men out to face the threat from the east and north, and Boise is ignoring it altogether."

"That's bad strategy," one of de Aguirre's barons said, a forty-something man with a scarred face that looked as if it had been adzed out of a stump, and very cold eyes. "Dividing their forces in the face of converging attacks? They're risking being weak everywhere. They'd be better advised to defend against us and throw everything they have east. Or the other way 'round, of course, my lady."

The abbess spoke again: "The CUT are diabolists. They serve the Adversary, the lord of Evil. And the ultimate definition of Evil is *futility*. It may appear strong for a time, but in the end it destroys itself."

That brought a moment of uneasy silence; the archbishop looked a little annoyed that she had beaten him to the punch, but not as if he disagreed. Tiphaine was glad she had. He would have been far more long-winded and less accurate.

Someone said: "We'd be a lot better off if Castle Campscapell hadn't fallen last year."

Tiphaine nodded; that had been at the old town of Pomeroy, and it had plugged the area between the northern slopes of the Blue Mountains and the deep canyon of the Snake River. Men had opened the gates of Campscapell and then killed themselves rather unpleasantly, for no reason anyone had been able to find, except that a redrobed magus of the CUT had stood there laughing as they did.

"We would. That was . . . whatever it is that the CUT does. Or did. Note that since this spring—when Artos took the Sword of the Lady in his hand and drew it by the light of common day—nothing similar has happened. And our holy men and women have rooted out a great deal of the CUT's evil since then."

The archbishop nodded. He had a soft plump face—a rarity these days—but his hazel eyes were extremely shrewd.

"Our exorcists have been busy. The compulsions their devils lay on the CUT's followers are foul, but we have detected many, and even cured some," he said.

"As important, no more castles have fallen . . . mysteriously," Tiphaine said; the thought of such things still offended her tidy soul and bleakly practical mind. "That doesn't mean they can't be stormed or undermined or battered down by trebuchets. The High King directs me to tell you that the defense of this city, and of the strongholds of the Eastermark more generally, are absolutely essential to his larger strategy for victory in this war. You *must* hold, and the whole Kingdom will do its best to see that you do."

"Artos!" someone shouted. *"Artos and Montival!"*

The others took it up; Tiphaine waited it out. High morale was important, and besides she agreed.

"The High King is mustering the whole strength of the Kingdom farther down the Columbia, and I've brought out a considerable force. I'll consult with your good Count as to the disposition of our field army here. What I'd like to talk to you about is your role in defending your own homes."

"We'll fight, my lady Grand Constable," one of the Guildmasters said in a growl. "We're not noble Associates, but by God and the Virgin and St. Amand our patron, we'll fight for our homes and our children and our city."

He bowed in his seat to de Aguirre and the archbishop. "And for the good lord who leads us, as his father did before him, and for Holy Church."

"Stoutly spoken!" she said. "I've brought out considerable equipment for you all, including fortress model catapults and flame-throwers stripped from the western castles, and their crews and ammunition."

Happy surprise showed at that; she winced slightly at the struggle it had taken. One or two instances had required walking the lord of the keep through the gates with a steel point held encouragingly close to his kidneys to remind him of his obligations as a vassal.

"And we've unloaded four thousand extra crossbows from the Portland armories."

That brought a puzzled silence. "My lady . . . that's more than our militias can use," one baron pointed out. "Considerably more."

Tiphaine nodded. "My thought exactly, but the High King showed me different. Now, we all know it takes a long time to train a soldier. Years for a man-at-arms, or a horse-archer, or for that matter a Mackenzie longbowman. However, you can learn to shoot a crossbow in a couple of weeks. Less, if it's at a big target. A couple of days, if it's just a matter of blazing away into the brown."

"That doesn't make a soldier!" came a protest from the scar-faced baron. "Not a *real* crossbowman."

"No, it doesn't, my lord. It doesn't mean being able to march twenty miles in armor and being fit to fight at the end of it, or knowing how to use sword and buckler, or maneuver in units to the word of command or fire volleys, or stand in ranks under fire and close up the files over the bodies of the wounded and the dead, or a hundred other things including being a genuine marksman. It *does* mean, however, that the one you've trained can run upstairs to the wall of a city, aim over the parapet, and shoot at a massed assault column. For that, all you have to be is able to walk and work the cocking lever and see something the size of a battalion in close ranks. Lioncel!"

The young squire had been standing motionless with Tiphaine's sword cradled in his arms. Now he laid it respectfully down on one of the side tables and opened a basket. The crossbow came out and he stood with it at port arms, his young face calm and attentive.

"This is my squire, Lioncel de Stafford. He's a very junior squire, a page until earlier today, and while he is in excellent training for his age and inches he's thirteen years old and as you can see far from his full growth. That is a standard-issue crossbow of the sealed pattern. Lioncel, span and fire!"

The youngster brought the weapon up before his face in the first move of the drill-book sequence. His right hand held the grip, and his left went to a metal loop set into the base of the forestock.

The weapon was still made as the Lord Protector's conscript engineers had designed it in the first weeks after the Change. The stock was hardwood, modeled after an old-time rifle called an M-14, with adjustable aperture sights over the trigger, a groove down the center for the bolt and a spring catch to hold it in place. The prod—the short horizontal bow bolted into a slot at the end—was a thirty-two-inch section of shaped automobile leaf spring.

Making the weapons was a Crown monopoly, and charging vassals for the ones they required to outfit their troops a source of revenue. The whole assemblage had a blunt, functional grace, rather like a war hammer.

Lioncel pulled on the loop, and the lever it was attached to pivoted down. Then he worked it, using his grip on the stock to make the two a scissors-style source of mechanical advantage. Click-*clack*, click-*clack*, click-*clack*, click-*clack*, click-*clack*, click-*clack*, as the pawl-and-ratchet mechanism in the stock forced the thick string back; then a louder *click!* as the trigger nut caught it.

The squire slapped the lever back into its slot and held the weapon by its forestock with his left hand as his right snapped down to an imaginary belt-quiver. He mimed pressing a short bolt into the groove, brought the weapon up to his shoulder and aimed at a snarling bear in the mural.

Tung, and a slight whapping sound as the string vibrated.

"Again."

He repeated the process. A crossbow didn't have the suave elegance of a Mackenzie longbow; the short prod had to draw at much more raw weight to give a bolt the same speed and range as the superbly efficient spring the long subtly curved yew stave made, and arrows were more aerodynamic than the stubby bolts. Even with the built-in spanning mechanism, a good bowman could get off three shots to the crossbow's one. But it had the supreme virtue that you didn't need to start at age six and practice all your life to master it, and at short range the bolts had a brutal authority that would make nothing of most armor.

"Again."

When Lioncel had fired three imaginary bolts he came to port arms again. Tiphaine looked around the table.

"Reverend Mother, may I borrow your attendant Sister . . ."

"Sister Fatima."

"Sister Fatima for a moment."

"Yes, my lady," the abbess said.

Sister Fatima stood immediately, standing with her eyes slightly cast down and hands linked before her. Tiphaine nodded approval; she'd seen soldiers less disciplined.

"Sister Fatima, you are . . . what, twenty?"

"Nineteen, my lady."

Nineteen, and of no more than middling height and slim, though healthy-looking, as far as you could tell with the voluminous habit.

"Your birth?"

"My father has a fief-minor in sergeantry on a manor of the Count's, a day's travel south of the city, my lady. Ferndale Manor."

That put him in the lowest class of Associate. As an infantry reservist called up a month a year in peacetime he would have a double-sized peasant farm and pay less rent and labor service; his sons would spend a couple of years in the Count's garrisons as young men. Such families were as close to a rural middle class as the Association had.

"Have you ever handled a crossbow?"

"No, my lady. My father and brothers are spearmen."

"Your occupation?"

"I helped with all the usual farm chores, my lady. Now in God's service I am an orderly at our hospital, and a student of medicine, and assist with clerical duties in the Mother Superior's office as needed."

"Excellent, Sister. Lioncel, give the good Sister the crossbow. Sister Fatima, please span and shoot three times."

Lioncel presented the weapon across his palms with a polite bow. The nun's eyes went a little wide as she accepted it, and it wobbled slightly as she adjusted to the solid nine pounds of weight. Then she settled it in a rather clumsy copy of Lioncel's posture and went through the loading procedure. She was awkward, and made elementary mistakes—holding the butt away from her shoulder in a way that would have given her a painful thump if there had been a bolt to launch. But it was obvious that she was handling the basic effort without much strain.

"Thank you, Sister, Reverend Mother," Tiphaine said, as Lioncel retrieved the weapon, replaced it in the basket and retrieved the sword.

"And there you have it," she went on to the room at large as he took up his position behind her. "You can quickly identify the natural shots. Bolts are reusable, so there's no limit on practice. Any laborer, any healthy peasant girl, can load. Have two or three behind the shooter handing forward loaded crossbows. That will augment your firepower quite a bit, especially here with the large circuit of the city walls to hold, and let you use your trained men where you really need them. The enemy are not going to sit down to two-year sieges, or an artillery and combat-engineering duel. If they come, they'll try ramps, siege towers, and plain old ladders, to swamp you with massed assaults regardless of costs. Shoot the guts out of them, break their hearts with losses, and you can stop them. Then your walls will be the anvil against which we'll hammer them to death."

Eventually, she thought but did not say.

The commoners were nodding enthusiastically. She thought she saw signs of hidden stomach cramps among some of the nobles, though not the Count, and the Countess was beaming and nodding herself. The Association had conquered as far and fast as it had because its leaders had quickly grasped the consequences of the Change, equipped their forces with effective gear based on pre-gunpowder weapons and armor, and given them at least some training from their own experience as hobbyists. That expansion had slowed and then stopped when the PPA ran into others who'd had variations on the same idea and time to recover from the shock of the Change and implement it. A lot of the nobles here were survivors of encounters with massed Mackenzie longbowmen or Bearkiller lancers or Corvallan or Yakiman pike-hedges, or the children and younger siblings of those who *hadn't* survived the experience. She let them take the full force of her glacier-colored eyes for a moment.

There was still a good deal of indigestion at the thought of letting too many of the lower classes have weapons which could penetrate the armor of a knight.

"This program will be implemented immediately and fully. So the High King in his wisdom has decreed," she said.

Which settles that, her glance said. *Or* I *will settle* you.

The silver notches in the hilt of the long sword that was in Lioncel's arms once more reinforced the message. When the civilians and the clerics had left, the staff came in and removed the lower table. Lioncel and Armand set up the map easel in its place, and a baron tried again while they were at it:

"My lady Grand Constable, are you sure about the crossbows—"

"Yes, my lord. I am. More to the point the Lady Regent, Her Majesty Mathilda, and His Majesty Artos the First are sure. Any questions?"

He subsided and she went to the map, drawing her dagger to use as a pointer.

"Everything I said to the good burghers was true. What I didn't dwell on—this sort of thing is how we're supposed to earn our keep, my lords—is that we estimate that the enemy are still going to be coming straight at us with between one hundred thousand and one hundred twenty thousand men."

Grunts of frank dismay at the numbers, which were horrific; even a generation after the Change, the far interior was still much more densely populated than the areas towards the coast where the big cities had been, and that translated into more fighting men. She was, within limits, glad that nobody here was gasconading about wading ankle-deep in enemy blood. But then these men had been on the front line for more than a year now. She nodded, a crisp gesture of acknowledgment:

"They're out to break us this year because if they don't they won't be in a position to try again. This has been a slow, cautious, methodical war so far. On our part, it was a delaying action. It won't be anymore."

Saints were invoked—which might actually do some

good now—and there was a flicker of men crossing them-selves. Maugis de Grimmond shrugged and spoke lightly:

"At least the High King didn't have to sneak into the Prophet's domains and throw something into a volcano."

That broke the momentary dismay, and turned it to grim amusement. Tiphaine nodded thoughtfully to the young nobleman, took a sip from her brandy-spiked cof-fee cup, put it down and went on. The point of her weapon traced lines above the silk of the map.

"That's the good part; the bad is that the Temple in Corwin isn't going up in smoke or falling into a pit and his armies aren't going to flee in despair either, even though the High King has the Sword. They're massing *here* outside Spokane, and *here* at Lewiston on the Snake, we think to keep their horses from stressing the grazing too badly in either place. They can't move directly west out of Spokane; too dry once you leave the Palouse and hit the Columbia plateau."

The red-haired baron of Tucannon nodded: "I hunted antelope there with my father a few years ago. I saw the skeleton of a jackrabbit lying beside an empty water can-teen it had been carrying."

A few chuckles at that; a lot of that country had been irrigated from Grand Coulee, but while the dams still stood the giant pumps that filled the canals had stopped flowing at six fifteen p.m. Pacific time, 1998. Those of the population who'd survived had ended up in places like this, where rainfall or windmills or simple gravity-flow ditches provided enough water. Nobody went there anymore except a few hunters.

Tiphaine waited impassively a moment and then went on: "There's no fodder there this time of year either. We could hold the north-south line of the Columbia above the bend forever, especially with the Free Cities backing us up and supplies and reinforcements easily available from the Yakima Valley and the baronies in the east-slope valleys and the Okanagan."

Her pointing dagger went south of the great river, into what had once been Oregon.

"The enemy occupied everything south of the Columbia last year, nearly as far as the boundaries of County Odell, after that cluster-fuck at Pendleton—which doesn't seem to care we now have their precious Bossman prisoner. And Bend fell a bit later, along with the rest of the Central Oregon Rancher's Association territories. Then the enemy spent months trying to force the passes of the High Cascades into the Willamette, and got nothing but bloody noses from the Mackenzies, Bearkillers and Corvallans. Then they died by the thousands in the winter blizzards because they didn't pull back in time."

A set of shark grins, or in a few cases winces; this time they were trying to imagine light horsemen riding into the teeth of those singing clouds of bodkin-pointed death the Mackenzie longbows could produce. Or caught cold and foodless in the huge snowfalls that stretched from October to May at those elevations, with the raiding parties of the Clan slipping through the forests around them like the wolves of Hecate they called themselves.

"Meanwhile the forces that the CORA left behind are waging a cavalry guerilla all over the range country and the foothills east of the Cascades, every inch of which they know, with their families safe in the Willamette and the forts for supplies and refuge. So now it's our turn. We have strong castles at all the crossings of the Columbia from the Wallula Gap to the Gorge, so they can't try to cross in strength to the north bank—incidentally, my lords, does anyone want to complain again about the way the Lady Regent forced everyone to spend money and sweat on fortifications and stockpiles the last fifteen years? No? Good."

Her knife-point moved again, through the rolling lands between the Blue Mountains and the Snake River.

"They have only one option; out of the Palouse and down old Highway 12 from Lewiston to Walla Walla, then to the Wallula Gap and west north of the river."

"How are they going to get past the river at the Gap?" Tucannon asked. "The castles there are very strong. Not much point in sweeping down Highway 12 and then sitting and watching the fish jump and trying to catch round shot and bolts with your teeth."

"Invest the castles and then use barges and pontoons to cross the river," she said. "Unless they can take the bridges up near Kennewick. We have castles covering those, but we couldn't build enough to cover all possible water crossings."

The fighting-men looked at each other; a few smiles flickered into being.

Good. They're starting to see the enemy's *problems, not just ours.*

"Well, good luck supporting a hundred thousand men on the other side of the Columbia *that* way," de Grimmond said.

Tiphaine nodded. "That's why we can't fight the decisive battle here in the Eastermark—"

"Why not?" a baron whose estates were near Dayton said.

"Here they'll still be close to their bases and they can use the railway and the Snake River to bring up supplies. I'm going to fight one or two battles, making them come to me because they're in a hurry, bleed them, and then withdraw westward north of the Columbia, harassing them with the river to guard my right flank, and ultimately joining up with the force the High King is putting together back around Goldendale in Aurea County. You will hold this city and your keeps; if they leave enough men to invest you closely . . . Good."

"Good?" someone asked.

"Good because anyone sitting in front of your gate is out of the fight just as much as if you'd chopped his head off. Or better, because the enemy still has to feed him. If they don't invest you closely, come out and raid their lines of supply. And we're going to scorch the earth; I don't want one kernel of grain or one sheep left for them—"

That led to howls; they subsided quickly faced with the obvious necessity, especially since the Count backed her energetically, along with de Grimmond. When they were listening again she continued:

"That's why we've built all those castles; castellation makes an attacker's life a misery. We'll draw them west, and each mile they advance will make them weaker and drive them mad with frustration, like chewing on meat full of gristle. Then, when they're stretched out and worn down, the High King will bring all our forces against them in a position he chooses and that they can't get around. By then they'll be desperate, with winter coming on and a hostile wasteland behind them; they'll have to go all-out to beat us so that they can get at our supplies. They won't be able to refuse battle, which means that they'll have to fight on our ground and our terms. We estimate that His Majesty, Artos, will be able to muster around eighty-five thousand for the decisive battle. If we win that, we win the war—though it won't be over that day. And that, gentlemen, is our strategy."

And I hope nobody is stupid enough to ask exactly where and when Artos plans to hit them. Athena, gray-eyed De-

*fender of the Polis, you who love the warrior's skill and care
and craft in defense of home and hearth and those we are
sworn to protect, let this work!*

That brought a slight mental stutter; it was the first
time she could ever recall spontaneously praying about
anything without a deliberate decision, even now that she
knew there was something to it. And something *touched*
her then, a feeling of chill relentless clarity like the flicker
of a great spear moving faster than a beam of pure light.
It was gone before she could be certain it was anything
more than her own mind functioning in total focus.

Then she went on:

"Lord Forest Grove has been screening against their
advanced elements, and will give you the details on their
dispositions and probable intentions. Lord Rigobert, the
floor is yours. And I believe Lord Maugis has some
thoughts on how we can act against the enemy's rear elements and transport."

She sat and waited out the discussion that followed,
which lasted until everyone was yawning despite the rare,
nerve-jolting treat of unlimited coffee. It was focused on
details in any case; nobody was trying to talk her into a
monumental last stand in defense of their favorite vineyards. At last the meeting broke up, most of the men
looking reasonably satisfied, or at least knowing what
they were supposed to do and understanding the reasons
for it, which would do. She stopped the Count on his way
out.

"Your lordship, there's something else that my lord de
Stafford and I must speak with you about. Something
more immediate."

"Yes, my lady?" de Aguirre said.

His eyes were haunted with the knowledge of what
was about to come crushing through his people's lands,

regardless of how the ultimate strategy worked. He'd probably be glad to have something more immediate to worry about.

"My lord Count, the entire military leadership of the Eastermark, plus myself and Lord Forest Grove, are here in your palace tonight. It's a very tempting target. Or I would think so, if I was on the other side and I got my start in clandestine operations. Walls keep out armies, not black-operations teams."

His face changed, and de Stafford set a hand on his shoulder. "Here's our plan, my lord," he began.

CHAPTER EIGHTEEN

COUNTY OF THE EASTERMARK
CHARTERED CITY OF WALLA WALLA
CITY PALACE OF THE COUNTS PALANTINE
PORTLAND PROTECTIVE ASSOCIATION
(FORMERLY SOUTHEASTERN WASHINGTON STATE)
HIGH KINGDOM OF MONTIVAL
(FORMERLY WESTERN NORTH AMERICA)
AUGUST 24, CHANGE YEAR 25/2023 AD

Now this is like old times, Tiphaine thought, with a hint of grim amusement. *Except that in the day it was usually me sneaking in through the window to kill someone.*

She had to admit it was well done. There had been hardly any noise at all, nothing like as loud as the occasional call of *all's well* from the watchmen in the town's streets, or the challenge-and-response from the completely useless guards patrolling the outer perimeter of the palace. Being that quiet while you were hanging upside down from a silk rope and sawing through steel bars with a diamond-dusted flexible saw was not easy.

A flicker of light crossed her closed lids, some lantern reflecting upward. The bed was extremely comfortable and the day had been long, but she had no difficulty staying in a half trance, breathing deeply and completely relaxed but in a stable state halfway between waking and sleep. She'd learned the trick of that not long after the Change, when she and Kat had to keep watch and watch. An instructor of Sandra's, a Korean so silent she'd never even learned his name, had taught her how to do it consciously at will later as one part of a training program designed to strengthen the strong and destroy the weak.

It was nearly as restful as real sleep, and had the advantage that your senses were if anything more acute than in the normal waking world.

A squeak. That would be the diamond cutter on the windowpane, now that the bars were out of the way. Her new-minted knights had been precisely right so far on the way the enemy would come. It was a compliment to her training of them.

In the darkness she grinned like a wolf.

Lady Sandra's school has left a legacy that will travel down the generations.

The sheets and pillows smelled of clean linen and lavender, and felt crisp and smooth under her fingers as she slowly pulled the coverings off. She was in working clothes, dark trews and shirt and jerkin, sock-shoes of glove-soft leather with doubled soles that gripped like fingers. Light mesh lined the jerkin, but for this sort of work you relied on speed.

It's actually more pleasant than being a general, she thought. *Straightforward, in a sneaky sort of way. But to acknowledge the absolute truth, I'm sick of both. I have been for years.*

She opened her eyes, keeping them down; she was facing away from the windows. Starlight and a little moonlight were perfectly adequate if you didn't try to close-focus on anything. They painted the room in shades of pale gray and sliver and blue. One leg moved out, and she caught her left heel on the edge of the mattress and bent the knee.

Of course, this could go wrong. You're never quite certain with knives, but we need them alive. You know, when I was in my twenties, I used to positively enjoy this sort of thing. Now I just worry about leaving Delia a widow . . . damn, she could be widowed twice *in this war.*

The thought was very distant. So was the knowledge that she rather liked the Count Palantine and his wife, and that if it had been peacetime she would have enjoyed visiting the Eastermark with Delia and Rigobert and the children. They had some astonishing falconry here, if you could call using great golden eagles to hunt pronghorn antelope that.

And the Count had mentioned a hunting and skiing lodge in the Blue Mountains that he'd be glad to lend her sometime, obviously one of his favorite haunts. Bear hunts, and sleigh rides, and cross-country skiing in cold that was dry and hard and bracing, not the damp bone-chill of the Willamette. Lioncel and Diomede would love that; they'd tire themselves out, shovel down big dinners and sleep like the dead, and she and Delia could make love on tigerskins before a great roaring fire.

I am *going soft in my old age.*

She smiled and slid the dagger a little closer under the pillow. There was something about the approach of a knife aimed at you that you could *feel.* And there was a shadow of a shadow on the wall away from the windows, a suggestion of movement. It would vanish if she tried to focus on it, but if you *didn't* try to do that it was clear as noon; and also the back of her right hand itched. That might be . . .

What was the old word? Ah, psychosomatic. Or it might not.

"Now," she said conversationally.

And flipped herself out of the bed, pulling at her heel and twisting herself around in midair to land in a fighting crouch, knife out with the point low and left forearm across her body with the palm and fingers stiffened into another weapon.

The dagger in the assassin's hand was already streaking down towards the spot where her back had been an instant before. The man had his full weight behind it, flinging himself forward and down to drive the length of watered steel all of its twelve inches deep and hard enough that the flaring edges would slice apart the ribs.

Good professional stroke, Tiphaine thought. *That would have done it nicely. You want to kill someone with a knife, don't waste time on fancy.*

Two more Cutters in dark clothing were climbing in through the windows. Armand and Rodard dropped silently from where they'd been waiting, heels braced on the little ledges above. Both struck the men below feetfirst, and the crossbows the assassins had been carrying dropped; one went off, and the bolt struck the plaster and board of an interior wall with a crunching *whap*. The sworn killers of the Church Universal and Triumphant always operated in threes; it was one of the few things they had in common with the Mackenzies.

The knifeman ignored the flurry of blows and thudding sounds from behind him. He wrenched the knife free and came over the bed in a silent rush, the blade held low and reversed with his thumb on the pommel and the blade jutting out from the right side of the fist.

Somewhere in the Cutter lands there's a school not entirely unlike the one I attended, she thought as she backed easily, moving with soft sure strides, the weight on the balls of her feet.

He didn't waste time; this wasn't a duel, not even the ghastly slashing frenzy of a knife fight, where the winner went to the healers for six months. The two knights would be on his back in instants. A feint high, a backhand slash to the face, and then a stab towards her thigh, aiming for the great vessel that ran up the inside towards the groin.

Fast, she thought. *But he's relying on it and I've got a third of a second on him.*

Her body sank and turned before the thought was complete, her hips swaying aside. Her own knife cut, upward, under the armpit, she couldn't chance whether he wore a mail vest. Cloth parted, and something else between; a spray of blood went up in the night, black drops in blackness. The arm went limp and the knife fell from it. The man hissed with a gobbling undertone and snatched at the weapon with his left, his fingertips touching the dimpled bone hilt before it struck the floor.

He never grasped it. She fell across him in a diving body check, and the breath wheezed out of him as his ribs hit the floor with her on his back. She drove her left elbow down into the base of his skull as they landed, the hard *thud* sending a shooting pain up her arm.

"Light," she said, shaking her hand and working the fingers.

The man wasn't quite limp, but he was twitching and moving with the vague undersea slowness of someone who'd had his bell truly rung. The lamps flared. Both the other assassins were down and bound, ankles and wrists lashed together and good thick gags in their mouths; she wanted no more fanatics biting out their tongues and drowning in their own blood before they had every scrap of information wrung out of them.

"See to this one," she said as she rose, kicking his knife

aside and wiping hers on the man's hair. "Don't let him bleed out. Pity about the rug."

She slipped her blade into the sheath along the inside of her left forearm as she walked through the doors into the other room. That one looked considerably messier; there was a triad of assassins lying just inside the windows. Two had been struck as they climbed over the sills—one had a leg still on his, with that spilled awkwardness that only the suddenly and violently dead could show. Both those two were riddled with crossbow bolts. At this range the armor-smashers buried themselves to the fletching, and one of the men had been pitched back and pinned upright to the wall like a butterfly in a display case. His body, limp and leaking on the tiles, slid off the shaft and struck the floor with a *thump* as she came in.

The third was three paces into the room, lying on his side with the kill-dagger just beyond his twitching fingertips, and, unfortunately from his point of view, still alive. The human body was astonishingly resilient sometimes. A single bolt had struck him, and his face was like a contorted carving of hardwood with blood seeping past his clenched teeth and out his nostrils in bubbles. Sound trickled out as well.

The sergeant of the crossbowmen saluted. "That one was clever, my lady," he said admiringly. "He backflipped into the room, must've dropped straight down and caught the sill and bounced in like a rubber ball. We missed him clean, everyone except young master . . . except Squire Lioncel de Stafford, I mean, my lady. He nailed him good, right in the brisket, which ain't easy when things go south and it's all noisy and confusing, like."

"No, it isn't," she said; it was astonishing how many bolts were used per hit in a combat situation. "Thank you, Sergeant. A very creditable job. A week's pay bonus to you and your squad for losing a night's sleep."

The man grinned, and she nodded again. She'd meant it. Missing number three hadn't been serious. A man with a knife wasn't going to do much against eight with swords and bucklers and wearing three-quarter armor, no matter how good he was with a blade. Assassination and straight-up fighting were quite different things. And one thing she'd learned from Sandra was never to stint praise or reward where they were really due. Being a cheapskate that way always left you with the bill coming due at the worst possible time.

Norman was a bit of a niggard now and then. Sandra, I note, is still alive and still in power long after he's dead.

Lioncel was staring at the dying Cutter, his crossbow still in his hands, motionless.

"Lioncel!" she said, and he started and seemed to come to himself.

Well, it is his first, I think . . . yes, definitely. About the same age I was, at that. Of course, these Cutters didn't intend to rape him before they killed him and eat his flesh afterwards. Still, it's traumatic.

"We . . . caught them by surprise, my lady," he said. "It all happened just like you said it would."

"Good. And Lioncel?"

He looked at her, his blue eyes a little wild.

"They came to kill us in our sleep. If your mother or little sister were here, they'd have killed *them*. We were defending them. Fight knights like knights, and stamp on a weasel."

He took a deep breath. "Yes, my lady."

"And he's too far gone for questioning. Finish it quickly. That's your responsibility, whether it's a beast or a man."

"Yes, my lady."

The boy was pale but steady as he drew his knife and did what was needful, and followed her back into the bedroom. The two knights had the Cutter she'd disabled in a chair, finishing up a field dressing and binding his arm before tying him up.

"Good," she said; the Cutter was reviving, a vicious clarity in his eyes. "We'll need this one for questioning. I think he's one of the leaders on this mission, and we'll have a nice little talk."

The Cutter laughed, and then opened his mouth at her. Lioncel crossed himself, Armand swore, and even Tiphaine blinked. Only the stub of a tongue remained in the man's mouth, and he laughed again, a thick odd sound. The wound was healed, but recent; this had been done deliberately by a surgeon and by the man's own choice, to keep him from talking if he was taken.

Then Tiphaine smiled. At first because she was trying to imagine torturing a man into *writing* out his answers. And then because of another thought.

"Keep him very safe," she said coolly. "Keep him for the High King. I think the Sword of the Lady can get secrets even from a tongueless man."

The mad glee dropped off the assassin's face, and he began to struggle and scream wordlessly. They were equipped for that; Rodard twisted open a metal canister, and held the damp pad of cloth within over the man's face. The struggles died away as his eyes rolled up in his head.

Lioncel was looking revolted, but he had her sword belt ready. She buckled it on as they walked out into the hallway, twice around her unarmored waist; the corridor was dim, with only a few lanterns gleaming on the armor and weapons. Rigobert had just arrived, with blood on his naked sword and a scratch down the front of the breastplate lames of his full suit.

"We didn't take any alive, and I lost a man, dammit," he said, handing his blade to a squire for cleaning without looking around. "You, my lady ninjette?"

"Killed three, took three prisoners, no losses. You are so depressingly straightforward sometimes, de Stafford."

Though my methods had substantially more downside risk. You roll the dice . . .

The nobleman made a disgusted sound as he took the blade again and sheathed it, before replying, "The ones who attacked us all had their tongues cut out. Which would render them useless for interrogation, and even more so on dates. I doubt even the Lady Regent's experts could do much with interrogation via sign language. Or in epistolary form."

"Ours had oral circumcision too. But remember who we work for now, Rigobert. Matti's guy? The one with the *magic sword*?"

"Ah!" A slow smile, and one which echoed hers. "Yes, there *is* a point to that observation. A point with an edge to it."

"I mentioned it to him, and he seemed rather upset."

"Good. I'm not looking forward to telling Jurian's family how he died."

"Dead's dead, Rigobert, tonight or next week from an arrow or a lance head. And"—she poked a finger at the scratch on his armor—"I don't think you were leading from behind."

He shook his head. "I still don't like it, we shouldn't have had losses when we were expecting them. Let's go call on our host."

They clattered down the staircase towards the family quarters—though in fact the Countess was now in a hidden safe room, not the chamber she usually shared with her husband. Apparently the Count's father had been a firm believer in having a secret passage out, of which Tiphaine heartily approved; Todenangst was riddled with them. A household knight met them before they reached the landing, panting and looking a little wild-eyed.

The freckle-faced young man stopped and started to salute with fist to breastplate, then realized he was hold-ing a red-running long sword in that hand and brought the hilt up before his face instead.

"My lady Grand Constable, my lord de Stafford."

"Is the Count your master unharmed?" she snapped.

"Yes. That is . . . this way, please!"

She exchanged a glance with her second-in-command. Their own swords came out, and sped up to a trot; silent with her party, and a ramming clank from de Stafford's, there was no way to move fast and quietly in armor. They went past the guard detail, who, she was pleased to see, were keeping their eyes front, and not turning around to look behind them except for a designated cover man—there were any number of classic misdirection ploys which relied on the natural impulse to focus on the place the noise was coming from.

The family quarters of the Counts were splendid but not ostentatious by the upper nobility's standards. Subtle signs showed recent modifications, including more locally made post-Change work, including several small elegant bronzes of wildlife, probably to mark the switch from the first count to his son—or to his son's wife, which was often the case. A library-study full of wood paneling and leather furniture and glass-fronted bookcases showed the first signs of the attack; bodies being carried away, blood, furniture overturned and scorch marks where fires started by overset lanterns had been hastily stamped out. The broad windows needed for light were probably why the enemy had picked this room for entry.

Tiphaine pursed her lips. "I'm glad I advised him to go overboard on numbers," she said, absently rubbing the back of her right hand.

Rigobert jerked his blond head in agreement. "I can think of a lot of operations which failed because not enough force was used," he said. "But other things being equal—timing mainly, and concealment—I can't think of a single damned one that failed because *too much* force was used. Subtle buys no bread."

Tiphaine nodded. A pair of crossbowmen were being given emergency care near the big doors from the library into the rest of the suite, and another lying on his back looked as if someone had grabbed his helmeted head and twisted until he was looking out over his shoulder blades. She bared her teeth.

Heard about that before, she thought.

Through a corridor, with two dead Cutters in it; these ones had shetes, the broad-tipped slashing swords favored in the far interior, and they were wearing cloth masks that covered everything but the eyes. Next was a door with firing loopholes that had been hit so hard that it sagged on one hinge; she bent slightly to check as she went by. The pattern of splintering around the lock confirmed what she'd thought; someone had slammed their hand into it.

"They thought they could pin them in this corridor and shoot them down," Rigobert said thoughtfully. "Didn't work, for some reason."

"Their point man broke the trap open from the inside," Tiphaine said.

Rigobert's fair brows went up. The chamber beyond was some sort of social space. Probably mainly a ballroom, judging from the superb parquet floor and the mirrors and spindly tables around the edge and the brilliantly lit crystal gas-chandeliers above. This was where the killing had mainly been, pitilessly illuminated by the lights designed to bring out jewels and bright cloth; her nostrils flared at the familiar scents, and the floors were never going to be the same. The local dead had been dragged out and laid in a row with their arms folded, and she saw stretchers disappearing out the other side of the big chamber as she entered.

Count Felipe was sitting on one of the chairs near the three-deep pile of enemy fallen. The spindly seat creaked dangerously under his armored weight. Two men with bolt cutters were working on the bevoir of his suit of plate, which had been bent so badly beneath his chin that the usual hinges and clasps were all irredeemably stuck; it came free with a clang, and another got the equally damaged gauntlet off his left hand.

Felipe swore again, his handsome swarthy young face showing as much chagrin and anger as pain. A chirurgeon began to work on the hand. By then the two western nobles were close enough to see that the fleshy pad at the base of the thumb there was mangled, besides the bruising where the little overlapping plates had been bent; the doctor was examining it carefully, and then got to work with tweezers and a small very sharp pair of scissors, and a spray of disinfectant.

At mere pain the Count's face went impassive, though a film of sweat covered it. He started to speak, and then something gripped Tiphaine's left ankle with crushing force and *jerked*.

Reflex saved her; she had the sword coming down before she hit the ground, curling up and using the grip that anchored her leg as a brace to strike. The edge of the long sword hit and bit, and the fingers started to relax as tendons cut. Another slash and she was free, rising in a flickering shoulder roll. Half-free at least; it took a stamp and the use of her point to get the hand off her ankle. Blades were rising and falling, amid half-hysterical shouts of loathing. She tested the ankle and found it only a little sore.

She looked up. A man had risen from the pile of bodies, half-risen at least. Six crossbow bolts studded his torso, and one eye was dangling down his cheek, and an arm ended in an oozing stump. The sole remaining eye *looked* at her.

"*I . . . see . . . you . . . forever. . . .*"

The voice was a rasping guttural, and air wheezed out of the chest from the other openings as well. If cinders could speak, they would use that tone. For a moment it was as if she were locked in endless hot stone, and then there was a dry wind and a rustle that might have been broad wings hunting in the night or the wind in narrow olive leaves of silver-gray, and the world returned.

Rigobert's long sword was up in the two-handed grip with the hilt beside his face. He stepped and struck, pivoting his torso in a beautiful *suihei* horizontal cut and follow-through. The head toppled away from the body, and the torso fell back with a thud.

Thank you, Lady of the Owl! Tiphaine thought.

Men were crossing themselves all around her, touching their crucifixes or saint's amulets. Her own hand had gone to her throat, for the owl medallion hidden there, and she grinned for an instant at the tinge of scorn she'd have felt for the others only a few years ago.

I'm finally a full-fledged Changeling, not caught betwixt and between, she thought. *Poor Sandra! She got the world of her dreams and she'll never really be at home here.*

Aloud she went on: "You men! Get that head and body, wrap them in mats and blankets, and take them away. Wear gauntlets. Burn the body and everything that's touched it, somewhere where you're upwind of the smoke. Don't touch it if you can help it. Wash afterwards. Wash *thoroughly* and discard your clothes and gloves. Have the floor here ripped up, cautiously. Scrub everything with lye and bleach, burn the wood. And get a priest to do an exorcism. Do it all *now*."

The Walla Walla men hesitated, looking at their lord. He flushed and snapped, "She's the Grand Constable, you fools, do what you're told! Do it all, do it right! Sir Budic, take charge and see that the Grand Constable's instructions are followed to the letter. Now! And get the rest of this carrion out of the palace."

A little more gently: "You've all done well and bravely, and I will not forget who stood with me this night. Now show good vassalage once more, and keep your mouths shut about this until I give out what's happened. We don't want a panic."

The men scattered about their tasks, though Tiphaine doubted any secrecy would last more than about fifteen minutes. When they had some small degree of privacy Felipe looked at her and ducked his head.

"I am in your debt, my lady. I and my House. But for you, I and my wife and our unborn child might have been caught by surprise by that . . . that *thing* and its minions. Even as it was—"

He looked around.

"I thought you were being overcautious when you recommended so many men waiting. Remind me not to doubt you again."

Lioncel silently returned her sword, clean once more, dropped a cloth into the pile that the Count's men were getting ready to burn, and then stripped off his gloves and added them as well.

She nodded, sheathed the weapon and went on to her host. "I don't claim to be infallible, but I've had some experience with this. With those creatures in particular, and I've made it my business to investigate. And the High King told me more."

"What *was* it? I . . . I had my sword through its belly, I swear I did, and then it put its hands around the bevoir of my suit and started to squeeze as if it were trying to throttle me through the metal, and I could feel the steel begin to buckle! I was holding it off with one hand against its face and stabbing it, and it *chewed* through the bison hide on the palm of my gauntlet!"

"That," Tiphaine said, "was a High Seeker out of Corwin. You don't really need the red robe to recognize them once they get into action; and if you kill them . . . well, you kill the man that was. But the . . . whatever . . . lingers, even stronger, for a few moments. Be flattered, my lord; the enemy have paid you a great compliment."

Her face was glacier-calm; inwardly she was cursing herself for overconfidence. Her little trap had worked perfectly . . . against normal assassins. It had been only marginally acceptable at what had shown up, and that only because the main effort had happened to hit here. If the Seeker had come after *her*—

"The High King had a similar experience on his quest," she said. "And Lady Juniper a little east of here, though she was better prepared."

Then she looked at the palm, stopping the chirurgeon for a second. "This was a bite?"

"He'd have had the thumb off in another moment, but someone hit him on the head with a war hammer."

"That would be what popped out the eye. Well, my lord, if you're going to be taking my advice from now on, after it's dressed I'd send for the Mother Superior."

The doctor gave her an offended stare. She glanced back at him and he opened his mouth, closed it, finished his work and left with a deep bow to join the others working on the casualties.

Felipe's face changed as he followed her thought.

No, he's not a genius as a field commander, but he's not stupid.

"My lady, my lord," he said. "I think we need to consult."

Rigobert's squires removed his armor as the Count's did his, and then they walked after him as he went, limping slightly. Their path led farther into the family quarters; when they stopped at a door that looked as if it had a solid steel core, so did the reinforced guard detail. When the door closed behind them the noiseless *whuff* and the abrupt silence confirmed her suspicions; she blessed his parents' paranoia. The room within was probably his wife's, from the decorations, which included a big oil painting of a snowbound landscape realistic enough to make Tiphaine shiver a little at the black pines shedding wisps of ice crystals. Certainly his wife was in the chamber, dressed in a thick night-robe trimmed with marten fur. The only windows were narrow and thickly barred, though open to the air. She started up, reached for his hand, and then stopped at the bandage.

"I'm fine," he said.

They embraced a little cautiously, for his bruises and injuries and her pregnancy, and he kept the bandaged left hand well clear of her. Ermentrude followed the words with close attention as he spoke, then curtsied to Tiphaine, and again to Rigobert.

"Please, be seated, my lady, my lord," she said, gracious but pale. "Refreshments?"

Felipe grinned at her, a tired expression. "I think we could all use a stiff brandy, my beloved," he said.

"Not for me," she said, and touched the slight swell of her stomach for a moment. "But how I wish I could."

She did the honors, poured herself a cordial, and they all sat around a table that bore some sewing gear and a copy of *Sense and Sensibility* with a tooled leather cover and a silk ribbon marking a place. It rested on another with the title *Birds of North America*.

You never knew everything about another human being. Tiphaine sipped at the brandy, which was excellent, not quite as smooth as the pre-Change salvage Sandra preferred, but demonstrably on the same road. Though at present raw hooch distilled from potatoes by peasants would have been welcome.

"You said that I should send for the Mother Superior of the house of the Sisters of Charity here," Felipe said, and raised his injured hand. "I presume not for their medical skills, excellent as those are?"

"No," Tiphaine said. "We are contending with . . . I think the expression is *principalities and powers*, my lord. And I'm not a superstitious person by natural inclination, as you may have heard."

He'd probably heard scandalized whispers that she was the next thing to an atheist, which, until fairly recently, would have been absolutely correct.

Not that I'm a good Catholic now either!

"Not the archbishop?" Ermentrude said curiously, but she sounded curious about Tiphaine's reasons rather than disagreeing with the judgment, from the tone.

"No. I'm sure he's a pious and learned man"—which took care of the formalities—"but what you need right now are certain . . . personal qualities. An archbishop is inevitably something of a politician and that is not what's required."

Felipe and his wife exchanged a glance, and he went on.

"Very well, my lady Grand Constable, I will do as you recommend, and light candles and pray to St. James, the patron of my House. Could you tell me exactly *what* we're facing? I know in general terms that the Church has denounced the CUT as diabolists and done everything but proclaim a Crusade . . . they'd need His Holiness for that, of course, and Badia is so far away . . . but could you give me some details? It would be very much appreciated."

Tiphaine hesitated; she was operating at the limits of her discretion here, and Sandra had always preferred need-to-know. On the other hand . . .

I'll edit things as I go along, just give him the gist. Certainly I'll take out the personal bits! And I'll be vague on exactly who *helped me out. But he* does *need to know; the war effort requires that he be brought up to speed. Plus I think Ermentrude is his closest adviser. And unlike their men-at-arms, I think they can keep secrets.*

"I was in charge of the Mary Liu matter," she said.

"Dowager Baroness Liu? Lord Odard de Gervais' mother?" Felipe said. "She was arrested for treason, wasn't she? I'd heard she was under house arrest at Fen House. But there was a rumor she died . . ."

"Yes. That wasn't simply a case of treason. What happened after her arrest has a bearing on your wound and what needs to be done to make sure it heals. The King had such a hurt on his quest from an arrow, and I did last spring, and now you. That May I rode to Fen House—"

INTERLACHEN PRISON
THE NEW FOREST, CROWN DEMESNE
(FORMERLY NORTHERN OREGON)
PORTLAND PROTECTIVE ASSOCIATION
HIGH KINGDOM OF MONTIVAL
(FORMERLY WESTERN NORTH AMERICA)
MAY 28, CHANGE YEAR 24/2022 AD

It was the dawn of a fine spring day when Tiphaine d'Ath rode out of the East Gate of Portland, taking the carefully maintained Banfield north to the I-205 interchange, towards the Columbia.

If anyone had been ill-advised enough to ask where she was going or why, she would have jerked her head back towards her squires and the mounted varlets carrying nets and boar spears and the half a dozen shaggy slothounds panting and padding in their wake. The dark green tunic and trews and shirt she wore, and the peaked Montero hat with a partridge feather in the livery badge would bear that out. It was well known that the Baroness of Ath had the rare and valued privilege of hunting in the Crown Preserves of New Forest and Government Island.

New Forest had once been Forest Park and Metro Portland's outer suburbs, before the firestorms and the plagues and then the Lord Protector's spearmen had emptied them.

Government Island to the east was still Government Island; the government had changed . . . but not the restricted status. They passed through the new agricultural zone quickly. Truck gardens and specialty orchards had been planted where once houses had crowded cheek by jowl.

Once off the old highways, Tiphaine relaxed a bit. Trees arched over Airport Way for a while. Then they opened out to reveal shaggy, intensely green meadow thick with blooming thickets of purple lilac and wild roses gone feral into impenetrable tangles and making the air heavy with sweetness. Then a stand of young garry oaks and black walnuts planted by the Crown's foresters, thirty or forty feet high, with here and there the snag of a scorched brick wall, or a reedy pond where a basement had been, and then self-sown woods ranging from the tall poplar trees and copper beeches of some park or suburb to tangled saplings poking their way through the monstrous barbed chevaux-de-frise of blackberry vines around a chimney. A generation's rapid growth in this moist mild climate had drawn a haze across the past, as if it were trying to turn the Change into something in a story or a song or a picture in an illuminated book.

Now and then a taller building poked through, a green mound overrun with vines, but most of those had been torn down for their materials in the program that had rebuilt Portland and sown the land with castles. It had been policy to clear these areas first. Now they helped feed and fuel the Crown city of Portland and provided hunting for its lords.

Practical, and I think Norman wanted to wipe out the remains of a world he hated. Maybe one man in a hundred thousand welcomed the Change, knowing full well what it was and what it would do. And they were the ones who did best.

The sounds of life were thick—the air full of northbound wings, murmurous with bees, squirrels chattering and scolding, now and then the slap of a beaver's tail, or a glimpse of a raccoon. Once an elk bounded across the roadway, and she saw the tracks of mule deer, whitetails, antelope and feral cattle and bison and the churned patches where wild boar had fed, besides smaller game innumerable. There were wolf and bear and cougar here too, and sometimes tiger wandered in for a while from the mountains or the river swamps, though the predators were fewer and wary.

Like me, she thought. *I'm rare and wary, all right. And I still don't like this area. It's even better hunting ground than Barony Ath's share of the Coast Range forests, but . . .*

In her lands in the Tualatin Valley you could pretend the Change had happened centuries ago, that it was a legend. Most people preferred that, and she did too. She had been young then, after all, still flexible, able to get on with her life. Well over half of it had been lived since then.

But Portland was where she'd been born, and lived all her life until the Change. That was long ago, but every so often something around here would jog her memory— the precise silhouette of Mt. Hood's white cone over some trees—and the ghosts of buildings and cars and people would return in her mind's eye.

Though it is good hunting ground. Most animals like the edge of a forest better than the depths, and this is all edge. When Heuradys is an old lady dandling her grandchildren, it'll be like Sherwood and the roots will have ground most of the ruins into the dirt.

Sandra Arminger did a little genteel hawking now and then for form's sake, or rode to hounds in the sense that she sat on a small gentle horse for an hour or so while other people chased the game, and then she went home. She'd also been known to remark that most hunting was far too much like wallowing in the mud with wild animals for her taste. The New Forest had other uses, though. Interlachen Prison was one, another of Norman Arminger's mad whims.

He was an evil bastard, but not a stupid one, Tiphaine

thought. *And there was a touch of demented brilliance to him at times. Well, fairly often, in fact.*

She'd always hated the man with excellent reason and she'd inwardly rejoiced when he was killed, along with the better part of a million other people, for all her loyal service to House Arminger. The only sorrow in it for her had been the grief Sandra had had to suffer through. But there were occasions when she thought she understood a little of what Sandra had seen in him—which was a disturbing thing in itself.

The forest thinned out a little as she approached the Columbia. The narrow spit of land known as Interlachen lay between Blue Lake and Fairview Lake, each sixty acres or better of shallow water. Wide channels had been dug at either end of the ridge to turn it into an island in the middle of a shallow marshy swale of water and reed beds and trees.

Guard towers loomed on both sides of the eastern channel; the western channel had two courses of walls. Tiphaine approved as her bona fides were scrupulously checked before the spear points and crossbows went up, and she was rowed across, with the horses and her party stashed in a barn on the shore. The Grand Constable leapt out of the boat onto the narrow bench and waited for the postern beside the main gates to be opened; it was all rather like a castle, but focused mainly inward rather than outward. The medium-security prisoners were all in the main building closest to her, which had a conventional enough layout for a jail, plus the quarters of the Seneschal and the guards and their families. A large bare cobbled yard separated it from the maximum-security block, known as Fen House. Norman had said the best place to hide a prison was inside a prison.

And laughed. It was a joke after his own heart.

Sir Stratson came to meet her and escorted her through the next few doors to the exercise yard and across it. He looked as mournful as ever. She couldn't imagine *living* here and not going insane, though the garrison seemed contented enough. They had boating and fishing, and poaching she supposed, and their families cultivated gardens nearby. Otherwise . . .

"So, have there been any changes since you sent that dispatch, Sir Stratson?"

There was no need to specify *which* prisoner she was inquiring after.

"No, about the same since she came out of her fugue. She works on that white-work embroidery . . . there's more than enough light in there most of the day. Eats, takes care of herself. She's a boring prisoner, to be sure. Whines and frets, demands and puts on airs. Nothing out of the ordinary for one of the upper-upper caught out in their peculations."

"And what does she remember of the missing months?"

"Nothing. She was truly annoyed about my cutting her hair. She doesn't remember anything. And she doesn't believe it, either. Thinks I drugged her like they did at Castle Gervais, won't believe what month it really is even with the weather and all."

Tiphaine studied the Warden as they waited for the guards to open the inner gates. He was a very fair-skinned man and only slightly taller than she, ruddy faced with a grizzled ring around the bald dome of his head, merging into whiskers and a floppy mustache. His dark eyes were alert enough, but the long lines on his horsey face told of a weariness that wasn't really physical.

He's what, late forties, early fifties. He'd have been younger than I am now at the Change, she thought clini-

cally. Younger than Delia is now, in fact, though a man grown. He didn't go mad back when like so many, but my guess is he's never forgotten or completely adapted and he's been perfectly content to rusticate here, keeping watch and doing the occasional session of questioning and watching the grass grow and the birdies fly. Norman did know how to find the right man for the right job. It's not just politics now, though. There's a . . . call it religious aspect. I don't know how he'll react to that.

They entered the high-security wing of the prison. Tiphaine grimaced.

Fen House. Norman's joke.

Everyone assumed that Fen House was a *house*, as in *house arrest.* It helped keep the families quiet.

Not least by soothing their consciences. Most of them don't like the ones who end up here, if only because they put their kin at risk by lethally pissing off the Crown. They can think they're in comfortable detention and forget about them. No, Norman was not stupid.

She stood in a broad room, three stories tall. The south wall behind her was mostly seven clerestory windows each stretching up two of the three. Directly in front of her was a large clear space. Two half-levels were above. Each contained three cells. Bare bars left them completely open to sight. The men walking a measured beat on the archers' walkways around the empty space at the second- and third-story levels could see every detail of each cell, and reach them with their crossbows at need. The place smelled of damp and lye soap; the spring light came in, but it didn't seem to really rest on the cheerless brick and concrete.

Here on the ground floor under the cells was a kitchen with a battered-looking woodstove and bunk beds slung for the guards. Once again, the line of sight was completely open. There were toilets and a urinal, tucked under the stairs that climbed the east and west walls. A quiet woman sat in the middle cell, a large sheet of white over her lap. Tiphaine frowned; Mary looked so *ordinary*.

Well, not every mad evil bitch has mad evil bitch written on her face.

"Has she said anything of a religious nature?"

Stratson looked uneasy. "I'm not much for religion, never was . . ."

Which is probably one reason he likes to be alone out here, Tiphaine thought. *I can sympathize to a certain extent. This High Medieval Holy Church thing always grated on me, not to mention Delia, even after I got to pay antiPope Leo a visit.*

"Is it relevant?" he continued. Then he sighed. "This Church Universal and Triumphant thing, right?"

"Right. Either she chose treason as a way to keep her family on what she thought was the winning side, or she *actually* converted. You have to understand people's motives to predict what they'll do."

"England had considerable troubles that way, under the Tudors and Stuarts," Stratson said, surprising her a little. "But, well, no. Nothing religious. She's just a rather stupid woman . . . How old was she at the time of the Change?"

Tiphaine reflected. "Young. I think, maybe fourteen, not that much older than I was. I remember that the Regent was quite angry when Eddie Liu proposed. But the Protector insisted that it was a good match and a different time, so her age wasn't so much an issue. It turned out to be a match made in heaven."

Stratson surprised her again, this time by laughing. "Or in hell, if those two suited each other," he said. At her look: "I met Eddie Liu . . . Eddie Scar-face . . . a few times, m'lady. He was here a fair bit in the Lord Protector's day."

Tiphaine nodded; even by the standards of the early years of the Protectorate Eddie had been ripe. And not as smart as he thought he was, though he'd had the elemental good sense not to presume on his close relationship with Norman to step on Sandra's toes. Norman had always backed Sandra in the end, against anyone.

"Hopefully her children will turn out better," Tiphaine said.

Stratson shook his head and sighed. "She's never asked, never mentioned either of the younger ones, Yseult and Huon. Once in a while she'd say something about Odard, but it was just snippets. Nothing concrete."

Tiphaine sighed; a disagreeable piece of work didn't get any better for waiting herself. If things went quickly, she actually *could* do some hunting and get back to Portland in the evening, which would be good protective coloration.

"Open her door," she said. "We need to have a chat."

Mary looked up from her embroidery when the barred door opened and clanged to behind Tiphaine. She quickly looked down again.

"Good day, my lady."

The Grand Constable studied the white-work; she'd lived with an expert needlewoman for fifteen years, and had an observant spectator's grasp of it. She even appreciated it, though she'd rather eat toads than do it herself. There was no accounting for tastes; Delia actually *liked* being pregnant, for instance.

"That's very neat work. Yseult mentioned it. Can I see it?"

Mary kept her gaze on the cloth for a few more seconds and then looked up.

"Yseult? How is she?"

Tiphaine nodded. "She's in fosterage in a noble household, at a place where her status as your daughter won't cause her trouble. Doing very well, from what I've heard, and well liked. Huon is still page to Lord Mollala. He was at the battle of Pendleton last year, running messages and so forth. Lord Chaka thinks well of him."

"Last year! You mean last month!"

Tiphaine shook her head. "It's been a long time. It's almost June. You've been in some sort of a fugue state since your arrest for treason. Do you remember your brother coming to you in September, just after the battle?"

Mary looked at her; there was something distinctly odd in her blue eyes, a desperation.

"You're trying to drive me mad!"

"*Drive* you?" said Tiphaine dryly. "No, you were arrested when news came that Vinton failed to give the Princess to the CUT and your late brother did a bunk. As far as we know, Odard is still alive, still with the Princess and they are somewhere on the Great Plains. Take a look out the window and tell me if you see fall or late spring."

Mary hesitated and then thrust the cloth into Tiphaine's hands and walked to the window. She stood there for what seemed like a very long time, gripping the bars and pressing her face against them. When she turned her eyes were full of tears, and the marks of the iron were white on her skin.

"So long, so long. Where was I?"

"Well, here, in body, but your mind was wandering. That's why Stratson had to cut your hair. It was getting badly snarled. I'd like to know where your mind wandered. According to the guards, you kept saying something about *hidden* and *eyes that couldn't see*."

Mary shook her head and took back her embroidery and began to ply her needle.

"I couldn't see Odard," she said, in an almost conversational voice. "They promised I'd always be able to see him and I could and then he went away, and they couldn't bring him back."

"They?"

"He, the Priest. He said God would grant me this miracle and . . ."

Mary snapped her mouth shut. Tiphaine waited. Mary shot her a sly glance. "He said . . . that . . . he'd pray that Odard got his desire, to marry the Princess."

Tiphaine frowned down at the woman. *Something is off,* she thought.

"And now you can see him?"

"Yes, he's traveling with them, there was grass, so much grass, and buffalo, and fights. There's a city, a great city, and a golden dome. I think he spent the winter hidden . . . But how? How did he escape the eye of the Sun?"

Tiphaine pondered the answer; the Cutters used a solar disk as one of their important symbols.

That's data. Next dispatch we can compare the dates and see if they match.

"Which priest told you this?"

"One from over the mountains. He was a true priest, not a schismatic like Pope Leo or the Mount Angel monks. He asked me to make a cloth for the altar of the Lord and promised me my prayers would be answered."

Tiphaine looked at the cloth with its odd symbols. "Did he give you a pattern?"

"No. He put it in my head, as proof he could do miracles."

Tiphaine nodded, taking a corner of the cloth and looking at it.

"You know," she said in a conversational tone of voice, "that wasn't a priest of Holy Mother Church. He was a Priest of the Church Universal and Triumphant out of Corwin."

"What do I care, so long as I get my revenge for Eddie's and Jason's deaths? And *my* son will rule Oregon!"

Mary stuck the needle in her mouth and sucked it, a moment. She cast another of those sly looks upward and Tiphaine stared, frozen.

Her eyes were black, like windows into . . . not even emptiness. Tiphaine clenched her stomach muscles against a sudden wave of nausea. She blinked. Mary Liu was there, but somehow it *wasn't* her. She tossed the cloth aside, and Mary's hand darted out, jabbing the needle point at Tiphaine. Tiphaine jerked back and the point slid down the back of her right hand, brushing along it ever so gently.

"Hee, hee, hee," giggled the thing that had been Mary Liu. "Bad cess to you and yours!"

Tiphaine walked over to the door and signaled it open. She turned back.

"Bad cess, bad cess, bad cess . . . You didn't help Jason out of that cell before the Rangers killed him."

As a matter of fact, they didn't kill him. I did. Sandra wanted his mouth shut and the blame put elsewhere. But that was just damage control after he screwed the pooch with your little scheme to use the bandits to attack the Dúnedain. Despite specific orders *not to do anything until we were* ready *to start the Protector's War. Did you think you wanted Astrid Loring's head more than I did, you* stupid *bitch? We* weren't *ready. That screwup of yours may well be why Corvallis came in at the worst possible moment, why the Association lost and Norman died.*

Tiphaine waited and watched the sitting woman with her idle needle. Slowly the eyes leached out and became blue again and she took up her needle and began the careful, neat, quick stitches of an expert. Tiphaine turned and went downstairs.

Did I actually just see that? Would it be more logical to assume I'm going crazy . . . no. I did just see that.

Then she looked at the sunlight; it was easy to see precisely how far the beams from the windows had moved across the bare floor.

"How long did I stand by the gate?" she asked.

Sir Stratson shook his head. "I didn't time it, but at least seven or eight minutes. Thought you were thinking deeply, m'lady."

Tiphaine scratched the back of her hand and looked down and cursed. A painful red welt ran from her wrist to the first knuckle.

How could that happen and I not feel it? And how could Mary Liu *move faster than I could withdraw my hand? Something very odd is going on here.*

"I think," said Tiphaine, with elaborate calm. "That you'd better not go into the cell again, unless you put her out with laudanum in wine."

"She did that?"

"Sucked a needle and tried to jab me with it. I didn't think she'd managed to scratch me. I really, really, suggest that any physical contact be kept to a minimum. In fact, I order it."

She met Stratson's eyes. He looked . . .

Spooked, scared as hell, thought Tiphaine. *Good, so am I.*

A year and a little more peeled away. Tiphaine looked at her right hand, holding it up and moving the fingers, marveling at the precise articulation of it, the exquisite symmetry and action. Then she bunched it. The forearm ran smoothly into the lower part of the hand without much indentation at the wrist; a gymnast's hand, or a swordswoman's.

"There was . . . a problem with the hand, after that scratch?" Countess Ermentrude de Aguirre said carefully.

"Problem?" Tiphaine said. "Well, yes, your grace. The first problem was that I didn't take it seriously enough at first."

Rigobert poured himself another brandy. "You always were stubborn, my lady," he said.

"If I weren't stubborn, I'd have been dead before my fourteenth birthday," Tiphaine said. "But in this case . . . yes, there was a downside. Fortunately I'm not *stupid*. I . . . went to see someone, you might say. In Bend."

CHAPTER NINETEEN

CITY OF BEND

OFFICES OF THE PLODDING PONY EXPRESS COMPANY

CENTRAL OREGON RANCHERS ASSOCIATION TERRITORY

(FORMERLY CENTRAL OREGON)

HIGH KINGDOM OF MONTIVAL

(FORMERLY WESTERN NORTH AMERICA)

JUNE 3, CHANGE YEAR 24/2022 AD

*B*end is hot in the summer.

Tiphaine kept the spurt of laughter behind a bland facade. The fact that she nearly didn't was a bad sign.

Bend is hot. I could just say, water is wet, she thought.

Her head buzzed. The joints of her body all ached as well. She'd felt a little like this with the flu once, when she was ten. Her mother had made her go to bed, and she'd missed school and hadn't even been able to read, just lying there hurting.

"My lady?"

Armand's face. So like Kat's. She shook her head. "Armand, get the horses taken care of. Set up camp with the rest of the Association forces. Have my tent placed next to whoever is in charge."

"Sir César Obregón de Lafayette," Armand said, alarm in his tone. "You're here to—"

"Ream him out, yes. Later."

That, she thought as things cleared, *really wasn't fair of me. But I have a little grudge to work off on the very puissant Sir César Obregón de Lafayette.*

She lifted her helm a bit to feel fresher air on her sweat-sopped hair; it helped her aching head, too, for an instant, but she put it back on. In spite of the heat, she was wearing full plate; if you didn't have your arms on it, that was about the best disguise anyone had ever invented. You couldn't even really tell someone's gender easily. She'd left off the sabatons and gauntlets, but wore dark suede gloves; and was sweating copiously into them.

"My lady, you're not well!" Armand said.

She started to laugh, and then stopped herself. That would *really* convince him that she was off her head.

I am, she thought, which threatened more laughter. *I am definitely not well.*

The will commanded the body; she'd learned *that* early, and Sandra's schools had ground it home.

The strong grow stronger. The weak die.

"I *know* I'm not well, Armand," she said, her voice lucid. "I'm going to get something done about it. This has to be confidential. Believe me, it *has* to be. Now cover for me. I'll be in contact later."

He nodded unwillingly, and stepped back. She slid the visor down and made her legs move; the bright sunlight dimmed to a slit, which helped a little, but it made the smell of sickness-sweat worse. She focused into the town past the grossly slack gate-guards, down the block, on the next street sign.

Walk a careful path.

It was a little like being drunk, but without the fun part. People tended to avoid her, perhaps because of the blank menace of the visor overlapping the bevoir. There were plenty of hostile looks, and occasionally a swaggering cowboy would spit on her shadow after she'd passed.

Present alliances or no, plenty of festering grudges remained. Raiding parties from Castle Odell had reached nearly this far, in the old wars. She'd been on a few of those herself.

I'm alone, she thought. *And it hurts too much to enjoy it.*

Pages, squires, tirewomen, men-at-arms, retainers and servants, there was no escaping them once you were a noble; doubly so as Grand Constable. Walking alone down a busy street wasn't on her agenda very often.

Armand really wanted to stop me. I wonder if he thought about knocking me over the head? In his position, I certainly would have. I didn't train him to blind obedience.

Her destination was north on Colorado Avenue, in the old industrial section. The bright summer sunlight made her squint, trying to read the street signs, lancing into her head. She'd visited the offices of the Plodding Pony Express several times before; always discreetly. She was fairly confident of finding it again. Given the burden of bad news from all fronts, she wanted to make sure that she wasn't followed or have rumors spark along her backtrail.

I'm pretty sure she's still here. And she's probably at the warehouse. I hope she manages to think fast on her feet. Though, when has BD ever been less than quick on the uptake?

Tiphaine found her steps wandering a bit along the sidewalk. A cowboy reached out to shove her away, met her eyes through the slit of the visor, clearly rethought his actions, and swerved around her.

Blowing the cover of the Meeting's spymistress would be a bad thing. A rumor that the Grand Constable has a magi-

*cal wound! God's wounds! But she got out of that infiltra-
tion mission in Pendleton back during the Great
Cluster-Fuck. That took real ability. And she's supposed to
be good at . . . the sort of thing I'm dealing with. Christ, off
to a witch doctor, literally.*

*And did I really swear God's wounds, like some kid
brought up by Society retreads who took a nosedive into their
personas at the Change and never came out again?*

That was funny too; Sandra *was* a Society retread, and
she *had* slipped into her Catherine-de-Medici-Eleanor-of-
Aquitaine persona . . . or slipped out of her twentieth-
century one, like a snake shedding its skin. Tiphaine
paused to pant and controlled the impulse to laugh at the
way her mind had used the oath. It was a warm day, but
she was shivering, again, like a winter chill that got into
your bones after riding all day through sleet and the
campfire afterwards smoking and hissing.

*I'm not going back to Montinore until I know I'm not
dragging fecal matter along behind. Delia might be able to
handle this, but I'm not risking her or the children. Whoever
or Whatever is out there, give me a hand here!*

She turned in at the gaping purple and teal sheet-metal
doors of the "Plodding Pony" headquarters into a warm
fug of smells with horse and mule the strongest. The
huge warehouse was dark and spots danced before her
eyes as they tried to adjust to a light level much less irritating than the clear high-altitude summer glare in Bend.
She made her way back through the gloom, dodging
packed cases on pallets, carts, straw bales and unidentified
miscellaneous pieces sitting ready to trip her up. At the
far back she could see some stairs, lit by a few dusty windows of ancient glass. Hopefully, the offices were up
there.

"Can I help you?"

Tiphaine jumped and looked to her right. *Someone snuck up on me without my noticing anything. I am sick. I am very sick.*

"Oh!" said BD, coming out of the gloom, wiping her hands on a filthy rag.

She was a weathered woman in her sixties, tough and thickset and moving as if she was still strong but creaked a bit. Tiphaine pushed up the visor and blinked in the non-light.

"Grand . . ."

She stopped at Tiphaine's urgent gesture and said: "Well, well, well, what can I do for the nobility today?" BD's voice was light but there was a bite in it. BD, Beatrize Dorothea, businesswoman, big wheel in the autonomous Kyklos villages, intelligence agent and enemy-become-ally of the Association. Witch.

"Little help with a problem shipping contaminated goods. Hoping you'll be able to give me good advice. Someone in a kilt said you were the best for some sorts of problems."

BD clicked her tongue and then waved Tiphaine to the side and ducked out a short door, down an alley, across a street and up some rickety stairs. The apartment was small and shabby, but comfortable, and BD quickly drew the curtains over the window. The stairs left Tiphaine panting.

"What contamination?" she asked tersely. "It's bad tradecraft for you to come and visit me like this."

"I wouldn't if it wasn't urgent and I couldn't make it seem ordinary. Because it isn't ordinary. See . . ."

Tiphaine stripped off her right glove and hissed. The pus had soaked through the gauze pad and into the soft suede and dried. It tore as she pulled off the glove.

BD pushed her into a chair and pulled back a bit of the

curtain. She took Tiphaine's elbow and maneuvered the hand into the stream of sunlight. The long, weeping, inflamed welt stood out, gaping deep into the back of her hand. There were shiny white flashes peeking through the leaking sera, the pinpricks of blood and green and yellow pus. Tiphaine felt a dry gag at the back of her throat.

"I've seen . . . most things in the world," she said. "I've had some wounds I considered extremely serious. But this makes me . . . ill. Why?"

BD looked up from the trauma at Tiphaine and frowned. She put a hand on the Grand Constable's forehead and scowled.

"How long have you been running a fever?" she asked.

Tiphaine frowned right back. "A fever?" she asked. "How would I know? Or even notice, unless it was bad?"

"You're an idiot, Lady d'Ath," said BD. "I don't know what you call bad—but it's bad. Bide a wee. I'll need some help, and you're staying right here."

"I can't! I've got to be seen . . . I have business with that fool . . ."

"Obregón? Good. He can stand to be kicked, and he can stand to wait. But you can come up with a story. I'll send for Armand; that's your squire, no? And Velin? Marks is in Campscapell, right? Is Velin here?"

"Armand is here, but not Velin. He'll be in Upper Boring right about now, tracking down a red herring, I think. This has to be *confidential*. Things are hanging by threads. I can't afford a panic. And Sandra would stick me in a hospital and I . . . suspect this involves things she wouldn't believe. I wouldn't either except I was *there*."

BD frowned at her. "I need you out of that plate and into some light clothes. I'll guess you don't have anything like a chemise in your saddlebags."

"You guess rightly, O mighty witch-woman. A pair of trews and a small shirt is my usual camp nightwear. Delia insists I wear a chemise at home, but it wouldn't do on campaign."

Gnarled old fingers pressed against her lips. "Lean back and rest, as best you can."

After a minute a glass was pressed into her left hand. "Drink, slow sips. You're dehydrated. You need to be flushed out."

BD lifted off the heavy sallet. "Unconquered Sun, how does this thing around your neck come off?"

"The bevoir?" Tiphaine mumbled. "Undo . . . the chain and hooks. Buckles underneath and open hinges. Lift it out. *Shit!*"

That as the older woman's inexpert hands jerked her head back and forth. She fiddled with the vambraces, found the trick and slid them down and off her forearms.

"Most of the rest is buckled . . . tied to the point strings on the doublet . . . the leather cords. Just cut 'em, woman!"

Tiphaine sighed as BD picked up the bits and pieces of ironmongery and walked out. She sipped at the tart, cold herbal tea and slowly felt herself relax; her heart stopped beating so fast, though she hadn't noticed it while it did. Her head throbbed and so did her arms and joints; aches she'd ignored in all the jangle of pain and strain that wearing armor every day for weeks on end caused. Even just having a helmet on every day gave you a savage headache more often than not.

It crept up on me, dammit.

A little of the office came clear. Before her was BD's altar. The figurine of the God danced oddly before her eyes, reaching his hands out to her and beckoning. The huge round carving of a woman seemed to rock back and forth, winking at her with every swaying move. She closed her eyes and sipped again.

When she opened her eyes, the sun had wandered off to another part of the sky; the quality of the light had changed.

I'm not wearing my armor? When, how long? What?

She blinked and focused on BD, standing in the door talking to a deep-voiced man. "Armand?" she asked.

BD turned and nodded. "He came to get you out of that tin can you wear. Thierry Renfrew came into camp yesterday and I've told him you're quite ill and that nobody is to know. Conrad introduced us a while back, so he's in the know. He's taking over the camp as your second for now. When you can use a pen, you can write up the necessary documents for him."

Tiphaine glared at the old woman, but it didn't seem to work. BD gave her a small sour smile.

"When you can muster a real, glacial, Lady Death glare, then I'll know you're better."

She took the aching hand in her own, a hand like a claw carved from horn, shaped by a generation of reins and tools.

"How did this happen?"

"As best I can make out, Mary Liu spit on her needle and touched me with it. And cursed me. While her eyes turned to something that looked like black tar."

She met BD's skeptical eyes defiantly.

"So, tell me the whole story," said the woman. Tiphaine did, and BD went on: "You sure Fen House was clean? It is a prison in the middle of a lake."

Tiphaine shook her aching head. "How do *you* know that?" she demanded.

"Don't be an idiot, Grand Constable. I'm the spymaster for the Mackenzies, Bearkillers and Mount Angel. Of course I know what Fen House is. And where."

"Oh, of course. No," said Tiphaine. "No, it's usually fairly clean. They scrub down every second day. Disinfectant. No lice. Even *Norman* hated lice, no matter how period they were, and he was the original Period Nazi. Rats and lice."

"Everyone did, after the epidemics," BD said grimly. "Nearly as many died of typhus as the Black Death."

"Yeah, I remember. They scared even him, he couldn't intimidate germs . . . I checked back with Stratson three times now. She's not scratched anybody else and nobody else who has gotten a scratch or burn has an infection like this."

She hesitated and then gritted her teeth. "I've been very careful to touch nobody and burn all the dressings and anything it drips onto, but a dog snatched one of my gloves yesterday. I had a lance follow it. It died within an hour, bubbling green and yellow mucus out its nose and mouth. I made them use shovels to move it and burned it completely."

"Well, you remember enough germ theory from before the Change to be useful. Sounds like you've been doing a good job keeping it from spreading. What have you been doing to your hand, itself?"

"Soaking it in hot water morning and night and then dripping pure alcohol on it. I'm afraid of what will happen if I take it home. Mary said . . . she said . . . *'Bad cess to you and yours.'*"

"Delia would probably have been able to keep it from getting this bad," BD grumbled. "People forget what it was like, before the Change. They think it was miracles, but it wasn't. Most of what we could do then was asepsis; cleanliness. A lot was supportive care. And then there were antibiotics. And when they didn't work people were betrayed and angry, because we'd beaten death, hadn't we?"

Tiphaine felt her eyes crossing. "I don't know. I don't think I'm following you . . ."

"You're running a fever of a hundred and four degrees. Of course your brain isn't following me! So, yes, I can do something and hopefully your body can do more. As for the rest . . . In all your years in the Association have you picked a special saint to protect you? The Virgin?"

"No. I'm . . . not really religious," Tiphaine said. "Haven't been since I was a kid. My mother put me off it."

"Ummm," said BD. "This is one thing Lady Sandra's teaching isn't going to help you with."

Tiphaine felt her eyes drooping. "She taught me to face things whether they were what I wanted to see or not."

"A point. First, let's change what you are doing. Hot water and pure alcohol are keeping the inflammation high. Cool water right now. Later we'll soak it in warm water with Epsom salts dissolved in it, three times a day . . . I'll get you the Epsom salts and some gentian violet. We'll continue to burn all the dressings. Don't touch people until you aren't producing scabs or pus. In fact, until you see the welt going down."

"How long?"

"If this were a normal infection, I'd say three days will do the trick. I think, however, that there is a magical component on it. So, I don't know. Will you try a spell?"

Tiphaine looked at her blankly. "Have somebody *pray* over me?" she asked, her voice rising.

"Ummm, if that's what you want to call it? I was going to ask you to dance your healing; I'm sure praying isn't your cuppa tea."

Tiphaine swallowed. "I don't believe . . . but something took over Mary Liu's body and spoke to me. And it really wasn't Mary Liu, though it was using her mind and memories and personality as some sort of . . . *pattern*. That wasn't a psychological collywobbles. There was something there and it hated me. I think it hated *everything*."

BD nodded. "So you do believe; you're just not up to admitting it yet. Back to the healing part. You are running a fever. You have a persistent infection and you have a generalized irritation of the skin because of the very harsh methods you've been using to fight the infection. There's going to be scarring."

This time Tiphaine let the half-hysterical laughter out. "I've been getting cut and bashed and abraded for twenty-three years. Parts of me look like a mad seamstress used me for practice!"

"Internal scarring could weaken your sword-hand."

That brought her up, though the buzzing was loud.

"We need you to do things that will enhance your immune system. Good food, good rest, freedom from worry. So I'm thinking that you should dance. I wish you did have a saint or patron or Goddess, I'd feel better if you petitioned for healing. When you get home, maybe Delia can help with that."

"They all work?" Tiphaine said.

"Oh, yes. But They play favorites. So, you need to petition to an aspect you can believe in. Which I suppose is why you didn't go to Doctor Robsvert, who's assigned to your camp. He's seventy, the most pre-Change man I've ever met, and if a stick turned into a snake in his hands, he'd claim it was paralyzed and he just didn't notice the scales while he was whittling on it. Then there's Doctor Methlin, who fights with Doctor Robsvert at the drop of a pin. He's a faith healer; Church of God, Scientist, who thinks walking on water isn't just possible but *easy* with a little positive thinking . . ."

Tiphaine tried to shake her head, but it was aching too much. "Neither sounds like a winner."

"I'd send you into Portland, or Mount Angel, or down to the Mackenzies if I thought we had time, but I don't think we do have time. When the infection's brought down, go to Bethany Refuge outside Portland; by then things will be un-alarming enough for you to pass it off as an ordinary battlefield injury that needs treatment . . . like football players in the old days. The Sisters of Compassion will get you started on physiotherapy for the hand, get it back to strength. We're going to need that strong right hand, Grand Constable. So now, *rest*."

COUNTY OF THE EASTERMARK
CHARTERED CITY OF WALLA WALLA
CITY PALACE OF THE COUNTS PALANTINE
PORTLAND PROTECTIVE ASSOCIATION
(FORMERLY SOUTHEASTERN WASHINGTON STATE)
HIGH KINGDOM OF MONTIVAL
(FORMERLY WESTERN NORTH AMERICA)
AUGUST 24, CHANGE YEAR 25/2023 AD

Tiphaine moved her hand again, looking at the white scar. The Countess cleared her throat. Felipe was looking at *his* hand. He spoke first. "The dog *died*? With green and yellow foam coming out of its nostrils? From swallowing the *bandage*?"

"Yes, my lord, it did. You can imagine how *I* felt about it. You're getting help earlier; on the other hand, it's an actual bite. Be cautious."

Ermentrude said thoughtfully, "You went to a pious

wisewoman, and she sent you to Bethany to the Sisters . . . and then you sought a spiritual patron to protect you against the evils of the CUT?"

Tiphaine smiled slightly. *Evidently I'm keeping things general efficiently while also getting across the essentials they do need to know.*

"Yes. As I said, I've never been particularly pious. But I found a real expert to . . . guide my meditations. One I trusted implicitly. And I had quite a, ummm, change of heart."

MONTINORE MANOR, BARONY ATH
TUALATIN COUNTY, PORTLAND PROTECTIVE
ASSOCIATION
WILLAMETTE VALLEY
(FORMERLY WESTERN OREGON)
HIGH KINGDOM OF MONTIVAL
(FORMERLY WESTERN NORTH AMERICA)
AUGUST 15, CHANGE YEAR 24/2022 AD

It was late by the time Tiphaine d'Ath and Delia de Stafford waved good-bye to their guests from the verandah of the manor house, a warm summer's night with bright stars and a great near-full moon rising over the forested Coast Range a little to the west, full of the scents of cut grass and roses and honeysuckle and a faint tinge of woodsmoke and fir sap. The steel wheels of the black carriage crunched on the crushed rock of the driveway, and then the lanterns at its rear faded down the long road that glittered white beneath the moon, flickering as they passed behind the wayside oaks. The lance heads of the escort swayed after them, until it all faded into the night. Moths battered against the big silver-framed lights above, and the wind moved quietly in the trees.

"My lady?" the house steward asked.

"Leave us," Tiphaine said.

"That will be all, Terrin, for the night," Lady Delia de Stafford added gently, with a smile. "And tell Goodwife Catrain that the Lord Chancellor Conrad said he'd weigh twice what he does if she ran the kitchens at Castle Odell, and the Lady Regent added that she had never eaten better slow-cooked spring lamb, even in Todenangst or Portland."

Tiphaine added a slight sideways jerk of the head. Young Terrin—his uncle-predecessor had retired last year—bowed and motioned the other servants away with his white wand and followed them.

And Delia managed to get all the ladies-in-waiting and pages and assorted highborn suchlike out of the house for the night, one way or another, without even offending them. A seldom-repeated miracle. Here I am, overlord of Ath in my own right, land and woods and water and villages and manors and a thousand families over whom I have the Low, Middle and High Justice, and I actually had more privacy when I was living in a two-bedroom apartment with my single-parent mom. Mind you, the wealth and power and land and so forth go a long way to compensate. Still.

Montinore had been a mansion before the Change, built long ago on mining profits as a country retreat and then the headquarters of a vineyard in the days of the Pinot Noir boom, a neoclassical house with white walls and tall pillars in front. Not many modifications had been necessary to make it the manor of the home estate at the core of the barony; adding a Great Hall at the rear, and outbuildings. The village a little to the east on the flats adjacent to the Five Great Fields was nearly all new, though. You could see the bell tower of the church, and a little of its red-tile roof, which was near enough for the outdoor servants to live there. The house faced southeast, but if she had walked out onto the lawn she could have seen the watch lights on the grim square towers of Castle Ath, on its hill half a mile west.

"Glad I finally talked you into moving down from the castle?" Delia said. "And it took a *year*."

"You're always right, sweetie. Though I have fond memories of the place; we met there, after all. And it was wartime."

The gardens and rolling lawns were still here around the mansion; better, if anything, under Delia's supervision. And the vineyards to the north that were the most valuable part of the manor's demesne farm. Delia had always been good at keeping the reeves and bailiffs and castellans and stewards honest and up to the mark.

"Always nice to see Conrad and Sandra in a setting that isn't *entirely* business," Tiphaine said, looking after the coach.

Though they'd come out here with her partly to occupy the traveling time with consultations.

Strictly speaking I should be going back with them. Damned if I'll cut the flying visit that short, though. I'm going to spend at least forty-eight hours with my sweetie, after all this time in the field!

"I wish they could have stayed longer," Delia said. "And that Conrad could have brought Valentinne and the children."

"We're all a little busy right now," Tiphaine said as they turned to go back in; she offered her arm, and Delia slid hers through it.

I'd have made the same call. The situation is just too volatile right now. I'll be leaving soon and leaving Delia alone again. Rehab in Bethany took a lot longer than I thought it would. And it's going to cost something fierce, the

Sisters put the screws to the nobility so they can heal the poor for free. Delia will have a cow if I don't warn her before the bill gets here. She manages the place well and that means she cares about the details.

The ceremonial keys tinkled gently at Delia's silver chain belt, the mark of her status as Châtelaine across from the equally ceremonial dagger that marked her as an Associate. She was in noblewoman's *at home* dress, what could be worn when dining *en famille*, a short over-tunic of cream silk, elaborately tucked and embroidered with a royal blue ankle-length under-tunic. It suited her, which it should, since she'd invented and spread the fashion.

Most things did suit her; she had a curling mane of night-black hair that torrented down from her light wimple, huge eyes of a blue like the sky on a spring morning, and a tip-tilted nose, and a scent that was like flowers. Just now her figure was a little riper from the birth of her daughter.

And I still haven't talked to Delia about Bend and BD. It's time and past time, even if I'd rather pull out my toenails with my teeth. What a tangled web I've found; tangling up my life.

"Odd thing, that," she said to Delia as they came into their sitting room.

"What?" asked Delia, turning away from Heuradys' crib and putting a finger to her lips.

Tiphaine grinned. "It'd take a bell ringing over her head to wake her up. You know that. This love seat is big enough for two, if they're friendly."

Musing, she went on: "The odd thing was learning that Jason Mortimer was betrothed to the older Reddings girl. Things got very rough for her, being pregnant and her prospective groom subtracted."

"Oh, yes. What brought that to your mind?"

"I've been thinking about the ramifications of things. I killed Jason, on orders from Sandra; that's why the Reddings chit ended up in the family way with no family."

"Why should that eat at you? You've killed enough men and even a few women. Every one of them probably had relatives and obligations. What's special about Jason?"

Tiphaine winced slightly; Delia had come to terms with her profession, but never really *liked* it. Though to be fair she didn't make any distinction between her black-ops beginnings and her current status. As she said, dead was dead.

"It's mostly just how miserable the entire Mortimer family seems to have been. And then I learn something good about them . . . *and* something bad. Did you know Jason offered to marry *me*? If I got him out of that place in Corvallis the Dúnedain had him stashed. Practically begged."

Delia turned in her arms and looked up at her from her shoulder. "Were you tempted?" she said, with a wicked grin. "You were a landless minor Associate then, after all, and he was a knight."

"Hardly. He didn't realize I'd been sent to kill him, but I'd have been tempted to off him anyway after that; he thought he was offering to do me a *favor*. But the odd thing is that Guelf and Mary Liu blamed me *anyway*, even though they think the Dúnedain did it . . . which they were intended to do, of course. Idiots. They screwed the entire timing of the Protector's War with their little scheme for vengeance and then their not-even-idiotic brother got *caught*. I increased the average intelligence of the human race by getting him before he could successfully breed. Still, it's a pity about the girl."

She sighed and took a deep breath. Before she could

speak, Delia murmured: "You know, darling, that's a familiar look. It sort of reminds me of the time we were at Forest Grove and Diomede and Lioncel walked in on us and their eyes bugged out and you had to tell them about the birds and the bees . . . and the birds and the birds and the bees and the bees, and then Rigobert came in looking for *them* and he heard and he started laughing and I thought you were going to strangle him, standing there in your bathrobe. Or the time Lioncel was all indignant about the song accusing me of being a witch and we had to tell him I *am* a witch and explain about *real* witches."

"Speaking of which, witch . . . it's time for a talk about religion."

"And you'd rather pull your toenails out with your teeth," Delia observed, and then gurgled laughter at her start. "I'd be a very unobservant witch if I didn't know you well after fifteen years, love. You don't just let sleeping dogs lie, you prefer to bury them and plant a tree on the grave. For someone so brave you can be so *chicken* sometimes."

Tiphaine knelt on the rug and extended her right hand, twitching back the fall of the houppelande. The overlong cuff on her shirt slid up, exposing the seamed pucker of white on the back of her right hand. Delia's face went pale, throwing the spray of freckles across her cheeks into high relief. She gasped as she pulled it across her lap for a better look.

"Why haven't you shown it to me?" demanded Delia, bending the hand and carefully tracing the length of the scar. "What happened! You were talking about *idiots* and then keeping this secret?"

"I was afraid it was a danger to you . . . and Heuradys," Tiphaine said, which halted Delia's tirade in midword. "And it *was*. Dangerous to you and her; which means I was entirely justified; plus reasons of state. Mary Liu did this."

"*What?* In person?"

"With her embroidery needle."

Tiphaine winced again at her look; this time it was her professional vanity that twinged. It was rather like a wolf confessing to a rabbit bite on the buttocks.

"With a *sewing needle?*"

Delia's callused fingertips stroked the length of the scar. Her strong fingers turned the sword-hand towards the light. Tiphaine nodded grimly.

Great. We could be running around the bed playing The Lustful Knight and the Innocent Country Maid *and what are we doing? Discussing wounds and prisoners in Fen House.*

"I don't think it actually *scratched* the skin, just ran down it . . . but by the time I walked back down the stairs it was a welt and it was hurting. It got badly infected and I wouldn't let anybody touch it. Mary said, *Bad cess to you and yours*, and I believe that she meant what she said and knew what would happen. That's magic, Delia. Real magic!"

Delia didn't look any calmer, and her grip on Tiphaine's hand was hurting. "Damned right, that's *magic!* Why didn't you get help! What did you do! Why haven't you . . ."

"I went to BD. You know, of the Kyklos."

"Oh." A hesitation. "I'm . . . well, she is a witch, I know that. I've met her, of course. And a good field-competent healer. I just wish . . ."

"I know. If it had been an ordinary wound, I would have come to you."

Tiphaine gently put a forefinger over Delia's parted lips. "Sweetheart, listen. This is very hard for me to talk about."

Delia closed her mouth, let go of her hand and walked

over to the crib in the corner. She picked up the sleeping Heuradys and held her close. "I'll be quiet, but you'd better tell me everything!"

Tiphaine nodded. "Gods do live and walk among us and . . . I don't believe in the Christian god, His son or His mother."

"They're real enough," Delia observed—not enthusiastically, but readily; her arms cradled the infant and she stroked a cheek.

"Yes, they're *real*. Oh, what my mother would have given to hear me say it! But I don't . . ."

"I understand. Actually it's probably your mother's fault you don't *like* them, after she tried to force-feed you. That's just not how your heart inclines. But now you want someone you *can* believe in, a guardian and pillar. Of course that means They must want *you*."

Delia kissed Heuradys and the baby stirred. She frowned as she put her back in the crib and turned to Tiphaine.

"I'm not going to yell . . . but there's a very big yell in me. Why didn't you go to Mount Angel or the main hospital in Portland, or Bethany? BD may be a witch, but she's not a doctor. Good field-grade healer, but not a professional, at that."

She went over to the sideboard and pulled out the stopper of the brandy, reaching for a glass.

Tiphaine sighed.

"Mostly because I just let the infection get worse and worse. I was doing stupid things to it, too. At Bethany they told me I nearly lost the hand. I think . . . what Mary Liu did to me may have made me act that way; pushed me to be . . . even more stubborn than I am naturally. Like a budo move, a come-with, using your opponent's strength against them."

"Lost the *hand*?"

Delia handed a brandy and soda to her and took a long pull on her own drink. Then she coughed and choked and coughed again.

"It looks a lot easier when you or Rigobert do it!"

Tiphaine had to laugh at Delia's disgusted expression.

"We get hardened to it. You've never drunk much and that must have gone straight to your head."

Delia peered at her glass and then set it carefully on the sideboard.

"It did," she observed. "I don't think I need any more, or I won't be able to have this conversation with you . . . BD is Apollo's priestess. But I think you'd be better with a Goddess. There are many different pantheons—"

"Greek," said Tiphaine. "I don't know too much about them, but I think they're the ones I could put up with. And vice versa!"

"Why?" Delia asked.

"Because of the Olympics. I dreamed about it so long . . . used to have actual dreams about Olympia."

"There's Artemis the Virgin Huntress."

"No," Tiphaine said thoughtfully.

I'm actually feeling better about this. If it has to be done, do it right. And remember those eyes looking at you at Fen House. I know when I need a friend who can operate in the same league! Poor Sandra again; she just couldn't do this. Well, she's got me.

Aloud, she went on: "No, I like hunting, but it's not what I am and I'm *definitely* not a virgin. I'm . . . I'm a warrior. I'm fighting for my home, the people who depend on me. For you and the kids."

"Athena," Delia said firmly. "Though she is a virgin too, I'm afraid. But she's a war Goddess."

636 S. M. STIRLING

"I thought Ares was the Greek God of war?"

"Ares is a God of frenzy; he drives men to battle and reaps them like grain on a bloody field. Achilles was His, and died young and childless and alone, trading length of days for everlasting fame. Athena is the defender of the polis, of art and skill, including the *art* of war. Odysseus had Her for a patron; the man of cunning mind who wanted nothing to do with Troy, but who *ended* the Trojan war and spent ten years scheming and fighting to get home to his wife and son so that he could end his days among his own people, by Penelope's side."

"That sounds a lot better than Mr. Frenzy."

Delia nodded soberly: "Athena gave Her people the olive and the high fortress that was their strength; she carries a spear and a shield and a tall crested helm. Her symbol is the owl, for wisdom and clever plans. And . . ."

Delia looked at her, blue eyes suddenly a little laughing as they met her glacier-colored ones.

"And?"

"And she was the Gray-Eyed One."

Tiphaine found herself laughing. There weren't many people she did that easily with, and only one when anything serious was happening.

"It's a natural."

"Then let us go on a journey . . ."

Somehow they had reversed positions and Tiphaine was lying in Delia's arms, not vice versa, and she was feeling lazy and floaty; much more pleasantly than when it had been fever induced.

Delia's voice ran on, like a spring wind through the treetops, while you lay and looked up and made stories in the clouds.

"And Ouranos wed Gaia . . . Metis was swallowed by

fearful Zeus and their daughter Athena who was born from the bloody head . . ."

Umbrella pines growing twisted on a rocky headland with asphodel blooming beneath them, a sea dark purple stretching to a horizon of islands. Sails, and a white froth where the oars stroked and the water curled back from a bronze ram. The smell of dry spicy dust and the taste of wine; a tower of rock and the gleam of marble atop it and the scent of incense. Water-broken light glittering on a great helmed form, ivory and gold, the shield leaned against her knee with the contorted Gorgon face and Victory poised in Her palm, up and up to the calmness like stars in her eyes. Chanted prayer and the music of the aulos. *A bull with golden horns pacing to the altar before robed and flower-garlanded maidens who lifted a great embroidered cloth in their hands and sang . . .*

Tiphaine came to herself with a start and looked up at Delia's face hanging over her and blinked.

"You witched me!" she said.

"Not so much," said Delia with a smile, and kissed her. "I relaxed you with the brandy. And then I put you in a hypnotic state; so you could hear and see the Gods as I spoke to you of them. And then She spoke."

"I think you're right."

Delia wiggled away, checked the cradle, and then propped the door to the bedchamber open so that a baby's cry would carry through.

"Ah, I wouldn't know," she said from the doorway and put the back of her hand theatrically to her forehead. "I am but an innocent country maid . . ."

Then she turned and darted inside.

COUNTY OF THE EASTERMARK
CHARTERED CITY OF WALLA WALLA
CITY PALACE OF THE COUNTS PALATINE
PORTLAND PROTECTIVE ASSOCIATION
(FORMERLY SOUTHEASTERN WASHINGTON STATE)
HIGH KINGDOM OF MONTIVAL
(FORMERLY WESTERN NORTH AMERICA)
AUGUST 24, CHANGE YEAR 25/2023 AD

Rigobert gave her a slight ironic look and tilt of brow. She didn't think Count Felipe caught it, but Ermentrude did; though she wouldn't know exactly what to make of it.

Right, Rigobert, so I gave them a heavily edited version. They're both good Christians; no need to shock them.

Felipe was frowning and looking at his bandaged hand. "Did finding a spiritual patron help you with . . . with this sort of thing?" Then he snorted and laughed. "It's really like something in a romaunt. Except that I just saw a dead man get up and fight."

"One of the nastier romaunts," the Countess agreed. "And did it, my lady d'Ath? Help, that is?"

She was afraid, but completely in control of it. Tiphaine inclined her head in respect; she knew from Delia's pregnancies that they made emotional control more difficult.

"Oh, yes, my lady Countess. Shortly thereafter, I was back at Fen House, on the Lady Regent's orders, just at the end of Winter Court this year. Then—"

INTERLACHEN PRISON
THE NEW FOREST, CROWN DEMESNE
(FORMERLY NORTHERN OREGON)
PORTLAND PROTECTIVE ASSOCIATION
HIGH KINGDOM OF MONTIVAL
(FORMERLY WESTERN NORTH AMERICA)
JANUARY 8, CHANGE YEAR 25/2023 AD

Tiphaine shook herself violently, water splattering all over the plain concrete floor from her hooded cloak of greased wool. It stank of wet lanolin, and the peculiar smell of chilly mud. There was mud spattered up her legs as well, cold and gelid, and her suit of plate armor was performing its usual miracle of being as shivering-miserable in cold weather as it was sweating-miserable in hot. At least she could afford stainless steel, not as likely to rust. All that was familiar enough; the Black Months were like this, except when they were honestly frigid and you got snow.

"Close behind me," she said to her page.

It was as close to midnight as made no matter, but the prison was awake and humming. The guards milled around in the common areas and the prisoners called to one another from their cells overlooking the panopticon. The smells were fairly rank, much worse than the last time she'd been here, and the ordinary damp winter chill was even worse than in most places. Chill moisture seemed to be flowing up from the floor into her legs, as well as leaking down her collar.

The lamplight flickered, and somewhere a man was beating something metallic on the bars of his cell and shrieking, "It was Tom, not me! Tom! Tom did it! You've got to believe me! Why won't you believe me!"

"Oh, shut up, you silly bastard, nobody gives a damn!" a guard shouted back.

I wish I'd had time to bring Armand or Rodard with me. Velin would have been even better! It's not like Sandra to be hasty like this; she's tight-stretched.

A few of the guards were finally noticing that a high-ranking agent of the Crown was there, which was fortunate.

For them, she thought.

None of them seemed to know what to do about it.

I am not a happy camper. I could be on my way back home with Delia, sitting with my feet by the fire watching Rigobert do that stupid macho trick he learned from Conrad where he cracks walnuts in his hand and then tapping one open with my dagger hilt. Instead I'm wading through a lunatic asylum in a swamp.

Then she drew a deep breath. *Gray-Eyed One, give me patience and wit.*

"Where's Sir Stratson?" she demanded, grabbing a man by the collar.

"He's over there in the other block."

"That's, *The noble knight is over there in front of the other block, my lady Grand Constable.*"

He repeated it as she twisted the collar, raising him on his toes. From the chevrons on his sleeve, he was supposed to be a sergeant.

"Get this place quieted down. *Now.*"

She released the man and turned to the page with her; he was thirteen, and looking cold and miserable but alert, his tow hair darkened with the half sleet, half rain and sticking to his face under the steel cap.

"Henriot, you stay here. I may send messages back to you, or you may see things . . . go very wrong. If they do, your mission is to get back to Portland. This is the code word you'd use."

She leaned close and made him repeat it.

"Good. You'll be taken immediately to the Lady Regent with that. Tell her: *Nuclear meltdown. Interdict and burn.* Answer any other questions she has, but that first."

The youngster hesitated, took a deep breath and said, "Code, then *nuclear meltdown. Interdict and burn.*" He walked over to a barred window and nodded. "I can see the courtyard, Grand Constable. They've got a lot of torches out there. I'll wait."

Old for a page, but a much better choice for this mission than Mollala's cousin.

She'd left young Brendan Carey with the horses. Because he was very good with horses, but inclined to be reckless. A natural impulse to run towards trouble rather than away from it was good in itself, but learning to control it was hard for a pubescent boy. Henriot was serious and more naturally disciplined.

This page-squire system has its good points and its bad. The good one is it starts them young. The bad one is that you're pretty well stuck with them once you've taken them on unless you want to expend political capital offending the little rat's kinfolk.

The courtyard was worse than the main block. Guards jostled each other, and torches flared: pine knot torches, gas torches, lanthorns swung and the wind blew and the rain gusted past, and shadows passed gigantic and distorted on the dim rain-wet walls. Crossbowmen stood, sheltered by minimum-security prisoners holding tarps and umbrellas. Stratson was striding back and forth, issuing orders.

Those she could catch mostly seemed to contradict each other. The rest would cause a good many deaths if anything set a light to this soggy tinder; the crossbowmen were all in each other's fields of fire, for example, and by their uneasy glances some of them had realized it, despite the darkness and chaos and rain.

He caught sight of Tiphaine and strode over. "My lady Grand Constable. Glad to see you. What should we do? I'm ready to fire the building."

Tiphaine took a deep breath. "*What* exactly has happened since your last dispatch, Sir Stratson?"

He drew back and hesitated. Tiphaine looked closely at the face lit by the flickering gaslight. He was more than ever like a spooked horse as the whites of his eyes showed, rising and sinking on the balls of his feet. His head was jerking up and down slightly, too. She didn't remember that.

Mary Liu, she knew. *This is worse than I thought. What did Delia tell me? "You have to make them do something nice, or at least dutiful. It breaks the hold on their minds."*

Tiphaine nodded to herself.

"Wonderful job, Stratson, wonderful!" she said.

She turned to the men, pitching her voice to cut through the burr of noise and the hiss of the rain.

"Men of the guard detail! I am impressed by how well Sir Stratson has coped, and all of you. Thank you. I'm sure Sir Stratson will express his gratitude in ways that you will very much appreciate. Stay alert and maintain your present positions. Help each other stay awake. Buddy up, partner up and stay alert."

To Sir Stratson: "Good man!"

She smacked him on the shoulder, gauntlet to the overlapping lames of a backplate, a genial gesture . . . and much more tactful than a slap on the face but just as likely to jar a mind out of a rut.

"The Lady Regent and old Norman certainly knew how to pick the right man for a job that might turn deadly. Let's go to the maximum-security wing and assess the situation."

The horse-faced man hesitated, his shoulders slowly

straightening up. He closed his toothy grimace and blinked. Tiphaine relaxed the least little bit, and Sir Stratson never knew how her hand had ghosted towards the hilt of her long sword.

I'm no witch, but I can see this man's come back from whatever corner of the void he was sitting in.

The guards were quieting down too, watching their commander and the Grand Constable approach Fen House. A few of them looked around, and began shouting or pushing the others into ranks.

Tiphaine spoke in a quiet voice, easily drowned by the hiss of the rain at a few paces: "Something happened to you, Stratson. You had your men set up in positions that were an invitation to friendly fire, and I saw some of the guard talking with your more dangerous prisoners. Do you remember anything?"

He shook his head dolefully. "Not a thing, Grand Constable. I was talking with Mary Liu, and then suddenly I was outside trying to make sure that the men were . . . it sounds bad, doesn't it? And then you."

"Talking?" asked Tiphaine. "You wrote me you drugged her with laudanum. Did she wake up?" She shook the arm a little. "Focus, focus . . . I need you all here. We're going to be in trouble pretty soon."

Stratson turned his face from the door and said, "Scared; I'm right scared of that place. Never liked it. Now it scares me."

Tiphaine thought hard for a moment. *You can't muscle this, you have to finesse it.*

"Stratson, listen, what did your mother call you?"

The wandering, watery brown eyes suddenly stilled. He looked at her intently. "Stanley. It's been a long time since somebody called me Stanley."

Tiphaine frowned. "No wife? No kids? No friends?"

"I'm the warden. Just never seemed right for me." He shook his head for a few minutes. "Was going to marry. Nice girl. Had the date all set, planned everything, hotel, judge, invitations . . . all set up for May 10th, 1998. And then the Change happened. I never did find my Mary. And I figured I'd never get that kind of a chance again."

He did go crazy after the Change, just in an inconspicuous, relatively functional way like a lot of other people. But it left him vulnerable.

"Once we've got this situation under control, you're going to take a long vacation and come east with us. POW guard duty is one of the hardest to do well. See some new landscapes. And then I think the Lady Regent might have something long-term for you, a nice little manor not too far from town. You've served long and faithfully and it won't be forgotten."

She looked at the man, his jaw hanging slightly. "We on?" she asked, in the vernacular of her childhood.

He closed his mouth firmly and his eyes gleamed and he nodded. "We're on, Grand Constable. Let's take care of this situation."

Tiphaine was cat-quiet as they entered, but everything seemed ordinary enough. The tall windows were dark holes, reflections bouncing off them as the rain streaked across them. The wind made the glass bulge and flex unpredictably. Gaslights hissed all around the lower level, their flames more or less steady. Tiphaine grimaced at the smell. Human and cattle feces produced the biogas. Most of the odor burned away, but unless the gas was expensively scrubbed before use enough escaped to make the building unpleasantly smelly. Fen House didn't rate scrubbers.

"She didn't stay drugged, my lady. She came out of the drug trance twice and I forbore to give her more.

Medic told me it would kill her. So I strapped her to the bed."

Stratson hesitated. "Then she started to talk. Her eyes turned black again. That's when I . . ." The man turned to her, confusion spreading over his face.

"Stanley," she said softly. He blinked and nodded.

"Dangerous woman. Well, not a woman, I don't think. But she didn't stay drugged; and she's got those black eyes again. I evacuated most of the men. Who could I trust?"

Tiphaine looked up at the prison tier. "Good question, Stanley."

She remembered a long dispatch from Princess Mathilda, detailing a night of chaos in Des Moines, and the Bossman's most trusted guards turning on him. Of a man ramming his head through a door, and grinning through mutilated ruin. Of another dying when a High Seeker of the CUT told him his belt was a rattlesnake.

"We'll just have to trust each other to get through this together," she said.

She reached down to tug off her right gauntlet and stopped. The owl talisman . . .

Am I imagining that? No. No, I'm not.

She pulled the gauntlet back on.

Stay armed and armored, then, girl. You Know Who says so. Yes, my lady!

"Right. Stanley, you're my backup. I'm going in there and dealing with this. If my eyes turn black, you fill me with arrows and burn the body until there isn't even ash . . . and do the same to that creature of the Ascended Masters, too. Got it?"

The man gave her the kind of look sergeants reserved for recruits and Tiphaine grinned in a way that showed fangs.

"Let's get this over with!"

She snatched the key ring from Stratson and ran lightly up the narrow stairs. The middle cell felt like a looming cave, with two gas flambeaux waving wildly.

Where's the draft coming from? she wondered.

She stuck the key in the lock and turned. The gate opened with a grating shriek.

Tiphaine laid a bet with herself. "Lady Mary," she said, striding over to the cot, shoving the barred door shut. The eyes opened—blue, and filled with anger.

"Slut! Dyke! He's dead! You killed him!"

"How would I have done that?" asked Tiphaine, testing the straps that bound the slight figure to the bed. Thick double-ply cowhide. John Hordle would have trouble breaking them, with no more leverage than that; Tiphaine herself would have been completely helpless.

"You taught that Princess to hate him!"

"Nobody ever taught Mathilda good judgment, she was born with it. I always thought her friendship with Odard was stupid, but I certainly never talked with her about it. Who actually killed Odard? Or didn't you see?"

"A man. A Saracen." Mary turned her face away. "He had a club and . . . he was so big and . . . my son killed him but he hit him going down . . . Odard never had a chance."

Tears fell out of the blue eyes and ran down the faded cheeks and ran into her ears. She shook her head, trying to dislodge them. Tiphaine didn't step closer.

"A club! Not even a duel with a sword! Or a joust! Just a stupid street melee with *pirates* in Kalksthorpe. The ravens, the ravens are laughing on the back of the chair! The old man is laughing!"

Tiphaine tensed. The light wasn't all that good, but she was pretty sure the eyes were getting darker. As if something bubbled up from within. *Like road tar*, BD had said. *And it stinks even worse, if you know how to smell it.*

"Mathilda kissed him good-bye and said she loved him like a brother. Odard *smiled* at her and said he was content."

Mary's voice was rising. "Content!" she shrieked. "She was supposed to marry him! And that awful priest from Mount Angel gave him last confession and absolution! He was sealed to the Ascended Masters! *I* promised them he would be theirs if he wed Mathilda! He did not belong to the Sacrificed God!"

The eyes . . .

Tiphaine backed away from the bed, and heard the thick doubled-ply leather straps creaking. *She* couldn't have broken those, not from that position. Mary Liu hadn't lifted anything heavier than a needle or a wineglass for most of her life, but they were creaking, standing harder than iron against the steel buckles.

Mathilda's alive, then, and the fellowship intact enough. They must have won that fight, wherever the hell Kalksthorpe is . . . never heard of it . . . Sandra would know. She'll be so relieved. They could tend to Odard rather than leave him fallen on the field. And it sounds like the little bastard died well. I never trusted him . . .

"Do you know where this happened?" she asked; the Lady Regent would want to know.

"Kalksthorpe, if that means anything to you!" The voice coming out of Lady Mary's throat was thicker and darker, deeper. "On the ocean, the ocean, so cold and gray . . . ships with the heads of dragons . . ."

The Atlantic. They got that far! Ships with the heads of dragons? What the fuck?

Then the words turned into a howl. The sound was pain rammed into her ears; it was like barbed hooks thrust through and turning in her head, tearing at her brain. She stumbled back and jammed her hands up under the flare of her sallet to cover her ears. The visor fell down, and her vision suddenly became a narrow slit, like a glowing window on a dark night.

She wasn't prepared for the sudden heave and snap as *something* within forced the small body past its limits. It came up and off the cot, directly at her like a cast-iron round shot from a catapult. The impact staggered her, even a small person was still a hundred-pound weight and Mary Liu or the thing that wore her was moving *fast*.

The lames of the breastplate spread the impact, and she went back into a crouch, grunting as if she'd been hit with a war hammer. Black beat at her vision, a black place where cindered suns collapsed inward upon themselves.

"Don't come in!" she shouted, and the sound echoed through the cavern that was Fen House. "Don't come in! If she wins, shoot her dead and fire the prison!"

She fought for breath. The chill was gone; hot, heavy darkness crested over her. Then a flash of light, a spear of light, and she was back in the cell. Teeth were reaching for her eyes, wet and yellow. Tiphaine ducked her head and reared back, then butted the brow of her sallet into them. Something cracked, something howled. Arms gripped her with astonishing strength and broken teeth grated on the steel of the bevoir over the throat, squealing and catching on the metal as they *chewed* at the steel.

Don't try to respond conventionally, something within prompted her. *You're not fighting little Mary Liu. Use your head, and not just as a battering ram.*

She didn't try to break the hold; instead she turned and rammed herself three steps into the iron bars. Tiphaine weighed a hundred and fifty pounds. Her armor was a third again more; and she could throw that weight into the saddle with a flex of her legs. The impact rattled her head but the arms dropped away. Mary leapt across the cell and grabbed at the mesh of welded rebar across the outer window, legs braced with monkey agility. Tendons stood out in her pale soft forearms, and one ripped loose. The steel did too, and she turned and *hit* the Grand Constable with it.

Tiphaine could feel the alloy steel of her armor flex under the blow and tasted her own blood. She stepped into the next strike, grabbed the bar on the downswing. The grinning meat-puppet gripped it in both hands and twisted. Tiphaine held on grimly, counter-twisting, pain shooting through her right hand.

This thing is stronger than a human being has any right to be. But it still only weighs *as much as Mary Liu.*

And suddenly the *thing* was aloft, hoisted by its own grip on the thick iron, over and about . . . and the warrior moved, putting her back, shoulder and arms into the swing. Tiphaine could hear a molten voice roar. Each time it did the world shook and blackness came over her sight. And then a cool soprano would sing out a great bell-like note and she could see again.

"Glaukopis! Nikephore!" she heard herself shout, and she knew no Greek, and yet knew the meaning of the words: *"Gray-Eyed! Victory-Bearer!"*

Swing and momentum and precision. The creature struck dead center in the glass and it shattered behind her, hands still reaching for Tiphaine's throat. The slender body folded and flew back, into the lintel, and over and out through the shattered window, receding as if she were watching it through the wrong end of a telescope, vanishing down a spiral into infinity.

Tiphaine turned frantically to the cell's gate. "Don't go out, don't go out, nobody go out or come in here. Let me handle it!"

She raced down the stairs, jumping sideways off that last ten steps, landing bent-kneed and rolling in a clash of plates and using her moving weight to push herself back onto her feet. Stratson opened the rear door by the kitchen and she raced out into the dark waste yard behind Fen House, splashing through puddles ankle deep, fighting for her balance on the soaking sagging marshy growths. Light came from some of the windows.

Before she could call, more lights came on; Stratson doing just the right thing. She could see a little figure covered in soaking white rags trying to heave itself up on its arms through the downpour. The legs didn't seem to be moving.

All right, Rudi, you sent us the story on how to deal with this . . .

The warden staggered out. She turned to him: "There's a wall around this piece of bog, right?"

"Yes." Stratson craned to look at the struggling figure. "What next?"

She swallowed and answered, her voice as hard as diamonds, the bell chiming in her head and the black held at bay, but heaving and twisting with dreadful strength. Her long sword came out, a fugitive gleam in the rain and darkness.

"I'm going to dismember the thing. Then we're going to clean everything. With fire."

"Aye, Lady. Whatever the Crown gives you, it isn't enough and I don't envy you."

Tiphaine could see the figure's legs begin to move.

Odd, almost like each is under the control of a different nervous system. Like she's being puppeted by a swarm of . . . things . . . crawling around inside her.

She let the thought go and filled her mind with a simple mantra she'd composed over the past few months with Delia's help.

Her sword went up. "Io, Io, *paean!*"

The creature moved, rolling in the mud. *Cut. You know how. Two-handed grip, turn, pivot, loose grip and then hard when it hits!*

Striking at shoulders, elbows, wrists, like butchery in a nightmare abattoir where the flesh under the steel wouldn't *die*.

Then the head lay looking up, dangling from a flap of muscle and skin. The eyes were open and looking at her; Mary's spiteful, angry, blue eyes.

Cut.

The head rolled free. Tiphaine knocked up her visor, went to one knee and set the sword point down, bracing herself on the hilt and dragging in one raw cold breath after another. It was a bad thing to do to a good sword, but it would have to go too. Her body was streaming sweat under the armor, but shivering with chill at the same time. Bits of hair and matter and skin spattered her armor and gauntlets, but the rain was still coming down. She turned her face up to its cleanness, let the water flow into her mouth, spat, did it again.

Stratson came to her. "My lady?" he asked.

He looked more like a horse than ever, his long yellow teeth bared by a grimace that pulled back his lips, his eyes wide open and staring.

He looks like he expects the pieces of her to come back together. I'm not surprised.

"Listen, she gets cremated tonight and everything with her."

He nodded, the whites of his eyes showing. "I thought you might, m'lady. Got things going while you were busy."

He signaled, and men came forward with barrels of the wood-alcohol mix used for lanterns; others dragged out a hose connected to the biogas plant, and still others made a chain to bring wood from the sheds that kept it more-or-less dry.

"Should I also . . . burn the room?"

"Probably. Spit, blood, hair, anything. Don't touch *anything* with your bare hands. I'm going to strip when I'm done and we'll burn even my armor and sword. It's a good thing my Associate's dagger is in my saddlebags. I'd burn that too if I'd been wearing it, and it's a gift from the Lady Regent."

The rain came down, but the wind was easing off. The prison guards rigged tarps to cover the soggy yard that sloped down to the swamp. One of them came forward with a torch and looked at her. She nodded curtly.

Whump! The alcohol caught, and then the wood below it as the heat drove out moisture and the gas played across it like a dragon's breath. More wood, more barrels of alcohol, blue and red flames soaring up. Men came bearing the contents of the cell, handling them with gingerly reluctance and heavy gloves.

"What about this?" asked Stratson, showing her the white altar cloth. He grasped one corner and cursed.

"What!"

"This!" A needle dangled from the leather gauntlet he wore. Tiphaine pulled the alcohol lamp closer. "Did it touch you?"

"No; but the whole cloth is run through and through with needles!"

She frowned down at it. "Put it down on the bed, strip the glove, make sure not to drop the needle and put it on top. The mattress is a bag of corn husks, right? Over a rope webbing?"

"Yes." Stratson did as he was told and eased back as Tiphaine carefully studied the length of cloth draped over the little bed. Needles twinkled in the waving flames.

"That sewing box of hers, too," he said. "It was set just so on the little table and it fell over. We caught it in time, but the boxes of pins opened up. Fortunately they all fell *in*, not out, but still . . . When did she have time to set this up?"

Tiphaine shook her head. "Shovels, oil . . . it's going to be a long night."

Then she looked at the spread of cloth and studied the designs; the odd symbology seemed to make her eyes slide along faster and faster . . .

She wrenched her gaze away. *No, I don't think I'll take this along for study.*

"Throw it on. All of it."

"Got some priests," Stratson said. "There's a hermitage in the woods. They come over and hear confessions and say Mass. Your page had someone run for them, smart kid."

Tiphaine realized he had an entourage, standing at a slight distance. Five of them were wearing habits, brown Dominican robes. The one who came forward wore the bright red cincture of the Hounds of God, which she hadn't seen in many years. Tiphaine bared her teeth, but the man raised a hand, palm-out to her. It was impossible to tell his age, but she thought the lines in his face were those of suffering as much as age.

"Peace, sister. Peace. After Pope Leo died, we were disbanded by orders of the Lady Regent. Bishop Maxwell tracked us down several years ago. All of us have had training in detecting the enemy's works. We have stayed disbanded; but at the orders and service of the secular authorities. Thus we do penance."

Tiphaine growled. *That's unexpected! Did Sandra know? But, if they are now on the side of the Angels . . . we need a few doughty warriors in the spiritual realm.*

"You've got me at a disadvantage, Father . . ."

"Lucien Blat. I am at your orders. What can we do?"

Stratson interrupted. "Tell me what will make this safe!" he demanded.

And Tiphaine found herself sharing a sympathetic glance with a Hound of God. The irony bit.

"What is . . . who is . . . what can you tell me?"

Tiphaine looked around and realized the priest hadn't overheard her conversation. Tersely she explained, and was reassured and oddly disturbed when the priest simply nodded acknowledgment.

Oh, damn. This sort of story is credible *now. It's good that he believes the truth, but the truth is so Not Good.*

"I think that we need to hallow and sanctify this land," the cleric said thoughtfully. "And not bringing anybody vulnerable here sounds like a very good idea. In the future; I'm afraid I agree, this entire place should be destroyed and interdicted. Possibly burned over in the late summer when it dries out enough, for several years running."

He turned and went to the other priests standing in the wind, as motionless as they might have been standing in the shade of an oak on a hot day, their hands tucked into the broad sleeves of their robes.

Disciplined, Tiphaine thought with approval.

As Father Lucien turned back to her the three paced the precincts, waving censers and sprinkling water, praying and chanting. One stood and sang the "Kyrie Eleison." His powerful baritone fought the wind and rain. The other four picked up the descant and response.

Father Lucien signed the cross before her.

Did I just feel something from my amulet? Damn, but I'm not used to this. I don't like *it.*

"Shall we pray for her soul?" he asked, between verses. "Christ died for us all. Even her."

"I don't know. She was born in the Church. She turned apostate and traitor for personal power. Probably about ten years ago. I could say her soul was stolen from her. With her permission, I think, but still."

"It's going to take a long time to reduce this to ashes," observed Father Lucien. "I and my fellow priests will stay here, watch and make sure that all is consumed. And we will pray."

Stratson cleared his throat. "Did you say you wanted to strip and bathe, Grand Constable?"

"Yes," she said, and closed her eyes for an instant with a crushing weariness that made her bones ache. "Everything I have on goes on the fire. The bathwater to be poured out by the marsh; the towels on the fire."

Father Lucien smiled at her. It was a small smile, and a bit tight. "Not taking any chances, I see, my lady Grand Constable."

Tiphaine looked at her sword and sighed. She pitched it carefully into the center of the flames. It stood, quivering. Then she pulled off her helm and tossed it carefully to land at the foot of the blade, wincing as she thought of the cost of a new suit of plate armor. Stratson gave her reasonably knowledgeable assistance with the parts you simply couldn't handle yourself. She turned to Lucien as she pulled off her right gauntlet. The scar stood out, inflamed, with a white rope of scar tissue down the center.

"She did that to me in May. It nearly cost me my hand. All it took was her sucking one of her needles and running it down my hand. She didn't even scratch the flesh; just touched it."

He looked carefully, but forbore to touch her. Then he nodded and strode forward, to stand by the cantor at the fire. By the time she had all the plate and mail off and was stripping the gambeson, tunic and trews, Stratson had all the men facing outwards.

I feel stupid doing this Lady Godiva with gooseflesh thing. But I was the one grappling with . . . that . . . and splattering its gore all over. If I inhaled her blood, or spit got through the armor and gambeson . . . I might wake up tomorrow losing my guts or showing pustules or carbuncles. Better get really clean.

The amulet was warm and comforting between her breasts. *This is probably a good thing to do.*

"My lady."

Father Lucien bowed before her and kept his eyes firmly over her left shoulder.

"Your page is inside with Father Manuel. They've prepared three baths for you. The boy has towels all warmed up and we really can't have our Grand Constable sick. And I assure you, we are taking extreme care. We will hold the vigil and not let even a spark or scrap get loose."

He frowned up at the security block. "I'm going to insist, as hard as I can, that the whole building be burned. Burned, exorcised, then let nature cleanse it for generations."

Tiphaine looked at him. *I am finding myself thinking good thoughts about a former Inquisitor. The world is a very strange place.*

"You are probably right. I'll speak to the Lady Regent and strongly recommend that we do so. God knows we're broke, with the war, and we will be for years to come. But this . . . needs doing."

COUNTY OF THE EASTERMARK
CHARTERED CITY OF WALLA WALLA
CITY PALACE OF THE COUNTS PALANTINE
PORTLAND PROTECTIVE ASSOCIATION
(FORMERLY SOUTHEASTERN WASHINGTON STATE)
HIGH KINGDOM OF MONTIVAL
(FORMERLY WESTERN NORTH AMERICA)
AUGUST 24, CHANGE YEAR 25/2023 AD

Countess Ermentrude looked at her husband. When he nodded confirmation, she pulled the night-robe around her more closely and shivered.

"*That* was what you fought?" she asked him. "Or something even *worse*? Merciful mother of *God*, Felipe!"

Tiphaine held out her glass. "Rigobert, do the honors, would you? That isn't my favorite memory and I have some . . . doozies."

He poured from the decanter he'd moved to within arm's reach. She drank again, ignoring the quiet speech in the background while she let the smooth fire of the brandy relax the knot in her gut.

But Delia was able to help with the nightmares. Reason to love, number seven thousand one hundred forty-two: doesn't freak out when I wake up sweating and shaking and grinding my teeth.

Felipe set down his own snifter, rose and bowed, the full formal gesture.

"My lady d'Ath, House Arminger and the Protectorate are very well served in their Grand Constable. House Artos and the High Kingdom of Montival will be as well."

"It needed doing, your grace," she said with a shrug. "I was there, and I did it."

He exchanged another glance with his wife.

"My lady Grand Constable, I cannot repay your aid with gifts, but I would give you one, if I might, as a symbol of our regard and a pledge of future friendship between our Houses. We spoke of my hunting lodge of *High Halleck*, in the mountains—my mother had it built and named it."

Tiphaine inclined her head. "I was thinking just a little earlier of asking for the loan of it," she said. "When the war is over."

He shook his head. "Not a loan. I . . . we would gift it to you, my lady, lodge and land and forest right. In free socage, not asking vassalage, of course."

Tiphaine put down the brandy snifter and made her mouth not drop open. House de Aguirre didn't do things by halves!

Sandra would be pleased. And Rudi and Mathilda would, too. I've certainly nailed down the Eastermark politically, the way they wanted. But I don't think . . . I'm Grand Constable, accepting a princely gift like that might . . .

She stood and bowed in return. "My lord, my lady, my office forbids that I accept such a gift in my own person."

Felipe began to frown slightly, but Ermentrude touched his sleeve and spoke, "But you have an heir, I believe, Lady d'Ath?"

"Yes. My adopted son, Diomede. Born to Lord Rigobert and his wife Lady Delia."

"Second son," Rigobert said helpfully.

Which gave a perfectly reasonable excuse for his welcoming a son taking the name of another House; it solved the inheritance problem rather neatly. Arrangements of that sort weren't at all uncommon, where a fief-holder had no heir of the body.

Count Felipe's face cleared, and he beamed. "Which

enables me to express my gratitude to you both," he said. "I must insist."

Gisarme-butts stamped in the corridor outside. Rigobert opened the door, and the Mother Superior of the Walla Walla abbey swept in. She made a curtsy: "My lord Count?" she said. "I came as quickly as possible."

Tiphaine stood. "I leave you in very capable hands, your Grace," she said.

She and de Stafford shook the nobleman's hand and bowed over Ermentrude's.

"And that is that," she murmured, as they walked back through the family quarters.

Bewildered work crews were already tearing up the bloodstained parquetry. The Baron of Forest Grove nodded approval.

"Except for winning the war, of course," he said. "And now we have to manage a fighting retreat for the High King."

CHAPTER TWENTY

ARMY HQ
THE HIGH KING'S HOST
HORSE HEAVEN HILLS
(FORMERLY SOUTH-CENTRAL WASHINGTON)
HIGH KINGDOM OF MONTIVAL
(FORMERLY WESTERN NORTH AMERICA)
OCTOBER 28, CHANGE YEAR 25/2023 AD

A knight was singing, alone at first and then joined by a dozen others:

> *"Morning red, morning red*
> *Will you shine upon me dead?*
> *Oliphants will soon be blowing,*
> *Then must I to death be going,*
> *I and many merry friends!"*

Rudi Mackenzie looked up from the map, remembering to keep the bacon and fried onions folded in a wheat cake aside so that it wouldn't drip grease on the precious document. The tall young man was one of the Protector's Guard, helping his squire to groom his destrier a little down the slope from the royal command pavilion; he wove ribbons into its mane, and it snuffled at him and lipped his yellow curls until he fed it an apple.

Around him his friends and comrades were finishing

bowls of porridge and bannocks and bacon, many already in their war-harness and the others in the midst of donning it, laughing as they sang, a few waving their spoons to the chorus:

"I and many merry friends!"

"Nothing like a little pessimism," Rudi said in a dull tone, and took another bite.

"It's not pessimistic," Mathilda said seriously. "It's a happy song, a young man's . . . Oh, you got me *again*!"

She thumped him in the ribs; a largely theoretical gesture, since he was in full plate, but her gauntlet made a satisfying *whunk* against the steel and he grinned and winked.

The air was full of the sounds and scents of an army getting ready to move; men's voices, the clank of metal, the creak of leather and wood, the occasional snort or neigh from a horse. Sweat and scorched bacon and dung, but also the clear cool fall air, and the first rains had laid the dust and left a dusting of green across the rolling hills. Banners snapped and fluttered, their points streaming towards the east and the enemy. Long shadows stretched westward, from the hills and the odd tree. Mostly the land here was tawny wilderness, even the herds of wild horses and antelope and bison fled. The birds waited overhead, though, crow and raven and buzzard, riding the air and waiting patiently.

They would have their victory today, whatever passed among humankind.

"The sun will be in our eyes for the morning," Bjarni Ironrede said, looking at the map. "Here?" he added, pointing.

"But the wind will be at our backs all day," Oak Barstow said. "Fifty, a hundred feet extra range, and the cloth yards will hit harder."

"Here is where we deploy," Rudi agreed, tapping his left forefinger on the map where Bjarni had indicated. "But if they've any wisdom, they won't force a full engagement while we hold that position. They'll push a little and then try to work around us."

He turned his head. "Lord Chancellor, you will continue to function as Chief of Staff here," he went on.

The warrior cleric looked happier in armor than he had the last time the High King saw him, which had been shepherding a supply convoy and looking very much as if he wanted to curse.

Rudi looked around the circle, with a particular eye on the Associate lords; there were a round dozen, but Conrad Renfrew looked to have them well in hand.

"My lords, this is the last of our preliminaries. We must fold the Grand Constable's force into the body of this army, and pass them to the rear where they will form our main reserve, and also get a chance to rest. We will offer battle this day, but only if the enemy accepts it on our terms. This will require the most precise attention to my orders. I will not fight except at an advantage; but there will be battle, either today, or in the next few days. The dance ends soon. Is all that understood?"

They all bowed their heads and thumped their breastplates in salute.

"General Thurston?" he went on.

"Two full regiments of my troops are ready, Your Majesty," the dark young man said. "Six battalions and field artillery. We'll anchor the archers, and Ironrede will fill any gaps."

"Excellent. Eric—"

The Bearkiller commander nodded.

"—my gut, not to mention my testicles, gives me a feeling that they'll try to work around our right and push

us away from the Columbia. Be wary of that, but not fix-
ated on it. We may backpedal, but if we do it will be
straight west. We will *not* allow ourselves to be forced
away from the river. There isn't enough water for an army
this size, otherwise."

"Yes, Your Majesty," he said. Then a grin, and a flourish of the steel fist. "They'll regret it if they try."

"See that they do."

A thunder of hooves, and a challenge-and-response
from below the hill. They all looked down. One of the
Dúnedain was riding a dappled gray Arab up towards
the command party, and a man on a good but not spectacular horse beside, carrying a long light lance with a
pennant marked with the crowned mountain and Sword
of Montival. As they approached Rudi recognized his
half sister Ritva; she was in the gear Rangers wore for a
real battle, a black brigandine with the Stars-and-Tree
picked out in silver rivets, mail sleeves and breeches, a
spired helm with cheek-pieces, a gray hooded cloak beneath.

There was a long bright scratch across the brow of the
helmet, the type an arrow would make, and the broken-
off stub of another in the cantle of her saddle.

*Ah, the one in the kettle helm and the red coat under his
mail shirt will be her Drumheller Canuk, then, and carrying my banner,* Rudi thought. *Good luck to them both this
day. Lug strengthen their arms, and the Crow Goddess beat
Her wings above them.*

They swept to a stop, and before the hooves had
stopped moving Ritva come out of the saddle in a showy
vault-dismount and went to one knee before him, bowing with hand to heart for a moment, and then extending
a dispatch.

Some of the others snorted a little at the showiness.

He didn't mind; such things kept hearts strong, and battles were won in the heart as much as on the field.

"Rise, and give me the report verbally, sister," he said.

She'd been sent for more than carrying an envelope; not least, to give an account that even the most birth-proud Associate lords would listen to carefully. He handed the document to Mathilda and then finished the sandwich with one last large bite, relishing the salty smoky tang of the cured meat and the sharp onion with it. He did not think he would die this day, but even with the Sword of the Lady there was no such thing as certainty.

Mathilda opened it and began to read it quickly while Ritva stepped up to the map.

"The Grand Constable's rearguard are making a stand *here*," she said. "Four Yakima infantry regiments and about three thousand horse, a thousand lancers and the rest light cavalry. The rest of the expeditionary force have broken contact and should be *here*"—she tapped the map to the northward, where the Horse Heaven Hills turned higher and sharper before they fell away to the Yakima Valley—"any minute now. They've got what's left of the baggage train, mostly field ambulances and the wounded . . . the ones who haven't been wounded in the last hour or two. We burned the rest of the wagons two days ago. A lot of the troops haven't eaten in twenty-four hours."

"Lord Chancellor," Rudi said.

Ignatius nodded, turning and giving orders in a low voice. Messengers knelt to listen to him, lean men and a few women in leather, Church couriers, many of them of the Order of the Shield. Clerks were writing as he spoke; the orders were folded, stamped and on their way while Ritva was still speaking.

"Enemy forces?" Rudi asked.

"Mostly light cavalry, their vanguard, trying to pin us. About ten thousand men. That's not counting their casualties, they've been pushing it hard and paying the butcher's bill."

Someone whistled softly; ten thousand *was* a stunning number for the mere lead element. Ritva went on: "But the *Hír i Dúnedain* says there's *at least* one brigade of Boise troops only about two hours by bicycle behind them and he strongly suspects more within striking distance."

Her finger traced an arc farther east, converging on the force that had been delaying and harassing the advance of the CUT and Boise.

"Ah," Rudi said. "Time and force and space. If that rearguard is not pulled out before the enemy are there in force enough to invest it, they are lost."

"The *Hír i Dúnedain* thinks you have very little time, Your Majesty."

"Ritva Havel, if Alleyne Loring-Larsson says that, I will believe it as I would sky-tall letters of fire, written in Ogham by Lug's spear. For now they hold, though?"

"Yes, my liege. The infantry are standing off the horse-archers but the Grand Constable says she doesn't have enough cavalry left to rock them back on their heels long enough for the infantry to break contact. She had to keep this many to cork the bottle while the rest of her force got away."

"A hard choice the Grand Constable had, but she made the right one," Rudi said. "Best to risk some than lose all."

His hand caressed the crystal hilt of the Sword. Time and force and space . . . maps and symbols moved before his eyes.

666   S. M. STIRLING

Decision formed. "Matti, you'll be in charge of the Protector's Guard. We'll take all of them. Edain, mount up the High King's Archers, the lot of them also. And . . . Viscount Chenoweth."

"Your Majesty?"

"Your *menie*?"

The eldest son of Conrad Odell nodded; a squire was behind him with a sheet of paper, but he didn't need it.

"One thousand six hundred, and ready to move immediately."

"Leave the spearmen; just the lancers and mounted crossbows."

"A thousand, then, Your Majesty."

"Get them here. Fast."

He bowed his head, turned, and was in the saddle within three paces. Ignatius was already handing a note to his own aides.

"The ambulances will be moving by the time you leave, Your Majesty," he said.

"Good." *Good man*, he thought. "My lords, ladies. I suggest you go prepare a welcome for our guests."

Edain was near, leading a horse. It was a mare, seventeen hands of night-black sleekness, deep-chested, arch-necked. She was middle-aged for a horse, especially a warm-blood—but the more closely you looked the less like an ordinary warm-blood of the destrier breed she looked, and even experienced horsemen would have taken a decade or so off her total if they were asked.

"My lady Epona," Rudi said to her, blowing into her nose in the kiss of the horse-kind. "Are you ready to dance with me this day?"

"Sure, and she'd stamp you into mush if you didn't," Edain said, grinning at him. "For didn't she travel all the way to the Sunrise lands with you and back?"

"Riding in a horsecar on the rails most of the way back," Rudi said lightly.

And glad I was of it. The strain was showing on her. Now she looks splendid.

He swung into the saddle.

"Let's go," he said.

"They're charging again," Alleyne Loring said. "Here."

Rudi took the heavy binoculars in one hand. Their picture was uncannily sharp, some art of the ancient world that prevented the picture that leapt to his eyes from wobbling and the magnification made little of the near two thousand yards' distance.

The Yakima infantry were deployed in a triangular formation on a low swale. It was the best position around, chosen with a good eye for ground; the eastern side was shielded by a steeper section of rising earth, almost like a bank. Rain or no, dust hung over them where hooves and wheels and thousands of hobnailed boots had torn the thin bunchgrass, and he hoped they'd had a chance to fill their water wagons. He could taste the dry papery flavor of it on his lips now, along with the salt of sweat. This was better fighting weather than high summer, though.

The formation on the rise bristled with pikes; the front four ranks had theirs down into the *prepare to receive cavalry* position, the front row on one knee and bracing each butt against a boot, the next three at shoulder or chest or waist height, a forest of sharp points. Behind them the next three stood with the weapons upright, and behind them was a double rank with glaives ready to stop any breakthrough.

It took strength to hold the sixteen-foot weapons like that. And a cold considered courage to spit on your hands and brace the pike and stand under arrows and bolts, closing up the holes as men fell silent or screaming and the earth shook under the charging hooves. The crossbows were interspersed between the blocks of pikes, three deep—prone and kneeling and standing. The silent menace was less showy, but just as real. So was that of the springalds and scorpions that were spaced along the lines.

"Cavalry in the center for now," Rudi noted. "Now, that is a position I would not care to assault, Alleyne."

"They have been, though, Sire."

He nodded agreement without taking the binoculars from his eyes. You could see the bodies of men and horses scattered back from each side of the triangle, out several hundred yards but thicker as you approached up to a wavering line at fifty yards or so, then a thinner scattering and a few right under the pike points. Some lying still, others still moving. He could see one man crawling away, legs motionless and a bolt standing in his back.

War, he thought. *Not a pretty sight nor a pretty thing, for all that we dress it.*

The enemy were going to try again, though. He could see them dispersed across miles around; most were in clumps around trains of packhorses.

"Filling their quivers. Rancher levies from the far interior, I make them for the most part, but not altogether savages."

Alleyne nodded. "Sire. Ah, there they go."

The horsemen from over the mountains moved towards the ranks on the hill. It was like watching water spatter on a pane of glass, but running backward so that the clots and streams flowed together, building around banners that bore odd spiky sigils—the brands of their Ranchers—or the rayed sun of the Church Universal and Triumphant, gold on scarlet.

Rudi looked over his shoulder. The solid block of the Protector's Guard waited, black armor and bright lance heads, the Lidless Eye on every shield and pennant, five hundred strong. The chivalry of Odell was about as numerous, but in armor bright or dark, each vassal lord with his men. Their lances swayed overhead, a forest of steel. He waved, and three horses trotted up the slope to pull up beside him.

"Now, my King?" Érard Renfrew said.

"Not quite yet, my lord Viscount," Rudi said. "Timing is all. But better to labor to restrain the stallion than prod the mule. Edain, when we go we're going in straight."

The clansman looked a little unhappy, but he couldn't be at the High King's side in a horseman's fight, and the best way he could safeguard Rudi would be to get the fight won, and as quickly as possible.

Rudi held out his left fist, then extended the little finger on that hand. "You like this, and the Odell crossbowmen with you. Turn the enemy back towards the lances. My lord Alleyne, you and your Rangers will screen our right."

The fair man in black nodded. "You're depending on . . . the Grand Constable to do the right thing," he said neutrally.

Ah, put the feud aside, man. Yes, she wished your Astrid dead these fifteen years and more, but she had no part in her end. The which was like something from her Histories, and just exactly as she would have wished, poor lady.

"She has so far. Now to your places, all of you."

"And mine's by you," Mathilda said.

Their hands touched in their gauntlets. Below the plainsmen were moving to the attack, slowly, which was wise. You saved the speed for when it was needed. Then there was a stir, an eddy, and they were in motion towards the point of the triangle on the hill, spreading around it in a swirling mass, and even across the distance you could hear the hooves.

And the chorus of yelping war cries, *Cut! Cut! Cut!*

The artillery spat at them, bolts and round shot; there were blackened patches on the grass, but no globes of fire went out. Then the little horizontal flicker of the crossbow bolts, and the ripple in the dun mass of the horsemen as each rose in the saddle to draw his bow . . .

Mathilda extended a hand. "Huon, lance."

The lad was there, and the long ash-wood shaft slapped into her gauntlet.

"Now," Rudi said. He slipped his arm into the loops of his shield and drew the Sword.

Shock ran through the world.

And over his voice, the high call of the oliphants. Behind him a rising thutter of hooves, as the lancers crested the rise a thousand strong.

"Morrigú!" he screamed.

"Artos and Montival!"

"Very neat timing," he gasped a half hour later, and forced his breathing to slow.

The ground beneath them was actually muddy with blood; he'd heard of that in songs, but never seen it before, and the smell was rank and metallic. Men were stabbing downward with their lances to give the mercy-stroke, mostly to wounded horses. Tiphaine d'Ath reined in across from him, limned by the morning sun; her mount snorted at Epona, then tossed its barded head aside, eyes rolling beyond the brow ridges of the steel peytral that warded its head as the big mare ignored him.

Rudi raised his voice a little to carry as he leaned over and extended his hand.

"Well done, and very well done, Grand Constable. I gave you a task, and you did it. Very well done indeed."

They gripped forearms for a moment. "The main column, Your Majesty?" she asked. "I had Lord Rigobert in command of it while I held the rear."

"Safe and back to our lines by now, eating barley bannock and bean soup by the field kitchens."

A very slight sigh. *Don't be overwhelming me with shouts of joy, now,* he thought. Another man came up beside her, the commander of the Yakima foot.

"Brigadier Wheedon, an impressive display of courage and cool discipline from your troops. Get your men on their bicycles and moving right now. Directly west will do, it's not steep."

"My wounded, ah, your lordship High King?"

"I've brought up a column of field ambulances. But waste no time. Abandon any gear that can't follow quickly; goods we can replace more easily than brave men. Move!"

"Yessir!" he said, and went off at a run.

Rudi looked at the tattered ranks of the knights behind the Grand Constable. One man had a helm with half an ostrich-feather plume, the rest sheared away; he recognized the olive face of the Count Palantine of the Eastermark when the visor was raised and the splintered shield's heraldic symbols: *Or, a tree vert with a wolf passant sable, on a tree brun.*

"My lord Count Felipe," he called. "Well-met. There's news from Walla Walla via the heliograph net. Your good lady is a notable war-captain; they beat off another assault there from the enemy yesterday, and inflicted heavy loss."

The man beamed. Rudi turned to the others. "Colonel Vogeler, Lord Alleyne, Rick, you'll screen the heavy horse. They'll be at us before we're back. Make them bunch and we'll punch at them again; or if they don't, we'll keep withdrawing."

Three Bears was grinning beneath his black-and-white war paint; he'd stopped with three strings of scalps, and they dripped onto the hide of his horse.

"Damned if we didn't finish off every third one, Strong Raven," he said.

"Damned if they won't come on again anyway," Rudi said grimly.

He glanced around for Matti, and his heart lurched when he saw her destrier standing empty-saddled, but then he realized Huon Liu was holding it. She was on foot, and a man knelt before her. It was Conrad's youngest son.

". . . arise, Sir Ogier!" she finished.

He did, managing a tired smile. Rudi leaned, and Epona pivoted. Nobody was left on the rise the pikemen had held, nobody but the dead. Far above a glider turned, the near-noon sun flashing from its polished canopy, a brightness among the black wings of the carrion birds.

And eastward—

He gasped, and then shook his head as the others looked at him. His hand clasped the hilt of the Sword.

"He is coming," he heard himself say. "The Prophet. Sethaz is coming."

New York Times **bestselling author**

S. M. STIRLING

"FIRST-RATE ADVENTURE ALL THE WAY."
—HARRY TURTLEDOVE

s922

AVAILABLE NOW IN HARDCOVER

FROM

New York Times bestselling author
S. M. STIRLING

The Given Sacrifice
A Novel of the Change

Rudi Mackenzie has led his army to victory over the
legions of the Church Universal and Triumphant. Now,
he must confront the forces behind the Church—the
Powers of the Void. Yet even a victory will not end the
conflict forever. The Powers of the Void threaten Rudi not
only in the present, but also in the future represented by
his children. As Rudi's heir, Princess Órlaith grows up in
the shadow of her famous father—and she realizes that
the enemy will do anything to see that she does not live
to fulfill her parents' dream...

"Nobody wrecks a world better than S. M. Stirling."
—*New York Times* bestselling author Harry Turtledove

**Available wherever books are sold or at
penguin.com**

facebook.com/acerocbooks